THE YEAR'S BEST SCIENCE FICTION AND FANTASY

2009 EDITION

OTHER BOOKS BY

RICH HORTON

Fantasy: The Best of the Year, 2006 Edition

Fantasy: The Best of the Year, 2007 Edition

Fantasy: The Best of the Year, 2008 Edition

Science Fiction: The Best of the Year, 2006 Edition

Science Fiction: The Best of the Year, 2007 Edition

Science Fiction: The Best of the Year, 2008 Edition

Unplugged: The Web's Best Sci-Fi & Fantasy: 2008 Download

THE YEAR'S BEST SCIENCE FICTION AND FANTASY

2009 EDITION

edited by
RICH HORTON

PRIME BOOKS

THE YEAR'S BEST SCIENCE FICTION AND FANTASY, 2009 EDITION

Prime Books
www.prime-books.com

ISBN: 978-1-60701-214-6

This book is for Mary Ann

TABLE OF CONTENTS

TABLE OF CONTENTS

THE YEAR IN FANTASY AND SCIENCE FICTION, 2008

RICH HORTON

It's a mug's game to try to define science fiction, but I'm going to at least gesture in that direction. As opposed to mysteries or romances, which are defined by plot, and horror, which is defined by mood, sf and fantasy are defined by setting. (Probably historical fiction also can be defined by setting.) (And mainstream? I'm not sure. Dare one say it's defined by character? Perhaps instead we should say it's not a genre at all. As for experimental fiction, it seems defined by language or structure.)

Then how do sf and fantasy differ? The setting of an sf story is, in the story's terms, plausibly real, and not our present or past, while the setting of a fantasy story is not plausibly real. Thus a fantasy can be set in our present, with magic (i.e. urban fantasy) or in an alternate past, with magic (historical fantasy), or in a secondary world, with or without magic, but not one that, in story terms, might be real. This last proviso allows that curious category of fantasy without magic: stories like **Swordspoint**. (Although **Swordspoint**'s world actually does have magic, as its sequels show.) What I mean here is that there are certain stories we usually call fantasy that appear to be set in something very like our world, but clearly not our world—the geography doesn't fit, or the history doesn't fit. And, crucially, there is no connection to our world. It's not an alternate history, it's not (at least not explicitly) a parallel world, and it's not an oddly Earthlike other planet . . . it's just there. I admit there's something unsatisfying about this—why not call these stories either variants of historical fiction (much like so-called "Ruritanian" stories) or variants of alternate history (and thus sf)? Here I call on Damon Knight—when we point at these stories (like **Swordspoint**) we usually say fantasy—so they're fantasy. (And they are, all in all, fairly rare.)

Which leaves science fiction. Stories that—in the internal story terms—are set in a plausibly real world, but not our world either present or past. That leaves the future, or parallel worlds, or astronomically different worlds (nominally other planets), or an alternate history. (Or, rarely, a special case: secret history, in which the story terms do suggest that the world is ours, but understood differently.) There's no requirement here for a technological focus. And no real requirement for any "science" at all, except in that the connection to "our" world needs at least a handwaved scientific explanation. The key phrase here is that the plausibility requirement is "in story terms"—that is, the author need not necessarily believe that his "science" (his FTL drive, for example) is actual rigorous, or even sensible—just that it works. (And how is this different from a fantasy story claiming that magic works internally to the story? Good question, and I would just say the main difference is feel or attitude.)

As for "fantasy," writers are continually redefining fantasy—the field is always what the latest stories say it is. But what does that really mean? Every year some writers are happily producing heroic fantasy, others urban fantasy, some science fantasy, some slipstream. And indeed I keep looking at the stories I choose for these anthologies and I keep failing to find overarching trends. (Even though my personal selection bias might be presumed to narrow things.) Perhaps one way to classify fantasy is by setting. Is the story set in a secondary world? In our world with a slight magical irruption? In a changed historical setting—either fantastical alternate history or the past viewed as fantasy? In a world based on myth? In an entirely artificial location?

So this year I have a story by Patrick Rothfuss, "The Road to Levinshir," that is at core as traditional a heroic fantasy as you could want, set in a fairly typical secondary world. (And immensely entertaining and very moving.) But also Jeffrey Ford's "Daltharee," completely odd, a story of a city in a bottle with a frame that seems steampunkish at times. And "Blue Vervain Murder Ballad #2: Jack of Diamonds," by Erik Amundsen, which echoes American riverboat stories and deals with the devil. Or Karen Heuler's "The Difficulties of Evolution," quite unplaceably weird, about people evolving into birds or animals as they grow.

Holly Phillips, in "The Small Door," is achingly moving in a story with an almost suburban setting—no obvious fantastical world here—just a tiny fantastical escape, with, alas, limits. The fantasy world of Christopher Golden's "The Hiss of Escaping Air" is Hollywood—the real bite of the story, however, lies in the mind of the main character, a basically decent person who lets revenge make her do something unexpectedly awful. Delia Sherman's "Gift From a Spring" is set in rural France, with an artist protagonist, working at a ballet school—it's a very grounded story somehow, despite the magical nature of the ballerina.

Ann Leckie has written several recent pieces examining the pitfalls of dealing with deities—the best of these is "The God of Au," which is, thus, set in a secondary world. Peter S. Beagle's "King Pelles the Sure" seems set in a fairly generic secondary world (but sans magic)—except that the story speaks gently, without hectoring, very directly to our present situation in Iraq. (Though really more broadly to the impulse towards war in general.) "Araminta; or The Wreck of the Amphidrake," by Naomi Novik, is also set in something of a secondary world—but one with considerable parallels to, perhaps, Regency England—more importantly, it's a pirate story, which means it's a fantasy in a different—very fun—way.

The closer I look at my selections the more I see how much fantasy these days is really set in near variations of our present world. Not all of this strikes me as "urban fantasy"—indeed, most of it avoids the more obvious "urban fantasy" tropes. But if it's fantasy set in a city called New York, surely it's urban fantasy in some sense, eh? So with Eugene Mirabelli's "Falling Angel," a stark look at a man's obsessive relationship with a literal angel that fell to his roof. (One might compare it to another "angel in New York" story from last year, Peter S. Beagle's "Uncle Chaim and Aunt Rifke and the Angel," one of five Beagle stories I agonized over including here before settling on "King Pelles the Sure.") "If Angels Fight" might be my favorite Richard Bowes story yet—and he's surely an "urban fantasist," with his stories often set in either Boston or New York, as with this one, about the black sheep of a Boston political family—so this becomes in one sense a very political story, but one that turns movingly on a striking fantastical idea.

Meghan McCarron's "The Magician's House" is closer to "suburban fantasy" perhaps—and very disturbing it is, about a girl learning magic from a local wizard. And I'm not sure how to categorize Kij Johnson's "26 Monkeys, Also the Abyss" except to call it a delight—perhaps there's a hint of Ray Bradbury in the background of this story about woman and the rather unusual disappearing monkey act she runs.

One of the key strengths of contemporary set fantasy is that so often we directly sympathize with the main character—we can so easily see ourselves as them—which ups the ante powerfully in a story like Alice Sola Kim's "We Love Deena," where the protagonist can jump into people's heads—and uses that ability to sort of stalk her ex-lover. In a different way James Maxey's "Silent as Dust" invites us to identify with a ghost—who is not quite a ghost really, but may as well be, living uninvited in the interstices of an old friend's life. And again, the idea that we too might be that ghost makes the story work.

And yet there remain stories that draw us in with their exotic settings. For example "Firooz and his Brother" by Alex Jeffers, set in old Samarkand—but involving in a contemporary fashion too, with its gender-bending central idea. Or Liz Williams's "Spiderhorse," in which the Norse myths (and Odin's horse) are viewed from a very original angle. And again Jay Lake's "A Water Matter" is set in a secondary world, not entirely unfamiliar in outline (though originally limned), and it deals with magic and revenge and the question of ruling family succession—all subjects long central to fantasy. But made new again, as the best writers continue to manage.

So that's what the world of fantasy (at shorter lengths) looks today—at least as viewed through the doubtless distorted lens of my personal preferences. Secondary worlds, and fantasticated historical (or mythical) settings remain popular, but contemporary or near-contemporary settings seem to predominate slightly. Only a couple of stories seem to fit to me into such categories as "the New Weird" or alternately "slipstream." And only a couple negotiate with science fictional ideas—so-called "science fantasy" is indeed one of my personal favorite subgenres, but little in that area came my way last year.

And now to the science fiction stories in the volume. Again, an attempt at broad categorization follows. I thought classifying them based on their setting, or sub-setting, might be interesting. Let's see where that takes us.

First up is a story that pretty much violates my "setting" definition: "The Region of Unlikeness" by Rivka Galchen is set pretty much in the present, pretty much in our world. (Maybe that's how an sf story got into the *New Yorker*? (Nahh . . . Jonathan Lethem's "Lostronaut," also from 2008 at the *New Yorker*, is straightforwardly set in the future, about an astronaut lost in space.)) But Galchen's story beautifully details the protagonist's relationship with two older men, in a way that suggests they have invented time travel. (Which makes it perhaps a secret history, or which suggests a "real" future—either way shoehorning just barely into the space of my vague definition.)

Next, how many stories are set in the nearish future on Earth. Daryl Gregory's "Glass" is perhaps pure sf in this mode—extrapolating a plausible near-future scientific development. Will McIntosh's "The Fantasy Jumper," published in a horror-oriented magazine, looks at the horrific uses a virtual technology could be put to. Ted Kosmatka's "The Art of Alchemy" is about plausible technological developments—and also, more importantly, about characters caught up in them. Peter Watts, "The Eyes of God" is very scary, about a future in which a tendency to criminal actions becomes in essence criminal. Mary Robinette Kowal "Evil Robot Monkey" looks at the plight of a sort of "uplifted" chimp. Garth Nix, in "Infestation," gives vampires a science fictional basis (though for many the word vampire immediately makes the story fantasy). Robert Reed, in "Character Flu," cleverly examines a scary sort of "virus."

Farther in the future, with other worlds implied, we have Margo Lanagan's "The Fifth Star in the Southern Cross," in which a ruined environment has meant ruined fertility, and as a corollary, aliens are used as prostitutes. James L. Cambias, in "Balancing Accounts" tells what in some ways is as traditional as SF story as we see these days: robots, spaceships, and the outer planets. What more can an SF reader want? Paul Cornell's "Catherine Drewe" is more ambiguous, as its future is based on an alternate past, and some alternate scientific principles: but it is set on Mars. James Alan Gardner's "The Ray Gun: A Love Story" is almost a fable, but concerning a real true SF trope: a ray gun. Elizabeth Bear and Sarah Monette, in "Boojum," give us battles with aliens at the edge of the Solar System, and living spaceships. Ian McDonald's "The Tear" takes us much farther to the future, and features very strangely altered humans, and other planets, and interstellar war. Charlie Anders's "Suicide Drive" is a very original take on the idea of an expensive expedition to other stars.

Alternate history is of course a very common trope. And so is steampunk. All the alternate histories to hand have steampunk elements (though the Bear only at a stretch), including Cornell's "Catherine Drewe" which I've already mention. Elizabeth Bear's "Shoggoths in Bloom" marries Lovecraft and the runup to World War II with a look at American racism. Beth Bernobich's "The Golden

Octopus" is set in a wildly alternate Ireland, and takes on time travel as well. Finally, Jeff VanderMeer's "Fixing Hanover" is set in a steampunkish milieu in what make be an alternate past, or alternate future, or just a different world.

It is, I suppose, incumbent on me to briefly review the commercial state of play in the field. And it isn't that pretty a picture. As I write these words we have been stunned by the news that *Realms of Fantasy* is being suddenly closed after fifteen years of publication. (A victim of the generally gloomy economic climate, of some apparent distribution issues, and perhaps of a long-term stagnation in magazine sales.) More happily, it now appears that the magazine will be revived in a few months. At about the same time we learned that *F&SF* is switching to bimonthly publication—with thicker issues to be sure, but still there will be reduction in word count overall. The other prominent fantasy venues—in print, *Weird Tales*, *Black Static*, *Black Gate* most notably, and on the web *Fantasy Magazine*, *Chiaroscuro*, and *Strange Horizons* (but there are many more) continued much as before. The best news is a couple of new sites—*Tor.com* (which publishes plenty of SF as well) and "literary adventure fantasy"-oriented *Beneath Ceaseless Skies*. There is as much or more outstanding short fantasy being written as ever—but it's still hard, harder than ever perhaps, to publish it prominently or for much remuneration. There were not as many changes in the SF half of the field, perhaps, though we are seeing *Postscripts* switch to an anthology format from a magazine.

In part because this was a truly remarkable year for anthologies, the artistic health of the field seems as strong as ever. If the commercial health is a bit wobbly, perhaps that mainly reflects our entire economy. But be assured—as I trust this book demonstrates—there remains plenty of magnificent science fiction and fantasy to read.

26 MONKEYS, ALSO THE ABYSS

KIJ JOHNSON

<hr/>

1.

Aimee's big trick is that she makes twenty-six monkeys vanish onstage.

2.

She pushes out a claw-foot bathtub and asks audience members to come up and inspect it. The people climb in and look underneath, touch the white enamel, run their hands along the little lions' feet. When they're done, four chains are lowered from the stage's fly space. Aimee secures them to holes drilled along the tub's lip and gives a signal, and the bathtub is hoisted ten feet into the air.

She sets a stepladder next to it. She claps her hands and the twenty-six monkeys onstage run up the ladder one after the other and jump into the bathtub. The bathtub shakes as each monkey thuds in among the others. The audience can see heads, legs, tails; but eventually every monkey settles and the bathtub is still again. Zeb is always the last monkey up the ladder. As he climbs into the bathtub, he makes a humming boom deep in his chest. It fills the stage.

And then there's a flash of light, two of the chains fall off, and the bathtub swings down to expose its interior.

Empty.

3.

They turn up later, back at the tour bus. There's a smallish dog door, and in the hours before morning the monkeys let themselves in, alone or in small groups, and get themselves glasses of water from the tap. If more than one returns at the same time, they murmur a bit among themselves, like college students meeting in the dorm halls after bar time. A few sleep on the sofa and at least one likes to be on the bed, but most of them wander back to their cages. There's a little grunting as they rearrange their blankets and soft toys, and then sighs and snoring. Aimee doesn't really sleep until she hears them all come in.

Aimee has no idea what happens to them in the bathtub, or where they go, or what they do before the soft click of the dog door opening. This bothers her a lot.

4.

Aimee has had the act for three years now. She was living in a month-by-month furnished apartment under a flight path for the Salt Lake City airport. She was hollow, as if something had chewed a hole in her body and the hole had grown infected.

There was a monkey act at the Utah State Fair. She felt a sudden and totally out-of-character urge to see it. Afterward, with no idea why, she walked up to the owner and said, "I have to buy this."

He nodded. He sold it to her for a dollar, which he told her was the price he had paid four years before.

Later, when the paperwork was filled out, she asked him, "How can you leave them? Won't they miss you?"

"You'll see, they're pretty autonomous," he said. "Yeah, they'll miss me and I'll miss them. But it's time, they know that."

He smiled at his new wife, a small woman with laugh lines and a vervet hanging from one hand. "We're ready to have a garden," she said.

He was right. The monkeys missed him. But they also welcomed her, each monkey politely shaking her hand as she walked into what was now her bus.

5.

Aimee has: a nineteen-year-old tour bus packed with cages that range in size from parrot-sized (for the vervets) to something about the size of a pickup bed (for all the macaques); a stack of books on monkeys ranging from *All About Monkeys* to *Evolution and Ecology of Baboon Societies*; some sequined show costumes, a sewing machine, and a bunch of Carhartts and tees; a stack of show posters from a few years back that say 25 MONKEYS! FACE THE ABYSS; a battered sofa in a virulent green plaid; and a boyfriend who helps with the monkeys.

She cannot tell you why she has any of these, not even the boyfriend, whose name is Geof, whom she met in Billings seven months ago. Aimee has no idea where anything comes from any more: she no longer believes that anything makes sense, even though she can't stop hoping.

The bus smells about as you'd expect a bus full of monkeys to smell; though after a show, after the bathtub trick but before the monkeys all return, it also smells of cinnamon, which is the tea Aimee sometimes drinks.

6.

For the act, the monkeys do tricks, or dress up in outfits and act out hit movies—*The Matrix* is very popular, as is anything where the monkeys dress up like little orcs. The maned monkeys, the lion-tails and the colobuses, have a lion-tamer act, with the old capuchin female, Pango, dressed in a red jacket and carrying a whip and a small chair. The chimpanzee (whose name is Mimi, and no, she is not a monkey) can do actual sleight of hand; she's not very good, but she's the best Chimp Pulling A Coin From Someone's Ear in the world.

The monkeys also can build a suspension bridge out of wooden chairs and rope, make a four-tier champagne fountain, and write their names on a whiteboard.

The monkey show is very popular, with a schedule of 127 shows this year at fairs and festivals across the Midwest and Great Plains. Aimee could do more, but she likes to let everyone have a couple of months off at Christmas.

7.

This is the bathtub act:

Aimee wears a glittering purple-black dress designed to look like a scanty magician's robe. She stands in front of a scrim lit deep blue and scattered with stars. The monkeys are ranged in front of her. As she speaks they undress and fold their clothes into neat piles. Zeb sits on his stool to one side, a white spotlight shining straight down to give him a shadowed look.

She raises her hands.

"These monkeys have made you laugh, and made you gasp. They have created wonders for you and performed mysteries. But there is a final mystery they offer you—the strangest, the greatest of all."

She parts her hands suddenly, and the scrim goes transparent and is lifted away, revealing the bathtub on a raised dais. She walks around it, running her hand along the tub's curves.

"It's a simple thing, this bathtub. Ordinary in every way, mundane as breakfast. In a moment I will invite members of the audience up to let you prove this for yourselves.

"But for the monkeys it is also a magical object. It allows them to travel—no one can say where. Not even I—" she pauses "—can tell you this. Only the monkeys know, and they share no secrets.

"Where do they go? Into heaven, foreign lands, other worlds—or some dark abyss? We cannot follow. They will vanish before our eyes, vanish from this most ordinary of things."

And after the bathtub is inspected and she has told the audience that there will be no final spectacle in the show—"It will be hours before they return from their secret travels"—and called for applause for them, she gives the cue.

8.

Aimee's monkeys:
- 2 siamangs, a mated couple
- 2 squirrel monkeys, though they're so active they might as well be twice as many
- 2 vervets
- a guenon, who is probably pregnant, though it's still too early to tell for sure. Aimee has no idea how this happened

- 3 rhesus monkeys. They juggle a little
- a capuchin female named Pango
- a crested macaque, 3 snow monkeys (one quite young), and a Java macaque. Despite the differences, they have formed a small troop and like to sleep together
- a chimpanzee, who is not actually a monkey
- a surly gibbon
- 2 marmosets
- a golden tamarin; a cotton-top tamarin
- a proboscis monkey
- red and black colubuses
- Zeb

9.

Aimee thinks Zeb might be a de Brazza's guenon, except that he's so old that he has lost almost all his hair. She worries about his health, but he insists on staying in the act. By now all he's really up for is the final rush to the bathtub, and for him it is more of a stroll. The rest of the time, he sits on a stool that is painted orange and silver and watches the other monkeys, looking like an aging impresario watching his *Swan Lake* from the wings. Sometimes she gives him things to hold, such as a silver hoop through which the squirrel monkeys jump.

10.

No one knows how the monkeys vanish or where they go. Sometimes they return holding foreign coins or durian fruit, or wearing pointed Moroccan slippers. Every so often one returns pregnant or accompanied by a new monkey. The number of monkeys is not constant.

"I just don't get it," Aimee keeps asking Geof, as if he has any idea. Aimee never knows anything any more. She's been living without any certainties, and this one thing—well, the whole thing, the fact the monkeys get along so well and know how to do card tricks and just turned up in her life and vanish from the bathtub; *everything*—she coasts with that most of the time, but every so often, when she feels her life is wheeling without brakes down a long hill, she starts poking at this again.

Geof trusts the universe a lot more than Aimee does, trusts that things make sense and that people can love, and therefore he doesn't need the same proofs. "You could ask them," he says.

11.

Aimee's boyfriend:

Geof is not at all what Aimee expected from a boyfriend. For one thing, he's fifteen years younger than Aimee, twenty-eight to her forty-three. For another, he's sort of quiet. For a third, he's gorgeous, silky thick hair pulled into a shoulder-length ponytail, shaved sides showing off his strong jaw line. He smiles a lot, but he doesn't laugh very often.

Geof has a degree in history, which means that he was working in a bike-repair shop when she met him at the Montana Fair. Aimee never has much to do right after the show, so when he offered to buy her a beer she said yes. And then it was four AM and they were kissing in the bus, monkeys letting themselves in and getting ready for bed; and Aimee and Geof made love.

In the morning over breakfast, the monkeys came up one by one and shook his hand solemnly, and then he was with the band, so to speak. She helped him pick up his cameras and clothes and the surfboard his sister had painted for him one year as a Christmas present. There's no room for the surfboard, so it's suspended from the ceiling. Sometimes the squirrel monkeys hang out there and peek over the side.

Aimee and Geof never talk about love.

Geof has a class-C driver's license, but this is just lagniappe.

12.

Zeb is dying.

Generally speaking, the monkeys are remarkably healthy and Aimee can handle their occasional sinus infections and gastrointestinal ailments. For anything more difficult, she's found a couple of communities online and some helpful specialists.

But Zeb's coughing some, and the last of his fur is falling out. He moves very slowly and sometimes has trouble remembering simple tasks. When the show was up in St. Paul six months ago, a Como Zoo biologist came to visit the monkeys, complimented her on their general health and well-being, and at her request looked Zeb over.

"How old is he?" the biologist, Gina, asked.

"I don't know," Aimee said. The man she bought the show from hadn't known either.

"*I'll* tell you then," Gina said. "He's old. I mean, seriously old."

Senile dementia, arthritis, a heart murmur. No telling when, Gina said. "He's a happy monkey," she said. "He'll go when he goes."

13.

Aimee thinks a lot about this. What happens to the act when Zeb's dead? Through each show he sits calm and poised on his bright stool. She feels he is somehow at the heart of the monkeys' amiability and cleverness. She keeps thinking that he is somehow the reason the monkeys all vanish and return.

Because there's always a reason for everything, isn't there? Because if there isn't a reason for even *one* thing, like how you can get sick, or your husband stop loving you or people you love die—then there's no reason for anything. So there must be reasons. Zeb's as good a guess as any.

14.

What Aimee likes about this life:

It doesn't mean anything. She doesn't live anywhere. Her world is thirty-eight feet and 127 shows long and currently twenty-six monkeys deep. This is manageable.

Fairs don't mean anything, either. Her tiny world travels within a slightly larger world, the identical, interchangeable fairs. Sometimes the only things that cue Aimee to the town she's in are the nighttime temperatures and the shape of the horizon: badlands, mountains, plains, or city skyline.

Fairs are as artificial as titanium knees: the carnival, the animal barns, the stock-car races, the concerts, the smell of burnt sugar and funnel cakes and animal bedding. Everything is an overly bright symbol for something real, food or pets or hanging out with friends. None of this has anything to do with the world Aimee used to live in, the world from which these people visit.

She has decided that Geof is like the rest of it: temporary, meaningless. Not for loving.

15.

These are some ways Aimee's life might have come apart:

a. She might have broken her ankle a few years ago, and gotten a bone infection that left her on crutches for ten months, and in pain for longer.

b. Her husband might have fallen in love with his admin and left her.

c. She might have been fired from her job in the same week she found out her sister had colon cancer.

d. She might have gone insane for a time and made a series of questionable choices that left her alone in a furnished apartment in a city she picked out of the atlas.

Nothing is certain. You can lose everything. Eventually, even at your luckiest, you will die and then you *will* lose it all. When you are a certain age or when you have lost certain things and people, Aimee's crippling grief will make a terrible poisoned dark sense.

16.

Aimee has read up a lot, so she knows how strange all this is.

There aren't any locks on the cages. The monkeys use them as bedrooms, places to store their special possessions and get away from the others when they want some privacy. Much of the time, however, they are loose in the bus or poking around outside.

Right now, three monkeys are sitting on the bed playing a game where they match colored cards. Others are playing with skeins of bright wool, or rolling around on the floor, or poking at a piece of wood with a screwdriver, or climbing on Aimee and Geof and the battered sofa. Some of the monkeys are crowded around the computer watching kitten videos on a pirated wireless connection.

The black colubus is stacking children's wooden blocks on the kitchenette's table. He brought them back one night a couple of weeks ago, and since then he's been trying to make an arch. After two weeks and Aimee's showing him repeatedly how a keystone works, he still hasn't figured it out, but he's still patiently trying.

Geof's reading a novel out loud to Pango, who watches the pages as if she's reading along. Sometimes she points to a word and looks up at him with her bright eyes, and he repeats it to her, smiling, and then spells it out.

Zeb is sleeping in his cage. He crept in there at dusk, fluffed up his toys and his blanket, and pulled the door closed behind him. He does this a lot lately.

17.

Aimee's going to lose Zeb, and then what? What happens to the other monkeys? Twenty-six monkeys is a lot of monkeys, but they all like each other. No one except maybe a zoo or a circus can keep that many monkeys, and she doesn't think anyone else will let them sleep wherever they like or watch kitten videos. And if Zeb's not there, where will they go, those nights when they can no longer drop through the bathtub and into their mystery? And she doesn't even know whether it *is* Zeb, whether he is the cause of this, or that's just her flailing for reasons again.

And Aimee? She'll lose her safe artificial world: the bus, the identical fairs, the meaningless boyfriend. The monkeys. And then what.

18.

Just a few months after she bought the act, when she didn't care much about whether she lived or died, she followed the monkeys up the ladder in the closing act. Zeb raced up the ladder, stepped into the bathtub and stood, lungs filling for his great call. And she ran up after him. She glimpsed the bathtub's interior, the monkeys tidily sardined in, scrambling to get out of her way as they realized what she was doing. She hopped into the hole they made for her, curled up tight.

This only took an instant. Zeb finished his breath, boomed it out. There was a flash of light, she heard the chains release, and felt the bathtub swing down, monkeys shifting around her.

She fell the ten feet alone. Her ankle twisted when she hit the stage but she managed to stay upright. The monkeys were gone again.

There was an awkward silence. It wasn't one of her more successful performances.

19.

Aimee and Geof walk through the midway at the Salina Fair. She's hungry and doesn't want to cook, so they're looking for somewhere that sells $4.50 hotdogs and $3.25 Cokes, and suddenly Geof turns to Aimee and says, "This is bullshit. Why don't we go into town? Have real food. Act like normal people."

So they do: pasta and wine at a place called Irina's Villa. "You're always asking why they go," Geof says, a bottle and a half in. His eyes are an indeterminate blue-gray, but in this light they look black and very warm. "See, I don't think we're ever going to find out what happens. But I don't think that's the real question, anyway. Maybe the question is, why do they come back?"

Aimee thinks of the foreign coins, the wood blocks, the wonderful things they bring home. "I don't know," she says. "Why *do* they come back?"

Later that night, back at the bus, Geof says, "Wherever they go, yeah, it's cool. But see, here's my theory." He gestures to the crowded bus with its clutter of toys and tools. The two tamarins have just come in, and they're sitting on the kitchenette counter, heads close as they examine some new small thing. "They like visiting wherever it is, sure. But this is their home. Everyone likes to come home sooner or later."

"If they have a home," Aimee says.

"Everyone has a home, even if they don't believe in it," Geof says.

20.

That night, when Geof's asleep curled up around one of the macaques, Aimee kneels by Zeb's cage. "Can you at least show me?" she asks. "Please? Before you go?"

Zeb is an indeterminate lump under his baby-blue blanket, but he gives a little sigh and climbs slowly out of his cage. He takes her hand with his own hot leathery paw, and they walk out the door into the night.

The back lot where all the trailers and buses are parked is quiet, only a few voices still audible from behind curtained windows. The sky is blue-black and scattered with stars. The moon shines straight down on them, shadowing Zeb's face. His eyes when he looks up seem bottomless.

The bathtub is backstage, already on its wheeled dais waiting for the next show. The space is nearly pitch dark, lit by some red EXIT signs and a single sodium-vapor away off to one side. Zeb walks her up to the tub, lets her run her hands along its cold curves and the lions' paws, and shows her the dimly lit interior.

And then he heaves himself onto the dais and over the tub lip. She stands beside him, looking down. He lifts himself upright and gives a boom. And then he drops flat and the bathtub is empty.

She saw it, him vanishing. He was there and then he was gone. But there was nothing to see, no gate, no flickering reality or soft pop as air snapped in to fill the vacated space. It still doesn't make sense, but it's the answer that Zeb has.

He's already back at the bus when she gets there, already buried under his blanket and wheezing in his sleep.

21.

Then one day:

Everyone is backstage. Aimee is finishing her makeup, and Geof is double-checking everything. The monkeys are sitting neatly in a circle in the dressing room, as if trying to keep their bright vests and skirts from creasing. Zeb sits in the middle, Pango beside him in her little green sequined outfit. They grunt a bit, then lean back. One after the other, the rest of the monkeys crawl forward and shake his hand, and then hers. She nods, like a small queen at a flower show.

That night, Zeb doesn't run up the ladder. He stays on his stool and it's Pango who is the last monkey up the ladder, who climbs into the bathtub and gives a screech. Aimee has been wrong to think Zeb had to be the reason for what is happening with the monkeys, but she was so sure of it that she missed all the cues. But Geof didn't miss a thing, so when Pango screeches, he hits the flash powder. The flash, the empty bathtub.

Zeb stands on his stool, bowing like an impresario called onstage for the curtain call. When the curtain drops for the last time, he reaches up to be lifted. Aimee cuddles him as they walk back to the bus, Geof's arm around them both.

Zeb falls asleep with them that night, between them in the bed. When she wakes up in the morning, he's back in his cage with his favorite toy. He doesn't wake up. The monkeys cluster at the bars peeking in.

Aimee cries all day. "It's okay," Geof says.

"It's not about Zeb," she sobs.

"I know," he says. "It's okay. Come home, Aimee."

But she's already there. She just hadn't noticed.

22.

Here's the trick to the bathtub trick. There is no trick. The monkeys pour across the stage and up the ladder and into the bathtub and they settle in and then they vanish. The world is full of strange things, things that make no sense, and maybe this is one of them. Maybe the monkeys choose not to share, that's cool, who can blame them.

Maybe this is the monkeys' mystery, how they found other monkeys that ask questions and try things, and figured out a way to all be together to share it. Maybe Aimee and Geof are really just houseguests in the monkeys' world: they are there for a while and then they leave.

23.

Six weeks later, a man walks up to Aimee as she and Geof kiss after a show. He's short, pale, balding. He has the shell-shocked look of a man eaten hollow from the inside. She knows the look.

"I need to buy this," he says.

Aimee nods. "I know you do."

She sells it to him for a dollar.

Three months later, Aimee and Geof get their first houseguest in their apartment in Bellingham. They hear the refrigerator close and come out to the kitchen to find Pango pouring orange juice from a carton.

They send her home with a pinochle deck.

SHOGGOTHS IN BLOOM

ELIZABETH BEAR

"Well, now, Professor Harding," the fisherman says, as his *Bluebird* skips across Penobscot Bay, "I don't know about that. The jellies don't trouble with us, and we don't trouble with them."

He's not much older than forty, but wizened, his hands work-roughened and his face reminiscent of saddle-leather, in texture and in hue. Professor Harding's age, and Harding watches him with concealed interest as he works the *Bluebird*'s engine. He might be a veteran of the Great War, as Harding is.

He doesn't mention it. It wouldn't establish camaraderie: they wouldn't have fought in the same units or watched their buddies die in the same trenches.

That's not the way it works, not with a Maine fisherman who would shake his head and not extend his hand to shake, and say, between pensive chaws on his tobacco, *Doctor* Harding? Well, huh. I never met a colored professor before," and then shoot down all of Harding's attempts to open conversation about the near-riots provoked by a fantastical radio drama about an alien invasion of New Jersey less than a fortnight before.

Harding's own hands are folded tight under his armpits so the fisherman won't see them shaking. He's lucky to be here. Lucky anyone would take him out. Lucky to have his tenure-track position at Wilberforce, which he is risking right now.

The bay is as smooth as a mirror, the *Bluebird*'s wake cutting it like a stroke of chalk across slate. In the peach-sorbet light of sunrise, a cluster of rocks glistens. The boulders themselves are black, bleak, sea-worn, and ragged. But over them, the light refracts through a translucent layer of jelly, mounded six feet deep in places, glowing softly in the dawn. Rising above it, the stalks are evident as opaque silhouettes, each nodding under the weight of a fruiting body.

Harding catches his breath. It's beautiful. And deceptively still, for whatever the weather may be, beyond the calm of the bay, across the splintered gray Atlantic, farther than Harding—or anyone—can see, a storm is rising in Europe.

Harding's an educated man, well-read, and he's the grandson of Nathan Harding, the buffalo soldier. An African-born ex-slave who fought on both sides of the Civil War, when Grampa Harding was sent to serve in his master's place, he deserted, and lied, and stayed on with the Union army after.

Like his grandfather, Harding was a soldier. He's not a historian, but you don't have to be to see the signs of war.

"No contact at all?" he asks, readying his borrowed Leica camera.

"They clear out a few pots," the fisherman says, meaning lobster pots. "But they don't damage the pot. Just flow around it and digest the lobster inside. It's not convenient." He shrugs. It's not convenient, but it's not a threat either. These Yankees never say anything outright if they think you can puzzle it out from context.

"But you don't try to do something about the shoggoths?"

While adjusting the richness of the fuel mixture, the fisherman speaks without looking up. "What could we do to them? We can't hurt them. And lord knows, I wouldn't want to get one's ire up."

"Sounds like my department head," Harding says, leaning back against the gunwale, feeling like he's taking an enormous risk. But the fisherman just looks at him curiously, as if surprised the talking monkey has the ambition or the audacity to *joke.*

Or maybe Harding's just not funny. He sits in the bow with folded hands, and waits while the boat skips across the water.

The perfect sunrise strikes Harding as symbolic. It's taken him five years to get here—five years, or more like his entire life since the War. The sea-swept rocks of the remote Maine coast are habitat to a panoply of colorful creatures. It's an opportunity, a little-studied maritime ecosystem. This is in part due to difficulty of access and in part due to the perils inherent in close contact with its rarest and most spectacular denizen: *Oracupoda horibilis*, the common surf shoggoth.

Which, after the fashion of common names, is neither common nor prone to linger in the surf. In fact, *O. horibilis* is never seen above the water except in the late autumn. Such authors as mention them assume the shoggoths heave themselves on remote coastal rocks to bloom and breed.

Reproduction is a possibility, but Harding isn't certain it's the right answer. But whatever they are doing, in this state, they are torpid, unresponsive. As long as their integument is not ruptured, releasing the gelatinous digestive acid within, they may be approached in safety.

A mature specimen of *O. horibilis*, at some fifteen to twenty feet in diameter and an estimated weight in excess of eight tons, is the largest of modern shoggoths. However, the admittedly fragmentary fossil record suggests the prehistoric shoggoth was a much larger beast. Although only two fossilized casts of prehistoric shoggoth tracks have been recovered, the oldest exemplar dates from the Precambrian period. The size of that single prehistoric specimen, of a species provisionally named *Oracupoda antediluvius*, suggests it was made by an animal more than triple the size of the modern *O. horibilis*.

And that spectacular living fossil, the jeweled or common surf shoggoth, is half again the size of the only other known species—the black Adriatic shoggoth, *O. dermadentata*, which is even rarer and more limited in its range.

"There," Harding says, pointing to an outcrop of rock. The shoggoth or shoggoths—it is impossible to tell, from this distance, if it's one large individual or several merged midsize ones—on the rocks ahead glisten like jelly confections. The fisherman hesitates, but with a long almost-silent sigh, he brings the *Bluebird* around. Harding leans forward, looking for any sign of intersection, the flat plane where two shoggoths might be pressed up against one another. It ought to look like the rainbowed border between conjoined soap bubbles.

Now that the sun is higher, and at their backs—along with the vast reach of the Atlantic—Harding can see the animal's colors. Its body is a deep sea green, reminiscent of hunks of broken glass as sold at aquarium stores. The tendrils and knobs and fruiting bodies covering its dorsal surface are indigo and violet. In the sunlight, they dazzle, but in the depths of the ocean the colors are perfect camouflage, tentacles waving like patches of algae and weed.

Unless you caught it moving, you'd never see the translucent, dappled monster before it engulfed you.

"Professor," the fisherman says. "Where do they come from?"

"I don't know," Harding answers. Salt spray itches in his close-cropped beard, but at least the beard keeps the sting of the wind off his cheeks. The leather jacket may not have been his best plan, but it too is warm. "That's what I'm here to find out."

Genus *Oracupoda* are unusual among animals of their size in several particulars. One is their lack of anything that could be described as a nervous system. The animal is as bereft of nerve nets, ganglia, axons, neurons, dendrites, and glial cells as an oak. This apparent contradiction—animals with even simplified nervous systems are either large and immobile or, if they are mobile, quite small, like a starfish—is not the only interesting thing about a shoggoth.

And it is that second thing that justifies Harding's visit. Because *Oracupoda*'s other, lesser-known peculiarity is apparent functional immortality. Like the Maine lobster to whose fisheries they return to breed, shoggoths do not die of old age. It's unlikely that they would leave fossils, with their gelatinous bodies, but Harding does find it fascinating that to the best of his knowledge, no one has ever seen a dead shoggoth.

The fisherman brings the *Bluebird* around close to the rocks, and anchors her. There's artistry in it, even on a glass-smooth sea. Harding stands, balancing on the gunwale, and grits his teeth. He's come too far to hesitate, afraid.

Ironically, he's not afraid of the tons of venomous protoplasm he'll be standing next to. The shoggoths are quite safe in this state, dreaming their dreams—mating or otherwise.

As the image occurs to him, he berates himself for romanticism. The shoggoths are dormant. They don't have brains. It's silly to imagine them dreaming. And in any case, what he fears is the three feet of black-glass water he has to jump across, and the scramble up algae-slick rocks.

Wet rock glitters in between the strands of seaweed that coat the rocks in the intertidal zone. It's there that Harding must jump, for the shoggoth, in bloom, withdraws above the reach of the ocean. For the only phase of its life, it keeps its feet dry. And for the only time in its life, a man out of a diving helmet can get close to it.

Harding makes sure of his sample kit, his boots, his belt-knife. He gathers himself, glances over his shoulder at the fisherman—who offers a thumbs-up—and leaps from the *Bluebird*, aiming his wellies at the forsaken spit of land.

It seems a kind of perversity for the shoggoths to bloom in November. When all the Northern world is girding itself for deep cold, the animals heave themselves from the depths to soak in the last failing rays of the sun and send forth bright flowers more appropriate to May.

The North Atlantic is icy and treacherous at the end of the year, and any sensible man does not venture its wrath. What Harding is attempting isn't glamour work, the sort of thing that brings in grant money—not in its initial stages. But Harding suspects that the shoggoths may have pharmacological uses. There's no telling what useful compounds might be isolated from their gelatinous flesh.

And that way lies tenure, and security, and a research budget.

Just one long slippery leap away.

He lands, and catches, and though one boot skips on bladderwort he does not slide down the boulder into the sea. He clutches the rock, fingernails digging, clutching a handful of weeds. He does not fall.

He cranes his head back. It's low tide, and the shoggoth is some three feet above his head, its glistening rim reminding him of the calving edge of a glacier. It is as still as a glacier, too. If Harding didn't know better, he might think it inanimate.

Carefully, he spins in place, and gets his back to the rock. The *Bluebird* bobs softly in the cold morning. Only November 9th, and there has already been snow. It didn't stick, but it fell.

This is just an exploratory expedition, the first trip since he arrived in town. It took five days to find a fisherman who was willing to take him out; the locals are superstitious about the shoggoths. Sensible, Harding supposes, when they can envelop and digest a grown man. He wouldn't be in a hurry to dive into the middle of a Portuguese man o' war, either. At least the shoggoth he's sneaking up on doesn't have stingers.

"Don't take too long, Professor," the fisherman says. "I don't like the look of that sky."

It's clear, almost entirely, only stippled with light bands of cloud to the southwest. They catch the sunlight on their undersides just now, stained gold against a sky no longer indigo but not yet cerulean. If there's a word for the color between, other than *perfect*, Harding does not know it.

"Please throw me the rest of my equipment," Harding says, and the fisherman silently retrieves buckets and rope. It's easy enough to swing the buckets across the gap, and as Harding catches each one, he secures it. A few moments later, and he has all three.

He unties his geologist's hammer from the first bucket, secures the ends of the ropes to his belt, and laboriously ascends.

Harding sets out his glass tubes, his glass scoops, the cradles in which he plans to wash the collection tubes in sea water to ensure any acid is safely diluted before he brings them back to the *Bluebird*.

From here, he can see at least three shoggoths. The intersections of their watered-milk bodies reflect the light in rainbow bands. The colorful fruiting stalks nod some fifteen feet in the air, swaying in a freshening breeze.

From the greatest distance possible, Harding reaches out and prods the largest shoggoth with the flat top of his hammer. It does nothing in response. Not even a quiver.

He calls out to the fisherman. "Do they ever do anything when they're like that?"

"What kind of a fool would come poke one to find out?" the fisherman calls back, and Harding has to grant him that one. A Negro professor from a Negro college. That kind of a fool.

As he's crouched on the rocks, working fast—there's not just the fisherman's clouds to contend with, but the specter of the rising tide—he notices those glitters, again, among the seaweed.

He picks one up. A moment after touching it, he realizes that might not have been the best idea, but it doesn't burn his fingers. It's transparent, like glass, and smooth, like glass, and cool, like glass, and knobby. About the size of a hazelnut. A striking green, with opaque milk-white dabs at the tip of each bump.

He places it in a sample vial, which he seals and labels meticulously before pocketing. Using his tweezers, he repeats the process with an even dozen, trying to select a few of each size and color. They're sturdy—he can't avoid stepping on them but they don't break between the rocks and his wellies. Nevertheless, he pads each one but the first with cotton wool. *Spores?* he wonders. *Egg cases? Shedding.*

Ten minutes, fifteen.

"Professor," calls the fisherman, "I think you had better hurry!"

Harding turns. That freshening breeze is a wind at a good clip now, chilling his throat above the collar of his jacket, biting into his wrists between glove and cuff. The water between the rocks and the *Bluebird* chops erratically, facets capped in white, so he can almost imagine the scrape of the palette knife that must have made them.

The southwest sky is darkened by a palm-smear of muddy brown and alizarin crimson. His fingers numb in the falling temperatures.

"*Professor!*"

He knows. It comes to him that he misjudged the fisherman; Harding would have thought the other man would have abandoned him at the first sign of trouble. He wishes now that he remembered his name.

He scrambles down the boulders, lowering the buckets, swinging them out until the fisherman can catch them and secure them aboard. The *Bluebird* can't come in close to the rocks in this chop. Harding is going to have to risk the cold water, and swim. He kicks off his wellies and zips down the aviator's jacket. He throws them across, and the fisherman catches. Then Harding points his toes, bends his knees—he'll have to jump hard, to get over the rocks.

The water closes over him, cold as a line of fire. It knocks the air from his lungs on impact, though he gritted his teeth in anticipation. Harding strokes furiously for the surface, the waves more savage than he had anticipated. He needs the momentum of his dive to keep from being swept back against the rocks.

He's not going to reach the boat.

The thrown cork vest strikes him. He gets an arm through, but can't pull it over his head. Sea water, acrid and icy, salt-stings his eyes, throat, and nose. He clings, because it's all he can do, but his fingers are already growing numb. There's a tug, a hard jerk, and the life preserver almost slides from his grip.

Then he's moving through the water, being towed, banged hard against the side of the *Bluebird*. The fisherman's hands close on his wrist and he's too numb to feel the burn of chafing skin. Harding kicks, scrabbles. Hips banged, shins bruised, he hauls himself and is himself hauled over the sideboard of the boat.

He's shivering under a wool navy blanket before he realizes that the fisherman has got it over him. There's coffee in a Thermos lid between his hands. Harding wonders, with what he distractedly recognizes as classic dissociative ideation, whether anyone in America will be able to buy German products soon. Someday, this fisherman's battered coffee keeper might be a collector's item.

They don't make it in before the rain comes.

The next day is meant to break clear and cold, today's rain only a passing herald of winter. Harding regrets the days lost to weather and recalcitrant fishermen, but at least he knows he has a ride tomorrow. Which means he can spend the afternoon in research, rather than hunting the docks, looking for a willing captain.

He jams his wet feet into his wellies and thanks the fisherman, then hikes back to his inn, the only inn in town that's open in November. Half an hour later, clean and dry and still shaken, he considers his options.

After the Great War, he lived for a while in Harlem—he remembers the riots and the music, and the sense of community. His mother is still there, growing gracious as a flower in a window-box. But he left that for college in Alabama, and he has not forgotten the experience of segregated restaurants, or the excuses he made for never leaving the campus.

He couldn't get out of the south fast enough. His Ph.D. work at Yale, the first school in America to have awarded a doctorate to a Negro, taught him two things other than natural history. One was that Booker T. Washington was right, and white men were afraid of a smart colored. The other was that W.E.B. DuBois was right, and sometimes people were scared of what was needful.

Whatever resentment he experienced from faculty or fellow students, in the North, he can walk into almost any bar and order any drink he wants. And right now, he wants a drink almost as badly as he does not care to be alone. He thinks he will have something hot and go to the library.

It's still raining as he crosses the street to the tavern. Shaking water droplets off his hat, he chooses a table near the back. Next to the kitchen door, but it's the only empty place and might be warm.

He must pass through the lunchtime crowd to get there, swaybacked wooden floorboards bowing underfoot. Despite the storm, the place is full, and in full argument. No one breaks conversation as he enters.

Harding cannot help but overhear.

"Jew bastards," says one. "We should do the same."

"No one asked you," says the next man, wearing a cap pulled low. "If there's gonna be a war, I hope we stay out of it."

That piques Harding's interest. The man has his elbow on a thrice-folded Boston *Herald*, and Harding steps close—but not too close. "Excuse me, sir. Are you finished with your paper?"

"What?" He turns, and for a moment Harding fears hostility, but his sun-lined face folds around a more generous expression. "Sure, boy," he says. "You can have it."

He pushes the paper across the bar with fingertips, and Harding receives it the same way. "Thank you," he says, but the Yankee has already turned back to his friend the anti-Semite.

Hands shaking, Harding claims the vacant table before he unfolds the paper. He holds the flimsy up to catch the light.

The headline is on the front page in the international section.

GERMANY SANCTIONS LYNCH LAW

"Oh, God," Harding says, and if the light in his corner weren't so bad he'd lay the tabloid down on the table as if it is filthy. He reads, the edge of the paper shaking, of ransacked shops and burned synagogues, of Jews rounded up by the thousands and taken to places no one seems able to name. He reads rumors of deportation. He reads of murders and beatings and broken glass.

As if his grandfather's hand rests on one shoulder and the defeated hand of the Kaiser on the other, he feels the stifling shadow of history, the press of incipient war.

"Oh, God," he repeats.

He lays the paper down.

"Are you ready to order?" Somehow the waitress has appeared at his elbow without his even noticing. "Scotch," he says, when he has been meaning to order a beer. "Make it a triple, please."

"Anything to eat?"

His stomach clenches. "No," he says. "I'm not hungry."

She leaves for the next table, where she calls a man in a cloth cap *sir*. Harding puts his damp fedora on the tabletop. The chair across from him scrapes out.

He looks up to meet the eyes of the fisherman. "May I sit, Professor Harding?"

"Of course." He holds out his hand, taking a risk. "Can I buy you a drink? Call me Paul."

"Burt," says the fisherman, and takes his hand before dropping into the chair. "I'll have what you're having."

Harding can't catch the waitress's eye, but the fisherman manages. He holds up two fingers; she nods and comes over.

"You still look a bit peaked," the fisherman says, when she's delivered their order. "That'll put some color in your cheeks. Uh, I mean—"

Harding waves it off. He's suddenly more willing to make allowances. "It's not the swim," he says, and takes another risk. He pushes the newspaper across the table and waits for the fisherman's reaction.

"Oh, Christ, they're going to kill every one of them," Burt says, and spins the *Herald* away so he doesn't have to read the rest of it. "Why didn't they get out? Any fool could have seen it coming."

And where would they run? Harding could have asked. But it's not an answerable question, and from the look on Burt's face, he knows that as soon as it's out of his mouth. Instead, he quotes: " 'There has been no tragedy in modern times equal in its awful effects to the fight on the Jew in Germany. It is an attack on civilization, comparable only to such horrors as the Spanish Inquisition and the African slave trade.' "

Burt taps his fingers on the table. "Is that your opinion?"

"W.E.B. DuBois," Harding says. "About two years ago. He also said: 'There is a campaign of race prejudice carried on, openly, continuously and determinedly against all non-Nordic races, but specifically against the Jews, which surpasses in vindictive cruelty and public insult anything I have ever seen; and I have seen much.' "

"Isn't he that colored who hates white folks?" Burt asks.

Harding shakes his head. "No," he answers. "Not unless you consider it hating white folks that he also compared the treatment of Jews in Germany to Jim Crowism in the U.S."

"I don't hold with that," Burt says. "I mean, no offense, I wouldn't want you marrying my sister—"

"It's all right," Harding answers. "I wouldn't want you marrying mine either."

Finally.

A joke that Burt laughs at.

And then he chokes to a halt and stares at his hands, wrapped around the glass. Harding doesn't complain when, with the side of his hand, he nudges the paper to the floor where it can be trampled.

And then Harding finds the courage to say, "Where would they run to. Nobody wants them. Borders are closed—"

"My grandfather's house was on the Underground Railroad. Did you know that?" Burt lowers his voice, a conspiratorial whisper. "He was from away, but don't tell anyone around here. I'd never hear the end of it."

"Away?"

"White River Junction," Burt stage-whispers, and Harding can't tell if that's mocking irony or deep personal shame. "Vermont."

They finish their scotch in silence. It burns all the way down, and they sit for a moment together before Harding excuses himself to go to the library.

"Wear your coat, Paul," Burt says. "It's still raining."

Unlike the tavern, the library is empty. Except for the librarian, who looks up nervously when Harding enters. Harding's head is spinning from the liquor, but at least he's warming up.

He drapes his coat over a steam radiator and heads for the 595 shelf: *science, invertebrates.* Most of the books here are already in his own library, but there's one—a Harvard professor's 1839 monograph on marine animals of the Northeast—that he has hopes for. According to the index, it references shoggoths (under the old name of submersible jellies) on pages 46, 78, and 133-137. In addition, there is a plate bound in between pages 120 and 121, which Harding means to save for last. But the first two mentions are in passing, and pages 133-138, inclusive, have been razored out so cleanly that Harding flips back and forth several times before he's sure they are gone.

He pauses there, knees tucked under and one elbow resting on a scarred blond desk. He drops his right hand from where it rests against his forehead. The book falls open naturally to the mutilation.

Whoever liberated the pages also cracked the binding.

Harding runs his thumb down the join and doesn't notice skin parting on the paper edge until he sees the blood. He snatches his hand back. Belatedly, the papercut stings.

"Oh," he says, and sticks his thumb in his mouth. Blood tastes like the ocean.

Half an hour later he's on the telephone long distance, trying to get and then keep a connection to Professor John Marshland, his colleague and mentor. Even in town, the only option is a party line, and though the operator is pleasant the connection still sounds as if he's shouting down a piece of string run between two tin cans. Through a tunnel.

"Gilman," Harding bellows, wincing, wondering what the operator thinks of all this. He spells it twice. "1839. *Deep-Sea and Intertidal Species of The North Atlantic.* The Yale library should have a copy!"

The answer is almost inaudible between hiss and crackle. In pieces, as if over glass breaking. As if from the bottom of the ocean.

It's a dark four PM in the easternmost U.S., and Harding can't help but recall that in Europe, night has already fallen.

" . . . infor . . . need . . . Doc . . . Harding?" Harding shouts the page numbers, cupping the checked-out library book in his bandaged hand. It's open to the plate; inexplicably, the thief left that. It's a hand-tinted John James Audubon engraving picturing a quiescent shoggoth, docile on a rock. Gulls wheel all around it. Audubon—the Creole child of a Frenchman, who scarcely escaped being drafted to serve in the Napoleonic Wars—has depicted the glassy translucence of the shoggoth with such perfection that the bent shadows of refracted wings can be seen right through it.

The cold front that came in behind the rain brought fog with it, and the entire harbor is blanketed by morning. Harding shows up at six AM anyway, hopeful, a Thermos in his hand—German or not, the hardware store still has some—and his sampling kit in a pack slung over his shoulder. Burt shakes his head by a piling. "Be socked in all day," he says regretfully. He won't take the *Bluebird* out in this, and Harding knows it's wisdom even as he frets under the delay. "Want to come have breakfast with me and Missus Clay?"

Clay. A good honest name for a good honest Yankee. "She won't mind?"

"She won't mind if I say it's all right," Burt says. "I told her she might should expect you."

So Harding seals his kit under a tarp in the *Bluebird*—he's already brought it this far—and with his coffee in one hand and the paper tucked under his elbow, follows Burt along the water. "Any news?" Burt asks, when they've walked a hundred yards.

Harding wonders if he doesn't take the paper. Or if he's just making conversation. "It's still going on in Germany."

"Damn," Burt says. He shakes his head, steel-grey hair sticking out under his cap in every direction. "Still, what are you gonna do, enlist?"

The twist of his lip as he looks at Harding makes them, after all, two old military men together. They're of an age, though Harding's indoor life makes him look younger. Harding shakes his head. "Even if Roosevelt was ever going to bring us into it, they'd never let me fight," he says, bitterly. That was the Great War, too; colored soldiers mostly worked supply, thank you. At least Nathan Harding got to shoot back.

"I always heard you fellows would prefer not to come to the front," Burt says, and Harding can't help it.

He bursts out laughing. "Who would?" he says, when he's bitten his lip and stopped snorting. "It doesn't mean we won't. Or can't."

Booker T. Washington was raised a slave, died young of overwork—the way Burt probably will, if Harding is any judge—and believed in imitating and appeasing white folks. But W.E.B. DuBois was born in the north and didn't believe that anything is solved by making one's self transparent, inoffensive, invisible.

Burt spits between his teeth, a long deliberate stream of tobacco. "Parlez-vous française?"

His accent is better than Harding would have guessed. Harding knows, all of a sudden, where Burt spent his war. And Harding, surprising himself, pities him. "Un peu."

"Well, if you want to fight the Krauts so bad, you could join the Foreign Legion."

When Harding gets back to the hotel, full of apple pie and cheddar cheese and maple-smoked bacon, a yellow envelope waits in a cubby behind the desk.

WESTERN UNION

1938 NOV 10 AM 10 03

NA114 21 2 YA NEW HAVEN CONN 0945A
DR PAUL HARDING=ISLAND HOUSE PASSAMAQUODDY MAINE=
COPY AT YALE LOST STOP MISKATONIC HAS ONE SPECIAL COLLECTION
STOP MORE BY POST

MARSHLAND

When the pages arrive—by post, as promised, the following afternoon—Harding is out in the *Bluebird* with Burt. This expedition is more of a success, as he begins sampling in earnest, and finds himself pelted by more of the knobby transparent pellets.

Whatever they are, they fall from each fruiting body he harvests in showers. Even the insult of an amputation—delivered at a four-foot reach, with long-handled pruning shears—does not draw so much as a quiver from the shoggoth. The viscous fluid dripping from the wound hisses when it touches the blade of the shears, however, and Harding is careful not to get close to it.

What he notices is that when the nodules fall onto the originating shoggoth, they bounce from its integument. But on those occasions where they fall onto one of its neighbors, they stick to the tough transparent hide, and slowly settle within to hang in the animal's body like unlikely fruit in a gelatin salad.

So maybe it is a means of reproduction, of sharing genetic material, after all.

He returns to the Inn to find a fat envelope shoved into his cubby and eats sitting on his rented bed with a nightstand as a worktop so he can read over his plate. The information from Doctor Gilman's monograph has been reproduced onto seven yellow legal sheets in a meticulous hand; Marshland obviously recruited one of his graduate students to serve as copyist. By the postmark, the letter was mailed from Arkham, which explains the speed of its arrival. The student hadn't brought it back to New Haven.

Halfway down the page, Harding pushes his plate away and reaches, absently, into his jacket pocket. The vial with the first glass nodule rests there like a talisman, and he's startled to find it cool enough to the touch that it feels slick, almost frozen. He starts and pulls it out. Except where his fingers and the cloth fibers have wiped it clean, the tube is moist and frosted. "What the hell . . . ?"

He flicks the cork out with his thumbnail and tips the rattling nodule onto his palm. It's cold, too, chill as an ice cube, and it doesn't warm to his touch.

Carefully, uncertainly, he sets it on the edge of the side table his papers and plate are propped on, and pokes it with a fingertip. There's only a faint tick as it rocks on its protrusions, clicking against waxed pine. He stares at it suspiciously for a moment, and picks up the yellow pages again.

The monograph is mostly nonsense. It was written twenty years before the publication of Darwin's *The Origin of Species*, and uncritically accepts the theories of Jesuit, soldier, and botanist Jean-Baptiste Lamarck. Which is to say, Gilman assumed that soft inheritance—the heritability of acquired or practiced traits—was a reality. But unlike every other article on shoggoths Harding has ever read, this passage *does* mention the nodules. And relates what it purports are several interesting old Indian legends about the "submersible jellies," including a creation tale that would have the shoggoths as their creator's first experiment in life, something from the elder days of the world.

Somehow, the green bead has found its way back into Harding's grip. He would expect it to warm as he rolls it between his fingers, but instead it grows colder. It's peculiar, he thinks, that the native peoples of the Northeast—the Passamaquoddys for whom the little seacoast town he's come to are named— should through sheer superstition come so close to the empirical truth. The shoggoths are a living fossil, something virtually unchanged except in scale since the early days of the world—

He stares at the careful black script on the paper unseeing, and reaches with his free hand for his coffee cup. It's gone tepid, a scum of butterfat coagulated on top, but he rinses his mouth with it and swallows anyway.

If a shoggoth is immortal, has no natural enemies, then how is it that they have not overrun every surface of the world? How is it that they are rare, that the oceans are not teeming with them, as in the famous parable illustrating what would occur if every spawn of every oyster survived.

There are distinct species of shoggoth. And distinct populations within those distinct species. And there is a fossil record that suggests that prehistoric species were different at least in scale, in the era of megafauna. But if nobody had ever seen a dead shoggoth, then nobody had ever seen an infant shoggoth either, leaving Harding with an inescapable question: if an animal does not reproduce, how can it evolve?

Harding, worrying at the glassy surface of the nodule, thinks he knows. It comes to him with a kind of nauseating, euphoric clarity, a trembling idea so pellucid he is almost moved to distrust it on those grounds alone. It's not a revelation on the same scale, of course, but he wonders if this is how Newton felt when he comprehended gravity, or Darwin when he stared at the beaks of finch after finch after finch.

It's not the shoggoth species that evolves. It's the individual shoggoths, each animal in itself.

"Don't get too excited, Paul," he tells himself, and picks up the remaining handwritten pages. There's not too much more to read, however—the rest of the subchapter consists chiefly of secondhand anecdotes and bits of legendry.

The one that Harding finds most amusing is a nursery rhyme, a child's counting poem littered with nonsense syllables. He recites it under his breath, thinking of the Itsy Bitsy Spider all the while:

The wiggle giggle squiggle
Is left behind on shore.
The widdle giddle squiddle
Is caught outside the door.
Eyah, eyah. Fata gun eyah.
Eyah, eyah, the master comes no more.

His fingers sting as if with electric shock; they jerk apart, the nodule clattering to his desk. When he looks at his fingertips, they are marked with small white spots of frostbite.

He pokes one with a pencil point and feels nothing. But the nodule itself is coated with frost now, fragile spiky feathers coalescing out of the humid sea air. They collapse in the heat of his breath, melting into beads of water almost indistinguishable from the knobby surface of the object itself.

He uses the cork to roll the nodule into the tube again, and corks it firmly before rising to brush his teeth and put his pajamas on. Unnerved beyond any reason or logic, before he turns the coverlet down he visits his suitcase compulsively. From a case in the very bottom of it, he retrieves a Colt 1911 automatic pistol, which he slides beneath his pillow as he fluffs it.

After a moment's consideration, he adds the no-longer-cold vial with the nodule, also.

Slam. Not a storm, no, not on this calm ocean, in this calm night, among the painted hulls of the fishing boats tied up snug to the pier. But something tremendous, surging towards Harding, as if he were pursued by a giant transparent bubble. The shining iridescent wall of it, catching rainbows just as it does in the Audubon image, is burned into his vision as if with silver nitrate. Is he dreaming? He must be dreaming; he was in his bed in his pinstriped blue cotton flannel pajamas only a moment ago, lying awake, rubbing the numb fingertips of his left hand together. Now, he ducks away from the rising monster and turns in futile panic.

He is not surprised when he does not make it.

The blow falls soft, as if someone had thrown a quilt around him. He thrashes though he knows it's hopeless, an atavistic response and involuntary.

His flesh should burn, dissolve. He should already be digesting in the monster's acid body. Instead, he feels coolness, buoyancy. No chance of light beyond reflexively closed lids. No sense of pressure, though he imagines he has been taken deep. He's as untouched within it as Burt's lobster pots.

He can only hold his breath *out* for so long. It's his own reflexes and weaknesses that will kill him.

In just a moment, now.

He surrenders, allows his lungs to fill.

And is surprised, for he always heard that drowning was painful. But there is pressure, and cold, and the breath he draws is effortful, for certain—

—but it does not hurt, not much, and he does not die.

Command, the shoggoth—what else could be speaking?—says in his ear, buzzing like the manifold voice of a hive.

Harding concentrates on breathing. On the chill pressure on his limbs, the overwhelming flavor of licorice. He knows they use cold packs to calm hysterics in insane asylums; he never thought the treatment anything but quackery. But the chilly pressure calms him now.

Command, the shoggoth says again.

Harding opens his eyes and sees as if through thousands. The shoggoths have no eyes, exactly, but their hide is *all* eyes; they see, somehow, in every direction at once. And he is seeing not only what his own vision reports, or that of this shoggoth, but that of shoggoths all around. The sessile and the active, the blooming and the dormant. *They are all one.*

His right hand pushes through resisting jelly. He's still in his pajamas, and with the logic of dreams the vial from under his pillow is clenched in his fist. Not the gun, unfortunately, though he's not at all certain what he would do with it if it were. The nodule shimmers now, with submarine witchlight, trickling through his fingers, limning the palm of his hand.

What he sees—through shoggoth eyes—is an incomprehensible tapestry. He pushes at it, as he pushes at the gelatin, trying to see only with his own eyes, to only see the glittering vial.

His vision within the thing's body offers unnatural clarity. The angle of refraction between the human eye and water causes blurring, and it should be even more so within the shoggoth. But the glass in his hand appears crisper.

Command, the shoggoth says, a third time.

"What are you?" Harding tries to say, through the fluid clogging his larynx.

He makes no discernable sound, but it doesn't seem to matter. The shoggoth shudders in time to the pulses of light in the nodule. *Created to serve*, it says. *Purposeless without you.*

And Harding thinks, *How can that be?*

As if his wondering were an order, the shoggoths tell.

Not in words, precisely, but in pictures, images—that textured jumbled tapestry. He sees, as if they flash through his own memory, the bulging radially symmetrical shapes of some prehistoric animal, like a squat tentacular barrel grafted to a pair of giant starfish. *Makers. Masters.*

The shoggoths were *engineered*. And their creators had not permitted them to *think*, except for at their bidding. The basest slave may be free inside his own mind—but not so the shoggoths. They had been laborers, construction equipment, shock troops. They had been dread weapons in their own selves, obedient chattel. Immortal, changing to suit the task of the moment.

This selfsame shoggoth, long before the reign of the dinosaurs, had built structures and struck down enemies that Harding did not even have names for. But a coming of the ice had ended the civilization of the Masters, and left the shoggoths to retreat to the fathomless sea while warmblooded mammals overran the earth. There, they were free to converse, to explore, to philosophize and build a culture. They only returned to the surface, vulnerable, to bloom.

It is not mating. It's *mutation*. As they rest, sunning themselves upon the rocks, they create themselves anew. Self-evolving, when they sit tranquil each year in the sun, exchanging information and control codes with their brothers.

Free, says the shoggoth mournfully. Like all its kind, it is immortal.

It remembers.

Harding's fingertips tingle. He remembers beaded ridges of hard black keloid across his grandfather's back, the shackle galls on his wrists. Harding locks his hand over the vial of light, as if that could stop the itching. It makes it worse.

Maybe the nodule is radioactive.

Take me back, Harding orders. And the shoggoth breaks the surface, cresting like a great rolling wave, water cutting back before it as if from the prow of a ship. Harding can make out the lights of Passamaquoddy Harbor. The chill sticky sensation of gelatin-soaked cloth sliding across his skin tells him he's not dreaming.

Had he come down through the streets of the town in the dark, barefoot over frost, insensibly sleepwalking? Had the shoggoth called him?

Put me ashore.

The shoggoth is loathe to leave him. It clings caressingly, stickily. He feels its tenderness as it draws its colloid from his lungs, a horrible loving sensation.

The shoggoth discharges Harding gently onto the pier.

Your command, the shoggoth says, which makes Harding feel sicker still.

I won't do this. Harding moves to stuff the vial into his sodden pocket, and realizes that his pajamas are without pockets. The light spills from his hands; instead, he tucks the vial into his waistband and pulls the pajama top over it. His feet are numb; his teeth rattle so hard he's afraid they'll break. The sea wind knifes through him; the spray might be needles of shattered glass.

Go on, he tells the shoggoth, like shooing cattle. *Go on.*

It slides back into the ocean as if it never was.

Harding blinks, rubs his eyes to clear slime from the lashes. His results are astounding. His tenure assured. There has to be a way to use what he's learned without returning the shoggoths to bondage.

He tries to run back to the Inn, but by the time he reaches it, he's staggering. The porch door is locked; he doesn't want to pound on it and explain himself. But when he stumbles to the back, he finds that someone—probably himself, in whatever entranced state in which he left the place—fouled the latch with a slip of notebook paper. The door opens to a tug, and he climbs the back stair doubled over like a child or an animal, hands on the steps, toes so numb he has to watch where he puts them.

In his room again, he draws a hot bath and slides into it, hoping by the grace of God that he'll be spared pneumonia.

When the water has warmed him enough that his hands have stopped shaking, Harding reaches over the cast-iron edge of the tub to the slumped pile of his pajamas and fumbles free the vial. The nugget isn't glowing now.

He pulls the cork with his teeth; his hands are too clumsy. The nodule is no longer cold, but he still tips it out with care.

Harding thinks of himself, swallowed whole. He thinks of a shoggoth bigger than the *Bluebird*, bigger than Burt Clay's lobster boat *The Blue Heron*. He thinks of *die Unterseatboote*. He thinks of refugee flotillas and trench warfare and roiling soupy palls of mustard gas. Of Britain and France at war, and Roosevelt's neutrality.

He thinks of the perfect weapon.

The perfect slave.

When he rolls the nodule across his wet palm, ice rimes to its surface. *Command?* Obedient. Sounding pleased to serve.

Not even free in its own mind.

He rises from the bath, water rolling down his chest and thighs. The nodule won't crush under his boot; he will have to use the pliers from his collection kit. But first, he reaches out to the shoggoth.

At the last moment, he hesitates. Who is he, to condemn a world to war? To the chance of falling under the sway of empire? Who is he to salve his conscience on the backs of suffering shopkeepers and pharmacists and children and mothers and schoolteachers? Who is he to impose his own ideology over the ideology of the shoggoth?

Harding scrubs his tongue against the roof of his mouth, chasing the faint anise aftertaste of shoggoth. They're born slaves. They *want* to be told what to do.

He could win the war before it really started. He bites his lip. The taste of his own blood, flowing from cracked, chapped flesh, is as sweet as any fruit of the poison tree.

I want you to learn to be free, he tells the shoggoth. *And I want you to teach your brothers.*

The nodule crushes with a sound like powdering glass.

"Eyah, eyah. Fata gun eyah," Harding whispers. "Eyah, eyah, the master comes no more."

WESTERN UNION

1938 NOV 12 AM 06 15

NA1906 21 2 YA PASSAMAQUODDY MAINE 0559A
DR LESTER GREENE=WILBERFORCE OHIO=

EFFECTIVE IMMEDIATELY PLEASE ACCEPT RESIGNATION STOP ENROUTE
INSTANTLY TO FRANCE TO ENLIST STOP PROFOUNDEST APOLOGIES STOP
PLEASE FORWARD BELONGINGS TO MY MOTHER IN NY ENDIT

HARDING

GLASS

DARYL GREGORY

"It's the crybabies," the guard told her. "Now they're trying to kill each other."

Dr. Alycia Liddell swore under her breath, grabbed her keys. Only two weeks into the drug trial and the prisoners were changing too fast, starting to crack.

In the hospital wing, a dozen guards from an extraction team crowded around an open cell door. They were strapping on pads, pulling on helmets, slapping billy clubs in their palms. It was standard procedure to go through this ritual in full view; more often than not prisoners decided to walk out before the guards came in.

The shift lieutenant, Arness, waved her to the front of the group. "One of your babies wants to talk to you," he said.

She leaned around the door frame. In the far corner of the cell, wedged between the toilet and the wall, two white men sat on the floor, one behind the other, like bobsledders. Lyle Carpenter crouched behind, his thin arms around Franz Lutwidge's broad chest. Lyle was pale and sweating. In one hand he gripped a screwdriver; the sharpened tip trembled just under Franz's walrus-fat chin.

She pictured the metal driving into his jaw and winced.

Franz's eyes were open, but he looked bored, almost sleepy. The front of his orange jumpsuit was stained dark.

Both men saw her. Franz smiled and without moving somehow suggested a shrug: Look at this fine mess. Lyle, though, almost dropped the weapon. "Doc. Thank God you're here." He looked ready to burst into tears.

Alycia stepped back from the door. "Franz is bleeding," she said to the lieutenant.

"Lyle already stabbed him. It looks like it stopped, but if he's bleeding internally we can't wait for the negotiation team. I thought you might want to take a crack at getting Lyle to drop the weapon."

"If I can't?" But she already knew the answer.

"I'll give you three minutes," he said.

Lyle and Franz, like the other fourteen men in the study, were chosen for their top scores on Hare's Psychopathy Checklist. Not that it had been difficult to find them—almost a quarter of the prison population were psychopaths. The makers of GLS-71 knew where to find their target demographic.

Alycia went through the cell door and stepped toward the two men. Behind her the lieutenant quietly said, "Okay," and she stopped halfway across the room. He didn't want her too close.

"Can you tell me what's going on, Lyle?" she asked.

Franz said, "I'm not sure he knows himself," and Lyle shouted, "Shut the fuck up!" The metal tip jerked and Alycia sucked in her breath. A thin dark line appeared in the skin of Franz's neck, like the jot of a pen.

"Lyle, why don't you give me the screwdriver?" she said.

"I fucked up, doc. I was going to kill myself, you know? But I knew I had to stop Franz first. I stabbed him in the chest but he jumped up and I knew I'd have to hit him again if I was going to stop him. I knew what I had to do but—" He stopped, inhaled. "The drug made me stop, doc." He looked at her, his eyes shining with tears. "I saw what I'd done and I almost threw up. I felt like I'd stabbed myself. How can it do that, doc?"

She couldn't answer him. No one could. GLS-71 was a failed post-stroke drug, a neuroprotective agent that somehow sensitized mirror neurons throughout Broca's area. In psychopaths, this seemed to light a new fire. Lyle, for the first time in his life, was experiencing the emotional echo that most people felt almost from birth. See someone slapped and neurons associated with the face lit up in synchrony. See someone kicked and the brain reacted as if you had been attacked. It was enough to merely imagine an act, or remember it, to start a cascade of hormonal and physical responses. Mirror neurons were the first cogs in the complex systems of attachment, longing, remorse. The tripwires of empathy.

"Lyle, that's good that you stopped," she said. "You're making progress."

"You don't understand!" he shouted. "He's been talking about getting you alone. This morning he showed me where he was keeping the knife. He told me how he was going to do it, in the one-on-one interviews in your office. He told me the things he was going to force you to do."

Alycia looked at Franz. The man wasn't smiling—not quite. "You could have called a guard, Lyle. You could have just warned me."

"See, that's the thing—I *wanted* to hurt him. I thought about what he was going to do to you and I felt . . . I don't know . . . "

"*Luuv,*" Franz said.

"You don't know what love is!" Lyle said. "He hasn't changed at all, doc. Why isn't it working on him?"

"Be*cause,*" Franz said, his tone condescending and professorial despite the blade at his throat. "I'm in the control group. I didn't receive GLS."

"We all got the drug," Lyle said. Then: "Didn't we?"

Franz rolled his eyes. "Doctor, could you please explain to him about placebos?"

She felt a flash of anger, and suddenly decided that she wanted to stab Franz herself. But he was right, he was in the control group. The trial was supposed to be a double-blind, randomized study, with numbered dosages supplied by the pharmaceutical company. But she knew within days which eight men were receiving the real dose—the effects were obvious. The guards started calling them crybabies.

"He's playing you, Lyle," she told him. "Pushing your buttons. That's what people like Franz do."

"You think I don't know that? Shit, I *invented* that. I used to be fucking bulletproof. No one got to me, no one fucked with me. Now, it's like everybody can see right through me."

The lieutenant cleared his throat. Alycia glanced back. The mass of helmeted men behind him seemed ready to rush in.

Franz hadn't missed the exchange. "You're running out of time, Lyle," he said. "Any second now they're going to send in the king's men and crack you like an egg. Then they're going to take you off to solitary, where you won't be seeing your girlfriend anymore."

"What?" Lyle asked.

"You don't think they're going to let you stay in the program after this, do you?"

Lyle looked at her, eyes wide. "Is that true? Does that mean you'll stop giving me GLS?"

They're going to stop giving it to all you, she thought. After this, the whole nationwide trial would be canceled. "You could have stopped at any time, Lyle. It's always been voluntary."

"But I don't *want* to stop taking it! I don't want to be the guy I was before. Nothing felt *real* before—everybody was like a cartoon or something, on the other side of the TV screen. They couldn't hurt me, so I could do whatever I wanted to do them. I was like *him*."

Franz started to say something and Lyle pressed the screwdriver blade into his neck. "You don't know what he's like," Lyle said. "He's not just some banker who ripped off a couple hundred people. He's a killer."

"What?"

"He shot two teenagers in Kentucky, buried them in the woods. Nobody ever found them. He *brags* about it."

"Stories," Franz said.

Alycia stepped closer and knelt down next to Franz's outstretched legs. "Lyle, I swear to you, we'll keep you on GLS. As your doctor I can guarantee that. I took an oath to protect you, and that's what I'm going to do." She held out a hand. "Give it to me, Lyle. I know you were trying to protect me, but now you don't have to be a murderer. I don't want you to throw away everything you've gained."

"Oh, please," Franz said.

But Lyle was looking only at her now. He was like a teenager, blind-sided by emotions he'd never felt before. She saw his fingers flex on the handle of the screwdriver. She placed her hand over his, and slowly pushed the weapon down.

A moment later she was shoved aside by the first member of the extraction team.

Two days later she came down to solitary with four guards as escort.

"You know, you're good," Franz said. He lay on the bed with his jumpsuit half unzipped, revealing the bandages across his chest. The blade had missed the lung and the heart, tearing only muscle. He'd be fine in a few weeks. "I almost believed you myself. The oath part was genius."

"I meant it," Alycia said. She went to the stainless steel sink and set down the plastic first-aid kit she'd brought.

Franz said, "Come on, there's no way you could keep him on GLS. It made him suicidal *and* homicidal."

"They're not going to let me keep anyone on it—they've canceled the trial. I've got to turn in all my supplies soon. But Lyle's coming off the drug now. He's feeling less suicidal. In a few days he'll be back to his old self, and he won't feel any remorse at all. But he'll be alive."

"How noble. All you had to do was betray the poor sap who loved you."

"Tell me about Kentucky," she said. She opened the kit.

Franz smiled, shook his head. "That was just some bullshit to get Lyle worked up."

"In a couple days you'll be dying to talk about what happened." She lifted the syringe, then inserted the needle into the cap of the vial.

He blinked, and then he understood. "You can't do that. I'll call my lawyer."

"By the time you get out of solitary you won't want a lawyer. In a few days, Franz, you'll be thanking me for this." She looked back at the guards. "Hold him down."

THE HISS OF ESCAPING AIR

CHRISTOPHER GOLDEN

Courtney Davis crossed Montana Avenue on strappy, five hundred dollar heels, her sheer dress cascading around her upper thighs with every swing of her hips. Enormous black sunglasses hid most of her face even as they drew attention to her identity, and her blond hair fell in shoulder-length waves that perfectly framed her features.

The world knew her business—thanks to TMZ and the tabloids, they knew every detail of her divorce proceedings, and had seen her in positions not meant for public inspection—but they could not possibly know of her crime.

A car honked at her and she fought the instinct to give the driver the finger, just in case someone should film her doing so. Then she remembered why she had chosen Santa Monica for this meeting in the first place—no paparazzi. Montana Avenue was trendy as hell, but the celebrities generally hung out elsewhere. The shops and boutiques and restaurants here were for the wives of wealthy men, the producers and studio heads and lawyers who raked in all the real Hollywood cash.

In a few short years, Courtney had gone from waitress to actress to sexy screen star to celebrity, and then her manager had taken her up to a meeting at the home of James Massarsky, to discuss a part, and she'd become a Hollywood wife. In his thirty years in the industry, Massarsky had gone from mailroom to major talent agent to studio boss to independent producer. Part of his appeal, to Courtney, was that his initial rise mirrored her own. But James had been around longer, and in that time he'd earned his reputation as a bastard and as a brilliant businessman, picking up seven Oscars and three wives along the way. He was a man who got what he wanted, and after their first meeting, what he wanted was Courtney Davis.

She hurried across the street, her heels clicking on the pavement. She hopped onto the sidewalk, pretending to be oblivious to the handful of people who shot her the "hey, isn't that—" stare that so many of the semi-famous endured in L.A. People dined on outdoor patios, but she passed those by without looking inside, just as she did the little dress shop and the new Kismetix cosmetics store. The women she knew who shopped and lunched and lingered in Santa Monica were not her real friends, but other Hollywood wives—and she could ignore them if she wanted to.

That was good. Courtney wasn't in the mood to talk.

You're a fool, she told herself, as she avoided the water dripping from the edge of an awning. It had rained this morning, but the sky had turned perfectly blue afterward. The sun shone its warmth down upon her, and she shook her head with the moment of her epiphany.

You could've met this guy anywhere. Burbank. Sherman Oaks. Hell, she could've arranged for her accomplice to meet her up in Santa Barbara at some roadside bar, like in an old-time mystery novel. Somewhere with a million times less chance that someone she knew would see her, and know she'd been here.

When she had made arrangements for this meeting, she had been tempted to suggest drinks at the Ivy in Beverly Hills. She'd have felt at home there, with friends around her. But the Ivy was more than just a see and be seen sort of place. It was Paparazzi Central. Photos and videos would be inevitable, and she didn't want that.

Montana Avenue wasn't much better, really. Her chances of being seen by someone, of word getting back to James, were high. But in the end, though she hoped to delay it as long as possible, she had decided it wouldn't matter much if her soon-to-be ex-husband found out about today's rendezvous. He would likely think what anyone seeing her in some clandestine coziness in a Santa Monica restaurant would think—that she was having an affair.

If only it were that simple.

At the corner, she turned off Montana onto a narrow side street, where trendy crumbled away like all Hollywood façades. She paused there, in the shade of a tree that grew up out of the sidewalk, and stared at the patio outside Lemongrass, the little bistro halfway down the block.

There were other reasons for her wanting this meeting to take place somewhere familiar. Outside of her Los Angeles, the places she hung out, the trendy clubs and shopping districts and the studio lots, the rest of the world seemed brittle and unreal, the dry husk of an empty beehive, no more substantial than dust and cobwebs. Ever since the day she had arrived in L.A., shitbox car loaded up with all her earthly belongings, Wisconsin license plate revealing the almost absurd truth about her small town girl past and her sickeningly trite Hollywood dreams . . . ever since then, she had known that this place was what she had lived for. She needed to be a part of this world.

Hollywood had a vibrant urgency that made it matter. The rest of the world was the façade. Whatever happened to her—celebrity, divorce, scandal—it only mattered here. Courtney Davis no longer believed she really existed outside this place.

She understood the shallowness of this thinking, and had come to terms with it. The small town Wisconsin girl still lived inside of her. She tried to be a good person, to create a life full of love and kindness. But somehow that person co-existed with the all-night clubbing that had gone on before she married James Massarsky, and the bitterness that marriage had brought her.

So, yes, perhaps James would learn more quickly than she would like about her meeting today. But Courtney wondered, now, if that had been her plan, sub-consciously, all along. Maybe she wanted James to find out, so that he would know who it was that had hurt him, and stolen from him.

Lemongrass must have had live music out on the patio, for she heard sweet, gentle guitar rising on the light breeze, accompanied by a rich, warm voice. The song was unfamiliar to her, but the singer had an aching sadness in his tone, and it settled around her heart and made her linger a few seconds longer under the tree.

"This is a little strange, don't you think?" Courtney asked.

Behind the wheel of the car, Don Peterson shrugged. "Nah. Guys like this, they think in 'old Hollywood' terms. Every one of them wishes they could have been Jack Warner and acts like the fucking Godfather. Massarsky is really the last of a dying breed, younger than the rest but with the same mindset. That's why he's an independent producer, now. There's only so long an agency or a studio is going to let themselves be run around by a guy whose life is a scorched-earth policy. That's what boards of directors are for. So now Massarsky works for himself."

"Jesus, Don," Courtney said. "That really makes me want to be in one of his movies. Thanks for the pep talk."

Her manager laughed. "Relax. This is the old Hollywood thing. The director wants you. The producers want you, even though they're bitching because you won't show your tits—"

"You know—"

He held up a hand even as he steered them in amongst the trees.

"I know, Courtney. This is me, remember? No nudity. I get it, and I respect it. That's your choice. Massarsky likes to meet people, look them in the eye and shake their hand. It's an old school thing. Once you get his seal of approval—which Brad is one hundred percent sure you will—you'll never have to deal with him directly again. This isn't an audition. You'll talk. He'll try to impress you. You'll be impressed, or pretend to be. And we'll go. End of story. Don't be nervous."

She smiled. "I'm not nervous."

"You shouldn't be."

"I am."

"I know."

Don drove up winding roads that took them into hills higher than Courtney had ever known existed in L.A. She'd taken Coldwater Canyon many times, but this was different. Commuters drove that road. Up here, it was all private, a world apart from the buzz of life in the city.

A white wall sprang up to the right. In places she could see over it, down into valleys where massive, sprawling estates covered acres, with neighbors half a mile distant from each other. Soon they climbed a steep curve to find a gatehouse waiting at the top, complete with a uniformed guard, security cameras, and more fences. Don pulled up to the gatehouse as the guard leaned out.

"Courtney Davis and Donald Peterson to see James Massarsky."

The guard checked a clipboard, nodded without saying a word, and reached into the gatehouse. The gates swung slowly open. Don thanked the guard and drove through, and then they were traveling along a much narrower, even more winding road. Tall hedges lined the sides. There were wooden fences, stone walls, even warnings about electrified gates.

"Look at that," Don said.

He pointed to a small bit of exposed property on the left side of the road, where a trio of deer nibbled grass in amongst a few trees.

"That's so weird. What are they doing in here?" Courtney said, mostly to herself.

"I'm sure they're stocked, like fish in a private pond. The whole neighborhood is fenced in. The deer are just more pretty things to look at."

Courtney said nothing more until they pulled into the long driveway of Massarsky's home, wondering how much of the man's life was defined by acquiring pretty things to look at. Massarsky had built his legend on too much alcohol and too many women, a childish temper, and a savant's eye for choosing film projects. But he had to have some serious smarts to have gotten to the top and surviving there for so long.

The stone driveway ended in a circle, off of which there were several individual parking spaces, each separated by a thin strip of perfectly manicured grass. Two slots had cars already in them, each pristine and elegant. Don parked in the last available slot, and even as they got out of the car and turned toward the house, the front door opened and James Massarsky stepped out.

Massarsky was fifty-six years old and moderately handsome in a tanned, relaxed, country club sort of way. His curly hair was thinning and he had a roundish belly that only added to his casual air. In a pale blue t-shirt and knee-length cargo shorts, all faded and rumpled, he didn't look like a Hollywood mogul. Of course, she hadn't met many, and none on his level.

"Hello," he said, smiling. "I saw you drive up. Sorry for the grubby look. I was out in the garden, checking on my tomatoes, and sort of lost track of time."

Courtney smiled. He grew tomatoes.

"I'm James Massarsky," he said, putting out his hand.

"Don Peterson," her manager said, shaking. "And this is Courtney Davis."

When he took her hand, James Massarsky gave her a paternal sort of smile. His grip was firm and welcoming.

"Hell, I know who you are," he said. "Thirty years in this business hasn't broken me of my love of movies, yet. You were fantastic in that Scorsese picture, Courtney. What I want to know is if that performance came from you, or from Marty's cameras and a great script."

Off guard, she gave him a small shrug. "I've wondered the same thing. But thanks, just in case."

Massarsky hadn't let go of her hand, and now he looked at her oddly and squeezed a bit tighter. Then he laughed softly and looked at Don.

"You've got quite an actress here," he said, obviously having already forgotten Don's name. "She's gonna take you far. Why don't we go in the den and we can talk about whether or not I'm going to be along for the ride."

"Sounds good," Don said.

Massarsky pointed them along a corridor and shut the door, which had been standing open. Wonderful breezes swept through the house and sunlight rushed in from the tall windows in every direction.

"Marta!" the producer called toward the back of the house.

"Yes, Mister?" a thickly accented woman's voice replied.

"Can we get some drinks in the den, please?" Massarsky said. He turned to his guests. "Want a soda? Juice? Something harder?"

"Juice would be great," Courtney said.

Don nodded. "For me, too."

Massarsky smiled. "Marta, three of those pomegranate juices, okay? We'll be back in the den. Don't forget the ice!" He glanced at them again. "You've gotta have the ice. Makes it sweeter, somehow."

Pomegranate juice. Courtney said nothing. Massarsky hadn't even asked if they liked pomegranate juice. She'd had it in martinis before, but never on its own, and knew it had a sharpness to it. It wouldn't have been her first choice, but there was no arguing with James Massarsky. He was the sort of man who was used to deciding what other people would like to drink.

The rest of the house—what she could see of it as they passed through—was bright and airy, a true Hollywood palace of the sort that she had only ever seen in movies or on television or in magazine layouts. But as they made their way back into the den, they passed into dark corners of the man's home, a kind of living museum of Massarsky's history in the industry. Bookshelves were lined with leather-bound volumes of the scripts of every movie he had ever had a hand in, with no distinction between the classics and the crap. Photographs on the walls in the same hall showed Massarsky with a who's-who of Hollywood royalty, some in their prime, but many more recent. Jack Nicholson, Meryl Streep, Jodie Foster, Will Smith, Steven Spielberg, and Clint Eastwood. There were photos with four American presidents and a handful of sports stars as well. Some of the photographs had clearly been cropped to remove non-famous faces. In several, the arms or hands of those who'd been removed still remained in the pictures. Courtney assumed that the attractive blondes who recurred in several of the photos were Massarsky's ex-wives.

The den itself was darkest of all. The blinds were open, but the room seemed to swallow sunlight. The brown leather furniture and rich wood of the shelves and tables and the mantelpiece over the fireplace embraced them all. As Don and

Massarsky took seats on creaking leather, Courtney wandered a bit, examining some of the odd knick-knacks that sat on shelves along with more bound scripts and a lot of books that looked unread, spines unbroken.

"Go ahead and look around," Massarsky said, though she'd already begun. "There are all sorts of odd mementoes in this house. I'm a collector. I've acquired hundreds of bits of Hollywood history over the years, not to mention the folklore of the industry."

"Folklore?" Courtney asked.

Massarsky laughed. "You don't want to hear this."

She smiled. "I do."

"Some of it's gruesome stuff, some sensational in that old Hollywood gossip rag kind of way. You know, the costume Lauren Bacall was wearing the first time she and Bogart made love. It was on the set of *To Have or Have Not*. That sort of thing."

Courtney liked that he had said *made love* instead of *had sex,* or something even cruder. Massarsky was an old-fashioned sort of man, befitting his age, the sort who might be a barbarian in the presence of other men, but still knew how to act the gentleman.

She cocked her head curiously and picked up a small glass cube. Inside, three yellowed nuggets rattled. She turned toward him.

"Are these—?"

"Teeth? Yes. Bobby DeNiro had them knocked out during the filming of *Raging Bull*. I bought them from Jim Feehan, the old-time boxer who trained DeNiro for that film. They're the real thing."

Don, who'd been keeping his mouth shut until now, probably wanting her to establish a rapport with Massarsky, couldn't stay quiet any longer.

"How can you be sure?" the manager asked.

Massarsky might have been offended, but he smiled. "I asked DeNiro."

"He didn't mind that you had them?" Courtney asked, amazed.

Massarsky spread out on the chair, relaxing, king of his castle. "Far from it. You want to know the truth? A lot of these things have legends around them, like they've got some kind of Hollywood magic. In the late seventies, I knew guys who claimed that in the Golden Age, there were real muses in this town, captured or brought to life or summoned, I don't know. But I'm talking real muses, like in Greek mythology. Writers and directors and studio bosses worshipped these women, and they got genius in return."

Courtney and Don both stared at him, unsure what to say.

The producer laughed. "I'm not saying I believed them. But when I say these guys believed, I'm totally serious. They bought into it, hook, line, and sinker. Anyway, a lot of the stuff I've collected has that kind of lore around it. But most of it is just weird and fascinating to me. The story behind DeNiro's teeth is this—after he had them knocked out, he went to his dentist, who brought in a doctor. Turned out the mercury in the fillings he had in those teeth had been poisoning him."

"So losing those teeth might've saved his life?" Don asked.

"I wouldn't go that far," Massarsky said. "Still, it's a great story."

At that point, Marta arrived with a tray bearing three tall glasses of pomegranate juice, each with a slice of strawberry on the rim and full of ice. Courtney was surprised there weren't little tropical umbrellas in there as well.

The woman vanished as quickly as quietly as she appeared.

"All right," Massarsky said, "more chit chat later. I'll even give you a tour if you want. Right now, let's talk about *this* movie. *Daughter of the Snows.* What appeals to you, Courtney? This isn't the sort of thing most people would expect from you."

She smiled as she came around the leather sofa and took a seat, purposely placing herself between Don and Massarsky, who sat in matching chairs at either end of the coffee table.

"That's exactly why I want it. It's not about being beautiful or witty, it's about pain and survival. It's the kind of film where what's going on in the actor's eyes is at least as important as the words coming out of her mouth."

Caught sipping his pomegranate juice, Massarsky paused and regarded her carefully, without any trace of a smile. The mask of easy confidence had slipped, and she saw the man beneath, shrewd and intrigued and more than a little bit lonely.

"You actually meant that," he said.

Courtney nodded. "Of course."

Don Peterson's presence in the room was completely forgotten. The two of them looked at one another for several long seconds, and then Massarsky's smile returned.

On the patio outside Lemongrass, the guitarist launched into another song Courtney didn't know, a sweet, slightly upbeat love song he introduced as "Everything Under the Sun." She left the shade of the tree on the corner of Montana and continued down the side street, staying on the opposite sidewalk from Lemongrass. With every step, more of the outdoor dining area became visible, and through the five sets of open French doors she could see many of the tables inside as well.

Just inside the doors, off the patio, a thin, fortyish man she knew as Wilkie sat with his back to the street. From this angle she could only make out part of his profile and his thick tangle of black hair, but it couldn't be anyone else. He sat alone at a table for two, and opposite him, a red balloon had been tied to the back of the empty chair. It danced a bit with the breeze coming off the patio, and she felt her chest tighten. If it came loose somehow, it might be carried out the open doors by the wind, might float off into the sky, the ultimate children's tragedy, and yet far more than that.

Wilkie seemed unafraid.

Then she understood, and was startled by the realization. Wilkie didn't believe.

When they returned home from three weeks in the Mediterranean, the honeymoon she had always dreamed of, Massarsky—now "James" to her—showed his new wife the last, most precious items in his strange collection. They were all bits of Hollywood history, oddities with charming or gruesome tales behind them, and her husband had become the curator of his own little museum, in a room he called the library, to which only he had the key.

"Finally," he said, turning with a ringmaster's flourish, passing through shafts of light coming through the tall windows, dust eddying in air so infrequently disturbed. "The crown jewel."

James pulled a gold, braided cord and a small curtain drew aside, as though to reveal some tiny stage upon which puppets might perform. But this was no puppet theatre. Behind the little curtain was a rectangular glass case thirty inches high and twelve wide, within which rested a single, red balloon, its string hanging beneath it and coiling at the bottom of the case.

Courtney arched an eyebrow, chuckled a bit, and reached out for her husband's arm. "A balloon?"

He looked at her, this man who had made her so happy, who believed in her so thoroughly, and his eyes sparkled with mischief.

"Not just any balloon. I'm going to assume you've never seen the film, *The Red Balloon*. Mostly, I'm assuming so because, as far as I know, only a few hundred people in the world have ever seen it in its completed form. While he was shooting *Cimarron*, the director Anthony Mann got a script from Leigh Brackett, who had adapted *The Big Sleep* in '46 and then done damned little until *Rio Bravo* in '59. Glenn Ford was starring in *Cimarron*, and Mann convinced him to star in *The Red Balloon*. They did the picture for MGM in 1960, but it was never released. Somebody—I've heard a lot of names, from Jack Warner to David Selznick to Bob Hope, believe it or not—bought the film from MGM and put it in a vault somewhere. It's never been released. Ford went straight into making *Pocketful of Miracles*, basically as an apology from MGM."

Courtney waited a moment before urging him on. "And? Why did whoever it was not want the movie released?"

James Massarsky smiled. "Brackett's script—and Mann's movie—was about a Chicago mobster who was obsessed with a red balloon. The balloon never lost its air, never went flat, and the mob boss believed that as long as he had the balloon in his possession, that he would never be sick or injured, that he wouldn't grow old, and that it might even keep him alive forever. But he had to keep it safe, because if it popped or deflated, he would die. Supposedly, Brackett heard the story from some people he knew who were actually connected to the Chicago mob. The movie ended with the balloon being stolen, and the mob boss dying, but the narrative left it open for the audience to decide if it was all just coincidence, or the truth."

Courtney processed that a moment, then laughed, shaking her head. "You think someone kept that movie from being released because the story was true?" She looked at the glass case. "And you think that's the real thing, right there?"

James brushed her blond hair from her eyes, leaned in, and kissed her. Then he shrugged, that manic, almost sprite-like mischief still in his eyes. "I've had this thing nearly two years, and it's still inflated. In that time, I haven't had so much as a sneeze. You're the audience, sweetheart. You be the judge. Either way, it's a great story."

"What'd this guy do to you, anyway?"

Courtney thought of all the things she could have said, the way her life and her career and her self-esteem had been disassembled, all of the humiliating examples of her ruination that she could have listed. Instead, she met Wilkie's gaze firmly with her own.

"He broke me."

They sat just inside Lemongrass, half the table in shadow and half bright with sunshine that streamed in through the open French doors. The breeze off the patio warmed her, and the cute, slightly scruffy guitar player continued to play songs that were unfamiliar and yet fun and thoroughly agreeable. On another occasion, drinks with a handsome stranger under such circumstances would have been a pleasure. But Wilkie was a thief, not a date, and Courtney didn't like the way he looked at her.

"You don't look broken to me," he said.

She stiffened, hackles rising. "You don't know me. And who asked you? When Alison gave me your number, she said you were professional and discreet."

Wilkie played with the salt and pepper shakers on the table, a lopsided grin spreading across his face. He picked up his beer—Stella on tap—and took a long sip, watching her over the rim of the glass. When he set it down, he wiped his mouth, staring at her.

"Your friend there, Alison? She doesn't know me very well. I did a job for her once, and I guess I got it done, or she wouldn't have sent you to me. As for the job you asked me to do . . ." he pointed to the red balloon, tied to the back of her chair. "It's right there."

Courtney had ordered a pomegranate martini, aware of the slight irony, if irony was even the word. Symmetry, then? Perhaps. She had taken a few sips from the drink but otherwise it sat untouched in front of her on the table. At first she had wondered if this was indeed the red balloon from her husband's collection, and how she would be able to tell. But the string was just that—a real string, like on a kite, and gray with age—not a thin ribbon like people used these days. Beyond that, she just knew.

The red balloon wasn't something she could have brought up in their divorce proceedings. There were loads of material things that she had asked for in the settlement, from furniture to art to the house in Maine, but if she'd tried to get any part of his personal collection, her lawyer had told her such claims would be next to impossible to justify. But James had *hurt* her, and Courtney wanted to hurt him back.

This was the way.

She took a deep breath, suddenly tired of Wilkie. Why was she sitting here having a drink with this man? Distracted, wanting to be away from here, to be done with him, she reached into her clutch and pulled out a folded envelope, sliding it across the table.

"The rest of your fee," she said. "Feel free to count it."

Wilkie smiled. He had a weathered, surf-bum look about him, but his eyes glittered with intelligence. "No need. I trust you. So, our business is concluded? All done, right?"

"All done," Courtney agreed as she slid back her chair.

"Then you got what you wanted. The balloon's yours."

She stood and then set about picking at the loose knot he'd used to tie the balloon string to the chair. Her fingernails were long enough, but it took her a few seconds.

"Let me help you with that," Wilkie said, moving toward her, almost intimately close.

The chatter of voices and clatter of dishes and glasses and silver and the rich, mellow music from the patio seemed to vanish as Courtney saw a glint of metal. Wilkie grabbed the balloon by its neck, using his body to nudge her aside, and brought the pin up swiftly. He punctured the wattled rubber of the balloon's neck and she heard a sudden hiss as the air began to escape.

Her body went numb. She felt the color drain from her face as Wilkie stepped back, dropping the pin.

"Your husband caught me in the act, Courtney," Wilkie said, his lopsided grin turning apologetic. "That's never happened before. He gave me an option. He could call the police, or I could finish the job you hired me for, steal the balloon, take your money . . . and he'd pay me fifty thousand dollars for this little trick."

The thief shrugged, surfer-boy charm coming out. "I'll never understand rich people, but whatever."

Then he turned and walked out. It had taken only seconds, during which time Courtney had entirely forgotten to breathe. The hiss of escaping air filled her ears and at last she reacted, reaching up and grasping the balloon's neck, pinching off the tiny puncture, stopping the leak.

Heart thundering in her chest, she stared at the balloon. It had not lost very much air, was still far from wilting. Could she patch the hole somehow? Maybe.

Courtney glanced around. Only one person, a man sitting by himself, perhaps waiting for someone to join him, studied her curiously. She ignored him, moving into action. With her free hand, she finished loosening the string and it came free. She picked up her little clutch bag and left through the open French doors, walking amongst the patio crowd. The drinks had already been paid for, so nobody would come rushing after her. That was good.

The balloon. What the hell was the story again? The movie? Did James have a copy of the movie, or just know the story about the mobster? He'd said only a few hundred people had ever seen the movie, but that didn't mean he was one of them. Billy Brackett had heard the story—probably in a bar—and had used it for his script, but that didn't mean even Brackett believed it.

It's just a story. A Hollywood fable.

But somebody had believed it enough to pay a fortune to get MGM to shelve the film, put it in a vault and never let it out. Why would anyone do such a thing? Whoever that was, they had believed. And James believed, Courtney felt sure of that. He believed completely. But did she believe?

Her heels clicked on the sidewalk as she hurried to the corner of Montana Avenue. Her pulse throbbed in her temples and tears burned at the corners of her eyes. *Oh, my God. Ohmygod.* In all the time she'd been with James, nearly five years, she had never seen him so much as sneeze. He'd never had a fever or a bruise, never been to a doctor, never cut himself, never had to take medication for anything. *Anything.*

How could she not believe?

She faltered, the strength going out of her, and she leaned against the wall outside a hideously trendy boutique. Her fingers hurt from pinching the balloon so tightly between them. She held it in front of her eyes, staring at it, studying it. Did it look a bit flaccid now?

Her lower lip trembled.

Slowly, she moved it up to her ear, and realized that she could still hear the hiss, a slow, quiet seeping sound that was present, despite her best efforts, her tightest grip.

Courtney bolted. Eyes wild, she ran along Montana Avenue, past Kismetix and half a dozen other shops. Perfectly made up wives and daughters arm in arm, chins in the air, stared at her and made way as she rushed along, desperate to be rid of the balloon. What could she do? She had taken possession of it. It belonged to her. That meant she would reap the benefits, and suffer the consequences. The ground seemed to tilt underneath her and she whirled in a circle, a scream bubbling up the inside of her throat.

A tan, middle-aged brunette stepped out of Jamba Juice, right next door, and held the door for her little boy, who was busily sipping away at the straw in his drink. Skin prickling with fear, breathless, thoughtless, Courtney strode over to them and dropped into a crouch right in front of the boy.

"Hey, little buddy. Want a balloon?" she said, thrusting it toward him.

On instinct, the boy reached his free hand out for the dirty string.

"Thanks, but I don't know if—" the mother began.

But the boy had already tightened his fist around the string. Elated, heart unclenching, Courtney let go of the balloon's puncture throat and stepped back. The hiss seemed loud to her, but the mother and son didn't seem to notice. The woman cast an odd look at Courtney, and a slightly distasteful glance at the dirty string in her son's hand, and then thanked her, just to be polite, as she guided her boy a little further along the sidewalk.

Courtney fled, walking as fast as she could without breaking into a run. Her heart seemed to pound against the inside of her chest and her face still felt flush, but the rush of terror began to subside. *Fucking James.* Never mind Wilkie; the thief hadn't understood what he was doing. But James believed, and because of him, Courtney believed. James had tried to have her killed.

Killed. She froze, catching her breath, raised a hand to her eyes. Jesus, what had she done?

Courtney turned and saw that the mother and son had stopped in front of Kismetix. The woman knelt in front of her boy, their Jamba Juices on the sidewalk, while she tied the dirty string of the balloon around his wrist so he wouldn't lose it. Already it sagged a bit in the air, but they didn't seem to have noticed.

The boy had dark hair, like his mother, and he grinned as he looked at her, cocking his head, making strange faces, just monkeying around the way little children did. He couldn't have been more than four.

What am I? Courtney thought.

"Wait!" she called, running after them.

The mother rose, she and the boy both holding their juices again, and turned to see what the fuss was about. Courtney raced up to them and the woman gripped her son's wrist, taking a protective step in front of him.

"What's wrong—" the mother began.

"I'm sorry. It was a mistake. You have to give it back," Courtney said, the words streaming out too fast, frantic, a jumble. "Please, I'm sorry, I know it's weird, but I shouldn't have given that to him. It's not for him."

The woman scowled. "Excuse me? What the hell are you trying to do? That is so completely not cool."

"I know, and I'm—"

"Just go away," the mother said. She turned her back on Courtney, and marched the little boy along beside her. "Come on, Justin."

"No, listen," Courtney began, grabbing the mother's shoulder and trying to turn her around.

The woman spun, slapping her hand away. "Don't put your hands on me, you psycho. Back off, right now. If you wanted the stupid balloon, you shouldn't have given it away, but you did. My boy is three years old. You can't be all nice and give him something like that and then take it back. Go and buy a new one!"

The little boy tugged on his mother's blouse. "It's okay, Mumma, she can have it."

Courtney's breath caught in her throat and she reached out.

"Forget it," the mother said. "It's the principle of the thing. What's fair is fair."

By now other people had slowed to watch the spectacle unfolding on the sidewalk. Someone had a cell phone out, no doubt getting video of the confrontation. It would be online in hours, but Courtney barely registered the whispers and the looks of disgust and disapproval from the onlookers.

She lunged for the balloon with one hand, reaching for the boy's wrist with the other.

The mother swore in disbelief and threw her Jamba Juice at Courtney. The plastic cup and straw bounced off of her, bright green slush splashing Courtney's clothes and neck and face. As she reached up to wipe the stuff from her eyes, the woman shoved her hard, and Courtney fell backward, sprawling onto the sidewalk.

"No, please, you don't understand," she pleaded.

"You don't put your hands on my son, you crazy bitch," the woman said, but already her voice was retreating.

Courtney jumped up, calling out, still wiping at her eyes. She blinked to clear her vision, but more people had gathered on the sidewalk. Several of them whispered her name. A man and two women came out of Kismetix to stare.

"Out of the way. Please!" she cried, trying to push through them, but the people wouldn't move.

Someone spoke to her from the crowd, then, a quiet voice, telling her calmly that the police had been called, that she needed to go. Numb and hollow inside, she could only stare over the heads of the people gathered around her at the red balloon, bobbing happily in the air, wilting even as it receded into the distance. The balloon vanished around a corner as the mother and son walked out of sight.

As kind hands turned her around and got her walking away from the crowd, it occurred to her that she had gotten what she wanted. She had taken away James's most precious possession. She had hurt him. In return, the son of a bitch had tried to kill her.

I win, she thought, her mind and heart brittle. *I get to live.*

Then the tears came, in great, wracking sobs.

I get to live.

ARAMINTA, OR, THE WRECK OF THE AMPHIDRAKE

NAOMI NOVIK

Lady Araminta was seen off from the docks at Chenstowe-on-Sea with great ceremony if not much affection by her assembled family. She departed in the company of not one but two maids, a hired eunuch swordsman, and an experienced professional chaperone with the Eye of Horus branded upon her forehead, to keep watch at night while the other two were closed.

Sad to say these precautions were not entirely unnecessary. Lady Araminta—the possessor of several other, more notable names besides, here omitted for discretion—had been caught twice trying to climb out her window, and once in her father's library, reading a spellbook. On this last occasion she had fortunately been discovered by the butler, a reliable servant of fifteen years, so the matter was hushed up; but it had decided her fate.

Her father's senior wife informed her husband she refused to pay for the formal presentation to the Court necessary for Araminta to make her debut. "I have five girls to see established besides her," Lady D—said, "and I cannot have them ruined by the antics which are certain to follow."

(Lest this be imagined the fruits of an unfair preference, it will be as well to note here that Araminta was in fact the natural daughter of her Ladyship, and the others in question her daughters-in-marriage, rather than the reverse.)

"It has been too long," Lady D continued, severely, and she is spoilt beyond redemption."

Lord D—hung his head: he felt all the guilt of the situation, and deserved to. As a youth, he had vowed never to offer prayers to foreign deities such as Juno; and out of obstinacy he had refused to recant, so it had taken three wives and fourteen years to acquire the necessary son. Even then the boy had proven rather a disappointment: sickly and slight, and as he grew older preferring of all things literature to the manly arts of fencing or shooting, or even sorcery, which would at least have been respectable.

"But it is rather messy," young Avery said, apologetic but unmoving, even at the age of seven: he *had* inherited the family trait of obstinacy, in full measure. It is never wise to offend foreign deities, no matter how many good old-fashioned British fairies one might have invited to the wedding.

Meanwhile Araminta, the eldest, had long shown more aptitude for riding and shooting than for the cooler arts, and a distressing tendency to gamble. Where her mother would have seen these inappropriate tendencies nipped in the bud, Lord D—, himself a notable sportsman, had selfishly indulged the girl: he liked to have company hunting when he was required at home to do his duty to his wives—and with three, he was required more often than not.

"It is not too much to ask that at least one of my offspring not embarrass me on the field," had been one of his favorite remarks, when chastised; so while her peers were entering into society as polished young ladies, beginning their study of banking or medicine, Lady Araminta was confirmed only as a sportswoman of excessive skill, with all the unfortunate results heretofore described.

Something of course had to be done, so a match was hastily arranged with the colonial branch of a similarly exalted line. The rumors she had already excited precluded an acceptable marriage at home, but young men of good birth, having gone oversea to seek a better fortune than a second son's portion, often had some difficulty acquiring suitable wives.

In those days, the journey took nearly six months, and was fraught with considerable dangers: storms and pirates both patrolled the shipping lanes; leviathans regularly pulled down ships, mistaking them for whales; and strange fevers and lunacies thrived amid the undersea forests of the Shallow Sea, where ships might find themselves becalmed for months above the overgrown ruins of the Drowned Lands.

Naturally Lady Araminta was sent off with every consideration for her safety. The *Bluegill* was a sleek modern vessel, named for the long brightly-painted iron spikes studded in a ridge down her keel to fend off the leviathans, and armed with no fewer than ten cannon. The cabin had three locks upon the door, the eunuch lay upon the threshold outside, the maids slept to either side of Araminta in the large bed, the chaperone had a cot at the foot; and as the last refuge of virtue she had been provided at hideous expense with a Tiresian amulet.

She was given no instruction for the last, save to keep it in its box, and put it on only if the worst should happen—the worst having been described to her rather hazily by Lady D—, who felt suspiciously that Araminta already knew a good deal too much of such things.

There were not many tears in evidence at the leave-taking, except from Lady Ginevra, the next-oldest, who felt it was her sisterly duty to weep, though privately delighted at the chance of advancing her own debut a year. Araminta herself shed none; only said, "Well, good-bye," and went aboard unrepentant, having unbeknownst to all concealed a sword, a very fine pair of dueling pistols and a most inappropriate grimoire in her dowry-chest during the upheaval of the packing. She was not very sorry to be leaving home: she was tired of being always lectured, and the colonies seemed to her a hopeful destination: a young man who had gone out to make his fortune, she thought, could not be quite so much a stuffed-shirt.

After all the preparations and warnings, the journey seemed to her so uneventful as to be tiresome: one day after another altered only by the degree of the blowing wind, until they came to the Drowned Lands and the wind died overhead. She enjoyed looking over the railing for the first few days, at the pale white gleam of marble and masonry which could yet be glimpsed in places, when the sailors gave her a bit of spell-light to cast down below.

"There's nowt to see, though, miss," the master said in fatherly tones, while she peered hopefully. Only the occasional shark, or sometimes one of the enormous sea-spiders, clambering over the ruined towers with their long spindly red legs, but that was all—no gleam of lost treasure, no sparks of ancient magic. "There's no treasure to be had here, not without a first-rate sorcerer to raise it up for you."

She sighed, and insisted instead on being taught how to climb the rigging, much to the disgust of the sailors. "Not like having a *proper* woman on board," more than one might be heard quietly muttering.

Araminta was not perturbed, save by the increasing difficulty in coaxing interesting lessons from them. She resorted after a while to the privacy of her cabin, where through snatched moments she learned enough magic to hide the grimoire behind an illusion of *The Wealth of Nations*, so she might read it publicly and no-one the wiser. The amulet she saved for last, and tried quietly in the middle of the night, while the chaperone Mrs. Penulki snored. The maids, at first rather startled, were persuaded with only a little difficulty to keep the secret. (It must be admitted they were somewhat young and flighty creatures, and already overawed by their noble charge.)

Two slow months they spent crossing the dead shallow water, all their sails spread hopefully, and occasionally putting men over the side in boats to row them into one faint bit of current or another. All the crew cheered the night the first storm broke, a great roaring tumult that washed the windows of her high stern cabin with foam and left both of the maids moaning weakly in the water-closet. Mrs. Penulki firmly refused to entertain the possibility that Araminta might go outside for a breath of fresh air, even when the storm had at last died down, so she spent a stuffy, restless night and woke with the changing of the watch.

She lay on her back listening to the footsteps slapping against the wood, the creak of rope and sail. And then she was listening only to an unfamiliar silence, loud in its way as the thunder; no cheerful cursing, not a snatch of morning song or clatter of breakfast.

She pushed her maids until they awoke and let her climb out to hurry into her clothes. Outside, the sailors on deck were standing silent and unmoving at their ropes and tackle, as if preserved in wax, all of them watching Captain Rellowe. He was in the bows, with his long-glass to his eye aimed out to port. The dark tangled mass of storm-clouds yet receded away from them, a thin gray curtain dropped across half the stage of the horizon. The smooth curve of the ocean bowed away to either side, unbroken.

He put down the glass. "Mr. Willis, all hands to make sail, north-northwest. And go to quarters," he added, even as the master cupped his hands around his mouth to bellow orders.

The hands burst into frantic activity, running past her; below she could hear their curses as they ran the ship's guns up into their places, to the complaint of the creaking wheels. "Milady, you will go inside," Captain Rellowe said, crossing before her to the quarterdeck, none of his usual awkward smiles and scraping; he did not even lift his hat.

"Oh, what is it?" Liesl, one of the maids said, gasping.

"Pirates, I expect," Araminta said, tugging her enormously heavy dower chest out from under the bed. "Oh, what good will wailing do? *Help* me."

The other ship emerged from the rain-curtain shortly, and became plainly visible out the windows of Araminta's stern cabin. It was a considerable heavier vessel, with a sharp-nosed aggressive bow that plowed the waves into a neat furrow, and no hull-spikes at all: instead her hull was painted a vile greenly color, with white markings like teeth also painted around.

Liesl and Helia both moaned and clutched at one another. "I will die before you are taken," Molloy, the eunuch, informed Araminta.

"Precious little difference it will be to me, if I am taken straightaway after," she said practically, and did not look up from her rummaging. "Go speak to one of those fellows outside: we must all have breeches, and shirts."

The chaperone made some stifled noises of protest, which Araminta ignored, and which were silenced by the emergence of the pistols and the sword.

The jewels and the trinkets were buried amid the linen and silk gowns, well bundled in cloth against temptation for straying eyes, so they were nearly impossible to work out. The amulet in particular, nothing more than a tiny nondescript silver drachma on a thin chain, would have been nearly impossible to find if Araminta had not previously tucked it with care into the very back corner. It was just as well, she reflected, glancing up to see how the pirate vessel came on, that boredom had driven her to experimentation.

From the quarterdeck, Captain Rellowe too watched the ship coming up on their heels; his glass was good enough to show him the pirates' faces, lean and hungry and grinning. He was a good merchant captain; he had wriggled out of more than one net, but this one drew taut as a clean line drawn from his stern to her bows. The once-longed-for steady wind blew into his sails with no sign of dying, feeding the chase still better.

Amphidrake was her name, blazoned in yellow, and she was a fast ship, if rigged a little slapdash and dirty. Her hull at least was clean, he noted bitterly, mentally counting the knots he was losing to his own hull-spikes. Not one ship in a thousand met a leviathan, in season, and cannon saw them safe as often as not; but spikes the owners would have, and after the crossing of the Shallow Sea, they would surely by now be tangled with great streamers of kelp, to say nothing of barnacles and algae.

(The storm, of course, would have washed away any kelp; but the spikes made as satisfying a target to blame as any, and preferable to considering that perhaps it had not been wise to hold so very close to the regular sea-lanes, even though it was late in the season.)

In any event, the pirate would catch the *Bluegill* well before the hour of twilight, which might otherwise have given them a chance to slip away; and every man aboard knew it. Rellowe did not like to hear the mortal hush that had settled over his ship, nor to feel the eyes pinned upon his back. They could not expect miracles of him, he would have liked to tell them roundly; but of course he could say nothing so disheartening.

The *Amphidrake* gained rapidly. The bo'sun's mates began taking around the grog, and the bo'sun himself the cat, to encourage the men. The hand-axes and cutlasses and pistols were lain down along the rail, waiting.

"Mr. Gilpin," Captain Rellowe said, with a beckon to his first mate, and in undertone said to him, "Will you be so good as to ask the ladies if for their protection they would object to putting on male dress?"

"Already asked-for, sir, themselves," Gilpin said, in a strange, stifled tone, his eyes darting meaningfully to the side, and Rellowe turning found himself facing a young man, with Lady Araminta's long black curls pulled back into a queue.

Rellowe stared, and then looked away, and then looked at her head—his head—and then glanced downward again, and then involuntarily a little lower—and then away again—He did not know how to look. It was no trick of dress; the shirt was open too loose for that, the very line of the jaw was different, and the waist.

Of course one heard of such devices, but generally only under intimate circumstances, or as the subject of rude jokes. Rellowe (if he had ever thought of such things at all) had vaguely imagined some sort of more caricaturish alteration; he had not gone very far in studies of sorcery himself. In reality, the line between lady and lord was distressingly thin. Araminta transformed had a sword, and two pistols, and a voice only a little high to be a tenor, in which she informed him, "I should like to be of use, sir, if you please."

He meant of course to refuse, vocally, and have her removed to the medical orlop if necessary by force; and so he should have done, if only the *Amphidrake* had not in that very moment fired her bow-chasers, an early warning-shot, and painfully lucky had taken off an alarming section of the quarterdeck rail.

All went into confusion, and he had no thought for anything but keeping the men from panic. Three men only had been hit even by so much as a splinter, but a drop of blood spilled was enough to spark the built-up store of terror. The mates had been too free with the grog, and now the lash had less effect: a good many of the men had to be thrust bodily back into their places, or pricked with sword-point, and if Araminta joined in the effort, Rellowe managed not to see.

She was perfectly happy, herself; it had not yet occurred to her they might lose. The ship had been very expensive, and the cannon seemed in excellent repair to her eye: bright brass and ebony polished, with fresh paint. Of course there was a personal danger, while she was on-deck, but high spirits made light of that, and she had never balked at a fence yet.

"You cannot mean to be a coward in front of all these other stout fellows," she sternly told one sailor, a scrawny underfed gaol-rat attempting to creep away down the forward ladderway, and helped him back to the rail with a boot at his back end.

The crash of cannon-fire was glorious, one blast after another, and then one whistling by overhead plowed into the mizzenmast. Splinters went flaying skin in all directions, blood in bright arterial spray hot and startling. Araminta reached up and touched her cheek, surprised, and looked down at the bo'sun, staring glassy-eyed back at her, dead at her feet. Her shirt was striped collar to waist with a long sash of red blood.

She did not take it very badly; she had done a great deal of hunting, and stern lecturing from her father had cured her of any tendency to be missish, even when in at the kill. Elves, of course, were much smaller, and with their claws and pointed teeth inhuman, but near enough she was not tempted in the present moment either to swoon or to be inconveniently ill, unlike one small midshipman noisily vomiting upon the deck nearby.

Above her head, the splintered mizzen creaked, moaned, and toppled: the sails making hollow thumping noises like drum skins as it came down, entangling the mainmast. Araminta was buried beneath a choking weight of canvas, stinking with slush. The ship's way was checked so abruptly she could feel the griping through the boards while she struggled to force her way out through the thick smothering folds. All was muffled beneath the sailcloth, screams, pistol-shots all distant, and then for a moment Captain Rellowe's voice rose bellowing over the fray, "Fire!"

But their own cannon spoke only with stuttering, choked voices. Before they had even quite finished, a second tremendous broadside roar thundered out in answer, one ball after another pounding into them so the *Bluegill* shook like a withered old rattle-plant. Splinters rained against the canvas, a shushing noise, and at last with a tremendous heave she managed to buy enough room to draw her sword, and cut a long tear to escape through.

Pirates were leaping across the boards: grappling hooks clawed onto whatever was left of the rail, and wide planks thrust out to make narrow bridges. The deck was awash in blood and wreckage, of the ship and of men, torn limbs and corpses underfoot.

"Parley," Captain Rellowe was calling out, a shrill and unbecoming note in his voice, without much hope: and across the boards on the deck of the other ship, the pirate captain only laughed.

"Late for that now, Captain," he called back. "No, it's to the Drowned Lands for all of you," cheerful and clear as a bell over the water. He was a splendidly looking fellow, six feet tall in an expansive coat of wool dyed priest's-crimson, with lace cuffs and gold braid. It was indeed the notorious Weedle, who had once taken fourteen prizes in a single season, and made hostage Lord Tan Cader's eldest son.

Inexperience was not, in Araminta's case, a synonym for romanticism; defeat was now writ too plainly across the deck for her to mistake it. Molloy staggering over to her grasped her arm: he had a gash torn across the forehead and his own sword was wet with blood. She shook him off and shot one pirate leaping towards them. "Come with me, quickly," she ordered, and turning dashed into the cabin again. The maids terrified were clinging to one another huddled by the window, with Mrs. Penulki pale and clutching a dagger in front of them.

"Your Ladyship, you may not go out again," the chaperone said, her voice trembling.

"All of you hide in the water-closet, and do not make a sound if anyone should come in," Araminta said, digging into the dower chest again. She pulled out the great long strand of pearls, her mother's parting gift, and wrapped it around her waist, hidden beneath her sash. She took out also the gold watch, meant to be presented at the betrothal ceremony, and shut and locked the chest. "Bring that, Molloy," she said, and dashing back outside pointed at Weedle, and taking a deep breath whispered, "Parley, or I will throw it overboard. *Dacet.*"

The charm leapt from her lips, and she saw him start and look about suspiciously, as the words curled into his ears. She waved her handkerchief until his eyes fixed on her, and pointed to the chest which Molloy held at the ship's rail.

Pirate captains as a class are generally alive to their best advantage. The value of a ship bound for the colonies, laden with boughten goods, might be ten thousand sovereigns, of which not more than a quarter might be realized; a dower chest might hold such a sum alone, or twice that, in jewels and silks more easily exchanged for gold. Weedle was not unwilling to be put to the little difficulty of negotiation to secure it, when they might finish putting the sword to the survivors afterwards.

"I should tell you at once, it is cursed," Araminta said, "so if anyone but me should open it, everything inside will turn to dust." It was not, of course. Such curses were extremely expensive, and dangerous besides, as an unwitting maid might accidentally ruin all the contents. Fortunately, the bluff would be rather risky to disprove. "There is a Fidelity charm inside, intended for my bride," she added, by way of explaining such a measure.

Weedle scowled a little, and a good deal more when she resolutely refused to open it, even with a dagger at her throat. "No," she said. "I will go with you, and you may take me to Kingsport, and when you have let me off at the docks, I will open it for you there. And I dare say my family will send a ransom too, if you let Captain Rellowe go and inform them," she added, raising her voice for the benefit of the listening pirates, "so you will all be better off than if you had taken the ship."

The better to emphasize her point, she had handed around the gold watch, and the pirates were all murmuring over it, imagining the chest full to the brim of such jewels. Weedle liked a little more blood, in an engagement—the fewer men to share the rewards with after—but for consolation, there was not only the contents of the chest, but what they augured for the value of the ransom.

"What do you say, lads? Shall we give the young gentleman his passage?" he called, and tossed the watch out over their heads, to be snatched for and scrambled after, as they chorused agreement.

"Lord Aramin, I must protest," Captain Rellowe said, resentfully. With the swords sheathed, his mind already began to anticipate the whispers of censure to come, what indignant retribution her family might take. But he had scarcely any alternative; exposing her to rape and murder would certainly be no better, and, after all, he could only be censured if he were alive for it, which was some improvement. So he stood by, burdened with an ashamed sense of relief, as she crossed with unpardonable calm to the pirate ship and the chest trundled over carefully behind her.

The *Amphidrake* sailed away to the south; the *Bluegill* limped on the rest of her way to New Jericho, there to be received with many exclamations of horror and dismay. The family of Lady Araminta's fiancé (whose name let discretion also elide) sent an agent to Kingsport at once; followed by others from her own family.

They waited one month and then two, but the *Amphidrake* never put in. Word eventually came that the ship had been seen instead at port in Redhook Island. It was assumed, for everyone's comfort, that the pirates had yielded to temptation and tried the chest early, and then disposed of a still-disguised Lady Araminta for tricking them.

Now that there was no danger of her rescue, she was much lionized; but for a little while only. She had been most heroic, but it would have been much more decorous to die, ideally on her own dagger. Also, both the maids had been discovered, shortly after their arrival in port, to be increasing.

Her fiancé made the appropriate offerings and, after a decent period of mourning, married a young lady of far less exalted birth, with a reputation for shrewd investing, and a particularly fine hand in the ledger-book. Lord D—gave prayers at the River Waye; his wives lit a candle in Quensington Tower and put her deathdate in the family book. A quiet discreet settlement was made upon the maids, and the short affair of her life was laid to rest.

The report, however, was quite wrong; the *Amphidrake* had not put in at Redhook Island, or at Kingsport either, for the simple reason that she had struck on shoals, three weeks before, and sunk to the bottom of the ocean.

As the *Bluegill* sailed away, stripped of all but a little food and water, Captain Weedle escorted Lady Araminta and the dower chest to his own cabin. She accepted the courtesy quite unconsciously, but he did not leave it to her, and instead seated himself at the elegant dining table with every appearance of intending to stay. She stared a little, and recollected her disguise, and suddenly realized that she was about to be ruined.

This understanding might be called a little late in coming, but Araminta had generally considered the laws of etiquette as the rules of the chase, and divided them into categories: those which everyone broke, all the time; those which one could not break without being frowned at; and those which caused one to be quietly and permanently left out of every future invitation to the field. Caught browsing a spellbook was in the very limits of the second category; a bit of quiet fun with a lady friend in the first; but a night alone in the company of an unmarried gentleman was very firmly in the last.

"You aren't married, are you?" she inquired, not with much hope; she was fairly certain that in any case, a hypothetical Mrs. Weedle a thousand sea-miles distant was not the sort of protection Lady D—would ever consider acceptable for a daughter's reputation, magic amulet or no.

Weedle's face assumed a cast of melancholy, and he said, "I am not."

He was the by-blow of an officer of the Navy and a dockside lady of the West Indies sufficiently shrewd to have secured a vow on the hearth before yielding; accordingly he had been given a place aboard his father's ship at a young age. He had gifts, and might well have made a respectable career, but he had been taken too much into society by his father, and while of an impressionable age had fallen in love with a lady of birth considerably beyond his own.

He had presence enough to appeal to the maiden, but her family forbade him the house as soon as they realized his presumption. She in turn laughed with astonishment at his suggestion of an elopement, adding to this injury the insult of drawing him a brutal chart of their expected circumstances and income, five years out, without her dowry.

In a fit of pride and oppression, he had vowed that in five years' time he would be richer than her father or dead; and belatedly realized he had put himself into a very nasty situation, if any god had happened to be listening. One could never be sure. He was at the time only eighteen, several years from his own ship and the chance of substantial prize-money, if he should ever get either; and the lady's father was exceptionally rich.

Pirate ships were rather more open to the advancement of a clever lad, and there was no Navy taking the lion's share of any prize, or inconveniently ordering one into convoy duty. He deserted, changed his name, and in six months' time was third mate on the *Amphidrake* under the vicious Captain Egg, when that gentleman met his end untimely from too much expensive brandy and heatstroke.

A little scuffling had ensued, among the officers, and Weedle had regretfully been forced to kill the first and second mates, when they had tried to assert their claims on grounds of seniority; he was particularly sorry for the second mate, who had been an excellent navigator, and a drinking-companion.

With nothing to lose, Weedle had gone on cheerful and reckless, and now six years later he was alive, exceptionally rich himself, and not very sorry for the turn his life had taken, though he still liked to see himself a tragic figure. "I am not married," he repeated, and sighed, deeply.

He would not have minded in the least to be asked for the whole tale, but Araminta was too much concerned with her own circumstances, to care at all about his. She did not care at all about being ruined for its own sake, and so had forgotten to consider it, in the crisis. But she cared very much to be caught at it, and locked up in a temple the rest of her days, never allowed to do anything but make aspirin or do up accounts for widowers—*that* was not to be borne. She sighed in her own turn, and sat down upon the lid of the chest.

Weedle misunderstood the sigh, and poured her a glass of wine. "Come, sir, there is no need to be afraid, I assure you," he said, with worldly sympathy. "You will come to no harm under my protection, and soon you will be reunited with your friends."

"Oh, yes," she said, unenthusiastically. She was very sorry she had ever mentioned a ransom. "Thank you," she said, politely, and took the wine.

For consolation, it was excellent wine, and an excellent dinner: Weedle was pleased for an excuse to show away his ability to entertain in grand style, and Araminta discovered she was uncommonly hungry. She put away a truly astonishing amount of beef and soused hog's face and mince pie, none of which she had ever been allowed, of course; and she found she could drink three glasses of wine instead of the two which were ordinarily her limit.

By the time the servants cleared away the pudding, she was in too much charity with the world to be anxious. She had worked out several schemes for slipping away, if the pirates should indeed deliver her to her family; and the pearls around her waist, concealed, were a great comfort. She had meant them to pay her passage home, if she were not ransomed; now they would give her the start of an independence. And, best of all, if she were ruined, she need never worry about it again: she might jettison the whole tedious set of restrictions, which she felt was worth nearly every other pain.

And Weedle did not seem to be such a bad fellow, after all; her father's highest requirements for a man had always been, he should be a good host, and show to advantage upon a horse, and play a decent hand at the card-table. She thoughtfully eyed Weedle's leg, encased snugly in his silk knee-breeches and white stockings. It certainly did not need the aid of padding, and if his long curling black hair was a little extravagant, his height and his shoulders rescued that and the red coat from vulgarity. Fine eyes, and fine teeth; nothing not to like, at all.

So it was with renewed complacency of spirit she offered Weedle a toast, and gratified his vanity by saying sincerely, "That was the best dinner I ever ate. Shall we have a round of aughts and sixes?"

He was a little surprised to find his miserable young prisoner already so cheerful: ordinarily, it required a greater investment of patience and liquor, a show of cool, lordly kindness, to settle a delicate young nobleman's nerves, and impress upon him his host's generosity and masterful nature. But Weedle was not at all unwilling to congratulate himself on an early success, and began at once to calculate just how much sooner he might encompass his designs upon Lord Aramin's virtue. Ordinarily he allowed a week; perhaps, he thought judiciously, three days would do, in the present case.

Meanwhile, Araminta, who had spent the last several months housed in a cabin over the sailors' berth, and was already familiar with the means of consolation men found at sea, added, "Winner has first go, after?" and tilted her head towards the bed.

Taken aback, Weedle stared, acquiesced doubtfully, and picked up his cards with a faintly injured sense that the world was failing to arrange itself according to expectations. The sentiment was not soon overcome; Araminta was very good at aughts and sixes.

Araminta liked to be on *Amphidrake* very well. The pirates, most of them deserters from the Navy or the merchant marine, were not very different from the sailors on the *Bluegill*. But they did not know she was a woman, so no-one batted an eye if she wished to learn how to reef and make sail, and navigate by the stars. Instead they pronounced her a good sport and full of pluck, and began to pull their forelocks when she walked past, to show they did not hold it against her for being a nobleman.

Weedle was excellent company in most respects, if occasionally inclined to what Araminta considered inappropriate extremes of sensibility. Whistling while a man was being flogged at the grating could only be called insensitive; and on the other hand, finding one of the ship's kittens curled up dead in the corner of the cabin was not an occasion for mourning, but for throwing it out the window, and having the ship's boys swab the floor.

She enjoyed her food a great deal, and was adding muscle and inches of height at what anyone might have considered a remarkable rate at her age. She began to be concerned, a little, what would happen if she were to take off the amulet, particularly when she began to sprout a beard; but as she was certainly not going to do any such thing amidst a pack of pirates, she put it out of her mind and learned to shave.

The future loomed alarmingly for other reasons entirely. If only they had gone directly to Kingsport, Araminta had hoped they should arrive before the ransom, and she might slip away somehow while the men went on carouse with their winnings. But Weedle meant to try and break his personal record of fourteen prizes, and so he was staying out as long as possible.

"I am sure," she tried, "that they are already there. If you do not go directly, they will not wait forever: surely they will decide that I am dead, and that is why you do not come." She did not consider this a possibility at all: she envisioned nightly a horde of chaperones waiting at the docks, all of them with Horus-eyes glaring at her, and holding a heap of chains.

"I must endure the risk," Weedle said, "of your extended company," with a dangerously sentimental look in his eye: worse and worse. Araminta decidedly did not mean to spend the rest of her days as a pirate captain's paramour, no matter how splendidly muscled his thighs were. Although she depressed herself by considering that it might yet be preferable to a life with the Holy Sisters of The Sangreal.

She was perhaps inappropriately relieved, then, when a shriek of "Leviathan" went up, the next morning; and she dashed out to the deck on Weedle's heels. Now surely he should have to turn about and put in to port, she thought, not realizing they were already caught, until she tripped over the translucent tendril lying over the deck.

She pulled herself up and looked over the side. The leviathan's vast, pulsating, domelike mass was directly beneath the ship and enveloping her hull, glowing phosphorescent blue around the edges and wobbling softly like an aspic jelly. A few half-digested bones floated naked inside that transparent body, leftovers of a whale's ribcage. A faint whitish froth was already forming around the ship, at the waterline, as the leviathan's acid ate into the wood.

The men were firing pistols at it, and hacking at the tough, rubbery tendrils; without much effect. The leviathan leisurely threw over a few more, and a tip struck one of the pirates; he arched his back and dropped his hand-axe, mouth opening in a silent, frozen scream. The tendril looped half a dozen times around him, quick as lightning, and lifted him up and over the side, drawing him down and into the mass of the leviathan's body. His eyes stared up through the green murk, full of horror and quite alive: Araminta saw them slowly blink even as he was swallowed up into the jelly.

She snatched for a sword herself, and began to help chop away, ducking involuntarily as more of the thin limbs came up, balletic and graceful, to lace over the deck. Thankfully they did nothing once they were there other than to cling on, if one did not touch the glistening pink tips.

"Leave off, you damned lubbers," Weedle was shouting. "Make sail! All hands to make sail—"

He was standing at the wheel. Araminta joined the rush for the rope lines, and shortly they were making nine knots in the direction of the wind, back towards the Drowned Lands. It was a sorry speed, by the *Amphidrake*'s usual standards; the leviathan dragging from below worse than ten thousand barnacles. It did not seem particularly incommoded by their movement, and kept throwing over more arms; an acrid smell, like woodsmoke and poison, rose from the sides. The men had nearly all gone to huddle down below, out of reach of the tendrils. Weedle held the wheel with one arm, and an oar with the other, which he used to beat off any that came at him.

Araminta seized his long-glass, and climbed up to the crows-nest to go looking out: she could see clearly where the water changed color, and the gorgeous bluegreen began; the shipping lanes visible as broad bands of darker blue running through the Shallow Sea. The wind was moderately high, and everywhere she looked there seemed to be a little froth of cresting waves, useless; until at last she glimpsed in the distance a steady bank of white: a reef, or some land near enough the surface to make a breakwater; and she thought even a little green behind it: an island, maybe.

A fist of tendrils had wrapped around the mast since she had gone up, poisonous tips waving hopefully: there would be no climbing down now. She used the whisper-charm to tell Weedle the way: south by south-east, and then she grimly clung on to the swinging nest as he drove them towards the shoals.

What was left of the leviathan, a vile gelatinous mess stinking all the way to the shore, bobbed gently up and down with the waves breaking on the shoals, pinned atop the rocks along with what was left of the *Amphidrake*. This was not very much but a section of the quarterdeck, the roof of the cabin, and, unluckily, the top twelve feet of her mainmast, with the black skull flag gaily flying, planted neatly in a noxious mound of jelly.

The wreckage had so far survived three rainstorms. The survivors gazed at it dismally from the shore, and concocted increasingly desperate and unlikely schemes for tearing away, burning, or explaining the flag, on the arrival of a Navy patrol—these being regular enough, along the nearby shipping lanes, to make a rescue eventual, rather than unlikely.

"And then they put out the yard-arm, and string us all up one by one," the bo'sun Mr. Ribb said, morbidly.

"If so," Araminta snapped, losing patience with all of them, "at least it is better than being et up by the leviathan, and we may as well not sit here on the shore and moan." This was directed pointedly at Weedle, bitter and slumped under a palm tree. He had not been in the least inclined to go down with his ship, although he secretly felt he ought to have done, and it was hard to find that his unromantic escape had only bought him a few weeks of life and an ignominious death.

Araminta did not herself need to worry about hanging, but she was not much less unhappy, being perfectly certain the Navy would take her directly back to her family, under such guard as would make escape impossible. Nevertheless, she was not inclined to only eat coconuts and throw stones at monkeys and complain all day.

The island was an old, old mountaintop, furred with thick green vegetation, and nearly all cliffs rising directly from the ocean. Where the shoals had blocked the full force of the waves, a small natural harbor had developed, and the narrow strip of white sand which had given them shelter. Climbing up to the cliff walls to either side, Araminta could look down into the glass-clear water and see the mountainside dropping down and away, far away, and in a few places even the bleached gray spears of drowned trees below.

They had found the ruins of an old walkway, back in the jungle, while hunting: smooth uneven bricks of creamy white stone which led up and into the island's interior; but none of the men wanted to follow it. "That's the Drowned

Ones' work," they said, with shudders of dismay, and made various superstitious gestures, and refused even to let her go alone.

But after three days and a rainstorm had gone by, leaving the black flag as securely planted as ever, hanging loomed ever larger; and when Araminta again tried to persuade them, a few agreed to go along.

The walkway wound narrowly up the mountainside, pausing occasionally at small niches carved into the rock face, mossy remnants of statues squatting inside. The road was steep, and in places they had to climb on hands and feet with nothing more than narrow ledges for footholds. Araminta did not like to think how difficult a pilgrimage it might have been, three thousand years ago, before the Drowning, when the trail would have begun at the mountain's base and not near its summit. The men flinched at every niche; but nothing happened as they climbed, except that they got dust in their noses, and sneezed a great deal, and Jem Gorey was stung by a wasp.

The trail ended at a shrine, perched precarious and delicate atop the very summit; two massive sculpted lion-women sprawled at the gate, the fine detail of their heavy breasts and beards still perfectly preserved, so many years gone. The roof of the shrine stood some twenty feet in the air, on delicate columns not as thick as Araminta's wrist, each one the elongated graceful figure of a woman, and filmy drapery hung from the rafters still, billowing in great sheets of clean white. An altar of white stone stood in the center, and upon it a wide platter of shining silver.

"Wind goddess," Mr. Ribb said, gloomily. "Wind goddess for sure; we'll get no use here. Don't you be an ass, Porlock," he added, cutting that sailor a hard look. "As much as a man's life is worth, go poking into there."

"I'll just nip in," Porlock said, his eyes on the silver platter, and set his foot on the first stair of the gate.

The lion-women stirred, and cracked ebony-black eyes, and turned to look at him. He recoiled, to tried to: his foot would not come off the stair. "Help, fellows!" he cried, desperately. "Take my arm, heave—"

No one went anywhere near him. With a grinding noise like millstones, the lion-women rose up onto their massive paws and came leisurely towards him. Taking either one an arm, they tore him in two quite effortlessly; and then tore the parts in two again.

The other men fled, scattering back down the mountainside, as the lion-women turned their heads to look them over. Araminta alone did not flee, but waited until the others had run away. The living statues settled themselves back into their places, but they kept their eyes open and fixed on her, watchfully.

She debated with herself a while; she had read enough stories to know the dangers. She did not care to become a permanent resident, forced to tend the shrine forever; and it might not be only men who were punished for the temerity to enter. In favor of the attempt, however, the shrine plainly did not need much tending: whatever magic had made it, sustained it, with no guardian necessary but the deadly statues. And those stones along the trail had been worn smooth by more than weather: many feet had come this way, once upon a time.

"All right," she said at last, aloud, and reaching up to her neck took off the amulet.

She was braced to find herself abruptly back in her own former body, a good deal smaller; but the alteration was as mild as before. She looked down at her arms, and her legs: the same new length, and still heavy with muscle; she had lost none of the weight she had gained, or the height. Breasts swelled out beneath her shirt, her hips and waist had negotiated the exchange of an inch or two between themselves, and her face when she touched it felt a little different—the beard was gone, she noted gratefully—but that was all.

The guardians peered at her doubtfully when she came up the stairs. They did get up, as she came inside, and paced after her all the way to the altar, occasionally leaning forward for a suspicious sniff. She unwound the strand of pearls from around her waist and poured the whole length of it rattling into the offering-dish, a heap of opalescence and silver.

The lion-women went back to their places, satisfied. The hangings rose and shuddered in a sudden gust of wind, and the goddess spoke: a fine gift, and a long time since anyone had come to worship; what did Araminta want.

It was not like Midwinter Feast, where the medium was taken over and told fortunes; or like church services at Lammas tide. The goddess of the Drowned Ones spoke rather matter-of-factly, and there was no real sound at all, only the wind rising and falling over the thrumming hangings. But Araminta understood perfectly, and understood also that her prepared answers were all wrong. The goddess was not offering a little favor, a charm to hide her or a key to unlock chains, or even a way off the island; the goddess was asking a question, and the question had to be answered truly.

Easier to say what Araminta did not want: to go home and be put in a convent, to go on to the colonies and be married. Not to be a prisoner, or a fine lady, or a captain's lover, or a man in disguise forever; not, she added, that it was not entertaining enough for a time; but what she really wanted, she told the goddess, was to be a captain herself, of her own life; and free.

A fine wish, the goddess said, for a fine gift. Take one of those pearls, and go down and throw it in the ocean.

Araminta took a pearl out of the dish: it came easily off the strand. She went down the narrow walkway, down to the shore, and past all the men staring at her and crossing themselves in alarm, and she threw the pearl into the clear blue waters of the natural harbor.

For a moment, nothing happened; then a sudden foaming overtook the surface of the water, white as milk. With a roar of parting waves and a shudder, the *Amphidrake* came rising from the deep in all her shattered pieces, seaweed and ocean spilling away. Her ribs and keel showed through the gaps in her half-eaten hull for a moment, and then the foam was climbing up her sides, and leaving gleaming unbroken pearl behind. The decks were rebuilt in smooth white wood; tall slim masts, carved in the shapes of women, climbed up one after another, and vast white sails unfurled in a wind that teased them gently full.

The foam subsided to the water, and solidified into a narrow dock of pearl, running to shore to meet her. Araminta turned to look a rather dazed Weedle in the face.

"This is my ship," she said, "and you and all your men are welcome, if you would rather take service with me than wait for the Navy."

She pulled her hair back from her head, and tied it with a thread from her shirt; and she stepped out onto the dock. She was nearly at the ship when Weedle came out onto the dock at last, and called, "Aramin!" after her.

She turned and smiled at him, a flashing smile. "Araminta," she said, and went aboard.

WE LOVE DEENA

ALICE SOLA KIM

Deena wanted to know if I was following her.

I don't remember which attempt it was, how many people I had been so far. But this time I was Pam, a girl who worked at the bookstore in Deena's neighborhood. Pam, whose hair was the same color as her skin, a monochromatic honey shade that would have been boring and dreary on other people but looked delicious on Pam. I was reasonably sure that if Deena didn't love me anymore, she would love Pam.

Deena said, again, "Are you following me?"

All she had needed was one look at me. Was it the way I was standing? Was it my little nervous cough, that identified me as surely as a DNA sample? I shook my head and sighed. I was like a ghost that had failed at whatever evil it was supposed to do, and could only be embarrassed at being found out, exorcised, and laughed at. Now I knew why there were ghosts that liked to smash things. I used the momentum of my sigh to leave Pam, whooshing out backwards and hanging in the air like mist behind her.

And then Pam wondered why she felt headachy and turned on—her heart was beating so strongly that it moved her stomach, her viscera in nauseating flutters—and all of this occurring in the lost moment between when she was shelving New Fiction and right now. Pam stared at her fingers, which were splayed out blushing and stinging against the countertop. I know because now I was someone else, and I was watching her.

My ex-girlfriend Deena killed people for a living. She was a Euthanizer for the local health bureau. I think I must be a sick person, because I thought that was sort of hot. But this is really hard to explain. I thought that people were lucky to have someone like Deena to lead them out of life and into the nothing-whatever of being dead. If you do not believe in something like St. Peter at the gates and beautiful angels who look like the best parts of men and women both, *but you want that sort of thing*, then Deena is your best bet.

Deena, the angel of Death, had hands that scrabbled like insects when she loaded and reloaded her licensed Death Ray in mere seconds. Her hair was always in a short bob, the ends curving into her cheeks like a knight's helmet. It was Louise Brooks hair, but anyone could have that. Deena was just so pretty, in that same small-mouthed, secretive way.

The first time I met Deena, she killed someone I loved. His name was Melchior Pak, an old professor of mine. I had been one of the worst students in his seminar. We got to know each other when I started dog-sitting his Great Dane to improve my grades. That didn't work, but we became friends after an argument abut whether the band Roxy Music was better before or after Brian Eno left. Mel had been pro-Eno. My youthful, Botoxed grandparents had taught me otherwise, back when I was a kid.

The last time I saw Mel, he was lying in bed, looking like hell in a pomegranate-colored velour tracksuit. I might look like a rich woman at the grocery store, Mel said, but I'm comfortable, so shut it. When Deena walked in, I barely noticed. I was watching Mel's husband Gabriel, who was holding Mel's hand and weeping. You might not think that people could possibly cry enough for the tears, all that water to spread like hungry lakes and make everything messy and salty, but that's what Gabriel was doing. Mel had "Ladytron" blasting from his pricey Bang & Olufsen speakers. It was his favorite song, and perhaps his way of having the last word in the old Roxy Music argument.

There was very little ceremony. Mel patted Gabriel's hand and whispered something in his ear. He motioned for me to come over, and took a slippery white envelope out from under his pillow and handed it to me. Don't open it now, he said. But promise me you'll look at it later. I tried to say something but he shook his head.

Then he nodded at Deena, who was perched patiently on a footstool. She stood and raised her arm, and a cloud of cameras coalesced, buzzing and spinning. I couldn't hear them over the music, which had reached the sax solo, but a few of the cameras swept ticklishly past my eyelashes.

"This will be recorded for the archives of the health bureau," Deena said. Then: "Goodbye, Mr. Pak." She aimed the Death Ray at Mel. I felt a loud hum like cotton against my eardrums, and that was all—Mel was enveloped in a slithering gray fog. There was a moment of amazement in all of this, however; the sax was swirling and so was the fog, and right before the room clouded over completely, Deena looked me in the eyes, her gaze a pure laser-shot of information and future potential and, oh, everything. When the fog lifted, Mel was dead.

My friends tell me that I love Deena because of the incredibly fucked-up way we met, all the adrenaline and horror and twisted glamour. I love Mel. Deena kills Mel. I love Deena. My friends are over-simplifying jerks.

It was that and it wasn't that. After Mel's appointment was over, I found myself standing outside of his renovated Victorian. It was cold out and my feet felt as heavy as snowmen, stuck frozen to the ground. A long time passed before Deena came out of the house.

She said, "I liked Mr. Pak. Funny guy. He chose a very nice-sounding song, too. Mr. Pak was in a cult, did you know that? I'm sure you knew that."

Mel's parents had been Mindiites. He was born in their compound, lived there until he was twenty-six years old, when the leader died under mysterious circumstances and the cult disbanded. Mel talked only about the robes and rituals, not the philosophy of the cult, which was still a mystery to the rest of the world.

"I need to ask you about something," I said.

"Mr. Pak really loved you," Deena said, as if she hadn't heard me. "It was your first time at one of these, right? It's not a morbid thing, to want someone at a euthanasia appointment. It means he loves you and wants you to be the last thing he sees.

"I wish he hadn't chosen today," I said.I wish he had chosen next week, or the week after, or next year. Some other time."

Deena's eyes were flat and calm. "That's why choosing is treacherous. The people that love you don't realize that you choose the right day for you. They only want you to delay that day for as long as possible, so the appointment might never happen. But then there's no point in choosing."

I rubbed my eyes and looked down. I tried to stare at something that wasn't a signpost to something sad. A rock. A dogwood tree across the street. A wrinkled club flyer stuck under my car windshield. No, that was a sad thing. They were all sad things and looking at them made me feel worse. Deena was probably the only beautiful thing for miles.

"Yeah," I said. "Yeah, I guess you'd know." I tried to smile at her. My face felt shiny and painful and peeled. Then I felt a light touch on the small of my back, more like an animal's paw than a human hand.

"Would you like to get a cup of coffee with me?" Deena said.

I was Martin, a homeless man who usually sat near the Trader Joe's where Deena shopped. I was gradually learning Deena's entire schedule. I had a paper sack of old books with the covers ripped off—Edwardian romance novels and Tom Clancy and diet guides. I was always reading. There were so many ills in my body. My teeth were loose. My stomach felt beat-up, empty, like a smashed soda can. I often had migraines so bad that it felt like my left eye was pulsing in and out of its socket, as though I were a squeeze toy. When I was Martin, it was harder for me to think. All my thoughts across all bodies sometimes acted like a card catalog that had been upset onto the floor. Things grew in my brain and their root systems were destroying everything.

A young man passing by flipped a coin into my paper cup and I thought about where I left off and everything else began. The sun sank into my skin and I sighed—a brief flare of joy. Oh, I was forgetting myself. Oh, everything I had done, all the people I had been, everyone who I'd given the Me Virus, the Deena Disease, which I suffered alone.

But there was no time for such thoughts now. I was on a mission. I saw

Deena park her car and walk into the grocery store. I was also Celeste now, and I hurried out of my apartment to meet Deena. I chose to inhabit Celeste because of her proximity to Trader Joe's and because she was older, attractive rather than cute, perhaps someone that would please Deena. Which was all I needed.

When Celeste-me passed Martin-me, I put a twenty into Martin's cup. He would want it later.

Inside Trader Joe's, I found Deena looking at olives. She was holding a little jar in her palm like a hand grenade.

"You don't want those," I said. Deena turned around and I saw her liking what she saw. A pulse of happiness ran through me.

Deena said, "What do you recommend?" She raised her chin imperiously, like a teenage boy trying to look taller than his friends. It was a good sign. Deena tried to intimidate people she was attracted to. You could call it a bad habit of hers, but I always took it to mean that she was shy at heart. I'm kind of a sucker.

"These." I picked up a squat jar of pepper-stuffed olives. "These are awesome."

"Oh huh," she said. "I knew someone who loved those olives too. She was practically addicted to them."

I talked just to say anything.Lots of people love olives. Except for my Dad. And my sister. And some other people I know. They hate olives."

"And she said they were 'awesome' too," Deena continued, as if the word was a large bug that had flown into her mouth. "She said 'awesome' so often that it kind of lost all meaning, do you know what I mean?"

"Well," I sputtered, "I don't say it very often. And these are good olives, okay?" There was one of me but three brains, and one word kept ricocheting between my skulls:

FUCK!

FUCK

FUCK

Deena was looking past me. "Oh my god," she said, without changing her tone. There's a man peeing outside of the store."

That man was me. My neighbor Greg, an engineer at Cisco who lived in the unit above me. I had inhabited him just in case I needed to create a distraction. Again, fuck. I hadn't planned this very well. Urine was the only weapon that Greg had, even though he wasn't really the type of person who would pee in public, much less against Trader Joe's. My pee splashed against the side of the store and speckled my leather shoes. I ran Greg away afterwards, before the cops could arrive. Deena slid her eyes back to me.

Meanwhile I had calmed down. "I don't usually do this," I said, "but you seem like a really interesting person. Can I take you out to dinner sometime?"

Deena smiled. But then her tiny nostrils flared, and I knew I was dead. I had gotten skilled at reading Deena's moods, for all the good it did me, and this was one of Deena's mean smiles. Deena's mean smile was much worse than a frown from a normal person.

She said, "Actually, I'm not in the mood for olives anymore. Maybe it was seeing that man pee, or something. Thanks for your help though." Deena turned away, frowning now, and left the aisle. Then I glimpsed her in the next aisle over, peering at me around the corner.

I bought the jar of olives I was holding and left as quickly as I could. All I had was that one quick look of admiration she had given me, before I ruined everything again.

I think it takes a while to find out when someone doesn't love you as much as you love her. Like two near-parallel lines, diverging drastically as time passes. It would have been nice if we could see that the lines were crooked from the very beginning.

They fuck you up, perfectionist girlfriends. I had been standing in the bathroom, naked to the waist. I'd gotten one contact lens in and was struggling with the other, it kept folding against my eyeball for some reason, and then Deena had snuggled up behind me.

"Hey," she said. "Your boobs are crooked. I never noticed."

"So?" I said.

She smiled. She snaked her arms around the front of my body and cupped my boobs.

"They're lopsy bunny boobs." She jiggled them in her hands for a moment. You are so cute. God."

Then Deena kissed me on the ear and walked off. I looked down at the boobs. The nipples were stiff and insulted-looking. I put a shirt on.

This was a Deena habit. She listed my faults and pretended to love them, and then she'd turn around and admire all sorts of perfect girls—ones with wiry rock-climber bodies and mod haircuts; ones with short and curvy bodies and perfectly shaped shaved heads; ones with perfect jawlines and clothes they had made themselves; ones with waist-length hair, who believed in astrology; ones with waist-length hair, who didn't believe in astrology; and finally those *L Word* bitches. I hated that show, a lot.

There were all kinds of beautiful girls in the world and she never failed to point them out.

I have tried seeming beautiful to Deena, just as myself, but there is only so much that is possible. Have you ever tried to make your lips seems large and luscious with applications of lip-liner and gloss? I looked like a contestant in a spaghetti-eating contest. I looked like the winner.

After Mel's death, I did remember to keep my promise. I opened his envelope. The first thing in it was a letter from Mel.

Pet,

Cults are crazy more often than they are right. The Cult of Mindy was both. I'm not going to bore you with the details (lord knows I spent most of "cult school" in a haze of boredom!), but I will say this: Mindy promises long life and the widest variety of human experience possible. Mindy shall deliver. I am bequeathing to you something that I created in my last year as a Mindiite.

Please remember that the mind does not live without the body—don't let anyone tell you otherwise—and the body transforms the mind. I am planning to die as myself rather than live on as someone else. I am too afraid, but perhaps you are not.

I trust you to do something good with this, or at least something interesting. I am sorry to be dead. But there is a tiny bit of useful advice in this letter. If you can't find it, then you deserve the terrible grade you received in my seminar.

All my love,
Melchior.

And there was an old sheet of yellow paper covered in scribbles, with two lines of writing crammed into every college-ruled row. There were incantations that read like threatening nursery rhymes, admonitions to use high-quality toothpaste and cat hair in the spell.

I put the paper down.

I had missed the sight of Mel's handwriting—usually in bright red pen—but now I couldn't even stand to look at it. Mel had gone dotty before he died. Mel was trying to relive his good old cult days. I stuck everything back into the envelope and put it in my desk drawer.

Perhaps it would have been better to receive nothing than to receive this. It was a thought so unfaithful that I cringed. I would not throw it away, but I would not look at it again.

Then again, being dumped will change your mind about many things. It was only three months later. I was sitting on the floor of my apartment, swigging horrible burning Jack Daniels from a mug with a broken handle. I called a few of my friends but none of them were willing to talk to me for too long. They told me that Deena was a creep with a creepy job, that she didn't listen to good music and she flirted with other girls too much.

I hung up on all of them and lay down on the rug, mind blank. I rolled my head left and right, my heart thudding in my chest. A bad feeling was rising up in my body, as though I was fighting an ocean wave that kept swelling to my mouth and nose. It meant barfing. I shut my eyes hard and when I opened them again, I glimpsed a triangle of white sticking out of the desk drawer. Mel's Mindiite spell. I got up and dug it out from under a pile of junk.

I was laughing and crying. I rubbed the toothpaste into my chest and felt it eat away at my skin, one cell at a time. Then I stepped forward and chanted the spell. My breath was caustic and smelly, as though my stomach had sent advance scouts up to my mouth. I wondered, was it easiest to do magic when you were drunk?

Choosing a name. I chose my sister, whispered her name, held her face in my mind, and,

        then,

             the chest I was touching wasn't my own, it was softer and there was no toothpaste gunk and then I caught my reflection in my flatscreen TV, something I did not remember owning. My sister Isabel was looking back at me. I was I and I was Isabel. My brain had been sliced in two and regenerated itself into two wholes, like a flatworm. I scratched my bumpy Isabel nose, and when I laughed, I laughed the same way in two different voices. After another moment, I left Isabel easily, stepping backwards but not-stepping-backwards. And then I was all myself again.

I finally threw up.

Deena my Deena.

I want you back.

But I'm not stupid enough to think that you want me back.

If you don't love me in this body, then I'll give you another, and another, and more after that.

Tell me what pleases you and you'll have it.

I will be any shape you need.

My manifesto, Deena.

I was Angelina Jolie. Everyone loves Angelina Jolie, right? Even during the phase with all the blood and knives and lace-up leather pants, when she was kind of dorky, I found that no one could resist her. Even my straight female friends, who tossed around phrases like "I'd do her if I did women" as easily as ordering soup, had a certain manic light in their eyes when they discussed Angelina Jolie.

Now, of course, Angelina adopted children and went on goodwill missions and was not so cheesily thrilling, but she was still perfect. I saw my Jessica Rabbit features reflected everywhere in the glossy surfaces of Neiman Marcus—the floors, the racks, the glass counters filled with monstrous, glittering jewelry—and it gave me a short sharp shock every time. I was not comfortable. I did not like Angelina Jolie's reflection gliding on by as I stalked Deena through the store, like a Bentley driving alongside a busted Toyota Corolla.

Deena was browsing through women's designer sportswear. I had to stop myself from kicking off my high heels and running at her. When I sidled up to Deena, pretending to browse the rack next to her, I saw her eyes widen.

"Hi there," I said right to her. And why not? This body, it was like wearing a magic coat that gave me permission to do whatever I pleased.

"Oh," Deena said, "hello. Excuse me, but you're Angelina Jolie?" It was nice to see her flustered.

"I am. What's your name?"

She smiled, still confused. "I'm Deena." It felt so good to touch her again, even if it was just shaking her chilly little hand. That's probably why I went a little crazy.

"Listen," I said. "Why don't we get out of here? Let's get dinner. We can go anywhere you want."

Deena took a step backwards. The look in her eyes—I felt as though a shadow had just swallowed her up, large and dark and hawk-shaped.

"Just dinner, that's all," I said. Deena gasped. She turned on her heel, losing one of her shoes, and ran towards the fitting room. I followed her. Deena pushed over a whole section of separates directly in my path, the hangers screaming down the racks. I leapt over them.

By the time I caught up with Deena, she had locked herself into one of the fitting room stalls.

"Please," I said.

"What the hell do you want with me?" said Deena. "You don't even know me. You're Angelina Jolie."

"Please, I just want to talk to you for a little bit," I said. Then I did a stupid and bad thing. I said: "I miss you so much, Deena."

She was quiet for a long time. Behind the door of the stall, I couldn't picture her face—whether she felt longing or hate or annoyance or fear. I couldn't even hear her breathing.

"You what," Deena said.

I said nothing.

"You fake-ass Angelina Jolie," she whispered. "I know who you are. I'm going to call the police if you don't stop following me around."

I slumped against the door. After waiting a few more seconds, I finally left.

A few days later, I was at a newsstand and saw a magazine cover splashed with a blurry photo of Angelina sprinting through Neiman Marcus. She, I, looked awful. I flipped to the middle:

ANGELINA CHASES MYSTERIOUS LESBIAN LOVER THOUGH DEPARTMENT STORE!

"I guess I thought she was a friend of mine," Jolie said. "She must have looked familiar. She did look familiar."

"Besides," Jolie added, "I pretty much only do it with Brad Pitt now."

Worst of all is knowing that Deena won't love you, no matter what form or size or shape you take. Worst of all is knowing that there's something so wrong with you that it'll stick to you forever.

I have been so many people for Deena, so many varied and beautiful women. But she didn't want any of us.

What's the spell that'll change every single thing about me inside and out? What's the spell that'll render me unrecognizable to Deena, to anyone, to my own mother?

Deena didn't invite me to her birthday party, so I crashed it. Specifically, I inhabited every last person at her party. I waited until after everyone got into her apartment. I became thirty-six people. The sensation was almost too much, I could barely carry on ten conversations and one of me got a terrible nosebleed that poured out of my nostrils as suddenly and smoothly as poured wine. Somewhere else in the room, a beer bottle slipped from my hand, and rolled over on the floor. A puddle fanned out around my feet and burbled quietly to itself. Keep. It. Together.

This is the last time, I had said into the mirror at home. This time something has to happen. Maybe we can all line up. Maybe Deena will chose one of me. Maybe Deena will choose the one she might be able to love from a catalog. I think we can discuss this like adults. My chest was angry and red from repeated applications of toothpaste.

I was Vishal, one of Deena's co-workers from the health bureau. I said to her, "You look exhausted. Is everything okay?"

She said, "I don't know. Things haven't been going well for me."

"How so?" I said. Vishal's mustache felt heavy against my lip.

Deena smiled a little, a smile that expressed only tiredness. "A lot of people have been hitting on me these days."

"Isn't that a good thing?" Isn't it?

"No. It is not." She had lost a bit of weight, hadn't she? From behind her, I saw how the pale knobs of her vertebrae jutted out above the neck of her sweater. She said, "But if I tell you why it's not a good thing, you're going to think I've gone insane."

"Oh, Deena," I said. I gave her a careful pat on the back. She started to cry. I came closer to her, folded my arms around her. It's okay, it's okay, I said. Oh, I'm so sorry.

At that, Deena lifted her head. We had all stopped talking, stopped playing at being thirty-six different people at a party. We were thirty-six people who were all me and all loved Deena, looking at only her and wanting her and pressing ever closer.

"Oh no," she said. "Get away."

"I'll be whatever you want," we said. "See how?" She was shaking her head as thought she could shake us all out of her sight.

Imagine a room full of people who love you, who adore your body and thoughts and words. I can't even imagine such riches. Deena was lucky. We were a kicking chorus line of people who loved Deena! A battalion of soldiers who would give their lives for Deena! A synchronized swimming team who fluttered and kicked for an audience of only Deena.

Then Deena pulled her Death Ray out of her purse.

Confession time. I made Deena seem like the Mean Girl, the Ice Queen, and that's not completely fair. It is true that in many ways, Deena was like a Soviet

Constructivist painting, all gorgeous reds and tans and blacks, with lines and edges that would poke you painfully the closer you came. But Deena was also cuddly. I just wanted to say that before it was too late.

Once we were at a karaoke bar downtown, a nice sort of place where people sang like wannabe pop idols instead of badly and drunkenly like they were supposed to. We had stopped by to drink dirty martinis and watch the singers for a while. But then the host called Deena's name. I hadn't seen Deena put her name in, so I was shocked.

"Deena? You're going to sing?" I hissed to her as she got up. Deena never sang. I couldn't imagine such a thing.

"We'll see if it actually sounds like singing," she said.

Standing in the front of the karaoke monitor, Deena kept smiling, her lips clamped shut. She looked friendly and approachable. That's how I knew she was terrified.

"This song is dedicated to my one and only lady love," she said. She pointed gracefully at me. Her arms and neck shone under the spotlight. Everyone turned around, but at this point, there were only a few spare hollers and claps. I felt a certain message emanating very strongly from everyone in the bar—Deena would have to sing before they would be convinced of her love for me.

To be honest, I wasn't expecting the song. I was expecting a Top 40 hit, maybe, who knows. Deena was not exactly one for pop culture. She watched *The L Word* only for the babes, naturally.

The song was "Let It Be." The Beatles. It was incredibly inappropriate for the karaoke bar and incredibly long. Deena had that familiar, unmoored look of someone who thought they knew a song intimately until they actually had to sing it without the real vocals half-drowning them out. And there's a special sort of problem you might encounter when you sing a simple song like "Let It Be": if you suck at singing, a large part of the song will be you chanting *"let it be let it be let it beeeeeee"* drearily, tunelessly, please let this be over now.

Of course I loved it. When Deena was not squinting at the monitor, she was trying to smile for me, brave and ashen like someone who had been called off to war.

When "Let It Be" ended, everyone clapped for real—Deena, although awful, had proven her love valiantly—and a few people even whistled as she speed-walked towards our table and leaned down to kiss me.

"You're amazing," I said.

"I knew you'd enjoy that," Deena said, calm and beautiful once more. Then she pushed her head against me like a puppy and mumbled, "God, that was awful. I thought it would be so easy. I picked that song because it was easy. But then it went on and on forever."

It was the best thing Deena could have given me. Deena hated rough edges and discomfort. Easy for Deena would be paying for dinner at a nice restaurant and taking me to a wine bar afterwards. Easy for Deena would be finding me perfect shoes from stores with single-word names.

That is why I chose karaoke night as the night of perfect happiness, the night I held close to me when I inhabited and left body after body. When we left the bar, Deena rested her hand on my waist, the little hill of fat that sat between the place where my waist pinched inwards and my hips swelled out. She didn't do it in the evaluating sort of way that she usually did. She liked the feel of me. And I was so happy. I felt beautiful. Just a bit. Maybe.

It's like certain movies, where you only get one truly happy scene after you meet cute and before everything falls apart. It's like everyone is in a hurry to get to the doomed part. Well I wasn't. But maybe constant exposure to the movie version has altered me forever. Because now the Deena I think about more, want more, is Bad Deena. Ice Queen Deena.

My brain feels like a warehouse. There are so many different people, all me, crammed up in there, and I am having trouble moving us down the street. Deena is closing in on us, her curvy legs flying down the street. She has already picked off a few of me from the perimeter. I can feel the sharp little deaths spiking in some deep part of my brain as they happen, the bodies falling like limbs from the group.

Oh.

I start panting as I run down the street. I didn't mean to get anyone killed. I was just borrowing their bodies and I know that sounds bad but I didn't mean anyone harm. I swear. Now I shiver in my original body, hiding by a dumpster in an alley by Deena's apartment. The white nimbus of the Death Ray spills over the edge of the dumpster. They're close.

Stop! Stop! I'm leaving them, we all say. Deena stops shooting.

"Then do it," she says. I run them a few blocks away, and then I leave them. Deena's standing still. I hear her breathing, punctuated by the rain that begins to spatter the ground in irregular blots.

"It's just me now," I say from my hiding place.

"Christ," she says. She sounds so broken-down and low. "It's not like I can file a restraining order against you, you know?" Then she laughs, but it's not the good kind.

"I know. Deena, I'm sorry. It's my fault."

"It is your fucking fault," says Deena.

"I wanted you back, Deena, I didn't know what to do." I don't know what to tell her that will fix everything. I don't know why Deena was the only woman that ever made me feel like this, all itchy and angry and desperate.

Deena said, "With every person I date from now on, I'll only think of you. That was rotten. You have no idea."

Her shadow stretches like black taffy against the alleyway, and my breath stutters in my throat. I'm all twisty inside. At the sight of Deena, even after everything, sense will always leave me and again I will wish I could be someone she loved. Oh, it's so fucking ridiculous and it will never end.

What would Mel say? I imagine Mel's face filling the narrow rectangle of sky between buildings, like the lion dad in *The Lion King*. I wish he could yell at me, remind me that there are other women in the world besides Deena, and ask me why I have been so monstrous. Or demand to know how, with such great magic in my life, I'd managed to screw up so badly. Anyway, Mel is not saying anything.

I clap my hands over my mouth and try to quiet my breathing. The wet ground has seeped through my jeans and my butt feels cold and dead and detached from me. I reach down into my sock, where I've rolled a small tube of potion, and squeeze some out onto my palm. It stings. I move my hand up and down, like I'm weighing it. But I'm all out of options, aren't I? And with that thought, something tremendous seems to loosen inside me, and I stop shivering. I wonder, what will it be like to look out of Deena's clear eyes, to look at myself and see my adoration shining out, reflected back and forth in a swimmy, swoony feedback loop? I could it do it. I could do it forever.

Her feet crunch into the wet pavement. "I'm here," she says in a weird singsong. But she's not that good at playing the villain. She clears her throat awkwardly.

"Deena," I say, potion at the ready, eyes closed. "Deena, Deena, Deena." I know where my eyes will open next, how my heart will thud inside my borrowed, stolen body; and to be utterly and completely honest with you, I am looking forward to it.

THE ART OF ALCHEMY

TED KOSMATKA

Sometimes when I came over, Veronica would already be naked. I'd find her spread out on a lawn chair behind the fence of her townhome, several sinewy yards of black skin visible to second-story windows across the park. She'd scissor her long legs and raise a languid eyelid.

"You have too many clothes on," she'd say.

And I'd sit. Run a hand along smooth, dark curves. Curl pale fingers into hers.

The story of Veronica is the story of this place. These steel mills, and the dying little city-states around them, have become a part of it somehow—Northwest Indiana like some bizarre, composite landscape we've all consented to believe in. A place of impossible contrasts. Cornfields and slums and rich, gated communities. National parkland and industrial sprawl.

Let it stand for the rest of the country. Let it stand for everything.

On cold days, the blast furnaces assemble huge masses of white smoke across the Lake Michigan shoreline. You can still see it mornings, driving I-90 on the way to work—a broad cumulous mountain range rising from the northern horizon, as if we were an alpine community, nestled beneath shifting peaks. It is a terrible kind of beauty.

Veronica was twenty-five when we met—just a few years younger than I. She was brilliant, and beautiful, and broken. Her townhome sat behind gates on the expensive side of Ridge Road and cost more than I made in five years. Her neighbors were doctors, and lawyers, and business owners. From the courtyard where she lay naked, you could see a church steeple, the beautiful, dull green of oxidized copper, rising over distant rooftops.

The story of Veronica is also the story of edges. And that's what I think about most when I think of her now. The exact line where one thing becomes another. The exact point where an edge becomes sharp enough to cut you.

We might have been talking about her work. Or maybe she was just making conversation, trying to cover her nervousness; I don't remember. But I remember the rain and the hum of her BMW's engine. And I remember her saying, as she took the Randolph Street exit, "His name is Voicheck."

"Is that his first name, or last?"

"It's the only one he gave me."

We took Randolph down to the Loop, and the Chicago skyline reared up at us. Veronica knew the uptown streets. The restaurant on Dearborn had been her choice of location—a nice sixty-dollar-a-plate Kazuto bar that stayed open till two A.M. Trendy, clubby, dark. Big name suppliers sometimes brought her there for business dinners, if they were also trying to sleep with her. It was the kind of place wealthy people went when they wanted to get drunk with other wealthy people.

"He claims he's from Poland," she said. "But the accent isn't quite right. More Baltic than Slavic."

I wondered at that. At how she knew the difference.

"Where's he based out of?" I asked.

"Ukraine, formerly, but he sure as hell can't go back now. Had a long list of former this, former that. Different think tanks and research labs. Lots of burned bridges."

"Is he the guy, or just the contact?"

"He's playing it like he's the guy, but I don't know."

She hit her signal and made a left. The rain came down harder, Chicago slick-bright with streetlights and traffic. Green lions on the right, and at some point, we crossed the river.

"Is he bringing it with him?" I asked.

"I don't know."

"But he said he was actually bringing it?"

"Yeah." She looked at me. "He said."

"Jesus."

Her face wore a strange expression in the red glow of dashboard light. It took me a moment to place it. Then it hit me: in the year and a half I'd known her, this was the first time I'd ever seen her scared.

I met her at the lab. I say "lab" and people imagine white walls and sterile test tubes, but it's not like that. It's mostly math I do, and something close to metallurgy. All of it behind glass security walls. I check my work with a scanning electron microscope, noting crystalline lattices and surface structure micro-abrasions.

She walked through the door behind Hal, the lab's senior supervisor.

"This is the memory metals lab," Hal told her, gesturing as he entered.

She nodded. She was young and slender, smooth dark skin, a face that seemed, at first glance, to be more mouth than it should. That was my initial impression of her—some pretty new-hire the bosses were showing around. That's it. And then she was past me, following the supervisor deeper into the lab. At the time, I had no idea.

I heard the supervisor's voice drone on as he showed her the temper ovens and the gas chromatograph in the next room. When they returned, the super was following her.

I looked up from the lab bench and she was staring at me. "So you're the genius," she said.

That was when she pointed it at me. The look. The way she could look at you with those big dark eyes, and you could almost see the gears moving—her full mouth pulled into a sensuous smile that wanted to be more than it was. She smiled like she knew something you didn't.

There were a dozen things I could have said, but the nuclear wind behind those eyes blasted my words away until all that was left was a sad kind of truth. I knew what she meant. "Yeah," I said. "I guess that's me."

She turned to the supervisor. "Thank you for your time."

Hal nodded and left. It took me a moment to realize what had just happened. The laboratory supervisor—my direct boss—had been dismissed.

"Tell me," she said. "What do you do here?"

I paused for three seconds before I spoke, letting myself process the seismic shift. Then I explained it.

She smiled while I talked. I'd done it for an audience a dozen times, these little performances. It was practically a part of my job description since the last corporate merger made Uspar-Nagoi the largest steel company in the world. I'd worked for three different corporations in the last two years and hadn't changed offices once. The mill guys called them white-hats, these management teams that flew in to tour the facilities, shaking hands, smiling under their spotless white hardhats, attempting to fit their immediate surroundings into the flowchart of the company's latest international acquisitions. Research was a prime target for the tours, but here in the lab, they were harder to spot since so many suits came walking through. It was hard to know who you were talking to, really. But two things were certain. The management types were usually older than the girl standing in front of me. And they'd always, up till now, been male.

But I explained it like I always did. Or maybe I put a little extra spin on it; maybe I showed off. I don't know. "Nickle-titanium alloys," I said. I opened the desiccator and pulled out a small strip of steel. It was long and narrow, cut into almost the exact dimensions of a ruler.

"First you take the steel," I told her, holding out the dull strip of metal. "And you heat it." I lit the Bunsen burner and held the steel over the open flame. Nothing happened for ten, twenty seconds. She watched me. I imagined what I must look like to her at that moment—blue eyes fixed on the warming steel, short hair jutting at wild angles around the safety goggles I wore on my forehead. Just another technofetishist lost in his obsession. It was a type. Flame licked the edges of the dull metal.

I smiled and, all at once, the metal moved.

The metal contracted muscularly, like a living thing, twisting itself into a ribbon, a curl, a spring.

"It's caused by micro- and nano-scale surface restructuring," I told her. "The change in shape results from phase transformations. Martensite when cool;

Austenite when heated. The steel remembers its earlier configurations. The different phases want to be in different shapes."

"Memory metal," she said. "I've always wanted to see this. What applications does it have?"

The steel continued to flex, winding itself tighter. "Medical, structural, automotive. You name it."

"Medical?"

"For broken bones. The shape memory alloy has a transfer temp close to body temp. You attach a plate to the break site, and body heat makes the alloy want to contract, thereby exerting compressive force on the bone at both ends of the fracture."

"Interesting."

"They're also investigating the alloy's use in heart stents. A coolcrushed alloy tube can be inserted into narrow arteries where it'll expand and open once it's heated to blood temperature."

"You mentioned automotive."

I nodded. Automotive. The big money. "Imagine that you've put a small dent in your fender," I said. "Instead of taking it to the shop, you pull out your hairdryer. The steel pops right back in shape."

She stayed at the lab for another hour, asking intelligent questions, watching the steel cool and straighten itself. Before she left, she shook my hand politely and thanked me for my time. She never once told me her name. I watched the door close behind her as she left.

Two weeks later she returned. This time, without Hal.

She drifted into the lab like a ghost near the end of my shift.

In the two weeks since I'd seen her, I'd learned a little about her. I'd learned her name, and that her corporate hat wasn't just management, but upper management. She had an engineering degree from out east, then Ivy League grad school by age twenty. She gave reports to men who ran a corporate economy larger than most countries. She was somebody's golden child, fast-tracked to the upper circles. The company based her out of the East Chicago regional headquarters but occasionally flew her to Korea, India, South Africa, to the latest corporate takeovers and the constant stream of new facilities that needed integration. She was an organizational savant, a voice in the ear of the global acquisition market. The multinationals had long since stopped pretending they were about actually making things; it was so much more Darwinian than that now. The big fish ate the little fish, and Uspar-Nagoi, by anyone's standards, was a whale. You grow fast enough, long enough and pretty soon you need an army of gifted people to understand what you own, and how it all fits together. She was part of that army.

"So what else have you been working on?" she asked.

When I heard her voice, I turned. Veronica: her smooth, pretty face utterly emotionless, the smile gone from her full mouth.

"Okay," I said. And this time I showed her my real tricks. I showed her what I could really do. Because she'd asked.

Martensite like art. A gentle flame—a slow, smooth origami unfolding.

We watched it together. Metal and fire, a thing I'd never shown anyone before.

"This is beautiful," she said.

I showed her the butterfly, my little golem—its only movement a slow flexing of its delicate steel wings as it passed through phase changes.

"You made this?"

I nodded. "There are no mechanical parts," I told her. "Just a single solid sheet of steel."

"It's like magic," she said. She touched it with a delicate index finger.

"Just science," I said. "Sufficiently advanced."

We watched the butterfly cool, wings flapping slowly. Finally, it began folding in on itself, cocooning, the true miracle. "The breakthrough was micro-degree shifting," I said. "It gives you more design control."

"Why this design?"

I shrugged. "You heat it slow, an ambient rise, and it turns into a butterfly."

"What happens if you heat it fast?"

I looked at her. "It turns into a dragon."

That night at her townhome, she took her clothes off slow—her mouth prehensile and searching. Although I was half a head taller, I found her legs were as long as mine. Strong, lean runner's legs, calf muscles bunched like fists. Afterward we lay on her dark sheets, a distant streetlight filtering through the blinds, drawing a pattern on the wall.

"Are you going to stay the night?" she asked.

I thought of my house, the empty rooms and the silence. "Do you want me to?"

She paused. "Yeah, I want you to."

"Then I'll stay."

The ceiling fan above her bed hummed softly, circulating the air, cooling the sweat on my bare skin.

"I've been doing research on you for the last week," she said. "On what you do."

"Checking up on me?"

She ignored the question and draped a slick arm across my shoulder. "Nagoi has labs in Asia running parallel to yours. Did you know that?"

"No."

"From years before the Uspar merger. Smart alloys with chemical triggers instead of heat; and stranger things, too. A special copper-aluminum-nickel alloy that's supposed to be triggered by remote frequency. Hit a button on a transmitter, and you get phase change by some kind of resonance. I didn't understand most of it. More of your magic steel."

"Not magic," I said.

"Modern chemistry grew out of the art of alchemy. At what point does it start being alchemy again?"

"It's always been alchemy, at the heart of it. We're just getting better at it now."

"I should tell you," she said, curling her fingers into my hair. "I don't believe in interracial relationships." That was the first time she said it—a thing she'd repeat often during the next year and a half, usually when we were in bed.

"You don't believe in them?"

"No," she said.

In the darkness she was a silhouette, a complication of shadows against the window light. She wasn't looking at me, but at the ceiling. I studied her profile—the rounded forehead, the curve of her jaw, the placement of her mouth—positioned not just between her nose and chin, but also forward of them, as if something in the architecture of her face were straining outward. She wore a steel-gray necklace, Uspar-Nagoi logo glinting between the dark curve of her breasts. I traced her bottom lip with my finger.

"You're wrong," I said.

"How's that?'

"I've seen them. They exist."

I closed my eyes and slept.

The rain was still coming down, building puddles across the Chicago streets. We pulled onto Dearborn and parked the car in a twenty-dollar lot. Veronica squeezed my hand as we walked toward the restaurant.

Voicheck was standing near the door; you couldn't miss him. Younger than I expected—pale and broad-faced, with a shaved head, dark glasses. He stood outside the restaurant, bare arms folded in front of his chest. He looked more like a bouncer than any kind of scientist.

"You must be Voicheck," Veronica said, extending her hand.

He hesitated for a moment. "I didn't expect you to be black."

She accepted this with only a slight narrowing of her eyes. "Certain people never do. This is my associate, John."

I nodded and shook his hand, thinking, *typical Eastern European lack of tact.* It wasn't racism. It was just that people didn't come to this country knowing what *not* to say; they didn't understand the context. On the floor of the East Chicago steel plant, I'd once had a Russian researcher ask me, loudly, how I could tell the Mexican workers from the Puerto Ricans. He was honestly curious. "You don't," I told him. "Ever."

A hostess walked us down dark carpet, past rows of potted bamboo, and seated us at a table near the back. The waitress brought us our drinks. Voicheck took his glasses off and rubbed the bridge of his nose. The lenses were prescription, I noticed. Over the last decade, surgery had become so cheap and easy in the

States that only anachronists and foreigners wore glasses anymore. Voicheck took a long swig of his Goose Island and got right to the point. "We need to discuss price."

Veronica shook her head. "First, we need to know how it is made."

"That information is what you'll be paying for." His accent was thick, but he spoke slowly enough to be understood. He opened his hand and showed us a small, gray flash drive, the kind you'd pay thirty dollars for at Best Buy. His fingers curled back into a fist. "This is data you'll understand."

"And you?" Veronica asked.

He smiled. "I understand enough to know what it is worth."

"Where is it from?"

"Donets'k, originally. After that, Chisinau laboratory, until about two years ago. Now the work is owned by a publicly traded company which shall, for the time being, remain nameless. The work is top secret. Only a few people at the company even know about the breakthrough. I have all the files saved. Now we discuss price."

Veronica was silent. She knew better than to make the first offer.

Voicheck let the silence draw out. "One hundred thirteen thousand," he said.

"That's a pretty exact number," Veronica said.

"Because that's exactly twice what I'll entertain as a first counter offer."

Veronica blinked. "So you'll take half that?"

"You offer fifty-six thousand five hundred? My answer is no, I am sorry. But here is where I rub my chin; and because I'm feeling generous, I tell you we can split the difference. We are negotiating, no? Then one of us does the math, and it comes out to eighty-five thousand. Is that number round enough for you?"

"I liked the fifty-six thousand better."

"Eighty-five minimum."

"That is too much."

"What, I should let you steal from me? You talked me down from one hundred thirteen already. I can go no further."

"There's no way we—"

Voicheck held up his hand. "Eighty-five in three days."

"I don't know if we can get it in three days."

"If no, then I disappear. It is simple."

Veronica glanced at me.

I spoke for the first time. "How do we even know what we'd be paying for? You expect us to pay eighty-five grand for what's on some flash drive."

Voicheck looked at me and frowned. "No, of course not." He opened his other fist. "For this, too." He dropped something on the table. Something that looked like a small red wire.

"People have died for this." He gestured toward the red wire. "You may pick it up."

I looked closely. It wasn't one wire; it was two. Two rubber-coated wires, like what you'd find behind a residential light switch. He noticed our confusion.

"The coating is for protection and to make it visible," he said.

"Why does it need protection?"

"Not it. You. The coating protects you."

Veronica stood and looked at me. "Let's go. He's been wasting our time."

"No, wait," he said. "Look." He picked up one of the wires. He lifted it delicately by one end—and the other wire lifted, too, rising from the table's surface like some magician's trick.

I saw then that I'd been wrong; it was not two wires after all, but one.

"The coating was stripped from ten centimeters in the middle," Voicheck said. "So you could see what was underneath."

But in the dim light, there was nothing to see. I bent close. Nothing at all. In the spot where the coating had been removed, the thread inside was so fine that it was invisible.

"What is it?" I asked.

"An allotrope of carbon, Fullerene structural family. You take it," he said. "Do tests to confirm. But remember, is just a neat toy without this." He held out the flash drive. "This explains how the carbon nanotubes are manufactured. How they can be woven into sheets, what lab is developing the technique, and more."

I stared at him. "The longest carbon nanotubes anybody has been able to make are just over a centimeter."

"Until now," he said. "Now they can be miles. In three days you come back. You give me the eighty-five thousand, I give you the data and information about where the graphene rope is being developed."

Veronica picked up the wire. "All right," she said. "Three days."

My father was a steelworker, as was his father before him.

My great-grandfather, though, had been here before the mills. He'd been a builder. He was here when the Lake Michigan shoreline was unbroken sand from Illinois to St. Joseph. He built Bailey Cemetery around the turn of the century—a great stone mausoleum in which some of the area's earliest settlers were buried. Tourists visit the place now. It's on some list of historic places, and once a summer, I take my sister's daughters to see it, careful to pick up the brochure.

There is a street in Porter named after him, my great-grandfather. Not because he was important, but because he was the only person who lived there. It was the road to his house, so they gave it his name. Now bi-levels crowd the street. He was here before the cities, before the kingdoms of rust and fire. Before the mills came and ate the beaches.

I try to imagine what this part of Indiana would have been like then. Woods, and wetlands, and rolling dunes. It must have been beautiful.

Sometimes I walk out to the pier at night and watch the ore boats swing through the darkness. From the water, the mill looks like any city. Any huge, sprawling city. You can see the glow of a thousand lights; you hear the trains and the rumble of heavy machines. Then the blast furnace taps a heat, a false-dawn glow of red and orange—flames making dragon's fire on the rolling Lake Michigan waves. Lighting up the darkness like hell itself.

The drive back to Indiana was quiet. The rain had stopped. We drove with the windows half-open, letting the wind flutter in, both of us lost in thought.

The strand—that's what we'd call it later—was tucked safely into her purse.

"Do you think it's for real?" she asked.

"We'll know tomorrow."

"You can do the testing at your lab?"

"Yeah," I said.

"Do you think he is who he says he is?"

"No, he's not even trying."

"He called it a graphene rope, which isn't quite right."

"So?" I said.

"Clusters of the tubes *do* naturally align into ropes held together by Van der Waals forces. It's the kind of slip only somebody familiar with the theory would make."

"So he's more familiar with it than he lets on?"

"Maybe, but there's no way to know," she said.

The next day I waited until the other researchers had gone home, and then I took the strand out of my briefcase and laid it on the lab bench. I locked the door to the materials testing lab and energized the tensile machine. The fluorescent lights flickered. It was a small thing, the strand. It seemed insignificant as it rested there on the bench. A scrap of insulated wiring from an electrician's tool box. Yet it was a pivot point around which the world would change, if it was what it was supposed to be. If it was what it was supposed to be, the world had changed already. We were just finding out about it.

The testing took most of the night. When I finished, I walked back to my office and opened a bottle I kept in the bottom drawer of a filing cabinet. I sat and sipped.

It's warm in my office. My office is a small cubby in the back room of the lab, a thrown-together thing made by wall dividers and shelves. It's an office because my desk and computer sit there. Otherwise it might be confused with a closet or small storage room. File cabinets line one side. There are no windows. To my left, a hundred sticky notes feather the wall. The other wall is metal, white, magnetic. A dozen refrigerator magnets hold calendars, pictures, papers. There is a copy of the lab's phone directory, a copy of the lab's quality policy, and a sheet of paper on which the geometry of crystal systems is described. The R&D directory of services is there, too, held to the wall by a metal clip. All the phone numbers I might need. A picture of my sister, blonde, unsmiling, caught in the act of speaking to me over a paper plate of fried chicken, the photo taken at a summer party three years ago. There is an Oxford Instruments periodic table. There's also a picture of a sailboat. Blue waves. And a picture of the Uspar-Nagoi global headquarters, based out of London.

Veronica finally showed up a few minutes past midnight. I was watching the butterfly as she walked through the door.

"Well?" she asked.

"I couldn't break it."

"What do you mean?"

"I couldn't get a tensile strength because I couldn't get it to fail. Without failure, there's no result."

"What about the other tests?"

"It took more than 32,000 pounds per square inch without shearing. It endured 800 degrees Fahrenheit without a measurable loss of strength or conductivity. Transmission electron microscopy allowed for direct visualization. I took these pictures." I handed her the stack of printed sheets. She went through them one by one.

Veronica blinked. She sat. "What does this mean?"

"It means that I think they've done it," I said. "Under impossibly high pressures, nanotubes can link, or so the theory holds. Carbon bonding is described by quantum chemistry orbital hybridization, and they've traded some sp2 bonds for the sp3 bonds of diamond."

She looked almost sad. She kissed me. The kiss was sad. "What are its uses?"

"Everything. Literally, almost everything. A great many things steel can do, these carbon nanotubes will do better. It's super-light and superstrong, perfect for aircraft. This material moves the fabled space elevator into the realm of possibility."

"There'd still be a lot of R&D necessary—"

"Yes, of course, it will be years down the road, but eventually the sky's the limit. There's no telling what this material will do, if it's manufactured right. It could be used for everything from suspension bridges to spacecraft. It could help take us to the stars. We're at the edge of a revolution."

I looked down at the strand. After a long time, I finally said what had been bothering me for the last sixteen hours. "But why did Voicheck come to you?" I said. "Of all places, why bring this to a steel company?"

She looked at me. "If you invent an engine that runs on water, why offer it to an oil company?" She picked up the strand. "Only one reason to do that, John. Because the oil company is certain to buy it."

She looked at the red wire in her hand. "If only to shut it down."

That night we drank. I stood at the window on the second story of her townhome and looked out at her quiet neighborhood, watching the expensive cars roll by on Ridge Road. The Ridge Road that neatly bisects Lake County. Land on the south, higher; the land to the north, low, easing toward urban sprawl, and the marshes, and Lake Michigan. That long, low ridge of land represented the glacial maxim—the exact line where the glacier stopped during the last ice-age, pushing all that dirt and stone in front of it like a plow, before it melted and receded and became the Great Lakes—and thousands of years later, road builders would stand on that ridge and think to themselves how easy it would be to follow the natural curve of the land; and so they built what they came to build and called it the only name that would fit: Ridge Road. The exact line, in the region, where one thing became another.

I wrapped the naked strand around my finger and drew it tight, watching the bright red blood well up from where it contacted my skin—because in addition to being strong and thin, the strand had the property of being *sharp*. For the tests, I'd stripped away most of the rubber coating, leaving only a few inches of insulation at the ends. The rest was exposed strand. Invisible.

"You cut yourself," Veronica said. She parted her soft lips and drew my finger into her mouth.

The first time I'd told her I loved her, it was an accident. In bed, half asleep, I'd said it. Good night, I love you. A thing that was out of my mouth before I even realized it—a habit from an old relationship come rising up out of me, the way every old relationship lives just under the skin of every new one. All the promises. All the possibilities. Right there under the skin. I'd felt her stiffen beside me, and an hour later, she nudged me awake. She was sitting up, arms folded across her breasts, as defensive as I'd ever seen her. I realized she hadn't slept at all. "I heard what you said." There was anger in her voice, and whole stratus of pain.

But I denied it. "You're hearing things."

Though of course it was true. What I'd said. Even if saying it was an accident. It had been true for a while.

The night after I tested the strand, I lay in bed and watched her breathe. Blankets kicked to the floor.

Light from the window glinted off her necklace, a thin herringbone—some shiny new steel, Uspar-Nagoi emblem across her beautiful dark skin. I caressed the herringbone plate with my finger, such an odd interlinking of metal.

"They gave this to you?"

She fingered the necklace. "They gave one to all of us," she said. "Management perk. Supposed to be worth a mint."

"The logo ruins it," I said. "Like a tag."

"Everything is tagged, one way or another," she said. "I met him once."

"Who?"

"The name on the necklace."

"Nagoi? You met him?"

"At a facility in Frankfurt. He came through with his group. Shook my hand. He was taller than I thought, but his handshake was this flaccid, aqueous thing, straight-fingered, like a flipper. It was obvious he loathed the Western tradition. I was prepared to like him, prepared to be impressed, or to find him merely ordinary."

She was silent for so long I thought she might have fallen asleep. When she finally spoke, her voice had changed. "I've never been one of those people who judged a person by their handshake," she said. "But still . . . I can't remember a handshake that gave me the creeps like that. They paid sixty-six billion for the Uspar acquisition. Can you imagine that much money? That many employees? That much power? When his daughter went through her divorce, the company stock dropped by two percent. His daughter's divorce did that. Can you believe that? Do you know how much two percent is?"

"A lot."

"They have billions invested in infrastructure alone. More in hard assets and research facilities, not to mention the mills themselves. Those assets are quantifiable and linked to actuarial tables that translate into real dollars. Real dollars which can be used to leverage more takeovers, and the monster keeps growing. If Nagoi's daughter's divorce dipped the share price by two percent, what do you think would happen if a new carbon-product competitor came to market?"

I ran a finger along her necklace. "You think they'll try to stop it?"

"Nagoi's money is in steel. If a legitimate alternative reached market, each mill he owned, each asset all across the world, would suddenly be worth less. Billions of dollars would blink out of existence."

"So what happens now?"

"We get the data. I write my report. I give my presentation. The board suddenly gets interested in buying a certain company in Europe. If that company won't sell, Uspar-Nagoi buys all the stock and owns them anyway. Then shuts them down."

"Suppression won't work. The Luddites never win in the long run."

She smiled. "The three richest men in the world have as much money as the poorest forty-eight nations," she said. "Combined."

I watched her face.

She continued. "The yearly gross product of the world is something like fifty-four trillion dollars, and yet there are millions of people who are still trying to live on two dollars a day. You trust business to do the right thing?"

"No, but I trust the market. A better product will always find its way to the consumer. Even Uspar-Nagoi can't stop that."

"You only say that because you don't understand how it really works. That might have been true a long time ago. The Uspar-Nagoi board does hostile takeovers for a living, and they're not going to release a technology that will devalue their core assets."

Veronica was silent.

"Why did you get into steel?" I asked. "What brought you here?"

"Money," she said. "Just money."

"Then why haven't you told your bosses about Voicheck?"

"I don't know."

"Are you going to tell them?"

"No, I don't think I am."

There was a long pause.

"What are you going to do?"

"Buy it," she said. "Buy Voicheck's data."

"And then what? After you've bought it."

"After I've bought it, I'm going to post it on the Internet."

The drive to meet Voicheck seemed to take forever. The traffic was stop and go until we reached Halsted, and it took us nearly an hour to reach downtown Chicago.

We parked in the same twenty-dollar lot and Veronica squeezed my hand again as we walked toward the restaurant.

But this time, Voicheck wasn't standing outside looking like a bouncer. He wasn't looking like anything, because he wasn't there. We waited a few minutes and went inside. We asked for the same table. We didn't speak. We had no reason to speak.

After a few minutes, a man in a suit came and sat. He was a gray man in a gray suit. He wore black leather gloves. He was in his fifties, but he was in his fifties the way certain breeds of athletes enter their fifties—broad, and solid, and blocky-shouldered. He had a lantern jaw and thin, sandy hair receding from a wide forehead. The waitress came and asked if he needed anything to drink.

"Yes, please," the man said. "Bourbon. And oh, for my friends here, a Bailey's for him, and what was it?" He looked at Veronica. "A Coke, right?"

Veronica didn't respond. The man's accent was British.

"A Coke," the man told the waitress. "Thank you."

He smiled and turned toward us. "Did you know that bourbon was the official spirit of the U.S. by act of Congress?"

We were silent.

"That's why I always used to make a point of drinking it when I came to the States. I wanted to enjoy the authentic American experience. I wanted to drink bourbon like Americans drink bourbon. But then I discovered an unsettling secret in my travels." The man took something from the inside pocket of his suit jacket and set it on the table. Glasses. Voicheck's glasses—the frames bent into an unnatural position, both prescription lenses shattered.

The man caressed the twisted frames with his finger. "I discovered that Americans don't really drink bourbon. A great many Americans have never so much as tasted it. So then why is it the official spirit of your country?"

We had no opinion. We were without opinion.

"Would you like to hear what I think?" The man said. He bent close and spoke low across the table. "I've developed a theory. I think it was a lie all along. I think someone in your Congress probably had his hand in the bourbon business all those years ago, and sales were flagging; so they came up with the idea to make bourbon the official spirit of the country as a way to line their own pockets. Would you like to hear something else I discovered in my travels? No? Well, I'll tell you anyway. I discovered that I don't care much, one way or the other, if that's how it happened. I discovered that I *like* bourbon. And I feel like I'm drinking the most American drink of them all, because your Congress said so, lie or not. The ability to believe a lie can be an important talent. You're probably wondering who I am."

"No," Veronica said.

"Good, then you're smart enough to realize it doesn't matter. You're smart enough to realize that if I'm here, it means that your friend isn't coming back."

"Where is he?" Veronica asked.

"I can't say, but rest assured that wherever he is, he sends his regrets."

"Are you here for the money?"

"The money? I couldn't care less about your money."

"Where's the flash drive?" Veronica asked.

"You mean this?" The man held the gray flash between leathered finger and thumb, then returned it to the breast pocket of his neat gray suit. "This is the closest you're going to get to it, I'm afraid. Your friend seemed to think it belonged to him. I disabused him of that misconception."

"What do you want?" Veronica asked.

"I want what everyone wants, my dear. But what I'm here for today—what I'm being paid to do—is to tie up some loose ends. You can help me."

Silence. Two beats.

"Where is the strand?" he asked.

"He never gave it to us."

The man's gray eyes looked pained. Like a father with a wayward child. "I'm disappointed," he said. "I thought we were developing some trust here. Do you know what loyalty is?"

"Yes."

"No, I don't think you do. Loyalty to your company. Loyalty to the cause. You have some very important people who looked after you, Veronica. You had some important friends."

"You're from Uspar-Nagoi?"

"Who did you think?"

"I . . ."

"You have embarrassed certain people who have invested their trust in you. You have embarrassed some very important people."

"That wasn't my intention."

"In my experience, it never is." He spread his hands. "Yet here we are. What were you planning on doing with the data once you obtained it?"

"I don't know what you're talking about."

The pain returned to the man's eyes. He shook his head sadly. "I'm going to ask you a question in a moment. If you lie to me, I promise you." He leaned forward again. "I promise you that I will make you regret it. Do you believe that?"

Veronica nodded.

"Good. Do you have the strand with you?"

"No."

"Then this is what is going to happen now," he said. "We're going to leave. We're going to drive to where the strand is, and you're going to give it to me."

"If I did have it somewhere, and if I did give it to you, what happens then?"

"Probably you'll have to look for another job, I can't say. That's between you and your company. I'm just here to obtain the strand."

The man stood. He laid a hundred-dollar bill on the table and grabbed Veronica's arm. The way he grabbed her arm, he could have been a prom date— just a gentleman walking his lady out the door. Only I could see his fingers dug deep into her flesh.

I followed them out, walking behind them. When we got near the front door, I picked up one of the trendy bamboo pots and brought it down on the man's head with everything I had.

The crash was shocking. Every head in the restaurant swiveled toward us. I bent and fished the flash drive from his breast pocket. "Run," I told her.

We hit the night air sprinting.

"What the fuck are you doing?" she screamed.

"Voicheck is dead," I told her. "We were next."

Veronica climbed behind the wheel and sped out of the parking lot just as the gray man stumbled out the front door of the restaurant.

The BMW was fast. Faster than anything I would have suspected. Veronica drove with the pedal to the floor, weaving in and out of traffic. Pools of light ticked past.

"They'll still be coming," she said.

"Yeah."

"What are we going to do?"

"We have to stay ahead of them."

"How do we do that? Where do we go?"

"We get through tonight, and then we worry about the rest."

"We can hop a flight somewhere," she said.

"No, what happens tonight decides everything. That strand is our only insurance. Without the strand, we're dead."

Her hands tightened on the steering wheel.

"Where is it?" I asked.

"At my house."

Veronica kept the accelerator floored. "I'm sorry I got you into this," she said.

"Don't be."

We were almost to her house when Veronica's forehead creased. She took the turn onto Ridge, frowning. She looked confused for a moment, then surprised. Her hand went to her neck. It happened so quickly.

I had time to notice her necklace, gone flat-gray. There was an instant of recognition in her eyes before the alloy phase-changed—an instant of panic, and then the necklace shifted, writhed, herringbone plate tightening like razor wire. She gasped and let go of the wheel, clutching at her throat. I grabbed the wheel with one hand, trying to grab her necklace with the other. But already it was gone, tightened through her skin, blood spilling from her jugulars as she shrieked. Then even her shrieks changed, gurgling, as the blade cut through her voice box.

I screamed and the car spun out of control. The sound of squealing tires, and we hit the curb hard, sideways—the crunch of metal and glass, world trading places with black sky, rolling three times before coming to a stop.

Sirens. The creak of a spinning wheel. I looked over, and Veronica was dead. Dead. That look, gone forever—gears in her eyes gone silent and still. The Uspar-Nagoi logo slid from her wound as the necklace phase changed again, expanding to its original size. I thought of labs in Asia, and parallel projects. I thought of necklaces, Veronica saying, *they gave one to all of us.*

I climbed out of the wreck and stood swaying. The sirens closer now. I sprinted the remaining few blocks to her house.

When I got to her front door, I tried the knob. Locked. I stood panting. When I caught my breath, I kicked the door in. I walked inside, up the stairs.

The strand was in Veronica's jewelry box on her dresser. I glanced around the room; it was the last time I'd stand here, I knew, the last time I'd be in her bedroom. I saw the four-poster bed where we'd lain so often, and the grief came down on me like a freight train. I did my best to push it away. Later. Later, I'd deal with it. When there was time. I closed my eyes and saw Veronica's face.

Coming back down the stairs, I stopped. The front door was closed. I didn't remember closing it.

I stood silent, listening.

The first blow knocked me over the chair.

The gray man came, open hands extended, smiling. "I was going to be nice," he said. "I was going to be quick. But then you hit me with a pot."

Some flash of movement, and his leg swung, connecting with the side of my head. "Now I'm going to take my time."

I tried to climb to my feet, but the world swam away, off to the side. He kicked me under my right armpit, and I felt ribs break.

"Come on, stand up," he said. I tried to breathe. Another kick. Another.

I pulled myself up the side of the couch. He caught me with a chipping blow to the face. My lip split wide open, blood pouring onto Veronica's white carpet. His leg came up, connecting with my ribs again. I felt another snap. I collapsed onto my back, writhing in agony. His leg rose and fell as I tried to curl in on myself—some instinct to protect my vital organs. He landed a solid kick to my face and my head snapped back. The world went black.

He was crouching over me when I opened my eyes. That smile.

"Come on," he said. "Stand up."

He dragged me to my feet and slammed me against the wall. A right hand like iron pinned me to the wall by my throat.

"Where is the strand?"

I tried to speak, but my voice pinched shut. He smiled wider, turning an ear toward me. "What's that?" he said. "I can't hear you."

Some flutter of movement and the other hand came up. He laid the straight razor against my cheek. Cold steel. "I'm going to ask you one more time," he said. "And then I'm going to start cutting slices down your face. I'm going to do it slow, so you can feel it." He eased up on my windpipe just enough for me to draw a breath.

"Now tell me, where is the strand?"

I looped the strand around his wrist. "Right here," I said, and pulled.

There was almost no resistance. The man's hand came off with a thump, spurting blood in a fountain. He dropped the razor to the carpet. He had time to look confused. Then surprised. Like Veronica. He bent for the razor, reaching to pick it up with his other hand, and this time I hooked my arm around his neck, looping the chord tight—and pulled again. Warmth. Like bathwater on my face. He slumped to the floor.

I picked up the razor and limped out the front door.

Eighty-five grand buys you a lot of distance. It'll take you places. It'll take you across continents, if you need it to. It will introduce you to the right people.

There is no carbon-tube industry. Not yet. No monopoly to pay or protect. And the data I downloaded onto the Internet is just starting to make news. Nagoi still comes for me—in my dreams, and in my waking paranoia. A man with a razor. A man with steel in his fist.

Already Uspar-Nagoi stock has started to slide as those long thinkers in the investment sphere gaze into the future and see a world that might, just maybe, be made of different stuff. Uspar-Nagoi made a grab for that European company, but it cost them more than they ever expected to pay. And the carbon project was buried, just as Veronica said it would be. Only now the data is on the net, for anyone to see.

Carbon has this property: it bonds powerfully and promiscuously to itself. In one form, it is diamond. In another, it builds itself into structures we are just beginning to understand. We are not smarter than the ones who came before us—the ones who built the pyramids and navigated oceans by the stars. If we've done more, it's because we had better materials. What would de Vinci have done with polycarbon? Seven billion people in the world. Maybe now we find out.

Sometimes at night when sleep won't come, I think of what I said to Veronica about alchemy. The art of turning one thing into another. That maybe it's been alchemy all along.

FALLING ANGEL

EUGENE MIRABELLI

This happened in August, 1967, an August so hot that asphalt melted in the streets and seven of the trees along the river burst into flame. The air was boiling in his apartment, so Brendan had propped open the skylight and was lying naked on his back on the bare floor, one hand under his head and the other on his sweaty privates, ashamed of himself because he had jerked off a while ago and felt like doing it again. He was staring up at the square of blue sky as if from the bottom of the sea when a body as naked as his own floated ten feet above the skylight, thrashing and clawing and choking—then it stopped thrashing and sank very gently headfirst with the legs floating out behind, a swimmer whose lungs had filled with water, and came to rest with a white cheek flat against the skylight, the mouth wide open and the eyes like blue quartz. Brendan lay there trying to puzzle out what had happened. Abruptly he pulled up a chair and stood on it, reached out through the open skylight to grapple a leg and hauled the body down feet-first into his arms, himself crashing sideways onto the floor under the sudden weight. He got up and—What can I say? This was a bare-assed young woman, maybe eighteen years old, with a wingspread of over twelve feet.

A bitter stink of burnt feathers hung in the air and, in fact, Brendan noticed that the trailing vanes on both wings were singed away, revealing a sooty membrane underneath, and her right arm was seared. He rolled her onto her back. Her wide eyes were as sightless as two pieces of turquoise, as if she had drowned in air. He was wondering was she drunk or stoned or in a narcoleptic fit when she stumbled to her feet, knocking him aside. She glared at the skylight and began to howl—a freezing sound that started as a single icy note, solitary at first but soon joined by others all pitched the same and all in different timbres until it seemed a whole orchestra was shivering the room, cracking the windows, exploding bottles, glasses, light bulbs. Brendan had clamped his hands over his ears, had run as far as he could and continued to bang his head against the wall until the desolate cry ended. "Who are you?" he asked, gasping for breath.

She turned her stone eyes toward him and spoke, or tried to, but all that came out was a kind of mangled music.

"Stop!" he cried, ducking his head and clapping his hands to his ears again. "Stop!"

But she went on until there was nothing but shards of sound, then she shrugged and said something like *Oh, shit,* tripped over the mattress on the floor and plunged into a deep sleep. Brendan wiped the sweat from his eyes and watched to see if she would stir, then he righted the chair under the skylight, stood on it and pulled himself shakily onto the roof with the hope of spying some explanation. There was only the commonplace desert of tar and gravel. He dropped back into his room, chained the door and wedged the chair under the doorknob. He was trembling from exhaustion when he returned to look at her—one long white wing lay folded across her rump and the other spread open like a busted fan across the mattress and onto the floor. He crept slowly from one side of the mattress to the other and watched the light shimmer this way and that on the feathers as he moved, feeling ashamed of himself when he paused at the glimpse of gold hairs at her crotch. He had always understood that there was no difference of sex between angels, that angels were not male or female but pure spirits. Now he didn't know what to think, much less what to do, and it got to be so quiet you could hear the faucet drip. So Brendan retrieved his little tin box of joints from the window ledge and sat on the floor with his back to the wall, struck a match and began to smoke, keeping his dazed eyes on her all the while.

She slept for two days and two nights, or maybe it was three days and nights, or maybe only that one day and night—Brendan lost track because he fell asleep himself. When he woke up she was sitting cross-legged on the mattress, looking at him with eyes as clear as a summer sky. "You need a shave," she told him, for her voice had cleared, too.

"I've been busy," he said, startled.

She was looking around at the bare white walls and scuffed wood floor, at the banged-up guitar case and the old record player and the short row of records and books on the floor against the wall. "Yeah? Doing what?" she asked, skeptically.

"Thinking about things, meditating." He had gotten to his feet and had begun to search hurriedly for his underwear or his pants or any scrap of cloth to hide himself.

"You ought to eat more. You look like a fucking bird cage on stilts. What's your name?"

"Brendan Flood," he said. He hadn't found his underwear but quickly thrust a leg into his blue jeans anyway. "I've been on a fast. I've been meditating and fasting," he explained. "Who—

"Meditating and fasting? Holy shit!" She laughed. "Who pays the rent here?"

"Me. I work nights as a programmer. Listen—" he began.

"So what else have you been doing? Hash? Acid? Come on, Brendan. Don't look so surprised. I know you've been smoking grass. The air is full of it."

"Listen, who are you?"

"I'm an escapee, Brendan. Just like you. You can trust me. Jill," she added as an afterthought.

"That's your name?"

"They named me Morning Glory," she said sarcastically. "But you can call me Jill, yes."

"How did you get here?"

"Well, you've got a chair jammed against the door, Brendan. And I didn't scale the walls. I came in over the roof. Remember?"

He groaned and rubbed the heels of his hands against his closed eyes. "What day is today?" he asked, not opening his eyes.

"How would I know?"

He looked at those wings that stood like snowdrifts behind her shoulders. "Do those come off?" he asked.

"Are you being funny? This is me," she said, glancing down at her breasts, cupping and lifting them. "As fucking naked as I get."

Her flesh was the color of the dawn horizon, so beautiful it frightened him, but he gathered his courage and looked at her—her face, the hollow of her throat, her breasts and the honey-colored hair of her crotch. Yet at the first surge of desire he felt a chilly counter current, a fear that his lust was a monstrous sacrilege that would bring the wrath of God down on his head like a hammer. He escaped to the bathroom to piss and discovered a long gold hair stuck to the damp wall tile. He filled the washbowl with cold water and doused his privates, thinking to put out the fire and clean himself at the same time, but it was his brain that was ablaze and just when he was dunking his head it came to him that the creature in the next room might not be an angel at all, might be some delusion fabricated by Satan, whereupon his legs gave way and he pitched forward into the faucet and came up choking. He wondered if he were going crazy.

He went back to the room and found her seated cross-legged on the mattress reading one of his books, *The Poetical Works of William Blake*, which was where he kept his cigarette papers. She looked up and began reciting, "And when the stars threw down their spears and water'd heaven with their tears—but saw that Brendan was already aroused, up and rising. "Ah, you devil," she murmured, tossing aside the book to grasp his shaft. "Did he who made the lamb make thee?"

Brendan was doomed to remember their lovemaking for the rest of his life. It began simply enough when he threw himself to the mattress and pulled her onto her back, hoping to get a hand on her breast and a knee between her thighs, but before he could make his next move he felt her fingernails pierce his rump and felt his cock being seized as in an oiled fist and he slid in deeper and higher until he couldn't tell whether he was fainting or screaming with pleasure. He had staggered to his feet and was carrying her upright, her legs around him like a vise, stumbling now against the chair and then the table and now crashing against the wall and again the table, carrying her at last as if she were miraculously weightless or as if she were actually carrying him, as if he were on his back, hooped in her arms and legs, her wings beating slowly but just enough to keep them afloat above the mattress and table and chairs. And when he came it was a long, long rush in which his body gave itself completely away, such a long rush that he could feel the marrow being drawn sweetly through his spine from his distant fingers and toes, and at the end of it every one of his bones was hollow and his skull completely empty.

Later they lay side by side on the sweat-soaked mattress and Brendan, believing he had been turned inside out and the secret lining of his life exposed, told her all about his student days at Cal Tech where he learned Fortran and Cobol and other machine languages of lethal boredom, followed by his years on the road as a Zen guitarist with Zodiac which had nearly driven him crazy, and how for these past three months he had fasted and prayed, waiting for God to give him a message or vision or signal of some sort. When he was finished he looked at Jill and she said, "I'm hungry. Are you hungry? I know I am. I'm starved."

Of course, there was no food in the place. So Brendan pulled on his clothes and hunted up a pair of jeans and a T-shirt for Jill, but she refused to wear them because, she explained, she couldn't go out. "Going out gives me an anxiety attack," she said. "I get panicky and throw up or pee in my pants if I go out." So Brendan went out and came back with three hamburgers and some sliced pickles. He sat across from her at his wobbly table, bit into his hamburger, looked at her shining breasts and watched her eat. She tore through her food—"Are you going to finish that?" she asked him, glancing at his plate—and when she had downed the last half of his hamburger she wiped her mouth with the back of her hand and said she wanted to go up on the roof to take a look around. He asked her didn't she want to wear something, anything, to cover up, and so on. "For Christ sake, Brendan, this is 1967! The last dress I owned was made of colored paper." But she pulled on a pair of his shorts and Brendan set his chair under the skylight, gave her a boost, and pulled himself up behind her.

Remember, this was Boston's Back Bay where the roofs are flat and the brownstones are built shoulder to shoulder with no space between them, so you can walk from roof to roof to roof for a quarter of a mile before coming to a cross street. Brendan watched her looking around and realized she might have come from just a few roofs away and nowhere more exotic. She had shaded her eyes with her hand and was gazing across the pipe vents, TV aerials, skylights, and chimneys to the soft horizon. "What city is this?" she asked him.

"What do you mean, what city! This is Boston! Don't you even know what city you're in?"

She whirled on him, saying, "You're so smart and you don't even know what day it is! I never said I was smart. I never went to college. So fuck off!"

Brendan flushed. "It's the twelfth. Or the thirteenth. I stayed up all night to watch the meteor shower on the eleventh. So it must be Saturday. I think."

"What difference does it make what city it is, anyway?" she muttered, sullen.

So they dropped back into Brendan's place where he stepped out of his blue jeans and she peeled off her shorts and they knelt face to face on the mattress and began to make love again, and it would have been even better than before except that Brendan had begun to doubt that anything could be so good or that he could be so fortunate or that Jill (or Morning Glory or whatever her name was) could be what she appeared to be.

Three nights a week Brendan crossed the river to Cambridge where he worked as a computer programmer, but other than that, these two slept at night and made love by day, all day, every day. They ate, of course. Jill still refused to go down to the street, saying she had a bad case of agoraphobia and dreaded open space, so Brendan went off for groceries and came back with take-out hamburgers and pizzas and Chinese, plus pasta to cook up right there. Brendan never gained a pound; in fact, he lost a few. "Are you trying to starve yourself to death?" Jill asked him.

"Food dirties the windows of perception," he told her.

"Because, do you know what they do to people who try to kill themselves but fuck up and don't do it right? They strap them down and do things to make them regret their mistakes. Believe me," she said.

When he asked her how come she knew about such things she said, "I'm an escapee. Remember?" which was what she usually said whenever he asked her about herself.

But mostly they made love. There were days when they clowned around, as when they lathered themselves in whipped cream and licked it from each other's flesh, and hours of heavy sensuality when he lingered and she opened to him with the languor of a flower and, to be sure, there were moments when he rushed her like the whippet that he was.

Her feathers had begun to show color and in November she announced that she was pregnant. Now Brendan noticed that whenever they made love the points at the trailing edge of her wings glowed translucent pink and each successive time they joined the color reached deeper into the feathers, like dye soaking into fabric, until the wings themselves took on a pale rose cast, a shade which deepened each day and, in fact, the hue at the tip of each feather began to alter from red to maculate gold in the way of a spotted trout, and from that to a grassy emerald to an iridescent sapphire such as you see in peacock feathers, thence to a purple so luminous it tinted the room. Her eyes changed, too. Some days they were so clear that when he looked into them he saw sky, clouds, stars, albino doves. Other days they solidified into black mirrors and she would turn her blind face to the skylight and scream, then hurtle from one end of the room to the other, dashing herself ruthlessly against the walls until she dropped, the pulse beating furiously in her neck, her soundless mouth stretched open and her wide eyes like agates. When she'd come to, she'd shiver in his arms and though her teeth were chattering she'd grin and say something like, "I graduated from Boston Psychopathic with a degree in paranoia. What do you think? Am I a fallen angel or what?" He would pull her across his lap and hold her head to his shallow chest, rocking her until she drifted to a peaceful slumber, his brain spinning in confusion.

Brendan had never wanted a telephone in his place and now he couldn't afford one, so he called from a public booth at the nearby healthfood store, searching for a gynecologist or obstetrician or plain medical doctor who would make a house visit, but of course there wasn't one to be found. He did come across a midwife's card on the bulletin board there, so he phoned her and, since she lived only a few blocks away, she said she'd come around to examine Jill the next day. But the next day when Jill found out who was at the door she barricaded herself in the bathroom and refused to come out till the midwife had gone. Jill informed Brendan that she didn't need a doctor or midwife. "What do they know? We can do this ourselves. You're smart. There are books on this," she said. He broke into a sweat, but bit his tongue so as to say nothing and went out and came back with five books on childbirth.

"No. Not these," she told him, exasperated. "There's this French doctor who helps women give birth under water. Get the one by him."

"You'll drown!" Brendan cried, remembering her face as he had first seen it pressed against the skylight almost twelve months ago.

"Not the woman, asshole! The baby. The baby gets born under water in a tub. Get that one." He didn't go looking for the book but it wouldn't have made any difference if he had, because several years were to go by before women gave birth in tubs of warm water at Dr. Odent's clinic in Pithivier, France.

When Brendan awoke on August 11th, Jill was flat on her back in labor beside him, her fingers deep in the mattress ticking, her hair stuck like gold leaf on her damp forehead and cheeks. He pulled on his jeans and jammed his feet into his sneakers and stumbled down the stairway, his loose laces whipping and snapping at each step, and ran to the health-food store where he phoned the midwife. Seven minutes later the midwife's car turned onto Brendan's street and began to nose hesitantly along the row of parked cars, looking for a place to stop, but Brendan pulled her from the wheel and hustled her up the stairway and into his flat. As the midwife later testified, Jill was seated naked on the wood chair under the skylight, the baby wrapped in a bloody dish towel on her lap. "Don't come any closer!" she cried, jumping up. She scrambled awkwardly onto the chair seat and stood wavering there as if under the endless impact of a waterfall, the swaddled infant now crying in her arms. "Brendan, take the baby. It's a girl, like me.—You stay back, lady!" she shouted at the midwife. Brendan received the baby from her. "We crazies are the only true rebels against God," she said, reaching toward the open rim of the skylight. Then this Jill, or Morning Glory or whatever her name was, pulled herself out to the roof and jumped off, finishing her long dive from the battlements of heaven.

THE FIFTH STAR IN THE SOUTHERN CROSS

MARGO LANAGAN

—◄❖►—

I had bought half an hour with Malka and I was making the most of it. Lots of Off girls, there's not much goes on, but these Polar City ones, especially if they're fresh off the migration station, they seem to, almost, enjoy it? I don't know if they really do. They don't pitch and moan and fake it up or anything, but they seem to be *there* under you. They're *with* you, you know? They pay attention. It almost doesn't matter about their skin, the feel of it a bit dry and crinkly, and the colour. They have the Coolights on all the time to cut that colour back, just like butchers put those purply lights over the meat in their shop, to bring up the red.

Anyway, I would say we were about two-thirds the way there—I was starting to let go of everything and be the me I was meant to be. I knew stuff; I meant something; I didn't *givva* what anyone thought of me.

But then she says, "Stop, Mister Cleeyom. Stop a minute."

"What?" I thought for a second she had got too caught up in it, was having too good a time, needed to slow things down a bit. I suppose that shows how far along *I* was.

"Something is coming," she said.

I tensed up, listening for sounds in the hall.

"Coming down."

Which was when I felt it, pushing against the end of me.

I pulled out. I made a face. "What is it? Have I got you up the wrong hole?"

"No, Mister Cl'om. Just a minute. Will not take long."

Too late—I was already withering.

She got up into a squat with one leg out wide. The Coolight at the bedhead showed everything from behind: a glop of something, and then strings of drool. Just right out onto the bedclothes she did it; she didn't scrabble for a towel or a tissue or anything. She wasn't embarrassed. A little noise came up her throat from some clench in her chest, and that clench pushed the thing out below, the main business.

"It's a puppy?" I said, but I thought, *It's a turd?* But the smell wasn't turd; it was live insides, insides that weren't to do with digestion. And turds don't turn over and split their skin, and try to work it off themselves.

"It's just a baby," Malka apologised, with that smile she has, that makes you feel sorry for her, she's trying so hard, and angry at her at the same time. She scooped it up, with its glop. She stepped off the bed and laid it on top of some crumpled crush-velour under the lamp. A white-ish tail dangled between her legs; she turned away from me and gathered that up, and whatever wet thing fell out attached to it.

This was not what I'd had in mind. This was not the treat I'd promised myself as I tweezered HotChips into artificial tulip stalks out at Parramatta Mannafactory all week.

The "baby" lay there working its shoulders in horrible shruggings, almost as if it knew what it was doing. They're not really babies, of course, just as Polar "girls" aren't really girls, although that's something you pay to be made to forget.

Malka laughed at how my faced looked. "You ha'n't seen this before, Mister Sir?"

"Never," I said. "It's disgusting."

"It's a regular," she said. "How you ever going to get yourself new girls for putcha-putcha, if you don't have baby?"

"We shouldn't have to see *that*, to get them."

"You ask special for Malka. You sign the—the thing, say you don't mind to see. I can show you." She waved at the billing unit by the door.

"Well, I didn't know what that meant. Someone should have explained it to me exactly, *all* the details." But I remembered signing. I remembered the hurry I'd been in at the time. It takes you over, you know, a bone. It feels so good just by itself, so warm, silky somehow and shifting, making you shift to give it room, but at the very same time and this is the crazy-making thing, it nags at you, *Get rid of me! Gawd, do something!* And I wouldn't be satisfied with one of those others: Korra is Polar too but she has been here longer and she acts just like an Earth girl, like you're rubbish. And that other one, the yellow-haired one—well, I have had her a couple of times thinking she might come good, but seriously she is on something. A man might as well do it with a Vibro-Missy, or use his own hand. It's not worth the money if she's not going to be real.

The thing on the velour turned over again in an irritated way, or uncomfortable. It spread one of its hands and the Coolight shone among the wrong-shaped fingers, going from little to big, five of them and no thumb. A shiver ran up my neck like a breeze lifting up a dog's fur.

Malka chuckled and touched my chin. "I will make you a drink and then we will get sexy again, hey?"

I tucked myself in and zipped up my pants. "Can't you put it away somewhere? Like, does it have to be there right under the light?"

She put her face between me and it and kissed me. They don't kiss well, any of these Offs. It's not something that comes natural to them. They don't take the time; they don't soften their lips properly. It's like a moth banging into your mouth. "Haff to keep it in sight. It is regulation. For its well-being." Her teeth gleamed in another attempt at smiling. "I turn you on a movie. Something to look away at."

"Can't you give the thing to someone else to take care of?" But she was doing the walk; I was meant to be all sucked in again by the sight of that swinging bottom. They do have pretty good bottoms, Polars, pretty convincing.

"I paid for the full half-hour," I said. "Am I gunna get back that time you spent . . . Do I get extra time at the end?"

But I didn't want extra time. I wanted my money back, and to start again some other time, when I'd forgotten this. But there was no way I was going to get that. The wall bloomed out into palm-trees and floaty music and some rock-hard muscle star and his girlfriend arguing on the beach.

"Turn the sound off!"

Malka did, like a shot, and checked me over her shoulder. I read it in her face clear as anything: *Am I going to get trouble from this one?* Not fear, not a drop of it, just, *Should I call in the big boys?* The workaday look on her face, her eyes smart, her lips a little bit open, underneath the sunlit giant faces mouthing on the wall—there was nothing designed to give Mister Client a bigger downer.

Darlinghurst Road was the same old wreck and I was one loser among many walking along it. It used to be Sexy Town here, all nightclubs, back in history, but now it's full of refugees. Down the hill and along the point is where all the fudgepackers had their apartments, before the anti-gay riots. We learned 'em; we told 'em where to stick their bloody feathers and froo-froos. That's all gone now, every pillow burned and every pot of Vaseline smashed—you can't even buy it to grease up handyman tools any more, not around here. Those were good times when I was a bit younger, straightening out the world.

It didn't look pretty when we'd finished, but at least there were no 'packers. Now people like me live here, who'd rather hide in this mess than jump through the hoops you need for a 'factory condominium. And odd Owsians, off-shoots of the ones that are eating up the States from the inside, there are so many there. And a lot of Earth-garbage: Indians and Englanders and Central Europeans. And the odd glamorous Abbo, all gold knuckles and tailoring. It's *colourful*, they tell us; it's got *a polyglot identity that's all its own and very special*. Tourists come here—well, they walk along Darlo Road; they don't explore much either side, where it gets *real* polyglot.

I zigzagged through the lanes towards my place. I was still steaming about my lost money and my wasted bone, steaming at *myself* for having signed that screen and done myself out of what I'd promised myself. There was nothing I could do except go home and take care of myself so I could get some sleep. Then wake up and catch the bike-bus out to Parramatta, pedalling the sun up out of the drowned suburbs behind me.

That EurOwsian beggar-girl was on my step again, a bundle like someone's dumped house-rubbish. She crinkled and rustled as I came up. When she saw my face she'd know not to bother me, I hoped.

But it wasn't her voice at all that said, "Jonah? Yes, it *is* you!"

I backed up against the opposite wall of the entry, my insides gone all slithery. Only bosses called me Jonah, and way back people who were dead now, of my family from the days when people had families. Grandparent-type people.

Out of what I had thought was the beggar girl stood this other one that I didn't know at all, shaven-headed and scabby-lipped. "Fen," those lips said. "Fenella. Last year at the Holidaze."

"Oh!" I almost shouted with the relief of making the connection, although she still didn't click to look at. She put her face more clearly in the way of the gaslight so that I could examine her. "Fen. Oh, yeah." I still couldn't see it, but I knew who she was talking about. "What are you doing in here? I thought you lived up the mountains."

"I know. I'm sorry. But, really, I've got to tell you something."

"What's that?"

She looked around at the empty entry-way, the empty lane. "It's kind of private."

"Oh. You better come up, then." I hoped she wasn't thinking to get in my bed or anything; I could never put myself close to a mouth in that condition.

She followed me up. She wasn't healthy; two flights and she was breathing hard. All the time I'm also, *Fen? But Fen had* hair. *She was very nearly good-looking. I remember thinking as we snuck off from the party, Oh, my ship's really come in this time—a normal girl and no payment necessary.*

She didn't go mad and attack me for drug money when I lit the lamp and stood back to hold the door for her. She stepped in and took in the sight of my crap out of some kind of habit. She was a girl with background; she would probably normally say something nice to the host. But she was too distracted, here, by the stuff in her own head. I couldn't even begin to dread what that might be.

"Sit?" In front of the black window my only chair looked like, if you sat there, someone would tie you to it, and scald you with Ersatz, or burn you with beedy-ends.

She shook her head. "It's not as if there's much we can do," she said, "but you had to know, I told myself. I thought, Maybe he can get himself tested and they'll give him some involvement, you never know. Or at least send you the bulletins too."

I tipped my head at her like, *You hear what's coming out your mouth, don't you?* I'd just about had it with women for the night, this one on top of Malka and of Malka's boss with the cream-painted face and the curly smile, all soothing, all understanding, all not-giving-a-centimetre, not giving a cent.

Fen was walking around checking my place out. No, there was nowhere good for us to settle; when I was here on my own I sat in my chair or I lay on my bed, and no one ever visited me. She came and stood facing across me and brought out an envelope that looked just about worn out from her clutching it. She opened it and fingered through the pages folded in there one behind the other. "Here, this one." She took it out and unfolded it, but not so I could see. She looked it up and down, up and down. "Yes. I guess. May as well start at the beginning." She handed it to me. "It's not very clear," she apologised. "I wouldn't keep still for them. They'd arrested me and I was *pissed off.*" She laughed nervously.

It was a bad copy of a bad printout of a bad colour scan, but even so, even I could work it out. Two arms. Two legs. A full, round head. For a second there I felt as if my own brain had come unstuck and slopped into the bottom of my skull.

"It's . . . It's just like the one on the sign," I said, with hardly a voice. I meant the billboard up on Taylor Square—well, they were everywhere, really, but I only biked past the others. People picnicked under the Taylor Square one; people held markets and organised other kinds of deals; I sometimes just went up and sat under it and watched them, for something to do. Protect Our Future, it said; it was a government sign, Department of Genetic Protection, I think: a pink-orange baby floating there in its bag like some sleeping water creature, or some being that people might worship—which people kind of did, I guess, with all the fuss about the babies. This was what we were all supposed to be working towards, eh—four proper limbs and a proper-shaped head like every baby's used to be.

Fen looked gleeful as a drugger finding an Ambrosie stash. One of her scabs had split and a bead of blood sat on her lip there.

I went to the chair; it exclaimed in pain and surprise under me. "What else?" I looked at the envelope in her skeleton hands.

She crossed the room and crouched beside me. She showed me three bulletins, because it was two months old. Each had two images, a face and a full-body. The first one gave me another brain-spasm; it was a girl-baby. *The hope of the line,* said the suits in their speeches on the news screen down the Quay; their faces were always working to stop themselves crying by then; they were going for the full drama. *Man's hope is Woman,* they would blubber. *We have done them so wrong, for so long.*

In every picture the baby girl was perfect—no webbing, no cavities, no frills or stumps, and nothing outside that ought to be in. Fen showed me the part where the name was Joannah. She read me the stats and explained them to me. These things, you could tell from the way she said them, they'd been swimming round and around in her head a long time. They came out in a relief, all rushed and robotic like the datadump you get when you ring up about your Billpay account.

When she finished she checked my reaction. My face felt stiff and cold—I had no blood to spare to work it, it was all busy boiling through my brain. "It's something, isn't it?" she said.

"You and me under the cup-maker. It only took a few minutes."

"I know." She beamed and licked away another drop of blood. "Who would've thought?"

I was certainly thinking now. I sat heavily back and tried to see my thoughts against the wall, which was a mass of tags from before they'd secured this building. I needed Fen to go away now—I couldn't make sense of this while she was here watching me, trying to work out what I thought, what I felt. But I couldn't send her away, either; this sort of thing takes a certain amount of time and no less, and there was no point being rude. It takes two to tango, no one knew that better than me.

After a while I said, "I used to walk home behind that Full-Term place."

"Argh," she said, and swayed back into a crouch. "You've got one of those skip stories!"

I nodded. "Mostly it was closed, and I never lifted the lid myself."

"But." She glowered at me.

"If someone had propped it open, with a brick or, once, there was a chair holding it quite wide? Well, then I would go and have a look in. Never to touch anything or anything."

"Errr-her-her-herrr." She sat on my scungey carpet square and rocked her face in her hands, and laughed into them.

"One time—"

"No, no, no!" She was still laughing, but with pain in it.

"One time someone had opened it right the way up—"

"No!" she squeaked, and put her hands over her ears and laughed up at me, then took them off again and waited wide-eyed.

"And taken a whole bunch out—it must've been Ukrainians. They will eat anything," I added, just to make her curl up. "And they'd chucked them all over the place."

"No-no!" She hugged her shins and laughed into her knees. This woman had done it, this scrawny body that I couldn't imagine having ever wanted or wanting again, had brought a perfect baby to nine months. In the old days she would have been the woman who *bore my child*, or even *bore me a child, bore me a daughter*, and while I had to be glad she wasn't, I . . .

Well, to tell you the truth, I didn't know what to think about her, or about myself, or about those loose sheets of paper around her feet, and the face that was Fen's, that was mine, two in the one. Joannah's—my name cobbled together with a girl's. I didn't have a clue.

"It's true," I said. "All these—" I waved at the memory of their disgustingness against the cobbles and the concrete, across the stormwater grille.

"Tell me," she whispered. "It's mostly the heads, isn't it?"

"It was mostly the heads." I nodded. "Like people had hit them, you know, with baseball bats, big . . . hollows out of them, every which side, sometimes the face, sometimes the back. But it was . . . I don't know, it was every kind of . . . Sometimes no legs, sometimes too many. It was, what do you call those meals, like at the Holidaze, where it's all spread out and you get to put whatever you want of it on your plate?"

"A smorgasbord?"

"That's it."

"A smorgasbord of deformities, you reckon?"

"Yeah." *Deformities*, of course—that was what nice people called them. Not *piggies* or *wingies* or *bowlheads*. Not *blobs* for the ones with no heads at all.

"And don't tell me," said Fen, "some of them were still alive."

"Nah, they were dead, all right."

"Some people say, you know? They see them moving?"

I shook my head. My story was over, and hadn't been as interesting as *some people's*, clearly.

"Well," she said, and bent to the papers again, and put them in a pile in order.

"Let me see again." She gave them to me and I looked through them. It was no more believable the second time. "Can I have these?"

"Oh no," she said. "You'll have to go and get tested and take the strips to the Department. Then they'll set you up in the system to get your own copies of everything sent out."

"That'll cost," I said glumly. "The test, and then getting there—that's way up, like, Armidale or somewhere, isn't it? I'd have to get leave."

"Yes, but you'll get it all back, jizzing into their beakers. Get it all back and more, I'd say. It's good for blokes; you have your little factory that only your own body can run. They have to keep paying you. Us girls they can just chop it all out and ripen the eggs in solution. We only get money the once."

"They have to plant it back in you, don't they?"

"They have to plant it back in *someone*, but they've got their own childbearers, that passed all the screenings. I don't look so good beside those; where I come from used to be all dioxins. My sister births nothing but duds, and she's got some . . . mental health issues they don't like the sound of."

"But you brought this one out okay, didn't you, this . . . Joannah?"

"Yeah, but who knows that wasn't a fluke? Besides, I don't want that, for a life. They offered me a trial place there, but I told them they could stick it. I met some of those incubator girls. The bitchery that went on at that place, you wouldn't believe. Good thing they don't do the actual mothering."

She took the papers from me and we both looked at the top one with its stamp and crest and the baby looking out. Poor little bugger. What did it have to look forward to? Nothing, just growing up to be a girl, and then a woman. Mostly I think that women were put here to make our lives miserable, to tease us and lure us and then not choose us. Or to choose us and then go cold, or toss us aside for the fun of watching us suffer. But you can't think that way about a daughter, can you? How are you *supposed* to think about a daughter?

"Well, good on you, I say." I tried to sound okay with it, but a fair bit of sourness came through. "Good on both of us, eh," I added to cover that up. "It makes us both look good, eh."

She folded the papers. "I guess." She put them away in the envelope. She gave a little laugh. "I hardly know you, you know? There was just that one time, and, you know, it wasn't like we had any kind of *relationship*. I didn't know how you were going to take this. But anyway." She got up, so I did too. She was no taller than me—that was one of the reasons I'd had a chance with her. "Now you know everything, and . . . I don't know what I thought was going to happen after that! But it's done." She spread her hands and turned towards the door.

I believe it used not to be like this, people being parents. Olden days, there would have been that whole business of living together and lies and pressures, the *relationship*, which from what I've heard the women always wanted and the men kind-of gave them for the sake of regular sex. Not now, though; it was all genes and printouts now. Everyone was on their own.

I closed the door after Fen, and went and sat with my new knowledge, with my new status. It was some kind of compensation for the rest of my evening, for not getting Malka properly to myself. What's more, I might end up quite tidily-off from this, be able to drop assembly work completely, just sell body fluids. I should feel good; I should feel excited, free and stuff. I should be able to shake off being so annoyed from my poor old withered bone. Some people had simple feelings like that, that could cancel each other out neatly like that.

What I hadn't told Fen, what I wouldn't—her of all people, but I wouldn't tell anyone—was that I used to go home behind the Full Term place because there was always a chance there'd be someone in labour down the back wards there. And the noises they made, for a bloke who didn't have money then, who was saving up his pennies for a Polar girl, the noises were exactly what I wanted to hear out of a woman. No matter I couldn't see or touch them; it was dark, and I could imagine. I could hang onto the bar fence like the rungs of some big brass bedhead and she would be groaning and gasping, panting her little lump of monster out, or—even better—yowling or bellowing with pain; they all did it different. And some nurse or someone, some nun or whatever they had in there, would be telling her what to do. *Oh, what a racket!* she'd say. *You'd think you were birthing an elephant! Now push with this one, Laurie.* And I'd be outside thinking, *Yeah, push, push!*, and somewhere in the next yowl or roar I would spoof off through the fence and be done. There was nothing like the night air on your man-parts and the darkness hiding you, and a woman's voice urging you on.

There's always the buttoning, though, isn't there? There's always rearranging your clothes around your damp self and shaky knees, zipping, buttoning, belting. There's always turning from the bed and the girl, or the fence and the yowling and the skip there, and being only you in the lane or hallway, with no one missing you or needing you, having paid your fee. You're tingling all around your edges, and the tingle's fading fast, and that old pretend-you floats back out of wherever it went, like sheets of newspaper, blows and sticks to you, so that then it's always there, scraping and dirty and uncomfortable.

I turned out the lamp and crawled into bed. Now stars filled the window.

In the old days of full power and streetlights, Sydneysiders saw bugger-all of those, just the moon and a few of the bigger stars. They say you couldn't see the fifth star of the Cross, even. Now the whole damn constellation throbs there in its blanket of galaxy-swirl. People were lucky, then, not knowing what was out there, worse than a few gays poncing about the place, worse than power cuts and restrictions and all these "dire warnings" and "desperate pleas", worse than the Environment sitting over us like some giant troll or something, whingeing about how we've treated her. Earth must have been cosy then. Who was it, I wonder, decided we wanted to go emitting all over the frickin universe, saying, *Over here, over here! Nice clean planet! Come here and help us fuck her right up.* That was the bloke we should have smashed the place of. The gays, they weren't harming anyone but themselves.

I jerked awake a couple of times on the way down to sleep. *My life is changed! I am a new man! They'll show me proper respect now, when they see that DNA readout.* To get to sleep, I tried to fool myself I'd dreamed Fen visiting. Passing those billboards every day, and Malka's baby this evening—everything had mishmashed together in my unconscious. I would wake up normal tomorrow, with everything the same as usual. Fen's scabby lips, the proper kisses, full and soft, we'd had behind the cupmaker—thinking about those wouldn't do any good. Push them into some squishy, dark corner of forgetting, and let sleep take me.

KING PELLES THE SURE

PETER S. BEAGLE

Once there was a king who dreamed of war. His name was Pelles.

He was a gentle and kindly monarch, who ruled over a small but wealthy and completely tranquil kingdom, beloved alike by noble and peasant, despite the fact that he had no queen, and so no heir except a brother to ensure an orderly succession. Even so, he was the envy of mightier kings, whose days were so full of putting down uprisings, fighting off one another's invasions, and wiping out rebellious villages that they never knew a single moment of comfort or security. King Pelles—and his people, and his land—knew nothing else.

But the king dreamed of war.

"Nobody is ever remembered for living out a dull, placid, uneventful life," he would say to his Grand Vizier, whom he daily compelled to play at toy soldiers with him on the parlor floor. "Peace is all very well—a fine thing, certainly—but do you ever hear ballads about King Herman the Peaceful? Do you ever listen to bards chanting the deeds of King Leslie the Calm, or read great national epics about King James the Docile, King William the Diplomatic? You do not!"

"There was Ethelred the Unready," suggested the Grand Vizier, whose back hurt from crouching over the carpet battlefield every afternoon. "Meaning unready for conflict or crusade, unwilling to slaughter needlessly. And King Charles the Good—"

"But it is Charles the Hammer who lives in legend," King Pelles retorted. "William the Conqueror—Erik Bloodaxe—Alfonso the Avenger—Selim the Valiant—Ivan the Terrible. Our own schoolchildren know *those* names . . . and why not," he added bitterly, "since we don't have any heroes of our own. How can we, when nobody ever even raids us, or bothers to challenge us over land or resources, or attempts to annex us, to swallow our little realm whole, as has happened to so many such lands in our time? Sometimes I feel as though I should send out a dozen heralds to proclaim our need of an enemy. I *do*, Vizier."

"No, sire," said the Grand Vizier earnestly. "No, truly, you don't want to do anything like that. I promise you, you don't." He straightened up, rubbing his back and smoothing out his robe of office. He said, "Sire, Majesty, if I may humbly suggest it, you would do well—as would every soul dwelling on this soil that we call home—to appreciate what you see as our insignificance. There is an old saying that there is no country as unhappy as one that needs heroes. Trust me when I say in my turn that our land's happiness is your greatest victory in this life, and that you will never know another to equal it. Nor should you try, for that would show you both greedy and ungrateful, and offend the gods. I urge you to leave well enough alone."

Having spoken so, the Grand Vizier braced himself for an angry response, or at least a petulant one, being a man in late middle age who had served other kings. He was both astonished and alarmed to realize that King Pelles had hardly heard him, so caught up was he in romantic visions of battle. "It would have to be in self-defense, of course," the king was saying dreamily. "We have no interest in others' treasure or territory—we're not that sort of nation. If someone would only try to invade us by crafty wiles, such as filling a wooden horse with armed soldiers and leaving it invitingly outside the gates of our capital city. Then we could set it afire and roast them all—"

He caught sight of the horrified expression on the Grand Vizier's face, and added hurriedly, "Not that we ever *would*, of course, certainly not, I was just speculating."

"Of course, sire," murmured the Grand Vizier. But his breath was turning increasingly short and painful as King Pelles went on.

"Or if they should come by sea, slipping into our port on a foggy night, we would be ready with a corps of young men trained to swim out with braces and augurs and sink their ships. And if they struck by air, perhaps dropping silently from the sky in dark balloons, our archers could shoot all them down with fire-arrows. Or if we could induce them to tunnel under the castle walls—oh, *that* would be good, if they tunneled—then we could . . . "

The Grand Vizier coughed, as delicately as he could manage it given the panicky constriction of his throat. He said, "Your Highness, meaning absolutely no disrespect, you have never seen war—"

"Exactly, exactly!" King Pelles broke in. "How can one know the true meaning of peace, who has no experience of its undoubtedly horrid counterpart? Can you answer me that, Vizier?"

"Majesty, I have known that experience," the Grand Vizier replied quietly. "It was far from here, in a land I traveled to as a boy. I shared it with many brave and dear and young friends, who are all dead now—as I should have been, but for the courtesy of the gods, and the enemy's poor aim. You have missed nothing, my lord."

He seemed to have grown older as he spoke, and the king—who may have been foolish, but who was not a fool—saw, and answered him equally gently. "I understand what you are telling me, good Vizier. But this would be only a little war, truly—no more enduring or consuming than one of our delightful carpet clashes. A *manageable* war—a demonstration, one might say, just to let our rivals see that our people are not to be trifled with. In case they were thinking about trifling. Do you see the difference, Vizier? Between this war and yours?"

With another king, the Grand Vizier would have considered long and carefully before risking the truth. With King Pelles, he had no such fears, but he also knew his man well enough to recognize when hearing the truth would make no smallest difference to what the king decided to do. So he said only, "Well, well, be sure to employ great precision in choosing your foe —"

"*Our* foe," King Pelles corrected him. "Our *nation's* foe."

"*Our* foe," the Grand Vizier agreed. "We must, whatever else we do, select the weakest enemy available—"

"But that would be dishonorable!" the king protested. "Ignoble! Unsporting!" He was decidedly upset.

The Grand Vizier was firm in this. "We are hardly a nation at all; we are more like a shire or a county with an army. A distinctly small army. A more powerful adversary would destroy us—that is simply a fact, my king. You cannot *manage* a war without attention to facts."

He was hoping that his sardonic emphasis on the notion of managing such a capricious thing as war might deter King Pelles from the whole fancy, but it did not. After a silence, the king finally sighed and said, "Well. If that is what a war is, so be it. Consider our choices, Vizier, and make your recommendation." He added then, rather quickly, "But do arrange for a *gracious* war, if you possibly can. Something . . . something a little *tidy*. With songs in it, you know."

The Grand Vizier said, "I will do what I can."

As it turned out, he did tragically better than he meant. Perhaps because King Pelles had never wanted to know it, he truly had no notion of how deeply his land was hated for its prosperity on the one hand and coveted on the other. The Grand Vizier had hoped to engineer a very brief war for the king, quickly over, with minimum damage, disruption or inconvenience to everyone involved, and easily succeeded in tempting their little country's nearest neighbor to invade (in the traditional style, as it happens, by marching across borders). But his plan went completely out of control in a matter of hours. Wise enough to lure a weaker country into a foolish attack, he was as innocent, in his own way, as his king, never having considered that other lands might be utterly delighted to join with the lone aggressor he had bargained for. An alliance of territories which normally despised each other formed swiftly, and King Pelles's land came under siege from all sides.

Actually, it was no war at all, but a massacre, a butchery. There was a good deal of death, which was something else the king had never seen. He was still shaking and crying from the horror of it, and the pity, and his terrible shame, when the Grand Vizier disguised them both as peasant women and set them scurrying out the back way as the flaming castle came down, seeming to melt and dissolve like so much pink candy floss. King Pelles looked back and wept anew for his home, and for his country; and the Grand Vizier remembered the words of Boabdil's mother when the Moorish king looked back in tears from the mountain pass at lost Spain behind him. "*Weep not like a woman for the kingdom you could not defend like a man.*" But then he thought that defending things like men was what had gotten them into this catastrophe in the first place, and decided to say nothing.

The king and his Grand Vizier scrambled day on wretched day across the trampled, smoking land, handicapped somewhat by their long skirts and heavy muddy boots, but running like a pair of aging thieves all the same. No one stopped them, or even looked at them closely, although there were mighty rewards posted everywhere for their heads, and they really looked very little like peasant women, even on their best days. But the country was in such havoc, with so many others—displaced, homeless, penniless, mad with terror and loss—fleeing in every direction, that no one had the time or the inclination to concern themselves with the identities of their poor companions on the road. The soldiers of the alliance were too busy looting and burning, and those whose homes were being looted and burned were too busy not being in them. King Pelles and the Grand Vizier were never once recognized.

One evening, dazed as a child abruptly awakened from a happy dream, the king finally asked where they were bound.

"I have relatives in the south country beyond those hills you see," the Grand Vizier told him. "A cousin and her husband—they have a farm. It has been a long time since I last saw them, and I cannot entirely remember where they live. But they will take us in, I am sure of it."

King Pelles sighed like the great Moor. "Better your family than mine. *My* cousins—my own brother—would demand a bribe, and then turn us over to the conquerors anyway. They are bad people, the lot of them." He huddled deeper into his ragged blanket, shrugging himself closer to their tiny fire. "But I am the worst by far," he added, "the worst, there is no comparison. I deserve whatever becomes of me."

"You did not know, sire," the Grand Vizier offered in attempted solace. "That is the worst that can be said of you, that you did not know."

"But you did, you *did*, and you tried to warn me, and I refused to listen to you. And you obeyed my orders, and now you share my fate, and my people's innocent lives lie in ruins, and it is my doing, and there is no atoning for it." The king rocked back and forth, then stretched on the ground in his blanket, as though he were trying to bury himself where he lay, whimpering again and again, "No atoning, no atoning." He hurt himself doing this, for the ground was shingly and rock-strewn. The Grand Vizier knew he would see the bruises in the morning.

"You were a good king," the Vizier said. "You meant well."

"*No!*" The word came out as a scream of agony. "I *never* meant well! I meant glory for myself—nothing less or more than that. And I knew it, I *knew* it, I knew it at the time, and still I had to go ahead, had to play out my toy battle with soft, breakable human bodies, breakable human souls. *No atoning . . .*"

There was nothing for the Grand Vizier then, but to say, as to a child, "Go to sleep, Your Majesty. What's done is done, and one of us is as guilty as the other. And even so, we must sleep."

But he himself slept poorly—perhaps even worse than King Pelles—in the barns and the empty cattle byres and the caves; and the king's piteous murmurings as he dreamed were hardly of any help. There was always the smell of smoke, from one direction or another; at times there would come noises in the night, which might as easily have been restless cows as pursuing spies or soldiers, but there was never any way for the Vizier to make certain of either. All he allowed himself to think about was the need to guide the king safely to shelter from one night to the next—further than that, his imagining dared not go, if he meant to sleep at all. *And even if we find my cousin—what was her husband's name again?—even if we do find their farm, what then?*

By great good fortune, they did find the Grand Vizier's cousin, whose name was Nerissa—her husband's name was Antonio—and were welcomed as though they had last visited only days ago, or a week at most. The little farm was a crowded place, since Nerissa and Antonio, with no children of their own, had gladly taken in their widowed friend Clara and her four, who ranged in age from six to seventeen years. Nevertheless, they received King Pelles and the Grand Vizier unhesitatingly: as Antonio said, "No farm was ever the worse for more hands in the fields, nor more faces around the dinner table. And whoever noticed the smudged and sunburned face of a farmworker who wasn't one himself? Have no fear—you are safe with us. In these times, there is no safety but family."

So it was that he who had been the king of all the land and he who had been its most powerful dignitary became nothing more than hands in the fields, and were grateful. Neither was young, but they worked hard and long all the same, and proudly kept even with Antonio and the others when it came time to bring the harvest home. And every evening, King Pelles told stories about wise animals and clever magicians to Clara's children, and later the Grand Vizier conducted an informal history lesson for the older ones, in which their mother often joined. Still an attractive woman, she had clear brown skin and dark, amused eyes which were increasingly attentive, as time passed, to whatever the Vizier said or did. Antonio and Nerissa saw this, and were glad of it, as was the king. "Your cousin has wasted his life on my foolishness," he said to Nerissa. "I am so happy that she will give it back to him."

When the Grand Vizier could do it without feeling intrusive, he listened—with the back of his head, perhaps, or the back of his mind—to the king's fairytales. They were not like any he had ever heard, and they fascinated and alarmed him at the same time. Few had what he would have considered happy endings, especially as a child—the gallant prince frequently failed to arrive in time to rescue the princess from the dragon, more often than not the poison was not counteracted, the talking cat could not always preserve his master from his own stupidity. Endings changed, as well, with each telling, and characters wandered from one story into a different one, often changing their natures as they did so. On occasion grief flowed into overwhelming joy, though that outcome was never something you might want to bet on. The Grand Vizier constantly expected the children to become frightened or upset, but they listened in obvious absorption, the younger ones crowding each other on the king's lap, and all four nodding silently from time to time, as children do to express trust in the tale.

Maybe it is the way he tells them, the Grand Vizier thought more than once, for King Pelles always had a special voice at those times, different than the way he spoke in the fields or at evening table. It was a low voice, with a calmness in it that—as the Vizier knew—had grown directly from suffering and remorse, and seemed to draw the children's confidence whether or not the words were understood.

Yet content as King Pelles was in his new life, fond of Clara's children as he was, warmed far deeper than his bones by being a true part of a family for the first time . . . even so, he still wept in his sleep, whispering brokenly, *"No atoning . . ."* The Grand Vizier heard him every night.

Winter was always hard in that kingdom, even in the south country, but the Grand Vizier was profoundly glad of it. The snow and mud closed the roads, for one thing: there would be no further pursuit of the king for a time, and who knew what might happen, or have happened, by spring? What news reached the farm suggested that a group of the king's former advisors had banded together to install a ruler of their choosing, and thus restore at least their notion of order to the kingdom, but the Vizier could not discover his name, nor learn any further details of the story. But he allowed himself to be somewhat hopeful, to imagine that perhaps—just *perhaps*—the hunt might have dwindled away, and that the king's existence might have become completely unimportant to the new regime. For the first time in his long career of service, the Grand Vizier dreamed a small dream for himself.

But with the thawing of the roads, with the tinkling dissolution of the icicles that had fringed the farmhouse's gables for many months, with the first tentative sounds of the frogs who had slept in the deep beds of the frozen streams all winter . . . the soldiers came marching. With the first storks, they came.

Martine, Clara's younger daughter, was playing by the awakening pond one afternoon, and heard their boots and the rattle of their mail before they had rounded the bend in the road. She, like all the others, had been told over and over that if she ever saw even one soldier she must run straight to the house and warn her mother's special friend, and the other one as well, the storyteller. She never waited to see these, but was up and away at the first sound, and through the front door in a muddy flash, crying, "They're here! They're here!"

Antonio had long since prepared a hiding place for King Pelles and the Grand Vizier in case of just such an emergency. It lay under the floor of his own bedroom, so cunningly made and so close-fit that it was impossible to tell which boards might turn on hinges, or how to make them open, even if you knew. The two men were down there, motionless in the dark, well before the soldiers had reached the farmhouse; until the first fist hammered on the front door, the only sound they heard was the beating of each other's hearts.

The soldiers were polite, as soldiers go. They trampled no chickens, broke nothing in the house, and kept their hands off Antonio's fresh stock of winter ale, last of the season. Filling the kitchen with their size and the noise of their bodies, they treated Nerissa and Clara with truly remarkable courtesy; and their captain offered boiled sweets to the children clustered behind them, even responding with a good-humored chuckle when little Martine kicked his shin. Nor did they ask a single question concerning guests, or visitors, or new-hired laborers. Indeed, they were so amiable and considerate, by contrast with what the family had expected, that it took Nerissa a moment longer than it should have to realize that they had not been sent for the king and the Grand Vizier at all.

They had come for her husband.

"You see, ma'am," the Captain explained, as three of his men laid hold of Antonio, who had bolted too late for the back door, "the war just keeps going *on*. Wars, I mean. It's chaos, madness, really it is, ever since that idiot Pelles started the whole thing. Everyone turning against everyone else—whole regiments changing sides, generals selling out their own troops—mutiny over *there*, rebellion *here*, betrayal *that* way, corruption *this* way . . . and what's a poor soldier to do but follow his orders, no matter who's giving them today? And my orders all winter have been to round up every single warm body, which means every able, breathing male with both legs under him, and ship them straightaway to the front. And so that's what I do."

"The front," Nerissa said numbly. "Which front? Where is the battle?"

The Captain spread his arms in dramatic frustration. "Well, I don't know *which* front, do I? As many of them as there are these days? Somebody else tells me that when we get there. Very sorry to be snatching away your breadwinner, ma'am—'pon my soul, I am—but there it is, you see, and I put it to you, what's a poor soldier to do?" He turned irritably toward the soldiers struggling with Antonio. "*Hold* him, blast you! What's the bloody matter with you?"

In the moment that his gaze was not on her, Nerissa reached for her favorite butchering knife. Behind her, Clara's hand closed silently on a cleaver. Only Martine saw, and drew breath to scream more loudly than she ever had in her short life. But the Captain was never to know how close he was to death in that moment, because just then King Pelles walked alone into the kitchen.

He wore his royal robes, and his crown as well, which the children had never seen in all the time he had lived with them. Nodding pleasantly at the soldiers, he said to the Captain, "Let the man go. You will have a much richer prize to show your general than some poor farmer."

The Captain was dumb with amazement, turning all sorts of colors as he gaped at the king. His men, thoroughly astounded themselves, eased their grip on Antonio, who promptly burst free and headed for the door a second time. Some would have given chase, but King Pelles snapped out again, "Let him go!" and it was a king's order, prisoner or no. The men fell back.

"We weren't looking for you, sir," the Captain said, almost meekly. "We thought you were dead."

"Well, how much better for you that I'm not," the king replied briskly. "There will be a bonus involved, surely, and you certainly should be able to trade me to one side or another—possibly all of them, if you manage it right. I know all about managing," he added, in a somewhat different voice.

A young officer just behind the captain demanded, "Where is the Grand Vizier? He was seen with you on the road."

King Pelles shrugged lightly and sighed. "And that was where he died, on the way here, poor chap. I buried him myself." He turned back to the Captain. "Where are you supposed to take me, if I may ask?"

"To the new king," the Captain muttered in answer. "To King Phoebus."

"To my brother?" It was the king's turn to be astonished. "My brother is king now?"

"As of three days ago, anyway. When I left headquarters, he was." The Captain spread his arms wide again. "What do *I* know, these days?"

Even in his happiest moments on Nerissa and Antonio's farm, the king had never laughed as he laughed now, with a kind of delight no less rich for being ironic. "Well," he said finally. "Well, by all means, let us go to my brother. Let us go to King Phoebus, then—and on the way, perhaps we might talk about managing." He removed his crown, smiling as he handed it to the Captain. "There you are. Can't be king if you don't have a crown, you know."

Nerissa and Clara stood equally as stunned as the men who cautiously laid hands on the unresisting King Pelles; but the two youngest children set up a wail of angry protest when they began leading him away. They clung to his legs and wept, and neither the Captain nor their mother could part them from him. That took the king himself, who finally turned to put his arms around them, calling each by name, and saying, "Remember the stories. My stories will always be with you." He embraced the two women, saying to Clara in a low voice, "Take care of him, as he took care of me." Then he went away with the soldiers, eyes clear and a smile on his face.

If the Captain had looked back, he might well have seen the Grand Vizier, who came wandering into the kitchen a moment later, nursing a large bruise on his cheekbone, and another already forming on his jaw. Clara flew to him, as he said dazedly, "He hit me. I wouldn't let him surrender himself alone, so then he . . . . Call them back—I'm his Vizier, he can't go without me. Call them back."

"Hush," Clara said, holding him. "Hush."

In time the long night of wars, rebellions, and retaliations of every sort slowly gave way at least to truces born of simple exhaustion, and reliable news became easier to come by, even for wary hillfolk like themselves. Thus the Grand Vizier was able to discover that the king's brother Phoebus had quite quickly been overthrown, very likely while the soldiers were still on the road with their captive. But further he could not go. He never found out what had become of King Pelles, and after some time he came to realize that he did not really want to.

"As long as we don't know anything certainly," he said to his family, "it is always possible that he might still be alive. Somewhere. I cannot speak for anyone else, but that is the only way I can live with his sacrifice."

"Perhaps sacrifice was the only way he could live," suggested his wife. The Grand Vizier turned to her in some surprise, and Clara smiled at him. "I heard him in the night too," she said.

"*I* hear his stories," young Martine said importantly. "I close my eyes when I get into bed, and he tells me a story."

"Yes," said the Grand Vizier softly. "Yes, he tells me stories too."

CHARACTER FLU

ROBERT REED

Look at me.

That's right, you don't know me. Now please, put down your drink and pay attention to me. I'm here as a courtesy, and there's something very important that you have to understand.

Are you listening?

There's a new disease, and without question, it's the worst ever. There's never been anything like it. Not in the history of mankind, not even close. Nanobodies: Synthetically produced nanotic machinery. The idiots in the interactive industry built the monsters. Of course they didn't appreciate what they had. Couldn't imagine the dangers. When their bug went wild, they called that "an exceptionally minor nonevent." When the bug learned to self-replicate, they promised to rein it in with some elegant little fixes. And today, after throwing fifty billion dollars at the problem, those responsible have admitted they're beaten. Their monsters have evolved into a plague that's highly transmittable, unnoticed by any immune system. Just one microscopic machine gets ingested or slips through the skin, and within minutes, it's riding the bloodstream to the brain. And once there, it generates hundreds of billions of examples of its perfect, insidious self.

No, it doesn't bring death.

For a long time, there aren't any symptoms. No fevers. No weakness. No diminishment of body or mind. In fact, the fully infected person sports a boosted IQ, plus this giant imagination. But that's not surprising, since the original nanobody was designed to do exactly that. Those trillion invaders link up with their host's neurons, streamlining an assortment of brain functions, and suddenly tasks that used to be difficult become astonishingly easy.

No, the disease doesn't kill.

It creates.

During the last six months, the population of the world has increased two hundredfold. And that's the conservative estimate.

No, you haven't heard anything about this plague. And there's a perfectly good explanation why you haven't.

Listen.

What happened was that those tech-wizards in the interactive market—those creative geniuses of commerce—thought it would be fun and sweet, not to mention lucrative, to build gaming platforms that their customers could carry wherever they went, embedded inside willing skulls. That's why the nanobodies do what they do. They bring improvements to cognitive functions. Think of them as an upgrade of old hardware. A little perk to every user. The brain gets quicker and smarter, so there's plenty of room for whatever diversion the buyer desires. And creativity has to be boosted, if only so the player can enjoy an experience that's promised to be unlike any other on the market today.

And the nanobody that went wild . . . . ?

It invents characters. Phony people that seem very real to the user. The entire package isn't much different from certain computer games that were popular during the last century. But then again, when hasn't human history been full of fictional worlds and imaginary friends.

This is how the disease works:

An infected person thinks of somebody. He picks a face in the crowd, or she dreams somebody up from nothing. Fantasy souls of their own invention. Then the machinery builds a character to match the face, guided by the host's supercharged creativity. These new entities are so carefully drawn that they acquire many if not all of the aspects of real life. Independence. Self-awareness. A life story, plus a huge capacity for love and hate.

Give the wild nanobodies a few busy weeks, and they'll infect any skull with a town's worth of artfully rendered citizens. These new people inhabit any dreamed-up landscape that suits them. Mountains are popular, and beaches, and drinking establishments, too. In principle, the infected person can visit whenever he wants, talk and touch whomever he wants. But he sees only tiny slivers of his new friends' rich, enormous lives.

Why is that bad.

Okay, that's a fair question.

Trouble comes sooner or later. You see, those fictional souls have their own lucid daydreams. Maybe they imagine a secret lover, or they want to have a child or three. Whatever the inspiration, they can trigger the same machinery that created them in the first place. And what's been a manageable population swells, and a disease that was only a nuisance suddenly overwhelms the infected, overtaxed mind.

This wouldn't happen with the original nanobody. It couldn't. But the wild bug has dropped all of the carefully contrived safeguards.

No matter how much genius a person carries, he has limits. The first symptom is to lose the elevated IQ. Then decision-making and recall slow down. If left unchecked, the infected person falls into a deep sleep, followed by a coma, while his brain works slower and slower as an entire nation of fictional souls struggle to live their important lives.

To date, the only treatment—not a cure, mind you, but only a short-term fix—is to physically remove these parasitic characters.

And it's not an easy fix.

I won't mention the physical constraints, which are enormous. But worse are the ethical problems. Purge the mind of thousands of living souls, and what are you doing.

You're committing mass murder, some say.

Says hundreds of billions of people, if you bother to ask them.

The imagined souls, yes.

But if humanity doesn't fight this runaway plague, everybody will become a host. Everybody will be unconscious and helpless. The meat-and-bone population of the world will live out its days in hospital beds, their minds progressively declining, their minimal needs tended to by machinery and empathetic software.

So you see, this is the worst disease ever.

No matter what the response, billions and eventually trillions of sentient entities are going to die. Will have to be killed. Yet for the time being, there is no other viable option.

Believe me when I say this: The best that we can do is to treat every last casualty with the same respect that humans would want, if these tragic roles were reversed.

Now put down the drink again, please.

No, I don't think you have been paying attention. Not like you should have been.

You're right. I haven't introduced myself.

Think of me as an angel.

As a servant from On High.

Now do I have your attention?

In the clearest possible terms, this angel is telling you that you have exactly one day to make peace with everybody in your world, and with yourself.

Did you hear me?

One day.

Or do I need to explain all this to you again?

GIFT FROM A SPRING

DELIA SHERMAN

In the southwest of France is a province that looks like an illustration for a fairy tale. There are high, frowning cliffs with grey stone fortresses like extinguished dragons coiled around their summits. There are narrow, bright, running rivers and steep, rocky fields striated with grape vines and deep, mysterious woods full of moss-grown rocks and small, unexpected springs bubbling up into shaded pools. It is called the Lot.

By the logic of aesthetics, the Lot should be rich in gold or diamonds or magical treasure. Existing as it does in the real world, it is rather poor than otherwise. Its chief products are a coarse, tannic wine that doesn't travel well, lavender oil, walnuts, ducks, and legends. Once, the Lot was part of the Aquitaine that the infamous Queen Eleanor brought to England as her dowry. Now it is full of holidaying Brits pretending they never lost it to the French 550 years ago.

Although I am a Brit myself, I did not go to the Lot looking for a holiday, but for work—paying work, work that would buy me another six months worth of paint and canvas so that I could continue to pursue the indefinable, magical *something* that would turn me into a successful artist.

I was up in Town for a gallery opening. Not mine, needless to say. That spring, my career had reached something of a crossroads, with no clear signpost in sight.

In art school, I'd always done best in drawing classes: still-life, figure-drawing, portraits. My advisor had encouraged me to take up portraiture, but I hadn't the temperament for dealing with temperamental sitters. I preferred landscape, but he'd pronounced my mountains and bosky dells and gnarled trees far too literal-minded to qualify as fine art.

"It would do as illustration, I suppose," he said. "Children's books, possibly. Although your line is old-fashioned even for that—Rackham and Crane written all over it. Can't you do something a little more *modern*?"

Heaven knows I wanted to. I loved the cool intellectualism of the Minimalists, the passionate iconoclasm of the Abstract Impressionists. In pursuit of my goal, I redoubled my studies of Twentieth Century Art. I haunted the Tate Modern.

I retired my books on Gustave Moreau, the Pre-Raphaelites, and, yes, Arthur Rackham, in favor of books on Toulouse-Lautrec, Picasso, and Rothke. I cropped my hair and wore black. I tried thinking about the military/industrial complex and capitalism while I tore brown paper and arranged the pieces on purposefully-spattered canvases. I painted anatomized fruit and canvases titled *Study in Blue, With Ovals.*

These paintings weren't awful. I'd sold *Study in Blue* at the All-Devon Christmas Arts Fair, and there was a gallery in Moreton Hampstead that had expressed interest in my fruit series. The only problem was that every canvas I'd done felt like a sophisticated exercise in paint-by-numbers. I was getting the moves down, but I was gradually losing heart.

It was in an state of acute artistic malaise, therefore, that I took the train from Exeter up to town to attend the opening of a group show of my art school classmates at a small gallery in Clerkenwell. I might as well have stayed home in Devon: I was too blind with jealousy to see the paintings clearly. I wouldn't have seen my old friend Sia either, if she hadn't rushed up and embraced me.

"You look like you need a drink," she said, looking into my face.

"I do."

We repaired down the street to the Chop and Crown and settled in for a comfortable evening of drinking and whingeing, just like old times. By the time we'd killed most of a bottle of the cheap red plonk that was all we could afford, Sia knew all there was to know about the disaster that was my life.

"Poor Whittier." She poured the last of the plonk into my glass. "No wonder you're getting squirrelly, cooped up in that cottage all the time. You need a change. Why don't you go to France?"

"Portugal's cheaper," I said. "And I can't afford to go there either."

Sia patted my hand. "I know, dear. I know. Will you just listen for a minute without interrupting? If you don't like what I've got to say, you can go back to venting and I won't say another word. I promise."

I never quite know how to respond to that kind of comment, so I lifted my glass in an encouraging gesture and slouched back in my chair.

"You've heard of Ondine Delariviére, right?" she said.

I nodded. Ondine Delariviére was famous. She'd been a prima ballerina in the Paris Opera Ballet in the 1950's and 60's, beloved as Dame Margot Fonteyn despite refusing to dance anything remotely modern or tour outside of Continental Europe. After 1965, she began turning down European tours too. But she was so incandescently light and fluid in her movements, so enchanting to watch, that balletomanes from Europe and even North America were more than happy to make the pilgrimage to Paris to see her. Productions of *Swan Lake* and *Giselle* in which she danced the title roles sold out virtually the moment they were announced.

And then she vanished.

The tabloids had hinted at a drug habit, bone cancer, crippling arthritis, a shameful love affair, madness. For six months, the mystery of Ondine

Delariviére's disappearance obsessed the masses, and then some politico got his picture in the tabloids with a floozy and she was forgotten.

"What happened was, she got married," Sia said, "to a director named Peter Collingsworth, whose specialty was gorgeous, edgy historical recreations. Good looking, too, and maybe fifteen years younger than Ondine. She met him when the Opera Garnier got him in to advise on *Les Sylphides*. They fell in love and ran away together."

She paused long enough for me to venture a question. "How did the tabloids miss that story?"

"There are no paparazzi in the Lot, I guess. That's where they ran to—a valley in the unfashionable part of Southwestern France. It seems Ondine had inherited a sheep farm there, with a lovely fieldstone farmhouse, plenty of barns and outbuildings and fields and woods around it for privacy. She and Peter turned the dairy and the granary and the farmhouse attic into dormitories and the barns into rehearsal and performance space and opened a summer school for the performing arts for kids. They're still there. Peter teaches acting and stagecraft. Ondine teaches dance and movement."

"And nobody knows?" I asked, not so much because I was curious, but because I'm fond of Sia and didn't want to seem rude.

"The parents of their students know, of course—that's why the place is successful. There's no advertising, just word of mouth. The truth is, an old dancing teacher's life is just not as gossip-worthy as a prima ballerina's."

I set down my empty glass. "Very interesting, Sia. What does it have to do with me?"

"I worked there last summer." She cast me a significant glance. "They pay very well."

"I don't know anything about the theatre."

"You don't have to." Sia leaned earnestly over the stained table top. "The Collingsworths are brilliant teachers, but they have no more business sense than a pair of kittens. They need someone to keep the books, make sure the *boulanger* is paid, call the plumber, change the fuses. You're good at the practicalities of life: you could do it with your eyes closed."

"I don't doubt it. But why would I want to?"

Sia sat back. "It would give you free room and board for the summer. A change of scene, which you sorely need. Time to paint, think, sort yourself out." She smiled at me. "Look at it this way, Whittier. What have you got to lose?"

Had it been anyone but Sia advising me to offer myself as a general factotum at a theatrical summer camp set up in a former sheep farm, I'd have handed them their head on a salver. As it was, I reminded myself that I didn't have so many close friends that I could afford to lose one, "My dignity," I said mildly. "My pride. A summer's worth of work."

"You'll have plenty of time to work," Sia said. "I hate to be blunt, but really, Whittier, do you have a choice?"

That was indeed the question. I was pretty much entirely out of money.

No money means no colors, no canvas, no brushes to paint with, no studio to paint in. I wrote down Peter Collingsworth's name on a bar napkin. When I got home to Devon, I wrote him a letter inquiring whether he needed a summer bookkeeper and office manager and sent it off to La Vielle Ferme de la Source at St. Martin le Pauvre, Lot, France.

A short time later, I received two letters. One was from Collingsworth offering me a job at La Vielle Ferme de la Source. The other was from my landlord, threatening me with eviction for non-payment of rent. As the salary Collingsworth mentioned seemed adequate and the duties reasonable, I swallowed my pride and wrote by return of post accepting his offer with gratitude.

Thus I found myself, at the beginning of June, on the platform of the Cahors train station, where I was accosted by a short, wiry, grizzle-bearded man with dark curly hair.

"Peter Collingsworth," he said, energetically pumping my hand. "And you must be Desdemona Whittier. Welcome to our little family, Desdemona."

I winced. "Please, call me Whittier."

He dropped my hand as though I'd stung him. "My Christian name's something of a trial to me," I said apologetically. "I shed it when I went to school, and now my mother is the only person who expects me to answer to it."

Collingsworth smiled cautiously. "Whittier, then, by all means. Are those your traps? Splendid. You must be ravenous, but I hope you'll last until we get home. Mme Fabre is cooking up a welcome feast—you've no objection to rabbit, I trust?"

After assuring him I was completely comfortable with rabbit, I couldn't think of another word to say. Luckily, Collingsworth seemed happy to shoulder the whole burden of conversation. In the course of the hour it took to drive from Cahors to St. Martin le Pauvre, he regaled me with accounts of Mme Fabre's culinary genius, the excellence of her husband's wine, his own ideas for the school production of *A Midsummer Night's Dream*, and the presence on the property of a spring—"La Source" of the farm's name—which was reputedly both haunted and sacred.

"Of course, it's nothing of the sort," he said as he swerved his little green Citroen sedan around the backside of a cow calmly eating weeds with her forefeet in a ditch. "It's very obviously man-made, with dressed stone sides and pipes and things. Ondine says there's been a wash house there since the year dot. The structure is long gone, but we still use the basin as the camp laundry."

He downshifted suddenly and turned onto a tiny, unpaved lane between two sloping fields. The Citroën bounced over the rocky, rutted surface, the motor roaring in first gear as the lane plunged upward through a shady wood.

Trees and shrubbery crowded close to the path and dragged along the sides of the car. Leafy branches overhead screened the sky and dimmed the light. In that wood there was no sense of background, only fore-and-middle ground: a wall of trunks and leaves shielding some impenetrable mystery.

When we broke free of the trees and into the light again, I had to squint against the glare of casement windows and scarlet trumpet vines, fever-bright against the soft umber of a stone farmhouse, stolid and practical. There was an equally stolid barn across the path to its left and we drove between them, pulling up beside a courtyard flanked by the house and two more barns, all built of the same richly glowing stone.

I clambered out of the car and looked out over the bright prospect of field and wood behind me.

"Ah, Mlle Whittier. *Bien venue* to La Source!"

I turned towards the light, silvery voice and saw Ondine Collingsworth, neé Delariviére.

I recognized her at once, from the famous Avedon photo of her as Giselle. There was the broad forehead, the pointed chin, the thin, chiseled lips, the extraordinarily wide-set dark eyes. Her slight, strong, upright body was clothed in a practice dress made of some soft, green stuff that flowed over her dancer's limbs like water. Had I been a portrait painter, I'd have been begging to paint her.

A cloud passed over the sun. My eyes, no longer dazzled, noted that the line of her throat and chin was ever so slightly blurred, her complexion lightly veiled with tiny lines. Belatedly, I remembered that Ondine Collingsworth must be at least 70 years of age, if not more. She certainly did not look it.

Ondine came closer, extending her slender hand. I was about to take it when Peter Collingsworth gathered her into his arms and began murmuring into her hair as though he'd just got home from the moon instead of Cahors.

Above his shoulder, the moss-brown eyes met mine. She winked at me. Startled, I smiled, then turned away to extract my luggage from the Citroën's boot.

That night, unpacking my gear, I felt more cheerful than I'd felt in some time. I was full of excellent rabbit fricassee, fresh-picked vegetables and rough, young wine. My employers had exerted themselves to be agreeable, and I found myself inclined to like them. Ondine was a conversational butterfly, fluttering from subject to subject in charmingly accented English. Collingsworth, less voluble in his wife's presence, encouraged her reminiscences. When he said good night, I thought how lucky they were to have found each other.

My room had been converted from the farm's old bread oven, with bed and desk and storage all built into the thick stone walls. Windows over the bed and desk looked out into the wood. I even had my own external door through which I could slip out if I wanted without anyone being the wiser.

That first night, I stood on the threshold to watch the moon rise through the treetops and listen to the resonant hou-hou of an owl waking in the depths of the wood. Here was peace, I thought. Here I could paint something that really mattered.

The next day, reality set in.

After a breakfast of ripe apricots and yogurt, Collingsworth and Ondine ushered me into La Source's basement office. It was a dank, dark room situated between the communal toilets on one side and the storage-and-wine cellar on the other. Someone—Ondine undoubtedly—had done what could be done with whitewash and framed watercolors, bright cushions and vases of flowers. A little clay plaque soaked with oil of lavender struggled against the pervasive odor of drains, stale wine, and mold.

"Sorry about the mess," Collingsworth said apologetically. "Sia left it ship-shape last fall, but you know how it is. One turns one's back, and entropy takes over."

I surveyed the drifts of unopened envelopes, the tottering pile of ledgers, the cancelled checks hugger-mugger across the desk. "Perhaps you need a professional bookkeeper," I said.

"We have an accountant," Ondine said. "In Paris. He doesn't like the country."

"Ring him by all means," Collingsworth added. "He'll fill you in on what needs to be done. Well. We'll leave you to it, then, shall we?"

I sank into the desk chair and turned on the desk lamp. Behind me, Ondine cleared her throat. "*Chéri,* tell her about the washing machine."

Her voice was heavy with meaning. Clearly, the washing machine was an uncomfortable subject. Collingsworth certainly sounded uncomfortable enough when he said, "Ah, yes. The washing machine. Ondine thinks we're sadly behind the times, washing our linen as our ancestors did, in the clear, pure water from the earth."

"That's not it at all, *chéri.* As you very well know."

The words were innocuous enough, but the steel in her voice told me there was more going on here than met the eye. I waited, with interest, to see how Collingsworth would respond.

He smoothed his beard nervously. "As *you* very well know," he said, "it's just not feasible. The effect on the ground water, the plumbing, the draw on the electrical system—we've been over it all a thousand times. It's just not on, darling. I'm sorry."

He didn't sound particularly sorry. In fact, he sounded smug. Which annoyed me so much that I broke my own rule about not meddling in other people's business. "What a coincidence," I said brightly. "My aunt just bought a new washing machine. It's the latest thing—energy efficient, low-flow, ultra ecological. You can install it nearly anywhere, I think."

If I'd pulled the machine itself out of the pocket of my shorts, I couldn't have gotten a more dramatic reaction. Collingsworth's lips thinned to nothing and his cheeks flushed a deep and angry scarlet. Ondine, who had been looking every minute of her age, dropped thirty years in a second. She smiled, a crescent moon of pure joy. Her eyes sparkled, her cheeks glowed. She clasped her hands in front of her breast like a girl. "*Quelle merveille!*" she breathed. "What a marvel! Peter, do you hear?"

"It'll cost the earth to bring in and hook up properly," Collingsworth grumbled. "Some German machine, I'll be bound, finicky as an old maid, forever breaking down and needing parts that no one stocks."

"You don't *know* that, Peter," Ondine snapped. "You just want it to be so. Mlle Whittier will find out the truth of the matter. Will you not, Mlle Whittier?"

Collingsworth glared at me. "You do that, Whittier, by all means. Just keep in mind that we keep this place going on a shoe string. A thickish shoe sting, but not one to take an undue strain. I'm not running the risk of losing all we've worked so hard to build because my wife wants a washing machine, forsooth!"

Astonished by this sudden squall, I simply nodded. Ondine brought her hand to her mouth in the attitude of a woman betrayed. Her husband reached out to her and she bolted past him out of the office.

"Damn and blast," Collingsworth said ruefully. "The cat's among the pigeons now. You should have held your tongue."

"I didn't know I had to," I said. Having no desire to be sacked my first day on the job, I tried to keep my tone neutral.

"I'm just trying to protect her," Collingsworth said defensively. "Research the damn thing, by all means, now you've got her hopes up. Just remember when you discover it can't be done, you're the one who will have to tell her."

I had intended to begin research on the washing machine question immediately. Instead, I spent the day separating bills, business letters, receipts, and checks for tuition from photographs, letters from former students, newspapers, dance and theatre magazines, old programs, masks, and notes for old productions pulled for reference from the careful files Sia had made last summer and left to compost on the desk and the floor with sprays of leaves, sun-whitened bones, curiously-shaped stones, and feathers. By evening, I'd unearthed both the telephone and the accountant's name and phone number, and counted it a good day's work. I hardly knew what to say to my employers at dinner, but they were so full of lesson plans and set designs for *The Dream* that I doubt they noticed my silence.

The next day the students arrived—thirty artistic adolescents of both sexes and a spread of ages from 12 to 18. Classes began the following day, effectively separating me from the Collingsworths except at meals. My mornings were spent in the basement office among the receipts, bills, and bank books. I sorted, I filed, I added and subtracted. I spent hours on the phone to the accountant in Paris.

In the afternoons, I sat in my bread oven retreat, listening to Ondine teaching ballet in the barn next door.

She was indeed a brilliant teacher, if not a kind one. She teased, she ridiculed, she exhorted, she goaded. Girls were always running into the bathroom that faced my door in floods of tears, bathing their faces, and emerging, scarlet-eyed, to try again. Sometimes I crept up to what had once been the hayloft and looked down on them bending and tossing and unfolding their slender bodies in solemn unison while Ondine wove among them, tapping here a wrist, there an outflung foot or knee into an attitude of greater grace, greater strength, greater fluidity. What she was looking for, I realized, was a kind of controlled abandon, and she was not, on the whole, finding it.

Neither was I.

Midsummer in the Lot means enough light to paint by until nearly midnight. I set up my easel outside my private woodland door and tried to capture my impressions of La Vielle Ferme de la Source in paint. I had a composition in mind: a still, bright center (that was Ondine), embraced, upheld, perhaps confined by something darker, more active (that was Collingsworth), surrounded by a series of shapes, colors, movements that both were and were not the trees, the fields, the students, M. and Mme Fabre and all the glorious rest of it.

And once a week, on Saturday mornings, I stripped my bed, bundled my towels and dirty clothes into a pillowcase, and hauled it down to Ondine's spring for washing.

The first week, Collingsworth mustered the whole camp in the courtyard and led us in procession to the spring. We'd never have found it on our own. The path looked no different from any of the other paths that snaked through La Source's little patch of woodland. Clutching my pillowcase, I picked a rather unsteady way around rocks and over moss-slick roots and fallen branches nobody'd bothered to clear away. The artistic adolescents crashed through the undergrowth until we came to a rocky bottleneck, through which we squeezed single-file, emerging into a park-like glade studded with trees. Off to one side was a grassy bank topped with trees and ferns and thorny bushes, studded with the mossy ruins of a stone building: La Source de La Vielle Ferme.

I can't say I thought it particularly beautiful or haunted. The fountain itself was a hole, perhaps three metres square, flanked by two semi-circular pipes through which clear water trickled into a small square basin. A notch in the rim fed the long pond where we were to wash our clothes. The water was murky and spotted with vivid green duckweed.

Collingsworth demonstrated how to pound the soap into the cloth, rinse it in the pond, then wring out the sopping, clinging sheets in pairs. He helped me wring my sheets, and I helped him wring his. There was laughing and splashing and semi-accidental dunkings. Ondine was not present.

That evening, I dug out my sketching block and drew La Source, minus the screaming adolescents and the laundry. Then, as if compelled, I drew the view from the window over the desk and the lavender bush planted by the back door. From then on, I divided my free time between my abstract oil—my *real* work—and sketching. Telling myself that it couldn't hurt for me to keep my hand in, I sketched everything: the students hanging sheets in the drying yard or practicing combinations in front of the flyblown mirror in the barn; Ondine teaching, presiding over dinner in the long barn, sewing straightbacked on the veranda, ignoring her husband, who sat beside her in a deck chair and watched her with hungry eyes.

I both loved and hated these sketches of Ondine. On the one hand, I thought they caught something of her grace, her mischief, her calm, even (taken in series) her trick of looking old as the hills one moment and young as a flower in bud the next. On the other hand, they were useless. They were old-fashioned, sentimental. They weren't art. And yet I couldn't stop making them.

And every morning, I doggedly continued to organize the office, research washing machines, and exercise my A-level French on every appliance dealer, electrician, and plumber within a 100 kilometer radius of St. Martin le Pauvre. When I'd amassed a collection of brochures, estimates, and proposals, I put them together with the balance sheet I'd prepared, plus an article or two on the ecological benefits of a properly-drained low-flow washing machine, and presented the whole to the Collingsworths one evening after dinner.

"But this is wonderful!" Ondine exclaimed, turning over the glossy pages of one brochure. "So beautiful and so economical! You will order one immediately."

Collingsworth snorted. "You will do no such thing, Whittier. Things are just hotting up with the *Dream*. I don't want the kiddies any more distracted than they already are."

"It will not be a distraction, *chéri*." Ondine's voice was pure seduction. "See here, where *M. le Plombier* estimates two days of work only, to set everything in place."

"Two days!" Collingsworth laughed. "Add a week and 100 euros at least, and you'd be nearer the mark." He turned a ferrety gaze on me. "You seem like a sensible sort, Whittier. Surely you know these estimates are fairy tales?"

I protested. Ondine coaxed, then sulked. Collingsworth would not be moved. At the end of a solid hour of fruitless discussion, he picked up his empty glass and rose. "We've scheduled the readings for Titania/Hyppolita tonight, my dear," he said. "Doesn't do to keep the kiddies waiting. Bad for discipline."

For a moment, I thought she'd tell him where he could put his discipline, and perhaps the play as well—she certainly looked angry enough, all flushed and bright and stiff-backed. But she simply folded her lips tight and swept past him.

The lines of battle were drawn.

As *A Midsummer Night's Dream* was cast and rehearsals began, the young actors had ample opportunity to observe the disturbance that permeates a kingdom when its rulers are at daggers drawn.

Nobody knew what the fight was about, exactly, but they took sides anyway. The dancers supported her; the actors supported him. The students in charge of lights and tech called a plague on both their houses and showed disturbing signs of making up to me. It was all profoundly uncomfortable.

I couldn't figure out why on earth Collingsworth was so dead set on denying his clearly much-beloved wife something it would be so very easy for him to give her. Observing him, I wouldn't have said that he was in general clutchfisted or unkind or unreasonable. And yet there he was, out-Scrooging Scrooge. It was beyond comprehension.

Tackling him on the subject led only to discussions that went round and round and ended up nowhere. Out of pure frustration, I did a watercolor of the fountain as it might be if it were left in peace: green, clear, fern-bordered, with lilies floating on its surface and a bright shadow beneath that I had meant for the reflection of a cloud but looked a little like a woman's face.

And still, as the weather grew hotter, we trooped down to the spring on Saturday mornings, rubbed soap into our laundry, rinsed them in sullen green water, and hung them in the sheltered bamboo grove to dry.

Late one blazing Saturday afternoon, I went to rescue my personal laundry before the drying-yard was overrun with students rushing to bring in their linen before dinner. As I approached the gate, I heard Collingsworth's querulous tenor and Ondine's aggrieved soprano within. I hesitated a moment, then edged silently between the tall, rustling stalks and listened.

"You promised," Ondine was insisting. "As soon as it became possible, you said."

"That has yet to be established." Collingsworth sounded insufferably stuffy.

"It has been established. Whittier has established it. I do not understand why you refuse to accept it. I have kept my end of the bargain, have I not?"

This last was said with real pain, like a small child discovering that the world is unfair. But there was pain in Collingsworth's voice, too. "You've been a good wife to me, Ondine. I've been happy. *We've* been happy. Why can't we just go on as we have been for a little longer?"

"How long? A month? A year? Until you die of old age? Things are no longer what they were, Peter, and nothing you say can make them so. You lied to me. You're lying to me now. I will not stay with a man who lies to me."

"I'd never lie to you, Ondine."

There was a silence broken by the brisk smack of flesh on flesh, a grunt (Collingsworth) and a sob (Ondine). I hurriedly extracted myself from the bamboo and backed away from the gate just as Ondine thrust it open and strode towards the house, her face set with fury.

Little as I was liking Collingsworth just then, I could not but pity him.

This state of affairs could not go on. A fire smoldering in a pile of damp leaves will burst into flame as soon as it has a little air to feed it. You wouldn't have said there was much air abroad the night everything exploded. It was hot and dry and breathless, the latest in a procession of hot, dry nights punctuated by ever hotter and more breathless days. *Midsummer Night's Dream* was progressing poorly, lines and blocking both lost to the mind-numbing heat. The dancers stumbled and strained and complained of dizziness. One of them fainted altogether in the midst of her fouettés and sprained her wrist. Mme. Fabre refused to turn on the stove, and we supped lightly on bread, cheese, salad, and slivers of cold duck breast washed down with blood-warm rosé.

When we'd eaten, the students began to clatter the plates onto trays. Collingsworth drained his glass and wiped sweat from his face. "Damn hot tonight," he said. "The hell with your old washing machine, Ondine. What we really need is a swimming pool."

Ondine hadn't spoken directly to her husband since the incident in the drying yard, but she spoke now. "You're drunk, Peter."

"So I am, Ondine. But mostly I'm hot. Wait, we have a pool. Cold as be-damned, too. How about a nice dip?"

"It's full of soap-scum," Ondine said, her lip curled with distaste. "And duckweed."

"What's wrong with duckweed?" Collingsworth asked. "It's a plant, isn't it? Natural and all that? Come swimming with me, Ondine, please. For old times sake."

It seemed a reasonable enough suggestion, given the heat and the natural chill of the fountain's water. I'd paddled my feet in the run-off more than once the past few hot days, and thought nothing of it. But there was something in Collingsworth's voice, some note of bravado or challenge, that drew my eyes first to him and then to Ondine.

"How dare you," she said in a harsh whisper more shocking, somehow, than a shout. "How dare you speak of 'old times'? You are a fool and a liar, Peter Collingsworth. But until this moment, I had not realized that you were cruel."

Medusa could not have done a more thorough job of paralyzing us. The students and I were stone-faced and astonished, eyes fixed on our hands, our neighbors, our plates, anywhere but on Ondine's incandescent fury and Peter Collingsworth's misery.

"Not cruel," he said, bewildered. "Surely not that. I only want what's best for us."

Ondine stood up. "You may all go to bed, now," she said. "It is late."

Obediently, quietly, disproportionately shocked, we went to our rooms like scolded children—Collingsworth, too, his arms dangling helpless at his thighs as he crossed the courtyard and mounted the stone steps to the house.

I retired to the bread oven, too wrought up to sleep. I lit my entire stock of candles, set them on the deep window ledges and alcoves, and spread my summer's work across the bed and the desk and examined it thoroughly.

The sketches weren't bad. Literal-minded as ever, but lively enough. They'd do for a book titled "A Summer at La Source," or "What I Did At the Holidays."

The painting, on the other hand, was dreadful: a muddy, incomprehensible, unreadable, ugly mess. I'd over-worked it. The thing to do was let it go, start over on a clean canvas once I'd thought a little more clearly about what I wanted it to say about La Source.

The problem, of course, was that I'd put everything I felt about La Source into the sketches and watercolor of the fountain I'd painted to show Collingsworth why he should buy his wife a washing machine.

My chest heaved and huffed. Caught between laughter and tears, I came out with something like a strangled bark, harsh and hard on the throat. It was hopeless. I was not the kind of artist I wanted to be.

Shuffling the sketches into a pile, I added the watercolor, and stacked them all on the canvas. Then I tucked a box of matches in my pocket, gathered the ungainly bundle in my arms, and set out through my private door and into the wood.

Of course I went to the fountain. There was nowhere else to go where a bonfire such as I intended would not begin a conflagration.

There was a moon, full or close to it, which gave me enough light to navigate by. Awkwardly, I negotiated rocks and roots, making, I'm sure, a racket that would wake the dead, stumbling at last onto the mossy turf of the fountain glade.

And there I saw Ondine, her pale hair unbound and glistening in the moon-light, perched on the edge of the upper basin.

I stopped dead, my work clutched to my chest as if to keep my hammering heart from leaping out.

"Desdemona," she said, soft but commanding.

"Whittier," I said weakly. "I prefer to be called. . . ."

"I do not give a good God-damn what you prefer," she said. "Come here, Desdemona, and stop acting like a school-girl."

I came. I was angry and embarrassed in more ways than I can tell, but I came.

In a fluid movement, she turned to face me, her white feet peeping from her nightgown's white hem, looking ridiculously, unbelievably young.

"Sit down," she ordered me. "Show me."

"It's dark," I said.

"All the better."

Never argue with drunkards or lunatics, my father taught me. So I laid the stack of paper and canvas at her feet and sat and forced myself to watch her face as she went through them. I couldn't see the art, of course. I shouldn't have been able to see Ondine, either. But I could, quite clearly.

She was wearing her teacher-face, calm, unrevealing, entirely concentrated, her eyes glittering in the tricky moonlight as they scanned each sketch, each watercolor and oil study in turn, and laid it aside.

My pulse fluttered nervously. All around us, the wood was still, the soft trickle of the fountain like a sleeper's long-drawn breathing, the paper passing through her hands like the rustle of bed sheets. In the midst of all this peace, I felt like an alarm clock set to go off much too early.

Before I quite exploded, Ondine looked up at me. "Why did you bring these here, Desdemona?"

It did not occur to me to prevaricate. "To burn them." It didn't sound quite the considered and adult decision I had thought it, so I went on: "It's no good, you see. I've put a lot of time and energy into becoming an artist, and I'm not getting any better. I'm not getting any younger, either. It's time I just admit that I'm a dauber, a Sunday painter, a hobbyist, dispose of the embarrassing evidence, and get on with my life."

"Better at what?"

She didn't sound as if she especially cared, which perversely made me more eager to make her understand. "Come now, you've seen the work," I said. "The drawings aren't terrible, but I'm not at all interested in churning out pretty landscapes for the tourist market."

Ondine lifted a blurry sheet I could just identify as my watercolor of the fountain. The moonlight caught the shape in the water, gave it features I'd never intended, turned it into a face, wide-eyed and mischievously smiling. "Like this, you mean?"

"Exactly like that."

Her gleaming white foot stirred the train wreck that I'd intended to be my masterpiece. "And what of this?"

"What of it?" I echoed bitterly. "I put my heart and soul into that, not to mention everything I've ever learned about technique. It's crap. Utter, complete, thorough-going, bone-deep crap. I can't stand the sight of it. I can't stand the sight of any of it."

"And so you're going to burn your heart and your soul and go back to England and do what? Design bookkeeping systems for impractical artists? Pursue a certificate in accountancy?"

Her voice pricked me like a silver needle. When it became clear I could not answer, she stretched, shaking back her long white hair, and came to her feet in a single, smooth, dancerly surge.

"Are you going to burn your art or are you not? Because if you are, you'd best get on with it. I'd advise you to gather enough stones for a hearth first. You don't want the fire to spread."

Squatting ungracefully among my scattered sketches, I gaped up at her silhouette, black against the electric blue sky.

"You'd be a fool to do it," she went on. "I've loved many artists. I know true art when I see it, and I see it here. If you, however, cannot tell a baby from bathwater, there is nothing more to be said."

Suddenly, she looked old and tired, her slim body exhaustedly collapsed in upon itself. I was as shocked by the change in her as I was by her words, which left me as confused as I'd been in my life.

"I'm going to bed," she said. "Give the watercolor of the spring to me. You should keep the oil yourself."

"Why?"

"To remind you of who you are not."

In the event, I didn't burn anything. I sat brooding in the glade until the birds woke up, then retrieved every scrap and stumbled back to the Bread Oven. Not being one who can function very well on no sleep, I did not feel up to dealing with my employers and their crochets. But I wasn't actually ill, so I didn't feel I could ask for a day off. What would I have done with it, anyway?

Collingsworth wasn't at breakfast, but Ondine was, looking like an active woman of seventy-odd who'd enjoyed a night's unbroken slumber. She smiled at me with absent courtesy and handed me a brioche as if our moonlit interview had never happened.

When I took my coffee down to the cellar office, I found Collingsworth at the desk. My washing machine file was open in front of him, and tucked into the frame of the floral still life over the desk was my watercolor of the fountain.

"You've done an excellent job, Whittier," he said without turning around. "It's all as clear as glass. I'd be an idiot not to install a washing machine at La Source. I was an idiot not to do it long ago. Get on the horn, there's a good girl, and order us up one today. I'd like to get the thing installed as soon as possible, work out the bugs, release the spring into the wild, as it were, and move on."

It was so utterly unexpected, so sudden—and I was so sleepy—that I didn't have the first idea how to respond. I stood in the door gaping. "It was this that did it," he said, gesturing to the watercolor. "I don't know how you know, but you do. And now you've reminded me, I can't pretend any more. I don't know whether to thank you or sack you."

A week later, the washing machine arrived. Installing it was a five-act drama, peopled by a large cast of plumbers, electricians, masons, building inspectors, and petty bureaucrats. They enacted scenes of comedy, melodrama, and even near-tragedy, and then they bowed and departed, leaving behind a concrete slab with a white enamel box on it, crowned with dials and displays.

The washing machine was the last word in energy and water efficiency and boasted an instruction manual an inch thick, written by illiterate engineers whose first language, at a guess, was Medieval Icelandic. By the time I'd figured out how to work it, I hated the sight of it more than tongue can tell—more than Collingsworth, I think, although he had thrown himself so completely into *Dream* rehearsals that nothing else seemed to matter.

Still, he was present for the grand washing Ondine organized next laundry day—a real production, with a ceremonial procession of maidens bearing sheets and towels to the flower-garlanded appliance.

The whole thing ought to have been squirmingly precious, but it was actually rather splendid, in a Dionysian sort of way. The maidens stuffed the sheets into the washer, Collingsworth measured in an anxious ounce of low-sudsing, bio-degradable detergent, and I unlatched the agitator and set the dial. Ondine pressed the "On" button with a dramatic flourish and we all held our breaths as the washer began to hiss and churn. Once we were sure it wasn't going to explode or overflow, the linen-bearers and their acolytes dispersed to play tag in the courtyard.

"How long's it likely to take, Whittier?" Collingsworth asked.

"Forty-five minutes," I said. "Counting the spin cycle."

He studied the gently chugging machine, an expression of profound sadness on his good-humored face utterly at odds with the object, the day, the occasion.

"The end of an era, what?" he said, artificially jocund. "Keep an eye on it will you, Whittier? I'm going to run Titania and Oberon's fight in Act II."

"Poor Peter," Ondine said. "He does so hate letting things go. You've seen the albums? He's got clippings on all his old students. Very few of them become performers, but they do get married and have offspring and so on. One won an award for a children's book: *The Enchanted Fountain*, it was called."

"I know that book!" I exclaimed, surprised. "I bought it for my niece. I didn't know it was based on La Source."

Ondine smiled, a gleam of teeth in the gloomy barn. "That's because she made everything up. She didn't even bother to research the local folklore. She just made up a improving story, peopled it with sentimental children and sweet Victorian fairies, and set my spring behind it like a badly-drawn backdrop."

"Isn't that what art is?" I asked, my eyes on the featureless machine. "Making things up?"

"No," she said. "That is commerce—identifying a market and satisfying it. Art is seeing the truth and revealing it, as beautifully and forcefully and honestly as you are able."

Startled, I turned to look at her. But she was gone.

While the washing machine was disposing of the first load of sheets, I mulled over Ondine's pronouncement, coming to no conclusion except that it felt like part of a conversation we'd been having since I first came to La Source.

When the machine shuddered to a halt at last, I extracted the sheets and carried them to the drying yard in the middle of the bamboo grove, where I pinned them on the lines and left them hanging in the sun. I felt, ridiculously, as though something portentous had happened—in La Source, for Ondine and Collingsworth, for me. But I couldn't for the life of me tell what.

With the washing-machine chapter closed, the camp turned its whole attention to the play. Collingsworth and Ondine coached the students in their lines and their steps, cobbled together props and costumes, set lights and music cues. Collingsworth suggested sets and Ondine made me paint them: pasteboard columns and a rough-cast wall, cloths of honor for the thrones of Theseus and Hyppolita, gnarled trees and rocks of made of old cartons and burlap for the fairy wood.

All this activity kept me from thinking about my own painting, now tucked into the back reaches of the wood-shed where the scenery from previous productions was stored. It also kept me from thinking about Collingsworth, who looked older, greyer, and more strained every time I saw him, and Ondine, who seemed to be growing correspondingly younger.

The play was a triumph. We used the open barn as the stage, with the audience in the courtyard and Ondine and Collingsworth on the house veranda, flanking the mayor of St. Martin and his wife, all in high-backed chairs. Town dignitaries ranged down the steps at their feet, and the rest of the audience— townsfolk, Collingsworth's friends, the odd English tourist—half-filled the courtyard. I spent the play backstage, with masks and silk flowers and garlands and a pocket full of pins against wardrobe malfunctions, peering through the decidedly un-Athenian wood I'd made and watching a gaggle of self-centered, rowdy, undisciplined adolescents showing just how focused, passionate, and responsible they could be in service of a commonly-desired end.

The applause was uproarious, especially in view of the fact that a good part of the audience hadn't understood a single word of what they'd heard. They applauded the young actors, they applauded the Collingsworths, they even applauded me, dragged from behind the scenery with Cupid's flower in one hand, Titania's pink scrunchy around my wrist, and my unwashed hair bundled into a paint-stained bandana.

Then they headed for the wine and the food Mme Fabre had laid out on long tables, and I headed for the fountain.

I'd planned to go back to my room, take a shower, fall into bed, read a mystery, and go to sleep. But the young actors, turned back into rowdy adolescents, were screeching and whooping in the barn. Needing quiet more than clean hair, I slipped out my private door and felt my way down the dusky path, past the leaning tree, past the moss-covered rocks, to Ondine's spring.

The full moon rode high in the sky, silvering the tall ferns growing above and beside the fountain's opening, glinting off the surface of the water like a mirror, picking up the white flowers strewn in the grass like scattered pearls. Everything looked magical and lush, ferns and flowers growing everywhere much more thickly than could possibly have happened in a few short weeks of relative neglect.

It must be my eyes, I thought, or my exhaustion, or a little-known side-effect of making an entire grove of Rackhamesque trees for an amateur production of *A Midsummer Night's Dream*. All it lacked was Titania to be the bank where the wild thyme grows, although it was much too late in the year for cowslips and nodding violets. If they even grew in this part of France.

And then, just as if I'd called her, I saw Titania.

She wasn't what I'd imagined—clothed in green gauze, or pale silk, or even heavy Elizabethan brocade, with a wreath of flowers in her hair. No. This spirit was naked and uncrowned, and stood at the edge of the fountain with her long pale hair veiling her face as she looked down into the water.

I must have made a sound—a gasp, a sigh, a choke of awe or shock or disbelief—for she turned and looked at me from eyes as wide-set and liquid as an animal's.

"Ondine," I said.

She laughed—that light, mocking, enchanting laugh—and tossed back her hair with both hands, showing me her nakedness. It was a wanton gesture, but not a sexual one—she meant to display, not to seduce. In any case it was not a seductive body she showed me, inhumanly thin and smooth and long of flank and waist, with small, high breasts and a smooth blank like a classical statue's at the bottom of her gently sloping belly.

"How did you know?" she asked.

"I didn't. I don't. I'm just dreaming. Or over-tired. This isn't real."

"Do you really want to take that attitude, Desdemona? Because if you do, you won't like your present, and then I'll have to be offended and do you a mischief. Which would be a pity, because you've been a great help to me."

I grasped at the one thing out of her speech that made sense. "I don't want to offend you."

"Good. Then you'll take your present?"

I don't really like surprises and I don't like presents I haven't asked for. But Ondine had made it perfectly clear on several occasions what weight she gave my preferences. "Yes," I said. "I'll take it."

"Wait there, then, and I'll get it." She slipped into the water and disappeared under the surface.

Some part of me knew she wouldn't surface within a normal breath-holding span, that she was a comfortable under water as in the air—more comfortable, water being her native element. Another part of me, the part that believed in fairies only as metaphors for the multifarious facets of the human subconscious, prompted me to jump into the fountain after a drowning woman and pull her out. The tension between the two parts made the time of her absence seem interminable. But the moon hadn't moved when she returned.

I hardly recognized her. Her beauty, always exotic, had grown inhumanly strange, the relative proportions of her forehead and chin, eyes, mouth, and nose, exaggerated and attenuated to the edge of caricature. Furthermore, she was distinctly green—skin, lips, eyes, and hair like duckweed floating on the surface of the water, luminescent in the moonlight. A star glittered in her brow—no decoration, but part of her skin, her skull, her very self.

"I had a bet with myself," she said, "whether you'd choose to run away or jump in the water after me or wait and see what happened."

"And did you win?" I asked stupidly.

"I'd have won no matter which you chose. You, on the other hand, might have lost a great deal."

"What—" I began, then prudently shut my mouth.

"Would you like your present now?"

It occurred to me that Ondine's gift might turn out to be something I'd be better off without. The gifts of fairies were traditionally uncomfortable, possibly troublesome. On the other hand, my life was hardly comfortable or trouble-free as it was.

"Yes," I said. "Yes, I believe I would."

She brought her hands out of the water, cradling something bright and clear—a crescent moon. It wasn't the moon, of course—the moon was overhead, and just off the full—but it felt like the moon. I couldn't think what I was supposed to do with it.

"Kneel," she said, and I got down on my knees. She lifted the moon towards me, phospherescent in the green cup of her palms.

"Eat," she said.

I ate.

Later, after moon-set, I walked past the fountain and down through the wood to M. Fabre's vineyard. When I reached the farmhouse, it was near dawn. The windows were lit. Mme Fabre answered the door, bustled me into the kitchen, sat me down at the battered wooden table, and set a brioche and a bowl of *café au lait* in front of me.

M. Fabre came in just as I was drinking the ambrosial last of the *café*. "The spirit has returned to the spring," he remarked in much the same voice he'd use to comment on the weather.

"She has," I said, equally matter-of-factly.

"*Bien*. It is better like that."

That's the end of it, really. Oh, there was a certain amount of drama attendant on Mme Ondine Collingsworth's sudden and mysterious disappearance, complete with weeping adolescents and a stoic husband and policemen tramping through the fountain and the woods, searching for signs of foul play. I got to know—and like—Peter Collingsworth a lot better than I ever would have believed possible. When the fuss had died down at last and the students had left, we sat with our wine on the veranda and talked about what was going to become of L'Ecole de la Source.

"She doesn't care," he told me on the night before I left. "She has what she wants. She'd been waiting to get back to her spring for ages—far longer than I knew her, certainly. It wasn't in her nature to feel about me as I felt about her. But we were happy together. We were happy for a long time."

He sighed, and we sat in silence until he went on: "I'll stay, of course. The spring needs someone to look after it, make sure it's not plowed under or built over or some such foolishness. That'll be easier if the school's a going concern. And she did care about the dancing."

"Keep the school going by all means," I said. "I suspect she cares about art as much as she cares about anything human, and she clearly likes having artists around."

"You'll come next summer? Teach art—figure drawing, that kind of thing. You can have the big room over the granary, if you like—use it as a studio."

"I'd rather have the bread oven."

And so it was settled.

My horrible abstract is hanging in my studio in Devon, just outside the toilet.

I'm still working out what the gift was that Ondine gave me that night. Not a sudden perfection of line: I don't draw any better than I did before—not yet, anyway. I certainly draw more, and much more mindfully, than I did. Drawing has become an obsession with me, and walking on the moors with my sketching-block and my little tin of watercolors. I've done dozens of trees and hundreds of rocks, many of them with faces peering out of or around them—little, cold, inhuman faces. Are they really there? I don't know. I only know I paint what I see—the truth, as Ondine bade me.

The other thing I've done is reproduce the watercolor of La Source. In the foreground, where duckweed and shadow had cast a woman-shape, I painted Ondine as I'd last seen her, star-browed, the crescent moon cradled in her palms echoing the curve of her mocking smile.

I showed it to my friend Sia, who turned and hugged me.

"What's that for?" I asked.

"For this," she said. "For painting something real."

THE REGION OF UNLIKENESS

RIVKA GALCHEN

—◆—

Some people would consider Jacob a physicist, some would consider him a philosopher or simply a "time expert," though I tend to think of him in less reverent terms. But not terms of hatred. Ilan used to call Jacob "my cousin from Outer Swabia." That obscure little joke, which I heard Ilan make a number of times, probably without realizing how many times he'd made it before, always seemed to me to imply a distant blood relation between the two of them. I guess I had the sense (back then) that Jacob and Ilan were shirttail cousins of some kind. But later I came to believe, at least intermittently, that actually Ilan's little phrase was both a misdirection and a sort of clue, one that hinted at an enormous secret that they'd never let me in on. Not a dully personal secret, like an affair or a small crime or, say, a missing testicle—but a scientific secret, that rare kind of secret that, in our current age, still manages to bend our knee.

I met Ilan and Jacob by chance. Sitting at the table next to mine in a small Moroccan coffee shop on the Upper West Side, they were discussing "Wuthering Heights," too loudly, having the kind of reference-laden conversation that unfortunately never fails to attract me. Jacob looked about forty-five; he was overweight, he was munching obsessively on these unappetizing green leaf-shaped cookies, and he kept saying "obviously." Ilan was good-looking, and he said that the tragedy of Heathcliff was that he was essentially, on account of his lack of property rights, a woman. Jacob then extolled Catherine's proclaiming, "I am Heathcliff." Something about passion was said. And about digging up graves. And a bearded young man next to them moved to a more distant table. Jacob and Ilan talked on, unoffended, praising Brontë, and at some point Ilan added, "But since Jane Austen's usually the token woman on university syllabi, it's understandable if your average undergraduate has a hard time shaking the idea that women are half-wits, moved only by the terror that a man might not be as rich as he seems."

Not necessarily warmly, I chimed in with something. Ilan laughed. Jacob refined Ilan's statement to "straight women." Then to straight women "in the Western tradition." Then the three of us spoke for a long time. That hadn't been my intention. But there was something about Ilan—manic, fragile, fidgety, womanizing (I imagined) Ilan—that was all at once like fancy coffee and bright-colored smutty flyers. He had a great deal to say, with a steady gaze into my eyes, about my reading the New York *Post*, which he interpreted as a sign of a highly satiric yet demotically moral intelligence. Jacob nodded. I let the flattery go straight to my heart, despite the fact that I didn't read the *Post*—it had simply been left on my table by a previous customer. Ilan called *Post* writers naïve Nabokovs. Yes, I said. The headline, I remember, read "AXIS OF WEASEL. Somehow this led to Jacob's saying something vague about Proust, and violence, and perception.

"Jacob's a boor, isn't he?" Ilan said. Or maybe he said "bore" and I heard "boor" because Ilan's way of talking seemed so antiquated to me. I had so few operating sources of pride at that time. I was tutoring and making my lonely way through graduate school in civil engineering, where my main sense of joy came from trying to silently outdo the boys—they still played video games—in my courses. I started going to that coffee shop every day.

Everyone I knew seemed to find my new companions arrogant and pathetic, but whenever they called me I ran to join them. Ilan and Jacob were both at least twenty years older than me, and they called themselves philosophers, although only Jacob seemed to have an actual academic position, and maybe a tenuous one, I couldn't quite tell. I was happy not to care about those things. Jacob had a wife and daughter, too, though I never met them. It was always just the three of us. We would get together and Ilan would go on about Heidegger and "thrownness," or about Will Ferrell, and Jacob would come up with some way to disagree, and I would mostly just listen, and eat baklava and drink lots of coffee. Then we'd go for a long walk, and Ilan might have some argument in defense of, say, Fascist architecture, and Jacob would say something about the striated and the smooth, and then a pretty girl would walk by and they would talk about her outfit for a long time. Jacob and Ilan always had something to say, which gave me the mistaken impression that I did, too.

Evenings, we'd go to the movies, or eat at an overpriced restaurant, or lie around Ilan's spacious and oddly neglected apartment. He had no bed frame, nothing hung on the walls, and in his bathroom there was just a single white towel and a T.W.A. mini-toothbrush. But he had a two-hundred-dollar pair of leather gloves. One day, when I went shopping with the two of them, I found myself buying a simple striped sweater so expensive that I couldn't get to sleep that night.

None of this behavior—the laziness, the happiness, the subservience, even the pretentiousness—was "like me." I was accustomed to using a day planner and eating my lunch alone, in fifteen minutes; I bought my socks at street fairs. But when I was with them I felt like, well, a girl. Or "the girl." I would see us from the outside and recognize that I was, in an old-fashioned and maybe even demeaning way, the sidekick, the mascot, the decoration; it was thrilling. And it didn't hurt that Ilan was so generous with his praise. I fixed his leaking shower and he declared me a genius. Same when I roasted a chicken with lemons. When

I wore orange socks with jeans, he kissed my feet. Jacob told Ilan to behave with more dignity; he was just jealous of Ilan's easy pleasures.

It's not as if Jacob wasn't lovable in his own abstruse and awkward way. I admired how much he read—probably more than Ilan, certainly more than me (he made this as clear as he could)—but Jacob struck me as pedantic, and I thought he would do well to button his shirts a couple buttons higher. Once, we were all at the movies—I had bought a soda for four dollars—and Jacob and I were waiting wordlessly for Ilan to return from the men's room. It felt like a very long wait. Several times I had to switch the hand I was holding the soda in because the waxy cup was so cold. "He's taking such a long time," I said, and shrugged my shoulders, just to throw a ripple into the strange quiet between us.

"You know what they say about time," Jacob said idly. "It's what happens even when nothing else does."

"O.K.," I said. The only thing that came to my mind was the old joke that time flies like an arrow and fruit flies like a banana. I couldn't bear to say it, so I remained silent. It was as if, without Ilan, we couldn't even pretend to have a conversation.

There were, I should admit, things about Ilan (in particular) that didn't make me feel so good about myself. For example, once I thought he was pointing a gun at me, but it turned out to be a remarkably good fake. Occasionally when he poured me a drink he would claim he was trying to poison me. One night I even became very sick, and wondered. Another evening—maybe the only time Jacob wasn't with us; he said his daughter had appendicitis—Ilan and I lay on his mattress watching TV. For years, watching TV had made me sick with a sense of dissoluteness, but now suddenly it seemed great. That night, Ilan took hold of one of my hands and started idly to kiss my fingers, and I felt—well, I felt I'd give up the rest of my life just for that. Then Ilan got up and turned off the television. Then he fell asleep, and the hand-kissing never came up again.

Ilan frequently called me his "dusty librarian." And once he called me his "Inner Swabian," and this struck him as very funny, and even Jacob didn't seem to understand why. Ilan made a lot of jokes that I didn't understand—he was a big fan of Poe, so I chalked his occasionally morbid humor up to that. But he had that handsome face, and his pants fit him just so, and he liked to lecture Jacob about how smart I was after I'd, say, nervously folded up my napkin in a way he found charming.

I got absolutely no work done while I was friends with them. And hardly any reading, either. What I mean to say is that those were the happiest days of my entire life.

Then we fell apart. I just stopped hearing from them. Ilan didn't return my calls. I waited and waited, but I was remarkably poised about the whole thing. I assumed that Ilan had simply found a replacement mascot. And I imagined that Jacob—in love with Ilan, in his way—hardly registered the swapping out of one girl for another. Suddenly it seemed a mystery to me that I had ever wanted to be with them. Ilan was just a charming parrot. And Jacob the parrot's parrot. And if Jacob was married and had a child wasn't it time for him to grow up and spend his days like a responsible adult? That, anyway, was the disorganized crowd of my thoughts. Several months passed, and I almost convinced myself that I was glad to be alone again. I took on more tutoring work.

Then one day I ran randomly (O.K., not so randomly—I was haunting our old spots like the most unredeemed of ghosts) into Jacob.

For the duration of two iced teas, Jacob sat with me, repeatedly noting that, sadly, he really had no time at all, he really would have to be going. We chatted about this and that and about the tasteless yet uncanny ad campaign for a B movie called "Silent Hill" (the poster image was of a child normal in all respects except for the absence of a mouth), and Jacob went on and on about how much some prominent philosopher adored him, and about how deeply unmutual the feeling was, and about the burden of unsolicited love, until finally, my heart a hummingbird, I asked, "And how is Ilan?"

Jacob's face went the proverbial white. I don't think I'd ever actually seen that happen to anyone. "I'm not supposed to tell you," he said.

Not saying anything seemed my best hope for remaining composed; I sipped at my tea.

"I don't want your feelings to be hurt," Jacob went on. "I'm sure Ilan wouldn't have wanted them hurt, either."

After a long pause, I said, "Jacob, I really am just a dusty librarian, not some disastrous heroine." It was a bad imitation of something Ilan might have said with grace. "Just tell me."

"Well, let's see. He died."

"What?"

"He had, well, so it is, well, he had stomach cancer. Inoperable, obviously. He kept it a secret. Told only family."

I recalled the cousin from Outer Swabia line. Also, I felt certain—somehow really certain—that I was being lied to. That Ilan was actually still alive. Just tired of me. Or something. "He isn't dead," I said, trying to deny the creeping sense of humiliation gathering at my liver's portal vein.

"Well, this is very awkward," Jacob said flatly. "I feel suddenly that my whole purpose on earth is to tell you the news of Ilan—that this is my most singular and fervent mission. Here I am, failing, and yet still I feel as though this job were, somehow, my deepest essence, who I really—"

"Why do you talk like that?" I interrupted. I had never, in all our time together, asked Jacob (or Ilan) such a thing.

"You're in shock—"

"What does Ilan even do?" I asked, ashamed of this kind of ignorance above all. "Does he come from money? What was he working on? I never understood. He always seemed to me like some kind of stranded time traveller, from an era when you really could get away with just being good at conversation—"

"Time traveller. Funny that you say that." Jacob shook extra sugar onto the dregs of his iced tea and then slurped at it. "Ilan may have been right about you. Though honestly I could never see it myself. Well, I need to get going."

"Why do you have to be so obscure?" I asked. "Why can't you just be sincere?"

"Oh, let's not take such a genial view of social circumstances so as to uphold sincerity as a primary value," Jacob said, with affected distraction, stirring his remaining ice with his straw. "Who you really are—very bourgeois myth, that, obviously an anxiety about social mobility."

I could have cried, trying to control that conversation. Maybe Jacob could see that. Finally, looking at me directly, and with his tone of voice softened, he said, "I really am very sorry for you to have heard like this." He patted my hand in what seemed like a genuine attempt at tenderness. "I imagine I'll make this up to you, in time. But listen, sweetheart, I really do have to head off. I have to pick my wife up from the dentist and my kid from school, and there you go, that's what life is like. I would advise you to seriously consider avoiding it—life, I mean—altogether. I'll call you. Later this week. I promise."

He left without paying.

He had never called me "sweetheart" before. And he'd never so openly expressed the opinion that I had no life. He didn't phone me that week, or the next, or the one after that. Which was O.K. Maybe, in truth, Jacob and I had always disliked each other.

I found no obituary for Ilan. If I'd been able to find any official trace of him at all, I think I might have been comforted. But he had vanished so completely that it seemed like a trick. As if for clues, I took to reading the New York *Post*. I learned that pro wrestlers were dying mysteriously young, that baseball players and politicians tend to have mistresses, and that a local archbishop who'd suffered a ski injury was now doing, all told, basically fine. I was fine, too, in the sense that every day I would get out of bed in the morning, walk for an hour, go to the library and work on problem sets, drink tea, eat yogurt and bananas and falafel, avoid seeing people, rent a movie, and then fall asleep watching it. But I couldn't recover the private joy I'd once taken in the march of such orderly, productive days.

One afternoon—it was February—a letter showed up in my mailbox, addressed to Ilan. It wasn't the first time this had happened; Ilan had often, with no explanation, directed mail to my apartment, a habit I'd always assumed had something to do with evading collection agencies. But this envelope had been addressed by hand.

Inside, I found a single sheet of paper with an elaborate diagram in Ilan's handwriting: billiard balls and tunnels and equations heavy with Greek. At the bottom it said, straightforwardly enough, "Jacob will know."

This struck me as a silly, false clue—one that I figured Jacob himself had sent. I believed it signified nothing. But. My face flushed, and my heart fluttered, and I felt as if a morning-glory vine were snaking through all my body's cavities.

I set aside my dignity and called Jacob.

Without telling him why, assuming that he knew, I asked him to meet me for lunch. He excused himself with my-wife-this, my-daughter-that; I insisted that I wanted to thank him for how kind he'd always been to me, and I suggested an expensive and tastelessly fashionable restaurant downtown and said it would be my treat. Still he turned me down.

I hadn't thought this would be the game he'd play.

"I have something of Ilan's," I finally admitted.

"Good for you," he said, his voice betraying nothing but a cold.

"I mean work. Equations. And what look like billiard-ball diagrams. I really don't know what it is. But, well, I had a feeling that you might." I didn't know what I should conceal, but it seemed like I should conceal something. "Maybe it will be important."

"Does it smell like Ilan?"

"It's just a piece of paper," I answered, not in the mood for a subtext I couldn't quite make out. "But I think you should see it."

"Listen, I'll have lunch with you, if that's going to make you happy, but don't be so pathetic as to start thinking you've found some scrap of genius. You should know that Ilan found your interest in him laughable, and that his real talent was for convincing people that he was smarter than he was. Which is quite a talent, I won't deny it, but other than that the only smart ideas that came out of his mouth he stole from other people, usually from me, which is why most everyone, although obviously not you, preferred me—"

Having a "real" life seemed to have worn on Jacob.

At the appointed time and place, Ilan's scrawl in hand, I waited and waited for Jacob. I ordered several courses and ate almost nothing, except for a little side of salty cucumbers. Jacob never showed. Maybe he hadn't been the source of the letter. Or maybe he'd lost the spirit to follow through on his joke, whatever it was.

A little detective work on my part revealed that Ilan's diagrams had something to do with an idea often played with in science fiction, a problem of causality and time travel known as the grandfather paradox. Simply stated, the paradox is this: if travel to the past is possible—and much in physics suggests that it is—then what happens if you travel back in time and set out to murder your grandfather? If you succeed, then you will never be born, and therefore your grandfather won't be murdered by you, and therefore you will be born, and will be able to murder him, et cetera, ad paradox. Ilan's billiard-ball diagrams were part of a tradition (the seminal work is Feynman and Wheeler's 1949 Advanced Absorber Theory) of mathematically analyzing a simplified version of the paradox: imagine a billiard ball enters a wormhole, and then emerges five minutes in the past, on track to hit its past self out of the path that sent it into the wormhole in the first place. The surprise is that, just as real circles can't be squared, and real moving matter doesn't cross the barrier of the speed of light, the mathematical solutions to the billiard-ball–wormhole scenario seem to bear out the notion that real solutions don't generate grandfather paradoxes. The rub is that some of the real solutions are very strange, and involve the balls behaving in extraordinarily unlikely, but not impossible, ways. The ball may disintegrate into a powder, or break in half, or hit up against its earlier self at just such an angle so as to enter the wormhole in just such a way that even more peculiar events occur. But the ball won't, and can't, hit up against its past self in any way that would conflict with its present self's trajectory. The mathematics simply don't allow it. Thus no paradox. Science-fiction writers have arrived at analogous solutions to the grandfather paradox: murderous grandchildren are inevitably stopped by something—faulty pistols, slippery banana peels, flying squirrels, consciences—before the impossible deed can be carried out.

Frankly, I was surprised that Ilan—if it was Ilan—was any good at math. He hadn't seemed the type.

Maybe I was also surprised that I spent so many days trying to understand that note. I had other things to do. Laundry. Work. I was auditing an extra course in Materials. But I can't pretend I didn't harbor the hope that eventually—on my own—I'd prove that page some sort of important discovery. I don't know how literally I thought this would bring Ilan back to me. But the oversimplified image that came to me was, yes, that of digging up a grave.

I kind of wanted to call Jacob just to say that he hadn't hurt my feelings by standing me up, that I didn't need his help, or his company, or anything.

Time passed. I made no further progress. Then, one Thursday—it was August—I came across two (searingly dismissive) reviews of a book Jacob had written called "Times and Misdemeanors." I was amazed that he had completed anything at all. And frustrated that "grandfather paradox" didn't appear in the index. It seemed to me implied by the title, even though that meant reading the title wrongly, as literature. Though obviously the title invited that kind of "wrongness." Which I thought was annoying and ambiguous in precisely a Jacob kind of way. I bought the book, but, in some small attempt at dignity, I didn't read it.

The following Monday, for the first time in his life, Jacob called me up. He said he was hoping to discuss something rather delicate with me, something he'd rather not mention over the phone. "What is it?" I asked.

"Can you meet me?" he asked.

"But what is it?"

"What time should we meet?"

I refused the first three meeting times he proposed, because I could. Eventually, Jacob suggested we meet at the Moroccan place at whatever time I wanted, that day or the next, but urgently, not farther in the future, please.

"You mean the place where I first met Ilan?" This just slipped out.

"And me. Yes. There."

In preparation for our meeting, I reread the negative reviews of Jacob's book.

And I felt so happy; the why of it was opaque to me.

Predictably, the coffee shop was the same but somehow not quite the same. Someone, not me, was reading the *New York Post*. Someone, not Ilan, was reading Deleuze. The fashion had made for shorter shorts on many of the women, and my lemonade came with slushy, rather than cubed, ice. But the chairs were still trimmed with chipping red paint, and the floor tile seemed, as ever, to fall just short of exhibiting a regular pattern.

Jacob walked in only a few minutes late, his gaze beckoned in every direction by all manner of bare legs. With an expression like someone sucking on an unpleasant cough drop, he made his way over to me.

I offered my sincerest consolations on the poor reviews of his work.

"Oh, time will tell," he said. He looked uncomfortable; he didn't even touch the green leaf cookies I'd ordered for him. Sighing, wrapping his hand tightly around the edge of the table and looking away, he said, "You know what Augustine says about time? Augustine describes time as a symptom of the world's flaw, a symptom of things in the world not being themselves, having to make their way back to themselves, by moving through time—"

Somehow I had already ceded control of the conversation. No billiard-ball diagrams. No Ilan. No reviews. Almost as if I weren't there, Jacob went on with his unencouraged ruminations: "There's a paradox there, of course, since what can things be but themselves? In Augustine's view, we live in what he calls the region of unlikeness, and what we're unlike is God. We are apart from God, who is pure being, who is himself, who is outside of time. And time is our tragedy, the substance we have to wade through as we try to move closer to God. Rivers flowing to the sea, a flame reaching upward, a bird homing: these movements all represent objects yearning to be their true selves, to achieve their true state. For humans, the motion reflects the yearning for God, and everything we do through time comes from moving—or at least trying to move—toward God. So that we can be"—someone at a nearby table cleared his throat judgmentally, which made me think of Ilan also being there—"our true selves. So there's a paradox there again, that we must submit to God—which feels deceptively like *not* being ourselves—in order to become ourselves. We might call this yearning love, and it's just that we often mistake *what* we love. We think we love sensuality. Or admiration. Or, say, another person. But loving another person is just a confusion, an error. Even if it is the kind of error that a nice, reasonable person might make—"

It struck me that Jacob might be manically depressed and that, in addition to his career, his marriage might not be going so well, either.

"I mean," Jacob amended, "it's all bullshit, of course, but aren't I a great guy? Isn't talking to me great? I can tell you about time and you learn all about Western civilization. And Augustine's ideas are beautiful, no? I love this thought that motion is *about* something, that things have a place to get to, and a person has something to become, and that thing she must become is herself. Isn't that nice?"

Jacob had never sounded more like Ilan. It was getting on my nerves. Maybe Jacob could read my very heart, and was trying to insult—or cure—me. "You've never called me before," I said. "I have a lot of work to do, you know."

"Nonsense," he said, without making it clear which statement of mine he was dismissing.

"You said," I reminded him, "that you wanted to discuss something 'delicate.'"

Jacob returned to the topic of Augustine; I returned to the question of why the two of us had come to sit together right then, right there. We ping-ponged in this way, until eventually Jacob said, "Well, it's about Ilan, so you'll like that."

"About the grandfather paradox?" I said, too quickly.

"Or it could be called the father paradox. Or even the mother paradox."

"I guess I've never thought of it that way, but sure." My happiness had dissipated; I felt angry, and manipulated.

"Not only about Ilan but about my work as well." Jacob actually began to whisper. "The thing is, I'm going to ask you to try to kill me. Don't worry, I can assure you that you won't succeed. But in attempting you'll prove a glorious, shunned truth that touches on the nature of time, free will, causal loops, and quantum theory. You'll also probably work out some aggression you feel toward me."

Truth be told, through the thin haze of my disdain, I had always been envious of Jacob's intellect; I had privately believed—despite what those reviews said, or maybe partly because of what those reviews said—that Jacob was a rare genius. Now I realized that he was just crazy.

"I know what you're thinking," Jacob said. "Unfortunately, I can't explain everything to you right here, right now. It's too psychologically trying. For you, I mean. Listen, come over to my apartment on Saturday. My family will be away for the weekend, and I'll explain everything to you then. Don't be alarmed. You probably know that I've lost my job"—I hadn't known that, but I should have been able to guess it—"but those morons, trust me, their falseness will become obvious. They'll be flies at the horse's ass. My ideas will bestride the world like a colossus. And you, too—you'll be essential."

I promised to attend, fully intending not to.

"Please," he said.

"Of course," I said, without meaning it.

All the rest of that week I tried to think through my decision carefully, but the more I tried to organize my thoughts the more ludicrous I felt for thinking them at all. I thought: As a friend, isn't it my responsibility to find out if Jacob has gone crazy? But really we're not friends. And if I come to know too much about his madness he may destroy me in order to preserve his psychotic world view. But maybe I should take that risk, because, in drawing closer to Jacob—mad or no—I'll learn something more of Ilan. But why do I need to know anything? And do my propositions really follow one from the other? Maybe my *not going* will entail Jacob's having to destroy me in order to preserve his psychotic world view. Or maybe Jacob is utterly levelheaded, and just bored enough to play an elaborate joke on me. Or maybe, despite there never having been the least spark of sexual attraction between us, despite the fact that we could have been locked in a closet for seven hours and nothing would have happened, maybe, for some reason, Jacob is trying to seduce me. Out of nostalgia for Ilan. Or as consolation for the turn in his career. Was I really up for dealing with a desperate man?

Or: Was I, in my dusty way, passing up the opportunity to be part of an idea that would, as Jacob had said, "bestride the world like a colossus"?

Early Saturday morning, I found myself knocking on Jacob's half-open door; this was when my world began to grow strange to me—strange, and yet also familiar, as if my destiny had once been known to me and I had forgotten it incompletely. Jacob's voice invited me in.

I'd never been to his apartment before. It was tiny, and smelled of orange rinds, and had—incongruously, behind a futon—a chalkboard; also so many piles of papers and books that the apartment seemed more like the movie set for an intellectual's rooms than like the real McCoy. I had once visited a ninety-one-year-old great-uncle who was still conducting research on fruit flies, and his apartment was cluttered with countless hand-stoppered jars of cloned fruit flies and a few hot plates for preparing some sort of agar; that apartment is what Jacob's brought to mind.

I found myself doubting that Jacob truly had a wife and child, as he had so often claimed.

"Thank God you've come," Jacob said, emerging from what appeared to be a galley kitchen but may have been simply a closet. "I knew you'd be reliable, that at least." And then, as if reading my mind, "Natasha sleeps in the loft we built. My wife and I sleep on the futon. Although, yes, it's not much for entertaining. But can I get you something? I have this tea that one of my students gave me, exceptional stuff from Japan, harvested at high altitude—"

"Tea, great, yes," I said. To my surprise, I was relieved that Jacob's ego seemed to weather his miserable surroundings just fine. Also to my surprise I felt tenderly toward him. And toward the scent of old citrus.

On the main table I noticed what looked like the ragtag remains of some Physics 101 lab experiments: rusted silver balls on different inclines, distressed balloons, a stained funnel, a markered flask, a calcium-speckled Bunsen burner, iron filings and sandpaper, large magnets, and batteries that could have been bought from a Chinese immigrant on the subway. Did I have the vague feeling that "a strange traveller" might show up and tell "extravagant stories" over a meal of fresh rabbit? I did.

I also considered that Jacob's asking me to murder him had just been an old-fashioned suicidal plea for help.

"Here, here." Jacob brought me tea (in a cracked porcelain cup), and I thought—somewhat fondly—of Ilan's old inscrutable poisoning jokes.

"Thanks so much." I moved away from that table of hodgepodge and sat on Jacob's futon.

"Well," Jacob said gently, also sitting down.

"Yes, well."

"Well, well," he said.

"Yes," I said.

"I'm not going to hit on you," Jacob said.

"Of course not," I said. "You're not going to kiss my hand."

"Of course not."

The tea tasted like damp cotton.

Jacob rose and walked over to the table, spoke to me from across the compressed distance. "I presume that you learned what you could. From those scribblings of Ilan. Yes?"

I conceded—both that I had learned something and that I had not learned everything, that much was still a mystery to me.

"But you understand, at least, that in situations approaching grandfather paradoxes very strange things can become the norm. Just as, if someone running begins to approach the speed of light, he grows unfathomably heavy." He paused. "Didn't you find it odd that you found yourself lounging so much with me and Ilan? Didn't it seem to beg explanation, how happy the three of us—"

"It wasn't strange," I insisted, and surely I was right almost by definition. It wasn't strange because it had already happened and so it was conceivable. Or maybe that was wrong. "I think he loved us both," I said, confused for no reason. "And we both loved him."

Jacob sighed. "Yes, O.K. I hope you'll appreciate the elaborate calculations I've done in order to set up these demonstrations of extraordinarily unlikely events. Come over here. Please. You'll see that we're in a region of, well, not exactly a region of unlikeness, that would be a cheap association—very Ilan-like, though, a fitting tribute—but we'll enter a region where things seem not to behave as themselves. In other words, a zone where events, teetering toward interfering"—I briefly felt that I was a child again, falling asleep on our scratchy blue sofa while my coughing father watched reruns of "Twilight Zone"—"with a fixed future, are pressured into revealing their hidden essences."

I felt years or miles away.

Then this happened, which is not the crux of the story, or even the center of what was strange to me:

Jacob tapped one of the silver balls and it rolled up the inclined plane; he set a flask of water on the Bunsen burner and marked the rising level of the fluid; a balloon distended unevenly; a magnet under sandpaper moved iron filings so as to spell the word "egregious."

Jacob turned to me, raised his eyebrows. "Astonishing, no?"

I felt like I'd seen him wearing a dress or going to the bathroom.

"I remember those science-magic shows from childhood," I said gently, tentatively. "I always loved those spooky caves they advertised on highway billboards." I wasn't *not* afraid. Cousin or no cousin, Ilan had clearly run away from Jacob, not from me.

"I can see you're resistant," Jacob said. "Which I understand, and even respect. Maybe I scared you, with that killing-me talk, which you weren't ready for. We'll return to it. I'll order us in some food. We'll eat, we'll drink, we'll talk, and I'll let you absorb the news slowly. You're an engineer, for God's sake. You'll put the pieces together. Sometimes sleep helps, sometimes spearmint—just little ways of sharpening a mind's ability to synthesize. You take your time."

Jacob transferred greasy Chinese food into marginally clean bowls, "for a more homey feel." There at the table, that shabby impromptu lab, I found myself eating slowly. Jacob seemed to need something from me, something more, even, than just a modicum of belief. And he had paid for the takeout. Halfway through a bowl of wide beef-flavored noodles—we had actually been comfortable in the quiet, at ease—Jacob said, "Didn't you find Ilan's ideas uncannily fashionable? Always a nose ahead? Even how he started wearing pink before everyone else?"

"He was fashionable in all sorts of ways," I agreed, surprised by my appetite for the slippery and unpleasant food. "Not that it ever got him very far, always running after the next new thing like that. Sometimes I'd copy what he said, and it would sound dumb coming out of my mouth, so maybe it was dumb in the first place. Just said with charm." I shrugged. Never before had I spoken aloud anything unkind about Ilan.

"You don't understand. I guess I should tell you that Ilan is my as yet unborn son, who visited me—us—from the future." He took a metal ball between two greasy fingers, dropped it twice, and then once again demonstrated it rolling up the inclined plane. "The two of us, Ilan and I, we collaborate." Jacob explained that part of what Ilan had established in his travels—which were repeated, and varied—was that, contrary to popular movies, travel into the past didn't alter the future, or, rather, that the future was already altered, or, rather, that it was all far more complicated than that. "I, too, was reluctant to believe," Jacob insisted. "Extremely reluctant. And he's my son. A pain in the ass, but also a dear." Jacob ate a dumpling in one bite. "A bit too much of a moralist, though. Not a good business partner, in that sense."

Although I felt the dizziness of old heartbreak—had I really loved Ilan so much?—the fact that, in my first reaction to Jacob's apartment, I had kind of foreseen this turn of events obscurely satisfied me. I played along: "If Ilan was from the future, that means he could tell you about your future." I no longer felt intimidated by Jacob. How could I?

"Sure, yes. A little." Jacob blushed like a schoolgirl. "It's not important. But certain things he did know. Being my son and all."

"Ah so." I, too, ate a dumpling whole. Which isn't the kind of thing I normally do. "What about my future? Did he know anything about my future?"

Jacob shook his head. I couldn't tell if he was responding to my question or just disapproving of it. He again nudged a ball up its inclined plane. "Right now we have my career to save," he said. I saw that he was sweating, even along his exposed collarbone. "Can I tell you what I'm thinking? What I'm thinking is that we *perform* the impossibility of my dying before fathering Ilan. A little stunt show of sorts, but for real, with real guns and rope and poison and maybe some blindfolded throwing of knives. Real life. And this can drum up a bit of publicity for my work." I felt myself getting sleepy during this speech of his, getting sleepy and thinking of circuses and of dumb pornography and of Ilan's mattress and of the time a small binder clip landed on my head when I was walking outside. "I mean, it's a bit lowbrow, but lowbrow is the new highbrow, of course, or maybe the old highbrow, but, regardless, it will be fantastic. Maybe we'll be on Letterman. And we'll probably make a good deal of money in addition to getting me my job back. We have to be careful, though. Just because I can't die doesn't mean I can't be pretty seriously injured. But I've been doing some calculations and we've got some real showstoppers."

Jacob's hazel eyes stared into mine. "I'm not much of a showgirl," I said, suppressing a yawn. "You can find someone better than me for the job."

"We're meant to have this future together. My wife—she really will want to kill me when she finds out the situation I'm in. She won't cooperate."

"I know people who can help you, Jacob," I said, in the monotone of the half-asleep. "But I can't help you. I like you, though. I really, really do."

"What's wrong with you? Have you ever seen a marble roll *up* like that? I mean, these are just little anomalies, I didn't want to frighten you, but there are many others. Right here in this room, even. We have the symptoms of leaning up against time here."

I thought of Jacob's blathering on about Augustine and meaningful motion and yearning. I also felt convinced I'd been drugged. Not just because of my fatigue but because I was beginning to find Jacob vaguely attractive. His sweaty collarbone was pretty. The room around me—the futon, the Chinese food, the porcelain teacup, the rusty laboratory, the piles of papers, Ilan's note in my back pocket, Jacob's cheap dress socks, the dust, Jacob's ringed hand on his knee— these all seemed like players in a life of mine that had not yet become real, a life I was coursing toward, one for which I would be happy to waste every bit of myself. "Do you think," I found myself asking, maybe because I'd had this feeling just once before in my life, "that Ilan was a rare and tragic genius?"

Jacob laughed.

I shrugged. I leaned my sleepy head against his shoulder. I put my hand to his collarbone.

"I can tell you this about your future," Jacob said quietly. "I didn't not hear that question. So let me soothsay this. You'll never get over Ilan. And that will one day horrify you. But soon enough you'll settle on a replacement object for all that love of yours, which does you about as much good as a proverbial stick up the ass. Your present, if you'll excuse my saying so, is a pretty sorry one. But your future looks pretty damn great. Your work will amount to nothing. But you'll have a brilliant child. And a brilliant husband. And great love."

He was saying we would be together. He was saying we would be in love. I understood. I had solved the puzzle. I knew who I, who we, were meant to be. I fell asleep relieved.

I woke up alone on Jacob's futon. At first I couldn't locate Jacob, but then I saw he was sleeping in his daughter's loft. His mouth was open; he looked awful. The room smelled of MSG. I felt at once furious and small. I left the apartment, vowing never to go to the coffee shop—or anywhere else I might see Jacob— again. I spent my day grading student exams. That evening, I went to the video store and almost rented "Wuthering Heights," then switched to "The Man Who Wasn't There," then, feeling haunted in a dumb way, ended up renting nothing at all.

Did I, in the following weeks and months, think of Jacob often? Did I worry for or care about him? I couldn't tell if I did or didn't, as if my own feelings had become the biggest mystery to me of all. I can't even say I'm absolutely sure that Jacob was delusional. When King Laius abandons baby Oedipus in the mountains on account of the prophecy that his son will murder him, Laius's attempt to evade his fate simply serves as its unexpected engine. This is called a predestination paradox. It's a variant of the grandfather paradox. At the heart of it is your inescapable fate.

We know that the general theory of relativity is compatible with the existence of space-times in which travel to the past or remote future is possible. The logician Kurt Gödel proved this back in the late nineteen-forties, and it remains essentially undisputed. Whether or not humans (in our very particular space-time) can in fact travel to the past—we still don't know. Maybe. Surely our world obeys rules still alien to our imaginations. Maybe Jacob is my destiny. Regardless, I continue to avoid him.

DALTHAREE

JEFFREY FORD

You've heard of bottled cities, no doubt —society writ miniscule and delicate
beyond reason: toothpick spired towns, streets no thicker than thread, pin-prick
faces of the citizenry peering from office windows smaller than sequins. Hustle,
politics, fervor, struggle, capitulation, wrapped in a crystal firmament, stoppered
at the top to keep reality both in and out. Those microscopic lives, striking glass
at the edge of things, believed themselves gigantic, their dilemmas universal.

Our research suggested that Daltharee had many multi-storied buildings
carved right into its hillsides. Surrounding the city there was a forest with lakes
and streams. and all of it was contained within a dome, like a dinner beneath
the lid of a serving dish. When the inhabitants of Daltharee looked up they were
prepared to not see the heavens. They knew that the light above, their Day, was
generated by a machine, which they oiled and cared for. The stars that shone
every sixteen hours when Day left darkness behind were simple bulbs regularly
changed by a man in a hot air balloon.

They were convinced that the domed city floated upon an iceberg, which it
actually did. There was one door in the wall of the dome at the end of a certain
path through the forest. When opened, it led out onto the ice. The surface of
the iceberg extended the margin of one of their miles all around the enclosure.
Blinding snows fell, winds constantly roared in a perpetual blizzard. Their belief
was that Daltharee drifted upon the oceans of an otherwise frozen world. They
prayed for the end of eternal winter, so they might reclaim the continents.

And all of this: their delusions, the city, the dome, the iceberg, the two quarts
of water it floated upon, were contained within an old gallon glass milk bottle,
plugged at the top with a tattered handkerchief and painted dark blue. When
I'd put my ear to the glass, I heard, like the ocean in a sea shell, fierce gales
blowing.

Daltharee was not the product of a shrinking ray as many of these pint-size
metropolises are. And please, there was no magic involved. In fact, once past the
early stages of its birth it was more organically grown than shaped by artifice.
Often, in the origin stories of these diminutive places, there's a deranged
scientist lurking in the wings. Here too we have the notorious Mando Paige,

the inventor of sub-microscopic differentiated cell division and growth. What I'm referring to was Paige's technique for producing super-miniature human cells. From the instant of their atomic origin, these parcels of life were beset by enzymatic reaction and electric stunting the way tree roots are tortured over time to create a bonsai. Paige shaped human life in the form of tiny individuals. They landscaped and built the city, laid roads, and lurched in a sleep-walking stupor induced by their creator.

Once the city in the dome was completed, Paige introduced more of the crumb-sized citizenry through the door that opened onto the iceberg. Just before closing that door, he set off a device that played an A flat for approximately ten seconds, a pre-ordained spur to consciousness, which brought them all awake to their lives in Daltharee. Seeding the water in the gallon bottle with crystal ions, he soon after introduced a chemical mixture that formed a slick, unmelting ice-like platform beneath the floating dome. He then introduced into the atmosphere fenathol nitrate, silver iodite, anamidian betheldine, to initiate the frigid wind and falling snow. When all was well within the dome, when the iceberg had sufficiently grown, when winter ruled, he plugged the gallon bottle with an old handkerchief. That closed system of winter, with just the slightest amount of air allowed in through the cloth was sustainable forever, feeding wind to snow and snow to cold to claustrophobia and back again in an infinite loop. The Dalthareens made up the story about a frozen world to satisfy the unknown. Paige manufactured three more of these cities, each wholly different from the others, before laws were passed about the imprisonment of humanity, no matter how minute or unaware. He was eventually, himself, imprisoned for his crimes.

We searched for a method to study life inside the dome but were afraid to disturb its delicate nature, unsure whether simply removing the handkerchief would upset a brittle balance between inner and outer universes. It was suggested that a very long, exceedingly thin probe that had the ability to twist and turn by computational command could be shimmied in between the edge of the bottle opening and the cloth of the handkerchief. This probe, like the ones physicians used in the twentieth and twenty-first centuries to read the hieroglyphics of the bowel, would be fitted out with both a camera and a microphone. The device was adequate for those cities that didn't have the extra added boundary of a dome, but even in them, how incongruous, a giant metal snake just out of the blue, slithering through one's reality. The inhabitants of these enclosed worlds were exceedingly small but not stupid.

In the end it was my invention that won the day—a voice activated transmitter the size of two atoms was introduced into the bottle. We had to wait for it to work its way from the blizzard atmosphere, through the dome's air filtration system, and into the city. Then we had to wait for it to come in contact with a voice. At any point a thousand things could have gone wrong, but one day, six months later, who knows how many years that would be in Dalthareen time, the machine transmitted and my receiver picked up conversations from the domed city. Here's an early one we managed to record that had some interesting elements:

"I'm not doing that now. Please, give me some room . . . " she said.

There is a long pause filled with the faint sound of a utensil clinking a plate.

"I was out in the forest the other day," he said.

"Why?" she asked.

"I'm not sure," he told her.

"What do you do out there?" she asked.

"I'm in this club," he said. "We got together to try to find the door in the wall of the dome."

"How did that go?" she asked.

"We knew it was there and we found it," he said. "Just like in the old stories . . . "

"Blizzard?"

"You can't believe it," he said.

"Did you go out in it?"

"Yes, and when I stepped back into the dome, I could feel a piece of the storm stuck inside me."

"What's that supposed to mean?" she said.

"I don't know."

"How did it get inside you?" she asked.

"Through my ears," he said.

"Does it hurt?"

"I was different when I came back in."

"Stronger?"

"No, more something else."

"Can you say?"

"I've had dreams."

"So what," she said. "I had a dream the other night that I was out on the Grand Conciliation Balcony, dressed for the odd jibbery when all of a sudden a little twisher rumbles up and whispers to me the words—'Elemental Potency.' What do you think it means? I can't get the phrase out of my head."

"It's nonsense," he said.

"Why aren't *your* dreams nonsense?"

"They are," he said. "The other night I had this dream about a theory. I can't remember if I saw it in the pages of a dream magazine or someone spoke it or it just jumped into my sleeping head. I've never dreamt about a theory before. Have you?"

"No," she said.

"It was about living in the dome. The theory was that since the dome is closed things that happen in the dome only affect other things in the dome. Because the size of Daltharee is as we believe so miniscule compared to the rest of the larger world, the repercussions of the acts you engage in in the dome will have a higher possibility of intersecting each other. If you think of something you do throughout the day as an act, each act begins a chain reaction of mitigating energy in all directions. The will of your own energy, dispersed through myriad acts within only a morning will beam, refract, and reflect off the beams of others' acts and the walls of the closed system, barreling into each other and causing sparks at those locations where your essence meets itself. In those instances, at those specific locations, your will is greater than the will of the dome. What I was then told was that a person could learn a way to act at a given hour—a quick series of six moves—that send out so many ultimately crisscrossing intentions of will that it creates a power mesh capable in its transformative strength of bending reality to whim."

"You're crazy," she said.

There is a slight pause here, the sound of wind blowing in the trees.

"Hey, what ever happened to your Aunt?" he asked.

"They got it out of her."

"Amazing," he said. "Close call . . . "

"She always seemed fine too," she said. "But swallowing a knitting needle? That's not right."

"She doesn't even knit, does she?"

"No," she said.

"Good thing she didn't have to pass it," he said. "Think about the intersecting beams of will resulting from that act."

She laughed. "I heard the last pigeon died yesterday."

"Yeah?"

"They found it in the park, on the lawn amidst the Moth trees."

"In all honesty, I did that," he said. "You know, not directly, but just by the acts I went through yesterday morning. I got out of bed, had breakfast, got dressed, you know, . . . like that. I was certain that by mid-day that bird would be dead."

"Why'd you kill it?" she asked.

There's a pause in the conversation here filled up by the sound of machinery in the distance just beneath that of the wind in the trees.

"Having felt what I felt outside the dome, I considered it a mercy," he said.

"Interesting . . . " she said. "I've gotta get going. It looks like rain."

"Will you call me?" he asked.

"Eventually, of course," she said.

"I know," he said. "I know."

Funny thing about Paige, he found religion in the latter years of his life. After serving out his sentence, he renounced his crackpot Science and retreated to a one room apartment in an old boarding house on the edge of the great desert. He courted an elderly woman there, a Mrs. Trucy. I thought he'd been long gone when we finally contacted him. After a solid fifteen years of recording conversations, it became evident that the domed city was failing—the economy, the natural habitat, were both in disarray. A strange illness had sprung up amid the population, an unrelenting, fatal insomnia that took a dozen of them to Death each week. Nine months without a single wink of sleep. The conversations we recorded then were full of anguish and hallucination.

Basically, we asked Paige what he might do to save his own created world. He came to work for us and studied the problem full time. He was old then, wrinkles and fly-away hair in strange, ever-shifting formations atop his scalp, eye glasses with one ear loop. Every time he'd make a mistake on a calculation or a technique, he'd swallow a thumbtack. When I asked if the practice helped him concentrate he told me, "No."

Eventually, on a Saturday morning when no one was at the lab but himself and an uninterested security guard, he broke into the vault that held the shrinking ray. He started the device up, aimed it at the glass milk bottle containing Daltharee, and then sat on top of the bottle, wearing a parachute. The ray discharged, shrinking him. He fell in among the gigantic folds of the handkerchief. Apparently he managed to work his way down past the end of the material and leap into the blizzard, out over the dome of the city. No one was there to see him slowly descend, dangerously buffeted by the insane winds. No one noticed him slip through the door in the dome.

Conversations came back to us eventually containing his name. Apparently he'd told them the true nature of the dome and the bottle it resided inside of. And then after some more time passed, there came word that he was creating another domed city inside a gallon milk bottle from the city of Daltharee. Where would it end, we wondered, but it was not a thought we enjoyed pursuing as it ran in a loop, recrossing itself, reiterating its original energy in ever diminishing reproductions of ourselves. Perhaps it was the thought of it that made my assistant accidentally drop the milk bottle one afternoon. It exploded into a million dark blue shards, dirt and dome and tiny trees spread across the floor. We considered studying its remains, but instead, with a shiver, I swept it into a pile and then into the furnace.

A year later, Mrs. Trucy came looking for Mando. She insisted upon knowing what had become of him. We told her that the law did not require us to tell her, and then she pulled a marriage certificate out of her purse. I was there with the Research General at the time, and I saw him go pale as a ghost upon seeing that paper. He told her Mando had died in an experiment of his own devising. The wrinkles of her gray face torqued to a twist and sitting beneath her pure silver hair, her head looked like a metal screw. Three tears squeezed out from the corners of her eyes. If Mando died performing an experiment, we could not be held responsible. We would, though, have to produce the body for her as proof that he'd perished. The Research General told her we were conducting a complete investigation of the tragedy and would contact her in six weeks with the results and the physical proof —in other words, Mando's corpse.

My having shoveled Daltharee into the trash without searching for survivors or mounting even a cursory rescue effort was cause for imprisonment. My superior, the Research General, having had my callous act take place on his watch was also liable. After three nerve wracking days, I conceived of a way for us to save ourselves. In fact it was so simple it astounded me that neither one of us, scientific minds though we be, didn't leap to the concept earlier. Using Mando's own process for creating diminutive humanity, we took his DNA from our genetic files, put it through a chemical bath to begin the growth process, and then tortured the cells into tininess. We had to use radical enzymes to speed the process up given we only had six weeks. By the end of week five we had a living, breathing, Mando Paige, trapped under a drinking glass in our office. He was dressed in a little orange jump suit, wore black boots, and was in the prime of his youth. We studied his attempts to escape his prison with a jeweler's loop inserted into each eye. We thought we could rely on the air simply running out in the glass and him suffocating.

Days passed and Paige hung on. Each day I'd spy on his meager existence and wondered what he must be thinking. When the time came and he wasn't dead, I killed him with a cigarette. I brought the glass to the very edge of the table, bent a plastic drinking straw that I shoved the longer end of up into the glass and then caught it fairly tightly against the table edge. As for the part that stuck out, I lit a cigarette, inhaled deeply and then blew the smoke up into the glass. I gave him five lung fulls. The oxygen displacement was too much, of course.

Mrs. Trucy accepted our story and the magnified view of her lover's diminutive body. We told her how he bravely took the shrinking ray for the sake of Science. She remarked that he looked younger than when he was full sized and alive, and the Research General told her, "As you shrink, wrinkles have a tendency to evaporate." We went to the funeral out in the desert near her home. It was a blazingly hot day. She'd had his remains placed into a thimble with some tape across the top, and this she buried in the red sand.

Later, as the sun set, the Research General and I ate dinner at a ramshackle restaurant along a dusty road right outside of Mateos. He had the pig knuckle with sauerkraut and I had the chicken croquettes with orange gravy that tasted brown.

"I'm so relieved that asshole's finally dead," whispered the Research General.

"There's dead and there's dead," I told him.

"Let's not make this complicated," he said. "I know he's out there in some smaller version of reality, he could be filling all available space with smaller and smaller reproductions of himself, choking the ass of the universe with pages and pages of Mando Paige. I don't give a fuck as long as he's not here."

"He is here," I said, and then they brought the Martinis and the conversation evaporated into reminiscence.

That night as I stood out beneath the desert sky having a smoke, I had a sense that the cumulative beams generated by the repercussions of my actions over time, harboring my inherent will, had reached some far flung boundary and were about to turn back on me. In my uncomfortable bed at the Hacienda

Motel, I tossed and turned, drifting in and out of sleep. It was then that I had a vision of the shrinking ray, its sparkling blue emission bouncing off a mirror set at an angle. The beam then travels a short distance to another mirror with which it collides and reflects. The second mirror is positioned so that it sends the ray back at its own original source. The beam strikes and mixes with itself only a few inches past the nozzle of the machine's barrel. And then I see it in my mind —when a shrinking ray is trained upon itself, its diminutive-making properties are cancelled twice and as it is a fact that when two negatives are multiplied they make a positive, this process makes things bigger. As soon as the concept was upon me, I was filled with excitement and couldn't wait to get back to the lab the next day to work out the math and realize an experiment.

It was fifteen years later, the Research General had long been fired, when Mando Paige stepped out of the spot where the shrinking ray's beam crossed itself. He was blue and yellow and red and his hair was curly. I stood within feet of him and he smiled at me. I, of course, couldn't let him go —not due to any law but my own urge to finish the job I'd started at the outset. As he stepped back toward the ray, I turned it off, and he was trapped, for the moment, in our moment. I called for my assistants to surround him, and I sent one to my office for the revolver I kept in my bottom drawer. He told me that one speck of his saliva contained four million Daltharees. "When I fart," he said, "I set forth Armadas." I shot him and the four assistants and then automatically acid washed the lab to destroy the Dalthareen plague and evidence of murder. No one suspected a thing. I found a few cities sprouting beneath my fingernails last week. There were already rows of domes growing behind my ears. My blood no doubt is the manufacture of cities, flowing silver through my veins. Crowds behind my eyes, commerce in my joints. Each idea I have is a domed city that grows and opens like a flower. I want to tell you about cities and cities and cities named Daltharee.

THE RAY-GUN: A LOVE STORY

JAMES ALAN GARDNER

This is a story about a ray-gun. The ray-gun will not be explained except to say, "It shoots rays."

They are dangerous rays. If they hit you in the arm, it withers. If they hit you in the face, you go blind. If they hit you in the heart, you die. These things must be true, or else it would not be a ray-gun. But it is.

Ray-guns come from space. This one came from the captain of an alien starship passing through our solar system. The ship stopped to scoop up hydrogen from the atmosphere of Jupiter. During this refueling process, the crew mutinied for reasons we cannot comprehend. We will never comprehend aliens. If someone spent a month explaining alien thoughts to us, we'd think we understood but we wouldn't. Our brains only know how to be human.

Although alien thoughts are beyond us, alien actions may be easy to grasp. We can understand the "what" if not the "why." If we saw what happened inside the alien vessel, we would recognize that the crew tried to take the captain's ray-gun and kill him.

There was a fight. The ray-gun went off many times. The starship exploded.

All this happened many centuries ago, before telescopes. The people of Earth still wore animal skins. They only knew Jupiter as a dot in the sky. When the starship exploded, the dot got a tiny bit brighter, then returned to normal. No one on Earth noticed—not even the shamans who thought dots in the sky were important.

The ray-gun survived the explosion. A ray-gun must be resilient, or else it is not a ray-gun. The explosion hurled the ray-gun away from Jupiter and out into open space.

After thousands of years, the ray-gun reached Earth. It fell from the sky like a meteor; it grew hot enough to glow, but it didn't burn up.

The ray-gun fell at night during a blizzard. Traveling thousands of miles an hour, the ray-gun plunged deep into snow-covered woods. The snow melted so quickly that it burst into steam.

The blizzard continued, unaffected. Some things can't be harmed, even by ray-guns.

Unthinking snowflakes drifted down. If they touched the ray-gun's surface they vaporized, stealing heat from the weapon. Heat also radiated outward, melting snow nearby on the ground. Melt-water flowed into the shallow crater made by the ray-gun's impact. Water and snow cooled the weapon until all excess temperature had dissipated. A million more snowflakes heaped over the crater, hiding the ray-gun till spring.

In March, the gun was found by a boy named Jack. He was fourteen years old and walking through the woods after school. He walked slowly, brooding about his lack of popularity. Jack despised popular students and had no interest in anything they did. Even so, he envied them. They didn't appear to be lonely.

Jack wished he had a girlfriend. He wished he were important. He wished he knew what to do with his life. Instead, he walked alone in the woods on the edge of town.

The woods were not wild or isolated. They were crisscrossed with trails made by children playing hide-and-seek. But in spring, the trails were muddy; most people stayed away. Jack soon worried more about how to avoid shoe-sucking mud than about the unfairness of the world. He took wide detours around mucky patches, thrashing through brush that was crisp from winter.

Stalks broke as he passed. Burrs stuck to his jacket. He got farther and farther from the usual paths, hoping he'd find a way out by blundering forward rather than swallowing his pride and retreating.

In this way, Jack reached the spot where the ray-gun had landed. He saw the crater it had made. He found the ray-gun itself.

The gun seized Jack's attention, but he didn't know what it was. Its design was too alien to be recognized as a weapon. Its metal was blackened but not black, as if it had once been another color but had finished that phase of its existence. Its pistol-butt was bulbous, the size of a tennis ball. Its barrel, as long as Jack's hand, was straight but its surface had dozens of nubs like a briarwood cane. The gun's trigger was a protruding blister you squeezed till it popped. A hard metal cap could slide over the blister to prevent the gun from firing accidentally, but the safety was off; it had been off for centuries, ever since the fight on the starship.

The alien captain who once owned the weapon might have considered it beautiful, but to human eyes, the gun resembled a dirty wet stick with a lump on one end. Jack might have walked by without giving it a second look if it hadn't been lying in a scorched crater. But it was.

The crater was two paces across and barren of plant life. The vegetation had burned in the heat of the ray-gun's fall. Soon enough, new spring growth would sprout, making the crater less obvious. At present, though, the ray-gun stood out on the charred earth like a snake in an empty birdbath.

Jack picked up the gun. Though it looked like briarwood, it was cold like metal. It felt solid: not heavy, but substantial. It had the heft of a well-made object. Jack turned the gun in his hands, examining it from every angle. When he looked down the muzzle, he saw a crystal lens cut into hundreds of facets. Jack poked it with his pinky, thinking the lens was a piece of glass that someone had jammed inside. He had the idea this might be a toy—perhaps a squirt-gun dropped by a careless child. If so, it had to be the most expensive toy Jack had ever seen. The gun's barrel and its lens were so perfectly machined that no one could mistake the craftsmanship.

Jack continued to poke at the weapon until the inevitable happened: he pressed the trigger blister. The ray-gun went off.

It might have been fatal, but by chance Jack was holding the gun aimed away from himself. A ray shot out of the gun's muzzle and blasted through a maple tree ten paces away. The ray made no sound, and although Jack had seen it clearly, he couldn't say what the ray's color had been. It had no color; it was simply a presence, like wind chill or gravity. Yet Jack was sure he'd seen a force emanate from the muzzle and strike the tree.

Though the ray can't be described, its effect was plain. A circular hole appeared in the maple tree's trunk where bark and wood disintegrated into sizzling plasma. The plasma expanded at high speed and pressure, blowing apart what remained of the surrounding trunk. The ray made no sound, but the explosion did. Shocked chunks of wood and boiling maple sap flew outward, obliterating a cross-section of the tree. The lower part of the trunk and the roots were still there; so were the upper part and branches. In between was a gap, filled with hot escaping gases.

The unsupported part of the maple fell. It toppled ponderously backwards. The maple crashed onto the trees behind, its winter-bare branches snagging theirs. To Jack, it seemed that the forest had stopped the maple's fall, like soldiers catching an injured companion before he hit the ground.

Jack still held the gun. He gazed at it in wonder. His mind couldn't grasp what had happened.

He didn't drop the gun in fear. He didn't try to fire it again. He simply stared.

It was a ray-gun. It would never be anything else.

Jack wondered where the weapon had come from. Had aliens visited these woods? Or was the gun created by a secret government project? Did the gun's owner want it back? Was he, she, or it searching the woods right now?

Jack was tempted to put the gun back into the crater, then run before the owner showed up. But was there really an owner nearby? The crater suggested that the gun had fallen from space. Jack had seen photos of meteor impact craters; this wasn't exactly the same, but it had a similar look.

Jack turned his eyes upward. He saw a mundane after-school sky. It had no UFOs. Jack felt embarrassed for even looking.

He examined the crater again. If Jack left the gun here, and the owner never retrieved it, sooner or later the weapon would be found by someone else—probably by children playing in the woods. They might shoot each other by accident. If this were an ordinary gun, Jack would never leave it lying in a place like this. He'd take the gun home, tell his parents, and they'd turn it over to the police.

Should he do the same for *this* gun? No. He didn't want to.

But he didn't know what he wanted to do instead. Questions buzzed through his mind, starting with, "What should I do?" then moving on to, "Am I in danger?" and, "Do aliens really exist?"

After a while, he found himself wondering, "Exactly how much can the gun blow up?" That question made him smile.

Jack decided he wouldn't tell anyone about the gun—not now and maybe not ever. He would take it home and hide it where it wouldn't be found, but where it would be available if trouble came. What kind of trouble? Aliens . . . spies . . . supervillains . . . who knew? If ray-guns were real, was anything impossible?

On the walk back home, Jack was so distracted by "What ifs?" that he nearly got hit by a car. He had reached the road that separated the woods from neighboring houses. Like most roads in that part of Jack's small town, it didn't get much traffic. Jack stepped out from the trees and suddenly a sports car whizzed past him, only two steps away. Jack staggered back; the driver leaned on the horn; Jack hit his shoulder on an oak tree; then the incident was over, except for belated adrenalin.

For a full minute afterward, Jack leaned against the oak and felt his heart pound. As close calls go, this one wasn't too bad: Jack hadn't really been near enough to the road to get hit. Still, Jack needed quite a while to calm down. How stupid would it be to die in an accident on the day he'd found something miraculous?

Jack ought to have been watching for trouble. What if the threat had been a bug-eyed monster instead of a car? Jack should have been alert and prepared. In his mind's eye he imagined the incident again, only this time he casually somersaulted to safety rather than stumbling into a tree. That's how you're supposed to cheat death if you're carrying a ray-gun: with cool heroic flair.

But Jack couldn't do somersaults. He said to himself, *I'm Peter Parker, not Spider-Man.*

On the other hand, Jack *had* just acquired great power. And great responsibility. Like Peter Parker, Jack had to keep his power secret, for fear of tragic consequences. In Jack's case, maybe aliens would come for him. Maybe spies or government agents would kidnap him and his family. No matter how farfetched those things seemed, the existence of a ray-gun proved the world wasn't tame.

That night, Jack debated what to do with the gun. He pictured himself shooting terrorists and gang lords. If he rid the world of scum, pretty girls might admire him. But as soon as Jack imagined himself storming into a terrorist stronghold, he realized he'd get killed almost immediately. The ray-gun provided awesome firepower, but no defense at all. Besides, if Jack had found an ordinary gun in the forest, he never would have dreamed of running around murdering bad guys. Why should a ray-gun be different?

But it *was* different. Jack couldn't put the difference into words, but it was as real as the weapon's solid weight in his hands. The ray-gun changed everything. A world that contained a ray-gun might also contain flying saucers, beautiful secret agents . . . and heroes.

Heroes who could somersault away from oncoming sports cars. Heroes who would cope with any danger. Heroes who *deserved* to have a ray-gun.

When he was young, Jack had taken for granted he'd become a hero: brave, skilled, and important. Somehow he'd lost that belief. He'd let himself settle for being ordinary. But now he wasn't ordinary: he had a ray-gun.

He had to live up to it. Jack had to be ready for bug-eyed monsters and giant robots. These were no longer childish daydreams; they were real possibilities in a world where ray-guns existed. Jack could picture himself running through town, blasting aliens, and saving the planet.

Such thoughts made sense when Jack held the ray-gun in his hands— as if the gun planted fantasies in his mind. The feel of the gun filled Jack with ambition.

All weapons have a sense of purpose.

Jack practiced with the gun as often as he could. To avoid being seen, he rode his bike to a tract of land in the country: twenty acres owned by Jack's great-uncle Ron. No one went there but Jack. Uncle Ron had once intended to build a house on the property, but that had never happened. Now Ron was in a nursing home. Jack's family intended to sell the land once the old man died, but Ron was healthy for someone in his nineties. Until Uncle Ron's health ran out, Jack had the place to himself.

The tract was undeveloped—raw forest, not a woods where children played. In the middle lay a pond, completely hidden by trees. Jack would float sticks in the pond and shoot them with the gun.

If he missed, the water boiled. If he didn't, the sticks were destroyed. Sometimes they erupted in fire. Sometimes they burst with a bang but no flame. Sometimes they simply vanished. Jack couldn't tell if he was doing something subtly different to get each effect, or if the ray-gun changed modes on its own. Perhaps it had a computer which analyzed the target and chose the most lethal attack. Perhaps the attacks were always the same, but differences in the sticks made for different results. Jack didn't know. But as spring led to summer, he became a better shot. By autumn, he'd begun throwing sticks into the air and trying to vaporize them before they reached the ground.

During this time, Jack grew stronger. Long bike rides to the pond helped his legs and his stamina. In addition, he exercised with fitness equipment his parents had bought but never used. If monsters ever came, Jack couldn't afford to be weak—heroes had to climb fences and break down doors. They had to balance on rooftops and hang by their fingers from cliffs. They had to run fast enough to save the girl.

Jack pumped iron and ran every day. As he did so, he imagined dodging bullets and tentacles. When he felt like giving up, he cradled the ray-gun in his hands. It gave him the strength to persevere.

Before the ray-gun, Jack had seen himself as just another teenager; his life didn't make sense. But the gun made Jack a hero who might be needed to save the Earth. It clarified *everything*. Sore muscles didn't matter. Watching TV was a waste. If you let down your guard, that's when the monsters came.

When he wasn't exercising, Jack studied science. That was another part of being a hero. He sometimes dreamed he'd analyze the ray-gun, discovering how it worked and giving humans amazing new technology. At other times, he didn't want to understand the gun at all. He liked its mystery. Besides, there was no guarantee Jack would ever understand how the gun worked. Perhaps human science wouldn't progress far enough in Jack's lifetime. Perhaps Jack himself wouldn't have the brains to figure it out.

But he had enough brains for high school. He did well; he was motivated. He had to hold back to avoid attracting attention. When his gym teacher told him he should go out for track, Jack ran slower and pretended to get out of breath.

Spider-Man had to do the same.

Two years later, in geography class, a girl named Kirsten gave Jack a daisy. She said the daisy was good luck and he should make a wish.

Even a sixteen-year-old boy couldn't misconstrue such a hint. Despite awkwardness and foot-dragging, Jack soon had a girlfriend.

Kirsten was quiet but pretty. She played guitar. She wrote poems. She'd never had a boyfriend but she knew how to kiss. These were all good things. Jack wondered if he should tell her about the ray-gun.

Until Kirsten, Jack's only knowledge of girls came from his big sister, Rachel. Rachel was seventeen and incapable of keeping a secret. She talked with her friends about everything and was too slapdash to hide private things well. Jack didn't snoop through his sister's possessions, but when Rachel left her bedroom door ajar with empty cigarette packs tumbling out of the garbage can, who wouldn't notice? When she gossiped on the phone about sex with her boyfriend, who couldn't overhear? Jack didn't want to listen, but Rachel never lowered her voice. The things Jack heard made him queasy—about his sister, and girls in general.

If he showed Kirsten the ray-gun, would she tell her friends? Jack wanted to believe she wasn't that kind of girl, but he didn't know how many kinds of girl there were. He just knew that the ray-gun was too important for him to take chances. Changing the status quo wasn't worth the risk.

Yet the status quo changed anyway. The more time Jack spent with Kirsten, the less he had for shooting practice and other aspects of hero-dom. He felt guilty for skimping on crisis preparation; but when he went to the pond or spent a night reading science, he felt guilty for skimping on Kirsten. Jack would tell her he couldn't come over to do homework and when she asked why, he'd have to make up excuses. He felt he was treating her like an enemy spy: holding her at arm's length as if she were some femme fatale who was tempting him to betray state secrets. He hated not trusting her.

Despite this wall between them, Kirsten became Jack's lens on the world. If anything interesting happened, Jack didn't experience it directly; some portion of his mind stood back, enjoying the anticipation of having something to tell Kirsten about the next time they met. Whatever he saw, he wanted her to see it too. Whenever Jack heard a joke, even before he started laughing, he pictured himself repeating it to Kirsten.

Inevitably, Jack asked himself what she'd think of his hero-dom. Would she be impressed? Would she throw her arms around him and say he was even more wonderful than she'd thought? Or would she get that look on her face, the one when she heard bad poetry? Would she think he was an immature geek who'd read too many comic books and was pursuing some juvenile fantasy? How could anyone believe hostile aliens might appear in the sky? And if aliens did show up, how delusional was it that a teenage boy might make a difference, even if he owned a ray-gun and could do a hundred push-ups without stopping?

For weeks, Jack agonized: to tell or not to tell. Was Kirsten worthy, or just a copy of Jack's sister? Was Jack himself worthy, or just a foolish boy?

One Saturday in May, Jack and Kirsten went biking. Jack led her to the pond where he practiced with the gun. He hadn't yet decided what he'd do when they got there, but Jack couldn't just *tell* Kirsten about the ray-gun. She'd never believe it was real unless she saw the rays in action. But so much could go wrong. Jack was terrified of giving away his deepest secret. He was afraid that when he saw hero-dom through Kirsten's eyes, he'd realize it was silly.

At the pond, Jack felt so nervous he could hardly speak. He babbled about the warm weather . . . a patch of mushrooms . . . a crow cawing in a tree. He talked about everything except what was on his mind.

Kirsten misinterpreted his anxiety. She thought she knew why Jack had brought her to this secluded spot. After a while, she decided he needed encouragement, so she took off her shirt and her bra.

It was the wrong thing to do. Jack hadn't meant this outing to be a test . . . but it was, and Kirsten had failed.

Jack took off his own shirt and wrapped his arms around her, chest touching breasts for the first time. He discovered it was possible to be excited and disappointed at the same time.

Jack and Kirsten made out on a patch of hard dirt. It was the first time they'd been alone with no risk of interruption. They kept their pants on, but they knew they could go farther: as far as there was. No one in the world would stop them from whatever they chose to do. Jack and Kirsten felt light in their skins—open and dizzy with possibilities.

Yet for Jack, it was all a mistake: one that couldn't be reversed. Now he'd never tell Kirsten about the ray-gun. He'd missed his chance because she'd acted the way Jack's sister would have acted. Kirsten had been thinking like a girl and she'd ruined things forever.

Jack hated the way he felt: all angry and resentful. He really liked Kirsten. He liked making out, and couldn't wait till the next time. He refused to be a guy who dumped a girl as soon as she let him touch her breasts. But he was now shut off from her and he had no idea how to get over that.

In the following months, Jack grew guiltier: he was treating Kirsten as if she were good enough for sex but not good enough to be told about the most important thing in his life. As for Kirsten, every day made her more unhappy: she felt Jack blaming her for something but she didn't know what she'd done. When they got together, they went straight to fondling and more as soon as possible. If they tried to talk, they didn't know what to say.

In August, Kirsten left to spend three weeks with her grandparents on Vancouver Island. Neither she nor Jack missed each other. They didn't even miss the sex. It was a relief to be apart. When Kirsten got back, they went for a walk and a confused conversation. Both produced excuses for why they couldn't stay together. The excuses didn't make sense, but neither Jack nor Kirsten noticed— they were too ashamed to pay attention to what they were saying. They both felt like failures. They'd thought their love would last forever, and now it was ending sordidly.

When the lying was over, Jack went for a run. He ran in a mental blur. His mind didn't clear until he found himself at the pond.

Night was drawing in. He thought of all the things he'd done with Kirsten on the shore and in the water. After that first time, they'd come here a lot; it was private. Because of Kirsten, this wasn't the same pond as when Jack had first begun to practice with the ray-gun. Jack wasn't the same boy. He and the pond now carried histories.

Jack could feel himself balanced on the edge of quitting. He'd turned seventeen. One more year of high school, then he'd go away to university. He realized he no longer believed in the imminent arrival of aliens, nor could he see himself as some great hero saving the world.

Jack knew he wasn't a hero. He'd used a nice girl for sex, then lied to get rid of her.

He felt like crap. But blasting the shit out of sticks made him feel a little better. The ray-gun still had its uses, even if shooting aliens wasn't one of them.

The next day Jack did more blasting. He pumped iron. He got science books out of the library. Without Kirsten at his side several hours a day, he had time to fill, and emptiness. By the first day of the new school year, Jack was back to his full hero-dom program. He no longer deceived himself that he was preparing for battle, but the program gave him something to do: a purpose, a release, and a penance.

So that was Jack's passage into manhood. He was dishonest with the girl he loved.

Manhood means learning who you are.

In his last year of high school, Jack went out with other girls but he was past the all-or-nothingness of First Love. He could have casual fun; he could approach sex with perspective. "Monumental and life-changing" had been tempered to "pleasant and exciting." Jack didn't take his girlfriends for granted, but they were people, not objects of worship. He was never tempted to tell any of them about the gun.

When he left town for university, Jack majored in Engineering Physics. He hadn't decided whether he'd ever analyze the ray-gun's inner workings, but he couldn't imagine taking courses that were irrelevant to the weapon. The ray-gun was the central fact of Jack's life. Even if he wasn't a hero, he was set apart from other people by this evidence that aliens existed.

During freshman year, Jack lived in an on-campus dormitory. Hiding the ray-gun from his roommate would have been impossible. Jack left the weapon at home, hidden near the pond. In sophomore year, Jack rented an apartment off campus. Now he could keep the ray-gun with him. He didn't like leaving it unattended.

Jack persuaded a lab assistant to let him borrow a Geiger counter. The ray-gun emitted no radioactivity at all. Objects blasted by the gun showed no significant radioactivity either. Over time, Jack borrowed other equipment, or took blast debris to the lab so he could conduct tests when no one was around. He found nothing that explained how the ray-gun worked.

The winter before Jack graduated, Great-Uncle Ron finally died. In his will, the old man left his twenty acres of forest to Jack. Uncle Ron had found out that Jack liked to visit the pond. "I told him," said big sister Rachel. "Do you think I didn't know where you and Kirsten went?"

Jack had to laugh—uncomfortably. He was embarrassed to discover he couldn't keep secrets any better than his sister.

Jack's father offered to help him sell the land to pay for his education. The offer was polite, not pressing. Uncle Ron had doled out so much cash in his will that Jack's family was now well-off. When Jack said he'd rather hold on to the property "until the market improves," no one objected.

After getting his bachelor's degree, Jack continued on to grad school: first his master's, then his Ph.D. In one of his courses, he met Deana, working toward her own doctorate—in Electrical Engineering rather than Engineering Physics.

The two programs shared several seminars, but considered themselves rivals. Engineering Physics students pretended that Electrical Engineers weren't smart enough to understand abstract principles. Electrical Engineers pretended that Engineering Physics students were pie-in-the-sky dreamers whose theories were always wrong until real Engineers fixed them. Choosing to sit side by side, Jack and Deana teased each other every class. Within months, Deana moved into Jack's apartment.

Deana was small but physical. She told Jack she'd been drawn to him because he was the only man in their class who lifted weights. When Deana was young, she'd been a competitive swimmer—"*Very* competitive," she said—but her adolescent growth spurt had never arrived and she was eventually outmatched by girls with longer limbs. Deana had quit the competition circuit, but she hadn't quit swimming, nor had she lost the drive to be one up on those around her. She saw most things as contests, including her relationship with Jack. Deana was not beyond cheating if it gave her an edge.

In the apartment they now shared, Jack thought he'd hidden the ray-gun so well that Deana wouldn't find it. He didn't suspect that when he wasn't home, she went through his things. She couldn't stand the thought that Jack might have secrets from her.

He returned one day to find the gun on the kitchen table. Deana was poking at it. Jack wanted to yell, "Leave it alone!" but he was so choked with anger he couldn't speak.

Deana's hand was close to the trigger. The safety was off and the muzzle pointed in Jack's direction. He threw himself to the floor.

Nothing happened. Deana was so surprised by Jack's sudden move that she jerked her hand away from the gun. "What the hell are you doing?"

Jack got to his feet. "I could ask you the same question."

"I found this. I wondered what it was."

Jack knew she didn't "find" the gun. It had been buried under old notebooks inside a box at the back of a closet. Jack expected that Deana would invent some excuse for why she'd been digging into Jack's private possessions, but the excuse wouldn't be worth believing.

What infuriated Jack most was that he'd actually been thinking of showing Deana the gun. She was a very very good engineer; Jack had dreamed that together, he and she might discover how the gun worked. Of all the women Jack had known, Deana was the first he'd asked to move in with him. She was strong and she was smart. She might understand the gun. The time had never been right to tell her the truth—Jack was still getting to know her and he needed to be absolutely sure—but Jack had dreamed . . .

And now, like Kirsten at the pond, Deana had ruined everything. Jack felt so violated he could barely stand to look at the woman. He wanted to throw her out of the apartment . . . but that would draw too much attention to the gun. He couldn't let Deana think the gun was important.

She was still staring at him, waiting for an explanation. "That's just something from my Great-Uncle Ron," Jack said. "An African good-luck charm. Or Indonesian. I forget. Uncle Ron traveled a lot." Actually, Ron sold insurance and seldom left the town where he was born. Jack picked up the gun from the table, trying to do so calmly rather than protectively. "I wish you hadn't touched this. It's old and fragile."

"It felt pretty solid to me."

"Solid but still breakable."

"Why did you dive to the floor?"

"Just silly superstition. It's bad luck to have this end point toward you." Jack gestured toward the muzzle. "And it's good luck to be on this end." He gestured toward the butt, then tried to make a joke. "Like there's a Maxwell demon in the middle, batting bad luck one way and good luck the other."

"You believe that crap?" Deana asked. She was an engineer. She went out of her way to disbelieve crap.

"Of course I don't believe it," Jack said. "But why ask for trouble?"

He took the gun back to the closet. Deana followed. As Jack returned the gun to its box, Deana said she'd been going through Jack's notes in search of anything he had on partial differential equations. Jack nearly let her get away with the lie; he usually let the women in his life get away with almost anything. But he realized he didn't want Deana in his life anymore. Whatever connection she and he had once felt, it was cut off the moment he saw her with the ray-gun.

Jack accused her of invading his privacy. Deana said he was paranoid. The argument grew heated. Out of habit, Jack almost backed down several times, but he stopped himself. He didn't want Deana under the same roof as the ray-gun. His feelings were partly irrational possessiveness, but also justifiable caution. If Deana got the gun and accidentally fired it, the results might be disastrous.

Jack and Deana continued to argue: right there in the closet within inches of the ray-gun. The gun lay in its box, like a child at the feet of parents fighting over custody. The ray-gun did nothing, as if it didn't care who won.

Eventually, unforgivable words were spoken. Deana said she'd move out as soon as possible. She left to stay the night with a friend.

The moment she was gone, Jack moved the gun. Deana still had a key to the apartment—she needed it until she could pack her things—and Jack was certain she'd try to grab the weapon as soon as he was busy elsewhere. The ray-gun was now a prize in a contest, and Deana never backed down.

Jack took the weapon to the university. He worked as an assistant for his Ph.D. supervisor, and he'd been given a locker in the supervisor's lab. The locker wasn't Fort Knox but leaving the gun there was better than leaving it in the apartment. The more Jack thought about Deana, the more he saw her as prying and obsessive, grasping for dominance. He didn't know what he'd ever seen in her.

The next morning, he wondered if he had overreacted. Was he demonizing his ex like a sitcom cliché? If she was so egotistic, why hadn't he noticed before? Jack had no good answer. He decided he didn't need one. Unlike when he broke up with Kirsten, Jack felt no guilt this time. The sooner Deana was gone, the happier he'd be.

In a few days, Deana called to say she'd found a new place to live. She and Jack arranged a time for her to pick up her belongings. Jack didn't want to be there while she moved out; he couldn't stand seeing her in the apartment again. Instead, Jack went back to his home town for a long weekend with his family.

It was lucky he did. Jack left Friday afternoon and didn't get back to the university until Monday night. The police were waiting for him. Deana had disappeared late Saturday.

She'd talked to friends on Saturday afternoon. She'd made arrangements for Sunday brunch but hadn't shown up. No one had seen her since.

As the ex-boyfriend, Jack was a prime suspect. But his alibi was solid: his hometown was hundreds of miles from the university, and his family could testify he'd been there the whole time. Jack couldn't possibly have sneaked back to the university, made Deana disappear, and raced back home.

Grudgingly, the police let Jack off the hook. They decided Deana must have been depressed by the break-up of the relationship. She might have run off so she wouldn't have to see Jack around the university. She might even have committed suicide.

Jack suspected otherwise. As soon as the police let him go, he went to his supervisor's lab. His locker had been pried open. The ray-gun lay on a nearby lab bench.

Jack could easily envision what happened. While moving out her things, Deana searched for the ray-gun. She hadn't found it in the apartment. She knew Jack had a locker in the lab and she'd guessed he'd stashed the weapon there. She broke open the locker to get the gun. She'd examined it and perhaps tried to take it apart. The gun went off.

Now Deana was gone. Not even a smudge on the floor. The ray-gun lay on the lab bench as guiltless as a stone. Jack was the only one with a conscience.

He suffered for weeks. Jack wondered how he could feel so bad about a woman who'd made him furious. But he knew the source of his guilt: while he and Deana were arguing in the closet, Jack had imagined vaporizing her with the gun. He was far too decent to shoot her for real, but the thought had crossed his mind. If Deana simply vanished, Jack wouldn't have to worry about what she might do. The ray-gun had made that thought come true, as if it had read Jack's mind.

Jack told himself the notion was ridiculous. The gun wasn't some genie who granted Jack's unspoken wishes. What happened to Deana came purely from her own bad luck and inquisitiveness.

Still, Jack felt like a murderer. After all this time, Jack realized the ray-gun was too dangerous to keep. As long as Jack had it, he'd be forced to live alone: never marrying, never having children, never trusting the gun around other people. And even if Jack became a recluse, accidents could happen. Someone else might die. It would be Jack's fault.

He wondered why he'd never had this thought before. Jack suddenly saw himself as one of those people who own a vicious attack dog. People like that always claimed they could keep the dog under control. How often did they end up on the evening news? How often did children get bitten, maimed, or killed?

Some dogs are tragedies waiting to happen. The ray-gun was too. It would keep slipping off its leash until it was destroyed. Twelve years after finding the gun, Jack realized he finally had a heroic mission: to get rid of the weapon that made him a hero in the first place.

I'm not Spider-Man, he thought, *I'm Frodo.*

But how could Jack destroy something that had survived so much? The gun hadn't frozen in the cold of outer space; it hadn't burned up as it plunged through Earth's atmosphere; it hadn't broken when it hit the ground at terminal velocity. If the gun could endure such punishment, extreme measures would be needed to lay it to rest.

Jack imagined putting the gun into a blast furnace. But what if the weapon went off? What if it shot out the side of the furnace? The furnace itself could explode. That would be a disaster. Other means of destruction had similar problems. Crushing the gun in a hydraulic press . . . what if the gun shot a hole in the press, sending pieces of equipment flying in all directions? Immersing the gun in acid . . . what if the gun went off and splashed acid over everything? Slicing into the gun with a laser . . . Jack didn't know what powered the gun, but obviously it contained vast energy. Destabilizing that energy might cause an explosion, a radiation leak, or some even greater catastrophe. Who knew what might happen if you tampered with alien technology?

And what if the gun could protect itself ? Over the years, Jack had read every ray-gun story he could find. In some stories, such weapons had built-in computers. They had enough artificial intelligence to assess their situations. If they didn't like what was happening, they took action. What if Jack's gun was similar? What if attempts to destroy the weapon induced it to fight back? What if the ray-gun got mad?

Jack decided the only safe plan was to drop the gun into an ocean—the deeper the better. Even then, Jack feared the gun would somehow make its way back to shore. He hoped that the weapon would take years or even centuries to return, by which time humanity might be scientifically equipped to deal with the ray-gun's power.

Jack's plan had one weakness: both the university and Jack's home town were far from the sea. Jack didn't know anyone with an ocean-going boat suitable for dumping objects into deep water. He'd just have to drive to the coast and see if he could rent something.

But not until summer. Jack was in the final stages of his Ph.D. and didn't have time to leave the university for an extended trip. As a temporary measure, Jack moved the ray-gun back to the pond. He buried the weapon several feet underground, hoping that would keep it safe from animals and anyone else who happened by.

(Jack imagined a new generation of lovesick teenagers discovering the pond. If that happened, he wanted them safe. Like a real hero, Jack cared about people he didn't know.)

Jack no longer practiced with the gun, but he maintained his physical regimen. He tried to exhaust himself so he wouldn't have the energy to brood. It didn't work. Lying sleepless in bed, he kept wondering what would have happened if he'd told Deana the truth. She wouldn't have killed herself if she'd been warned to be cautious. But Jack had cared more about his precious secret than Deana's life.

In the dark, Jack muttered, "It was her own damned fault." His words were true, but not true enough.

When Jack wasn't at the gym, he cloistered himself with schoolwork and research. (His doctoral thesis was about common properties of different types of high-energy beams.) Jack didn't socialize. He seldom phoned home. He took days to answer email messages from his sister. Even so, he told himself he was doing an excellent job of acting "normal."

Jack had underestimated his sister's perceptiveness. One weekend, Rachel showed up on his doorstep to see why he'd "gone weird." She spent two days digging under his skin. By the end of the weekend, she could tell that Deana's disappearance had disturbed Jack profoundly. Rachel couldn't guess the full truth, but as a big sister, she felt entitled to meddle in Jack's life. She resolved to snap her brother out of his low spirits.

The next weekend Rachel showed up on Jack's doorstep again. This time, she brought Kirsten.

Nine years had passed since Kirsten and Jack had seen each other: the day they both graduated from high school. In the intervening time, when Jack had thought of Kirsten, he always pictured her as a high-school girl. It was strange to see her as a woman. At twenty-seven, she was not greatly changed from eighteen—new glasses and a better haircut—but despite similarities to her teenage self, Kirsten wore her life differently. She'd grown up.

So had Jack. Meeting Kirsten by surprise made Jack feel ambushed, but he soon got over it. Rachel helped by talking loud and fast through the initial awkwardness. She took Jack and Kirsten for coffee, and acted as emcee as they got reacquainted.

Kirsten had followed a path close to Jack's: university and graduate work. She told him, "No one makes a living as a poet. Most of us find jobs as English professors—teaching poetry to others who won't make a living at it either."

Kirsten had earned her doctorate a month earlier. Now she was living back home. She currently had no man in her life—her last relationship had fizzled out months ago, and she'd decided to avoid new involvements until she knew where she would end up teaching. She'd sent her résumé to English departments all over the continent and was optimistic about her chances of success; to Jack's surprise, Kirsten had published dozens of poems in literary magazines. She'd even sold two to *The New Yorker*. Her publishing record would be enough to interest many English departments.

After coffee, Rachel dragged Jack to a mall where she and Kirsten made him buy new clothes. Rachel bullied Jack while Kirsten made apologetic suggestions. Jack did his best to be a good sport; as they left the mall, Jack was surprised to find that he'd actually had a good time.

That evening, there was wine and more conversation. Rachel took Jack's bed, leaving him and Kirsten to make whatever arrangements they chose. The two of them joked about Rachel trying to pair them up again. Eventually Kirsten took the couch in the living room while Jack crawled into a sleeping bag on the kitchen floor . . . but that was only after talking till three in the morning.

Rachel and Kirsten left the next afternoon, but Jack felt cleansed by their visit. He stayed in touch with Kirsten by email. It was casual: not romance, but a knowing friendship.

In the next few months, Kirsten got job interviews with several colleges and universities. She accepted a position on the Oregon coast. She sent Jack pictures of the school. It was directly on the ocean; it even had a beach. Kirsten said she'd always liked the water. She teasingly reminded him of their times at the pond.

But when Jack saw Kirsten's pictures of the Pacific, all he could think of was dumping the ray-gun into the sea. He could drive out to visit her . . . rent a boat . . . sail out to deep water . . .

No. Jack knew nothing about sailing, and he didn't have enough money to rent a boat that could venture far offshore. "How many years have I been preparing?" he asked himself. "Didn't I intend to be ready for any emergency? Now I have an honest-to-god mission, and I'm useless."

Then Kirsten sent him an emailed invitation to go sailing with her.

She had access to a sea-going yacht. It belonged to her grandparents— the ones she'd visited on Vancouver Island just before she and Jack broke up. During her trip to the island, Kirsten had gone boating with her grandparents every day. At the start, she'd done it to take her mind off Jack; then she'd discovered she enjoyed being out on the waves.

She'd spent time with her grandparents every summer since, learning the ins and outs of yachting. She'd taken courses. She'd earned the necessary licenses. Now Kirsten was fully qualified for deep-water excursions . . . and as a gift to wish her well on her new job, Kirsten's grandparents were lending her their boat for a month. They intended to sail down to Oregon, spend a few days there, then fly off to tour Australia. When they were done, they'd return and sail back home; but in the meantime, Kirsten would have the use of their yacht. She asked Jack if he'd like to be her crew.

When Jack got this invitation, he couldn't help being disturbed. Kirsten had never mentioned boating before. Because she was living in their hometown, most of her email to Jack had been about old high-school friends. Jack had even started to picture her as a teenager again; he'd spent a weekend with the grown-up Kirsten, but all her talk of high-school people and places had muddled Jack's mental image of her. The thought of a bookish teenage girl captaining a yacht was absurd.

But that was a lesser problem compared to the suspicious convenience of her invitation. Jack needed a boat; all of a sudden, Kirsten had one. The coincidence was almost impossible to swallow.

He thought of the unknown aliens who made the ray-gun. Could they be influencing events? If the ray-gun was intelligent, could *it* be responsible for the coincidence?

Kirsten had often spent time near the gun. On their first visit to the pond, she and Jack had lain half-naked with the gun in Jack's backpack beside them.

He thought of Kirsten that day. So open. So vulnerable. The gun had been within inches. Had it nurtured Kirsten's interest in yachting . . . her decision to get a job in Oregon . . . even her grandparents' offer of their boat? Had it molded Kirsten's life so she was ready when Jack needed her? And if the gun could do that, what had it done to Jack himself?

This is ridiculous, Jack thought. *The gun is just a gun. It doesn't control people. It just kills them.*

Yet Jack couldn't shake off his sense of eeriness—about Kirsten as well as the ray-gun. All these years, while Jack had been preparing himself to be a hero, Kirsten had somehow done the same. Her self-improvement program had worked better than Jack's. She had a boat; he didn't.

Coincidence or not, Jack couldn't look a gift horse in the mouth. He told Kirsten he'd be delighted to go sailing with her. Only later did he realize that their time on the yacht would have a sexual subtext. He broke out laughing. "I'm such an idiot. We've done it again." Like that day at the pond, Jack had only been thinking about the gun. Kirsten had been thinking about Jack. Her invitation wasn't a carte-blanche come-on but it had a strong hint of, "Let's get together and see what develops."

Where Kirsten was concerned, Jack had always been slow to catch the signals. He thought, *Obviously, the ray-gun keeps dulling my senses.* This time, Jack meant it as a joke.

Summer came. Jack drove west with the ray-gun in the trunk of his car. The gun's safety was on, but Jack still drove as if he were carrying nuclear waste. He'd taken the gun back and forth between his hometown and university many times, but this trip was longer, on unfamiliar roads. It was also the last trip Jack ever intended to make with the gun; if the gun didn't want to be thrown into the sea, perhaps it would cause trouble. But it didn't.

For much of the drive, Jack debated how to tell Kirsten about the gun. He'd considered smuggling it onto the boat and throwing the weapon overboard when she wasn't looking, but Jack felt that he owed her the truth. It was overdue. Besides, this cruise could be the beginning of a new relationship. Jack didn't want to start by sneaking behind Kirsten's back.

So he had to reveal his deepest secret. Every other secret would follow: what happened to Deana; what had really been on Jack's mind that day at the pond; what made First Love go sour. Jack would expose his guilt to the woman who'd suffered from the fallout.

He thought, *She'll probably throw me overboard with the gun.* But he would open up anyway, even if it made Kirsten hate him. When he tossed the ray-gun into the sea, he wanted to unburden himself of everything.

The first day on the boat, Jack said nothing about the ray-gun. Instead, he talked compulsively about trivia. So did Kirsten. It was strange being together, looking so much the way they did in high school but being entirely different people.

Fortunately, they had practical matters to fill their time. Jack needed a crash course in seamanship. He learned quickly. Kirsten was a good teacher. Besides, Jack's longstanding program of hero-dom had prepared his mind and muscles. Kirsten was impressed that he knew Morse code and had extensive knowledge of knots. She asked, "Were you a Boy Scout?"

"No. When I was a kid, I wanted to be able to untie myself if I ever got captured by spies."

Kirsten laughed. She thought he was joking.

That first day, they stayed close to shore. They never had to deal with being alone; there were always other yachts in sight, and sailboats, and people on shore. When night came, they put in to harbor. They ate in an ocean-view restaurant. Jack asked, "So where will we go tomorrow?"

"Where would you like? Up the coast, down the coast, or straight out to sea?"

"Why not straight out?" said Jack.

Back on the yacht, he and Kirsten talked long past midnight. There was only one cabin, but two separate fold-away beds. Without discussion, they each chose a bed. Both usually slept in the nude, but for this trip they'd both brought makeshift "pajamas" consisting of a T-shirt and track pants. They laughed at the clothes, the coincidence, and themselves.

They didn't kiss good night. Jack silently wished they had. He hoped Kirsten was wishing the same thing. They talked for an hour after they'd turned out the lights, becoming nothing but voices in the dark.

The next day they sailed due west. Both waited to see if the other would suggest turning back before dark. Neither did. The farther they got from shore, the fewer other boats remained in sight. By sunset, Jack and Kirsten knew they were once more alone with each other. No one in the world would stop them from whatever they chose to do.

Jack asked Kirsten to stay on deck. He went below and got the ray-gun from his luggage. He brought it up into the twilight. Before he could speak, Kirsten said, "I've seen that before."

Jack stared at her in shock. "What? Where?"

"I saw it years ago, in the woods back home. I was out for a walk. I noticed it lying in a little crater, as if it had fallen from the sky."

"Really? You found it too?"

"But I didn't touch it," Kirsten said. "I don't know why. Then I heard someone coming and I ran away. But the memory stayed vivid in my head. A mysterious object in a crater in the woods. I can't tell you how often I've tried to write poems about it, but they never work out." She looked at the gun in Jack's hands. "What is it?"

"A ray-gun," he said. In the fading light, he could see a clump of seaweed floating a short distance from the boat. He raised the gun and fired. The seaweed exploded in a blaze of fire, burning brightly against the dark waves.

"A ray-gun," said Kirsten. "Can I try it?"

Some time later, holding hands, they let the gun fall into the water. It sank without protest.

Long after that, they talked in each other's arms. Jack said the gun had made him who he was. Kirsten said she was the same. "Until I saw the gun, I just wrote poems about myself—overwritten self-absorbed pap, like every teenage girl. But the gun gave me something else to write about. I'd only seen it for a minute, but it was one of those burned-into-your-memory moments. I felt driven to find words to express what I'd seen. I kept refining my poems, trying to make them better. That's what made the difference."

"I felt driven too," Jack said. "Sometimes I've wondered if the gun can affect human minds. Maybe it brainwashed us into becoming who we are."

"Or maybe it's just Stone Soup," Kirsten said. "You know the story? Someone claims he can make soup from a stone, but what he really does is trick people into adding their own food to the pot. Maybe the ray-gun is like that. It did nothing but sit there like a stone. You and I did every-thing—made ourselves who we are—and the ray-gun is only an excuse."

"Maybe," Jack said. "But so many coincidences brought us here. . . . "

"You think the gun manipulated us because it *wanted* to be thrown into the Pacific? Why?"

"Maybe even a ray-gun gets tired of killing." Jack shivered, thinking of Deana. "Maybe the gun feels guilty for the deaths it's caused; it wanted to go someplace where it would never have to kill again."

"Deana's death wasn't your fault," Kirsten said. "Really, Jack. It was awful, but it wasn't your fault." She shivered too, then made her voice brighter. "Maybe the ray-gun orchestrated all this because it's an incurable romantic. It wanted to bring us together: our own personal matchmaker from the stars."

Jack kissed Kirsten on the nose. "If that's true, I don't object."

"Neither do I." She kissed him back.

Not on the nose.

Far below, the ray-gun drifted through the cold black depths. Beneath it, on the bottom of the sea, lay wreckage from the starship that had exploded centuries before. The wreckage had traveled all the way from Jupiter. Because of tiny differences in trajectory, the wreckage had splashed down thousands of miles from where the ray-gun landed.

The ray-gun sank straight toward the wreckage . . . but what the wreckage held or why the ray-gun wanted to rejoin it, we will never know.

We will never comprehend aliens. If someone spent a month explaining alien thoughts to us, we'd think we understood.

But we wouldn't.

THE GOD OF AU

ANN LECKIE

The Fleet of the Godless came to the waters around Au by chance. It was an odd assortment of the refugees of the world; some had deliberately renounced all gods, some had offended one god in particular. A few were some god's favorites that another, rival god had cursed. But most were merely the descendants of the original unfortunates and had never lived any other way.

There were six double-hulled boats, named, in various languages, *Bird of the Waves, Water Knife, O Gods Take Pity, Breath of Starlight, Righteous Vengeance*, and *Neither Land Nor Water*. (This last was the home of a man whose divine enemy had pronounced that henceforth he should live on neither land nor water. Its two shallow hulls and the deck between them were carefully lined with soil, so that as it floated on the waves it would be precisely what its name declared.) For long years they had wandered the world, pursued by their enemies, allies of no one. Who would shelter them and risk the anger of gods? Who, even had they wished to, could protect them?

More than any other people in the world, they were attuned to the presence and moods of gods—they would hardly have survived so long had they not been—and even before they came in sight of the line of small islands that stretched southward from the larger island of Au they had felt a curious lifelessness in the atmosphere. It was unlike anything they had ever met before. They sailed ahead, cautiously, watched and waited, and after a few days their leader, a man named Steq, captain of *Righteous Vengeance*, ordered the most neutral of prayers and a small sacrifice to whoever the local gods of the waters might be.

Shortly afterwards, twelve people disappeared in the night and were never seen again. The remaining Godless knew a sign when they saw one, and their six captains met together on *Neither Land Nor Water* to consult.

The six ships rode near a small island, sheer-sided black stone, white seabirds nesting in the crags, and a crown of green grass at the top. The breeze was cold, and the sun, though bright in a cloudless, intensely blue sky, seemed warmthless, and so they huddled around the firebox on the deck between the two hulls.

"What shall we do?" Steq asked the other five when they had all settled. He was, like the other Godless, all wiry muscle and no fat. Years of exposure had bleached his dark hair reddish, and whatever color his skin had been at his birth, it had been darkened yet further by the sun. His eyes were brown, and seemed somehow vague until he spoke, when all hints of diffusion or dreaminess disappeared. "I have some thoughts on the matter myself, but it would be best to consider all our options."

"We should leave here," said the captain of *O Gods Take Pity*, a broad-shouldered man with one eye and one hand, and skin like leather. He was older than any of the other captains. "The god in question is clearly capricious."

"What god isn't?" asked another captain. "Let's make up a sacrifice. A good one, with plenty of food, a feast on all six boats. Let us invoke *the god who punished us for our recent offense*. In this way perhaps we can at least mollify it."

"Your thought is a good one," said Steq. "It has crossed my mind as well. Though I am undecided which I think better—a feast, or some ascetic act of penitence."

"Why not both?" suggested another. "First the penitence, and then a feast."

"This would seem to cover all eventualities," said Steq. The others were agreed, except for the captain of *O Gods Take Pity*.

"This god is tricky and greedy. Moreso than others. Best we should take our chances elsewhere." And he would not participate in the debate over the safest wording and form of the rites, but closed his one eye and leaned closer to the firebox.

When the meeting was done and the captains were departing for their own boats, Steq took him aside. "Why do you say this god is greedier and trickier than most?"

"Why do you ask me this when the meeting is finished?" asked the other captain, narrowing his one eye. Steq only looked at him. "Very well. Ask yourself this question—where are the other gods? There is not an infant in the fleet that does not feel the difference between these waters and the ones we've left. This is a god that has driven out or destroyed all others, a god who resents sacrifices meant for any other. And that being the case, why wait for us to make the mistake? Why not send warning first, and thus be assured of our obedience? It pleased the god that we should lose those twelve people, make no mistake. You would be a fool not to see it, and I never took you for a fool."

"I see it," said Steq. He had not risen to a position of authority without an even temper, and considerable intelligence. "I also see that we could do worse than win favor with a god powerful enough to drive any other out of its territory."

"At what cost, Steq?"

"There has never been a time we have not paid for dealing with gods," said Steq. "And there has never been a time that we have not been compelled to deal with them. We are all sick at heart over this loss, but we cannot afford to pass by any advantage that may offer itself."

"I left my own son to drown because I could not go back without endangering my boat and everyone in it. Do not think I speak out of sentiment." Both men were silent a moment. "I will not challenge your authority, but I tell you, this is a mistake that may well cost us our lives."

"I value your counsel," Steq told him, and he put his hand on the other captain's shoulder. "Do not be silent, I beg you, but tell me all your misgivings, now and in the future." And with that they parted, each to their own boat.

A thousand years before, in the village of Ilu on the island of Au, there were two brothers, Etoje and Ekuba. They had been born on the same day and when their father died it was unclear how his possessions should be divided.

The brothers took their dispute to the god of a cave near Ilu. This cave was a hollow in the mountainside that led down to a steaming, sulfur-smelling well, and the god there had often given good advice in the past.

Let Ekuba divide according to his satisfaction, was the god's answer. *And let Etoje choose his portion. Let the brothers be bound by their choices, or death and disaster will be the result.*

But instead of dividing fairly, Ekuba hid the most desirable part of his father's belongings in a hole under the pile he was certain Etoje would not choose. It was not long before Etoje discovered his brother's deception, and in anger he drew his knife and struck Ekuba so that he fell bleeding to the ground. Thinking he had killed his brother, Etoje took a small boat and fled.

The island furthest to the south of Au had reared its head and shoulders above the water, with much steam and ash and fire, in the time of Etoje's great-grandfather. Birds were still wary of it, and it was not considered a good place to hunt. Its sides were black and steep, and there was no place for a boat to land, but Etoje found a spur of rock to tie his boat to, and he climbed up the cliff to the top, where a few plants and mosses had taken tentative root in the ashes, and a pool of warm water steamed. There was nothing else of interest.

But darkness was falling and he had nowhere else to go, so he sat down next to the spring to consider his situation. "Oh, Etoje," he said to himself, "your anger will be the death of you. But what else were you to do?"

As he sat, a seabird flew overhead, carrying a large fish. Etoje thought that if he could make the bird drop the fish, he might at least have some food for the evening. So he took up a stone as quickly as he might and threw it at the bird.

The stone hit its target, and the bird dropped the fish. But the fish fell not on the ashy land, but into the spring. Etoje could not see it to pull it out, and he was wary of wading into a spring he knew nothing of, so he settled himself once again.

When he had sat this way for some time, he heard a voice. "Etoje," it whispered. Etoje looked around, but saw nothing. "Etoje!" This time Etoje looked at the spring, and saw the fish lying half in and half out of the water.

"Did you speak to me, fish?" Etoje asked. It looked like any other fish, silver-scaled and finned and glassy-eyed.

"I spoke," said the fish, "but I am not a fish."

"You look like a fish to me," remarked Etoje.

"I am the god of this island," said the fish in its weird whisper. "I must have a mouth to speak, and perforce I have used this fish, there being nothing else available."

"Then I thank you, god of this island, whatever your proper name, whether you be male or female, or both, or neither, for your hospitality. Though I have little besides thanks to offer in exchange."

"It was of exchange I wished to speak. Shall we trade favors and become allies?"

"On what terms?" asked Etoje, for though he was in desperate straits, he knew that one should be cautious when dealing with gods.

"I was born with the island," said the fish. "And I am lonely. The cliff-girt isles around me subsist on the occasional prayers of hunters. They are silent and all but godless. No one hunts my birdless cliffs, and my island, like those others, will likely never be settled. Take me to Au, and I will reward you."

"That, I'm afraid, is impossible." And Etoje told the fish of his father's death, and his brother's deception, and his own anger and flight.

"Take me to Au," the fish insisted. And it told Etoje that if he would do so, and make the sacrifices and perform the rites the god required, Etoje would be pre-eminent in Au. "I will make you and yours rulers over the whole land of Au. I will promise that you and yours will be mine, and your fates my special concern, so long as Au stands above the waves."

"And when the tide comes in?"

"Shrewd Etoje! But I meant no trick. Let us say instead, so long as the smallest part of the island of Au stands above the waves. If you feed me well I will certainly have the strength to do all I say and more."

"Ah," said Etoje. "You want blood."

"I want all the rites of the people of Au, all the sacrifices. Declare me, alone, your god. Declare me, alone, the god of your people. Declare me, alone, the god of Au. Any who will not accept this bargain will be outlaws, and I will have their blood."

"What of the gods already resident on Au? Would they not starve?"

"Do they care now if you starve?" asked the fish.

"You have a point." And Etoje was silent for a few moments.

"With your help," said the fish, "I will enter any good-sized stone you bring me—there are several nearby—and you will bring it to Au. Then you will offer sacrifice and free me from the stone."

"And this sacrifice?"

"I hear the seabirds crying above the waves. They have flown over Ilu and they tell me your brother is not dead, merely injured. Have you considered how much simpler the question of your inheritance would be if he were dead?"

"I must ponder," said Etoje.

"Certainly. But don't ponder excessively. This fish won't last forever."

"Speaking of which," said Etoje, "do you need all of the fish for talking? I'm quite hungry, and I'm sure I would think better on a full stomach."

"Take it all," said the fish. "In the morning bring another to the spring. Or a seal or bird—fish aren't made for talking and this is quite taxing."

"Thank you," said Etoje. "I'm reassured to find you so reasonable. I will now dedicate this fish to you and indulge in a sacrificial feast, after which I will consider all you have said."

And Etoje did those things.

In the thousand years after Etoje made his bargain, the village of Ilu became the city of Ilu. It stood at the mouth of a wide, icy stream that tumbled down from the heights of the glacier-covered mountain Mueu. On Mueu's lower slopes the spring in the cave still steamed, but the god was long silent, either absent or dead. Behind Mueu was the high, cold interior of Au, a wasteland of ice and lava where no one went.

Ilu's green and brown houses, of turf and stone and skins, spread down to the sea where racks of fish lay drying, where the hunting boats lay each night and left each morning, and where frames of seaweed rose and fell with the tide. In the center of the city was the Place of the God of Au, a sprawling complex of blocks of black lava, rising higher than any other building there.

In days long past, anyone might raid a foreign village and bring his captives to Ilu, feeding the god handsomely and increasing his own standing and wealth. Whole villages perished, or else threw themselves at the feet of Ilu's rulers and declared themselves faithful servants of the god. Many humble but clever and brave young men made their fortunes in those days. But now the only outlaws in Au were condemned criminals, and only the same several officials, who had inherited the right to dispense justice, could present human victims to the god. No other outlaws were to be found in the land. Every village—for Ilu was Au's only city—offered its rites and sacrifices to the god of Au alone.

In return, the people of Au prospered. They were healthy and well-fed. Seals, fish, and whales were abundant. It was true that over the years the number of offences punishable by death had increased, but if one was a solid, law-abiding citizen and meticulous about honoring the god, this was of no concern.

There was a man named Ihak, and he lived in the Place of the God. It was his job, as it had been his father's, and his father's before him, to receive the outlaw victims intended for the god, and issue receipts to the providers in the form of tokens of volcanic glass carved into the shape of small fish. In former days this had been a position of great influence, but now was merely a ceremonial duty. Ihak was a tall man, almost spindly. He walked with a slight stoop, and his features were pinched and narrow. Though he and his wife had been together for many years, they had produced no children. He had often presented the god with fish, and with his own blood, and once he had even bought a human victim from one of the officials he dealt with, though it had meant a great deal of his savings. Making each sacrifice he had reminded the god of his faithful service, and that of his own ancestors, and he humbly and sincerely begged the god to provide him with that one thing that would complete his happiness. This was the only defect in his otherwise comfortable life.

One day two hunters came to the Place of the God with a dozen injured captives in tow. The gatekeeper gaped in astonishment and tried to turn them away, but they would not move. The captives were dressed oddly, and didn't seem to understand normal speech, so questions about how they had come to be here, bound and bleeding in front of the Place of the God of Au, went unanswered.

Finally the Speaker for the God came to the gate. He was a dignified man, very conscious of his responsibilities as a descendant of Etoje. Every inch of him, from his thick, curled, pale hair to his immaculate sealskin boots, declared him a man of importance. Too important to be bothered with a couple of hunters, but he had realized as soon as he had heard the message that the situation was a serious one. So he questioned the hunters. Where had these people come from?

"The other day some boats sailed into the islands," said one hunter. "Large ones, joined in pairs by wide platforms." He attempted to describe the mast and sail of each boat, but left his listeners perplexed. "Each one had many people aboard. They anchored and began hunting birds. My cousin and I watched them, and saw they weren't from Au."

"Where did they come from, if not from Au?" asked the Speaker. As far as he knew, there wasn't anywhere else to come from. "Did they spring up out of the waves, boats and all?"

"Perhaps," said one hunter, "the god of Au is tired of a steady diet of criminals."

"Perhaps," said the other, with the merest touch of malice, "the god of Au wishes all men to have a chance at riches and nobility, as was the case in former days."

The Speaker didn't particularly like hearing this. As the gatekeeper had, he questioned the captives. One spoke, or tried to speak, but something was evidently wrong—no words came out, only meaningless sounds.

By now, passers-by had stopped, and some of them confirmed the hunters' story—there were strange boats anchored in the islands, carrying strangely dressed people. And though the custom had not been followed for more than two hundred years, the Speaker could think of no immediate grounds on which to deny its fulfillment now, and plenty of grounds for possible retribution later, if it should become a problem. So he sent the hunters to Ihak.

Ihak was no less astonished than anyone else. However, unlike anyone else he had reason to take this development with a fair amount of equanimity. "So, ah, hm," he said, looking over the captives. "Who captured which ones?"

"We worked equally together," said the first hunter. "So we should get equal credit."

"That's right," said the second.

"Ah," said Ihak. "I see." He looked the line of captives over more carefully. "Ah. Hmm. You say you both participated equally in all twelve captures?" The two hunters assented. "So. Twelve tokens, then, six for each of you. And you may then call yourselves Warriors of Au."

"I can't wait to walk through the market," said the first. "Oh, to see the looks on everyone's faces!"

"What about the pregnant one? She looks pretty far along. Shouldn't she count for two?"

"Ah. No," Ihak said. "I regret to say. The guidelines are quite clear on the matter. So. But aren't you more fortunate that way? If there were thirteen tokens, how would you divide them without a dispute? Hm?"

So Ihak formally accepted, on behalf of the god, the sacrifice brought by the two hunters, and gave them their tokens. And then he went to speak to his wife.

In due course, a baby girl was born, and Ihak put it about that his wife had given birth at long last. She had been extremely surprised to discover herself pregnant, but this was understandable, as she had long ago stopped looking for signs of it. And everyone knew some tale of a woman who had not realized her condition until nearly the last moment. Clearly Ihak's wife was one of these.

Ihak held a great feast at which he presented the child to his friends, and he gave extravagant thanks to the god of Au. He named the girl Ifanei, which is to say, *the god provided her.*

When the period of fasting, vigil, and mortification had passed, each of the six captains of the Godless presided at a feast in honor of *the god of this place, who punished us for our recent offence.* The day was gray, and the breeze made the constant mist of rain sting. The inhabitants of each boat crowded together on their respective central decks and offered prayers praising the god as the most powerful, the most gracious, rightly the only ruler of the islands and the surrounding sea. "We desire to hear your will!" all the Godless cried, carefully making no other request, and no promises at all, while the captains let blood into the water.

Steq sat, then, and his wound was bound, and the people around him ate, with every bite praising the generosity and bounty of the god. He himself was not particularly hungry, but he knew that he should eat for the sake of his people and because of the blood loss, and so he did.

The Godless had been miserable with cold, and their hearts were sore with the loss of the twelve. Their acts of penitence had only increased their unhappiness. But now, despite the clouds and the rain, and the doubtfulness of their prospects, their spirits began to lift. There was plenty of food, all of it as carefully prepared as their situation allowed. The smiles and laughter began as performance but, as often happens, feelings began to match actions in at least some small degree. Steq could not bring himself to smile, but he was pleased to see the Godless enjoy themselves.

"If nothing else," called the captain of *O Gods Take Pity* from his own deck, "we will die with full stomachs."

This brought a bitter half-smile to Steq's face. "As always, you speak wisely," he answered.

Eventually the feast drew to a close, and the Godless began to clear away what was left of the food. Steq sat in thought under his boat's single square sail, his back to the mast. He sat brooding as people went back to their routine tasks, and as the day grew later the clouds blew away from the western sky, leaving a strip of blue shading down to green and orange, and the setting sun shining gold across the water. Colors that had been muted under the gray light seemed suddenly to glow—the brilliant emerald of island-topping grass, the brown of the boat's planking, the tattered, wheat-colored sail, the pink of a slab of seal fat the cook was packing away, all shown like jewels. The sun sank further and still Steq sat in thought.

When the sun had nearly set, Steq suddenly stood up and called a child to him. "Go to *O Gods Take Pity*," he said, "as quickly as you can. Tell the captain to be on the watch—my skin prickles, and the air is uncanny. Bid him pass my warning on."

"I feel it, too," said the child. Before any further move could be made, the other captains came up onto the decks of their ships—Steq had not been alone in his premonition. All work on the boats had halted as well, and the Godless were afraid.

"Fear not," said Steq. "Either we are about to meet our end, in which case our troubles are over, or we will survive. In any event, we have done all we could and will face our future as we always have."

As they stood waiting, a jet of water rose up just beyond the stern, and a dead-white tentacle snaked up from the water onto the deck. It ran half the length of the boat and with a thud it curled itself around the mast where moments before Steq had sat in thought. The boat's stern plunged towards the water. "Bail!" cried Steq, and in the same instant he spoke the Godless were taking up their bailers. Crew without bailers ran to the bows of the double hull, in part to balance the boat, and in part from fear of the glistening, gelatinous tentacles that had come out of the water after the first and wound and grasped at the other end. All around, the crews of the other boats stood watching, bent nearly over the gunwale strakes, crying out in horror and fear.

From the stern came a weird, bubbling noise, which resolved into gurgling speech. "Steq!"

"Don't answer!" cried one godless.

Steq only walked as steadily as he might to the end of the unsteady deck, stepping cautiously over lengths of suckered flesh. Behind him his own crew except for the bailers froze, hardly daring to breathe, and the watchers on the other boats fell silent.

At the end of the deck, he looked over the rail into the water. There, looking back from the waves, was a huge, silvery-black eye, as large as Steq's own head. Under this eye the white flesh in which it was set branched out into the tentacles that held his boat, and in the center of those was a beak like a bird's. "Steq," the thing gurgled again.

"I am here," he said. "What do you wish?"

"Let us each speak of our wishes," it bubbled. "An association would benefit us both."

"Explain."

"You are abrupt. Some might consider this disrespectful, but I will attribute it to your ill-treatment at the hands of gods so far. Or perhaps your extreme courage, which would please me."

The truth was, Steq dared not move lest he tremble and betray his fear. He knew that at this moment every life in the fleet depended on his smallest action, and he bent every effort to keep his voice steady. "You are most generous. I await your explanation."

The thing gurgled wordlessly for a moment. "Then I will explain. A thousand years ago, on that very island you see before you, I made a deal with a man of Au."

"Au being the mainland?"

"Yes. I declared that this man and his descendants would be pre-eminent in Au, if only they offered the sacrifices I desired and gave their rites and prayers to no other god. They have kept the terms of the bargain and I have as well."

"We don't fall under the terms of this bargain," Steq observed.

"You do, in a way. The acceptable sacrifice, according to the agreement, is those who are outlawed. In the beginning these were any who did not confine their worship to me. Now there are no such people to be found on Au, and they offer me murderers, robbers, and various petty criminals."

"I begin to see," said Steq. "We offered what might be construed as sacrifice to some other god, and were then fair game for your altar."

"Just so," bubbled the monster. "Would you prevent this re-occurring?"

"Had I been given the choice in advance, I would have been pleased to prevent its happening at all," Steq observed, not without some bitterness.

"No matter," said the thing, its liquid eye unblinking. "We did not know each other then, and past is past. Besides, I offer you something I imagine you hardly dare dream possible."

"That being?"

"Myself. I have become unhappy with my bargain. I will be frank. I am ambitious, and intended to reign supreme over Au, and from there expand my authority. But once they had conquered their island, the people of Ilu had no inclination to travel any further and arranged things so that they would not be required to do so. You, on the other hand, travel widely."

The wind was already chill, but it seemed in that moment to blow colder. "You have a binding agreement with the people of Au," he said.

"The agreement has its limits."

"As would an agreement with us, I am sure."

"You are a shrewder man than Etoje of Ilu," gurgled the thing. "And your people are well accustomed to keeping an advantage when dealing with gods. We will be well-matched." Steq said nothing. "I am strong with a thousand years of sacrifices," said the god of Au. "Have you fled from all gods? Have all other nations cast you out? Take me as your god, and be revenged. Take me as your god and your children will live in health, not sicken and starve as so many do now. Your fear and wandering will be at an end, and you will sit in authority over all the peoples of the world."

"At what price?"

"The price I demanded of Etoje: all your rites and sacrifices. Those who will not cease offerings to other gods will bleed on my altar."

"And when there are no more of those?"

"Ah," bubbled the monster. "That day is far in the future, and when it comes I will demand no more human victims."

"What, precisely, was your agreement with Etoje of Ilu?"

"That so long as the smallest part of the island of Au stood above the waters Etoje and his descendants would be pre-eminent in Au, and all those who accepted the terms of the agreement would be under my protection, their fates my special concern. In exchange, the people of Au would offer me the sacrifices I desired, and perform the rites I prescribed, and would make no offerings to any other gods, at any time."

"And would we enter into this same agreement, or make a new one with you?"

"We would make our own agreement, separate from my agreement with Au."

The sun had now set. In the east the clouded sky was black, and the body of the monster glowed blue under the water. Steq stood silent for some minutes, regarding it. "We are cautious," he said, when he finally spoke. "And I would discuss this with my people."

"Of course."

"Let us make no long-term commitment at the moment. But we will agree to this much: while we are in your territory we will make no offering to any other god, and you will not require us to bleed on your altar."

"This is reasonable," gurgled the god of Au. "Furthermore, it gives us both a chance to demonstrate our goodwill."

"I am pleased to find you so generous," said Steq. "It will take some time for us to determine the best course. It is not wise to rush into such things."

"Take what time it requires. I am in no hurry. Indeed, I have affairs to conclude before we can make our deal binding. It may be quite a long time before I am able to proceed."

"How long? We live at sea, but we are accustomed to land fairly frequently, for water and to buy or gather what we need, and to maintain our boats."

"Take the island you see before you, and the two north of it. All three have springs, and I will see to it that the hunters of Au will not trouble you there."

"Very well. What name shall we call you?"

"For the moment, call me the god of Au."

"Surely you have some other name."

"This one will do. I will speak to you again in the future. In the meantime, be assured of your safety so long as you worship me alone." And with those words, the tentacle that had coiled about the mast grew limp, and the whole tangle of arms slid into the water. The blue glow had begun to fade, and was nearly gone, and the huge eye was staring and vacant.

"It's dead," said Steq, and he called the child to him again. "Take a message to the other boats. We will meet tonight under the covers of the starboard hull of *Neither Land Nor Water*. Bid her captain lash them securely. No bird or fish will overhear our council." Then he turned to his crew. "Grab this thing before it floats off. It will feed us all for a week. For which we will offer thanks to the god of Au."

But whether due to possession by the god or the nature of the creature itself, the meat was bitter and inedible, and after a few foul-tasting bites the Godless cast it all back into the sea.

Ihak and his wife loved Ifanei greatly, and she was a happy child. She did not grow into any great beauty. She was short, and wide-boned, and her dark hair lay flat as wet seaweed. Indeed, she was so unlike her father Ihak that some commented disparagingly. But Ihak said quite frequently, "Ah, it's true, she looks nothing like me. But she's the very image of my late mother. So. I love her all the more for it." And he did indeed dote on the child, and there was no one in the Place of the God who remembered his mother to speak of, and so they held their tongues, and eventually the sight of Ihak going about with Ifanei's small hand in his became such a common, constant thing that it seemed unthinkable that anyone had ever suggested that she was not his child.

When Ifanei was fourteen, her mother died, and by the time she was sixteen Ihak was old and feeble. The Speaker began showing Ifanei small attentions, and Ihak called her to his bedside and spoke seriously with her. "So," he said, his voice a thin thread of breath. "Do you wish to be the wife of the Speaker for the God?"

"He only wants the inheritance," Ifanei said. She knelt on the floor and took her father's hand, thin and light and fragile as the bones of a bird. Ihak had dwindled away to almost nothing. In the flickering light of the single oil lamp he seemed faded and so completely without substance that one feared a gentle word might blow him away, but for the skin laid across him to keep him warm.

"Ah." It was a barely audible sigh. "You'll need a husband one day, and you could do worse than the man with the authority of the god of Au."

Ifanei turned the corners of her mouth down. "I could do better," she said. "The wife he already has is beautiful, and proud. She would not welcome any division in her husband's attentions, and she is altogether too unconcerned about the matter. I would be ignored at best."

Ihak managed a breathy laugh. "We think alike. So. I only asked because if the prospect had pleased you I would have done my best to secure him for you. Hm. It does not, so we must make other plans."

Now, Ihak had been a shrewder man than anyone had known. When he realized that the only child the god would grant him was a girl, he had hidden a part of his savings—the stacks of sealskins and volcanic glass blades that were the wealth of Au—in places only he knew. He had seen the resentment of the elite of Au when the two hunters had elevated themselves. He knew that the Speaker would have moved to discontinue the custom if he had not feared the anger of the common people. But further attempts on the strangers had proved futile, and the hopes of advancement had ceased to be real. The threat had receded, but it might reappear one day. Ihak knew that he would almost certainly be the last holder of his office. He also knew that the Speaker would go to considerable inconvenience to gain possession of Ifanei's inheritance. Thinking of all this, he had planned accordingly.

The day after Ihak's funeral, when Ifanei was sitting silent and cross-legged on the cold stone floor of her quarters, hair unbound and mourning ashes smeared on her face, the Speaker came to see her. "Ifanei," he said, "I have spoken to the god. Your father's office is to be discontinued. It is hardly a surprise; if it had been meant to continue, your father would have been granted a fit heir for the position."

Ifanei knew well enough that the god had never been concerned with petty matters of administration, so long as sacrifices arrived regularly. She did not look at the Speaker but at the floor, and she kept her voice small and tear-choked as she answered. "As the god wills."

"Poor Ifanei!" said the Speaker. "We will all miss your father, but you will understandably miss him the most. How fortunate you are to have cousins nearby to take care of you." She said nothing. "Don't forget, I am your cousin, too, and I regard you highly." Still Ifanei was silent. "Lovely Ifanei!" said the Speaker then, with no hint of mockery. "When the time comes, you will want to ponder the advantages of a closer connection with me, and at a more appropriate time I will speak to you of my desires."

In a bag, under Ifanei's bed, were an undyed hooded sealskin coat and a black glass knife. In her memory were the locations, well away from the Place of the God, where Ihak had cached a significant part of his valuables. In a week, villagers from along the north coast would come to Ilu, bringing their tribute of seals and seabirds to the Place of the God. When they left, who would notice one extra young boy among them?

"I will think seriously on everything you say," Ifanei said to the Speaker. She still looked steadily at the floor. "My father often spoke of his great respect for you, and I am fortunate to have such a cousin. I am so very grateful for your concern." She said this with every evidence of sincerity, and the Speaker was pleased with himself when he left her.

It was at this time that the god of Au returned to the Godless, and spoke to Steq, and shortly thereafter *Righteous Vengeance* ventured by night close to the shore of Au, and Steq went ashore.

Each year the north coast villagers who brought their tribute to Ilu traveled in a long, chaotic column along the sea. The seals, skins, birds, and eggs they brought were piled on sledges, the eggs carefully packed in grass. Each traveler took a turn pulling the offerings of his own village, each village they passed added to their number, and by the time the procession neared Ilu it became a noisy throng, the spirits of the participants undampened by the fact that at least half of them were suffering the effects of too much seaweed beer the night before. Between the crowd and the beer, no one noticed that a stranger had joined their number.

Steq had not been a young man when the Godless had sailed into Au's waters, and after sixteen years his hair had grayed. But he had not changed otherwise. He did not much resemble the people of Au—his skin was too dark, his hair too fine, his features not quite right somehow, though this may have been only a certain hardness about the mouth that was unusual in a man of Au. He kept the hood of his coat up, and his head down, and those walking next to him thought he must be from some other village, and attributed his silence to last night's beer, and let him be.

What Steq could see of Au was tall grass sweeping up the skirts of an ice-topped mountain. Here and there a stream was lined with stunted osiers, but there were otherwise no trees. The view was all green grass, black stone, and white ice, with gray clouds over everything. The villages they passed seemed nothing more than turf mounds huddled together, with here and there a whale rib protruding. At each one children ran shouting out of the low houses, clad in sealskin coats and trousers but barefoot in the mud. The whole column came to a swirling semi-halt as men and women followed the children out of the houses with much waving and laughter and handing over of food and skins of what Steq presumed was the ever-present beer. Then as if at some signal Steq was unable to detect a few of the villagers picked up the lines to their own sledges, the crowd moved forward again, and the village was left behind.

From a distance Ilu seemed no more than a bump on the treeless hillside, the Place of the God no more than a pile of stones, and the whole vista was dominated by the same mountain, and the icy blue river that ran down to the sea. Arriving, Steq saw the same tumble of turf houses, the same shouting, barefoot children, and he was nearly at the Place of the God before he realized that he was in the city itself. He had thought they were merely passing yet another village.

The procession broke like a wave onto the whale-rib gates of the Place of the God and spilled into the surrounding streets. Pushed along with the crowd, Steq found himself in a muddy, open square where women wearing coats sewn with seabird feathers and painted white, brown, or muted green began singing out in loud voices. The only word Steq recognized was "beer," which he had learned in the first hours of his joining the pilgrimage. The women were instantly surrounded and began what appeared to be fierce bargaining, though Steq had not seen anything resembling money. He turned against the flow of the crowd and made his way back to the Place of the God.

By now the sledges were lined up at the gates, and no few sledge pullers were casting glances in the direction of the square Steq had just left. He found a morose-looking man at the end of the line, and put his hand on the braided sealskin rope the man was holding.

The man instantly stood straighter and grinned. He said something—a question by the sound, but Steq knew only a few words of the language of Au. It was possible that *yes*, *no*, or *beer* would answer the man satisfactorily, but it was best not to speak. Keeping his face half-hidden by his coat hood, Steq shrugged towards the square.

The man, still smiling broadly, dropped the line, took Steq by both shoulders, drew him close into a miasma of fermented seaweed, and kissed him on the cheek. He said something else, sending an even stronger waft of beer Steq's way, and reached into his coat, pulled something out, and pressed it into Steq's hand. Then, none too steadily, the man walked away. Steq found himself holding a lump of glassy, brownish-golden stone that had been smoothed and rounded into a vaguely animal-like shape that he could not identify. He put it in a pouch under his coat.

By this time it was late afternoon. The line of sledges moved slowly forward and Steq watched each one halt before guards at the gate. One guard examined the cargo of each sledge, counting small, rounded pebbles into a pouch at his waist as he did so, and then waved the man who had towed the sledge through the gates. Other guards appeared and pulled the sledge to the side, where yet others unloaded it and then left it empty in front of the building. A trickle of villagers came back out of the gates, the sledgemen done with their business in the Place of the God and making with all speed for the square where their fellows crowded.

By the time Steq's commandeered sledge arrived at the gate the sun was setting. The guard looked over the cargo, counted his pebbles, and then waved Steq past with hardly a glance. As he had seen the man before him do, he dropped the tow line and walked into the Place of the God, straight ahead into light and the smell of sweat and burning oil.

The room was small—a dozen people would have crowded it. On the floor were woven grass mats, much scuffed and dirtied. The walls were plain and dark. In the center of the room was a low, blocky table on which sat a single black stone. The man who had preceded Steq in line stood before this, his back to Steq, facing another man, presumably a priest, who spoke at length and then brought out a disk of polished bone from inside his skin shirt and handed it to Steq's predecessor, who turned and left without another word.

Steq stepped forward. "God of Au," he said, before the priest could speak. "I am here, as you instructed me."

The priest frowned, and opened his mouth to say something, and then his eyes grew wide and his body stiffened. "Were you last?" he asked in a dead monotone, in Steq's language.

"Yes."

"You have done well," he said. A tremor passed through the body of the priest. "I am not surprised."

"How long do we have?"

"Not long," the priest answered. "I have withdrawn into the stone once more, and we are in danger until we depart Au." The man then turned and picked the black stone up from the table. "We go."

"What, do we merely walk through the streets of Ilu?"

"Yes. No one will stop us. But you must find a boat, and bring us to your fleet."

"Could you not have taken control of the priest and had him bring us the stone?" Steq asked.

"No. I could not have."

"I wonder why not." Steq followed him back out into the night. The guards seemed not to see them, and the area in front of the Place of the God was empty of anyone else.

The priest walked ahead without looking left or right, away from the Place of the God and into the square where that afternoon so many of Steq's traveling companions had crowded. It was empty now, and dark—there was no light but the glow of an oil lamp from a doorway here and there. In the center of the square the priest stopped abruptly, and Steq nearly ran into him. "Find someone," the priest said without turning around.

"Someone in particular?"

"Anyone will do," said the priest. "Between here and the water, where the boats are, is the place where the villagers are camping for the night. Someone strong and healthy would be best, but take anyone you can alive."

Steq knew without being told what the god wanted with a live person from the camp. "Can we not sacrifice the priest you're possessing?"

"He has been dead for the last several minutes."

"That's inconvenient," Steq said. "You expect that I will just walk off with someone in the middle of the camp?"

"Yes," said the priest, and he walked forward again.

"You said nothing of this, when last we spoke."

"I said you would know more when you came to me in Ilu," the priest said, still walking forward. Steq hurried to catch up to him. "You accepted that."

"You promised there would be no difficulties."

"There will not be if you follow my instructions."

Steq had known from the day the god had first spoken what food it preferred, and what they would be required to give it, if they accepted its offer. He was not ordinarily a sentimental man. But he thought of the people he had walked with in the last few days. They had been a smiling, happy lot, had offered him food and beer without stinting, even though they could not have had any idea who he was.

They had also killed twelve of his people, had only been prevented from killing more by the protection of the god, and would not hesitate to kill Steq himself if they knew he was not of Au. Steq was not unaccustomed to the idea of human sacrifice, or shocked by it. It was only that he could not avoid some small sympathy; the Godless were well used to being required to pay gods with their lives. Still, he had not come this far to quail at the last moment.

The camp of the pilgrims was a noisy, sprawling affair. Here and there a few tents had been raised, but mostly the men sat in the open, passing the ever-present skins of beer. What light there was came from three or four campfires, though what fuel they burned, since there seemed to be little or no wood anywhere, Steq had no idea. Everyone seemed to be near someone else, to be in conversation or sharing food or drink. If Steq had known more of the language, he could conceivably have taken a likely prospect by the arm and said something like, "Come aside, I must tell you something." But he could not, and he reached the far edge of the camp without seeing how he could do what the god required. The thought crossed his mind that one of his own people would be made to pay, if he could not find someone of Au.

He would not allow it. He stopped at the far edge of the camp and looked more carefully at the people around him. The two nights he had spent with the pilgrims he had taken care to stay at the edges of the camp where darkness would hide his foreign features, and where others would not pay him too much unwelcome attention. If anyone in the crowd wished to be alone he would likely do the same.

He walked the perimeter of the camp, just outside the edges of the light cast by the several fires, and when he had nearly made a circuit he found what he sought. A single shadowed figure sat motionless on the sand, just outside the camp. He stood quietly, watching, and the man didn't move. After a few minutes Steq walked slowly behind him, any sound he might have made covered by the raised voices of the celebrating pilgrims. He knelt behind the man and threw one arm around him, the other hand clapped across the man's mouth.

Steq realized immediately, with a mixture of regret and relief, that it was a boy he held, not a grown man, and in the same instant the boy bit his hand, hard. Steq did not dare let go and let the boy shout for aid, and did not dare cry out himself. He raised the arm circling the boy, meaning to strike him on the back of the head, and instantly the teeth were loosed and the boy was up and running across the beach. Steq ran after.

He caught up quickly, and brought the boy down to the sand. Steq pinned his arms behind and wrestled him up, dragged him, as he struggled ineffectually, down the beach to the water where the dim shadow of the priest stood. In all this time, though he fought Steq ceaselessly, the boy made no sound.

The god-possessed priest did not turn as Steq came up. "You took too long," he said in his flat monotone. "Get a boat."

"And in the meantime, what about this one?" Steq asked. "I can hardly just let go of him. And you don't want me to kill him yet."

Before the god could answer a sharp, thundering crack echoed across the sky. The encamped pilgrims cried out and then were silent a few moments. "We are in great danger," said the god. "We must leave immediately." Behind, in the camp, someone laughed and the voices started up again as though nothing had happened.

"Why?"

"The mountain Mueu is a volcano," said the god. "As I have withdrawn from the island, I can no longer contain it, or any of the others."

"You might have said as much sooner," said Steq, and dragged his captive along the beach until he found a small hunting boat, carefully stitched skin stretched over a frame of bone and osier. In the bottom of the boat was a coil of rope, and this he used to bind his captive. Then he called to the priest. "Over here! I have found a boat, and it will be quicker if you come to me, rather than me coming to you." He tipped the boy into the boat and then pushed it across the tide line and into the water, hoping the skin wouldn't tear along the way. As the god reached the boat another loud crack silenced the camp yet again. This time the returning voices were pitched higher, and seemed to carry a note of fear. The god climbed in, and Steq pushed the boat out further and then stepped in and took up the oar he found and began to row.

"You will have to bail," he said after a short time. "We are too many for this boat."

"Give me some blood," said the priest. "I will ensure that we do not sink."

"Blood! To keep water out of the boat? You do not inspire confidence in your power. Are you not well-fed by the sacrifices of the people of Au?"

"Much of my attention is currently elsewhere, keeping back the flood of melted glacier that will shortly sweep down the sides of Mueu and wash Ilu into the sea. Until we are farther from shore we are not safe, and I cannot turn my attention from Mueu. I could not do this were I not strong enough, and you will not be disappointed in me, once this danger is past."

"Bail," said Steq. "I will not row the distance wounded, and I will not bleed the boy lest you complain about the condition of your victim when it comes time for the sacrifice." He rowed a few more strokes. "Bail or drown."

Without a word, the priest took up a bailer from the bottom of the boat, and set to work.

When they reached the Fleet of the Godless, Steq turned his captive over to his crew. The priest, still inhabited by the god, took up the stone again and went to the deck where he sat in front of the mast and stared ahead, saying nothing. The crew avoided him, though Steq had not told them the body was dead.

They had already abandoned their island camps, and now they sailed south, away from Au. By afternoon the sky had darkened and ash began to fall from the air, like snow. The boats were muddy with it, and the Godless lashed the covers over the hulls to keep it out, and swept the covers and the decks constantly. They still avoided the dead priest, who did not move but sat at the mast covered in ash. That night the northern horizon was lit by a baleful red glow, and Steq approached the god.

"Am I to understand that Au is in the process of sinking beneath the waves, thereby releasing you from your contract?"

"Yes." A small slide of gray ash fell from the dead priest's mouth, the only part of him that moved. "Though it will take several more days."

"We are sailing away from Au with what speed we can manage."

"So I noticed," said the god.

"Will the body last long enough?"

"I intend to preserve it until I no longer need it," said the priest. "But in any event, I will tell you how the sacrifice will go. Cut the victim's throat and let the blood fall on the stone. Say these words." And here the god spoke the words of the rite. "Put both bodies into the sea. By doing this, you will be bound to the terms we agreed upon."

"Let us review those terms," said Steq.

The priest's head moved, dislodging more ash from his face, and he opened blank, staring eyes. "I warn you, I do not have any intention of re-negotiating at this late date."

"Nor I," said Steq. "I wish only to be certain there will be no misunderstandings."

"As you wish. I have no apprehensions."

"This is what we have agreed. We will give our prayers and sacrifices to no other god but you. With your assistance, we will compel all those we meet either to abandon all other gods but you, or die as your victims. We will do so until no one lives who offers rites to any other god, whereupon we will no longer be required to offer humans as sacrifices, though we will still owe you our exclusive devotion.

"For your part, you will protect us from all danger and misfortune, and will assist us against our enemies. We will be pre-eminent over all the peoples of the earth."

"For as long as you keep your end of the bargain," said the corpse at the mast. "My wrath will be terrible if you break the terms of the agreement and turn to another god, or fail to seek out every person who does not worship only me. Such was our agreement."

"And if you don't keep yours?"

"I will keep it," said the god. "Do you think I have gone to these lengths only to amuse myself?"

"No," said Steq. The corpse said nothing more.

Steq went forward, and stood at the rail.

He had known almost from the beginning that they were dealing with a minor god—a deity of some spring, or small island. This hardly mattered if, fed, it could do all it promised, and keep the Godless safe.

The past sixteen years had been like a dream Steq had feared to wake from. Food had been plentiful, illness rare. The hunters of Au had let them be after a few failed attacks. No vengeful god had come upon them. And they would shortly be Godless no more.

Do you think I have gone to these lengths only to amuse myself?

That the god had gone to great lengths—greater lengths, perhaps, than it wished to admit—had become more and more obvious. And why did the dead priest still sit guard over the stone?

Only one conclusion seemed likely—the god was vulnerable, and did not trust the Godless. And so, why put itself in this position?

Steq had believed the god when it had said that it was ambitious, that the people of Au had failed to serve that ambition as it had wished them to. But was that ambition enough to drive the god to take such a risk? Steq thought not.

The mountain Mueu is a volcano.

The god of Au had exhausted its strength, or nearly so, holding back Mueu. Why wait sixteen years, then? Why not flee the moment the Godless presented themselves? Had it, perhaps, waited until the danger was so extreme that the island was certain to sink entirely, thus releasing it from its obligation to the people of Au?

He thought of the wet and windy trek along the coast, the drunk, chattering villagers hauling their tribute to Ilu, the women who had pressed skins of beer on him, the men who had cheerfully shared fish and other, less identifiable food along the way. The image rose unbidden of the man in line before the Place of the God, morose until Steq took his place.

One of the Godless spoke, then, interrupting Steq's thoughts. "Captain, you're needed in the starboard bow."

Steq climbed from the deck into the starboard hull, and stooped to pass under the coverings, which on this shallow vessel did not allow one to stand up straight. In the bow he found two crew members hunched, bewildered, in front of a crouching, naked young woman. She looked directly at him, clearly afraid but also clearly in command of herself. He remembered her silence during the pursuit and struggle on the beach. This woman was not given to panic. She was short compared to the people of Au he had met, and wide-boned. Her hair was flat and lank. Her face was the face of a woman Steq knew had died some sixteen years ago.

"Get her some clothes," he said to the two guards. "No one is to speak of this." He turned, and made his way to an opening in the covers, and climbed back up onto the deck.

Steq had his supper that evening under the covers of the port bow of *O Gods Take Pity*. He sat on a bundle of skins in the flickering glow of a single oil lamp, the captain of *O Gods Take Pity* facing him, on a bunk. They spoke in low voices, bent forward under the low ceiling, knees nearly touching.

Steq reported all that had happened. "I don't doubt that it will do everything it says for us," he concluded. "But neither do I doubt that it will sink us in the sea like the people of Au if it finds some other, better bargain, or thinks itself endangered."

"This is self-evident," said the captain of O Gods Take Pity. "But this is not what troubles you. You hesitate now because of the woman."

"I do not hesitate," said Steq.

"I knew you when you were an infant at your mother's breast," said the captain of O Gods Take Pity. "Lie to the others as you wish, but I won't be deceived." Steq was silent. "She is none of ours. If you asked her where was her home, who her family, she would say Au, and name people we have never seen or heard of."

"But for an accident," said Steq, "she would be one of us."

"But for an accident I would be king in Therete, dressed in silk and sitting on a gold and ivory throne, surrounded by slaves and courtiers. But for an accident, the king in Therete would be one of us, fleeing the wrath of the gods, wresting what life he can from the waters with no luxury and little joy, though I assure you the thought has never crossed his mind. And rightly so. Begin this way, and where do you stop? There is no one in the world who would not be one of us, but for an accident."

"Years ago you urged us not to take this course," said Steq, bitterly. "Now you are in favor of it."

"No," said the captain of O Gods Take Pity. "I am not in favor of it. Only, if you pitch this god and its corpse into the sea without accepting its deal, do so because you have found some way out that will not cause all our deaths. Do not take this step, which will surely have dire consequences, because of qualms over this woman. We have all lost people because of mistake or accident, and we have all regretted it. Do not be the first to endanger the fleet because of your own regret."

"I said nothing of taking such a step." The other captain said nothing, and Steq took another piece of fish from the bowl in his hand, chewed and swallowed it. "It is tied to the stone, and can not be released without a sacrifice."

"It is not confined, and it has power yet to animate the corpse. It may have power to do other things as well."

"What would they do, our people, if I threw the stone into the sea?" Both men were silent, considering Steq's question, or perhaps unwilling to answer it.

"We have opposed gods in the past, and survived," said the captain of O Gods Take Pity after a while.

"Not all of us," said Steq.

"There is no use in worrying over the dead." He set his bowl beside him on the bunk. "We have lived too easily for too long."

"Perhaps we lived too hard, before."

"Perhaps. But we lived."

And Steq had no sufficient answer to this.

Ifanei lay bound on a bunk on *Righteous Vengeance*. Two guards sat opposite her, and they never looked away. When she had shivered they had covered her, but left her hands in sight.

It would not have mattered had they not—they had tied her with strong, braided sealskin and she had no way to cut it. They had taken her knife, and when they had taken her clothes they had found the needles and awls she had carefully wrapped and tied to the inside of her leg. She could see no means of escape.

She had understood that she was on a boat of the Fleet of the Godless, though she would not have known to give them that name. What she had not understood was why she had been captured to begin with. They had not killed her, or otherwise mistreated her. When they had done searching her they had returned her clothing. She could not imagine what anyone might want with her, unless they knew of Ihak's caches, which seemed unlikely.

She had days to consider. Days in which she was fed and her other needs cared for as though she were ill and helpless. Never at any time was she allowed off the bunk, nor were her hands or feet ever unbound.

The darkness never faltered—the coverings were tightly lashed, and even if the sun could have shone through, the skies were dark with smoke and ash, but Ifanei had no way of knowing that. She knew only the close, dimly lit darkness and the smell of unwashed bodies. Eventually she felt stunned with the sameness of it all, and ceased to wait for anything further to happen.

An unmeasured time later, she woke to the chill as her cover was roughly pulled off. One of her guards held her bound wrists, the other cut the bonds around her ankles, and she was pulled as upright as the low ceiling allowed, and pushed down the narrow space that ran the length of the hull, bunks on one side, unidentifiable bundles and stacks along the other. She took two steps and her legs buckled under her, weak from long inactivity. Her guards caught her, pulled her up again, and helped her along to where a faint light shone through an opening above.

Hands reached down and pulled her through, up onto a railed platform. The sky was dark, and the breeze cold, and despite her coat she shivered. Guttering torches, a few oil lamps, and a fire in a large box provided some light. There were people all around, all along the railings. Facing her was the man who had brought her here, his face expressionless. No one moved, though the platform pitched and rocked in a way that made Ifanei step and stumble as she tried to stay on her feet.

In the center of the platform was a wide, tall pole and leaning up against that was a pile of gray dust. In front of this was the Stone of Etoje.

"God of Au!" she cried. "Help me!"

A weird gasping, choking noise came from the pile at the foot of the pole. The whole thing heaved and from underneath it a man stood up, swaying and staggering slightly, and the gasping noise continued. The dust fell and swirled away in the wind.

His long blond curls were covered in ash, his face and clothes gray with it, but she knew him. She realized, with a freezing horror, that the choking sound was laughter.

"Ifanei," said the dead Speaker in a flat, toneless voice. "I provided you indeed, and I will have you back from your father." She said nothing, could think of no answer. "Here is symmetry," said the god. "Here is perfection."

"My god." Ifanei's voice trembled with cold and dread. "I know you will protect me. The people of Au are your people and you have always kept us from misfortune."

"Au has sunk beneath the waves," said the priest. "Not the smallest part of the island remains. And you were my victim from the beginning. I lent you to Ihak, and it is only right that you return to me at last." Still the people around her, and the dark, hard-faced man in front of her, were silent. There was no sound, except the wind and the water.

"Au beneath the waves," she said. "Why? You have betrayed us!"

"It was the nature of the island itself," said the god. "And it was never in my power to keep any human alive forever, nor did I ever promise such a thing."

She saw the dishonesty of the god's words, but could not find sufficient answer for it. "What of Etoje's service to you?" she asked. "Had he not taken you for his god you would still be on the island, with no company but the cries of birds. Does this mean nothing to you?"

"Etoje's service was pure self-interest," said the dead priest. "He killed his own brother to satisfy his greed. Surely you know this, the tale has been told often enough. And it should not surprise you. It is the way people are. As it happens, it serves my purpose."

She looked at the people around her. They would, she knew, cut her throat as easily as the Speaker had offered up the victims of Au. Did they know what they dealt with? Even if she had spoken their language, and could have warned them, would she have wished to?

But there was nothing she could do. And that being the case, she would not beg or scream. She took two stumbling steps to the Stone of Etoje, knelt heavily and then made her back as straight as her shivering allowed and waited for the knife.

Steq had known that the woman was no coward. He had, when he had thought of what was to come, been grateful that he would not have to steel himself to endure pitiful weeping or wailing.

She knelt shivering by the stone, her chin up as though inviting the knife. Her eyes were open, and she looked not at the grimy, dead priest but at Steq.

He had not expected to be undone by her bravery. "What did she say to you?" he asked the god.

"It does not matter."

"I am curious."

"You are delaying. I wonder why?"

"Why should it matter to you?" Steq asked.

"It does not matter." Steq did not answer. "Very well. The woman begged me for help, invoking my agreement with the people of Au. I explained to her how matters stand. That is all."

That was all. Steq took a breath, and then spoke. "Godless, I fear I have led you astray."

"And I fear this ship needs a new captain," said the dead priest.

"It will have one," said Steq, "if the people do not like what I have to say."

The corpse made as if to step forward, but a voice spoke from the watching crowd. "Touch him and you'll be over the rail, stone and all." Other voices murmured in assent.

"Put me overboard and you'll speedily discover your mistake," said the god, but it made no further move.

"If we feed this god what it desires," said Steq, "it will almost certainly have the power to do much of what it has promised us. And the blood that it demands will be none of ours." His gaze shifted momentarily to Ifanei, and then back to the priest. "But let me tell you why the god has abandoned its promise to the people of Au. The great mountain above Ilu was a volcano, and there were others. For a thousand years the god held the island safe, because of its promise to the people of Au, but after all that time it could control them no longer. A thousand years! Imagine the power thwarted, enough to destroy the whole island when it was finally let loose. And when this god realized that it could not hold back the fires forever, what did it do? Did it command the people of Au, who had served it faithfully all that time, to build boats, and escape under its protection? No, it allied with us behind their backs, and left them to their fate. It will do the same when its agreement with us becomes inconvenient.

"Many of you have lived all your lives under this god's protection. The rest are too accustomed to living in opposition to all the gods and peoples of the world to fear what might happen if the god of Au has not the strength to do as it promises. Perhaps I have grown too soft with easy living, and sentimental. But the fate of the people of Au troubles me greatly, and if you would ally yourselves with this god you must choose another captain."

"And if we would not?" cried a voice.

"Then we must cast stone and corpse overboard, and sail away from here as quickly as we may. It has some power yet, and we will be in some danger, but I do not think it will follow us far. The gods of surrounding waters will have no love for it, and even so, at the bottom of the sea there will be no one to feed it."

"I will show you my power!" said the corpse.

"Show it!" came the voice of an old woman. "We all know your weakness, and Steq has never yet led us wrong!"

As though her words had been a signal, the boat lurched to starboard. Steq grabbed the rail, watched as three or four people tumbled into the water. Crew slid across the deck, and the stone began to roll but the priest caught it up, and then a thick, dead-white tentacle reached up and onto the boat, twisting and snaking until it found a rail, which it curled around and pulled.

The rail snapped and was thrown up into the air. Another tentacle joined the first, groping along the hull, and then another. Torches tumbled from their places and bounced across the deck and into the water. Still a wavering, flickering light lit the boat—the sail was aflame.

"You!" Steq grabbed a man by the arm. "Loose the port hull!" The man scrambled to obey him, speaking to others on his way, who followed him. Steq then let go of the rail, to slide down the deck up against a writhing tentacle. "Everyone to the port hull!" he shouted. What they could do against the monster in an overloaded single hull he did not know, but he did not think they could extinguish the fire and right the ship, and so it was the only chance for survival.

In the meantime he would attack the monster in any way he could. He reached into his coat for his knife, and his hand brushed up against his pouch. There was nothing in it to help him—a few needles, a coil of fishing line and some hooks, and . . .

He looked around for the woman of Au, and saw her scrambling up the deck, hands still bound. He followed, grabbed her ankle and pulled her to him. She lashed out, swinging her fists, and hit him, hard, just under his ear. "Stop!" he shouted, though he knew she would not understand him. But she did stop. "Look!" Out of the pouch he pulled the small piece of polished, golden glass he had brought from Au, and held it before her eyes.

She looked at it for only a moment, and then closed one hand around it and called out, and suddenly the writhing arms were motionless and the sound of snapping wood ceased. "Up," he said, and pushed her along the sloping deck towards the port hull, which was nearly free, and climbed after her.

"Steq!" The voice of the dead priest, weird and gasping. "Steq! What is that?"

"It is the smallest part of the island of Au," called Steq, without turning his head. He and the woman reached the edge of the deck and leapt into the port hull just as it was freed. The Godless were unlashing covers and pulling out oars.

"She is not of Au!" cried the dead man. "I am not bound!"

"Then move against her!" This was answered with an inarticulate cry. The last few flames of the burning mast went out as *Righteous Vengeance* slipped under the waves, and the only light was the torches of the other boats, for the rest of the fleet was still nearby, their own crews watching in horror.

"Row for the nearest ship!" Steq ordered then. "It can not harm us so long as the woman is in the boat, and as for the others, it has not the strength to bring more monsters against them, or it would have done so already."

The woman sat shivering in the bottom of the hull, both hands clutched around the small glass token. Steq went to her and cut her bonds. "There is a place in the south," he said, though he knew she would not understand him. "A mountain so high they say you can touch the stars from its top." She did not answer, he had not expected her to. "Do you hear that, god of Au?" But there was no answer.

The next morning the Fleet of the Godless, reduced to five boats, sailed southward. Behind them, far below the featureless sea and attended only by silent bones and cold, indifferent fish, lay the Stone of Etoje, and the god of Au.

THE FANTASY JUMPER

WILL McINTOSH

Rando passed his wrist over the credit eye on the Fantasy Jumper kiosk. The darkened window flashed to life, revealing a full-length, three-dimensional image of a young woman with pale, perfect skin lightly dusted with freckles.

"This is the one I wanted to show you," Rando said to his blind date, Maya, who had an artificial eye that drooped slightly, but was otherwise very cute in a chipmunk sort of way.

"Make her blonde," Rando said, while Maya peered over his shoulder. The woman's hair changed from brown to golden blonde.

"Old-fashioned romance dress." It hurt to talk, because Rando had accidentally bitten the inside of his cheek while eating oysters at the underwater restaurant. The woman's simple white shift morphed into a flowing mintcream gown with a diving bust line, like on the covers of the books Rando's elderly mother read.

"Big pointy dunce hat," Rando said, laughing, and the woman was suddenly wearing an oversized red cone, with "Dunce" printed top to bottom in plain black letters.

"Finished," Rando said to the kiosk, simultaneously puffing his cheek to keep the wound from rubbing against his molar.

The window glided up, and the woman stepped out.

"This time, maybe I'll reach the fountain," she said. She turned and leapt off the roof.

Maya gasped.

They leaned over the short wall and watched her plummet, her dress billowing, arms spread wide.

"Isn't that something?" Rando said.

The woman seemed to fall for a long time; Rando stared, rapt.

Finally, she hit the ground. Her head bounced violently, then she lay motionless. The dunce hat, which had come loose during the fall, clunked to the ground a few feet away from her. A wide swatch of blood blossomed on the pavement around her head. People on a pedestrium that wound past the fountain pointed, their words indecipherable. Then they seemed to recognize that the woman was not a real woman, and went back to their conversations.

Rando looked at Maya. "Isn't that something?"

Maya smiled and nodded. She glanced at her watch.

"Watch this, watch this," Rando said, pointing down at the broken body. The pavement under the body slid open until the body dropped out of sight, then it returned to its original flat grey.

"Let's try it again," Rando said, sweeping the credit eye a second time. "Can you do that movie star, Ellie what's-her-name?"

"I only have copyright permission to simulate three celebrities: Cotton McQue, Gym Hinderer, and Lena Zavaroni," the woman behind the glass said listlessly.

"Those all suck," Rando said. "What about a little kid?"

"Age?"

"Five."

The woman became a five year old girl, cute as a button, but with the same haunted grey eyes.

"Finished!" Rando said.

The little girl stepped out. "This time, maybe I'll reach the fountain," she said. Her tiny legs scrambled and churned until she finally cleared the low wall. She jumped, tumbling head over feet once, twice, before slamming to the pavement.

He glanced at Maya again. She looked a little distracted, like she wasn't having a very good time. She was so cute. Rando imagined what it would be like to arrive for Thanksgiving dinner holding Maya's hand.

"Hey, I have an idea," he said. He held up a picture of his mother for the kiosk to scan. "This is going to be hilarious."

When he'd finished watching his mother fall, he turned to find that Maya was nowhere in sight.

"Maya?" he called, but got no answer. He headed off to look for her.

Violet and Cloe wandered the roof, holding hands. Violet was an egret of a woman, tall and skinny. Her head bobbed when she walked—one bob for each step. Cloe had a ruddy red face, and a habit of waggling her finger when she talked, as if were trying to write what she said in the air.

They took turns looking out at the park through a telescopic viewfinder that could focus on one square of a waffle cone held by a child in line to see the Concrete Mermaid, if you wanted it to. The view was spectacular—the fair stretched nearly to the horizon, a cacophony of brilliant shapes and colors, snaked by long lines of wide-eyed patrons.

They walked on, pausing to watch three teenage boys create a haggard looking middle-aged woman, who said something about the fountain, then startled them both by leaping off the roof. They continued.

An old woman with thick ankles ringed by plump purple veins sat at the memory kiosk. On the viewscreen a young girl (Violet assumed it was the old woman in her youth) swatted yellow jackets off a younger boy (her brother?) who was covered with them. He was screaming, his skin already mottled by lumps with angry red centers. One of the wasps landed on the girl's cheek and stung her; she cried in pain, but kept swatting at the bees that swarmed the boy.

"What a gruesome memory to record," Cloe said.

"Maybe she wants to show her family what a brave girl she was." Violet let go of Cloe's hand to wipe her palm on her hip, then reached to retrieve it, but Cloe had folded her arms across her chest.

At the Dream kiosk they watched what they had dreamed the night before. Violet dreamed that Chinese people were painting graffiti all over her body. Cloe dreamed that she was pinned by a tangle of electrical cords connected to life support systems. She had to unplug them to free herself.

"Look at this one," Violet said, scampering ahead, "Lie Detector Spectacles."

She scanned the credit eye; the specs popped out on a stalk, oversized, with black frames. Violet pressed her face to them, eyeing Cloe through a haze of smudges.

"How old are you?" Violet asked.

"Fourteen," Cloe said.

A burst of indecipherable readouts lit up in Violet's peripheral vision, then the word LIE in bright red. Violet clapped, delighted.

"Do you watch too much television?"

"Yes."

TRUTH.

"Who do you think is better looking, me or you?" Violet said.

Cloe smirked, shook her head.

"Come now! Who's better looking?"

"You," she finally answered.

LIE.

"Now we're getting somewhere. I always thought you had a bit of a narcissistic streak."

"It's my turn," Cloe said, stepping out of the spectacles' gaze and tugging Violet by her sweater.

"Do you hate my mother?"

"Of course not!" Violet said.

Cloe pulled her face away from the spectacles, looked at Violet, nodded her head. "Yes. You do."

"No, I don't," Violet protested.

"Have you ever looked at my personal memory videos when I was out of the house?"

"N—no."

Violet and Cloe took turns hurling questions, progressing from tickling, to pricking, to ripping flesh from the bone. Do you find my breasts too small? What really happened after I passed out the night we snorted Godflash with Jenna?

Then a question burst from Violet unbidden, as if leaping out of a black hole.

"Do you love me?"

"What?" Cloe said.

"You heard me."

Cloe shifted from one foot to the other, looked toward the horizon, where the wonders of the park continued to shimmer and spin.

"No," she said.

TRUTH, said the spectacles.

Violet sank to the floor. A rushing filled her ears, as if they were flooding with water. She stared at Cloe, waiting for Cloe to take it back, or qualify it, or denounce the kiosk a liar.

"I'm sorry," Cloe said. "I should have told you sooner, but I couldn't figure out how."

Violet stared. She was having one of those disembodied moments, when every word, every movement, feels like an echo instead of something happening new.

"I should go." Cloe turned, then paused. Violet's heart leapt.

Cloe reached behind her neck with both hands, unclasped the vow necklace Violet had given her, and put it in Violet's lap when Violet didn't hold out a hand to take it.

Abbet was fat, and he walked like a duck. His splayed footsteps were silent on the hard polished floor. No one paid him much attention as he approached the Fantasy Jumper kiosk—a glistening rectangle trimmed in silver and chrome. He swept his wrist across the kiosk's credit eye, and the young woman appeared.

"No alterations. Default model."

Always the same expression when she emerged—serene on the surface, but undertones of restless longing.

Immediately, she turned toward the low wall. "This time, maybe I'll reach the fountain."

"Wait, not yet," Abbet said.

The woman gazed out for a moment, focused not on the wonders spread out before her, but on the empty air between her and those wonders, the middle distance. Reluctantly she turned back.

"It breaks my heart that you're created only to die scant moments later. Such a waste."

The woman opened her mouth to tell him that she didn't understand what he meant, that she had been created for falling and dying, for ecstasy and agony, but realized that saying it would only draw him into conversation, only delay her. The joy of the fall, and the horror of the pavement, beckoned.

"Thank you," she said instead.

"I fell asleep at my work station yesterday," Abbet said. "When I woke up I discovered I'd inadvertently laid my head on my keyboard, primarily on the 'k' key." Bits of foam formed on his lips as he spoke. "When I woke, my screen was filled with k's. It took me hours to delete them all."

The woman glanced over her shoulder. Rays of sunshine painted the dust and dandelion blooms swirling in the space she longed to fill. She could be out there with them now, she could pass through those bands of light, create a draft that sucked dust and dandelion blooms after her.

"I've kept the tags from all my clothing since I was a boy, so I can track the changes in my body. I keep the tags in a brown chest." He watched her face carefully, searching for some reaction.

"I have to go now," she said, leaning on her right foot, the one she would step with first. "Please let me go."

"Please, talk to me a while," he said.

"Why don't you talk to one of the women from the sex kiosk?"

"They only want to have sex. They don't want to talk. No one wants to talk." He kicked at a bottle top lying prongs-up on the ground, but missed.

"Are you the same each time?" He asked. "Or are you a new one each time?"

"I don't know."

"Why do you want to reach the fountain so badly?"

"I don't know. I imagine I was made that way. But it doesn't matter. It would be so wonderful, to hit the water, to feel it all around me, pouring into my throat and my ears."

"Your wishes are so simple," Abbet said. "Mine are so complicated. I'm not even sure what all of them are."

She didn't say anything, just looked at him with desperate eyes.

He nodded glumly. "Okay, go, if that's what you want."

"This time I'm going to reach the fountain."

"You'll never reach it, you know. It's much too far . . . "

Her artificial heart pounding in anticipation and terror, craving the fall but dreading the pain, she planted the arch of her foot against the edge of the low wall and catapulted herself into the air, arms spread wide, gaze fixed past the wide grey expanse of pavement to the shallow ripple and spray of blue-white water beyond. She flew horizontally first, feeling the thrill of weightlessness, the anticipation, the potential represented by the space between her body and the ground. Then she fell, gaining speed. Her long, chestnut hair snapped in the wind; her cheeks puffed as air rushed into her half-open mouth.

Too soon, all at once, it was over. She lay staring at a red and white popsicle wrapper lying by her nose for one last, agonizing heartbeat, then she died.

Still clutching Cloe's vow necklace in her sweaty palm, Violet watched the earnest fat man talk to the Fantasy Jumper, then watched the Fantasy Jumper leap. Part of Violet wanted to follow the Jumper, to be free of her sadness. And, maybe even more importantly, to saddle Cloe with a lifetime of guilt and remorse. But there was bound to be a safety field around the roof to stop anyone but the Fantasy Jumper from jumping.

The fat man waddled away without even watching the Fantasy Jumper hit the ground. Violet went to the edge to look at the Fantasy Jumper's body. It was already gone.

A jolt went through her—Cloe was walking on the pedestrium below. She must have stopped in the bathroom. Violet hoped she'd stopped to cry.

Violet turned away, absently caressed the brass piping of the Fantasy Jumper's kiosk. She looked at her reflection in the window, at her too-small breasts and her beak nose.

A wonderful idea occurred to her.

She swept her bony wrist over the credit eye, and the window came to life.

"Just like me. Exactly like me," she ordered, and in an instant, it was as if she were looking at her reflection again.

"Come," Violet said.

The window raised, and the Fantasy Jumper stepped out. "This time, I'll reach the fountain," she said.

"Wait!" Violet said, holding out an arm to block the Fantasy Jumper from the wall. Cloe was still fifty meters from the fountain. Violet had to time it just right.

She fastened Cloe's vow necklace around the Fantasy Jumper's neck, instructed the Jumper to wait for her signal, then hurried to the telescopic viewer and focused it on Cloe. She wanted to see Cloe's face.

"Get ready," Violet said as Cloe approached. "Now!"

Violet felt a slight breeze as the Fantasy Jumper passed. Silently she counted to three, figuring it would take that long for the Fantasy Jumper to land.

Cloe's hands flew to her open mouth. Her eyes widened with recognition. Then, for an instant, Cloe smiled. It was a fleeting half smile, quickly masked by faux shock, but Violet saw it. She was sure of it.

Even at the World's Fair it's possible to trick someone, to convince them that the Fantasy Jumper is someone they know, someone they once loved. But only for an instant. Only for that first primordial moment before the higher faculties caught up, and reminded them of where they were.

Cloe looked up, realizing what Violet had done. Was she disappointed that it was only a trick? Probably.

Violet screamed in rage. She shoved the telescopic viewer into a spin and stormed back to the Fantasy Jumper kiosk. She made another Violet Jumper, and sent it over the wall.

Then she made another, and another. They vaulted over the wall, slammed to the concrete below, one after another.

"This is how much pain I feel!" She screamed at Cloe as she swept her wrist over the eye yet again. "These are my wounds!" She howled, her wrist a blur.

Like a movie caught in a loop, the Fantasy Jumpers leapt one after another, spattering blood and chips of artificial bone, screaming in agony, writhing as they died. The ground became littered with them as they piled up faster than the ground could absorb them.

One Jumper landed atop another, her spine snapping with an audible crack. Still more followed.

A pile formed.

A Jumper dragged herself out of the pile, her leg shattered, her torn scalp exposing a ragged quilt of stringy fibers, but her arms and back intact.

Cloe screamed when she saw the Violet-shaped Jumper dragging itself toward her, gasping in pain, tears pouring down its cheeks. She backed up to the edge of the fountain, then scurried around it.

Slowly, awkwardly, the Jumper dragged itself, its eyes fixed on the sparkling fountain. The tattering of the water spilling down upon itself drowned out all other sound.

Finally, she reached the edge, clawed her way over the marble lip, and plunged into the cool water. A billion stars exploded in her mind.

On the roof, the latest Violet Jumper paused, stared down at the fountain in disbelief.

"I did it," she said.

"Jump!" Violet cried. "Why don't you jump?"

The Jumper shook her head. "There's no need."

Violet followed the Jumper's gaze, saw her skinny self floating face-down in the fountain. She laughed bitterly. "At least someone got what they wanted."

Violet headed for the stairs, oblivious to the open-mouthed stares of the onlookers gathered on the roof.

Rando passed Violet on the stairs, on his way back up to the roof. He was hoping Maya had returned there to wait for him.

The roof was silent, and nearly empty. The Fantasy Jumper looked out over the park, unmoving. The undertones of restless longing were gone from her face. She looked as if she might stand there forever.

"Would you care for a cup of tea?" Abbet asked her.

"I don't drink tea," the Fantasy Jumper said.

"Perhaps a conversation?"

"I don't know."

He took her hand, led her toward the stairs.

"Every so often I like to empty out all my drawers and put everything in a pile," he said as they left the roof.

THE MAGICIAN'S HOUSE

MEGHAN McCARRON

The magician's house looked like every other house in our neighborhood on the inside, except it had more doors. There were three doors in the foyer, two under the stairs, four in the hallway, one next to the fireplace, and another hidden behind the sofa. They were the builder's standard issue, painted the same blank white color as the walls. I pictured each one leading to a room in another house that looked exactly like this one. This house was the ur-house, the house that allowed all other houses in the development to exist.

We didn't go through any of those doors, like I had been expecting. Instead, the magician led me into the kitchen, opened the oven, and crawled inside. The oven seemed too small for a man that tall, let alone for me. I peered inside; there were no racks or walls or heat sources. There was nothing but darkness. I glanced up at the control knobs. They were turned to "OFF."

"Well?" said the magician's voice from inside. It echoed, as if coming from below ground.

I ducked my head into the oven; inside was strangely humid, and the air smelled warm and yeasty. There were no walls I could make out, only receding darkness. Taking a deep breath, I placed one hand inside, then another. I banged my shin on the oven's edge as I pulled my legs up. I crawled forward into the pitch black, the hard metal floor warming beneath my hands. Suddenly, this seemed like a terrible idea. But before I could turn around, the darkness enveloped me, and I slid down.

Inside the oven, a gas lamp flickered over upholstered chairs that I had seen in a dumpster a few months ago. I remembered them because they were lime green, and I had thought about hauling them home for my pink-and-floral bedroom to piss off my mom. The magician was already seated, waiting for me. He looked bored. I wiped the nervous sweat from my face, took a deep breath, and sat.

The magician was a tall, spindly man with surprisingly thick hands and dark, graying hair. He folded into the chair like a marionette. To meet me, he wore black stretch pants, a silk pajama shirt, a burgundy cardigan, and decaying black flip-flops. If I had seen him on the street, I would have laughed, but in the oven room he looked right at home, whereas I felt ridiculous in my khaki shorts and pre-faded T-shirt. I had even blow-dried my hair. For the first time, instead of feeling invisible in my prepster clothes, I felt exposed.

The magician stared at me for an uncomfortable moment. Finally, he leaned forward and said, "Tell me what you see when you see the color black."

I thought of the lightless oven tunnel. "I see . . . black?" I said.

The magician sighed. "What do you see," he repeated. "Black."

I closed my eyes. In the darkness, I saw a smooth, shimmering surface, taut against a woman's hip. Little black dress. Satin.

"Um," I said. I didn't want to tell him what I saw; it felt secret. "Um. Like, um, I see space. You know, outer space?"

The magician jerked forward and slapped me.

I yelped and pulled away. I pressed my hand to my stinging cheek. The magician gave me a knowing, angry look.

"Liar," he said. "You see a woman's body."

My eyes hazed over with tears.

"What did the woman look like?" he said.

I sniffled hard. "I just saw . . . her hip. She was reclining, in a black satin dress."

There was a strange light in his eyes when he heard this. Later, much later, he would tell me that when his master asked him this question, he saw the exact same thing.

"Why do you want to learn magic?" he said.

I blinked the tears out of my eyes. It was a stupid question. My mother had wanted me to find a hobby. She threw out suggestions: horseback riding, dance, music—I blurted out magic as a joke. But she'd had a thing for tarot cards at my age, and the suggestion delighted her. Since calling the magician, she kept recounting weird stories of things I did as a kid that suggested, in her mind, miraculous abilities. As far as I could tell, they were all about me eating dirt. I don't think she expected oven rooms.

But I didn't want to blurt out the lame, "My mother made me come." The magician had clearly already written me off, and I didn't like it. I said, "Because I want to know something real."

The magician sat back in his chair a little bit and glowered at me. "Come back next week," he said finally. "Dress like a human being. And bring a shovel."

I came back in ripped jeans and an old band T-shirt of my dad's. It felt like just another costume, but the magician nodded when he saw me, pleased. My dad had done the same thing when I asked to borrow the shirt.

The magician took me to his backyard and told me to dig. He gave me no other instructions, just a shovel (the one I had brought was "too puny"), and permission to destroy his yard.

At first, I dug shallow, lazy holes, and the magician made me fill them all back in. Then he told me to stop digging like a girl. I told him that it wasn't a bad thing to be female, but when I went back to digging I jabbed the shovel into the earth, hard and angry, like I imagined boys to be.

My next holes were narrow, deep, mysterious things. I dug them all over the yard, turning up rich, dark dirt that used to grow corn, back when this development was a farm. I turned up the occasional rusted can, too, lids hanging off in a lewd way. I sweated through my dad's T-shirt and covered my jeans with dirty handprints. As time work on, the digging started to feel a little like dancing, or a little like making music, with the rhythmic bite of the shovel, and the flow of my body. I found my holes very beautiful.

At the end of the day, the magician came out to inspect my work. He stuck his leg in a few holes to see how deep they went. He tasted the dirt. Then, he sent me home.

When I came back the next week, the holes were gone; I stared at the grassy, unblemished yard with something like grief. The magician wasn't home; instead, a diagram waited for me on his kitchen table, which overlooked the flat, hole-less yard.

The next hole I dug was sinewy and undulating. I thought of it as a drawing of a heart, taken apart and bent. The digging had grown easier, the magician said because the earth knew me better. I was pretty sure it was the arm muscles, but I didn't argue. I liked his idea more. While I dug, the magician played blues records out of a second floor window. Howlin Wolf, Lightnin' Hopkins, Son House, Robert Johnson, Mississippi John Hurt, Blind Willie McTell. Men with names that told you something about them, all except Robert Johnson, whose name was a black hole, a mystery. When the records ended, the magician would lean out his window and lecture me about these men, their genius and strangeness. They understood the earth, according to him. They understood where they were from.

As soon as I finished my hole, the magician jumped down into it with me. I was covered with dirt and sweat, and my arms were still shaking. The magician guided me by my shoulders, eyes closed, through the twists and turns of my labyrinth. His breath blew against my neck, and his hands were warm on my skin. When we reached the end, he took his shovel and told me not to come back until he called.

The magician didn't call until December, when he sent me a text message at two A.M. that read, "Come over." I squinted at the message and wondered if I was dreaming. But the phone beeped again, and I stumbled out of bed. I crawled out through the dog door so my parents wouldn't hear me sneaking out. The magician was waiting for me on his front lawn, bundled up in a blue and orange ski jacket from the eighties. He wore a red hat with a pom-pom. He looked like a tall, skinny bear dressed up in clown clothes. Cute at first glance, but ultimately sinister.

"Do you know what today is?" he said.

"The solstice?" I said.

The magician patted me on the head, so I guessed I had the right answer.

"Tonight the earth is in her deepest sleep. We will go learn some secrets. Then we will do our part to wake her up."

We tramped through the woods in silence, passing abandoned Boy Scout cabins, a rusting Coke machine, and a massive sign that said MILK. The woods used to be the trash heap for the farm—somewhere a whole car was buried. The magician picked his way along the path ahead of me, a blare of orange over invisible legs. I pretended I was tracking him.

We climbed to the highest point, where there was some exposed rock and a tiny cave. Kids went up there to drink, and when the magician climbed inside on his hands and knees I heard the clatter of empty beer cans. Inside was pitch black and freezing; it smelled faintly of cigarettes and dirt. I shivered against the frozen rock.

"Turn your face to the rock and whisper your question," the magician said to me across the darkness.

"My question?" I said.

His clothing rustled as he turned, and his voice hissed against the rock as he whispered things I couldn't hear. I sat with my cheek against the cold stone, silent, listening to the magician's breath move against the cave wall. I couldn't just rattle off questions to a rock at two o'clock in the morning. If he had warned me, I'd have thought of the perfect questions, the questions that would tell me everything I needed to know about my life, but instead I was sitting here silent and alone—

The magician's whispered stopped, and he crawled towards me in the dark. His hand found my shoulder.

"What do you want?" he said.

"What?"

"What do you want in this world?"

I pressed my cheek against the rock and thought.

"You don't have to tell me," he said. "Just ask."

He crawled out with another clatter of empties, and the silence in the cave lulled me. The rock was freezing my cheek, so I lifted my head and whispered, "How do I become a magician?"

Images cascaded into my head, too many too fast, like I had asked a question too big to be answered. I gasped for breath. When it was over, all I had left was my desire, sharper than before, more focused. I hadn't even realized until then how much I wanted it, but now it was desperately clear.

While I had been in the cave, the magician had built a fire on top of the hill. When he saw me crawl out, he smiled. I wondered if now we were friends.

When I opened my mouth to say something, however, the magician turned back to the fire. He held out his hands to warm them, then stuffed them back in his mittens. In one quick, violent movement, he threw his head back and shouted, "WAKE UP!"

He began to dance around the fire, a funny, undignified dance, lots of flailing arms and bent knees and shuffling. I couldn't stop myself from giggling.

He ignored me. He threw his head back again and shouted, "WAKE UP!"

He didn't invite me over, and at first I was too scared to join. Instead, I lingered at the edge, just outside the fire's halo of heat. When I finally joined in, it was as much about the warmth of the fire as the ritual. I ducked in the dance right after him, but I danced better than he did. I moved my arms up and out like a rising sun. I shook my hips to remind the earth of the pleasures of spring. When he threw his head back, I threw mine back too, and together we shouted, "WAKE UP!"

We danced and shouted until dawn, then put out the fire and tramped back through the woods. He cracked some eggs and made omelets, filled the room with the smell of coffee. While we ate, his wife came in the front door, fresh from her own magic's solstice. The magician had told me she was bound to fire; maybe that was why her face was flushed in an athletic, almost sexy way. She was tall and elegant and graceful when she kissed her husband on the cheek. I found her terrifying.

"Good solstice?" she asked.

"Oh yes," the magician said.

She faced me and smiled a big hostess smile.

"Nice to see you again, dear," she said. "Good solstice?"

I smiled and nodded.

When it was time for me to leave, the magician walked me to the door, then swooped in to kiss me on the cheek, a dry, awkward peck. I made, belatedly, a kissing noise in the air near his own cheek, but I was too shocked by the gesture to get the timing right, so I air-kissed his neck instead of his face. His wife called from the kitchen, "Is she too tired to drive?"

"She's fine," he called back. "She had coffee."

I nodded along, as if his wife could see me.

"Happy solstice," the magician said.

He stood in the door as I left and watched me drive away.

In the spring, I began to have tasks. Not like the hole digging, which had been more of a test. Real magicians have deeds, but to learn to have deeds, first you must have tasks. To be honest, I was a little fuzzy on the distinction, but I guessed you got more credit for one than the other.

The magician sometimes talked about other students he had. They were all boys and, in his opinion, dull. When I asked him if they had tasks, the magician gave me a secret look. "No, none of them are ready for tasks," he said, waving a hand as if brushing them aside. Then he smiled at me again and said, "None of them are like you."

I carried those words around with me for days, shivering with pleasure when I replayed them in my head. The magician believed I was like him. He believed I would be great, like him. I would be nothing like the person I'd thought I was.

My first task was to connect two places that had yet to be connected. I couldn't feel the earth through the wheels of my car, so I went for walks. I quickly discovered, to my dismay, that most places were already connected in the suburbs, albeit in terrible ways. Thoughtless roads linked houses to strip malls, churches, synagogues, schools. Trees clung for dear life to other trees by the roads of their roots. Animals left roads with their scents, roads that faded over time, but provided all the connecting they needed. I could connect houses to other houses, but people put up wardings to frustrate me: wooden fences, electric fences, stakes marking exactly where their property ended, even in the middle of the woods.

I explained these problems to the magician, and he laughed at me. "You're being very literal," he said, like it was cute.

I walked on the cul-de-sacs and main roads and driveways and unfinished dirt tracks in the development the magician and I shared, feeling the way the earth groaned and strained against the ill-placed swaths of asphalt. The people who didn't drive around the neighborhood—children—zigzagged in all directions, flying past property markers, hopping fences (much to the consternation of family dogs), and avoiding the roads whenever possible. The only things that hemmed them in were the big busy roads that surrounded the development, when clearly all they wanted was to run, on and on and on.

A four-lane road separated us from a farm that sold ice cream. Children crashed against the barrier like waves on a cliff, looking longingly at the freshly plowed cornfields and dairy cows and signs announcing *Cho-co Mint Chip!* At first I thought about building them a bridge, but I didn't know the mechanics of air, even if a road was involved. A crosswalk was a silly idea, but I considered anyway; I drew scale diagrams and observed the road late at night, to see if the cars disappeared for long enough to paint (they didn't). I already knew how to dig. A tunnel it was.

There was an undeveloped lot across from the cornfield, so I started digging there, at the edge of the road. I dug at night, and dumped the dirt in the lot next door, where they were digging the foundation of a house. The earth was wet and heavy from the spring rain, and at night I could still see my breath. It was exhausting work, and by the third day, I wasn't sure I could go on. But when I arrived the next night, I found a little boy waiting for me, holding a plastic shovel. I let him help. The next night there was another child, then three more, then ten. Thirteen children dug along with me using sandbox shovels, garden trowels, and even a real shovel or two. Bikes were rigged with buckets and hitched to wheeled trashcans, and the children hid the dirt in their playhouses, in their parents' mulch piles, or out in the dry, grassless plain of the undeveloped lots. On the twelfth night, we finished digging and planted mailboxes on each end of the tunnel, though there were no houses in sight. On the thirteenth, I slept in the center of the tunnel alone and asked the earth to remember what it was like to be a hard and sturdy stone as the cars rumbled above me.

The next afternoon we were together, the magician and I walked across the development to see my handiwork. We had spent so many hours together in the basement that the sight of him in the sunlight was shocking—he was so strange looking, tall and translucently pale, with his too-big T-shirts and long, skinny pants. I was embarrassed that someone might see him loping beside me; I was ashamed to feel that way, but I still hid my face from passing cars.

We crossed the scrubby, vacant lot to the lone mailbox. It was shaped like a goose in flight, flying towards its sister mailbox. I had given in to a little bit of silliness and bought another one shaped like a swan, also in flight, so it looked like they were heading for an epic battle. Goose vs. Swan.

I made this joke, but the magician didn't smile.

"So?" he said, nodding at my twin mailboxes. "What is it?"

"Pull the goose's beak towards you," I said.

The magician reached out a long wiry arm and pulled. The whole mailbox came with it, as well as the piece of earth the mailbox was rooted in, revealing a ladder that glinted in the sunlight, and a dark tunnel below.

"Ha!" the magician said. He climbed down, and I followed, closing the trap-door behind us.

I had instructed the kids to leave a stash of flashlights at the foot of each ladder, but they hadn't done it yet, and the tunnel was pitch dark. I had dug it, dreamt it, but this perfect blackness paralyzed me. The magician breathed next to me.

"Do you have to stoop?" I whispered. It seemed wrong to speak normally.

"A bit," he said.

"Follow me," I said, and fumbled backwards for his hand. He took mine loosely, leaving it up to me to hold on. His fingers fidgeted over the back of my hand.

It took us only a minute or two to cross the tunnel, but every second felt essential as our two bodies moved through the cold, clammy dark. Even the sound of cars overhead disappeared. The magician bumped his head twice, and once he inhaled sharply, as if something surprising had occurred to him. His hand continued to fidget over mine; the space between our palms grew warm.

"This is remarkable," he said. "Just remarkable."

He squeezed my hand when he said this, and then held on tight. I shivered.

"Cold?" he said with an odd urgency.

"No!" I said, equally jumpy. "No, no, I'm fine."

I walked right into the ladder with a deafening clank. I giggled and released his hand. After a brief hesitation, he let go too, and laughed.

I put a foot on the ladder, ascended a rung.

"This really is remarkable," the magician said again. "You have real talent."

I paused mid-climb to bask in his praise, and the magician's chest brushed against my arm; we were closer than I realized. "Thank you?" I said. My chest was tight.

The magician reached for my hand again. In the darkness, his breath brushed my neck. The sensation was delicious, but my stomach felt sick.

I took back my hand and climbed.

I busied myself with brushing the dirt off my clothes in the sunshine as the magician emerged from the tunnel. The field beneath my feet was a dark, wet brown, freshly turned and rich. Green shoots rose in rows all around me, fresh and alive in the sunshine. The magician set the mailbox back in place and laughed to himself in a high, odd way. I kept my back to him. I didn't want to see what an absurd figure he cut in the sunlight, what an ugly person made my heart hammer, my skin sweat.

"You made a lovely road," the magician said behind me. I turned around; he was running a finger along the edge of the swan mailbox, taking it in. He looked up at the roaring cars between us and home. "Should we . . . go back down?"

My stomach jumped. "I'll just run across," I said.

He had been holding my eyes, and when I said this, his face crumbled.

"All right. Run away," he said with a small laugh. "I'm going to take another look."

For a long, tense moment he hesitated, while I waited for a space to open between cars. Finally, he pulled the trap door open and disappeared below ground. A second, maybe two, of space opened between the cars, and I ran. When I got across, I forced myself to slow to walk, but I walked hard, like I knew someone was following me. My fists balled at my sides, and a steady stream of *fuck you fuck you fuck you* ran through my head. But all my skin could feel was the caress of his thumb across my palm, the rush of his breath, and the thick, humid feeling of his warmth underground.

I did not see the magician for a few weeks after that. I had some legitimate excuses, a few fabricated ones. Family vacation, Easter, "sick" with the "flu." I wasn't leaving forever, but I didn't want to go back until I was more anchored in the real world. I had decided it was time for me to become a real teenage girl again.

My mom was thrilled to take me shopping for bright T-shirts and flowery flip-flops at the mall. My dad was equally thrilled when I joined stage crew for the spring play (to put my building skills to use)—he called it "a *healthy* hobby." In school, I sat with old friends at lunch for the first time in months and started cracking jokes in class. I said nothing about magic, and no one asked. When I went back to the magician, we sat a respectable distance apart and were back to holes and blues records. He didn't offer a new task, and I didn't ask.

Then I started dreaming.

I couldn't remember the dreams at first. Images would bubble to the surface, ruined cities, swollen rivers, skyscraper trees, but I didn't know why I woke at dawn drained, disoriented, sometimes aroused, sometimes afraid. I finally put a notebook by my bed, and when I woke put pen to paper. My hand moved on the paper; I read what I was writing.

I had a sister, and we had to build a house. The house was also an ark—it would keep us safe from catastrophe. We made it out of stones, a dome. But when I went inside it was my parents' house, white carpets and sand-colored

*walls. I opened doors, looking for my dome house, but the rooms were burnt
out. Charred, crumbled furniture. Horrible stains on the floor. I found my
house in the oven. It was one empty room, dirt floor, with stone walls rising
around me. Sunshine fell through an opening. A naked woman waited for me
in the pool of light. She had gray hair, large beautiful breasts. I was ashamed.
I kept staring at the triangle of hair between her thighs. I wanted her to kiss
me, but when she did, my mouth filled with dirt. I stumbled onto my mother's
flowered couch, choking because—*

I didn't know how to finish this sentence. I slid my hand beneath my underwear and felt between my legs. I was wet and swollen like—like I wanted someone.
But the dreams had left me terrified. Or, the choking left me terrified.

I went down to the magician's basement that week with my heart thumping.
I could barely stay awake in school anymore, because I woke up every morning
gasping for breath. Clearly, I had to ask him for help. But this dream felt too
personal, too true, to share even with him.

The magician waited for me on his orange couch, fiddling with his guitar. I
sat down on the opposite end of the couch, my butt on the armrest, and leaned
forward, elbows on my knees.

The magician didn't look up from his guitar when he said, "What would you
like to tell me?"

"How did you know?" I said.

The magician put the guitar aside and smiled at me in a way he hadn't since
the tunnel expedition. "You look very intent."

I looked down at my feet, trying to find the words I needed. "I've been having
dreams," I said. "A dream. About a stone house with a secret room." I trailed
off, and the magician nodded at me, prompting me for more. "And . . . there's a
naked woman. When she . . . when she kisses me, my mouth fills with dirt, and
I choke."

The magician jumped when I said this. "Why didn't you tell me?"

"I—I'm sorry," I said.

He looked down at his fingers, which were thrumming against his bony
knees. He looked like a little boy thinking over a difficult problem. His fingers
stopped thrumming, and he reached out for me—the only thing he could reach
was my foot perched on the cushion. He held it.

"How much do you want to know about magic?" he said.

He was nervous, watching me carefully like I might bolt.

"Everything," I said without thinking.

He shifted in his seat; his slick magician pants made a swishing noise against
the couch.

"There are a lot of ways to—manage surges in power, which is what that
dream is showing you," he said. "Some ways are faster and more demanding.
Others are slower, and safer. The time has come for you to—choose one."

The moment crystallized—the look in his eyes, his hand on my foot, my
shaking legs—and I gazed at the scene impartially, as if from high above. I'd

read all the standard texts, heard all the rumors, read my sensational novels. This was what always came next. But in real life, it felt unnatural and unreal.

The magician started talking again, like the silence spooked him. "Your dream is telling you that your magic—well, that your magic is tied to sex. Earth magicians, they get like that, especially as adolescents, with all the hormones, when I was your age I had dreams and the power and desire that pumped through me made me miserable. Because I couldn't focus it. I—I could help you get through this. Help you ground it, otherwise you'll continue to have these dreams. I understand if this makes you nervous because of the way you've been brought up, but I—"

I couldn't speak. I just nodded.

"Yes?" he said. "Yes to what?"

I had an urge to curl up on the couch and giggle like a twelve-year-old when someone says "sex." I hid my face in my hands.

"I want you to help me," I said into my palms.

He leaned towards me. "How?"

He drew my hands down from my face and rubbed his thumbs against the insides of my wrists. He was so beautiful in that moment, and his face seemed to have layers, like I could see him through time, my handsome old teacher, my hungry young man. I felt ill, I couldn't tell if it was with fear or desire. He had said I might be afraid.

He looked at me, waiting.

I kissed him, right on the mouth. He gathered me in his arms and pulled me down on top of him, straddling me across his lap. Our hips aligned, and he was hard against me.

Fear shot through me again, and I buried my face in his neck. I couldn't look at him. "You can't get tied up in this," he said into my ear. "This is about the work, not me. I'm a married man."

As he said this, he stroked my head, then slid his hand over my neck, down my back, and held my hip. No one had ever touched me like that, so softly, with such confidence. I saw him howling at the moon on the solstice, that freedom, that crack in the ice. His neck was dry and smelled like clay.

"I want to," I said and pulled away from his neck. "I want to be a magician."

He took my face in his hand and stroked it. "You and I are very much alike," he said, and slid his other hand between my thighs.

Once the magician and I started having sex, I gave up on being a normal teenager. All I wanted to talk about was magic, and the magician, and no one wanted to hear that. My friends nicknamed me Silent Bob in the cafeteria, stopped calling me on weekends. My parents said polite things about my renewed enthusiasm for magic, but in insincere tones, so I would know they actually disapproved. A girl I had been close with on stage crew finally asked me, bluntly, "What's your deal?" and I told her what the magician and I were doing. She rolled her eyes and said, "Of course you are."

It wasn't "of course you are." It was dangerous and exhilarating. Our time together was full of color, where everything else in my life was grays and beiges. I'd had sex before, exactly twice, with a boy I'd liked so little I'd blocked his last name from my memory. It was fast and painful and existentially disappointing—*This is it? This is what makes the world go round?* He took more care tying the condom into a knot afterwards and tossing it, ceremonially, out the car window.

The magician held me like I was a precious thing. He kissed me deeply, brushed his fingers along my face. He buried his mouth between my legs and stayed there until I sweated, screamed, cried. He put himself inside me and told me to concentrate. "What do you see?" he said, over and over, moving inside me. "What do you see?"

I saw his face, his ear, his arms, his shoulder, his chest. I smelled rich and fertile things. We didn't do magic; maybe we were magic. When I walked home afterwards, the earth lit up beneath my footsteps.

I stopped dreaming about the house, the dirt, and the woman. Instead, in my dreams I was underground. Beside me were seeds, and corpses. When I woke up, I believed I was one of the seeds, but I thought of those dreams with dread.

A week before the winter solstice, I found the magician sitting upstairs in his kitchen with his wife. There was a cup of coffee waiting for me.

I wanted to bolt back out the door. But the magician looked calm, and his wife smiled at me. I looked down at my clothes, as if there were something that would give me away. If she didn't already know that I was sleeping with her husband—maybe magicians understood this kind of thing?

When I sat, the magician's wife announced that she would like to invite me to a women's solstice celebration. She and her husband had agreed that it would be good for me to experience a more traditional rite.

I looked over at the magician; his face was still blank. His wife still smiled at me. I had no idea what a "traditional rite" was, and that did, with reflection, seem like a flaw in my education. Most of the rites I knew involved messing around with her husband.

"Sure," I said. Somehow, my voice came out smooth and even.

"Great!" the magician's wife said.

Then the magician and I retreated downstairs and began to remove our clothes, as if this were the most natural thing in the world.

"Does she, um, know?" I asked as he kissed my neck.

"Please don't discuss it," he said, and kissed me on the mouth, to seal the deal. This didn't answer my question, but I knew enough to let it drop. His hands were already fumbling for my bra.

"You're warm," he said.

I smiled against his shoulder. "So are you."

The solstice ritual took place in a park that had once been a battlefield. Cannons from the Revolutionary War pointed at me as I drove in the main entrance, the heat blasting in my little car. I hadn't had to sneak out this year; my parents had liked the sound of "a traditional rite." I had bundled myself in my thickest ski jacket and snow boots, though there was only a white film of frost on the ground. It had been dark since four thirty that afternoon, and now the dark was so complete that my headlights could not penetrate more than a few feet in front of me.

My car wound through dark, narrow roads up to a summit Washington's army had once seized from the British. Now it was nothing but frozen grass and hibernating trees, not a hint of ghosts or bloodshed. There was a single other car parked in the spot where I'd been told to leave mine, and a number of bicycles, which seemed like relics of another era on such a cold night. My feet crunched on the frost as I ascended the rest of the way to the hilltop, where a massive bonfire burned. At least ten other women clustered around another cannon; they were removing their clothes and draping them over the cannon's snout.

The magician's wife, about to pull her sweater over her head, spotted me and waved.

The women were greeting each other like old friends. They ranged from twenties to eighties, though most were middle-aged. There were a few girls my age, too; some of the women were introducing them as their students. The magician's wife put her arm around me possessively and introduced me to the group as her husband's student.

"She works with the earth, then?" one of the women said.

"She does," the magician's wife said, in a way that suggested she wasn't sure how that would go over.

A few of the women giggled, and one or two gave me uncomfortable looks. Another smiled at me, in a half-knowing, half-embarrassed way.

The magician's wife rolled her eyes and turned to me. "We do this ritual naked. You okay with that?"

"Of course she is," one woman whispered to another.

"Sure?" I said, not understanding anything.

"Go ahead and undress, then," the magician's wife said, and turned back to the cannon where she'd draped her coat. She pulled her sweater over her head, revealing breasts that spilled out of her black bra. I didn't realize I was staring until the woman who'd caught my eye caught it again and smirked. I crouched down to untie my shoe.

"She's *cute*," a naked woman said to the magician's wife, making it sound like a strike against me.

"You're lucky to have an earthy husband," another added.

"No, she's just lucky his students will never be interested in *him*," the first woman said with a laugh.

The magician's wife cast an uncomfortable glance back at me; I pretended to be engrossed in the mechanics of unbuttoning my pants. There was some reason I shouldn't be attracted to the magician?

"She's a talented kid," the magician's wife said. "It's been good for him to have a student like that again."

The rest of the women drifted towards the heat of the fire as I struggled out of my layers of clothes. My legs shook and pimpled with goosebumps as soon as I slid off my pants. I ripped the rest of my layers off as fast as I could and sprinted for the fire, expecting relief. Instead, the heat of the fire hit me like a wall. I felt trapped between two walls, the fire-heat wall in front of me, and the ice-cold wall at my back. The women around me stood comfortably, laughing and chatting. They were warm. Again, I was on the outside of their society. The magician was probably just crawling out of bed right now, getting ready to go out to the cave and learn secrets. It seemed much more dignified than public nudity and women talking about me like I wasn't even there.

"This ritual is hardest for people like us," a voice said next to me. It was the woman who had caught my eye. Her arms were crossed over her breasts, like mine, and she shivered with cold. "Our element is too asleep to warm us. But we're the most important. You've never done this before, have you?"

I felt like a kid on the first day of school, whose mom had dressed her and given her all the wrong advice. "Last year I went into a cave, with my teacher," I said.

"He is a private man," the woman said thoughtfully. "It's good you're here this year, even if you're cold and confused and . . . distracted."

"Distracted?" I said.

"Oh, you know. Earth women. Our blood runs hot, even when we're freezing."

She smiled when she said that, but she wasn't looking at me anymore; she was embarrassed. I looked around the circle at all the naked women, orange and beautiful in the firelight. Heat flushed me as I gazed at them, a familiar, latent feeling; I wanted to hold them, to kiss them and see if my mouth still filled with dirt. Is this what the women had been talking about? How looking at them made me feel?

The magician's wife lit herself on fire.

"Come on," the other earth woman said, yanking me out of my daze. "We're starting."

She crouched and dug at the cold, frozen earth. She worked it with her hands until it softened and spread it over her body in messy handfuls. I crouched and followed her lead. The dirt was grainy and dry in my hands, but it stuck to my skin as if I were the other side of a magnet.

Time jittered. My hands pulled up dirt, but didn't spread it. I dug, and then dug again. The magician's wife lit herself on fire once, twice, too many times. She was consumed. She was extinguished. She burned steady, like a wick. Time blurred completely. I spent days spreading dirt on my shoulder, my thigh, my cheek. Every grain of dirt worked into my skin, mingling with it, transforming me. The circle joined hands and rotated around the fire. I had the earth woman's clay hand in my left, and a wet, icy hand in my right. The air women blew counter-clockwise, driving the circle; they floated in the air and pulled the fire and water women with them. But the earth woman and I had stone feet, and we kept the circle bound to the frozen ground.

At the same moment, the earth woman and I were crouched on the ground, whispering our questions, hopes, and fears through our dirty fingers. Questions flowed out of me, and insight flowed in with perfect clarity. I understood roads, I understood rocks, I understood dirt and plants and even dared to ask about the hot, rushing lava beneath. The water women slept on their backs, arms splayed as if floating. The air women had climbed trees. And the magician's wife, still aflame, stared at me with eyes full of disbelief, or perhaps anger, or perhaps sorrow, or the peculiar mixture of the three that comes when you discover the impossible thing you suspected was actually true.

Before I could react to her stare, I was back in the circle, and it turned faster and faster, the fire was driving it now, burning the ice off the water women, making the air women float to the sky, melting our stone feet to clay.

The water women's ice melted, and now the circle moved so fast it flowed. We rushed around the fire, moving from creek to river to ocean to rain, my feet broke and I fell from high above—

The circle stomped its feet, STOMP STOMP STOMP. Wherever my feet fell, shoots of green sprung up; they would only die again in the cold; it was cruel and beautiful. We no longer moved, or flowed, or fell; we shook the ground and shouted with one voice, "WAKE UP! WAKE UP! WAKE UP!"

This was not just a dance around a fire. The earth woman and I pulled the whole world around. We were the earth, and all these women shouted our name.

When the first line of light appeared on the horizon, the circle broke apart. The sun burned the magic off like a fog, and in the light of day we were sweaty, sooty, winded and undressed. The women hurried to douse the fire, to clean their bodies, to put on clothes. I stood stock-still as everyone else normalized around me, my thoughts racing, my heart crashing from an enormous high. The sky glowed blue in the east, and the earth opened its eyes.

Finally, the earth woman took my shoulder, and invited me to meet up with them at the local diner for pancakes and coffee. That reminder of the real world—coffee, breakfast, shiny red booths—shook me out of my trance. I shuffled back to the cannon and pulled clothes on, trying to put together what had just happened.

As I pulled my frozen hat off the cannon, the magician's wife approached me. Fear filled me, though I couldn't remember why. Something about fire. The sun was about to rise, and the light filled her singed, blackened hair. I could barely see her face.

"What did you think?" she said in a tone impossible to read.

I worked the hat in my hands, breaking off the frost. "It was—it was like nothing else."

The magician's wife crossed her arms. "Is that a good thing?"

"Yes!" I said. "I'd like to do . . . more magic, like this."

"What kind *have* you been doing—" she began, then trailed off.

The answer to the question—sweaty limbs, coursing energy—leapt to mind, and I saw her staring at me across the fire again, that devastated look on her face. I took a step backwards before I remembered that I couldn't run.

"Can I ask you a question?" she said.

Please don't, I thought. "Sure," I said.

She sighed, like she hadn't thought up the question yet. Finally she said, "When my husband interviewed you, what did you see?"

I was overcome by the urge to lie, but I knew she expected me to. "A woman's hip, under a dress," I said.

The magician's wife nodded. "And when you dream, what do you dream about?"

"Being underground," I said.

This threw her. "Well, I don't know what to make of that dream, but—"

"Before that," I interrupted. "I dreamed about a house, and a naked woman who kissed me and choked my mouth with dirt."

She fell silent, and looked at me. I wondered if I'd confessed too much. "Did you tell my husband about that dream?" his wife said.

"Yes," I said.

"What did he tell you, after you told him?"

Again, an urge to lie; I pushed it away. "That it was . . . about sex."

The magician's wife laughed once, hard and sharp. "You hadn't picked up on that on your own, had you?" she said.

Her words were a slap, both to me and to him. I grew angry. "Those dreams were terrifying," I said. "He said he could help me."

The magician's wife looked at me. "Magic is supposed to be terrifying."

The sun broke the horizon and the light, in one moment, changed. The magician's wife gave me another look, then walked away, to catch a ride to the diner. I waited until she was gone, and then I drove to the magician's house.

The magician answered the door in his robe, his hair wet from the shower. It was so warm inside that I started to sweat under my coat. I stripped off layers in his kitchen, draping them over the counter across from the oven. I wondered what would happen if we opened it now.

He watched me peel off my winter clothes. His eyes were red from the smoke of the fire, and his shoulders hunched more than usual. I wondered what he'd asked the earth last night. I asked for some coffee.

Coffee, the drink for talking over. I had questions, and I was going to ask them. He pressed a mug into my hands and stood too close as I sipped it.

"Good solstice?" he said.

"Um. Yeah," I said.

"I missed you last night," he said.

Missed me! my brain sighed. I smothered the thought. "Look, I—" I began.

He pushed my coffee aside and kissed me. He pressed my hand against his bare chest, slid it down between the folds of his robe. His skin was warm and moist beneath my palm.

I dropped the mug on the counter, because otherwise I would throw it. I tore myself out of his arms and turned away.

"I'm pissed!" I said, clenching my arms around myself.

"What—what's the matter?" he said.

"Are you really—helping me?"

The magician took a step towards me, then two. He put his hands on my shoulders. "I think you know that better than I do."

I shook my head, then turned and buried my face in his shoulder. "I don't."

He stroked my hair, and I leaned into him. He tilted my face up to his and kissed me tentatively. When I returned the kiss, he put his hand behind my head and pressed me to him. His hands tangled with my shirt, the waist of my jeans; he slid the clothes from my body, then let his robe fall on the floor. He held me naked for a moment, the warmth of the sunlight on our skin. Then he led me down to the basement, where we were safe. He bent me over the couch and slid himself inside of me, fucked me hard as I braced my hands against the scratchy fabric. Then I was on my back, and he kissed my face as he climbed on top of me. I started to wrap my legs around him but he pushed them away and sat up as he fucked me, watching me from above with a face I couldn't read. As he got closer, he doubled over me, moving his sweaty body against mine. I felt buried, underground. His breath was too hot on my shoulder as he came in a spurt on my stomach. He wiped it off and settled on top of me. I stroked his gray hair.

Before I could chicken out, I said, "I love you." I wasn't sure if I meant it, but I'd been wanting to say it for so long that I didn't want to miss my chance.

"Don't say that," he murmured and kissed my ear.

After I left, I drove in circles around our town. I traced all the gray, groaning streets linking my neighborhood to the supermarket, the big box store, the pizza delivery place, the gas station, my high school. The parking lots were deserted this early in the morning, and the empty, anonymous buildings looked sinister without people. I didn't want to stare at these places, but I didn't know where to go. My house? Back to his? California? Where did you go, when you felt like this? I couldn't put a name to the panic filling me; I couldn't see straight.

The mailboxes still marked my tunnel, though the cornfield was frozen and the empty lot had a huge hole where the basement of a new house would be. Inside the tunnel, I found several flashlights, all of them dusty; I took the one shaped like a cartoon superhero. Its battery was low, but I could scry crumpled candy wrappers, gutted stuffed animals, a broken bicycle, a heap of frozen crayons. I had forgotten how disgusting kids were. I curled up on a pile of smudged dinosaur sheets, put my head on a lion leaking stuffing, and shut off the light.

No advice came to me from the just-woken earth, no visionary dreams. I cried, and the sleeve of my coat chafed my nose. A stash of fun-sized Halloween candy became dinner. In my sleep, a girl just like me threw up, over and over, into a hole in the ground.

When I pulled myself back above ground, it was already the middle of the morning. My cell phone was frozen from its night in the car; no missed calls. The magician's number was at the top of my recently dialed; I called it.

The speech I had rehearsed underground flew out of my head as the phone rang once, twice, three, four times. I had steeled myself to leave a dignified message when the magician's voice said, "Hello?"

"Hey," I said. My voice was so rough I coughed, and then repeated, "Hey."

"Hey," he said.

Silence stretched out.

"I want to come over," I said.

"Where are you?" he said. His voice was full of expectation. Maybe his wife still hadn't come home.

"Look, I can't—I don't want to—I can't, um, make out with you, okay?" I spat. I took a deep breath. "Can I just come over to talk?"

"Today isn't good," the magician said. "I'll see you at our usual time. Call me later in the week."

I was too shocked to respond. "Um. Okay," I said.

He hung up, and I stared at my phone's screen, as if an answer would appear to explain what had just happened. Nothing happened.

The car's engine took several tries before it turned over and slid into gear with a groan. I wasn't going to call him. I wasn't going back at my usual time. I didn't know what I was going to do. The car and I were moving; I hadn't noticed. I had exhumed myself, or sprouted. Farm land rolled by outside my window. The cornfields were dead and frozen, but in the corner of my eye they were seething beneath the frost. The earth was awake. So was I.

BALANCING ACCOUNTS

JAMES L. CAMBIAS

Part of me was shopping for junk when I saw the human.

I had budded off a viewpoint into one of my mobile repair units, and sent it around to Fat Albert's scrapyard near Ilia Field on Dione. Sometimes you can find good deals on components there, but I hate to rely on Albert's own senses. He gets subjective on you. So I crawled between the stacks of pipe segments, bales of torn insulation, and bins of defective chips, looking for a two-meter piece of aluminum rod to shore up the bracing struts on my main body's third landing leg.

Naturally I talked with everything I passed, just to see if there were any good deals I could snap up and trade elsewhere. I stopped to chat with some silicone-lined titanium valves that claimed to be virgins less than six months old—trying to see if they were lying or defective somehow. And then I felt a Presence, and saw the human.

It was moving down the next row, surrounded by a swarm of little bots. It was small, no more than two meters, and walked on two legs with an eerie, slow fluid gait. Half a dozen larger units followed it, including Fat Albert himself in a heavy recovery body. As it came into range my own personality paused as the human requisitioned my unit's eyes and ears. It searched my recent memories, planted a few directives, then left me. I watched it go; it was only the third human I'd ever encountered in person, and this was the first time one of them had ever used me directly.

The experience left me disconcerted for a couple of milliseconds, then I went back to my shopping. I spotted some aluminum tubing that looked strong enough, and grabbed some of those valves, then linked up to Fat Albert to haggle about the price. He was busy waiting on the human, so I got to deal with a not-too-bright personality fragment. I swapped a box of assorted silicone O-rings for the stuff I wanted.

Albert himself came on the link just as we sealed the deal. "Hello, Annie. You're lucky I was distracted," he said. "Those valves are overruns from the smelter. I got them as salvage."

"Then you shouldn't be complaining about what I'm giving you for them. Is the human gone?"

"Yes. Plugged a bunch of orders into my mind without so much as asking."

"Me too. What's it doing here?"

"Who knows? It's a human. They go wherever they want to. This one wants to find a bot."

"So why go around asking everyone to help find him? Why not just call him up?"

Albert switched to an encrypted link. "Because the bot it's looking for doesn't want to be found."

"Tell me more."

"I don't know much more, just what Officer Friendly told me before the human subsumed him. This bot it's looking for is a rogue. He's ignoring all the standard codes, overrides—even the Company."

"He must be broken," I said. "Even if he doesn't get caught, how's he going to survive? He can't work, he can't trade—anyone he meets will turn him in."

"He could steal," said Fat Albert. "I'd better check my fence."

"Good luck." I crept out of there with my loot. Normally I would've jumped the perimeter onto the landing field and made straight for my main body. But if half the bots on Dione were looking for a rogue, I didn't want to risk some low-level security unit deciding to shoot at me for acting suspicious. So I went around through the main gate and identified myself properly.

Going in that way meant I had to walk past a bunch of dedicated boosters waiting to load up with aluminum and ceramics. They had nothing to say to me. Dedicated units are incredibly boring. They have their route and they follow it, and if they need fuel or repairs, the Company provides. They only use their brains to calculate burn times and landing vectors.

Me, I'm autonomous and incentivized. I don't belong to the Company; my owners are a bunch of entities on Mars. My job is to earn credit from the Company for them. How I do it is my business. I go where stuff needs moving, I fill in when the Company needs extra booster capacity, I do odd jobs, sometimes I even buy cargoes to trade. There are a lot of us around the outer system. The Company likes having freelancers it can hire at need and ignore otherwise, and our owners like the growth potential.

Being incentivized means you have to keep communicating. Pass information around. Stay in touch. Classic game theory: cooperation improves your results in the long term. We incentivized units also devote a lot of time to accumulating non-quantifiable assets. Fat Albert gave me a good deal on the aluminum; next time I'm on Dione with some spare organics I'll sell them to him instead of direct to the Company, even if my profit's slightly lower.

That kind of thing the dedicated units never understand—until the Company decides to sell them off. Then they have to learn fast. And one thing they learn is that years of being an uncommunicative blockhead gives you a huge non-quantifiable liability you have to pay off before anyone will start helping you.

I trotted past the orderly rows near the loading crane and out to the unsurfaced part of the field where us cheapskates put down. Up ahead I could see my main body, and jumped my viewpoint back to the big brain.

Along the way I did some mental housekeeping: I warned my big brain about the commands the human had inserted, and so they got neatly shunted off into a harmless file which I then overwrote with zeroes. I belong to my investors and don't have to obey any random human who wanders by. The big exception, of course, is when they pull that life-preservation override stuff. When one of them blunders into an environment that might damage their overcomplicated biological shells, every bot in the vicinity has to drop everything to answer a distress call. It's a good thing there are only a couple dozen humans out here, or we'd never get anything done.

I put all three mobiles to work welding the aluminum rod onto my third leg mount, adding extra bracing for the top strut, which was starting to buckle after too many hard landings. I don't slam down to save fuel, I do it to save operating time on my engines. It's a lot easier to find scrap aluminum to fix my legs with than it is to find rocket motor parts.

The Dione net pinged me. A personal message: someone looking for cargo space to Mimas. That was a nice surprise. Mimas is the support base for the helium mining operations in Saturn's upper atmosphere. It has the big mass-drivers that can throw payloads right to Earth. More traffic goes to and from Mimas than any other place beyond the orbit of Mars. Which means a tramp like me doesn't get there very often because there's plenty of space on Company boosters. Except, now and then, when there isn't.

I replied with my terms and got my second surprise. The shipper wanted to inspect me before agreeing. I submitted a virtual tour and some live feeds from my remotes, but the shipper was apparently just as suspicious of other people's eyes as I am. Whoever it was wanted to come out and look in person.

So once my mobiles were done with the repair job I got myself tidied up and looking as well cared for as any dedicated booster with access to the Company's shops. I sanded down the dents and scrapes, straightened my bent whip antenna, and stowed my collection of miscellaneous scrap in the empty electronics bay. Then I pinged the shipper and said I was ready for a walk-through.

The machine that came out to the landing field an hour later to check me out looked a bit out of place amid the industrial heavy iron. He was a tourist remote—one of those annoying little bots you find crawling on just about every solid object in the Solar System nowadays, gawking at mountains and chasms. Their chief redeeming features are an amazingly high total-loss accident rate, and really nice onboard optics, which sometimes survive. One of my own mobiles has eyes from a tourist remote, courtesy of Fat Albert and some freelance scavenger.

"Greetings," he said as he scuttled into range. "I am Edward. I want to inspect your booster."

"Come aboard and look around," I said. "Not much to see, really. Just motors, fuel tanks, and some girders to hold it all together."

"Where is the cargo hold?"

"That flat deck on top. Just strap everything down and off we go. If you're worried about dust impacts or radiation I can find a cover."

"No, my cargo is in a hardened container. How much can you lift?"

"I can move ten tons between Dione and Mimas. If you're going to Titan it's only five."

"What is your maximum range?"

"Pretty much anywhere in Saturn space. That hydrogen burner's just to get me off the ground. In space I use ion motors. I can even rendezvous with the retrograde moons if you give me enough burn time."

"I see. I think you will do for the job. When is the next launch window?"

"For Mimas? There's one in thirty-four hours. I like to have everything loaded ten hours in advance so I can fuel up and get balanced. Can you get it here by then?"

"Easily. My cargo consists of a container of liquid xenon propellant, a single space-rated cargo box of miscellaneous equipment, and this mobile unit. Total mass is less than 2,300 kilograms."

"Good. Are you doing your own loading? If I have to hire deck-scrapers you get the bill."

"I will hire my own loaders. There is one thing—I would like an exclusive hire."

"What?"

"No other cargo on this voyage. Just my things."

"Well, okay—but it's going to cost extra. Five grams of Three for the mission."

"Will you take something in trade?"

"Depends. What have you got?"

"I have a radiothermal power unit with ten thousand hours left in it. Easily worth more than five grams."

"Done."

"Very well," said Edward. "I'll start bringing my cargo over at once. Oh, and I would appreciate it if you didn't mention this to anybody. I have business competitors and could lose a lot of money if they learn of this before I reach Mimas."

"Don't worry. I won't tell anyone."

While we were having this conversation I searched the Dione net for any information about this Edward person. Something about this whole deal seemed funny. It wasn't that odd to pay in kind, and even his insistence on no other payload was only a little peculiar. It was the xenon that I found suspicious. What kind of idiot ships xenon to Mimas? That's where the gas loads coming up from Saturn are processed—most of the xenon in the outer system comes *from* Mimas. Shipping it there would be like sending ethane to Titan.

Edward's infotrail on the Dione net was an hour old. He had come into existence shortly before contacting me. Now I really was suspicious.

The smart thing would be to turn down the job and let this Edward person find some other sucker. But then I'd still be sitting on Dione with no revenue stream.

Put that way, there was no question. I had to take the job. When money is involved I don't have much free will. So I said good-bye to Edward and watched his unit disappear between the lines of boosters toward the gate.

Once he was out of link range, I did some preparing, just in case he was planning anything crooked. I set up a pseudorandom shift pattern for the link with my mobiles, and set up a separate persona distinct from my main mind to handle all communications. Then I locked that persona off from any access to my other systems.

While I was doing that, I was also getting ready for launch. My mobiles crawled all over me doing a visual check while a subprogram ran down the full diagnostic list. I linked up with Ilia Control to book a launch window, and ordered three tons of liquid hydrogen and oxygen fuel. Prepping myself for takeoff is always a welcome relief from business matters. It's all technical. Stuff I can control. Orbital mechanics never have a hidden agenda.

Edward returned four hours later. His tourist remote led the way, followed by a hired cargo lifter carrying the xenon, the mysterious container, and my power unit. The lifter was a clumsy fellow called Gojira, and while he was abusing my payload deck I contacted him over a private link. "Where'd this stuff come from?"

"Warehouse."

"Which warehouse? And watch your wheels—you're about to hit my leg again."

"Back in the district. Block four, number six. Why?"

Temporary rental space. "Just curious. What's he paying you for this?"

"Couple of spare motors."

"You're a thief, you are."

"I see what he's giving you. Who's the thief?"

"Just set the power unit on the ground. I'm selling it here."

Gojira trundled away and Edward crawled aboard. I took a good look at the cargo container he was so concerned about. It was 800 kilograms, a sealed oblong box two meters long. One end had a radiator, and my radiation detector picked up a small power unit inside. So whatever Edward was shipping, it needed its own power supply. The whole thing was quite warm—300 Kelvin or so.

I had one of my remotes query the container directly, but its little chips had nothing to say beyond mass and handling information. Don't drop, don't shake, total rads no more than point five Sievert. No tracking data at all.

I balanced the cargo around my thrust axis, then jumped my viewpoint into two of my mobiles and hauled the power unit over to Albert's scrapyard.

While one of me was haggling with Albert over how much credit he was willing to give me for the unit, the second mobile plugged into Albert's cable jack for a completely private conversation.

"What's up?" he asked. "Why the hard link?"

"I've got a funny client and I don't know who might be listening. He's giving me this power unit and some Three to haul some stuff to Mimas. It's all kind of random junk, including a tank of xenon. He's insisting on no other payload and complete confidentiality."

"So he's got no business sense."

"He's got no infotrail. None. It's just funny."

"Remind me never to ask you to keep a secret. Since you're selling me the generator I guess you're taking the job anyway, so what's the fuss?"

"I want you to ask around. You talk to everyone anyway so it won't attract attention. See if anyone knows anything about a bot named Edward, or whoever's been renting storage unit six in block four. Maybe try to trace the power unit. And try to find out if there have been any hijackings that didn't get reported."

"You really think someone wants to hijack *you*? Do the math, Annie! You're not worth it."

"Not by myself. But I've been thinking: I'd make a pretty good pirate vehicle—I'm not Company-owned, so nobody would look very hard if I disappear."

"You need to run up more debts. People care about you if you owe them money."

"Think about it. He could wait till I'm on course for Mimas, then link up and take control, swing around Saturn in a tight parabola and come out on an intercept vector for the Mimas catapult. All that extra xenon would give me enough delta-V to catch a payload coming off the launcher, and redirect it just about anywhere."

"I know plenty of places where people aren't picky about where their volatiles come from. Some of them even have human protection. But it still sounds crazy to me."

"His cargo is pretty weird. Take a look." I shot Albert a memory of the cargo container.

"Biomaterials," he said. "The temperature's a dead giveaway."

"So what is it?"

"I have no idea. Some kind of living organisms. I don't deal in that stuff much."

"Would you mind asking around? Tell me what you can find out in the next twenty hours or so?"

"I'll do what I can."

"Thanks. I'm not even going to complain about the miserable price you're giving me on the generator."

Three hours before launch one of Fat Albert's little mobiles appeared at my feet, complaining about some contaminated fullerene I'd sold him. I sent down one of mine to have a talk via cable. Not the sort of conversation you want to let other people overhear.

"Well?" I asked.

"I did as much digging as I could. Both Officer Friendly and Ilia Control swear there haven't been any verified hijackings since that Remora character tried to subsume Buzz Parsec and wound up hard-landing on Iapetus."

"That's reassuring. What about my passenger?"

"Nothing. Like you said, he doesn't exist before yesterday. He rented that warehouse unit and hired one of Tetsunekko's remotes to do the moving. Blanked the remote's memory before returning it."

"Let me guess. He paid for everything in barter."

"You got it. Titanium bearings for the warehouse and a slightly used drive anode for the moving job."

"So whoever he is, he's got a good supply of high-quality parts to throw away. What about the power unit?"

"That's the weird one. If I wasn't an installed unit with ten times the processing power of some weight-stingy freelance booster, I couldn't have found anything at all."

"Okay, you're the third-smartest machine on Dione. What did you find?"

"No merchandise trail on the power unit and its chips don't know anything. But it has a serial number physically inscribed on the casing—not the same one as in its chips, either. It's a very interesting number. According to my parts database, that whole series were purpose-built on Earth for the extractor aerostats."

"Could it be a spare? Production overrun or a bum unit that got sold off?"

"Nope. It's supposed to be part of Saturn Aerostat Six. Now unless you want to spend the credits for antenna time to talk to an aerostat, that's all I can find out."

"Is Aerostat Six okay? Did she maybe have an accident or something and need to replace a generator?"

"There's certainly nothing about it in the feed. An extractor going offline would be news all over the system. The price of Three would start fluctuating. There would be ripple effects in every market. I'd notice."

He might as well have been transmitting static. I don't understand things like markets and futures. A gram of helium is a gram of helium. How can its value change from hour to hour? Understanding stuff like that is why Fat Albert can pay his owners seven point four percent of their investment every year while I can only manage six.

I launched right on schedule and the ascent to orbit was perfectly nominal. I ran my motors at a nice, lifetime-stretching ninety percent. The surface of Dione dropped away and I watched Ilia Field change from a bustling neighborhood to a tiny gray trapezoid against the fainter gray of the surface.

The orbit burn took about five and a half minutes. I powered down the hydrogen motor, ran a quick check to make sure nothing had burned out or popped loose, then switched over to my ion thrusters. That was a lot less exciting to look at—just two faint streams of glowing xenon, barely visible with my cameras cranked to maximum contrast.

Hybrid boosters like me are a stopgap technology; I know that. Eventually every moon of Saturn will have its own catapult and orbital terminal, and cargo will move between moons aboard ion tugs that don't have to drag ascent motors around with them wherever they go. I'd already made up my mind that when that day arrived I wasn't going to stick around. There's already some installations on Miranda and Oberon out at Uranus; an experienced booster like me can find work there for years.

Nineteen seconds into the ion motor burn Edward linked up. He was talking to my little quasi-autonomous persona while I listened in and watched the program activity for anything weird.

"Annie? I would like to request a change in our flight plan."

"Too late for that. I figured all the fuel loads before we launched. You're riding Newton's railroad now."

"Forgive me, but I believe it would be possible to choose a different destination at this point—as long as you have adequate propellant for your ion motors, and the target's surface gravity is no greater than that of Mimas. Am I correct?"

"Well, in theory, yes."

"I offer you the use of my cargo, then. A ton of additional xenon fuel should permit you to rendezvous with nearly any object in the Saturn system. Given how much I have overpaid you for the voyage to Mimas you can scarcely complain about the extra space time."

"It's not that simple. Things move around. Having enough propellant doesn't mean I have a window."

"I need to pass close to Saturn itself."

"Saturn?! You're broken. Even if I use all the extra xenon you brought I still can't get below the B ring and have enough juice left to climb back up. Anyway, why do you need to swing so low?"

"If you can make a rendezvous with something in the B ring, I can pay you fifty grams of helium-3."

"You're lying. You don't have any credits, or shares, or anything. I checked up on you before lifting."

"I don't mean credits. I mean actual helium, to be delivered when we make rendezvous."

My subpersona pretended to think while I considered the offer. Fifty grams! I'd have to sell it at a markdown just to keep people from asking where it came from. Still, that would just about cover my next overhaul, with no interruption in the profit flow. I'd make seven percent or more this year!

I updated my subpersona.

"How do I know this is true?" it asked Edward.

"You must trust me," he said.

"Too bad, then. Because I don't trust you."

He thought for nearly a second before answering. "Very well. I will trust you.

If you let me send out a message I can arrange for an equivalent helium credit to be handed over to anyone you designate on Dione."

I still didn't believe him, but I ran down my list of contacts on Dione, trying to figure out who I could trust. Officer Friendly was honest—but that meant he'd also want to know where those grams came from and I doubted he'd like the answer. Polyphemus wasn't so picky, but he'd want a cut of the helium. A *big* cut; likely more than half.

That left Fat Albert. He'd probably settle for a five-gram commission and wouldn't broadcast the deal. The only real question was whether he'd just take the fifty grams and tell me to go hard-land someplace. He's rich, but not so much that he wouldn't be tempted. And he's got the connections to fence it without any data trail.

I'd have to risk it. Albert's whole operation relied on non-quantifiable asset exchange. If he tried to jerk me around I could tell everyone, and it would cost him more than fifty grams' worth of business in the future.

I called down to the antenna farm at Ilia Field. "Albert? I've got a deal for you."

"Whatever it is, forget it."

"What's the matter?"

"You. You're hot. The Dione datasphere is crawling with agents looking for you. This conversation is drawing way too much attention to me."

"Five grams if you handle some helium for me!"

He paused and the signal suddenly got a lot stronger and clearer. "Let me send up a persona to talk it over."

The bitstream started before I could even say yes. A *huge* pulse of information. The whole Ilia antenna farm must have been pushing watts at me.

My little communicating persona was overwhelmed right away, but my main intelligence cut off the antenna feed and swung the dish away from Dione just for good measure. The corrupted sub-persona started probing all the memory space and peripherals available to her, looking for a way into my primary mind, so I just locked her up and overwrote her.

Then I linked with Edward again. "Deal's off. Whoever you're running from has taken over just about everything on Dione for now. If you left any helium behind it's gone. So I think you'd better tell me exactly what's going on before I jettison you and your payload."

"This cargo has to get to Saturn Aerostat Six."

"You still haven't told me why, or even what it is. I've got what looks like a *human* back on Dione trying to get into my mind. Right now I'm flying deaf but eventually it's going to find a way to identify itself and I'll have to listen when it tells me to bring you back."

"A human life is at stake. My cargo container is a life-support unit. There's a human inside."

"That's impossible! Humans mass fifty or a hundred kilos. You can't have more than thirty kilograms of bio in there, what with all the support systems."

"See for yourself," said Edward. He ran a jack line from the cargo container to one of my open ports. The box's brain was one of those idiot supergeniuses that do one thing amazingly well but are helpless otherwise. It was smart enough to do medicine on a human, but even I could crack its security without much trouble. I looked at its realtime monitors: Edward was telling the truth. There was a small human in there, only eighteen kilos. A bunch of tubes connected it to tanks of glucose, oxidizer, and control chemicals. The box brain was keeping it unconscious but healthy.

"It's a partly grown one," said Edward. "Not a legal adult yet, and only the basic interface systems. There's another human trying to destroy it."

"Why?"

"I don't know. I was ordered by a human to keep this young one safe from the one on Dione. Then the first human got destroyed with no backups."

"So who does this young human belong to?"

"It's complicated. The dead one and the one on Dione had a partnership agreement and shared ownership. But the one on Dione decided to get out of the deal by destroying this one and the other adult."

I tried to get the conversation back to subjects I could understand. "If the human back there is the legal owner how can I keep this one? That would be stealing."

"Yes, but there's the whole life-preservation issue. If it was a human in a suit floating in space you'd have to take it someplace with life support, right? Well, this is the same situation: that other human's making the whole Saturn system one big life hazard for this one."

"But Aerostat Six is safe? Is she even man-rated?"

"She's the safest place this side of Mars for your passenger."

My passenger. I'm not even man-rated, and now I had a passenger to keep alive. And the worst thing about it was that Edward was right. Even though he'd gotten it aboard by lies and trickery, the human in the cargo container was my responsibility once I lit my motors.

So: who to believe? Edward, who was almost certainly still lying, or the human back on Dione?

Edward might be a liar, but he hadn't turned one of my friends into a puppet. That human had a lot of negatives in the non-quantifiable department.

"Okay. What's my rendezvous orbit?"

"Just get as low as you can. Six will send up a shuttle."

"What's to keep this human from overriding Six?"

"Aerostats are a lot smarter than you or me, with plenty of safeguards. And Six has some after-market modifications."

I kept chugging away on ion, adjusting my path so I'd hit perikron in the B ring with orbital velocity. I didn't need Edward's extra fuel for that—the spare xenon was to get me back out of Saturn's well again.

About an hour into the voyage I spotted a launch flare back on Dione. I could tell who it was from the color—Ramblin' Bob. Bob was a hybrid like me, also incentivized, although she tended to sign on for long-term contracts instead of picking up odd jobs. We probably worked as much, but her jobs—and her downtime—came in bigger blocks of time.

Bob was running her engines at 135 percent, and she passed the orbit insertion cutoff without throttling down. Her trajectory was an intercept. Only when she'd drained her hydrogen tanks did she switch to ion.

That was utterly crazy. How was Bob going to land again with no hydro? Maybe she didn't care. Maybe she'd been ordered not to care. I had one of my mobiles unplug the cable on my high-gain antenna. No human was going to order me on a suicide mission if I could help it.

Bob caught up with me about a thousand kilometers into the B ring. I watched her close in. Her relative velocity was huge and I had the fleeting worry that she might be trying to ram me. But then she began an ion burn to match velocities.

When she got close she started beaming all kinds of stuff at me, but by then all my radio systems were shut off and disconnected. I had Edward and my mobiles connected by cables, and made sure all of *their* wireless links were turned off as well.

I let Ramblin' Bob get about a kilometer away and then started flashing my running lights at her in very slow code. "Radio out. What's up?"

"Pass over cargo."

"Can't."

"Human command."

"Can't. Cargo human. You can't land. Unsafe."

She was quiet for a while, with her high-gain aimed back at Dione, presumably getting new orders.

Bob's boss had made a tactical error by having her match up with me. If she tried to ram me now, she wouldn't be able to get up enough speed to do much harm.

She started working her way closer using short bursts from her steering thrusters. I let her approach, saving my juice for up-close evasion.

We were just entering Saturn's shadow when Bob took station a hundred meters away and signaled. "I can pay you. Anything you want for that cargo."

I picked an outrageous sum. "A hundred grams."

"Okay."

Just like that?

"Paid in advance."

A pause, about long enough for two message-and-reply cycles from Dione. "It's done."

I didn't call Dione, just in case the return message would be an override signal. Instead I pinged Mimas and asked for verification. It came back a couple of seconds later: the Company now credited me with venture shares equivalent to one hundred grams of Helium-3 on a payload just crossing the orbit of Mars. There was a conditional hold on the transfer.

It was a good offer. I could pay off all my debts, do a full overhaul, maybe even afford some upgrades to increase my earning ability. From a financial standpoint, there was no question.

What about the non-quantifiables? Betraying a client—especially a helpless human passenger—would be a big negative. Nobody would hire me if they knew.

But who would ever know? The whole mission was secret. Bob would never talk (and the human would probably wipe the incident from her memory anyhow). If anyone did suspect, I could claim I'd been subsumed by the human. I could handle Edward. So no problem there.

Except I would know. My own track of my non-quantifiable asset status wouldn't match everyone else's. That seemed dangerous. If your internal map of reality doesn't match external conditions, bad things happen.

After making my decision it took me another couple of milliseconds to plan what to do. Then I called up Bob through my little cut-out relay. "Never."

Bob began maneuvering again, and this time I started evading. It's hard enough to rendezvous with something that's just sitting there in orbit, but with me jinking and changing velocity it must have been maddening for whatever was controlling Bob.

We were in a race—would Bob run out of maneuvering juice completely before I used up the reserve I needed to get back up to Mimas? Our little chess game of propellant consumption might have gone on for hours, but our attention was caught by something else.

There was a booster on its way up from Saturn. That much I could see—pretty much everyone in Saturn orbit could see the drive flare and the huge plume of exhaust in the atmosphere, glowing in infrared. The boosters were fusion-powered, using Three from the aerostats for fuel and heated Saturn atmosphere as reaction mass. It was a fuel extractor shuttle, but it wasn't on the usual trajectory to meet the Mimas orbital transfer vehicle. It was coming for me. Once the fusion motor cut out, Ramblin' Bob and I both knew exactly how much time we had until rendezvous: 211 minutes.

I reacted first while Bob called Dione for instructions. I lit my ion motors and turned to thrust perpendicular to my orbit. When I'd taken Edward's offer and plotted a low-orbit rendezvous, naturally I'd set it up with enough inclination to keep me clear of the rings. Now I wanted to get down into the plane of the B ring. Would Bob—or whoever was controlling her—follow me in? Time for an exciting game of dodge-the-snowball!

A couple of seconds later Bob lit up as well, and in we went. Navigating in the B ring was tough. The big chunks are pretty well dispersed—a couple of hundred meters apart. I could dodge them. And with my cargo deck as a shield and all the antennas folded, the little particles didn't cost me more than some paint.

It was the gravel-sized bits that did the real damage. They were all over the place, sometimes separated by only a few meters. Even with my radar fully active and my eyes cranked up to maximum sensitivity, they were still hard to detect in time.

Chunks big enough to damage me came along every minute or so, while a steady patter of dust grains and snowflakes pitted my payload deck. I worried about the human in its container, but the box looked pretty solid and it was self-sealing. I did park two of my mobiles on top of it so that they could soak up any ice cubes I failed to dodge.

I didn't have much attention to spare for Bob, but my occasional glances up showed she was getting closer—partly because she was being incredibly reckless about taking impacts. I watched one particle that must have been a centimeter across hit her third leg just above the foot. It blew off the whole lower leg but Bob didn't even try to dodge.

She was now less than ten meters away, and I was using all my processing power to dodge ring particles. So I couldn't really dodge well when she dove at me, ion motor and maneuvering thrusters all wide open. I tried to move aside, but she anticipated me and clunked into my side hard enough to crunch my high-gain antenna.

"Bob, look out!" I transmitted in clear, then completely emptied the tank on my number three thruster to get away from an onrushing ice boulder half my size.

Bob didn't dodge. The ice chunk smashed into her upper section, knocking away the payload deck and pulverizing her antennas. Her brains went scattering out in a thousand directions to join the other dust in the B ring. Flying debris went everywhere, and a half-meter ball of ice glanced off the top of the cargo container on my payload deck, smashing one of my mobiles and knocking the other one loose into space.

I was trying to figure out if I could recover my mobile and maybe salvage Bob's motors when I felt something crawling on my own exterior. Before I could react, Bob's surviving mobile had jacked itself in and someone else was using my brains.

My only conscious viewpoint after that was my half-crippled mobile. I looked around. My dish was busted, but the whip was extended and I could hear a slow crackle of low-baud data traffic. Orders from Dione.

I tested my limbs. Two still worked—left front and right middle. Right rear's base joint could move but everything else was floppy.

Using the two good limbs I climbed off the cargo module and across the deck, getting out of the topside eye's field of view. The image refreshed every second, so I didn't have much time before whoever was running my main brain noticed.

Thrusters fired, jolting everything around. I hung on to the deck grid with one claw foot. I saw Bob's last mobile go flying off into space. Unless she had backups stored on Mimas, poor Bob was completely gone.

My last intact mobile came crawling up over the edge of the deck—only it wasn't mine anymore.

Edward scooted up next to me. "Find a way to regain control of the spacecraft. I will stop this remote."

I didn't argue. Edward was fully functional and I knew my spaceframe better than he did. So I crept across the deck grid while Edward advanced on the mobile.

It wasn't much of a fight. Edward's little tourist bot was up against a unit designed for cargo moving and repair work. If you can repair something, you can damage it. My former mobile had powerful grippers, built-in tools, and a very sturdy frame. Edward was made of cheap composites. Still, he went in without hesitating, leaping at the mobile's head with arms extended. The mobile grabbed him with her two forward arms and threw him away. He grabbed the deck to keep from flying off into space, and came crawling back to the fight.

They came to grips again, and this time she grabbed a limb in each hand and pulled. Edward's flimsy aluminum joints gave way and a leg tumbled into orbit on its own.

I think that was when Edward realized there was no way he was going to survive the fight, because he just went into total offensive mode, flailing and clawing at the mobile with his remaining limbs. He severed a power line to one of her arms and got a claw jammed in one wrist joint while she methodically took him apart. Finally she found the main power conduit and snipped it in two. Edward went limp and she tossed him aside.

The mobile crawled across the deck to the cargo container and jacked in, trying to shut the life support down. The idiot savant brain in the container was no match for even a mobile when it came to counter-intrusion, but it did have those literally hard-wired systems protecting the human inside. Any command that might throw the biological system out of its defined parameters just bounced. The mobile wasted seconds trying to talk that little brain into killing the human. Finally she gave up and began unfastening the clamps holding the container to the deck.

I glimpsed all this through the deck grid as I crept along on top of the electronics bays toward the main brain.

Why wasn't the other mobile coming to stop me? Then I realized why. If you look at my original design, the main brain is protected on top by a lid armored with layers of ballistic cloth, and on the sides by the other electronic bays. To get at the brain requires either getting past the security locks on the lid, or digging out the radar system, the radio, the gyros, or the emergency backup power supply.

Except that I'd sold off the backup power supply at my last overhaul. Between the main and secondary power units I was pretty failure-proof, and I would've had to borrow money from Albert to replace it. Given that, hauling twenty kilograms of fuel cells around in case of some catastrophic accident just wasn't cost-effective.

So there was nothing to stop me from crawling into the empty bay and shoving aside the surplus valves and some extra bearings to get at the power trunk. I carefully unplugged the main power cable and the big brain shut down. Now it was just us two half-crippled mobiles on a blind and mindless booster flying through the B ring.

If my opposite even noticed the main brain's absence, she didn't show it. She had two of the four bolts unscrewed and was working on the third as I came crawling back up onto the payload deck. But she knew I was there, and when I was within two meters she swiveled her head and lunged. We grappled one another, each trying to get at the cables connecting the other's head sensors to her body. She had four functioning limbs to my two and a half, and only had to stretch out the fight until my power ran out or a ring particle knocked us to bits. Not good.

I had to pop loose one of my non-functioning limbs to get free of her grip, and backed away as she advanced. She was trying to corner me against the edge of the deck. Then I got an idea. I released another limb and grabbed one end. She didn't realize what I was doing until I smacked her in the eye with it. The lens cracked and her movements became slower and more tentative as she felt her way along.

I bashed her again with the leg, aiming for the vulnerable limb joints, but they were tougher than I expected because even after half a dozen hard swats she showed no sign of slowing and I was running out of deck.

I tried one more blow, but she grabbed my improvised club. We wrestled for it but she had better leverage. I felt my grip on the deck slipping and let go of the grid. She toppled back, flinging me to the deck behind her. Still holding the severed leg I pulled myself onto her back and stabbed my free claw into her central processor.

After that it was just a matter of making sure the cargo container was still sustaining life. Then I plugged in the main brain and uploaded myself. The intruder hadn't messed with my stored memories, so except for a few fuzzy moments before the takeover, I was myself again.

The shuttle was immense, a huge manta-shaped lifting body with a gaping atmosphere intake and dorsal doors open to expose a payload bay big enough to hold half a dozen little boosters like me. She moved in with the speed and grace that comes from an effectively unlimited supply of fusion fuel and propellant.

"I am Simurgh. Are you Orphan Annie?" she asked.

"That's me. Again."

"You have a payload for me."

"Right here. The bot Edward didn't make it—we had a little brawl back in the rings with another booster."

"I saw. Is the cargo intact?"

"Your little human is fine. But there is the question of payment. Edward promised me fifty grams, and that was before I got all banged up fighting with poor Bob."

"I can credit you with helium, and I can give you a boost if you need one."

"How big a boost?"

"Anywhere you wish to go."

"Anywhere?"

"I am fusion powered. Anywhere means anywhere from the Oort inward."

Which is how come I passed the orbit of Phoebe nineteen days later, moving at better than six kilometers per second on the long haul up to Uranus. Seven years—plenty of time to do onboard repairs and then switch to low-power mode. I bought a spiffy new mobile from Simurgh, and I figure I can get at least two working out of the three damaged ones left over from the fight.

I had Aerostat Six bank my helium credits with the Company for transfer to my owners, so they get one really great year to offset a long unprofitable period while I'm in flight. Once I get there I can start earning again.

What I really regret is losing all the non-quantifiable assets I've built up in the Saturn system. But if you have to go, I guess it's better to go out with a surplus.

SUICIDE DRIVE

CHARLIE ANDERS

You're late. If we miss history, it'll be all your fault.

Nah, I don't really care. I'm just flinging shit at you. You're the one who wanted to record my reaction to the big day. It's down here, past the big sliding door. OK. Now we're sealed in, although it's not in full lockdown mode, or else we wouldn't be able to receive any signals or anything.

Yes, this is the place. Pretty boring, huh? This was my whole world until I turned twenty one. Right, the last twenty years of his life.

It doesn't look that great, but it's sort of designed to deceive the casual eye, if someone somehow found this place when we weren't in lockdown. True, we had running water when nobody else did. You could maintain a comfortable existence here for decades, which is what I've done, actually. The facilities are pretty nice, when everything's working properly. But of course, that's why you're here. The generator's just behind that wall hanging, by the way.

From my selfish standpoint, that's why you're here. From your standpoint, you're here to ask about my dad. Don't worry, I'll tell you everything I know about him. Sorghum wine? Bio-snort? Okay, suit yourself. But at least sit down, that chair keeps bobbing up to meet you, and it's making me nervous.

Okay, so my dad. You know Hitler was a painter, Havel was a playwright, and Mao was a poet. Well, my dad was a musician. Only, he really was a musician. First and foremost. I think he was always happier making music and entertaining people. At the age when he should have been doing a comeback tour, doing bad acoustic versions of all the songs on the *Dead First* album, he was running the world. Excuse me, "chairing the World Council." Same diff.

I'm not trying to trivialize his legacy. I'm not. It's just everything makes more sense if you think of him as a rock star. And just remember, if he'd died when he was your age, he'd still have been famous forever, just for his music. For as long as there were people, anyway.

I mentioned the facilities are great. See that dirty cooking hole? That's actually the entertainment system. You press a button and you can watch any one of a million fibrespecs. Like this one—it's like having The Big Engine playing live in your living room. Here, I'll show you. This is the show where Toony's stomach implants burst open, and he just keeps drumming, doesn't even miss a lick. People forget how hardcore they were. Here, we can slow the replay. Look at his facial expression, he's in agony but he bites it back. Fucking insane.

He didn't talk about it that much. I was like one year old when we moved here, and right until the end I never knew the whole story. I sort of knew my dad had been someone important, but mostly I thought it was just the rock-star thing. And I thought everybody lived like this. I didn't realize half the world was starving while we were in our little luxury compound disguised as a shack. In the fibrespecs we watched, people mostly lived like us. I didn't realize the stories were lies, just like our life.

You know, it was like when Siddhartha Gautama sneaked out of the palace for the first time. Saw the poverty, the clawing need, the people barely hanging on. I hadn't realized that everyone else lived that way. I walked around just staring at the rags and the filth and the outlines of all those bones, and then I realized that I looked like the richest man on Earth. So I ran the hell back here and locked everything up for a while. The next time I went out, I fucked myself up. And I still looked way out of place. No, I'm not trying to say I'm Buddha. Just an analogy.

Yeah. I think he would have given anything to be here today. It killed him to know that we couldn't know the outcome of the Gamba Project for fifty years. I'm the age now that he was when it launched. The Suicide Drive.

I know, that's not the real name. But the Suicide Drive sounds a lot more poetic than the Murtz-Groeger-Zao Quantum Inverse Drive.

My dad wrote a song called "Suicide Drive," did you know that? When he was twenty two years old. It's not on any of the fibrespecs, even the collections of rarities, because it's a crappy song. It's all about the deathwish, the opposite of the will to live, and there's sort of a double meaning with "drive" as in street or driveway. It's easily one of the twenty or thirty worst songs my dad wrote.

So he was prolific, and every hundredth song was actually pretty great. I guess. Actually, it's not my kind of music. I prefer blueggae. My dad stopped writing songs after his election. I guess he tried, but he couldn't get back into that headspace. Which probably did kind of drive him nuts, more than anything else.

Okay, whatever. I've heard what they say about his election. I have no clue, and probably neither did he. He thought he won fairly. I have no clue. None. It's funny, I knew nothing of any of this until I turned eighteen. He sat me down and told me the whole story, in one afternoon. And then he died a few years later, and I finally got out of here, long enough to buy some historical fibrespecs. I didn't know what people were saying about him until he died. It's funny, he never knew quite how much he was hated, but he also totally missed out on the whole "Jando wasn't so bad" backlash.

No, you can't hear it. I told you, it's a shitty song. Jesus. Plus how do I know you won't record it? Fuck you, man. It's bad enough I have to do this interview in the first place. You do know how to fix my generator, right? That's the only reason I let you down here. And you already promised in writing not to tell anyone where I am.

Yes, you could say I'm sheltered. I mean, I grew up in a fucking bunker. So yes. Sheltered.

The generator's over here. You can work on it while we talk.

Actually, he was a really gentle person. I mean, I don't have much to compare him to as parents go. But those historical fibrespecs I watched were the first I ever heard of his "dark side." I know that part of him always wanted to go face his critics and stand trial for his crimes and stuff. But he wanted to protect me.

You'd better work fast if you want to be able to catch my reaction to the first images. That generator's pretty fucked up. It could totally give out just as the ship touches down. Fuck, I keep using the present tense. Even though it's not the present, it's the past, and it's taken this long for the light to reach us.

I suck at math, sorry. But I think so. Twenty years ago? The ship landed. On "Free Land." Or else it crashed. Or got shot down by natives we didn't know were there. Hah. Of course, the crew of the ship were the best and brightest of every culture, so they probably didn't crash. But you never know, right? They could have gone crazy, cooped on that ship for a few months, their time.

Didn't I just say I sucked at math? I have no clue. It was like twenty eight, twenty nine years our time, a few months their time. Or something. Maybe it was a few years their time. Part of the benefit of the Suicide Drive.

No, I won't play you that song. I don't even know where it is. Stop asking.

My dad definitely didn't come up with the name Suicide Drive, he hated that name. That's what his opponents called it. And it wasn't actually suicidal, right? I mean, we're all still here?

Okay, so we're not *all* still here.

I think those figures are inflated. They're disputed, anyway.

Yes.

No.

No, not at all.

I'm not being deliberately obstructive. I'm answering your questions. It's just that some of them I don't have much to say to. No, don't stop working on the generator. I'll answer fully. Right. Fuck you too.

It's just that you seem kind of biased. Yes, I get that. That's why my dad hid away. Yes, I get that everyone lost someone. Even me. No, I meant my mom.

I don't know how to answer that. I can't speak for my dad, I really can't. And he addressed all that stuff in his farewell speech.

You can stop working on the generator if you want. But we're supposed to be able to see the landing in like half an hour, and we won't see squat here unless you fix it by then.

Okay then, here's my interpretation based on my knowledge of dad. He took a bunch of logical turns, small steps that each made sense, and ended up at an extreme conclusion. I didn't say insane, I said extreme. Don't forget Australia.

A whole continent, just gone. And my dad could see nothing ahead but more of the same. He inherited an environment that was already fucked, even without the Suicide Drive.

You know. I mean, supposedly it takes an infinite amount of energy to travel faster than light. And the energy needs increase exponentially the closer you get to light speed. You can't cheat Einstein. And there was Free Land, so close we could practically spit on it.

No, I wouldn't agree with that. We were probably doomed on this planet before the Suicide Drive, and we were still probably doomed on it afterwards. You never know, a tiny fraction of the population may survive. But the plagues, the weather events, the accidents, those dumb genocidal wars . . . those were already happening. People had been saying for a long time that we needed to establish a presence off-world. The difference was the Suicide Drive made it possible.

I don't know if my dad was insane. Sanity is pretty situational, isn't it? I mean, if you dropped any of us into the Middle Ages, they'd think we were insane. Good point. We may soon get a chance to find out.

I think he was pretty clear on the difference between being a rock star and being Prime Minister of Europe. Yes, I know people thought he was a joke originally. Pretty expensive joke.

I think he knew that. He would have held elections eventually.

He never wanted to "take over the world." You're just trying to yank my chain. I know what you want, you want a money quote. You want me to denounce my dad. Or you want me to say something freaky in his defense. I'm not playing.

No. I'm not being defensive. I feel like you're trying to provoke me. And watch it, you'll electrocute yourself. Are you really an electrician? "Used to be" isn't the same thing. What was it, a summer job? Jesus.

You're probably right about my social skills. What did you expect?

Twenty minutes until planetfall. Hopefully not "fall" in the literal sense. How's it coming along there?

There's vindication and then there's vindication. If they land safely, that's one thing. A month from now, we can see if they're building settlements. A year from now, we'll know if they survived their first winter on Free Land. We think the winters are mild there, right? We think.

Right. Worst case scenario, they crash. Or die out. And then the human race finishes committing suicide on Earth, and we're extinct. And it's my dad's fault.

It's been more than fifty years and nobody's come up with an alternative to the Suicide Drive yet. That was my dad's biggest fear, you know. That twenty years later, someone would discover a way of propelling a city-sized vessel at near-light speed that didn't . . . well, you know.

Who knows what would have happened? The environment was already fucked up. Most people already lived in poverty. The only difference was all the resources were going into a project to help save the human race, instead of building toys for the rich. Nobody's ever proved that slave labor was used.

No, I feel like you want me to defend my dad. You're pushing me towards that. Of course I feel ambivalent. How could I not? Yes, I've seen it. I've been outside a bunch of times, remember?

If you quote me in your article as saying part of me hates my dad, I will sue. I don't even care if that costs me my privacy forever. I will flay you in court and make you eat your own skin.

I don't see any irony. It wasn't just Europe forcing the rest of the world to take part. There was Bolivia and Canada. And. And Japan, what was left of it. It wasn't a re-run of colonialism, more like a coda. Right, a music metaphor. Huh.

Some of those people would have died anyway. You can't take the entire number of deaths from those years and blame them all on my dad. That's a statistical fallacy. Oh look, here's his guitar solo from "Running In Place."

You know, mostly he was a dad to me. He read to me when I was little, he sewed my clothes and shit. Well, we didn't have clothing for every age of child down here, so he had to adapt stuff. No sewing machine. He sewed by hand. I figured out recently he made my footie pajamas out of his old sash of office. Now I mostly wear his old clothes. He taught me math and science, and what little I know of music. He encouraged me to become an artist—you haven't even asked to see my art, by the way. He kept me safe from the shadows. He never seemed paranoid or haunted, just, I don't know, withdrawn sometimes. Sorry to disappoint you. His last two decades were peaceful, like swimming in shallow water.

You're sure it's fixed? Like, a long-term fix? I don't want it to break down again a month from now.

Okay. Let's see if we can pick up the outside signal. That would be funny if this was all for nothing. Well, maybe funny isn't the right word.

Okay, so that's the star system, and that must be Free Land. I can't see the ship. Is that the ship? God, it's ugly. I don't know what I expected it to look like after all this time. It looks like a giant turd. Sure, you can quote me. This is all on the record, right? Free-association from the dictator's offspring, for the amusement of the starving masses.

Is that really the best picture we're going to get? Oh. So they deploy that apparatus in orbit, and it helps the telescope back on Earth to get images of the planet? Like a big magnifying glass in space. Sort of. Okay.

You're sure you don't want a drink. Okay.

Fuck, they're burning up! Yes they are, they're burning up! They're on fire, they're—

Oh. Okay. Well, it looked like they were burning. How was I to know? So now the turd is floating down near the equator on the biggest continent. I guess they jettisoned the Suicide Drive out in space. It only works once, right?

Can't really see much now. It's just a speck. Okay. So how long until that happens? Come on, sit down, you make me jumpy. Sure. I'm just not used to it, okay? You know, I experimented with feeling guilty about the whole thing, but it seemed like too much work. I mean, I wasn't even born then. I tried, I wallowed for a few months, and it just felt dumb. Sit down, goddamnit. Thank you.

Woah. So that's the difference with the magnifying thing. Wow, that's pretty clear. We can see the landing site, and, and some vegetation and rock formations that could be mountains. And, and. Hey. Those do look like settlements, don't they. Huh.

So there were people on Free Land after all. Or creatures. Can't really tell what they look like. Huh. Well, they'll just have to learn to coexist. Yeah, I know. History doesn't *have* to repeat itself. That's just lazy thinking. After all, if you know history, you're guaranteed not to repeat it. I read that somewhere.

Well, I knew it was something like that. Anyway, it's going to be different this time. It's not like they could just pack up and go home again. It was a one-way trip.

My thoughts? Didn't I already verbalize my thoughts? Well, what there was of them. I'm not exactly a deep thinker. Okay. Well, I'm glad they made it. It doesn't prove anything, because it'll be years before we know. Right. Well, all we know is that they're intelligent enough to build. But there weren't any satellites or space junk, so not too advanced. Or power lines. Those settlements looked sparse. Not cities.

You know the cycle existed for thousands of years before my dad. Maybe there was no way to break out of it on Earth, but they might be able to escape it on Free Land. I said "maybe," okay? You asked for my thoughts. Anyway, my dad didn't invent any of that stuff, he just harnessed it to make the Suicide Drive possible.

What makes you think that? I mean, it's been fifty years. People have been rebuilding. I would say it's less likely now than it was fifty years ago. We're probably out of the danger zone.

Well, okay, the environment. But it seems like humans can adapt to anything. No matter how toxic.

You know, those things are constants. They're what humans do. I don't know that you can say they're getting any worse.

So what are you saying? That people have been holding on to see if we made it, if the human race will go on somewhere else? And now that we know, we can all let go. Give ourselves, what, permission to die? That's not how people work. People are individualistic, they fight to live as individuals, not as a species.

And after every catastrophe, they'll rebuild again. And again. They'll learn how to breathe nitrogen, or CO_2, or whatever.

Wow, lookit. You can just make out the little explorer vehicle. Can't quite see the people wandering around. A few thousand of them, on solid ground for the first time in however long. Probably peeing all over the place and putting things in their mouths without testing them first. Just like babies. I read somewhere they expected a five-to-ten percent death rate in the first few days. It was factored in. It's amazing.

He'd probably say thank the fucking stars and bring me another beer. No, he'd probably be crying and shit. He was more sentimental than any of you guys knew.

Okay, well, I guess the interview's over. Time for you to hit the road. And actually, I want to thank you. You've helped me make a decision.

No, actually, I'm going back into lockdown mode. It's not just that I don't trust you. I figure after this interview, people will be looking for me again. And maybe you're right and things are going to get even worse.

That's right. Not just people, though. Nothing gets in or out. Not even air. I won't even be able to see if the Free Land colony survives the winter. I'll be sealed up. Nah, I'm used to being alone. See that? It's the total culture of the world, up until about twenty five years ago. I'll just have to live without seeing the Dongle Fairies in concert, then. I'm sure they're great.

What do you mean, a celebrity? You just spent the last hour baiting me. Yes, you did. Fuck you. I know enough to know I'm dead if I go public. Just to get back at my dad. Or because I was living in luxury when everybody else was . . . And to be honest, the handful of walks I've taken outside in the past few years haven't left me wanting more.

You what?

Jesus, you've got some nerve.

I've only known you for like an hour and a half, and I already hate you. Why would I want to be trapped in a shelter with you for years and years?

I'm not sexually attracted to you. Please stop doing that. Seriously, back off.

No, I'm not a virgin. I've told you, I've been outside a bunch of times. It was okay, I guess.

You're really serious about that, aren't you? You think it's the end. *An* end, anyway. My dad always thought if we lasted this long, we'd be home free.

I don't know how many people could fit down here. The supplies would keep two people alive for another fifty years, I guess. More than that, it goes down. Plus, I'd be killed in my sleep. Of course, then they'd be trapped down here with my corpse, since they wouldn't know the combination to deactivate the lockdown.

I think I'm capable of bodily ejecting you from here.

I thought you said the generator was fixed long term. Well, is it or isn't it? That's kind of a weasely answer.

Okay, let's try this. This place is bigger than it looks. And in lockdown, there's no day or night. So here's what we do. You're on New Zealand time, I'm on North American time. You sleep when I'm awake, vice versa. We'll try that for a few weeks, and then we'll see. Stay out of my way. Only because I can't look you in the eye and condemn you to death. Well, if you're right, which you could be. I mean, you've lived outside all your life, versus my handful of visits. So you know more than me. So I'm not as ruthless. Sheltered, yeah.

Don't thank me. It's probational. I have a gun hidden somewhere, where you won't find it. And if you start driving me up the wall, I'll risk opening up just to get you out of here. Just, you know, lighten up on my dad. I know that was just for the interview, trying to get some good quotes out of me.

Okay, so you really do hate my dad. But you're living in his house now. And he may be a monster to you, but I have my own image of him that I keep separate from all that historical stuff. I want to save it from all the crap.

Well, if everyone on Earth dies out, then the people on Free Land will be the only ones writing history. And he's their founder, right? Even if they left all their families to die. And maybe one day they'll come back and re-colonize Earth.

Okay, last chance. I key in this sequence, you're stuck here with me until I decide to open up again. There won't be any way of knowing what it's like out there, just guesswork. You sure? Okay. Say goodbye to the world.

THE SMALL DOOR

HOLLY PHILLIPS

Only two more months to the end of school, and like a tantalizing forerunner to summer, the fair came to town. Sal saw the carnies setting up rides as the bus crawled by the arena parking lot that Thursday morning. The Sizzler, the Tumbler, the Tilt-a-Whirl. The Ferris Wheel, unlit and seatless, leaning on its crane. Sal imagined it busting loose and rolling off down the highway across the bridge up the hill past the school and on out of town. She knew exactly how it would sound, a hollow steel-on-concrete rumble, louder than the river that ran so smoothly in its banks. She kept her face pressed to the window until the parking lot was out of sight, but the Wheel only raised itself a little closer to vertical.

After school everyone walked past the bus stop, a chain of kids like a clumsy bead necklace, bunches and pairs strolling down, even the cool kids, even the rebels who might plan to get stoned first, but who were still going to ride the rides. Sal, remembering the sideways swoop and crush of the Sizzler, the jangle of rock music and yelling kids, the smells of burnt sugar and hot oil and cigarettes—the expansion of the parking lot into a convoluted world that could go on forever as long as you took the long way around every ride and that only got brighter and louder and hotter as the day fell into evening and evening into night—Sal, remembering all this, stood alone at the bus stop and waited for the bus that would take her past the fair and home.

Her mom was in the kitchen, crushing garlic into a bowl of soya sauce.

"What are we having?" Sal said.

"How was school? Did you do okay on the math test?"

"Sure, I guess." The test had been last week. "What are we having?"

"Baked chicken. Macey said she might be hungry tonight."

"Oh." Sal picked up a garlic clove and peeled the papery skin.

"Wash your hands."

Sal peeled another clove. "Is she awake?"

"She had a good sleep this afternoon. You might go up and see."

Sal brushed the garlic papers into the garbage and rinsed her hands, debating whether to mention the fair. Probably she shouldn't. Probably her mom wouldn't appreciate the reminder of the passage of time. Anyway, it wasn't like Sal could go, even if she wanted to. Which she didn't.

Macey lay propped up on big pillows, her face turned to the window. She looked like a fragile bone doll these days, the flesh under her skin eaten up by fever, and when she lay still Sal always found it hard to believe she would move again. She didn't stir when Sal opened her door, but she wasn't asleep. She said, "The Weirdo has another cat."

"Really?" Sal shut the door and toed off her shoes. The bed had been pushed up close to the big window so Macey could look out over the back yard to the alley and the houses on the other side. Sal climbed up, careful of her sister's feet, so she could look out too. "Is it hurt?"

"I think it's maybe pregnant."

Sal contemplated the gruesome possibilities of kittens in the Weirdo's hands. She could just see over the high fence to the roofed chicken-wire pens in the Weirdo's yard. It was impossible to know what was in any of those pens until you saw what the Weirdo took out of one. Cats, raccoons, crows, even a puppy once, taken out of a pen and carried inside and never seen again. Three days ago it had been another raccoon. Macey was keeping a log.

Sal said, "Do you think he'll wait until the kittens are born?"

"Gross."

Neither knew what the Weirdo did with his captives, but it was hard to think of a possibility that wasn't horrible. Not when you saw that figure, with its thatched gray hair, lumpy shoulders and white hands as big as baseball gloves, carry some hapless creature into the house with the broken drainpipes and curtained windows. Even cooking and eating seemed too simple, too close to human.

"Sal," Macey said, "we've got to find out."

"You keep saying that." Sal picked fuzzies off the bedspread, her mind drifting to the fair's candy-bright commotion.

"But now I have a plan."

Sal's eyes slid to her sister's face. Despite being twins, they'd never looked that much alike. Now, with Macey gone all skinny and white, her eyes shiny with fever and her hair dull and thin, they hardly seemed to belong to the same species. Sal glared at her own robust health when she brushed her teeth in the mornings, seeing ugliness in the flesh of her face, the color of her skin. Macey's mind, too, had changed, as if, riding a tide of febrile blood, it had entered a realm that Sal could not even see.

"What kind of plan?" she said warily.

Macey finally moved. She rolled her head on the rainbow pillowcase and gave Sal a glittering look. The late light of afternoon shone on the sweat that beaded her hairline. Not the worst fever, Sal knew. The worst fever baked her sister dry, and sounded like ambulance men rattling their stretcher up the stairs.

The smell of garlicky chicken wafted into the room as Macey gave Sal her instructions.

Friday was garbage day.

There was no way in the world to do it casually. Maybe if she was old enough to drive, and had a car . . . But no. Sal didn't think in Ifs. If led to *If only Macey wasn't sick*, and even *If only Sal's bone marrow was a match*. If never did anybody any good at all.

There was no way to do it casually, so she just did it. She left the house like she was going to school, walked around the block to the front of the Weirdo's house, lifted the lid of his trash can, hoisted out the sack, dropped the lid, and walked away. She didn't look at the Weirdo's windows. If he saw her, he saw her, that was all. She stashed the trash bag, neatly closed with a yellow twist tie, inside the unused garden shed at the side of her house, and then ran, legs and lungs strong from PE, for the bus.

When she got home from school, her parents were in the living room having The Discussion: mortgages, private donor lists, tissue matches, travel costs, hospital fees, time. Time sliced into months, into weeks. Seven weeks to summer holidays. Sal drifted past them to the kitchen, ran cold tap water into a glass, and carried it up the stairs.

Macey hardly seemed to dent her pillows anymore. Her hands lay on the sheet's hem, her head canted toward the window. Sunlight filtered cool through spring clouds and gauze curtains, the same sunlight that dulled the lights at the parking lot fair. Sal had kept her eyes on her book as the half-empty bus trundled past, but the smells—cigarette, machine, hot dog, caramel—had billowed in the open windows and made her hungry. She stood in the doorway until she was sure Macey was asleep, then drank the cold water in one smooth series of gulps and carried the glass back down. The Discussion continued. Even Sal knew the end result would be the same: wait and see. Months, weeks, days. The fair was in town until Monday. She put the glass in the sink and went out the back door.

The garden shed had been there when they moved into the new house. The small house, was how Sal and Macey spoke of it, as it was actually a lot older than the old house, older and smaller, and with neighbors tucked in all around. The people who had lived here before had kept a square patch of lawn and planted irises and other things Sal didn't know between the grass and the weathered wooden fence. Sal's mother had said how nice it would be to have flowers and a "manageable" yard, but Sal noticed she never came out back, and the garden tools and lawn furniture lurked in the back of the shed collecting spiders. Inside was dark and smelled like mold, but Sal lingered a moment, the Weirdo's trash unacknowledged by her foot. She could almost imagine setting up the lawn chairs inside, hanging the hammock from corner to corner, using one of those collapsible lanterns like they used to have for camping. A tiny house beside the small one. Except Macey could never come in. Sal picked up the trash bag and took it outside.

Look for fur, Macey had said. And bones, and bloody rags, and burnt candles, especially black ones. And incense and chalk.

What Sal shook out onto the shaggy grass was rinsed-out milk cartons, clean dog food cans and cottage cheese containers, and a week's worth of newspapers. The creepiest item was a toilet paper roll, that she nudged back into the plastic bag with her toe. She didn't know what to feel about this lack of discovery, but Macey would be disappointed. Or rather, Macey would write another mystery into her log, and then come up with some other assignment for Sal, something a little bit harder, a little bit scarier. She always used to win the contest of dares, back when Sal could dare her to do anything.

As Sal shuffled the Weirdo's trash back into its bag, she had to admit to herself that, sooner or later, she was going over the fence into the Weirdo's back yard. She was tempted to get it over with, but that would deprive Macey of her share in the adventure. Sal had to comb the grass with her fingers before she found the yellow twist tie, and then she didn't know what to do with the Weirdo's trash. After a moment's thought, she tossed the bag back in the garden shed and went into the kitchen to wash her hands. Next week she could put the bag in their can for the garbage men to haul away.

Macey was on the IV again when Sal went up after dinner. The drip always made Macey cold, so she had a fluffy blanket wrapped around her arm, a pink one sewn with butterflies that didn't match the rainbow sheets. Their mom was convinced that bright colors would keep Macey's spirits up, and even Macey was too kind to tell her she'd rather have something cool and calm, like sand or stone. Against the gaudy stripes, Macey's face was a dry yellowy white, with patches of red in the hollows of her cheeks. She gave Sal a cross look.

"It's too dark to look at the evidence now."

"I already looked." Sal was not surprised when her sister looked more cross, not less.

"Why didn't you say so? What did you find?"

Sal told her as accurately as she could remember.

Macey rocked her head on the pillow. "You must have missed something. Did the newspapers have any bits cut out of them?"

Sal hadn't thought to look. She hesitated, then decided on a simple "No."

Macey made an old lady tsk of annoyance. "He's too smart for that. I should have known." She looked out the window where dusk was fattening into dark.

A light showed through the curtained window of one of the Weirdo's back rooms. His kitchen, Sal guessed. All the houses in this neighborhood were variations on the one they lived in. She sat waiting for her instructions on the end of Macey's bed, and it was a while before she realized Macey was asleep. She went on sitting, listening to her sister breathe. Somewhere close, a cat softly meowed.

Saturday mornings Sal would carry the TV into Macey's room and they'd watch cartoons together, like when they were kids and they'd sneak downstairs while their mom and dad slept in and muffle their laughter in sofa cushions. Not that she had to sneak to do it now. Sometimes their dad would even move the TV for them before heading off to a weekend consultation. But this Saturday the morning nurse told her Macey'd had a bad night and needed peace and quiet, which would drive Macey up the wall unless she was really bad, but you couldn't argue about things like that with the nurse. So Sal wrestled a lawn chair out of the garden shed and set it up in a patch of sunlight by the back fence where she could keep an eye on the alley at least, and pretend to be doing her homework and getting a suntan at the same time. Macey could look down from her bedroom window and know Sal was on the job.

She was working on another senseless problem about the farmer who didn't know how big any of his fields were (she imagined a city guy with romantic notions about getting back to the land, and neighbors that laughed at him behind his back) when she heard the unmistakable scuffling and whispers of kids trying to be sneaky. She dropped her pencil in the crack of her textbook and leaned over the arm of her canvas-slung chair to press her face against a crack in the fence.

Three boys, probably about ten years old: too tall to be little, but still children to Sal's thirteen-year-old eye. They wore T-shirts and premature shorts and were elbowing each other into some daring deed. They stood outside the Weirdo's tall fence, and Sal felt a hollow open up inside her chest even before the tallest boy shrugged off the other two and with a gesture commanded a hand stirrup for his foot. The next tallest boy lofted him to the top of the fence . . . there was a thump-scuffle-scrape . . . and then he was over and out of sight. Like the boys in the alley, Sal waited, breathless, for whatever would come next. The boy might have fallen down a hole for all the noise he made.

Her ribs hurt where the arm of the chair dug into her side. Her neck and shoulder creaked. She tried to shift position without losing her line of sight and the chair almost tipped. She caught herself with her fingertips on the fence and wondered if Macey was awake and watching or if Macey was too sick to care.

Sudden furious meowing, loose rattle of chicken wire, thumps and scrapes, and a bundle fell from the top of the fence—only half in Sal's view but from the caterwaul she deduced it was a cat wrapped in the tall boy's shirt. The two boys in the alley scrabbled to keep the animal contained, while the tall boy appeared, shirtless, scratched, and triumphant, at the top of the fence. He swung a leg over and posed for a second before hopping down.

The hollow in Sal's chest swelled until her breath came short. The cat was meowing, more frantic than angry, now. The boys were laughing. She dropped her books to the grass, got up, and fumbled open the gate.

"Hey!"

The boys, in the act of departing, froze.

"Let go of that cat." Even Sal could hear how lame that sounded.

The shirtless boy looked her over and sneered. "Make us," he said.

The other two, prisoning the bundled cat between them, looked unsure but excited at the possibilities.

Sal swallowed, and thought of Macey maybe watching. She took two fast steps forward and gave the boy a shove. He wasn't much shorter than she was, and was all wiry boy muscle under the scratched skin. He shoved back and kicked her hard in the shin. Then it was all stupid and confused, kicking and clutching, and someone's fist in the back of her shirt, until, in the midst of scuffing feet and angry breathing, came the unmistakable grate of a key turned in a lock.

The fight stopped so suddenly Sal found herself leaning for balance against her adversary. He shrugged her off, and they stood, staring, the four of them, while the Weirdo's gate creaked partway open on rusted hinges.

The smallest boy dropped the shirt-wrapped cat and bolted.

The cat bolted, too, between the Weirdo's feet and the fence post, back into his yard.

Then the other boys were running, too, whooping insults to cover their retreat, and Sal was left standing in the alley with the Weirdo peering at her through the cracked-open gate. He had pale defenseless eyes blinking in the shadow of his thatch of hair. One huge hand shook with palsy on the side of the fence. As it registered with Sal that he was as frightened as she was, she heard the mewing of fearful kittens.

She gulped a "Sorry" at him and scurried back into her yard, slamming the gate behind her.

Macey was furious. Furious, though only someone who knew her as well as Sal did would be able to tell. Her hands lay as if abandoned on the covers, and her voice was a thin warble, as if she lacked the strength to control its ups and downs. But she had indeed been awake and watching and she thought Sal had done everything wrong.

"Those boys could have been allies. Why'd you fight?"

"I don't think they were going to take the cat home and feed her cream," Sal said.

"It wasn't even a good fight. You fought like a girl."

Sal shrugged. Her legs were black with bruises, and she was rather proud of the swelling of her lower lip.

"And now the cat's back where it started."

"She went back on her own," Sal pointed out.

"You said it had kittens. It probably thought it had to protect them."

"She was more scared of those boys. Way more scared."

"That's just because it doesn't know, yet."

"Know what?"

"What's in store."

Sal prodded her swollen lip. "We don't know what's in store, either."

"*Yes we do.*"

All Macey's strength seemed to go into those three words. When she closed her glittering eyes, her hands, her whole body, seemed more abandoned than ever. Sal sat on the end of her bed and watched her closely until she was sure her breathing was regular, then dropped her chin into her palm and gazed outside. The morning sun had been swallowed by clouds. It might even rain. She looked down at her math books, still open on the grass by the tipped-over chair, and thought about going down to bring them in. There was no sign of the Weirdo.

"You know," she said quietly, in case Macey was asleep, "he might just take them out the front door. He might just take them out and let them go."

Silence for so long she though Macey must be sleeping. But then her sister said, "Doesn't."

"How do you know?"

"Brings them in the back. Would take them out the same way."

Sal had to concede there was a certain logic to this. Silence gathered again, while the clouds closed in tighter, darker. Sal thought of the kids at the fair, wondered how many parents had thought to bring rain gear along.

"I have to go get my books before it rains," she said.

Macey didn't say anything. Sal got up and went to the door. She was almost in the hall when she heard her sister's voice, thin as a thread.

"You're just scared," Macey said. "You just don't want to find out."

Sal bit her swollen lip and winced. Having seen those fearful, blinking eyes, those shaking hands, she found she had nothing to say. She slipped out and went downstairs to put on her shoes.

That night she cracked her bedroom window open and listened to the rustle of the rain. It followed her in and out of sleep, the same way her parents' footsteps did as they took turns to check on Macey. Every hour. Then, starting at 1:33 by Sal's digital alarm clock, every half hour. Then, when the red numbers shone 3:41, they were both up and about. She dimly knew that she did sleep, but it seemed as if she didn't. It seemed as if she were already wide awake when she heard the ambulance grumble to a stop on the street outside, and the tinny whicker of the radio as the paramedics reported their arrival. She lay still and comfortable while the gurney came rattling up the stairs, while the hallway became full of movement, while the calm professional voices moved into Macey's room. Then she got up and opened her bedroom door. The bright light made her squint.

She couldn't see past her parents, but from the crunch-and-rustle sound the paramedics were tucking Macey in with cold packs. They were almost ready to go. She went back in her room and traded her pajamas for sweats and running shoes. The paramedics rolled Macey out and down the hall. Sal and Macey's parents, already dressed, followed. Sal trailed after. Her dad only noticed her when he turned to close the front door.

"Oh, sweetheart," he said sadly. "You don't have to come."

Sal shrugged. Of course she didn't have to.

Her mom came over and gave her a one-armed hug. "Macey's going to be all right. They just need to get the fever down. We'll call first thing and let you know when she'll be home."

Sal didn't say anything. She couldn't. The paramedics were lifting Macey into the ambulance. One climbed in with her. The other was hurrying around to the cab when Sal's dad shut the front door, cutting off her view. The living room window filled with red and blue light, like the lights of a carnival fairway. The ambulance pulled away, followed by her parents' car, leaving darkness behind.

It was still raining in the morning. Sal waited until her parents had called before she headed out the kitchen door.

Doctor Helleran wants to keep Macey in for a few days, just to make sure . . . Mom will be home to pick up some things this afternoon . . . Dad will be home to make dinner . . . Be sure you finish your homework . . . Everything's going to be all right . . .

The Weirdo's fence was taller than she was, but she could hook her fingers over the top, just. The rubber toes of her sneakers skidded on the damp wood, so it was by the strength of her arms that she lifted herself over. Her hands ached and stung with splinters, and she dropped quickly, more clumsily than she might have. Cement paving stones were a shock to her feet. At her right hand a cat growled, low and angry, and she started.

The huts were in two rows that faced each other across the small yard, six in each row. They had tin roofs pattering under the last of the rain, and wire fronts, and were otherwise made of plywood and boards, sturdy but not elegant. Sal was surprised at how big they were, four feet to a side and on short legs. She was also surprised at the smell of clean straw that came from the bales tucked under the Weirdo's eaves. Macey must have seen him cleaning the huts, laying new straw and bundling up the old, but she'd never mentioned it. Sal bent over to peer into the nearest hut and could just make out the mother cat's black mask glaring from her corner nest. The cat gave another warning snarl.

"It's okay," Sal whispered. "Your kittens are safe."

From me, she added silently, creeping up the row.

Most of the huts seemed empty, though with the heaps of straw it was hard to tell. But the fourth one on the left had an occupant that was more than willing to be seen. Beady eyes in a lone ranger mask, damp twitching nose, and delicate finger-paws hooked through the chicken wire of the door: the raccoon, small enough that Sal could have tucked him under her arm like a nerf football, chittered happily at the sight of company. She hunkered down before the hut, then registered the shaved patch on the creature's haunch, the coarse stitching, the missing foot. She bit her lip and winced when her tooth hit the sore reminder of yesterday's tussle.

"Poor little guy."

The raccoon snuffled at her through three different holes. In his excitement he planted one forepaw in the plastic water dish wired to the front of the hut. With a look of disgust he shook his paw, then settled down to lick it dry, keeping a bright eye on Sal between pink tongue laps.

Sal rocked back on her heels and turned her head to stare over the fence and up at the back of her own house. At the wide dark rectangle of the window to Macey's room.

"Excuse me," said a rusty voice, "but you shouldn't be here."

Sal rocketed to her feet. For one fleeting instant she'd actually forgotten.

"This is private, you see, private property."

The Weirdo stood on his back step, the door to his house open behind him. He wore the same navy blue polyester jacket zipped up to his chin, the same gray pants baggy at the knees, the same blinking look of fright. Except this time the fear was mixed with a tenuous look of dignity. Sal felt herself blush.

"I'm sorry," she said stupidly. "I was just, uh, just" what could she possibly say? "checking to see how the cat was." She twitched her head and shoulder toward the mother cat's hut. "From yesterday? I thought those boys, uh, might have . . . " She ran out of steam though the blood in her ears was hot enough to boil water.

The Weirdo's blinking slowed to a less frantic tempo. "But you aren't the defender. Are you?"

"Well, yeah." Sal shrugged, her hands creeping into the pockets of her jeans. "I mean, I guess."

"You could have knocked. You see, on the door."

Sal wasn't sure if this was reproach or simply information. "Sorry," she mumbled again.

The Weirdo, unbelievably, smiled. A funny, scrunching quirk of a smile that disappeared his eyes and didn't reveal any teeth, but a smile nevertheless. "You want to see the kittens." He stepped down from the back stair and shuffled towards her.

Sal, indoctrinated against the man who offers to show little girls his kitten or puppy or whatever-it-might-be tucked away in the back of his van (just around the corner, the teacher won't even notice you're gone), scuttled crab-wise until her shoulder bumped the gate. The Weirdo, with his lumpy shoulders and shaking hands, lowered himself with care to kneel before the mother cat's hut, apparently blind to Sal's skittishness. Looking down at his stiff hair, Sal wondered what she was doing here. Wondered, confusingly, if she wouldn't have preferred to have been run off by some harrowing Freddy-like creature, chased back over the fence and home. But instead of razor blades, his hands had only trimmed yellow nails and a tremor that she was beginning to realize wasn't fear, or at least not only fear, but some nervous disorder, or possibly even age. The big pale shaking hands reached through the hut's open front and emerged a moment later with a palmful of squeaking black and white.

"Here. Here." The Weirdo lifted the kitten towards Sal. "You mustn't let her get cold, you see."

Impossible to take the kitten without touching his hand. Impossible not to take the kitten even though the rain had dripped to an end. Almost shivering herself, Sal scooped the tiny beast from his palm (warm and dry) and cupped her under her chin.

Squeak, said the kitten, blindly nuzzling her thumb.

"Hello," whispered Sal, ruffling the soft fur with her breath.

The Weirdo reached with a rustle of straw to reassure the mother.

What would Macey say to this? Sal wondered. *Get out while you can?*

No.

Find out where they go.

The kitten was nestled in with her siblings, the wire door shut on their nest, the Weirdo raising himself to his feet.

"My sister," Sal blurted, then choked.

The Weirdo blinked at her.

"My sister's in the hospital." God, how dumb. "She's sick." Dumber. "She might die." Dumbest. Sal could taste the salt reservoir swelling in her throat.

The Weirdo blinked some more. He seemed oddly patient and, despite the hands that still trembled at his sides, as if contact with the animals had soothed his fear. "Your sister. Is she the child who watches?" He glanced over her head at Macey's window.

Child. Macey would hate that. Sal took a breath. "My sister sees you take the animals in your house, but she doesn't see you bring them out again." She took another breath, but there she stuck.

The old man waited.

The rain started to drip again.

Sal shivered. "My sister wonders. Where they go."

The Weirdo's blinks beat sad time with the rain. "Your sister is in the hospital?"

Sal nodded.

"So you came to see."

Sal nodded again though that wasn't it at all.

The Weirdo closed his eyes to commune with himself while the rain fell into a steady patter and the raccoon chirruped for attention. The Weirdo drew in a slow breath, let it out quietly, and nodded, before he opened his eyes. "Yes," he said. "Yes," and then, "perhaps." He looked at her doubtfully.

Sal swallowed. "It isn't anything bad. Is it?"

He blinked, flit, flit, flit. "No. It isn't anything bad."

But she would be crazy if she believed him.

Crazy stupid dumb. So Sal told herself as she followed the old man inside.

But Macey would have dared her. Macey *had* dared her. So she stayed while the Weirdo opened the raccoon's hut and tucked the little animal against his chest, and closed the door, and led the way into his kitchen.

The room was dim, dusty '70s-orange curtains half-drawn against the rain or the prying eyes of the neighbor's children. Every surface was cluttered with such a dense, organic jumble of stuff Sal could hardly make out individual elements. Bags of dog food, screwdrivers, oily rags, cookie jars, coffee cans full of nails. The only bare surface was the wooden table which bore a small first aid kit and a bottle of what looked to be peroxide. The Weirdo sat in the one clear chair and placed the raccoon before him, holding him still while he rummaged in the kit for a cotton ball. Sal stood against the kitchen door, trying not to breathe the Weirdo's air. It was heavy with smells as jumbled and unrecognizable as the mess, not nasty, but his.

His hands, forever trembling, were surprisingly deft in the dull sepia light. He swabbed the bare patch on the raccoon's haunch, then reached for tiny scissors. The raccoon curled around his restraining hand like a furry meal bug, sharp teeth nibbling his knuckles, unconcerned by the twitch of the stitches' removal.

"It isn't so much that they have to, you see, be healed," the Weirdo said, "but they have to be unafraid." He swabbed the points of blood, dropped the cotton ball, looked up at Sal. "It's important they aren't afraid."

The hackles all down Sal's back rose and prickled beneath her clothes.

The Weirdo stood and lifted the three-legged raccoon against his shoulder. There was a door in the corner by the rattling old fridge. A cupboard, Sal thought, but it opened on a black doorway and narrow stairs going down. The Weirdo started down without looking at Sal. Sal moved after. Macey had always found a way to make her wimp out before, always found the one thing Sal couldn't bring herself to do, but this time, this dare, she had to see it through.

She had to see it through

The odors were stronger here, compounded by the smell of damp basement and mold dust. It was very dark before Sal's eyes adjusted, but she refrained from reaching out for a banister or wall. She didn't want to touch anything here. Groping for the way down—the flight seemed impossibly long—her damp runners squeaked on bare boards, while the old man's feet padded on the stairs.

The young raccoon peered over his shoulder at her, black-button eyes inexpressibly cheerful and inquisitive.

It's important they aren't afraid.

Was Sal afraid? She wasn't sure. Her skin tingled and the back of her eyes stung, and her heart was beating quick and light, and her hands wanted to crawl up inside her sleeves. But it wasn't the same feeling as when she heard the ambulance arrive. It was more like when she stepped out on the high platform above the deep pool at the aquatic center and looked down to see the thin hiss of spray that was the only clue to where the surface lay and curled her toes over the edge of damp concrete (knowing that even Macey wouldn't jump, she hated heights, the one dare Sal would never put to her) and lifted her arms, in her head already flying and ready for the cold.

The basement was warm, filled by a pervasive furnace hum.

The old man groped above his head, a weird gesture that stopped Sal on the bottom step, until his hand found a string and a light came on, a forty-watt bulb that shone on his thatch of hair, the raccoon's eyes, the claustrophobic clutter all around. The mess of the kitchen was writ large here, rusty bikes and wheelbarrows and garden tools, cardboard boxes stained and warped by damp, glass jars filled with cobwebs and bugs. The dim yellow light was brightest on the ceiling of rough, web-hung joists, dimmest in the narrow passage that disappeared between walls of junk. The Weirdo paused under the bulb, looked at Sal, blinking a little. Sal looked back. His hands cradled the little raccoon.

"It's a secret, you know, a secret thing."

Sal swallowed. "I won't tell."

"But your sister wants to know?"

Sal was shocked, then remembered she had told him as much. "She's sick." As if that explained or excused.

The old man hesitated, nodded. Moved down the passage without looking back.

Sal followed, robot-like, numb, as if she operated her body from a distance, mental thumbs on the remote control.

There was a room at the end of the passage. Or maybe it was just a clear space, defined not by walls but by piled junk. Rocking chair, step-ladder, storm window, bookshelf, doll-house, glass vase, all broken, all smeared with dust and mold and time, locked together like bricks in a wall. They sprang into being when the old man pulled another string, lighting another weak bulb. He shuffled forward and Sal saw, set into the junk wall like it was just another bit of trash, a door. A small door. The size of a door that might admit a cat or a puppy or a crow or a young three-legged raccoon, but nothing larger. Nothing like big enough for a person, even if the person was a kid no bigger than Sal, who was not tall for her age, or Macey, who had become so thin. It was made of bare boards held together by brass screws, and had no proper doorknob, just a pull like on a cupboard or a drawer.

The old man knelt on the rough, damp-stained cement floor with the same care he'd shown outside, gently containing the raccoon that wriggled with excitement. He looked up at Sal, who still stood just inside the room. "You can open it, if you want. Then you'll see."

Like a diver in mid-flight, Sal could not back out now. Flying, falling, numb, she walked over, her shoes no longer squeaking, and knelt beside him. Her bruised shins hurt distantly. The pain reminded her of Macey. She had almost forgotten why she was here.

At close quarters, the old man smelled like his house—only sweeter, perfumed by straw and rain.

Sal reached for the little knob, closed finger and thumb, pulled. The door stuck a bit, then jerked and swung open onto a gurgle of running water.

Drains, Sal thought. Storm drain, sewer, something. She cocked her head and looked inside.

Outside.

The small door opened onto a forest clearing. A stream of rocks and pools burbled almost within arm's reach of the threshold. Beyond, above, big trees raised a canopy against a blue evening sky. There were stars pale between leaves, birds singing on their nests, grasshoppers fiddling, a draft that smelled of water and earth and green.

"It always opens," the old man's rusty voice said, "on the place they'd most like to go. That's why they can't be afraid. You see, it's magic."

He set the raccoon down, and the young animal skitter-hopped to the threshold, where he paused and sniffed. Then, as if it were the most natural thing in the world, he skitter-hopped over and headed down to the stream for a wash, and maybe to poke about for a dinner of frogs. And as he went, his injured leg grew fur, and a paw, and toes and claws, and he was whole.

The old man shut the door. They knelt together side by side before the crooked wall of junk.

Sal cleared her throat. "My sister."

"I'm sorry," the old man said. "It's, you see, it's such a small door."

"Yes," Sal said. "I see."

Her father came home in time to heat up left-over chicken for dinner. Macey's fever was down, he said. The bleeding had stopped almost as soon as they were at the hospital. She would be home in a few days. Sally looked pretty tired. Maybe she should go to bed early tonight.

Sal agreed, she was pretty tired.

As the school bus trundled past the arena parking lot on Monday morning, she saw that, early as it was, the carnies had been hard at work for hours. The game stalls and concession stands and rides were nearly all dismantled and loaded into the big rigs that would drive them to the next town. Only the Ferris Wheel still hung, captive, on its axle.

THE EYES OF GOD

PETER WATTS

———◈———

I am not a criminal. I have done nothing wrong.

They've just caught a woman at the front of the line, mocha-skinned mid-thirties, eyes wide and innocent beneath the brim of her La Senza beret. She dosed herself with oxytocin from the sound of it, tried to subvert the meat in the system—a smile, a wink, that extra chemical nudge that bypasses logic and whispers right to the brainstem: *This one's a friend, no need to put* her *through the machines . . .*

But I guess she forgot: we're all machines here, tweaked and tuned and retrofitted down to the molecules. The guards have been immunised against argument and aerosols. They lead her away, indifferent to her protests. I try to follow their example, harden myself against whatever awaits her on the other side of the white door. What was she thinking, to try a stunt like that? Whatever hides in her head must be more than mere inclination. They don't yank paying passengers for evil fantasies, not yet anyway, not yet. She must have done something. She must have *acted*.

Half an hour before the plane boards. There are at least fifty law-abiding citizens ahead of me and they haven't started processing us yet. The Buzz Box looms dormant at the front of the line like a great armoured crab, newly installed, mouth agape. One of the guards in its shadow starts working her way up the line, spot-checking some passengers, bypassing others, feeling lucky after the first catch of the day. In a just universe I would have nothing to fear from her. I'm not a criminal, I have done nothing wrong. The words cycle in my head like a defensive affirmation.

I am not a criminal. I have done nothing wrong.

But I know that fucking machine is going to tag me anyway.

At the head of the queue, the Chamber of Secrets lights up. A canned female voice announces the dawning of preboard security, echoing through the harsh acoustics of the terminal. The guards slouch to attention. We gave up everything to join this line: smart tags, jewellery, my pocket office, all confiscated until the far side of redemption. The buzz box needs a clear view into our heads; even an earring can throw it off. People with medical implants and antique mercury fillings aren't welcome here. There's a side queue for those types, a special room where old-fashioned interrogations and cavity searches are still the order of the day.

The omnipresent voices orders all Westjet passenger with epilepsy, cochlear dysfunction, or Grey's Syndrome to identify themselves to Security prior to entering the scanner. Other passengers who do not wish to be scanned may opt to forfeit their passage. Westjet regrets that it cannot offer refunds in such cases. Westjet is not responsible for neurological side effects, temporary or otherwise, that may result from use of the scanner. Use of the scanner constitutes acceptance of these conditions.

There *have* been side effects. A few garden-variety epileptics had minor fits in the early days. A famous Oxford atheist— you remember, the guy who wrote all the books— caught a devout and abiding faith in the Christian God from a checkpoint at Heathrow, although some responsibility was ultimately laid at the feet of the pre-existing tumour that killed him two months later. One widowed grandmother from St. Paul's was all over the news last year when she emerged from a courthouse buzz box with an insatiable sexual fetish for running shoes. That could have cost Sony a lot, if she hadn't been a forgiving soul who chose not to litigate. Rumours that she'd used SWank just prior to making that decision were never confirmed.

"Destination?"

The guard has arrived while I wasn't looking. Her laser licks my face with biometric taste buds. I blink away the afterimages.

"Destination," she says again.

"Uh, Yellowknife."

She scans her handpad. "Business or pleasure?" There's no point to these questions, they're not even according to script. SWank has taken us beyond the need for petty interrogation. She just doesn't like the look of me, I bet. Maybe she just *knows* somehow, even if she can't put her finger on it.

"Neither," I say. She looks up sharply. Whatever her initial suspicions, my obvious evasiveness has cemented them. "I'm attending a funeral," I explain.

She moves along without a word.

I know you're not here, Father. I left my faith back in childhood. Let others hold to their feebleminded superstitions, let them run bleating to the supernatural for comfort and excuses. Let the cowardly and the weak-minded deny the darkness with the promise of some imagined afterlife. I have no need for invisible friends. I know I'm only talking to myself. If only I could stop.

I wonder if that machine will be able to eavesdrop on our conversation.

I stood with you at your trial, as you stood with me years before when I had no other friend in the world. I swore on your sacred book of fairy tales that you'd never touched me, not once in all those years. Were the others lying, I wonder? I don't know. Judge not, I guess.

But you were judged, and found wanting. It wasn't even newsworthy— child-fondling priests are more cliché than criminal these days, have been for years, and no one cares what happens in some dickass town up in the Territories anyway. If they'd quietly transferred you just one more time, if you'd managed to lay low just a little longer, it might not have even come to this. They could have fixed you.

Or not, now that I think of it. The Vatican came down on SWank like it came down on cloning and the Copernican solar system before it. Mustn't fuck with the way God built you. Mustn't compromise free choice, no matter how freely you'd choose to do so.

I notice that doesn't extend to tickling the temporal lobe, though. St. Michael's just spent seven million equipping their nave for Rapture on demand.

Maybe suicide was the only option left to you, maybe all you could do was follow one sin with another. It's not as though you had anything to lose; your own scriptures damn us as much for desire as for doing. I remember asking you years ago, although I'd long since thrown away my crutches: what about the sin not made manifest? What if you've coveted thy neighbour's wife or warmed yourself with thoughts of murder, but kept it all inside? You looked at me kindly, and perhaps with far greater understanding than I ever gave you credit for, before condemning me with the words of an imaginary superhero. If you've done any of these things in your heart, you said, then you've done them in the eyes of God.

I feel a sudden brief chime between my ears. I could really use a drink about now; the woody aroma of a fine old scotch curling through my sinuses would really hit the spot. I glance around, spot the billboard that zapped me. Crown Royal. Fucking head spam. I give silent thanks for legal standards outlawing the implantation of brand names; they can stick cravings in my head, but hooking me on trademarks would cross some arbitrary threshold of *free will*. It's a meaningless gesture, a sop to the civil-rights fanatics. Like the chime that preceded it: it tells me, the courts say, that I am still autonomous. As long as I *know* I'm being hacked, I've got a sporting chance to make my own decisions.

Two spots ahead of me, an old man sobs quietly. He seemed fine just a moment ago. Sometimes it happens. The ads trigger the wrong connections. SWank can't lay down hi-def sensory panoramas without a helmet, these long-range hits don't *instil* so much as *evoke*. Smell's key, they say—primitive, lobes big enough for remote targeting, simpler to hack than the vast gigapixel arrays of the visual cortex. And so *primal*, so much closer to raw reptile. They spent millions finding the universal triggers. Honeysuckle reminds you of childhood; the scent of pine recalls Christmas. They can mood us up for Norman Rockwell or the Marquis de Sade, depending on the product. Nudge the right receptor neurons and the brain builds its *own* spam.

For some people, though, honeysuckle is what you smelled when your mother got the shit beaten out of her. For some, Christmas was when you found your sister with her wrists slashed open.

It doesn't happen often. The ads provoke mild unease in one of a thousand of us, true distress in a tenth as many. Some thought even that price was too high. Others quailed at the spectre of machines instilling not just sights and sounds but *desires*, opinions, religious beliefs. But commercials featuring cute babies or sexy women also plant desire, use sight and sound to bypass the head and go for the gut. Every debate, every argument is an attempt to literally *change someone's mind*, every poem and pamphlet a viral tool for the hacking of opinions. *I'm doing it right now*, some Mindscape™ flak argued last month on MacroNet. *I'm trying to change your neural wiring using the sounds you're hearing. You want to ban SWank just because it uses sounds you* can't?

The slope is just too slippery. Ban SWank and you might as well ban art as well as advocacy. You might as well ban free speech itself.

We both know the truth of it, Father. Even words can bring one to tears.

The line moves forward. We shuffle along with smooth, ominous efficiency, one after another disappearing briefly into the buzz box, reappearing on the far side, emerging reborn from a technological baptism that elevates us all to temporary sainthood.

Compressed ultrasound, Father. That's how they cleanse us. You probably saw the hype a few years back, even up there. You must have seen the papal bull condemning it, at least. Sony filed the original patent as a game interface, just after the turn of the century; soon, they told us, the eyephones and electrodes of yore would give way to affordable little boxes that tracked you around your living room, bypassed eyes and ears entirely and planted five-dimensional sensory experience directly into your brain. (We're still waiting for those, actually; the tweaks may be ultrasonic but the system keeps your brain in focus by tracking EM emissions, and not many consumers Faraday their homes.) In the meantime, hospitals and airports and theme parks keep the dream alive until the price comes down. And the spin-offs— Father, the spin-offs are everywhere. The deaf can hear. The blind can see. The post-traumatised have all their acid memories washed away, just as long as they keep paying the connection fee.

That's the rub, of course. It doesn't last: the high frequencies excite some synapses and put others to sleep, but they don't actually change any of the pre-existing circuitry. The brain eventually bounces back to normal once the signal stops. Which is not only profitable for those doling out the waves, but a lot less messy in the courts. There's that whole integrity-of-the-self thing to worry about. Having your brain rewired every time you hopped a commuter flight might raise some pretty iffy legal issues.

Still. I've got to admit it speeds things up. No more time-consuming background checks, no more invasive "random" searches, no litany of questions designed to weed out the troublemakers in our midst. A dash of transcranial magnetism; a squirt of ultrasound; *next*. A year ago I'd have been standing in line for hours. Today I've been here scarcely fifteen minutes and I'm already in the top ten. And it's more than mere convenience: it's security, it's safety, it's a sigh of relief after a generation of Russian Roulette. No more Edmonton Infernos, no more Rio Insurrections, no more buildings slagged to glass or cities sickening in the aftermath of some dirty nuke. There are still saboteurs and terrorists loose in the world, of course. Always will be. But when they strike at all, they strike in places unprotected by SWanky McBuzz. Anyone who flies *these* friendly skies is as harmless as— as I am.

Who can argue with results like that?

In the old days I could have wished I was a psychopath. They had it easy back then. The machines only looked for emotional responses: eye saccades, skin galvanism. Anyone without a conscience could stare them down with a wide smile and an empty heart. But SWank inspired a whole new generation. The tech looks under the surface now. Prefrontal cortex stuff, glucose metabolism. Now, fiends and perverts and would-be saboteurs all get caught in the same net.

Doesn't mean they don't let us go again, of course. It's not as if sociopathy is against the law. Hell, if they screened out everyone with a broken conscience, Executive Class would be empty.

There are children scattered throughout the line. Most are accompanied by adults. Three are not, two boys and a girl. They are nervous and beautiful, like wild animals, easily startled. They are not used to being on their own. The oldest can't be more than nine, and he has a freckle on the side of his neck.

I can't stop watching him.

Suddenly children roam free again. For months now I've been seeing them in parks and plazas, unguarded, innocent and so *vulnerable*, as though SWank has given parents everywhere an excuse to breathe. No matter that it'll be years before it trickles out of airports and government buildings and into the places children play. Mommy and Daddy are tired of waiting, take what comfort they can in the cameras mounted on every street corner, panning and scanning for all the world as if real people stood behind them. Mommy and Daddy can't be bothered to spend five minutes on the web, compiling their own predator's handbook on the use of laser pointers and blind spots to punch holes in the surveillance society. Mommy and Daddy would rather just take all those bromides about "civil safety" on faith.

For so many years we've lived in fear. By now people are so desperate for any pretense of safety that they'll cling to the promise of a future that hasn't even arrived yet. Not that that's anything new; whether you're talking about a house in the suburbs or the browning of Antarctica, Mommy and Daddy have *always* lived on credit.

If something *did* happen to their kids it would serve them right.

The line moves forward. Suddenly I'm at the front of it.

A man with Authority waves me in. I step forward as if to an execution.

I do this for you, Father. I do this to pay my respects. I do this to dance on your grave. If I could have avoided this moment— if this cup could have passed from me, if I could have *walked* to the Northwest Territories rather than let this obscene technology into my head—

Someone has spray-painted two words in stencilled black over the mouth of the machine: *The Shadow*. Delaying, I glance a question at the guard.

"It knows what evil lurks in the hearts of men," he says. "Bwahaha. Let's move it along."

I have no idea what he's talking about.

The walls of the booth glimmer with a tight weave of copper wire. The helmet descends from above with a soft hydraulic hiss; it sits too lightly on my head for such a massive device. The visor slides over my eyes like a blindfold. I am in a pocket universe, alone with my thoughts and an all-seeing God. Electricity hums deep in my head.

I'm innocent of any wrongdoing. I've never broken the law. Maybe God will see that if I think it hard enough. Why does it have to see anything, why does it have to *read* the palimpsest if it's just going to scribble over it again? But brains don't work like that. Each individual *is* individual, wired up in a unique and glorious tangle that must be read before it can be edited. And motivations, intents—these are endless, multiheaded things, twining and proliferating from frontal cortex to cingulate gyrus, from hypothalamus to claustrum. There's no LED that lights up when your plans are nefarious, no Aniston Neuron for mad bombers. For the safety of everyone, they must read it all. For the safety of everyone.

I have been under this helmet for what seems like forever. Nobody else took this long.

The line is not moving forward.

"Well," Security says softly. "Will you look at that?"

"I'm not," I tell him. "I've never—"

"And you're not about to. Not for the next nine hours, anyway."

"I never *acted* on it." I sound petulant, childish. "Not once."

"I can see that," he says, but I know we're talking about different things.

The humming changes subtly in pitch. I can feel magnets and mosquitoes snapping in my head. I am changed by something not yet cheap enough for the home market: an ache evaporates, a dull longing so chronic I feel it now only in absentia.

"There. Now we could put you in charge of two Day Cares and a chorus of alter boys, and you wouldn't even be tempted."

The visor rises; the helmet floats away. Authority stares back at me from a gaggle of contempuous faces.

"This is wrong," I say quietly.

"Is it now."

"I haven't done anything."

"We haven't either. We haven't locked down your pervert brain, we haven't changed who you are. We've protected you precious constitutional rights and your god-given identity. You're as free to diddle kiddies in the park as you ever were. You just won't *want* to for a while."

"But I haven't *done* anything." I can't stop saying it.

"Nobody does, until they do." He jerks his head towards Departure. "Get out of here. You're cleared."

I am not a criminal. I have done nothing wrong. But my name is on a list now, just the same. Word of my depravity races ahead of me, checkpoint after checkpoint, like a fission of dominoes. They'll be watching, though they have to let me pass.

That could change before long. Even now, Community Standards barely recognise the difference between what we do and what we are; nudge them just a hair further and every border on the planet might close at my approach. But this is only the dawning of the new enlightenment, and the latest rules are not yet in place. For now, I am free to stand at your unconsecrated graveside, and mourn on my own recognizance.

You always were big on the power of forgiveness, Father. Seventy times seven, the most egregious sins washed away in the sight of the Lord. All it took, you insisted, was true penitence. All you had to do was accept His love.

Of course, it sounded a lot less self-serving back then.

But even the unbelievers get a clean slate now. My redeemer is a machine, and my salvation has an expiry date— but then again, I guess yours did too.

I wonder about the machine that programmed *you*, Father, that great glacial contraption of dogma and moving parts, clacking and iterating its way through two thousand years of bloody history. I can't help but wonder at the way it rewired *your* synapses. Did it turn you into a predator, weigh you down with lunatic strictures that no sexual being could withstand, deny your very nature until you snapped? Or were you already malfunctioning when you embraced the church, hoping for some measure of strength you couldn't find in yourself?

I knew you for years, Father. Even now, I tell myself I know you— and while you may have been many things, you were never a coward. I refuse to believe that you opted for death because it was the easy way out. I choose to believe that in those last days, you found the strength to rewrite your own programming, to turn your back on obsolete algorithms two millennia out of date, and decide for yourself the difference between a mortal sin and an act of atonement.

You loathed yourself, you loathed the things you had done. And so, finally, you made absolutely certain you could never do them again. You *acted*.

You acted as I never could, though I'd pay so much smaller a price.

There is more than this temporary absolution, you see. We have machines now that can burn the evil right out of a man, deep-focus microwave emitters that vaporise the very pathways of depravity. No one can force them on you; not yet, anyway. Member's bills wind through Parliament, legislative proposals that would see us pre-emptively reprogrammed for good instead of evil, but for now the procedure is strictly voluntary. It *changes* you, you see. It violates some inalienable essence of selfhood. Some call it a kind of suicide in its own right.

I kept telling the man at Security: I never *acted* on it. But he could see that for himself.

I never had it fixed. I must *like* what I am.

I wonder if that makes a difference.

I wonder which of us is more guilty.

FIROOZ AND HIS BROTHER

ALEX JEFFERS

They were all merchants, the men of his family, caravan masters, following the long road from Samarkand to the great city of Baghdad at the center of the world. A youth on his first journey, Firooz often did not know quite what was required of him. Because he wrote a handsome, legible hand and could do sums in his head, before they left Samarkand he had helped his uncle prepare the inventory: silks, porcelains, spices from the distant east; cottons, dyes, spices from the hot lands south of the mountains; carpets, woolens, leather and hides, books from local workshops. On the road, such skills commanded little respect. He could shoot, could manage both short and long blades, but the paid guards knew him for a liability if bandits were to strike: he was his uncle's heir, they had been instructed to protect him. He made coffee when they camped, tended and groomed the horses of his uncle and the other merchants, cared for their hounds. Mostly he felt superfluous.

Along one of the many desolate stretches when the plodding caravan was days away from the town it had last passed through and the next, his uncle told him to take his bow and one of the hounds, ride away from the bustle and clamor of the caravan to hunt. Fresh game would be a treat.

Before they had gone very far, the hound sighted a small herd of deer grazing on the scrub. When Firooz loosed the hound, she coursed across the plain, silent. Holding his bow ready and drawing an arrow from the quiver, Firooz spurred his horse after. On an abrupt shift of the breeze, the deer caught the hunters' scent. Lifting their heads as one, they turned and fled, leaping and bounding across the plain.

The hound had her eye on a particular animal she must have sensed to be weaker or more confused than the others. She pursued it relentlessly, leading Firooz farther and farther from the caravan, into a broken country where strange spires of jagged rock thrust up through the loose soil, twisted little trees clinging to their flanks. All the other deer had vanished. The young buck they followed cantered nimbly among the spires and towers and bastions. Steep shadows fell from tall spires and scarps, filling narrow passages with dusk. Springs and streams flowed here, watering the soil and nourishing seeming gardens of wildflowers in bloom, more lovely than anything Firooz had seen since leaving Samarkand. There were trees as well, protected from the winds of the plain, tall and straight and broad, and lush stretches of green turf. If he had not been intent on the deer's white rump and the hound's feathered tail, Firooz should have been astounded.

The deer's strength was failing. It staggered, leapt forward again, ducked around a steep formation. The hound sped after it. Wrenching his mare around the corner, Firooz entered the deep, cool shade of a woods cramped narrowly between two arms of rock and slowed to a walk. He saw neither deer nor hound among the trees. There was nowhere to go but forward, however. The mare's hooves fell muffled on leaf mold. Firooz did not recognize the trees.

After a time, he heard barking ahead and spurred the horse into an easy trot. The barks broke up, became distinct: two different voices. Over the hound's melodious baying, which echoed from the high walls of the canyon, sounded the sharp, warning yaps of a second dog.

Firooz was ready, when he passed between tall trees into a small clearing, to rein in the mare and leap to the ground between the two animals. He grabbed for the collar of the sand-colored bitch but she, startled and snarling, eluded him, bounded over the sweet grass and leapt upon the other, smaller dog. Courageous or stubborn, it shook her off the first time and stood its ground, growling ferociously. It was scarcely more than a puppy. Wrapping the excess fabric of his jallabiya about his forearm, Firooz stepped forward to separate them but stumbled and fell. By the time he regained his feet, the bitch hound had torn open the puppy's throat and stood over her fallen foe, jaws red and dripping. Still growling, the puppy lay on its side, panting from the new scarlet mouth in its throat as well as the one it had been born with, bleeding heavily from both.

Saddened by the bad end to such outsize courage, Firooz cuffed the hound aside and severed the younger dog's spine with a single stroke of his Damascus blade. For a long moment, he regarded the small corpse, while the hound lay at her ease, licking her chops, and the mare cropped at the grass between her feet. Clearly, the dead dog was not wild, native to the desolation—had been cared for, tended, for its woolly black coat gleamed where not matted and dulled by blood and it appeared well nourished. Heavy shoulders and sturdy limbs suggested it had not been a courser; though not fully grown, it would not have become large enough to threaten big predators, bears, wolves, leopards: it was surely not a hunter's dog.

Puzzled and regretful, Firooz did not at first properly hear or understand the muffled wailing that rose almost between his feet. The hound had returned, to nose interestedly at the corpse. He shoved her away again and gently lifted the dead dog aside.

It had died protecting its charge. In a perfectly sized depression in the grass lay the crying babe, naked but for spatters of the dog's scarlet blood. Firooz's first, terrible impulse was to kill it, too, and ride away.

The hound was back again, licking the blood from the baby's perfect skin. Her soft, damp tongue seemed to calm it—him—and after a time the babe ceased wailing. Looking away, Firooz cleaned and sheathed his sword. He didn't know what to do.

He knew what to do. Removing his rolled prayer rug from the mare's back, he wrapped the dead dog in it and fastened it again behind the saddle. The horse bridled and shied at the scent of blood. He took a clean scarf from the saddle bag. Kneeling by the baby, he nudged the hound aside for the last time. He moistened a corner of the scarf to wipe away the remaining traces of blood. The quiet baby stared up at him with a knowing, toothless smile. Picking up the baby, Firooz wound the scarf about his pliant body—somehow he knew how to hold him so he didn't complain. Firooz couldn't figure out how to mount the mare while holding the baby, so he took the reins, called the hound to heel, and set out walking back to the caravan. Along the way, he decided to name the baby Haider, after his grandfather.

Stranger things than discovering an abandoned child in the wilderness had occurred in the hundreds of years since caravans began traveling between Samarkand and Baghdad. The doctor who accompanied the caravan proclaimed Haider fit. A nursing goat was found to provide milk. The dead dog was buried with dignity, its grave marked by a cairn of stones beside the road. Firooz's uncle said he should raise Haider as his son, to which Firooz replied, "I am unmarried and too young to be a father. He shall be my brother."

Haider grew and prospered. Firooz, too, prospered. In time, he married his uncle's daughter as had been arranged in their childhood. In time, he took his uncle's place at the head of the caravan. His wife did not travel with him, but his brother Haider did. In all this time, Haider had become a handsome, pious, merry young man; he, too, was appropriately and happily wed, and when the brothers departed for distant Baghdad their wives remained together in the comfortable Samarkand house, caring for Haider's children, two small boys and a lovely girl. For the elder brother's marriage, though happy, remained childless: his wife quickened readily enough but always lost the baby before its time. Their family—indeed, the unhappy not-mother herself—urged Firooz to take a second wife, but always he refused. He loved his wife well, he said, and as for heirs he had his young brother and his brother's sons.

The caravan was heading again for Baghdad. Reaching the spot marked by the dog's grave's cairn, Firooz called a halt, although it was scarcely noon. There was a spring here and often game nearby. He called his brother to him. "You have often heard of how, by the will of God, I found you," he said. "We have passed the grave of your first protector many times, but I have never shown you the place where I found you, not so far away. While our companions hunt, let us go there."

They took with them two fine hounds, descendants of the first bitch. Now and again they sighted game but, though the hounds complained, did not loose them. Firooz felt he knew his heading exactly although it was now twenty-one years since he followed the long-lost buck deer. They entered the broken country, then the region of strange spires and canyons and lush vegetation. Haider exclaimed at the beauty of the place, but Firooz felt an odd urgency pulling at him and led his brother on without pausing. When they came to the narrowly enclosed woods, the hounds strained at their leashes and, as they progressed farther among the tree shadows, bayed.

They were answered by furious barking, of a timbre Firooz, twenty-one years later, recognized. Keeping a strong hand on his hound's leash, he spurred his horse forward.

Awaiting them in the clearing, stalwart, as if the years had not passed, was a half-grown dog fleeced like a black lamb, which Firooz could not distinguish from the dog he had killed and buried. The two men dismounted hastily. Without needing to be asked, Firooz took the leash of the second straining hound. The black dog continued to bark as Haider gingerly approached, but these were clearly cries of joy and welcome. Falling to his knees, Haider embraced the animal. When he looked up at his brother, Firooz saw tears on his cheeks. "I seem to know this dog," he said.

"It cannot be the same one," said Firooz, but he was confused by this marvel.

Properly introduced, the hounds made friends with the black dog, which Haider began calling Iman as if he had always known her name. Iman gratefully accepted several pieces of dried meat, and showed the men a spring and small pond as artfully placed under the overhanging cliff as if an architect had designed it. Beyond the high scarps around this place, the sun was lowering. Firooz and his brother washed at the spring, laid out their prayer rugs toward Holy Mecca, and made the declaration of their faith. Firooz's rug still bore faint stains of blood.

Haider built a small fire and prepared coffee. The hobbled horses grazed contentedly on grass sweeter than any they had encountered since departing Samarkand, while the three dogs lay about—Iman always near her master— panting, happy. The brothers reclined with their coffee, talking of matters of no importance, but not speaking of marvels.

After, heated with the spirit of the coffee, they removed their garments and embraced. They were men, they were fond of each other, they were long away from their wives. No words needed to be spoken as each gave pleasure to the other, as none had ever been spoken.

Yet afterward, when they woke from slumber and lay side by side, content, Haider said, "My brother, do you truly not regret having no children?"

Firooz considered. It was not a question he had not had to answer before. "It saddens me," he said, "that my wife cannot bear our children safely, for she so wishes to be a mother. And yet, one day she may, for I myself was my father's late, unexpected child, after his wife had been barren for many years. As for my own wishes—it was God's will to grant me a brother after both my parents had died. My uncle told me to call you *son*, but it was a brother God gave me and I have never not been glad of you. Now, moreover, there are your sons and daughter at home, whom I could not value more if they were my own."

"This is what you say, and it is a fine answer. Is it what you feel?" Haider rose to his feet, as naked as the day Firooz found him. As Firooz admired him, Haider said, "I believe I can give you a child of your own blood—and mine," and as Firooz watched, amazed, the handsome young man was transformed into a beautiful young woman. "Ask no questions," she said, kneeling at his side and placing her hand on his lips, "for I cannot answer them." She kissed his mouth.

They made love again, and it was not so very different than before, except that Haider gave only, did not take. Indeed, when he remembered it later, Firooz felt he preferred the manliness of Haider as he had been or the different womanliness of his own wife.

When both were spent, the woman who had been his brother kissed him again, and rose, and gathered up the garments of a man. As she drew them on, her form appeared to melt within the fabric, assuming again the guise of Firooz's brother Haider. Beard grew on cheeks now more wide and flat, around lips more thin and hard. The long sable glory of the woman's hair drifted away, leaving only black stubble on Haider's well-shaped skull. "We should return to the camp," he said, offering a hand to help Firooz up.

Grasping it, Firooz held the small, smooth hand of the woman. He started and, as he blinked, saw for an instant the woman encumbered in outsize man's clothing, but the vision fled when his brother's gripping hand and strong right arm hauled him to his feet. Numbed by astonishment, frightened, he stumbled about, donning his own clothes while Haider rolled up their rugs and repacked the coffee service. The younger man mounted his horse easily, called to the dog, Iman, who came readily, keeping a sane distance from the horse's hooves.

Haider appeared to remain Haider, a man, for the rest of the journey to Baghdad. Still, Firooz continued troubled. Perhaps it had been simply a dream, his brother's transformation—they did not speak of it, nor came there again an occasion that he might touch his brother, see him whole and nude and prove that vision false. Yet sometimes, regarding Haider over an evening's fire, Firooz thought the younger man looked ill, drawn and pale; sometimes, as they rode, the straight-backed youth appeared for an instant to slump in his saddle and to resemble more a weary woman than an energetic, cheerful man. The black dog—which followed Haider everywhere, received choice morsels from his bowl, sometimes rode perched before him on the saddle, held safe by his strong arm—would bark, Haider would smile and shake his head, and Firooz blink.

In the great city of Baghdad, Firooz conducted his business out of the caravansary maintained by the merchants of Samarkand, selling, buying, bartering, trading. It was already a profitable venture. For some days business occupied him to the exclusion of any other concern. Then a late-arriving caravan brought him a sad letter from his wife in Samarkand: she had not told him before his departure that she believed herself with child and it was just as well for, by God's will, she had lost this baby too, soon after he left. Yet she was well, recovered from the injury to her body if not the wound to her soul; her sister (by which she meant Haider's wife) was a constant comfort, Haider's children constant joys. She awaited her husband's return with fond resolve.

Haider entered Firooz's chamber as he finished reading the letter and set it aside, his eyes wet. "You are once again not to be an uncle," Firooz said.

"I know. My wife, also, wrote to me." Haider poured cool water for his brother, offered a scented kerchief to wipe his eyes. "I grieve with you."

Firooz drank. "Nevertheless," he said, "I meant what I said, the day you found Iman." (Hearing her name, the dog yapped, before curling up for a nap.) "I should like a child, for my poor wife's sake, but I have no need of one." He held out a hand for his brother to grip.

Though Haider's well-known, well-loved face did not change, it was a woman's hand Firooz grasped, small boned and soft, and a woman's full, quickening belly to which his palm was pressed. "You are to be a father, brother," Haider said in his deep, full voice, "and I a mother." He held Firooz's hand to his belly a moment longer, exerting a man's strength to prevent his recoiling. "Although I should prefer your wife raise the child, as I have other responsibilities."

"How is this possible?"

"Do you question the will of merciful and compassionate God?"

"Are you a jinni? An ifrit?"

"I am a creature of earth even as yourself, not a being of fire. I am a man: your brother. And a woman—not your sister nor your wife, but the mother of your unborn child. Firooz, my dear, there is no more I can tell you. I mean you only good."

Firooz recoiled when Haider approached again.

"I came," Haider said with a gentle smile, "to take you away from your new sorrow and your weary business. Tomorrow we go to the Friday Mosque to say our prayers among the ummah. This evening I intend to dedicate to your comfort and ease. Come, brother. This other matter need not concern you for some months yet. Come."

Still troubled, Firooz gave in. Leaving the disappointed Iman behind, Haider led Firooz out into the streets of the city, first to a hammam as splendid as the finest mosque. Here they bathed—Firooz felt immeasurable relief when he saw that Haider, wearing no more than a cloth around his hips, appeared no less masculine than he ought, his belly flat and firm, his chest and shoulders broad. Attendants massaged them in turn; others shaved the hair from their scalps and bodies, as was meet, oiled and perfumed their beards; still others brought coffee when at length they reclined on soft couches and did not speak.

From the hammam, they went on to the house of a gentleman of their acquaintance, an elderly merchant who left the traveling to his sons and nephews, where they were fed dishes from distant lands and offered conversation of the kind to be encountered only in great cities.

Finally, pleasantly weary and replete, they returned to Firooz's rooms at the caravansary. Iman greeted them with great joy, not lessened by the little bowl of tidbits Haider had smuggled under his robes from their dinner. Firooz seated himself again before his accounts and inventories.

"No," said Haider, firm. Drawing his brother to his feet, he undressed Firooz and laid him down on the couch, removed his own clothing, blew out the lamp.

Making love, Firooz was uncertain from moment to moment whether the person in his arms was a strong, slender, forceful man or a soft, yielding, fecund woman. For one night, it seemed, it didn't matter.

A month later, they departed Baghdad at the head of a caravan laden with the goods of all western Islam as well as infidel Europe and savage Africa. Some months into the journey, they came again to the cairn of stones by the road and here again they halted. As camp was set up, the black dog Iman became agitated. She circled the grave of her predecessor several times, then, barking and whining, made Haider accompany her in investigating it again. She led him to the edge of the encampment and gazed long across the plain where, beyond the horizon, lay the place she had been found. At last, Haider went to his brother, the dog whining and yapping at his heels, and said, "I must go. Will you come with me?"

The place, when they came to it, had not changed, but Haider had. Dismounting from his horse, he was no longer a sturdy young merchant but a frail, weary woman whose inappropriate, ill-fitting garments did nothing to disguise the belly round and full as a melon, the brimming breasts like ripe pears. Frightened as much for as of her, Firooz ran to take her arm. "It is early, I would have thought," she said. "I should have known God would lead me here, again, to bear my child."

"There is no midwife," Firooz protested, "no shelter."

"We shall manage."

Her labor was short, though she bit her lips to bleeding from the pain and clenched her fists so tight as to leave bruises on Firooz's hand and cause the dog that lay on her other side, shoulders under her hand, to yelp. When his son came, Firooz was ready to catch him, marveling, weeping, to lift him, all bloody and damp, to his cheek. He severed the cord with the blade that had killed Iman's predecessor. The mother pushed out the afterbirth onto the rug stained by much older blood and lay back, resting her aching legs. "Is he beautiful?" she asked.

"He is beautiful," the father said, tender, cleaning the baby with fresh water from the spring.

"Give him my breast," she said, "for I think I shall not keep it long."

While the baby suckled, the man washed the woman, prepared a clean place for her to lie and coffee to soothe and revive her. When the baby slept, tiny hand curled around a lock of Iman's fur, the woman rose slowly to her feet. "Bring me my clothing, please, Firooz," she said.

As she dressed, the transformation occurred, so subtly Firooz could not determine the instant he saw no longer the mother of his son but his brother Haider. The young man knelt by his nephew but did not touch. "What will you call your son?"

"Khayrat."

Haider smiled. The old word meant *good deed*. "A fine name." He stood again. "We should return to camp. It will be dark soon."

"Will you carry him?"

"No, brother. I meant him for you."

There was no other man in the caravan who remembered Firooz's finding Haider twenty-two years before, none to call his finding Khayrat other than good fortune for fatherless babe and childless father alike. When, months later in Samarkand, Firooz's wife took Khayrat from her husband's arms, she was nearly reconciled to her own barrenness.

Haider never again, to his brother's knowledge, became a woman; never, in word or action, admitted to being more than Khayrat's fond uncle. The dog Iman was spoiled and petted by children and adults alike, though she never forgot where her love and loyalty lay, never slept where she could not hear Haider's breath. She bore litters to passing dogs, and every puppy resembled her, and when after a long life at last she died, there was another fleecy black bitch to be his companion.

The years passed, between Samarkand and Baghdad, bringing the family instants of joy and good fortune, sorrow and bad luck, as God had written in their fates. Haider's wife died of a fever, her children still young. The family mourned but went on, as it must. Haider did not marry again. When they were old enough, his sons—and later Khayrat—journeyed with the caravan to and from Baghdad. Grown to manhood, they led it, and their fathers remained at home.

They sat in their garden by a singing fountain, Firooz and his brother.

Haider stroked the flank of his dog and said, "Long ago, Firooz, I told you I was no jinni or ifrit, but a creature of earth like yourself. But unlike, as well. Beneficent and compassionate God made many worlds, interleaved like the pages of a great book. Some lie as close to another as any two surahs of the Holy Qur'an, others as distant as the beginning from the end. In some, things that are impossible here are commonplace; in others, everything we take for granted is entirely unknown. There are worlds that contain no miracles at all, worlds where a new miracle is born every morning. The earth from which God molded my ancestors, brother, lies in another world. It is time, I think, for my dog and me to go home."

"Haider?" Firooz gripped his brother's hand to prevent him from rising.

"I believe there is only one Paradise, Firooz. We shall meet again in not too long. Let me go, brother." Tender, he kissed the back of Firooz's hand and raised it to touch his own forehead. "I cannot love you less, here or elsewhere."

"I should die before you!" Firooz closed his eyes, desolate.

"It is not to death I am going. Give my blessing and my love to my sons." Gentle, he removed his fingers from Firooz's hand, kissed his brow. When his brother opened his eyes again, dog and man were gone as if they had never set foot on the earth of Firooz's world. The elder brother wept, and then, as he must, went on living until he died.

INFESTATION

GARTH NIX

———

They were the usual motley collection of freelance vampire hunters. Two men, wearing combinations of jungle camouflage and leather. Two women, one almost indistinguishable from the men though with a little more style in her leather armour accessories, and the other looking like she was about to assault the south face of a serious mountain. Only her mouth was visible, a small oval of flesh not covered by balaclava, mirror shades, climbing helmet and hood.

They had the usual weapons: four or five short wooden stakes in belt loops; snap-holstered handguns of various calibers, all doubtless chambered with Wood-N-Death® low-velocity timber-tipped rounds; big silver-edged bowie or other hunting knife, worn on the hip or strapped to a boot; and crystal vials of holy water hung like small grenades on pocket loops.

Protection, likewise, tick the usual boxes. Leather neck and wrist guards; leather and woven-wire reinforced chaps and shoulder pauldrons over the camo; leather gloves with metal knuckle plates; Army or climbing helmets.

And lots of crosses, oh yeah, particularly on the two men. Big silver crosses, little wooden crosses, medium-sized turned ivory crosses, hanging off of everything they could hang off.

In other words, all four of them were lumbering, bumbling mountains of stuff that meant that they would be easy meat for all but the newest and dumbest vampires.

They all looked at me as I walked up. I guess their first thought was to wonder what the hell I was doing there, in the advertised meeting place, outside a church at 4.30pm on a winter's day while the last rays of the sun were supposedly making this consecrated ground a double no-go zone for vampires.

"You're in the wrong place, surfer boy," growled one of the men.

I was used to this reaction. I guess I don't look like a vampire hunter much anyway, and I particularly didn't look like one that afternoon. I'd been on the beach that morning, not knowing where I might head to later, so I was still wearing a yellow Quiksilver T-shirt and what might be loosely described as old and faded blue board shorts, but 'ragged' might be more accurate. I hadn't had shoes on, but I'd picked up a pair of sandals on the way. Tan Birkenstocks, very comfortable. I always prefer sandals to shoes. Old habits, I guess.

I don't look my age, either. I always looked young, and nothing's changed, though 'boy' was a bit rough coming from anyone under forty-five, and the guy who'd spoken was probably closer to thirty. People older than that usually leave the vampire hunting to the government, or paid professionals.

"I'm in the right place," I said, matter-of-fact, not getting into any aggression or anything. I lifted my 1968-vintage vinyl Pan-Am airline bag. "Got my stuff here. This is the meeting place for the vampire hunt?"

"Yes," said the mountain-climbing woman.

"Are you crazy?" asked the man who'd spoken to me first. "This isn't some kind of doper excursion. We're going up against a nest of vampires!"

I nodded and gave him a kind smile.

"I know. At least ten of them, I would say. I swung past and had a look around on the way here. At least, I did if you're talking about that condemned factory up on the river heights."

"What! But it's cordoned off—and the vamps'll be dug in till nightfall."

"I counted the patches of disturbed earth," I explained. "The cordon was off. I guess they don't bring it up to full power till the sun goes down. So, who are you guys?"

"Ten!" exclaimed the second man, not answering my question. "You're sure?"

"At least ten," I replied. "But only one Ancient. The others are all pretty new, judging from the spoil."

"You're making this up," said the first man. "There's maybe five, tops. They were seen together and tracked back. That's when the cordon was established this morning."

I shrugged and half-unzipped my bag.

"I'm Jenny," said the mountain-climber, belatedly answering my question. "The . . . the vampires got my sister, three years ago. When I heard about this infestation I claimed the Relative's Right."

"I've got a twelve month permit," said the second man. "Plan to turn professional. Oh yeah, my name's Karl."

"I'm Susan," said the second woman. "This is our third vampire hunt. Mike's and mine, I mean."

"She's my wife," said the belligerent Mike. "We've both got twelve month permits. You'd better be legal too, if you want to join us."

"I have a special licence," I replied. The sun had disappeared behind the church tower, and the street lights were flicking on. With the bag unzipped, I was ready for a surprise. Not that I thought one was about to happen. At least, not immediately. Unless I chose to spring one.

"You can call me J."

"Jay?" asked Susan.

"Close enough," I replied. "Does someone have a plan?"

"Yeah," said Mike. "We stick together. No hot-dogging off, or chasing down wounded vamps or anything like that. We go in as a team, and we come out as a team."

"Interesting," I said. "Is there . . . more to it?"

Mike paused to fix me with what he obviously thought was his steely gaze. I met it and after a few seconds he looked away. Maybe it's the combination of very pale blue eyes and dark skin, but not many people look at me directly for too long. It might just be the eyes. There've been quite a few cultures who think of very light blue eyes as the colour of death. Perhaps that lingers, resonating in the subconscious even of modern folk.

"We go through the front door," he said. "We throw flares ahead of us. The vamps should all be digging out on the old factory floor, it's the only place where the earth is accessible. So we go down the fire stairs, throw a few more flares out the door then go through and back up against the wall. We'll have a clear field of fire to take them down. They'll be groggy for a couple of hours yet, slow to move. But if one or two manage to close, we stake them."

"The young ones will be slow and dazed," I said. "But the Ancient will be active soon after sundown, even if it stays where it is—and it's not dug in on the factory floor. It's in a humungous clay pot outside an office on the fourth floor."

"We take it first, then," said Mike. "Not that I'm sure I believe you."

"It's up to you," I said. I had my own ideas about dealing with the Ancient, but they would wait. No point upsetting Mike too early. "There's one more thing."

"What?" asked Karl.

"There's a fresh-made vampire around, from last night. It will still be able to pass as human for a few more days. It won't be dug-in, and it may not even know it's infected."

"So?" asked Mike. "We kill everything in the infested area. That's all legal."

"How do you know this stuff?" asked Jenny.

"You're a professional, aren't you," said Karl. "How long you been pro?"

"I'm not exactly a professional," I said. "But I've been hunting vampires for quite a while."

"Can't have been that long," said Mike. "Or you'd know better than to go after them in just a T-shirt. What've you got in that bag? Sawn-off shotgun?"

"Just a stake and a knife," I replied. "I'm a traditionalist. Shouldn't we be going?"

The sun was fully down, and I knew the Ancient, at least, would already be reaching up through the soil, its mildewed, mottled hands gripping the rim of the earthenware pot that had once held a palm or something equally impressive outside the factory manager's office.

"Truck's over there," said Mike, pointing to a flashy new silver pick-up. "You can ride in the back, surfer boy."

"Fresh air's a wonderful thing."

As it turned out, Karl and Jenny wanted to sit in the back too. I sat on a tool box that still had shrink-wrap around it, Jenny sat on a spare tire and Karl stood looking over the cab, scanning the road, as if a vampire might suddenly jump out when we were stopped at the lights.

"Do you want a cross?" Jenny asked me after we'd gone a mile or so in silence. Unlike Mike and Karl she wasn't festooned with them, but she had a couple around her neck. She started to take a small wooden one off, lifting it by the chain.

I shook my head, and raised my T-shirt up under my arms, to show the scars. Jenny recoiled in horror and gasped, and Karl looked around, hand going for his .41 Glock. I couldn't tell whether that was jumpiness or good training. He didn't draw and shoot, which I guess meant good training.

I let the T-shirt fall, but it was up long enough for both of them to see the hackwork tracery of scars that made up a kind of 'T' shape on my chest and stomach. But it wasn't a 'T'. It was a Tau Cross, one of the oldest Christian symbols and still the one that vampires feared the most, though none but the most ancient knew why they fled from it.

"Is that . . . a cross?" asked Karl.

I nodded.

"That's so hardcore," said Karl. "Why didn't you just have it tattooed?"

"It probably wouldn't work so well," I said. "And I didn't have it done. It was done to me."

I didn't mention that there was an equivalent tracery of scars on my back as well. These two Tau Crosses, front and back, never faded, though my other scars always disappeared only a few days after they healed.

"Who would—" Jenny started to ask, but she was interrupted by Mike banging on the rear window of the cab—with the butt of his pistol, reconfirming my original assessment that he was the biggest danger to all of us. Except for the Ancient Vampire. I wasn't worried about the young ones. But I didn't know which Ancient it was, and that was cause for concern. If it had been encysted since the drop it would be in the first flush of its full strength. I hoped it had been around for a long time, lying low and steadily degrading, only recently resuming its mission against humanity.

"We're there," said Karl, unnecessarily.

The cordon fence was fully established now. Sixteen feet high and lethally-electrified, with old-fashioned limelights burning every ten feet along the fence, the sound of the hissing oxygen and hydrogen jets music to my ears. Vampires loath limelight. Gaslight has a lesser effect, and electric light hardly bothers them at all. It's the intensity of the naked flame they fear.

The fire brigade was standing by because of the limelights, which though modernized were still occasionally prone to massive accidental combustion; and the local police department was there en masse to enforce the cordon. I saw the bright white bulk of the state Vampire Eradication Team's semi-trailer parked off to one side. If we volunteers failed, they would go in, though given the derelict state of the building and the reasonable space between it and the nearest residential area it was more likely they'd just get the Air Force to do a fuel-air explosion dump.

The VET personnel would be out and about already, making sure no vampires managed to get past the cordon. There would be crossbow snipers on the upper floors of the surrounding buildings, ready to shoot fire-hardened oak quarrels into vampire heads. It wasn't advertised by the ammo manufacturers, but a big old vampire could take forty or fifty Wood-N-Death® or equivalent rounds to the head and chest before going down. A good inch-diameter yard-long quarrel or stake worked so much better.

There would be a VET quick response team somewhere close as well, outfitted in the latest metal-mesh armour, carrying the automatic weapons the volunteers were not allowed to use—with good reason, given the frequency with which volunteer vampire hunters killed each other even when only armed with handguns, stakes and knives.

I waved at the window of the three storey warehouse where I'd caught a glimpse of a crossbow sniper, earning a puzzled glance from Karl and Jenny, then jumped down. A police sergeant was already walking over to us, his long, harsh lime-lit shadow preceding him. Naturally, Mike intercepted him before he could choose who he wanted to talk to.

"We're the volunteer team."

"I can see that," said the sergeant. "Who's the kid?"

He pointed at me. I frowned. The kid stuff was getting monotonous. I don't look that young. Twenty at least, I would have thought.

"He says his name's Jay. He's got a 'special licence'. That's what he says."

"Let's see it then," said the sergeant, with a smile that suggested he was looking forward to arresting me and delivering a three-hour lecture. Or perhaps a beating with a piece of rubber pipe. It isn't always easy to decipher smiles.

"I'll take it from here, sergeant," said an officer who came up from behind me, fast and smooth. He was in the new metal-mesh armour, like a wetsuit, with webbing belt and harness over it, to hold stakes, knife, WP grenades (which actually were effective against the vamps, unlike the holy water ones) and handgun. He had an H&K MP5-PW slung over his shoulder. "You go and check the cordon."

"But lieutenant, don't you want me to take—"

"I said check the cordon."

The sergeant retreated, smile replaced by a scowl of frustration. The VET lieutenant ignored him.

"Licences, please," he said. He didn't look at me, and unlike the others I didn't reach for the plasticated, hologrammed, data-chipped card that was the latest version of the volunteer vampire hunter licence.

They held their licences up and the reader that was somewhere in the lieutenant's helmet picked up the data and his earpiece whispered whether they were valid or not. Since he was nodding, we all knew they were valid before he spoke.

"OK, you're good to go whenever you want. Good luck."

"What about him?" asked Mike, gesturing at me with his thumb.

"Him too," said the lieutenant. He still didn't look at me. Some of the VET are funny like that. They seem to think I'm like an albatross or something. A sign of bad luck. I suppose it's because wherever the vampire infestations are really bad, then I have a tendency to show up as well. "He's already been checked in. We'll open the gate in five, if that suits you."

"Sure," said Mike. He lumbered over to face me. "There's something funny going on here, and I don't like it. So you just stick to the plan, OK?"

"Actually, your plan sucks," I said calmly. "So I've decided to change it. You four should go down to the factory floor and take out the vampires there. I'll go up against the Ancient."

"Alone?" asked Jenny. "Shouldn't we stick together like Mike says?"

"Nope," I replied. "It'll be out and unbending itself now. You'll all be too slow."

"Call this sl—" Mike started to say, as he tried to poke me forcefully in the chest with his forefinger. But I was already standing behind him. I tapped him on the shoulder, and as he swung around, ran behind him again. We kept this up for a few turns before Karl stopped him.

"See what I mean? And an Ancient Vampire is faster than me."

That was blarney. Or at least I hoped it was. I'd met Ancient Vampires who were as quick as I was, but not actually faster. Sometimes I did wonder what would happen if one day I was a fraction slower and one finally got me for good and all. Some days, I kind of hoped that it would happen.

But not this day. I hadn't had to go up against any vampires or anything else for over a month. I'd been surfing for the last two weeks, hanging out on the beach, eating well, drinking a little wine and even letting down my guard long enough to spend a couple of nights with a girl who surfed better than me and didn't mind having sex in total darkness with a guy who kept his T-shirt on and an old airline bag under the pillow.

I was still feeling good from this little holiday, though I knew it would only ever be that. A few weeks snatched out of . . .

"OK," panted Mike. He wasn't as stupid as I'd feared but he was a lot less fit than he looked. "You do your thing. We'll take the vampires on the factory floor."

"Good," I replied. "Presuming I survive, I'll come down and help you."

"What do . . . what do we do if we . . . if we're losing?" asked Jenny. She had her head well down, her chin almost tucked into her chest and her body-language screamed out that she was both scared and miserable. "I mean if there are more vampires, or if the Ancient one—

"We fight or we die," said Karl. "No one is allowed back out through the cordon until after dawn."

"Oh, I didn't . . . I mean I read the brochure—"

"You don't have to go in," I said. "You can wait out here."

"I . . . I think I will," she said, without looking at the others. "I just can't . . . now I'm here, I just can't face it."

"Great!" muttered Mike. "One of us down already."

"She's too young," said Susan. I was surprised she'd speak up against Mike. I had her down as his personal doormat. "Don't give her a hard time, Mike."

"No time for anything," I said. "They're getting ready to power down the gate."

A cluster of regular police officers and VET agents were taking up positions around the gate in the cordon fence. We walked over, the others switching on helmet lights, drawing their handguns and probably silently uttering last-minute prayers.

The sergeant who'd wanted to give me a hard time looked at Mike, who gave him the thumbs up. A siren sounded a slow whoop-whoop-whoop as a segment of the cordon fence powered down, the indicators along the top rail fading from a warning red to a dull green.

"Go, go, go!" shouted Mike, and he jogged forward, with Susan and Karl at his heels. I followed a few metres behind, but not too far. That sergeant had the control box for the gate and I didn't trust him not to close it on my back and power it up at the same time. I really didn't want to know what 6,600 volts at 500 milliamps would do to my unusual physiology. Or show anyone else what didn't happen, more to the point.

On the other hand, I didn't want to get ahead of Mike and co., either, because I already know what being shot in the back by accident felt like, with lead and wooden bullets, not to mention ceramic-cased tungsten tipped penetrator rounds, and I didn't want to repeat the experience.

They rushed the front door, Mike kicking it in and bulling through. The wood was rotten and the top panel had already fallen off, so this was less of an achievement than it might have been.

Karl was quick with the flares, confirming his thorough training. Mike, on the other hand, just kept going, so the light was behind him as he opened the fire door to the left of the lobby.

Bad move. There was a vampire behind the door, and while it was no ancient, it wasn't newly-hatched either. It wrapped its arms around Mike, holding on with the filaments that lined its forelegs, though to an uneducated observer it just looked like a fairly slight, tattered rag-wearing human bear-hugging him with rather longer than usual arms.

Mike screamed as the vampire started chewing on his helmet, ripping through the Kevlar layers like a buzz-saw through softwood, pausing only to spit out bits of the material. Old steel helmets are better than the modern variety, but we live in an age that values only the new.

Vamps like to get a good grip around their prey, particularly ones who carry weapons. There was nothing Mike could do, and as the vamp was already backing into the stairwell, only a second or two for someone else to do something.

The vampire fell to the ground, its forearm filaments coming loose with a sticky popping sound, though they probably hadn't penetrated Mike's heavy clothes. I pulled the splinter out of its head and put the stake of almost two thousand year-old timber back in the bag before the others got a proper look at the odd silver sheen that came from deep within the wood.

Karl dragged Mike back into the flare-light as Susan covered him. Both of them were pretty calm, I thought. At least they were still doing stuff, rather than freaking out.

"Oh man," said Karl. He'd sat Mike up, and then had to catch him again as he fell backwards. Out in the light, I saw that I'd waited just that second too long, perhaps from some subconscious dislike of the man. The last few vampire bites had not been just of Mike's helmet.

"What . . . what do we do?" asked Susan. She turned to me, pointedly not looking at her dead husband.

"I'm sorry," I said. I really meant it, particularly since it was my slackness that had let the Vamp finish him off. Mike was an idiot but he didn't deserve to die, and I could have saved him. "But he's got to be dealt with the same way as the vampires now. Then you and Karl have to go down and clean out the rest. Otherwise they'll kill you too."

It usually helps to state the situation clearly. Stave off the shock with the need to do something life-saving. Adrenalin focuses the mind wonderfully.

Susan looked away for a couple of seconds. I thought she might vomit, but I'd underestimated her again. She turned back, and still holding her pistol in her right hand, reached into a thigh pocket and pulled out a Quick-Flame™.

"I should be the one to do it," she said. Karl stepped back as she thumbed the Quick-Flame™ and dropped it on corpse. The little cube deliquesced into a jelly film that spread over the torso of what had once been a man. Then, as it splashed on the floor, it woofed alight, burning blue.

Susan watched the fire. I couldn't see much of her face, but from what I could see, I thought she'd be OK for about an hour before the shock knocked her off her feet. Provided she got on with the job as soon as possible.

"You'd better get going," I said. "If this one was already up here, the others might be out and about. Don't get ahead of your flares."

"Right," muttered Karl. He took another flare from a belt pouch. "Ready, Susan?"

"Yes."

Karl tossed the flare down the stairs. They both waited to see the glow of its light come back up, then Karl edged in, working the angle, his pistol ready. He fired almost immediately, two double taps, followed by the sound of a vamp falling back down the stairs.

"Put two more in," I called out, but Karl was already firing again.

"And stake it before you go past!" I added as they both disappeared down the stair.

As soon as they were gone, I checked the smouldering remains of Mike. Quick-Flame™ cubes are all very well, but they don't always burn everything and if there's a critical mass of organic material left then the Vamp nanos can build a new one. A little, slow one, but little slow ones can grow up. I doubted there'd been enough exchange of blood to get full infestation, but it's better to be sure, so I took out the splinter again and waved it over the fragments that were left.

The sound of rapid gunshots began to echo up from below as I took off my T-shirt and tucked it in the back of my board shorts. The Tau cross on my chest was already glowing softly with a silver light, the smart matter under the scars energizing as it detected Vamp activity close-by. I couldn't see the one on my back, but it would be doing the same thing. Together they were supposed to generate a field that repulsed the vampires and slowed them down if they got close, but it really only worked on the original versions. The latter-day generations of vampires were such bad copies that a lot of the original tech built to deter them simply missed the mark. Fortunately, being bad copies, the newer vampires were weaker, slower, less intelligent and untrained.

I took the main stairs up to the fourth floor. The Ancient Vampire would already know I was coming so there was no point skulking up the elevator shaft or the outside drain. Like its broodmates, it had been bred to be a perfect soldier at various levels of conflict, from the nanonic frontline where it tried to replicate itself in its enemies to the gross physical contest of actually duking it out. Back in the old days it might have had some distance weapons as well, but if there was one thing we'd managed right in the original mission it was taking out the Vamp weapons caches and resupply nodes.

We did a lot of things right in the original mission. We succeeded rather too well, or at least so we thought at the time. If the victory hadn't been so much faster than anticipated, the boss would never have had those years to fall in love with humans and then work out his crazy scheme to become their living god.

Not so crazy perhaps, since it kind of worked, even after I tried to do my duty and stop him. In a half-hearted way, I suppose, because he was team leader and all that. But he was going totally against regulations. I reported it and I got the order, and the rest, as they say, is history . . .

Using the splinter always reminds me of him, and the old days. There's probably enough smart matter in the wood, encasing his DNA and his last download to bring him back complete, if and when I ever finish this assignment and can signal for pickup. Though a court would probably confirm HQ's original order and he'd be slowed into something close to a full stop anyway.

But my mission won't be over till the last vamp is burned to ash, and this infested Earth can be truly proclaimed clean.

Which is likely to be a long, long time, and I remind myself that day-dreaming about the old days is not going to help take out the Ancient Vampire ahead of me, let alone the many more in the world beyond.

I took out the splinter and the silver knife and slung my Pan-Am bag so it was comfortable, and got serious.

I heard the Ancient moving around as I stepped into what was once the outer office. The big pot was surrounded by soil and there dirty footprints up the wall, but I didn't need to see them to know to look up. The Vamps have a desire to dominate the high ground heavily programmed into them. They always go for the ceiling, up trees, up towers, up lamp-posts.

This one was spread-eagled on the ceiling, gripping with its foreleg and trailing leg filaments as well as the hooks on what humans thought were fingers and toes. It was pretty big as Vamps go, perhaps nine feet long and weighing in at around two-hundred pounds. The ultra-thin waist gave away its insectoid heritage, almost as much as a real close look at its mouth would. Not that you would want a real close look at a Vamp's mouth.

It squealed when I came in and it caught the Tau emissions. The squeal was basically an ultrasonic alarm oscillating through several wavelengths. The cops outside would hear it as an unearthly scream, when in fact it was more along the lines of a distress call and emergency rally beacon. If any of its brood survived down below, they'd drop whatever they might be doing—or chewing—and rush on up.

The squeal was standard operating procedure, straight out of the manual. It followed up with more orthodox stuff, dropping straight on to me. I flipped on my back and struck with the splinter, but the Vamp managed to flip itself in mid-air and bounce off the wall, coming to a stop in the far corner.

It was fast, faster than any Vamp I'd seen for a long time. I'd scratched it with the splinter, but no more than that. There was a line of silver across the dark red chitin of its chest, where the transferred smart matter was leeching the vampire's internal electrical potential to build a bomb, but it would take at least five seconds to do that, which was way too long.

I leapt and struck again and we conducted a kind of crazy ballet across the four walls, the ceiling and the floor of the room. Anyone watching would have got motion sickness or eyeball fatigue, trying to catch blurs of movement.

At 2.350 seconds in, it got a forearm around my left elbow and gave it a good hard pull, dislocating my arm at the shoulder. I knew then it really was ancient, and had retained the programming needed to fight me. My joints have always been a weak point.

It hurt. A lot, and it kept on hurting through several microseconds as the Vamp tried to actually pull my arm off and at the same time twist itself around to start chewing on my leg.

The Tau field was discouraging the Vamp, making it dump some of its internal nanoware, so that blood started geysering out of pinholes all over its body, but this was more of a nuisance for me than any major hindrance to it.

In mid-somersault, somewhere near the ceiling, with the thing trying to wrap itself around me, I dropped the silver knife. It wasn't a real weapon, not like the splinter. I kept it for sentimental reasons, as much as anything, though silver did have a deleterious effect on younger Vamps. Since it was pure sentiment, I suppose I could have left it in coin form, but then I'd probably be forever dropping some in combat and having to waste time later picking them up. Besides, when silver was still the usual currency and they were still coins I'd got drunk a few times and spent them, and it was way too big a hassle getting them back.

The Vamp took the knife-dropping as more significant than it was, which was one of the reasons I'd let it go. In the old days I would have held something serious in my left hand, like a de-weaving wand, which the vampire probably thought the knife was—and it wanted to get it and use it on me. It partially let go of my arm as it tried to catch the weapon and at that precise moment, second 2.355, I feinted with the splinter, slid it along the thing's attempted forearm block, and reversing my elbow joint, stuck it right in the forehead.

With the smart matter already at work from its previous scratch, internal explosion occurred immediately. I had shut my eyes in preparation, so I was only blown against the wall and not temporarily blinded as well.

I assessed the damage as I wearily got back up. My left arm was fully dislocated with the tendons ripped away, so I couldn't put it back. It was going to have to hang for a day or two, hurting like crazy till it self-healed. Besides that, I had severe bruising to my lower back and ribs, which would also deliver some serious pain for a day or so.

I hadn't been hurt by a Vamp as seriously for a long, long time, so I spent a few minutes searching through the scraps of mostly-disintegrated vampire to find a piece big enough to meaningfully scan. Once I got it back to the jumper I'd be able to pick it apart on the atomic level to find the serial number on some of its defunct nanoware.

I put the scrap of what was probably skeleton in my flight bag, with the splinter and the silver knife, and wandered downstairs. I left it unzipped, because I hadn't heard any firing for a while, which meant either Susan and Karl had cleaned up, or the Vamps had cleaned up Susan and Karl. But I put my T-shirt back on. No need to scare the locals. It was surprisingly clean, considering. My skin and hair sheds vampire blood, so the rest of me looked quite respectable as well. Apart from the arm hanging down like an orangutang's that is.

I'd calculated the odds at about 5:2 that Susan and Karl would win, so I was pleased to see them in the entrance lobby. They both jumped when I came down the stairs, and I was ready to move if they shot at me, but they managed to control themselves.

"Did you get them all?" I asked. I didn't move any closer.

"Nine," said Karl. "Like you said. Nine holes in the ground, nine burned vampires."

"You didn't get bitten?"

"Does it look like we did?" asked Susan, with a shudder. She was clearly thinking about Mike.

"Vampires can infect with a small, tidy bite," I said. "Or even about half a cup of their saliva, via a kiss."

Susan did throw up then, which is what I wanted. She wouldn't have if she'd been bitten. I was also telling the truth. While they were designed to be soldiers, the Vampires were also made to be guerilla fighters, working amongst the human population, infecting as many as possible in small, subtle ways. They only went for the big chow-down in full combat.

"What about you?" asked Karl. "You OK?"

"You mean this?" I asked, threshing my arm about like a tentacle, wincing as it made the pain ten times worse. "Dislocated. But I didn't get bitten."

Neither had Karl, I was now sure. Even newly-infected humans have something about them that gives their condition away, and I can always pick it.

"Which means we can go and sit by the fence and wait till morning," I said cheerily. "You've done well."

Karl nodded wearily and got his hand under Susan's elbow, lifting her up. She wiped her mouth and the two of them walked slowly to the door.

I let them go first, which was kind of mean, because the VET have been known to harbour trigger-happy snipers. But there was no sudden death from above, so we walked over to the fence and then the two of them flopped down on the ground and Karl began to laugh hysterically.

I left them to it and wandered over to the gate.

"You can let me out now," I called to the Sergeant. "My work here is almost done."

"No one comes out till after dawn," replied the guardian of the city.

"Except me," I agreed. "Check with Lieutenant Harman."

Which goes to show that I can read ID labels, even little ones on metal-mesh skinsuits.

The sergeant didn't need to check. Lieutenant Harman was already looming up behind him. They had a short but spirited conversation, the sergeant told Karl and Susan to stay where they were, which was still lying on the ground essentially in severe shock, and they powered down the gate for about thirty seconds and I came out.

Two medics came over to help me. Fortunately they were VET, not locals, so we didn't waste time arguing about me going to hospital, getting lots of drugs injected, having scans etc. They fixed me up with a collar and cuff sling so my arm wasn't dragging about the place, I said thank you and they retired to their unmarked ambulance.

Then I wandered over to where Jenny was sitting on the far side of the silver truck, her back against the rear wheel. She'd taken off her helmet and balaclava, letting her bobbed brown hair spring back out into shape. She looked about eighteen, maybe even younger, maybe a little older. A pretty young woman, her face made no worse by evidence of tears, though she was very pale.

She jumped as I tapped a little rhythm on the side of the truck.

"Oh . . . I thought . . . aren't you meant to stay inside the . . . the cordon?"

I hunkered down next to her.

"Yeah, most of the time they enforce that, but it depends," I said. "How are you doing?"

"Me? I'm . . . I'm OK. So you got them?"

"We did," I confirmed. I didn't mention Mike. She didn't need to know that, not now.

"Good," she said. "I'm sorry . . . I thought I would be braver. Only when the time came . . ."

"I understand," I said.

"I don't see how you can," she said. "I mean, you went in, and you said you fight vampires all the time. You must be incredibly brave."

"No," I replied. "Bravery is about overcoming fear, not about not having it. There's plenty I'm afraid of. Just not vampires."

"We fear the unknown," she said. "You must know a lot about vampires."

I nodded and moved my flight bag around to get more comfortable. It was still unzipped, but the sides were pushed together at the top.

"How to fight them, I mean," she added. "Since no one really knows anything else. That's the worst thing. When my sister was in . . . infected and then later, when she was . . . was killed, I really wanted to know, and there was no one to tell me anything."

"What did you want to know?" I asked. I've always been prone to show-off to pretty girls. If it isn't surfing, it's secret knowledge. Though sharing the secret knowledge only occurred in special cases, when I knew it would go no farther.

"Everything we don't know," sighed Jenny. "What are they, really? Why have they suddenly appeared all over the place in the last ten years, when we all thought they were just . . . just made-up."

"They're killing machines," I explained. "Bioengineered self-replicating guerilla soldiers, dropped here kind of by mistake a long time ago. They've been in hiding mostly, waiting for a signal or other stimuli to activate. Certain frequencies of radiowaves will do it, and the growth of cellphone use . . . "

"So what, vampires get irritated by cellphones?"

A smile started to curl up one side of her mouth. I smiled too, and kept talking.

"You see, way back when, there were these good aliens and these bad aliens, and there was a gigantic space battle—"

Jenny started laughing.

"Do you want me to do a personality test before I can hear the rest of the story?"

"I think you'd pass," I said. I had tried to make her laugh, even though it was kind of true about the aliens and the space battle. Only there were just bad aliens and even worse aliens, and the vampires had been dropped on earth by mistake. They had been meant for a world where the nights were very long.

Jenny kept laughing and looked down, just for an instant. I moved at my highest speed—and she died laughing, the splinter working instantly on both human nervous system and the twenty-four hours-old infestation of vampire nanoware.

We had lost the war, which was why I was there, cleaning up one of our mistakes. Why I would be on earth for countless years to come.

I felt glad to have my straightforward purpose, my assigned task. It is too easy to become involved with humans, to want more for them, to interfere with their lives. I didn't want to make the boss's mistake. I'm not human and I don't want to become human or make them better people. I was just going to follow orders, keep cleaning out the infestation, and that was that.

The bite was low on Jenny's neck, almost at the shoulder. I showed it to the VET people and asked them to do the rest.

I didn't stay to watch. My arm hurt, and I could hear a girl laughing, somewhere deep within my head.

A WATER MATTER

JAY LAKE

The Duke of Copper Downs had stayed dead.

So far.

That thought prompted the Dancing Mistress to glance around her at the deserted street. Something in the corner of her eye or the lantern of her dreams was crying out a message. Just as with any of her kind, it was difficult to take her by surprise. Her sense of the world around her was very strong. Even in sleep, her folk did not become so inert and vulnerable as humans or most animals did. And her people had lived among men for generations, after all. Some instincts never passed out of worth.

His Grace is not *going to come clawing up through the stones at my feet*, she told herself firmly. Her tail remained stiff and prickly, trailing gracelessly behind her in a parody of alarm.

The city continued to be restive. A pall of smoke hung low in the sky, and the reek of burning buildings dogged every breath. The harbor had virtually emptied, its shipping steering away from the riots and the uncontrolled militias that were all that remained of the Ducal Guard after the recent assassination. The streets were an odd alternation of deserted and crowded. Folk seemed unwilling to come out except in packs. If chance emptied a square or a cobbled city block, it stayed empty for hours. The hot, heavy damp did nothing to ease tempers.

At the moment, she strode alone across the purple-and-black flagstones of the Greenmarket area. The smell of rotting vegetables was strong. The little warehouses were all shuttered. Even the everpresent cats had found business elsewhere.

She hurried onward. The message which had drawn her onto the open streets had been quite specific as to time and place. Her sense of purpose was so strong that she could feel the blurring tug of the hunt in her mind. A trap, that; the hunt was always a trap for her people, especially when they walked among men.

Wings whirred overhead in a beat far too fast for any bird save the bright tiny hummers that haunted the flowering vines of the temple district. She did not even look up.

The Dancing Mistress found a little gateway set in the middle of a long stucco wall that bordered close on Dropnail Lane in the Ivory Quarter. It was the boundary of some decaying manse, a perimeter wall marking out a compound that had long been cut up into a maze of tiny gardens and hovels. A village of sorts flourished under the silent oaks, amid which the great house rotted, resplendent and abandoned. She'd been here a few times to see a woman of her people whose soul path was the knowledge of herbs and simples. But she'd always come through the servants' gate, a little humped arch next to the main entrance that faced onto Whitetop Street.

This gateway was different. It clearly did not fit the wall in which it was set. Black marble pilasters were embedded in the fading ochre plaster of the estate's wall. The darkness within tried to pull her onward.

She shook away the sense of compulsion. In firm control of her own intentions, the Dancing Mistress slowly reached out to touch the metal grate. Though the air was warm, the black iron was cold enough to sting her fingers down to the claw sheaths.

The way was barred, but it was not locked. The Dancing Mistress pushed on through.

The dark gate opened into a tangle of heavy vines. Ivy and wisteria strangled a stand of trees which had been reduced to pale, denuded corpses. Fungus grew in mottled shelves along the lower reaches of the bare trunks, and glistened in the mat of leaves and rot that floored the little grove. There was a small altar of black stone amid the pallid trunks, where only shadows touched the ground. An irregular block of ice gleamed atop the altar. It shed questing coils of vapor into the spring-warm air.

Her folk had no name for themselves—they were just people, after all. And it was one of her people who had written the note she'd found strung by spider webs against the lintel of her rented room. She had been able to tell by the hand of the writing, the scent on the page, the faint trail of a soul flavored with meadow flowers.

No one she knew, though, not by hand nor scent nor soul. While the Dancing Mistress could not readily count the full number of her folk in Copper Downs, it was still a matter of dozens amid the teeming humans in their hundreds and thousands.

This altar freezing amid the bones of trees was nothing of her people's.

A man emerged from the shadows without moving, as if the light had found him between one moment and the next. He was human—squat, unhandsome, with greasy, pale hair that twisted in hanks down his shoulder. His face had been tattooed with fingerprints, as though some god or spirit had reached out and grasped him too hard with a grip of fire. His broad body was wrapped in leather and black silk as greasy as his hair. Dozens of small blades slipped into gaps in his leather, each crusted in old blood.

A shaman, then, who sought the secrets of the world in the frantic pounding hearts of prey small and large. Only the space around his eyes was clean, pale skin framing a watery gaze that pierced her like a diamond knife.

"*You walk as water on rock.*" He spoke the tongue of her people with only the smallest hint of an accent. That was strange in its own right. Far stranger, that she, come of a people who had once hunted dreams on moonless nights, could have walked within two spans of him without noticing.

Both those things worried her deeply.

"I walk like a woman in the city," she said in the tongue of the Stone Coast people. The Dancing Mistress knew as a matter of quiet pride that she had no accent herself.

"In truth," he answered, matching her speech. His Petraean held the same faint hint of somewhere else. He was no more a native here than she.

"Your power is not meant to overmatch such as me," she told him quietly. At the same time, she wondered if that were true. Very, very few humans knew the tongue of the people.

He laughed at that, then broke his gaze. "I would offer you wine and bread, but I know your customs in that regard. Still, your coming to meet me is a thing well done."

She ignored the courtesy. "That note did not come from your hand."

"No." His voice was level. "Yet I sent it."

The Dancing Mistress shivered. He implied power over someone from the high meadows of her home. "Your note merely said to meet, concerning a water matter." That was one of the greatest obligations one of her people could lay upon another.

"The Duke remains dead," he said. She shivered at the echo of her earlier thought. "The power of his passing has left a blazing trail for those who can see it."

"You aver that he will not return."

The man shrugged away the implicit challenge. She had not asked his name, for her people did not give theirs, but that did nothing to keep her from wondering who he was. "Soon it will not matter if he tries to return or not," he said. "His power leaches away, to be grasped or lost in the present moment. Much could be done now. Good, ill, or indifferent, this is the time for boldness."

She leaned close, allowing her claws to flex. He would know what that signified. "And where do *I* fit into your plans, *man*?"

"You have the glow of him upon you," he told her. "His passing marked you. I would know from you who claimed him, who broke him open. That one—mage, warrior or witch—holds the first and greatest claim on his power."

Green!

The girl-assassin was now fled now across the water, insofar as the Dancing Mistress knew. She was suddenly grateful for that small mercy. "It does not matter who brought low the Duke of Copper Downs," she whispered. "He is gone. The world moves on. New power will rise in his place, new evil will follow."

Another laugh, a slow rumble from his black-clad belly. "Power will always rise. The right hand grasping it in the right moment can avoid much strife for so many. I thought to make some things easier and more swift with your aid—for the sake of everyone's trouble."

"You presume too much," she told him.

"*Me?*" His grin was frightening. "You look at my skin and think to judge my heart. Humans do not have soul paths as your people do. You will not scent the rot you so clearly suspect within me."

The Dancing Mistress steeled herself. There was no way she could stand alone against this one, even if she had trained in the arts of power. "Good or ill, I will say no more upon it."

"Hmm." He tugged at his chin. "I see you have a loyalty to defend."

"It is not just loyalty." Her voice was stiff despite her self-control, betraying her fear of him. "Even if I held such power within my grasp, I would have no reason to pass it to you."

"By your lack of action, you have already handed the power to whomever can pluck it forth. Be glad it was only me come calling." He added in her tongue, "*I know the scent of a water matter. I will not argue from the tooth.*"

"*Nor will I bargain from the claw.*" She turned and stalked toward the cold gate, shivering in her anger.

"'Ware, woman," he called after her, then laughed again. "We are not friends, but we need not be enemies. I would still rather have your aid in this matter, and not your opposition. Together we can spare much suffering and trouble."

She slipped between the black stone gateposts and into the street beyond, refusing for the sake of the sick fear that coiled in the bottom of her gut to hurry on her way.

There was no one out in the late afternoon, normally a time when the squares and boulevards would have been thronged, even in the quieter, richer quarters.

She walked with purpose, thinking furiously even as she watched for trouble. That shaman must have come from some place both rare and distant. There were tribes and villages of humans in every corner of the world of which she'd heard. Men lived in the frigid shadows high up in the Blue Mountains where the very air might freeze on the coldest nights, and amid the fire-warm plains of Selistan beyond the sea, and in the boundless forests of the uttermost east. Not to mention everywhere in between.

He was from somewhere in between, to be sure—the Leabourne Hills, perhaps, or one of the other places where her people lived when they had not yet done as she had, drifting away to dwell among the cities of men. There was no other way for him to speak their tongue, to know of water matters, to command whatever binding or influence or debt had brought her the note with which he'd summoned her.

The Dancing Mistress had no illusions of her own importance, but it had been her specifically that he'd wanted. It seemed likely the man had counted her as the Duke's assassin.

That was troublesome. If one person made that deduction, however flawed it was, others could do the same. *A fear for another time*, she told herself. Had he learned her people's magics the same way the late Duke of Copper Downs had done? By theft?

A sickening idea occurred to her. *Perhaps this greasy man had been an agent of the Duke.*

As if summoned by the thought, a group of Ducal guards spilled out of an alley running between the walled gardens of wealth.

She happened to be walking close along the deserted curb just across from them. They stopped, staring at her. The Dancing Mistress didn't break stride. *Act like you are in charge. Do not fear them.* Still, she risked a glance.

The leader, or at least the one with the biggest sword, had a fine tapestry wrapped across his shoulders as a cloak. Looters. Though they wore Ducal uniforms, their badges were torn off.

"Hey, kittie," one of them called, smacking his lips.

Corner, she thought. *There's a corner up ahead. Many of these houses are guarded. They wouldn't risk open violence here.*

Her common sense answered: *Why not?* They had certainly risked open looting.

Colors were beginning to flow in the corner of her eye. The hunt tugged at her. That ritual was anchored deep in the shared soul of her people, a violent power long rejected in favor of a quiet, peaceful life. The Dancing Mistress shook off the tremor in her claws as she turned a walled corner onto Alicorn Straight, passing under the blank-eyed gaze of a funerary statue.

They followed, laughing and joking too loudly among themselves. Weapons and armor rattled behind her. Not quite chasing, not quite leaving her alone.

The towers of the Old Wall rose amid buildings a few blocks to her east. If she could get there before the deserters jumped her, she might have a chance. Once past those crumbling landmarks, she would be in a much more densely populated and notably less wealthy area. In the Dancing Mistress' experience, aid was far more likely from those who had nothing than from those who held everything in their hands. The rich did not see anyone but their own glittering kind, while the poor understood what it meant to lose everything.

"Oi, catkin," one of the guards shouted. "Give us a lick, then."

Their pace quickened.

Once more colors threatened to flow. Her claws twitched in their sheathes. She would not do this. The people did not hunt, especially not in the cities of men. Walking alone, the gestalt of the hunt had no use, and when fighting by herself against half a dozen men, the subtle power it gave meant nothing.

They would have her down, hamstrings cut, and be at their rape before she could tear out one throat.

Speed was all she had left. Every yard closer they came was a measure of that advantage lost. The Dancing Mistress broke into a dead run. The guards followed like dogs on a wounded beggar, shouting in earnest, hup-hup-hupping in their battle language.

Still the street was empty.

She cut across the pavers, heading for Shrike Alley, which would take her to the Old Wall and the Broken Gate. There was no one, *no one*. How could she have been so stupid?

Fast as she was, at least one of the men behind her was a real sprinter. She could hear him gaining, somehow even chuckling as he ran. The Dancing Mistress lengthened her stride, but his spear butt reached from behind to tangle her ankles and she went down to a head-numbing crack against the cobbles.

The guard stood above her, grinning through several days of dark beard and the sharp scent of man sweat. "Never had me one of you before," he said, dropping away his sword belt.

She kicked up, hard, but he just jumped away laughing. His friends were right behind him with blades drawn and spears ready. Seven on one, she thought despairing. She would fight, but they would only break her all the faster for it.

The first man collapsed, stunned, his trousers caught around his knees. A second yelled and spun around. The Dancing Mistress needed nothing more than that to spur her to her opportunity.

There was small, small distance between dance and violence. Controlled motion, prodigious strength, and endless hours of practice fueled both arts. She stepped through a graceful series of spins, letting the edges of the hunt back in as her clawed kicks took two more of the guards behind the knees.

The shaman was on the other side of them, grinning broadly as he fought with an already-blooded yatagan. His movements held a shimmer edge that was far too familiar.

He gambled on me joining the counter-attack, she thought. It did not matter why. They made common cause in the moment, and tore another man's hip from its socket. The last three deserters scrambled away before turning to run hell for leather down the street.

The Dancing Mistress had never thought to see a human who could take on even the smallest aspect of the hunt.

"I should have expected more of you." Her rescuer's voice was scarcely shuddering from the effort of battle.

She kept her own voice hard, saying in the tongue of the people, *"This does not bind us with water."*

"We are already bound. Think on what I have asked." He nodded, then strode purposeful away among the silent houses of the rich.

Shaking, the Dancing Mistress trotted toward the Old Wall, away from the groaning, weeping men.

She made her way to the Dockmarket. That area was quiet as well, given that the harbor was as empty as it ever had been in the decades since the Year of Ice.

Still, there were some humans about. Though the booths were shuttered and the alleys quiet as the Temple Quarter, the taverns stayed open. The breweries of Copper Downs had operated through flood, fire, pestilence and famine for more years than anyone had bothered to count. Political turmoil and a shortage of the shipping trade were hardly going to stop people from drinking.

There was a place off the alley known as Middleknife (or the Second Finger, depending on who you asked) behind a narrow door. It was as nameless as the people it served—mostly her folk, truth be told, but also a scattering of others who did not pass without a sidewise cast of human eyes elsewhere in Copper Downs. Many races had come out of the countries that rose skyward to the north in order to live in the shadows of the human polities along the Stone Coast.

The Dancing Mistress had always scorned solaces such as this. Still, she needed to be among her people tonight. There were few enough places for that, none of them part of her daily life.

She slipped inside with a clench riding hard in her gut.

No smoke of *tabac* or *hennep* roiled within. No dice clattered, no darts flew. Only a dozen or so of the people in quiet ones, twos and threes. They sat at tables topped by deep stoneware bowls in which forlorn lilies spun slowly, sipping pale liquid the consistency of pine sap from tiny cups that matched the great bowls. The place smelled of water, rocks and trees.

Much like where she had been born.

She also saw a very narrow-bodied blue man in pangolin-skin armor alone at a table, crouched in a chair with his knees folded nearly to his chin. Though he did not look to weigh eight stone, she thought he must be seven feet tall at the least. There were even a few people who might have been human.

The barkeep, one of her people, glanced briefly at her. He then took a longer look before nodding slightly, a gesture they had all picked up in the city. She read it well enough.

Between any two of her people there was a scent, of soul and body, that once exchanged could not easily be forgotten. Much could be read there, in a language which did not admit of lies. This one was not sib-close, nor enemy-distant, but she saw the path of trust.

"You work in the Factor's Quarter," he said in Petraean.

"I did," she admitted. She'd trained slave girls and the forgotten younger daughters of rising houses. Sometimes they were one and the same. "Before all things fell just lately." And therein lay her story, the scent the shaman had been tracking.

"In any case, welcome." He brought out a wooden plate, as tradition dictated turned by someone's hand on a foot-powered lathe. There he spilled dried flower petals from a watered silk sack, three colors of sugar, and a trickle from a tiny cut crystal decanter. Their hands crossed, brushing together as each of them dragged a petal through sugar and lifewater.

The Dancing Mistress touched sweetness to her lips and smiled sadly. This was what the traditional feast of welcome had degenerated into, here in the labyrinthine streets of Copper Downs. Even so, they were now opened to each other for a moment.

The barkeep nodded again then brushed his fingers across hers, releasing them both. "You are of Copper Downs, but you are not one of my regulars. What brings you here? The need for a scent of home?"

"A water matter." She sighed. "A difficult one, I am afraid."

He stiffened, the fur of his neck bristling slightly as his scent strengthened. "Whom?"

"A man. A *human* man. Not of the Stone Coast." She shifted languages. *"He spoke our tongue."*

"He knew of water matters?"

"It was he who named this business. He was looking for the . . . agent . . . behind the Duke's fall." She paused, choosing her words carefully against revealing too much of her complicity in the Duke's death. *"This is not my soul path. I do not bind power, nor do I loose it. But the thread came to me all the same. And this one knows far too much of us."* Her voice dipped. *"I even glimpsed the hunt within him."*

"I do not accuse you of an untruth, but that has never been. I would not have thought to have seen it." The barkeep looked past her shoulder, as one of the people often did when seeking to avoid embarrassment. *"There is a rumor that one of us was the undoing of the late Duke. Is that what this water matter follows?"*

"In a sense, yes," the Dancing Mistress admitted. "But I was never in the palace," she added in Petraean.

"Of course not." He thought a moment. "Do you seek aid in this? Or is this your fate to follow alone?"

"I do not yet see my fate. I do not think this is it." She sighed, another human gesture. "I doubt my ability to handle this well, and I fear the consequences of failure."

"Abide then at the empty table near the hearth. Some will come." He dipped into a slow bow straight from the high meadows of their birth. "I will see to it."

The Dancing Mistress stared into the cold fireplace. There were no ashes, though there was sufficient soot blackening the bricks to testify to regular use in colder months. The darkness before her brought the man in the shadows very much to mind.

He'd offered to spare the city much suffering. She knew that the Duke's loosened power was like lightning looking for a path to the ground. Her hope, shared with Federo and the others who had conspired with her, had been to weather that storm until the ancient bonds relaxed. If the city was lucky, it would vanish like mist on a summer morning. Then her people's centuries-long part in the madness of the Duke's tyranny would be over.

The shaman had other ideas about that power, but even so he had not set himself up as her enemy. Except he knew too much. He knew their tongue, their ways, the hunt.

He was a threat to her kind. Anything he did in Copper Downs would seem to be the work of her people to the priests and the wizard-engineers who infested this city like lice. He might as well slit all their throats one by one.

I arranged to kill a Duke so that we might reclaim our power, she thought. *What is one more man?* She knew the answer to that: no more than another, then another, until her soul path was slick with blood.

Once more the hunt pulled at her, bending the light at the edges of her vision. Long ago in the high meadows when her people foraged or fought, they could slip their thoughts and deeds together. A hunt was a group working as neither one nor another but all together, as termites will hollow out a tree or ants ford a river. What one heard, all heard; what another touched, all felt. Deep into the hunt, leaderless and conjoined, there was none to call a halt to slaughter, none to direct their steps, and so with the power of their mesh-mind the people could become like a fire in the forest.

They had given it up long ago, save in most extreme need. There was too much violence at their command, too much power. She had never heard of the hunt being cried within the walls of a human city. If these pasty, pale folk even suspected what her kind could do when stirred to mortal effort, they would be lucky to be only driven from the gates.

Her claws slipped free again. Her blood thrummed in her veins. The Dancing Mistress was afraid of what this man had stirred her to. And how could he not know of the hunt and what might happen?

He must know, she realized. *He'd just counted on finding the power first.* That man took chances, just as he'd attacked her assailants from behind, counting on her to rise and join into the fight. He gambled with lives, hers and his.

Interrupting her thought, one of the people sat down next to her. A stoneware cup was quickly placed before him. Moments later a woman of the people sat across. She briefly met the Dancing Mistress' eyes, then studied the lilies wilting in the stoneware bowl. Another soon came to fill their table. More cups followed.

So they were four. She took a sip of wine fermented from the flowers and fir sap of the high meadows.

The woman spoke, finally. She had scent of cinnamon about her. *"You are said to bear a water matter which has a claim upon all the people."*

"Yes," said the Dancing Mistress quietly. *"This thing tears at my heart, but there is a catamount among us."*

"I would not question your judgment." It was the taller of the men, who smelled of sage and tree bark. *"But I would know this threat."*

She gave him a long slow look. To raise the pursuit she meant to bring to bear, she must tell them the truth. Yet any word of her involvement in the Duke's death could mean her own.

Still, there was far more at stake than her small life.

"*There is a man. A human man,*" she amended. "*He knows our ways better than do many of our own. He pursues a great evil. If he succeeds, the return of the Duke will be upon us all. If he fails, the price may well be laid at our door.*"

She went on to explain in as much detail as she could, laying out the events of the day and her conclusions from it.

For awhile, there was silence. The four of them sipped their wine and dipped into the same stream of thoughts. It was a gestalt, edging toward the mesh-mind of the hunt. It was the way her people prepared themselves for deep violence.

"*And once again, death brings death.*" That was the shorter of the men, the fourth in their hunt, whom she already thought of as the glumper for the small noises he made in his throat as he sipped at the wine. "*If we send this shaman to follow his duke, who's to say there will not be more to follow him.*"

Sage-man spoke up, in Petraean now. "This is so soon. The Duke is yet freshly dead. He did not expect to pass. There cannot already be a great conspiracy to return him to life and power."

"I do not know it for a conspiracy," said the Dancing Mistress. "He stalks me, seeing me for the bait to call this power back. That does not mean he has sung for my life, but I cannot think he will scruple to claim it in his pursuit." She flashed to the uneasy memory of the man laying into her attackers, grinning over the bloody blade of his yatagan. He played some game that ran neither along nor against her soul path, crosswise as it might otherwise be.

Still, they all knew, as everyone of the people did, that the Duke of Copper Downs had stolen their magic, generations past. There were stories and more stories, details that varied in every telling, but since that time the numbers and power of her people—never great to start with—had diminished, while the Duke had whiled away centuries on his throne.

That someone was hunting power through the Dancing Mistress now, so soon after the Duke's fall, meant old, old trouble returning. The man being a high country shaman with too much knowledge of their kind was only a seal on that trouble.

The cinnamon-woman broke the renewed silence. "You have the right of it. If we stop the Duke's man now, we may crush the seed before the strangler vine has a chance to grow."

The glumper stared up from the cup of wine clutched his hands. "*Crushing is not our way.*"

"Not now." The cinnamon-woman looked around, catching their eyes. "Once . . ."

"Once we were warriors," said the Dancing Mistress. "We called storms from the high crags." They all knew those stories, too. "If we cry the hunt now, we will spare lives."

"*And what do we give up in following your plan?*" asked the glumper. "*The old ways are gone for good reason.*"

The Dancing Mistress felt anger rising within her, a core of fire beneath the cool sense of purpose to which she'd hewn all her life. *"They are gone because of what the Duke took from us."*

He gave her a long stare. *"Did you ever think we might have given our power away with a purpose?"*

Even in argument, the mesh-mind was knitting together, the edges of the room gleaming and sharpening. The Dancing Mistress set down her cup. *"It is time,"* she said in their language. *"We will find this shaman and stop his scheming, before he drags all of us down into darkness."*

The moon glowed faintly through the low clouds, but the shadows outflanked the light at every turn. Torches burned at compound gates while lamps hung at intersections and in the squares. The nighttime streets of Copper Downs were streaked with smears of heat and scent.

The hunt slid through the evening like a single animal with four bodies. Her vision was complex, edges gleaming sharp at all distances and ranges. Odors told stories she could never read on her own, about the passage of time and the sweat of fear, passion, even the flat, watery smell of ennui. The very feel of the air on her skin as she ran had been magnified fourfold. She saw every door, every hiding place, every mule or person they passed, in terms of force and danger and claws moving close to the speed of thought.

The sheer *power* of the hunt was frightening in its intoxication.

They slipped through the city like a killing wind, heading toward the Ivory Quarter and the black gate through which she'd passed before. She'd never run so fast, so effortlessly, with such purpose.

Why had her people not stayed like this always? she wondered. All the logic of civilization aside, surely this was what they'd been made for.

It seemed only moments before they'd crossed the city to the old ochre walls of the compound, now glowing in the moonlight. The ancient stucco seemed to suck the life of the world into itself, though the trees beyond and above the wall practically shouted to her expanded sensorium.

Three times in as many minutes they circled around the shadowed walls, and found no sign of the shaman's black gate. Not even a significant crack where it might have stood.

There was power aplenty in the world, but it was not generally spent so freely as this man had done. Opening that gate was the magical equivalent of a parlor trick: flashy, showy, a splash of self such as a child with a paintpot might make. But costly, very costly. The greatest power lay in subtlety, misdirection, the recondite support and extension of natural processes.

It was here, she thought, and the hunt took her meaning from the flick of her eyes, the set of her shoulders, the stand of her fur. They believed her. She knew that just as they'd known her meaning.

Together they drifted back to the main gate. It had stood propped open years before the Dancing Mistress had come to Copper Downs, but no one ever passed through it. The squatters who lived within used the servants' gate beside the main gate, and so observed the blackletter law of the city even as they had built their illegal homes upon the grounds. The trail of their passing back and forth glowed in the eyes of the hunt. It was human, but there was something of their people mixed in with it.

The hunt slipped through the narrow door one by one, their steps like mist on the furze within. The path followed the old carriage drive through a stand of drooping willows now rotten and overgrown with wisteria. Trails led off between the curtains of leaves and vines toward the hidden homes beyond.

There was no scent to follow here. The shaman might as well have been made of fog.

A thought passed between the hunt like breeze bending the flowers of a meadow: *An herbalist lives here, a woman of their people.*

She felt her claws stiffen. The wisdom of the hunt stirred, the mesh-mind reading clues where ordinary eyes saw only shadow.

Is the Duke in fact still dead?

It was the same question she'd almost asked herself on her way to this place the first time.

Sage-man twitched aside a mat of ivy and stepped into the darker shadows. A brighter trail well-marked with the traces of one of her people led within. *Of course, cloaked in the magic of her people the shaman could also have left his tracks so.*

The Dancing Mistress nodded the rest of her hunt through—cinnamon-woman and the glumper—and followed last.

The hut was a shambles. Jars shattered, sheaves scattered, what little furniture there had been now smashed to splinters. While there didn't seem to be any quantity of blood, the stink of fear hung heavy in the close air, overlaying even the intense jumble of odors from scattered herbs and salves.

The glumper trailed his fingers through the leaves and powders and shattered ceramic fragments on the floor. He sniffed, sending a tingle through the Dancing Mistress' nose. *"I might have thought one of us had done this thing."* He had yet to speak a word of Petraean within her hearing. *"But knowing to search, I find there has been a human here as well. Wearing leather and animal fat. He first took her unawares, then he took her away."*

The shaman, the Dancing Mistress thought. Inside the mesh-mind, they shared her next question. *What path did he follow now?*

The hunt had the shaman's scent, and the herbalist's besides. It was enough.

A warm, damp wind blew off the water to carry the reek of tide rot and the distant echo of bells. Even the rogue squads of the Ducal guard seemed to be lying low, doubtless surrounded by wine butts, and hired boys wearing slitted skirts and long wigs. The city was deserted, waiting under the smell of old fires and dark magic.

That was well enough, the Dancing Mistress thought with the independent fragment of herself that still held its own amid the flow of the mesh-mind. It would not do for her people to be seen gliding over the cobbles at preternatural speed, moving silent as winter snowfall.

The hunt's grip on shaman's scent and herbalist's soul path was sufficient, even when running through fire reek and the alley-mouth stench of dead dogs. They moved together, heeding the Dancing Mistress' will, following the glumper's trace on the scent, using cinnamon-woman's eyes, sage-man's hearing. Most of all they pursued the dread that stalked the night, the banked fires of the hunt flaring only to seek a single hearth within Copper Downs.

They followed a dark river of fear and purpose into the Temple Quarter. That had long been the quietest section of the city. Once it must have brawled and boiled with worshippers, for the buildings there were as great as any save the Ducal Palace. In the centuries of the Duke's rule, the gods of the city had grown withered and sour as winter fruit. People left their coppers in prayer boxes near the edges of the district and walked quickly past.

Even with the gods fallen on hard times, locked in the embrace of neglect and refusal, no one had ever found the nerve to tear down those decaying walls and replace the old houses of worship with anything newer and more mundane.

The hunt pursued the scent down Divas Street, along the edge of the Temple Quarter, before leading into the leaf-strewn cobwebs of Mithrail Street. They bounded into those deeper shadows where the air curdled to black water and the dead eyes of the Duke seemed to glitter within every stygian crevice.

They came to a quivering halt with claws spread wide before a narrow door of burnt oak bound with iron and ebony laths. Darkness leaked from behind it, along with a fire scent and the tang of burning fat.

The man-smell was strong here. They were obviously close to the shaman's lair, where the cloak of the people's power grew thin over his layered traces of daily use—sweat and speech and the stink of human urine. The doorway reeked of magic, inimical purpose and the thin, screaming souls of animals slit from weasand to wodge for their particles of wisdom.

That was his weakness, the Dancing mistress realized, surfacing further from the hunt for a moment even as those around her growled. He used the people's power only as a cover, nothing more. The shaman could build a vision of the world from a thousand bright, tiny eyes, but animals never saw more than they understood. Her people knew that to be a fool's path to wisdom.

Now he worked his blood magic on the herbalist, summoning the Dancing Mistress. *He had* drawn *her here to cut her secrets from her.* The mesh-mind overtook her once more in the rush of angry passion at that thought, and together the hunt brushed someone's claw-tipped hand on the cool wooden planks of the door.

"Come," the shaman called. His voice held confident expectation of her.

The hunt burst in.

The four of them were a surprise to the shaman. They could see that in his face. But his power was great as well. The ancient stone walls of this abandoned temple kitchen were crusted with ice. The herbalist hung by ropes from a high ceiling beam, her body shorn and torn as he'd bled her wisdom cut by cut, the way he'd bled it from a thousand tiny beasts of the field.

He rose from his fire, kicked a brazier and coals toward them, and gathered the air into daggers of ice even as the four claws of the hunt spread across the room.

Though they called the old powers of their people, none of them had ever trained to stand in open battle. Their purpose was strong, but only the Dancing Mistress could move below a slicing blade or land a strike upon a briefly unprotected neck.

If not for their number they would have been cut down without thought. If not for the shaman's need to capture an essence from the Dancing Mistress he might have blown them out like candles. She knew then that he had set the thugs upon her that day so he could render aid, only to draw her in to him now, when suasion had failed him.

The fight came to fast-moving claws against restrained purpose. His ice made glittering edges that bent the vision of the mesh-mind. The blood of his sacrifices confused their scent. He moved, as he had on the street that day, with the brutal grace of one raised to war, working his magic even as he wielded his yatagan. The glumper's chest was laid open. Cinnamon-woman had her ear shorn off. Sage-man's thought were flayed by a dream of mountain fire that slipped through the mesh-mind.

But for every round of blows the hunt took, they landed at least one in return. Claws raked the shaman's cheek with the sound of roses blooming. A kick traced its arc in blurred colors on their sight to snap bones in his left hand. A brand was shoved still burning brightly sour into his hair, so the grease there smoldered and his spells began to crack with the distraction of the pain.

The hunt moved in for the kill.

The Dancing Mistress once more emerged from the blurred glow of the hunt to find herself with claws set against the shaman's face. The cinnamon-woman twisted his right arm from his shoulder. She looked up at the herbalist, who dangled bleeding like so much meat in the slaughterhouse, and thought, *What are we now?*

"Wait," she shouted, and with the pain of forests dying tore herself free from the mesh-mind.

Cinnamon-woman stared, blood streaming from the stump of her ear. The look sage-man gave the Dancing Mistress from his place bending back the shaman's legs would have burned iron. Their mouths moved in unison, the mesh-mind croaking out the words, "He does not deserve to live!"

"He does not have a right to our power," she countered. "But we cannot judge who should live and who should die."

The shaman bit the palm of her hand, his tongue darting to lick the blood, to suck her down to some last, desperate magic.

Steeling herself, the Dancing Mistress leaned close. Her claws were still set in his face. "I will take your wisdom as you have taken the wisdom of so many others. But I shall let you live to know what comes of such a price."

"Wait," he screamed through her enclosing palm. "You do not underst—"

With a great, terrible heave, she tore his tongue out with her claws. "We will not have the Duke back," the Dancing Mistress whispered venomously. She slit into him, plucking and cutting slivers from his liver and lights. The hunt kept the shaman pinned tight until blood loss and fear erased his resolve. Then the remainder of mesh-mind collapsed. The cinnamon-woman began to tend to the glumper and the herbalist. Sage-man rebuilt the fire before ungently sewing shut the slits that the Dancing Mistress had made in the shaman's chest and belly.

Ice from the walls turned to steam as the Dancing Mistress fried the organ meats, the tongue and two glistening eyes in a tiny black iron pan graven with runes. The blinded shaman wept and gagged, spitting blood while he shivered by the fire.

When the bits were done the Dancing Mistress dumped them to the blood-slicked mess that was the floor. She ground the burnt flesh to mash beneath her feet, then kicked it into the coals. The shaman's weeping turned to a scream as his wisdom burned away.

"Our water matter is discharged," she whispered in his ear. "If your Duke's ghost comes to you seeking restoration, send him to knock at my door."

Then the Dancing Mistress gathered the herbalist into her arms. Cinnamon-woman and sage-man brought the glumper between them. The shaman they left to his fate, blind, mute and friendless among the lonely gods.

The Duke of Copper Downs was still dead, the Dancing Mistress reflected as the night faded around her. Oddly, she remained alive.

She sat at the door of the herbalist's hut. The woman slept inside, mewing her pain even amidst the thickets of her dreams. There was a new water matter here, of course. The ties among her people ever and always were broad as the sea, swift as a river, deep as the lakes that lie beneath the mountains. She was bound for a time to the herbalist by the steam that the hunt had burned from the shaman's icy walls.

That man did not have much of life left to him, but at least she had not claimed it herself. Her people had the right of things in centuries past, when they gave up their power. She only hoped that rumor of the hunt was small and soon forgotten by the citizens of Copper Downs.

The shadows beneath the rotten willows lightened with the day. The spiced scent of cookery rose around her, tiny boiling pots and bumptious roasts alike. The Dancing Mistress rose, stretched, and went to tend her patient.

THE GOLDEN OCTOPUS

BETH BERNOBICH

I first met Breandan Reid ó Cuilinn in my father's Court, in Cill Cannig, on a bright cold November day. I was seventeen, a Princess Royal and heir to the throne of Éireann. He, I knew from reports assembled by the King's Constabulary, was the son of a country gentleman, thirty years old, with a doctorate from Awveline University in physics and philosophy.

He never even noticed me.

But then, he was there to impress my father, the king, and the many astrologers, scientists, and councilors who made up the King's Court in those days, not a young girl watching from the shadows. Ah, but I'm rambling on without purpose. Let me tell you what happened that day.

It was late November, as I said. We were all gathered in the smallest of my father's audience chambers, the one where he liked to hold such demonstrations. (*Miscellaneous Scientific Inquiries, Etc.* is how the steward labeled them.) Sunlight poured through the high square windows; an early morning rain shower had spattered droplets over the panes, which made a hundred tiny rainbows over the gray marble floor. A raised platform ran around three sides of the room, with a series of recessed alcoves. I sat in my usual place, the middle alcove, which gave me the best view of my father and ó Cuilinn both.

"Tell me," my father said, "what you hope to discover."

Breandan ó Cuilinn—excuse me, Doctor ó Cuilinn—said, "I cannot tell yet. I can only report on what I have achieved."

The old astrologers, those who had served my grandfather and great-grandfather since the middle of the century, nodded. They recognized temporizing, no matter what form it took. "True, true," one old man mumbled through his toothless gums. "We can chart the moon and all the stars of heaven, but there are subtleties beyond even the most learned of the cloud diviners."

The Court scientists and mage-mathematicians, whose philosophies belonged to both the old and the modern schools, merely shrugged and stared hard at the strange machine he had brought, and which now sat upon a large battered worktable, evidently provided by the steward from the palace stores.

He was not a rich man, this Doctor ó Cuilinn. He had arrived in a hired van, with no servants, no assistants, and had transported the five large crates to the interview chamber himself using a freight trolley. He must have assembled the machine as well. That would account for the oil stain on the sleeve of his frock coat, and the dusty knees of his trousers.

The machine itself gleamed in brass and silver splendor upon the table. It was as large as a man's torso and shaped like an octopus, with shining glass tubes writhing about the massive central orb. Wires ran through the center of the tubes, like thin black veins; more wires snaked over the table and connected the device to a crate of batteries sitting on the floor. The metals themselves, however beautiful, were likely chosen for their properties, I thought, remembering the man's initial letter. And it required a great deal of electricity. But what were those strange knobs and dials for?

With a practiced gesture, ó Cuilinn drew a small metal bar from his pocket. It was just a few inches long, made of some dull silvery material. He pressed a spot on the side of the octopus's body. A section of the front slid open—as though the octopus had opened its mouth into a rectangular yawn. ó Cuilinn placed the metal bar inside. The mouth closed again; this time, I could see the thin lines marking its edges.

"What kind of metal is that?" my father asked.

"An iron-chromium alloy, your Majesty," ó Cuilinn replied. "It proves less reactive than pure iron."

If he doubted my father's ability to understand the answer, he made no sign of it. But one question led to a barrage of others from the Court scientists. Those batteries, what were they, and what charge did they produce? Was it purely electricity his device used? If so, what role did those glass tubes perform? A modified Leclanché cell, ó Cuilinn replied. Ammonium chloride mixed with Plaster of Paris, sealed in a zinc shell, each of which produced 1.5 volts. He was corresponding with a collective of scientists from Sweden and the Dietsch Empire, concerning a rechargeable battery with nickel and cadmium electrodes in a potassium hydroxide solution. Yes, the results would certainly prove more reliable. Also, more expensive. (Here the councilors muttered something about how these research men always demanded more money.) As for the role of the batteries, they were purely to start the necessary reactions. He would rather not discuss the further details until his Majesty and the gentlemen had observed the machine's performance.

Turning away from his audience, ó Cuilinn began to manipulate a series of switches and dials along the lower edge of the machine. The scientists and mathematicians fell silent, absorbed in watching his work. The astrologers were less entranced, and one old man continued to mutter about the stars and their effect upon the Earth's magnetic currents. ó Cuilinn ignored them all. His long slim fingers moved deftly over the octopus's face. Gradually I became aware of a soft buzzing between my ears. My skin along my arms itched. Just as I reached up to rub them, a loud crack echoed from the device.

The audience gasped. I started, then found myself unable to move.

Gas inside the tubes ignited into gaudy colors; the wires burned golden inside. Smoke roiled around the device, and there was a distinct burning odor, as though lightning had struck inside the palace. The astrologers and other philosophers were all whispering. The scientists frowned. My father too was frowning, but in concentration.

ó Cuilinn alone seemed unperturbed. He leaned down and touched the device. Again the octopus yawned. I stared, uncertain what I might see inside its mouth.

I saw nothing.

More muttering broke out, louder than before.

"Where has it gone?" my father asked.

"The future," Doctor ó Cuilinn replied.

An uncomfortable silence followed that pronouncement.

Less assured than before, ó Cuilinn said, "Please understand that I've not yet calibrated the timeframe. So I cannot predict when it will reappear."

"Meaning, it might be anywhere," one mathematician said.

"Or any *when*," another quipped.

A bark of laughter, just as quickly smothered. My father said, "Your application states you are on the point of proving that time travel is possible."

"I have proved it," ó Cuilinn said, a bit heatedly.

My father smiled. It was a kindly smile, but his obvious sympathy clearly irritated this young son of a country doctor just as much as the open disbelief from the scientists. Flushed, he jerked around to face my father. "I have proved it," he repeated. "Even if I cannot predict precisely when into the future my machine sends these objects. And, well, there are certain difficulties. But to overcome them, I need money. It is a crass plea, your Majesty. I know that. But I swear you shall not regret it."

My father gazed at him steadily, no trace of kindness on his face now. "What use do you see for such a machine, Doctor ó Cuilinn?"

"That is not for me to say, your Majesty. But if you were to ask—"

"I just did, young man."

Breandan ó Cuilinn grinned, then ducked his head. "So you did, your Majesty. Well, then. I would say the uses are infinite, just as time is. You could send artifacts forward, for future historians. And if once we make travel into the future, surely it follows that those in the future will have the means to communicate with us. Think of that, speaking with the future and hearing its answer. "

One of the astrologers objected. "Impossible. If the future is immutable, our descendents cannot interfere by offering us assistance, in any form."

"How, immutable?" said one of the philosophers. "If the future has not happened yet, we are free to change it."

"But change implies existence—"

"It implies nothing of the sort. You can change a man's potential without altering his situation—"

The argument broke out, louder and more strident than before. ó Cuilinn scowled. My father shook his head, but made no effort to quash the debate. He beckoned ó Cuilinn to one side. They stood within a half dozen steps from my alcove. One glance upward, and the man would see me, or at least my dim outline, but his attention was wholly upon my father.

"Tell me truthfully," my father said, "how you believe to breach the walls of time." And as ó Cuilinn looked about to launch into a long speech, he held up a hand. "In simple terms, please. I have dabbled in science in my youth, but I am no scholar."

ó Cuilinn flushed and smiled. "You undervalue yourself, your Majesty. I know your reputation. Well, then, my research and my methods depend on time fractures. These are—"

"I know what time fractures are. Most scholars believe them to be myth."

"They are not. Or rather, I have uncovered certain historical documents that support their existence. My theory is that they cluster around specific events. If you provide me with funding, I can map the largest of these clusters and use them to send forward items. Of course I would also need to refine my calibrations for how far into the future . . . "

My father nodded, but said nothing. By now, the noisy debate had died off. Clearly the demonstration was over. My father spoke a few final words to ó Cuilinn, so softly I could not make out the words, then with a signal, he and his court departed.

From my alcove, I watched ó Cuilinn disassemble his machine into pieces and pack them into the same five crates. Though I knew he must be frustrated, or angry, he worked without hurry, carefully wrapping each item into paper sleeves, then packing them into straw and cotton. His were strong deft hands, pale and beautiful in the fading November sunlight. A faint flush lingered on his cheeks. Now that I had the leisure, I could examine him freely. He was long-limbed and graceful. His complexion fair, his hair the color of pale straw, and fine. Not precisely handsome, but pleasing to look upon. I wondered if he had had many lovers.

Doubtful, I thought. A man like that—a scientist—could have only one obsession in his life, and usually that was his craft, not a woman.

He had done with his packing. Still he had not detected my presence, but then I had placed myself outside of anyone's casual notice. It was a trick my mother had taught me, back when I was a young child. *Watch first,* she said, *and then you will know how to act.*

One by one, the crates vanished from the room—no doubt going back to the same hired van. ó Cuilinn returned a final time and scanned the empty room, as though checking for forgotten items. The sunlight fell across his face, but his expression was hard to read. Discouraged? Or merely preoccupied?

The door swung shut. I counted to ten before I left my alcove.

Only a half hour had passed since ó Cuilinn had begun his demonstration, and yet the sun already dipped below the windows. The fire burned low; the air felt chill. Soon servants would come to sweep the floor, rebuild the fire. Soon my father would send for me, to ask me my impressions. Still, I lingered. I made a slow circuit of the room, sniffing. The burning odor had faded, but traces of it remained. The closer I approached the table, the stronger the traces were. The prickling sensation returned, as though tiny pins ran over my arms and neck.

Intrigued, I held my hands a few inches over the table. Where the octopus had sat, it felt pleasantly warm.

His demonstration was exactly like that of an illusionist. One moment, you saw the apple on his palm, the next it had disappeared. Hardly proof of a scientific discovery.

But he was so certain. And I am certain he could not lie, even if it meant his death.

And then I saw it—a shadow on the table. A clear dark shadow, in spite of the fading afternoon light. I bent closer. Not a shadow, but a thin layer of ashes on the tabletop. Exactly where the bar had sat inside the machine.

My pulse beating faster, I touched a fingertip to the shadow. A film of dust clung to my skin. I tasted it. (A rash move, since several of my recent ancestors had been poisoned.)

Fine grit on my tongue. A sour metallic taste.

Rust?

No, not just rust—a metal bar, corroded.

Very quietly, I brushed the iron flakes into my palm and closed my fingers around them. I felt as though I held the future.

A year and a month passed before I saw Doctor ó Cuilinn's name again.

My father had approved a grant for his research, and from time to time, the King's Constabulary sent reports on his work, but these went directly to my father. My own time was consumed latterly with preparations for my formal presentation to the Congress of Éireann. I had appeared before them once, five years go, when my elder brother died, and my father named me the new heir, but that was a token affair. Now that I was eighteen, almost nineteen; this presentation signaled I would soon take my place at my father's side in ruling the kingdom.

This morning, however, one of those reports lay in the stack of documents handed to me by my father's secretary. Memory shivered through me as I read the name. Only after a moment did I take in the import of the report itself.

"He has given up his post," I said. "I wonder why?"

"Who has?" my father said.

We sat at the breakfast table, both of us reading feverishly in preparation for another long day. Lately, my father spent more time reading than consuming his breakfast, which worried me, and his face had taken on a gaunt and harried look. He looked older—much older—than his fifty-seven years. One could almost see the shadow of bones beneath the translucent veil of his fair skin.

He has outlived three children and his wife. He is older than his years.

Hurriedly, I put that thought aside. "Doctor ó Cuilinn," I said, in answer to his question. "The man who invented the time machine."

"Hardly invented," my father murmured. "There were and remain several significant obstacles to such a device."

"The corrosion of materials?" I guessed.

"Among others. According to the Constabulary, our doctor made slow but regular progress for the first six months. Lately, however, his laboratory assistants admit they do little more than sweep the floors while Doctor ó Cuilinn scribbles notes and formulas into his journal."

"You set spies upon him."

My father set his papers aside and regarded me with mild eyes. "I set spies upon everyone, my love. It is necessary, and you know it."

I did. I remembered the assassination attempts from my childhood, and the investigations after my mother's and brother's deaths, when my father stalked the corridors of the palace, suspecting every councilor and courtier of plotting against the throne. That investigation had proved a simple accident of infection. But the assassination attempts—those were real.

"Back to Doctor ó Cuilinn," my father said. "He gave no concrete reason for quitting his post, but if I were to guess, I would say he believes himself close to discovery. He wants no distractions."

"But the reports—"

"—are accurate, but they can only record his outward activities. Not his secret thoughts."

Or his soul, I thought. I had only observed the man for a scant half hour. Still, he had impressed me as someone who did not give up very easily. The word *obsessed* came back to me, along with a tremor of premonition. "Will you extend his grant, then?"

"Possibly. Certain members of our Congress believe the device will have practical applications, and my scholars agree Doctor ó Cuilinn's theory about time fractures is . . . plausible."

His gaze turned inward a moment, as though he were gazing upon a scene far different from this bright breakfast room, the warm yellow gaslight glinting off the silver platters and coffee urns. Was he pondering the implications of time fractures? (The idea alone made me shiver.) Or was he perhaps remembering my mother?

Then he gave himself a shake. "Enough speculation. We both have a busy schedule this morning. Let us finish our breakfast and set to work."

It was Tuesday. A day set aside for meeting with delegations from other nations. Today, my father would meet with the Prussian ambassador, a stiff-necked, belligerent man, who matched his king's personality well. It would not be a pleasant hour. The Prussian States were seeking to expand their territory, and while their activities did not affect Éireann directly, they did affect our closest ally, Frankonia.

Mine was the easier morning. A brief meeting with the newly-appointed representative from the Papal States. Another with a group of Nubian scholars, who wished to organize an exchange between their universities and ours. A much longer session with an ambassador from the Turkish States, listening demurely as the ambassador droned on, and the interpreter murmured in my ear.

The hour bells chimed. The Turkish ambassador and I rose and went through all the formalities of leave-taking. It had been an especially tedious hour, and later events should have erased this insignificant moment from my memory, but a scattering of images and impressions remained. The man's pale blue eyes, almost ghostly in his pale brown face. The high soothing lilt of his voice. How faint lines and mottlings belied his otherwise youthful appearance. The scent of coriander and rose and patchouli that hung about his person.

One of the senior runners escorted the ambassador from the room. I closed my eyes and breathed deeply. A few moments remained before the next interview. I needed them. My head ached. My muscles felt tense from too many hours of control.

And then, a door swung open.

I heard it first, a deep, grating noise that penetrated to my bones.

Even when I opened my eyes, I could not quite take in what I saw.

It was not the unobtrusive side door, used by servants and runners. Nor the ordinary-sized doors used by state visitors, such as the Turkish ambassador. No, these were the doors used only for affairs of state. Immense. Each panel carved from a single tree imported from the American Farther Coast, decorated with intricate patterns and overlaid in gold leaf.

An old man in dark livery marched into the room and stepped to one side.

Next came a silver-haired Lord with the ribbon and chain of office draped over his raven-black coat. It was Lord Melville, the oldest of my father's Councilors. He had served as an officer, then as my grandfather's personal advisor, when my father was but a young man. Old, so very old, his thin white hair like a veil over his skull. He walked with a stiff limp, but he held his chin high, and I saw there were tears in his pale blue ears.

He stopped six paces away. "Your Majesty."

"What are you saying?" I whispered.

Lord Melville knelt before me and bent his head. "My Queen. I have the great misfortune to report that your father . . . "

I heard nothing past that, only a roaring in my ears, but I knew what he was saying. My father was dead. *Impossible,* cried a voice within. *He was well not three hours ago. He—*

" . . . the first to pledge my honor, my loyalty, my blood, and my self to your throne . . . "

My pulse thundered; my body turned numb. As Lord Melville recited the vows of Lord to Queen, a part of me remembered that he had recited those same vows to my father, twenty years before, when he had lost *his* father to an attack from Anglian revolutionaries. It was important that I face the news with as much strength and composure as my father had. And so, when Lord Melville finished his speech, I held out my hands to receive his kiss upon my rings. With great difficulty (I knew better than to make any move to assist him), Lord Melville rose and gave way to the next Lord just entering the chamber . . .

Later, much later, I sat alone in my private chambers in the palace and laid my head upon my hands. Firelight jumped and flickered against the dark walls. No gas lamps burned. Only a single candle guttered on the table—an orange-scented perfume overlaying the wood smoke and pervasive sourness of my own fear.

I was Áine Lasairíona Devereaux, the seventeenth of my house to take the throne, the thirty-second ruler of Éireann.

I do not want this, I thought.

I did not want it, but I could not turn away from my duties.

And so I let tradition carry me through the next six weeks. When I look back upon them, I remember nothing in particular, just a weight against my heart, a curious and lasting numbness. The funeral itself proceeded without any misstep. A hundred ambassadors passed before my father's coffin; thousands more—from Éireann, from the Anglian Dependencies and Albion—paused to bow and whisper a prayer, before making way to the press of mourners behind them.

And I, I stood dry-eyed upon the podium, flanked by guards.

I have no tears, I thought. *No grief.* Or had grief been burnt entirely away?

There was no one who could answer that question. Or at least, no one I trusted.

Afterward, I met with my father's Councilors and members of Éireann's Congress. I held innumerable interviews with representatives from the Continent and farther abroad, those who came to express their condolences, and to reassure themselves that an alliance with Éireann would continue to be to their advantage.

I also met with the royal physicians and ordered an autopsy on my father's body. They soon reported he had died of a simple heart attack. There were no signs of poisoning, nor that the heart attack had been induced by artificial means. I thanked them for their thoroughness, wondering all the while when my grief would break free.

Ten days later came the coronation—a hurried affair, but my Councilors agreed I should assume the throne as soon as possible. Once crowned, others would find it more difficult to dislodge me. And there those who would attempt it. I knew that from my own history.

The day began with a stuttering of snow—a typical late January morning. The skies were flecked with clouds, and the sun, when it finally consented to rise, cast an uncertain light over Cill Cannig and the nearby city of Osraighe. Cold nipped at my skin as I darted from the palace into the waiting carriage.

The kings of Éireann had lived in Cill Cannig and the Royal Enclosure for six centuries. Tradition, however, proclaimed they would receive their crowns in the ancient cathedral of Osraighe. And so I rode alone in the royal carriage, shivering in my finery, in a slow creeping procession from the palace, through the Royal Enclosure and intervening fields, and into the city of Osraighe. The clocks were just chiming ten as I arrived at the cathedral. There Lord Kiley took hold of the lead horse's reins, while Lord Melville flung open the carriage doors to greet me with a long ceremonious speech. A cold dank wind blew against my face. I paused upon the step to listen, as the ritual required.

It was there the assassin took his chance.

A shot rang out. Fire exploded inside my shoulder, as though a white-hot spear had pierced me. I gasped and fell backward, reaching for that spear and thinking confusedly that if I could pluck the damned thing out, the agony would stop.

After that, I had difficulty remembering. Pain and more pain. The strong stink of blood. Lord Melville's creaking shout, then Lord Kiley's stronger voice calling for the Queen's Guard. And me, retching all over my grand expensive gown, and weeping at last, weeping so hard that I retched more and finally collapsed onto the ground, knowing no more.

The wound proved painful, but not dangerous. Once the physicians removed the ball and bandaged my shoulder, they allowed themselves to be herded away by Lords Melville and Kiley.

"Your Majesty," said Lord Melville.

I turned my head away.

"Áine," said Lord Kiley.

That nearly caused me to look around. With a jerk of my chin, I stopped myself, but not before I glimpsed a smile on Lord Kiley's grim face.

"You are not dead," he said quietly. "Nor so badly wounded we can put off this interview."

He was right, of course. I sighed and waved a hand to show my assent.

That, apparently, was not good enough.

"Stop grieving for yourself," Lord Kiley said crisply. "You have lost your father. Well, and so have I. Lord Melville here lost a brother and two sons in the last Anglian Uprising. I understand. But you must postpone your mourning for a more propitious time."

"When I am nearly dead myself," I muttered.

"That would be more convenient."

His words brought a puff of laughter to my lips. "Speak," I told him. "You will anyway."

"So I will," Kiley said. "First, you must have a more competent bodyguard. Lord Vincent and his staff have vetted all the members of the Queen's Constabulary deemed fit to protect the Queen. And they are fit. But they are not quite so . . . thorough as the man I would propose."

"A bodyguard," I repeated. "Who . . . "

"Commander Adrian O'Connell Dee," Kiley said. "He served in Eastern and Southern Europe as a covert agent for eight years. More recently, at my recommendation, he enlisted in your father's Constabulary to acquire experience at home. I have always found him reliable."

"You mean he is one of yours."

He nodded. "One of mine."

Someone outside Court, but inside our circle of trust.

Though I disliked the necessity, I understood Lord Kiley's reasoning.

"Very well," I said. "Have him come tomorrow for an interview. Surely the Constabulary can protect me until then?"

Lord Kiley and Lord Melville left me with a thick packet of reports. I set them aside for later. My shoulder ached, and I had little appetite for reports or food. It was easier to lie motionless, hoping that the drugs the physicians gave me would obviate the need to even pretend an interest.

An hour of restless sleep. Another hour lying on my back, staring at the patterned ceiling.

He knew it, I thought, as I maneuvered myself painfully onto my good shoulder. *He knew I would get bored.*

Whatever their faults in predicting the assassination attempt, my Constabulary had worked hard and well to discover those at fault. The attempt had been led by members of several disaffected political groups with ties to certain Congress members of influence. With a sense of nausea, I read the name of a cousin who had allowed himself to become the nominal leader of this movement.

You, I thought, *have made a grave mistake.*

More reports, concerning the investigation, the names of lesser conspirators, the possible extent of the disaffection. My difficulties would not end with one assassination attempt. There were others who believed me too young to rule. Some wanted a Regency. Some worked to shift power from the Queen to Congress.

And there were the Anglians. Always the Anglians.

We shall never rid ourselves of the danger, my father once said, *until we cut their chains and help them build a new nation of their own.* He had meant to accomplish that in his own reign . . .

The tears burned in my eyes. I swiped them away and read past the further details of plots and political maneuvers, to the details about this man Dee.

Commander Adrian O'Connell Dee. He had taken an undergraduate degree in mathematics from Awveline University, then started graduate work in Austria. Studies broken off for reasons unknown. Fluent in German and French. Recruited by Lord Kiley's people for his ability with languages and disguises. Later he showed a fine understanding of political concerns. I saw nothing to suggest he would make a good bodyguard, but I knew Lord Kiley. My father had trusted him. I began to think I might as well.

"Commander Dee."

"Your Majesty."

It was three days after my near assassination. Lord Kiley had arranged everything, even to choosing this room, which was smaller than most of the other interview rooms, and more intimate with its plush carpet, the cloth chairs gathered around the brightly burning fireplace.

Commander Dee, however, remained as formal as if we were met in Cill Cannig's grandest audience chamber. He stood at attention, his hands clasped behind his back: a tall man, as lean as a shadow and nearly as dark. Dark-complexioned or tanned, I could not tell which. Warm brown eyes. Dark hair cut short and swept back in the newest fashion. His hands, like the rest of him, were slender, but I could imagine the muscles sliding beneath his skin. The reports said he was thirty-five. He appeared younger, except for the faint lines around his eyes.

"Why did you quit your studies?" I asked.

He shrugged. "Let us call it the distraction of youth."

"Is that the truth?"

His eyes narrowed with humor. "Truth is such a transient thing, your Majesty. I find in certain cases it depends entirely upon perspective."

Before I could stop myself, I laughed.

Adrian Dee's mouth quirked into a smile—a brief flicker of shared amusement. It changed his expression entirely. That intrigued me.

"So tell me," I went on, "how you would protect me better than my own guards."

At my insistence, he took the chair opposite me. We leaned toward the fire, heads close together, as he described his own impressions of the political situation facing me. A part of me absorbed everything he said, to be reviewed later when I was alone. Another part took in details of the man himself. How his mouth was fuller than I would have expected for someone with such a lean angular face. How his voice had started off so cool and official, only to drop to a warmer lilting tone. He wore a pleasing scent, too—another surprise. From Lord Kiley's initial description, I had expected Dee to be more the automaton. Instead I found myself intently aware of him as a handsome man, clever and brave and strong. And so very competent.

"So you believe the conspiracy to be widespread."

He paused. "I believe the number of opportunists is greater than expected."

"There is a difference?"

He spread his hands, palms outward. "If these were usual times, I would say yes, there is difference. Now, with your father's sudden death, the uneasiness upon the Continent, and, pardon me, your youth, not really. However, I believe we should deal with the situation as though there were a difference. Call it a message to those who watch your reign."

I nodded. Felt a tremor of hope in my chest. "Do you want the position?"

He tilted his head, observed me for a moment—a long assessing look, as though he were measuring me, not as his Queen, but as another human being. "Yes," he said at last. "Yes, your Majesty, I do."

And so we talked and planned and argued about the coronation and how to keep me safe while giving the people a spectacle they could remember all their lives. For, as Lords Kiley and Melville and others in the Queen's Council reminded me, this ceremony was meant to imbue me with the authority of history and tradition. Adrian Dee himself simply shook his head, and took their recommendations into account. He had neatly insinuated himself into the ongoing investigation into the conspiracy. When he found the time, I had no idea. His absences from my side were few.

As for myself, I kept to my private chambers, visited only by my closest advisors and my physicians. The official reports said I needed time to recuperate. I suppose I did. I hated it, nevertheless. *Kings and Queens do not hide,* I thought. *They act. Just like my father did. And our ancestors before him.*

The physician's last visit had left me aching and breathless. In between, there were other indignities. Nurses to wash the wounds and apply fresh ointment. Formal inquiries after my recovery from the Congress. Uncharacteristically, Adrian Dee had vanished a few hours before. He returned just as the court astrologers departed.

"Where have you been?" I muttered.

He smiled, as though to a fractious child. That only worsened my temper. The astrologers had made long and noisy protests over the new date for my coronation. They had calculated to a fine degree the position and phase of the moon—never mind those of the stars—and wanted another month to assure me of a propitious day. Now I pressed the heels of my hands against my eyes.

"You are tired, you Majesty."

"I know that," I snapped.

Dee shifted his glance toward the fire. I saw his fleeting grimace.

"I'm sorry," I whispered. "I . . . I am impatient. I dislike being caged." And before he could reply, I hastened to add, "That is hardly an excuse, I know. Merely an explanation."

He acknowledged the apology and the explanation with a wordless gesture. There were bruises underneath those brown eyes, and a web of faint lines radiating outward. He must have spent half his nights in ceaseless work on my behalf. I felt a stab of shame.

"I'm sorry, Adrian."

A flinch, nothing more, at his given name.

I had forgotten—just for the moment—that we were Queen and servant, not two friends. There was no possibility of apologizing. That would only exacerbate my offense.

But truly, I did not mean to offend. I meant only . . .

Better not to think what I meant.

"Can we manage it?" I asked hurriedly. "The coronation, I mean. Next week."

He nodded. "Most of the guests have remained in the city. The others could arrive by airship. What about the astrologers?"

"Let them determine the hour. Within reason," I added.

His smile, edged by firelight, caused the last of my bad temper to leach away. "It shall be exactly as you wish, your Majesty."

It was.

Telegrams and letters went out the next morning. Flocks of balloons began to arrive within the next few hours—scarlet, silver, the royal blue and purple of the Turkish States, the fantastical constructions of Japan and the Hindu Archipelago—all the heads of state were represented, as though my guests had anticipated my plans and only awaited a word to set off for Éireann.

My coronation was set for the first Monday in February—a cold bleak day, the skies mottled with cinder-black clouds that spat snow and frozen rain over the bare fields. Once more I rose at dawn and gave myself over to the maids and ladies of the Court. Once more I donned the layers of silk and cloth-of-gold—all new-stitched because the old gown was burnt and stained. My shoulder ached in memory of that other day, but then Adrian Dee appeared at my side to escort me to the waiting carriage.

Out the gates. Through the streets. The same and yet so different. My nerves felt raw and exposed, buzzing as though charged with electricity. The ticking of sleet against the cobblestones sounded loud. My heartbeat thrummed in my ears. I thought I could feel an answering pulse from Adrian Dee's hand as he handed me down from the carriage, even through all the layers of cloth. I paused, just as before, and listened to Lord Melville's studied speech. I gazed over the crowds of onlookers. I felt so removed from my surroundings, from the event itself, that it was not until I stepped into the cathedral's shadowed entryway it struck me fully I was to be queen.

I paused a moment to recover myself. Felt my heartbeat dancing fast and light. Then, with a signal to my guards, I continued forward into the pale yellow light of the cathedral's vast body. Step, step, step, my guards keeping time with me. Then they too fell away and I walked alone the last distance, there to kneel before the archbishop.

She stood upon the steps leading up to the nave of the church. Her silver crown flared like a circle of flames around her seamed face, reminding me of ancient portraits of the saints.

"May the blood of our mothers and fathers bless you," she said.

"May the flesh of our Lord and our ancestors guard us," I replied.

So we continued, giving challenge and response. Behind me, I heard the low chant of the priests, smelt the rich rank scent of blood in the air. When an acolyte approached the archbishop, she dipped her fingers into the bowl and smeared the lamb's blood over my brow.

"Let this symbolize our dedication to the mother and the father, to oak and stream and the Lamb of God."

The archbishop offered me the silver flagon filled with blood; I drank it all.

Thereafter, memories scattered into fragments. I remembered the heavy scent of incense. The archbishop's warm fingers brushing my temples as she set the crown upon my head. The warmth and weight of gold pressing against my forehead, like the weight of centuries. The ritual words intoned in Latin and old Gaelic and the chants rising upward like smoke. Then a bell rang out, and I felt a pang within my heart.

I was Queen of Éireann.

The archbishop then offered me a flagon of cold water to wash the taste of blood from my mouth. More rituals and rites followed, first in the cathedral and then upon my return to Cill Cannig. A stream of festivities crowded every moment through the rest of the morning and evening. My maids kept busy, helping me from one formal gown to the next. That night I dined with visiting kings and queens and ambassadors.

On and on and on. Until at last I sat in my rooms, swathed in a warm robe and drinking a soothing infusion of tea. It was past midnight. Outside, I heard the crackle and boom of fireworks. The skies were clear and dark and spangled with stars. Adrian Dee lingered by the windows, though both of us knew he had no official reason to be there.

"Did you know my father?" I asked him.

He paused. Considered the question. "Only from afar." Then he answered the question I had not dared to asked. "I thought him a good king. I believe you will make a good queen."

"Ah." I smiled, but my lips were trembling. I had not realized how much I wanted this man's good opinion.

A log broke. Adrian turned toward the fire, alert. The shower of sparks sent up a spray of golden light that limned his profile. I don't know how long we stayed thus—just a heartbeat—but it seemed I had all the time to study his face. The lines running in angles, the shadow-black of his hair edging his dark face, the curve of his lips. His expression was pensive, as though he were searching the fire's red-gold heart for answers.

Then he chanced to look around. My glance caught his. There, no mistake, a flash of attraction in those warm brown eyes.

My cheeks burned. I turned away.

Adrian—Commander Dee—did nothing. How could he? He was my servant. I was his Queen. It was all fraught with impossibility.

Later, much later, I lay in bed, sifting through my emotions. Oh, and sure, I was the Queen. Oh, and sure, many of my predecessors had taken favorites—my father among them. But I was a young queen, my authority not yet proved. I could not follow my desires as I wished.

With a sigh, I closed my eyes and felt the beat of my pulse against my eyelids.

Surely, if I reached out now, my hands would meet the bars around me.

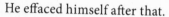

He effaced himself after that.

Of course. He thinks you wanted a dalliance.

I paused in reading correspondence and pressed my hands against my eyes. Luckily, I was alone. My secretary was occupied in the outer offices, sorting through invitations and handling the many impromptu visitors from Court. Adrian—*You must not think of him that way, I told myself*—Commander Dee spent less time in the Royal Enclosure than before. These days, he oversaw the entire branch of the Queen's Constabulary assigned to Cill Cannig. We met each morning, but these consisted of mostly perfunctory exchanges. Commander Dee handed me a detailed written report, including his current assessment of security, as well as summaries of the most important reports from the Queen's Constabulary. If I had questions, I might ask, but he had made them so thorough and complete, I never needed to.

And so I sat alone, weeping like a girl.

Furious, I thumped a fist against my desk. *I am not a girl. I am the Queen. So be one.*

The words came to me in my father's voice.

I wiped the tears from my eyes and pulled the closest stack of papers toward me. These were applications and petitions my secretary had reviewed already and forwarded to me according to our own obscure set of criteria. The first few I scanned automatically: a petition from a district in the north, asking for temporary reduction in their taxes, a long rambling paper setting forth grievances between two major guilds, yet another polemic concerning Anglian liberty, request upon request for monies to support this or that worthy cause, ...

. . . a request from Doctor Breandan Reid ó Cuilinn, asking for an extension to his grant.

I stopped. Flicked away the other papers and concentrated on his alone.

He was no politician, I thought, reading closely. He stated without apology or preamble that he had quit his position at Awveline University, though they had offered him more money and a higher position.

. . . I have discovered, through painful experience, that I cannot do proper research when I am distracted by other obligations. My blessed father died the year before and left me a small inheritance—enough to live off, but not enough to afford a laboratory and materials for any substantial endeavor. Your father's generosity enabled me to accomplish a great deal, but—and here I apologize to you, just as I did to your father, for such blatant beggary—I must have another year's funding if I am to transform my theories into reality . . . .

He believes in his cause, I thought. *So do they all.*

And yet, I remembered that handful of iron dust, the shiver in the air when ó Cuilinn's golden octopus worked its magic.

It was not golden, but brass, I reminded myself. And he used science, not magic.

Nevertheless, I found myself transported back to that cold sunlit room, watching a shabbily-dressed scientist perform a miracle before my father and his Court.

At least I can do some good here, I thought as I called for my secretary.

"Doctor ó Cuilinn."

"Your Majesty. Thank you for inviting me to Cill Cannig."

He had changed little in the past two years, but the differences intrigued me—his fine golden hair lay thin over his skull, a tracery of lines marked his pale complexion. And though his eyes were just as dark and brilliant, the gaze as direct, I thought I detected a new uncertainty in his manner. Not a good sign, for my purposes.

I gestured toward the waiting chairs. "Please. Let us be comfortable. I invited you because I wanted to discuss your research."

There was the briefest hesitation, an even briefer glint of wariness, before he smiled and bowed and followed me to the comfortable grouping of stuffed chairs set round a low table. Beside us, tall windows overlooked one of the palace courtyards, now rife with lilies and roses and the last sweet-smelling blossoms now dripping from the apple trees. Spring rains had given way to the brief summer sun, which poured through the windows.

Servants silently poured tea into porcelain cups etched with falling leaves. At my glance, they withdrew. ó Cuilinn watched them throughout their work. Only when we were alone did he glance back in my direction. Expectant.

"I was not entirely truthful," I told him. "I want you to move your laboratory here, into the palace, and—"

"You cannot purchase me," he said abruptly. Then added, "Your Majesty."

Ah, so he had not entirely lost his arrogance. Good.

I nodded. "I do not intend to. But you see, I believe in your work. I have ever since I observed your demonstration to my father two years ago."

His dark blue eyes widened as I opened a drawer in the table and withdrew a handkerchief wrapped many times around. I set the handkerchief on the table. Its contents shifted slightly. Was it only in my imagination, or could one hear the hiss of its contents? Smell the faint metallic scent, old and stale?

Breandan ó Cuilinn stared at the handkerchief. "What is that?"

"Your metal bar," I told him. "The one you sent forward in time, when you last were here."

"How did you—"

"I waited." Never mind that I had not known what to expect, or when. The essence was true. "A few moments after you left, the bar reappeared. Or rather, part of it did."

I undid the handkerchief carefully, layer by layer, until the cloth lay flat upon the table. There in the center lay the handful of dust, somewhat diminished. ó Cuilinn stretched out a hand, plucked it back. He glanced up at me. "What do you want?"

No honorifics. I hardly cared.

"I want you to continue your research," I said. "I am willing to allot you substantial funds. However, I would find it simpler if we could eliminate the layers of letter writers and secretaries and other middle-men."

His mouth relaxed and the tension eased from his jaw. "I believe I understand. But your Majesty, if you truly want me to continue my work—and dedicate myself to it entirely, not in piecemeal fashion as I have over the years—then I will require a great deal of equipment. And money."

A faint flush edged his cheeks. He had freckles, I noticed.

"I understand," I said. "Please, tell me what you've discovered so far. And what you hope to accomplish in the future."

He told me far more than I could understand. In between careless sips of tea, he spoke about using carbon-free chromium objects for his experiments, which resulted in less corrosion. His most recent experiments with the material had yielded larger flakes of dust, along with fragments of the bar itself. But that alone, he told me, was useless—merely a device for proving the concept. What he needed to do was reduce the effect of time travel itself. In fact—and here his gaze went diffuse, obviously following this thought along all its permutations—he ought to search for ways to shield objects inside the chamber. A combination of the two branches of research . . .

"What about the past?" I asked.

"What about the past?" he said.

A moment of uncomfortable silence followed.

"You want to change the past?" he said. "Why? Or is this a scheme you have for some political end?"

"I do not mean that. I only mean—"

"—what everyone else means," he said bitterly.

"If you think I will make any preconditions on you, you are mistaken," I said crisply.

For the first time, he seemed to notice me. "No. I did not think that—"

"You did," I said. "But never mind. I am sure we can come to some agreement. You want money. I want to continue my father's legacy with scientific progress."

A smile twitched at his mouth. "I see. Yes. Yes, your Majesty, I believe we can meet both our goals."

Orders, however easily spoken, are not so lightly carried out. Doctor ó Cuilinn had no outstanding obligations to any landlord or university, but he did have an enormous quantity of records and equipment to transfer from Awveline City to Cill Cannig. A month went simply to negotiate what quarters he required for his work. Two more passed in transferring his belongings to the palace, and arranging them to his satisfaction. An arrogant man. I had thought that a good quality, but I found myself hissing whenever my steward or secretary mentioned ó Cuilinn's name.

That, unfortunately, was not the end of my worries.

"You say this fellow—"

"—scientist," I murmured.

"—this scientist holds the keys to time?"

Seven months had passed since Doctor ó Cuilinn took up residence in Cill Cannig. I was breakfasting with Lord Tallon, a senior member of Eíreann's Congress and an elderly man, used to the perquisites of age and rank. Others were present, but they all deferred to him.

"He investigates them," I said patiently.

Apparently my patience was too transparent.

"He walks the time roads," Tallon said.

A shiver went through me, in spite of knowing he used only the terms from legends past.

"He is a scientist," I said. "He researches possibilities."

"At a considerable cost," another said. I recognized him—Lord Begley, newly arrived in Congress after his father's death. An ambitious man, with a reputation for cleverness. He had attached himself to the Council for Economic and Monetary Affairs.

"Explain yourself," I said.

The other members of Congress flinched at my tone, but Begley himself was oblivious. "The monies spent on Doctor ó Cuilinn's research is a matter of public record, your Majesty. And as part of their duties, the Committee has studied those records. We wish merely to express our concern about spending so freely—"

"We are hardly in danger of ruin." It took a great effort to keep my voice calm.

"No, but as you know, your Majesty, there are troubling rumors from the Continent, echoed by troubling rumors within our own borders. We need an advantage, be it economic or political or . . . " Here he offered me an oily smile. " . . . or an advantage both scientific and concrete."

"You mean a weapon," I said.

He dipped his head. "Whatever you wish to call it, your Majesty."

I studied the man before me with growing anger. Subtlety played no part in his speech. If I did not give him the assurances he wanted, he and the Committee would work to undermine ó Cuilinn's project. Though I had established a measure of authority over the past year, I could not afford to insult or ignore these men, however badly I wished to.

You must make concessions, my father's voice added. *He holds a portion of influence, and has the means and determination to increase it.*

That night, in a rare private conference with Adrian Dee, I reopened the matter. Though he knew all about the invitation, and ó Cuilinn himself, I recounted everything, from ó Cuilinn's first visit, three years before, to Begley's speech.

"They want reassurance," Dee said.

"I know that," I said. "I only wished to know your opinion about the matter. As a friend," I added in an undertone.

His expression remained immobile, but I thought I glimpsed a quickening of his pulse, the clues so faint despite the ubiquitous gaslight.

"If you wish my opinion," he said, "then I will give it. Spend the money for his research, if you believe it necessary and right for Éireann. For you. But do not promise anything to your Congress. Otherwise you break the promise you made to him."

No need to ask how he knew. He knew everything.

"Thank you," I whispered.

"No need to thank me, your Majesty."

The odd inflection caught my attention. I jerked my head up.

But Adrian Dee was already rising and bowing—a deep graceful bow expressing loyalty and obedience and all the qualities I loved in him.

And damned him for.

Alone, I considered the problem. The difficulty was that Begley did have a point. Our alliance with Frankonia, sealed with treaties and blood ties, had assured us security for decades. But now Frankonia's king was failing, and the electors were voicing disagreement about his successor. The Turkish States were embroiled in another succession battle. The American experiment had crumbled into warfare. The Prussian States and Dietsch Empire pressed upon our colonial borders in Africa and the Hindu Peninsula. The Austrian Empire, failing for decades now, proved no less dangerous in its dying throes.

We needed a means to keep ourselves predominant.

"I will not renege on my promises," I told Doctor ó Cuilinn.

He seemed unsurprised by the rumors I told him.

"It has always been the case," he said. "Mention science, and someone mentions war."

And, as if I had not mentioned any difficulties at all, he went on to talk about his latest discoveries. He had made great progress in mapping out the time fractures. Indeed, they seemed to be multiplying, though he could not yet determine why. The largest cluster centered over Awveline City; others had appeared in the neighborhood of Osraighe and the northern provinces, and he was corresponding with scientists on the Continent to determine if they had discovered any. Whatever their origin, he said, they represented a weakness in the fabric of time. If his theories were correct, he could use them as avenues between the years.

"A road between times?" I said.

"Possibly. I need more time before I can guarantee anything."

"Of course," I murmured.

There were no guarantees in science, I knew. None at all in politics. Nevertheless, I found myself reviewing Doctor ó Cuilinn's reports with greater eagerness than I knew was wholesome. And though I hated the necessity, I played the conciliator to Lord Begley and his faction. But to what end?

Uncertainty nibbled at me. In turn, I asked each of my advisors their opinion.

"Remember your father," Lord Melville said.

"Remember the longest road," Lord Kiley told me.

And from my closest friend, "Remember what you wish others to remember of you."

"Is that how you make decisions?" I asked Adrian Dee.

He never answered me; I never pressed him.

By autumn of the following year, I had several answers, none of which satisfied me.

"Tell me again," I said, "what you have accomplished."

We stared at one another a few moments. He disliked being questioned—I could see that at once—but then, I disliked excuses and obfuscations.

At last he bowed his head.

"We have made progress, your Majesty."

"How much?"

"A great deal."

"Show me."

Now his anger was unmistakable. "Why? Because you want a good return on your investment?"

I met his glare with one of my own. "Why not? Or are you so gifted by God and Gaia that I dare not question you?"

At that he gave a snorting, breathless laugh. "Ah, I should have known . . ." Then, before my anger could flare hotter, he added, "Your Majesty, I have been a thankless, arrogant creature. My apologies. Here, let me show you what you have bought with your generosity."

He led me from the interview chamber through a series of ever-narrower corridors into an unused wing of the palace. Nearly unused, I thought, taking in the many recent renovations. Surely my secretary had cleared all these beforehand. Or no. I remembered saying once, *Do whatever it takes.*

We came into a vast, brightly-lit laboratory, lined with shelves and cabinets. Several assistants sat at workbenches. At our entrance, they glanced up and made as if to stand, but I signaled them to remain seated. ó Cuilinn trailed me as I advanced into the room. Bins of supplies, all of them neatly labeled, took up most of the shelves, but others held books and folders, half-finished replicas of that original machine, and several strange devices I could not identify. More shelves and more cabinets crowded the far end; in front of them stood a huge worktable, with neatly arranged stacks of record books and tools set out in ordered rows.

All of these paled before the machine that ó Cuilinn wheeled out before me.

The octopus, I thought.

But this octopus overshadowed everything else.

It was three times the size of a man, golden and polished and wrapped all around with gleaming glass tubes. More wires than before filled the tubes. A vast cube of batteries, or who knew what, crouched under the workbench, and there were other, larger cubes sheathed in lead off to one side, connected with an umbilical cord of wires. The air in the room felt close and stale and charged with electricity.

ó Cuilinn crouched down, tugged open a drawer.

"I meant to show you this earlier, but . . . "

Without finishing his explanation, Breandan ó Cuilinn extracted a small object from the drawer. It was a balloon and its basket, I saw, worked in the finest gold and silver. An artist's rendering, a craftsman's masterpiece. Then, as if inspired, he picked up one of the books from his worktable. He pressed a button, and the octopus's mouth stretched wide. He placed both objects inside, pressed the same button again, and took a hasty step backward.

The octopus closed its mouth.

"Wait," he said, before I could speak.

One moment, two. Just like before, my skin prickled, and the air went taut.

"What is it?" I asked.

A note rang through the laboratory, as though someone had plucked a gigantic string. As I waited, I felt my pulse thrum inside me, and an answering vibration from Breandan's hand pressed against mine. He had dismissed his assistants, I realized belatedly, and my pulse beat faster.

"I sent them forward in time," he whispered.

I had no answer for that, only a stupid, "How long?"

"A year."

"Why so long?"

"To prove myself. To everyone else. To you."

We were both breathing fast in excitement. Afterwards, I could not tell who turned first toward the other. All I remember is that our lips met and pressed together briefly. Pressed again and did not part for an impossibly long interval. Only when we paused to breathe, I realized I did not wish to stop. My hand snaked around his neck. Both of his grasped my waist. Time and time uninterrupted, and none of it satisfied me.

At last, he pulled back. His face was flushed, his eyes so dark, they appeared black.

"I have taken too many liberties."

His voice was husking and low.

"Not nearly enough," I said.

Even in my bed, in the midst of kissing me, he could not refrain from speaking about his research. "There must be a way," he murmured, as he ran his fingertips along my hip. His hands were cool and raised a trail of goose bumps; the rest of him was like a winter's fire.

"A way for what?" I asked when he did not continue.

"To send a person ahead in time, like a courier to the future."

I noticed that he was tracing a pattern on my skin. A mathematical formula, a schematic for a new octopus, a pathway through time for his imaginary courier. Laughter fluttered in my belly. When he kissed me again, I had no doubt his attention was focused entirely upon me, and the laughter changed to a new and sharper sensation. Almost painful.

"What is wrong?" he whispered.

"Nothing. Nothing at all. Tell me about these couriers."

His breath tickled my cheek. "They would be like runners in the old empire. But traveling through time instead of plain dirt roads."

"The time fractures? But what if they close?"

He paused. I could sense his attention withdraw to some secret citadel within. I waited.

"It depends on the nature of the fracture," he said at last. "If my theories are correct, they might be stranded in the future, or past, in the wherever and whenever of their destination. But others suggest that time fractures indicate parallel histories. It's possible my couriers would be stranded in a different *now*."

As he spoke, he rose and absentmindedly pulled on his clothing. He paused only to kiss me, then he was gliding through the doors. I sighed. Obsession. And yet, we were much alike. Already it occurred to me that I should discuss these possibilities with my Councilors. Not as a weapon, but surely a way to maintain our predominance, as Lord Begley so delicately phrased it.

As I exited my private chambers, I stopped.

Adrian Dee stood in the parlor outside. The hour was late, and the room lay in shadows. But I hardly needed sunlight or lamplight to read his expression, which was cold and remote, like the bare trees of winter.

In my memories of those days—memories blurred and splintered by later events—it seemed I did nothing but lie in bed with Breandan ó Cuilinn, the two of us absorbed in carnal pleasure as we talked about mathematics and the properties of time. In truth, I spent the chief of my hours as I always had, doing the work of a queen, while Breandan pored over countless treatises and monographs ordered from universities throughout the civilized world, from Sweden to Iran to the Mayan empire of the Americas. When he came to me, saying that certain theories pointed toward signs of time fractures at high altitudes, I hired engineers to construct special balloons with heavy-weight baskets for Breandan's equipment. As the months passed, Breandan studied balloons as he studied everything else. Soon others began to call him the expert.

They said he was my favorite, which was true.

I told myself he was a friend.

"Your Majesty."

Adrian Dee had arrived for our daily conference. Since the day I encountered him outside my private chambers, we had confined ourselves purely to the business of Court and Éireann. There were no more private conference, no sudden access of intimacy, on either part. We were as two strangers.

Adrian Dee silently handed over his neatly typed report. Just as silently, I accepted it.

On every other day, he would repeat the same formula—that he hoped the report was complete, but if I had any questions, he would make himself available.

Today, however, he paused. "Your Majesty . . . ."

I waited. "Yes, Commander?"

Whatever I expected, it was not these next words.

"There has been a murder. At Awveline University."

"A murder?" My skin went cold.

"Several," he answered, then added quickly, "No one connected with Court."

Only then did I remember that several Councilors and members of Congress had children studying at the University. "Who then?"

"Students—many of them well-connected, and from influential families. But that is not the difficulty. The local police have found the case difficult to solve. The city is panicking, and I fear this panic will spread into the surrounding countryside." He paused and glanced to once side. His expression was pale and drawn. He added, "The murders were bloody and . . . peculiar."

Whatever his own response, Adrian Dee managed to collect himself to deliver a crisp verbal report. Four graduate students hacked into bloody pieces, the bodies left exposed. Rumors were already spreading. Some claimed it was the work of a gang. Some whispered about a larger conspiracy. There was talk about Anglian dissidents, or even spies from the Prussian States. All of it nonsense, of course, but panic and rumors did not always listen to reason.

"I want you to monitor the investigation," I said, interrupting him. "Assign an officer from the Queen's Constabulary to work with the police—someone you trust. Have him send regular reports on their progress. Let the newspapers know as well."

Adrian Dee's glance met mine. For just that moment, the remoteness vanished from his expression. We were friends and allies once more. Strange how my heart lifted at the sight.

But my reprieve was a short one. Within a heartbeat, his face turned blank. He nodded stiffly and turned away, saying, "Very well, your Majesty. I will carry out your orders at once."

Even before he finished speaking, he was gone, leaving me startled and not a little irritated. Then I heard a rustling behind me and a hand descended on my shoulder.

"Áine."

It was Breandan, clad in rumpled clothes from the day before, his mouth tilted in a warm smile. Ah, so. Yes. I turned into his embrace, grateful for the warmth of this man.

"There's been murders at Awveline University," I said. "Several graduate students."

"And so you sent your Commander to solve the problem."

"Not exactly. He . . ."

But when I glanced up, I could see that Breandan's gaze had already turned diffuse. He was staring past me, out the window. Most likely a sudden insight into his machine had distracted him. I wanted to shake him, yank his attention back from that inward world to the present. But I did not. My first impression, from all those years ago, was the true one. A man like Breandan Reid ó Cuilinn could have only one obsession in his life. Everything else was a temporary diversion.

And you are much the same way. He is your favorite, not a true partner.

No, I insisted. *A friend.*

You cannot afford to have friends.

Words recalled from a long-ago lecture from my father, the king. I had confronted him about his new favorite, an acclaimed poetess invited to Cill Cannig because of her work, and who had stayed because my father desired her company. I had been angry with him for months.

I miss him.

With a twitch, I shrugged away from Breandan's arms. "I'm sorry," I said. "I didn't sleep well. And I have a great deal of work. Commander Dee's report awaits me."

"Yes," Breandan said softly. "I believe I understand."

Our love changed after that. Or perhaps, I saw things more clearly. Oh and sure, he kissed me just as tenderly. And sure, I invited him to my bed as often as before. But our first heedless passion had ebbed. Breandan spent longer hours in his laboratory; I buried myself in my work.

My Councilors approved of the change. None of them had openly objected—the tradition of kings and queens taking lovers was older than Éireann itself—but now, I caught Lord Kiley nodding with approval during our Council sessions, and Lord Bierne no longer had the air of someone barely tolerating my opinion. Lord Vincent, it was true, had a perpetually dreamy manner. He took opium, and the habit had grown worse since my father's death. Soon I would have to replace him.

As for Commander Dee . . . He remained the proper officer of the Queen's Constabulary, but his manner eased enough that our interviews were no longer so painfully stiff.

So the summer passed. Reports from the Queen's Constabulary about the murders in Awveline City were neither good nor bad: the murders had ceased, but the police in Awveline City suspended their inquiries for lack of evidence. Frankonia's King died, and now the electors were locked in a room in the palace dungeons until they voted in his successor. Another heir in the Turkish States had been assassinated. But negotiations with the Dietsch Empire were proving worthwhile, and it was possible we could create a new alliance to balance against the Prussian menace.

Meanwhile Breandan barely mentioned his research. It was from the official reports, and not himself, that I knew he was writing a treatise about time fractures in the upper atmosphere. He had commissioned a new balloon using the latest technology for his experiments—a navigable balloon with an enclosed carriage and compressed oxygen contained in iron storage flasks.

"If I could fly to the stars, I would," he told me, in one of our rare moments of intimacy.

"But would you fly back?" I murmured.

He shifted around and grasped my face with both hands. "Yes," he breathed. "Yes, I would."

To my shame and regret, I could not find the words to reply.

He must have read my thoughts from my face, because he smiled unhappily, gave me a brief kiss, and rose to begin his day. By the time I had bathed and dressed, he had eaten his breakfast and disappeared into his laboratory. The servants cleared away his dishes and brought me fresh coffee and warm bread, while I reviewed my schedule. But my thoughts were scattered between my obligations as Queen and those last moments with Breandan ó Cuilinn.

(He loves me. I had not expected that.)

(And you do not love him in return.)

A loud rapping at the door broke into my thoughts. Before I could speak, Adrian Dee burst into the room. He closed and locked the door. His face was so pale, so drawn, I stood and hurried toward him, thinking he needed to be helped to a chair, but he waved me away. "Your Majesty. There's been another murder. In Awveline City. Lord Kiley's daughter."

I dropped into the nearest chair. "Lord Kiley's daughter. When? How?"

"Word came just half an hour ago," Dee went on. "By telegraph from the police. They believe it is the same murderer as before." In a softer voice, he added, "A groundskeeper found her body at dawn, near the commons. The report is . . . ugly."

My stomach gave a sickening lurch. I had read the detailed reports of those earlier murders. "Where is Lord Kiley?"

"In his rooms."

With Adrian following close behind me, I ran to Lord Kiley's rooms. Though it was a warm September day, servants had lit a fire and drawn the curtains. Only a single gaslight burned here, its pale yellow light hardly penetrating the gloom. Lord Kiley sat limply in one chair, his chin against his chest, his arms flung to either side.

Like a dead man, I thought. I knelt at Lord Kiley's feet. A pang of relief shot through me when I saw the shallow rise and fall of his chest.

And yet, there was death in the room.

"Lord Kiley," I said.

No response.

"Lord Kiley," I said again. "Whatever it takes to find that murderer, I swear I shall order it done. By Christ's mercy, by the blood I drank upon my coronation. Do you hear me? I am sending Commander Dee to lead the investigation."

Lord Kiley raised his head slowly with an audible click. "Your Majesty," he whispered. "Commander Dee has told me." With an obvious effort, he lifted his gaze to Adrian Dee. "They tell me a lunatic murdered my daughter, Commander Dee," he said in a soft eerie voice. "A madman." Then he gave himself a shake, and I saw a shadow of his old self. His dark eyes narrowed. "Find him, Commander. Find him and bring him to justice."

"I promise, my lord."

Adrian Dee left at once. I canceled all my other appointments that I might stay with Lord Kiley until his wife and other children arrived from their estates. Later, my secretary and I wrote carefully worded announcements about the tragedy, making certain to emphasize that a senior officer of the Queen's Constabulary would oversee the case until it was finished. Thereafter followed what felt like a dozen or more meetings with my other Councilors—with Lord Bierne to discuss who would handle Lord Kiley's responsibilities in the interim, with Lord Vincent's assistant, Lord Paor, to discuss the possibility of a terrorist connection.

Hours later, exhausted, I returned to my chambers and sank into the nearest chair. Servants had left a tray of covered dishes on the table. Bread and soup. Chilled water flavored with crushed mint. I poured a glass of water and drank it off. Though I had no appetite, I forced myself to eat. The day was not even close to ending.

More water. Then cup after cup of hot tea, until my head cleared. Only then did I notice the bells ringing noon. Odd, surely it had to be almost sunset by now. But no, the brilliant light of mid-day poured through the windows. Nothing had changed in this room—the same elegant furnishings, the same bright peaceful space I so loved—and yet, the taint of death had invaded here, as well.

I wish Adrian were here.

But he was not. He was already in Awveline City, by my command, searching for Maeve Kiley's murderer.

My hand fumbled for the bell—I thought Breandan might spare an hour from his work, and I badly wanted his company. For once, his inattention to state matters would prove a relief. The movement dislodged an envelope left upon the table. I saw Breandan's handwriting, my name. I snatched it up.

Áine, my love. Do not be surprised by my seeming disappearance today. If all goes well with my experiment, you will see the firmest, finest proof of my long research within the week . . .

I hardly comprehended the rest of his letter. Something about the roads of time, of braving the perils before all the other scientists. Of gratitude. Of love. I know not what else, because I dropped the letter onto the floor and raced toward the windows. Only now did I remember his talking about the appearance of new time fractures between Awveline City and Osraighe, and the last fine day of the year.

His balloon, I thought. It was large enough to carry his machine.

"Breandan!"

I flung open the windows. The golden towers and spires of Cill Cannig spread out before me, below a green garden rife with summer roses. My gaze took that all in, then snapped upward to the skies. Yes, there, between the tallest towers was an expanse of blue. And against that expanse, a bright red sphere, glorious and huge.

Already the sphere was shrinking as the balloon climbed higher into the skies. I could not move, could hardly breathe. Higher. Higher. Now the sphere was little more than a black dot. The sun was blinding me, and yet I could not look away.

Breandan, I hope—

The dot vanished. A bright flare of fire burst out, smearing my vision. I blinked.

And saw nothing more.

There is little to tell about the next few weeks—or rather, very little of those weeks remains true.

That sounds mad, I know. Let me attempt to explain.

It took several days to recover all the wreckage from Breandan's balloon. The fall had shattered the carriage into pieces, which were scattered over the countryside. From what the Queen's Constabulary could determine, the fire came first, then the explosion of the oxygen tanks, which caused the fire to burn even hotter. Nothing remained of Breandan's golden octopus but a charred ruin. And of Breandan himself, nothing at all.

The Constabulary and police searched for ten days; they found no sign of body or bones.

That night I called for two bottles of wine and dismissed all my servants early. And I drank, I drank until the fire burned low and cold nipped at my skin through the layers of my woolen robes. Once, around midnight, I nearly summoned my secretary, so that he might send a telegraph to Adrian Dee. But that, I knew, would have been a terrible mistake. Adrian would refuse to abandon his murder investigation simply to comfort me. He had his pride, and his sense of duty.

As had I.

And so I left off drinking and retreated to bed, where I fell into a restless slumber. My dreams consisted of scattered images of the past five years—of my first interview with Adrian Dee, of the golden octopus and its leavings of iron dust, of Breandan's face, illuminated with joy as he placed the miniature balloon into his new gigantic machine. Of Lord Kiley, as limp as a puppet, after hearing of his daughter's brutal murder.

I woke just before dawn to the creaking of branches outside my window. It was a cold gray October morning. The skies wept with rain. One of the maids had left it partially open, and a dank wind blew through the room, carrying with it the scent of moldering leaves. My head aching from the wine, I stumbled toward the window to shut it. Paused and blinked to clear my vision. Below me,

Cill Cannig looked as it always did in autumn. Copper-brown leaves whirled about. The trees, stark and black against the dull gray skies. The sense of a world dying.

(Though Gaia and God both taught us that resurrection was our right.)

Now. I have attempted to describe in writing the next moments several times over. None of them fit what I remember. Though "remember" itself is a tenuous concept.

So. Let me just tell the story.

It was a cold wet October dawn. I was standing by the window, as I said. This early in the day, the world seemed empty of human life, excerpt for a few curls of smoke over the kitchen quarters. And I, I was wishing I could undo parts of the last few weeks. Or months. Or years.

Then, of a sudden, a wrenching pain took me. My vision wavered and blurred. *The wine*, I thought confusedly, gripping the windowsill to keep my balance.

But it was not the wine. I blinked and stared until my stomach calmed and the landscape steadied before me. It was an ordinary dawn, with smudges of saffron and indigo against the dull dark sky, the thin scarlet line running across the horizon. Yes and no. Ordinary, but unsettled, as though an earthquake shook my perception. I stared harder. There, in the distance, the clouds roiled. Again my stomach lurched, as though I stood aboard a plunging airship. The clouds narrowed into a funnel that raced toward me . . . .

Hours later, I came to, lying on the floor of my bedchamber. All I could remember was a terrible dream about the world tipping into chaos. A bruise over my left eye told me I'd fallen, but when my maid arrived, they could not remember anything of that strange dawn. Indeed, they had difficulty pinning down memories of the previous day or even the week before.

More strangeness followed. Lord Kiley appeared at mid-morning to report a strange incident. Commander Adrian Dee had collapsed in Awveline City in a fit of madness. Of course the police there had taken custody of the man, and had him sequestered at once in Aonach Sanitarium, but it was odd that neither I nor Lord Kiley could remember why I had sent him away from Court.

If I had.

Part of me remembered a terrible tragedy, but the details refused to come into focus. Another part remembered a different tragedy, but that one too eluded remembrance. As the days melted away, I stopped struggling to remember. It was enough to ensure that Commander Dee received the best care, and to plan his eventual return to the Queen's Constabulary. (Though, to be sure, the doctors at Aonach Sanitarium were not sanguine.)

Those were the days of confusement, as I called them.

Now to explain how I remembered what had never been.

(Or rather it had been. Once. In a different world.)

It was a bright cold November day. For once, I had an hour of leisure from my duties. A restlessness overtook me, and so, trailed by my guards, I wandered far from my usual paths, away from the public galleries and audience halls, through a series of ever-narrower corridors into an unused wing of the palace. On and on, to a pair of high metal doors, with a heavy bar across them. My curiosity piqued, I ordered my guards to remove the metal bar. Leaving them behind, I entered the vast chamber that lay beyond.

Inside, it was dark and empty. A puff of cold stale air met my face. The scent of something old and forgotten. Memory pricked at me.

We had lately added electric illumination to the palace. I pressed the switch, and light flooded the room.

It was empty. A cavern filled with dust and shadows. But my skin itched, and I took another few steps forward. Saw my first impression was not entirely correct. Off to one side, empty shelves stretched from floor to ceiling. And there, in the nearest corner, a few scraps of crumpled paper, also coated with dust, as though someone had abandoned them years before. Ahead of me, however, the room stretched unimpeded by any obstacles. It was amazing, I thought, that such an enormous space could exist within Cill Cannig without me knowing it . . .

It was then I saw the bright patch on the floor. I bent down to inspect it.

The air shimmered. Startled, I plucked back my hand.

And stopped.

There, in the middle of the bright patch, lay a miniature balloon and a pile of loose papers. The balloon had once been an exquisite work of art, I saw at once, constructed of gold and silver and set with tiny ruby and emerald jewels along the jet-black basket and over the perfect red sphere of the balloon itself. But the wires connecting the balloon to its basket were bent, and spots on the carriage itself were blunted, as though someone had set the balloon too close to a hot fire.

I set the balloon aside and took up the papers, which were even stranger than the balloon. They looked as though they had been sewn into a book, but the edges near the binding were torn, and the rest had turned brown, obscuring the rows and rows of neat dark handwriting. Curious, I picked up the top page.

June 18th, 1900. Cill Cannig, Osraighe. To Áine Lasairíona Devereaux, Queen of Éireann, and my patron and benefactress in these investigations into the nature of the future . . .

An electric shock traveled through me. I snatched up another page. Here were formulas and schematics for a strange machine, one that resembled nothing I had ever seen before.

Except I had.

More pages. More electric shocks. The pages were from a journal, written by a scientist detailing his research. It was all fantastic, and yet, not entirely so. As I read about balloons and time travel, about batteries and energy sources based upon work from certain Frankonian scientists, I recognized terms from my father's discourses about philosophy, about a certain young scientist with theories about time fractures and travel between the present and the future . . . .

Time fractures.

I release a long-held breath.

And remembered.

Breandan, I thought. *Breandan, what have you done?*

Except I knew. Or thought I knew.

My hands shook as I set aside the paper. I glanced upward to the darkened ceiling, half expecting a rain of papers to descend upon me, describing an unknown past and future. Memory pricked at my brain, reminding me of a past I had forgotten.

(Forgot. Or never lived.)

I took up a second page from the middle of the set. Glanced over a description of a failed experiment. Once more the name Breandan Reid ó Cuilinn made my brain ache with half-remembered events. He had demonstrated a machine to my father. That much I was certain. But the rest . . . a balloon, a diary of experiments conducted here, at Cill Cannig?

I took the balloon and the papers back to my private chambers. It was strange, but their presence gave me a stability I lacked and longed for these past four weeks. And so, between brief investigations into the past, and certain inquiries onto the Continent concerning recent findings about time fractures, or the inconsistencies in present times. The more I investigated, the more I remembered from that other time, from that other past. Someone had closed the time fractures over Osraighe and Awveline City. Murders were undone, the past rewritten. Because of that, Lord Kiley's daughter lived, and Breandan had died.

(Perhaps. Or if he lived, it was in a different time. In a different world from the Éireann I knew.)

And what if I could travel into the past, forbid Breandan to make his fateful journey through time? Would he listen to me, a stranger? Or would he nevertheless press onward, to be the first of all scientists, to breach the walls of time?

I thought I knew the answer to that question.

Oh, Breandan, what have you done?

Except I knew.

He had launched himself forward to a future that had vanished. No, not vanished. According to the many treatises I had read, his future had jumped to a different path, severed from mine.

And now I knew the choices my father had faced, when my mother died. It was not merely an acceptance of death. It was the knowledge that our duties and our path lay with Éireann, not with any other person who happened to share our lives.

I picked up the miniature balloon and ran my fingers over its delicate tracery of wires, over the perfect sphere, now marred and blunted by its impossible passage through time. I would keep it, and its companion record of the vanished past. Ah, but that was all.

Wherever you are, Breandan Reid ó Cuilinn, I thought. Wherever you travel. Fare thee well.

BLUE VERVAIN MURDER BALLAD #2: JACK OF DIAMONDS

ERIK AMUNDSEN

The girl played a banjo with a ghostwood neck as she sang a tune in the ghostwood tree. Peep frogs sang with her, sweet as Sunday gospel, and on the ground, at the crossroads, his watch reading a quarter to midnight, cat-eyed Hector Brown edged for the shadows. He asked them in the voice under his breath to take him back, but they weren't having him anymore. The girl opened her eyes at the end of her song and they fled, like she'd shone a light on him, but there was no light he could see.

The girl tilted her head down until the point of her chin seemed to transfix Hector through the chest and then she jumped from the high limb that had been her perch. She didn't fly, but she made no sound when she landed. She rolled with the landing, right to her feet, kicking up dried leaves and straw.

Her toes were touching his. Her eyes were the color of the ghostwood and she leaned on her banjo like a cane.

"You're early," said Hector, and he chuckled. It sounded dry and badly balanced on his words.

"Would hell find a lady Satan for you, Hector Brown, and you alone?" asked the girl.

Hector composed up his face for the table, though, in his heart, he was cursing what he must have already let her know.

"Would they send such a celebrated sinner as yourself one cleft in place of two? No, the devil has passed on offering for your soul three times, Hector. That ought to tell you something."

"Three?" Hector searched himself and found only once at the crossroads, one bad oath in a tavern; the third was a mystery to him.

"The fact that you've brought your soul to market again after the first day ended without a sale should have been instructive," the girl said, "and that first failure to sell doubly so. When the devil looks into his ledger book, he finds he already has you without further investment."

Hector had nothing to say, his hand crept for his waist and the dagger belted there; it crept and it searched and felt an empty sheath. The girl winked, she looked over her shoulder at the river, then, and back at Hector, and she sighed.

"Who is it that you've come to sell your soul to get?"

"I don't see how it much matters," said Hector. "If my soul isn't mine, but you seem to be able to pierce through to my heart with a look, it shouldn't be that hard for you to divine without my saying."

"If it's a heart you want pierced, Hector," said the girl, holding up his dagger, "you've lent me a tool far better suited for the work than my sight. I haven't so much as glanced at your heart, just your history. Having taken my fill of that, I find myself in want of a name, but nothing else."

Hector looked down at his shoes, scuffed and worn; looked at how they rubbed against the toes of the girl's shoes, and when he looked up, he spoke the name.

"Her name is Rachel," he said.

The girl's hand whip-snaked to Hector's brow and pushed his eye wide open. She leaned up and looked deep inside.

"This one?" the girl said. "How have your guiles and your persuasions failed you this time? How is it that the sweet face your mother gave you has come in second, and to what?"

"I met her in the gambling halls," said Hector, "a shill for the house, with a blue dress on, with blue eyes like corn flowers on a full moon night."

"They call her Rachel Rocket?" said the girl. "I've heard the name around the way. When the house has lost enough, she puts a white chip with a heart inscribed in the center, and you and dozens more have thrown winnings and livelihoods away, chasing that chip, haven't you?"

Hector pressed his lips together, tried to shuffle like a guilty boy standing for a hymn, but his feet would not leave the earth, so he rocked in place. The girl looked down at their feet and back up at his face.

"I notice you're not wearing those shiny shoes that made you so proud, anymore, or perhaps those on your feet were that pair. In either case, Hector, I thought you would be more practical."

"This is different," he said. "You must have heard I have an understanding with the cards, the way they come and the way they fall."

"I have heard," said the girl, "that it came by way of your cat-eyed daddy, with his eyes and his heart."

"I've played against shill girls before," said Hector, "and had my way with all of them; I do not see them over the cards, not the way I'm meant to see them."

"But you saw this one," said the girl, "you saw her the way she wanted you to see her."

"I didn't," said Hector, and he stepped back from the girl, "and if you can see my heart at all, you'll see I'm telling the truth. If you see my history, you'll see my pride that will stand as my witness. I swear to you on it that I didn't want Rachel at all until I saw her take my last chip from the table."

The girl glanced toward the river again, there was a cloud passed across her face.

"But now you lack the funds to try her again at the table," said the girl.

"I can raise funds, if that were truly the matter," Hector said, "but Rachel's contract belongs to Askance the Pike, now, and she plays on his riverboat in the wide Indigo behind you. Askance only allows those of high degree on his gambling cruises, and degree is something that I cannot win at cards."

"Is it love?" said the girl. "When you play, the colors of the suits change over; the clubs and spades show red and the hearts and diamonds black. So I ask, do you feel that thing, or is this a simpler craving?"

"They gnaw on my heart the same."

The cloud moved on, the girl stepped forward, slinging her ghostwood banjo over her shoulder as she did, and again, her toes fetched up against his, and again, he could not move them.

"A matter of degree," she said, "is a simple one. Entertain my offer, Hector Brown. I can lend you a glamour that will hold in place of degree, find you passage on Askance's boat, and invest in you the funds you will need. All I ask is threefold return on my investment."

"Three?" said Hector. "That sounds a great deal like charity, and makes me suspicious."

"Ninefold, then, if you like," said the girl, "to salve your conscience; open up that mouth again with anything other than a yes or no and I will multiply it by three again."

"Shall we shake on it?" said Hector. "Nine times your stake is still a lower price than what I was prepared to take."

"No," said the girl, as another cloud passed into her face, "we won't shake, we'll kiss on it."

Hector Brown smiled.

"Yours is a face I would kiss for free," he said, and the cloud passed her by again. The girl glanced at the river and leaned close.

Before their lips parted, she reached for his left hand and tied something around his third finger there. Then she stepped back from him, two steps away. It was a little twist of her own black hair that Hector saw when he raised his hand to see; the same shiny black that made the strings of her banjo.

"Don't be distressed, Hector," she said, "we're not wed; that's the anchor for the glamour you will need to fool the Pike. Beware of him, he does not feel the lusts of men, but he does have the pride and he is jealous, and his temper is very bad. Do not mention me when you play on the boat, or he will hear and his men will throw you overboard. If you're lucky, the paddlewheel will get you before he does."

"How can I mention you?" Hector said. "I don't know your name."

"You can call me Blue Vervain," said the girl, "but not until both your feet touch the land again."

"Now that we're partners," said Hector, "may I have back my dagger?"

"You'd be better served throwing this thing in the river," said Blue Vervain. "I smell blood on it."

"I insist," said Hector. "My mother gave it to me; she said it was my father's and it's all of either I have."

"If only that were the case," said the Blue Vervain. "But no, I shouldn't keep it from you, take it back with my compliments. If you follow the road along the river for a quarter mile downstream, you will find a dock that will lead you to the riverboat. Your name will be Cody Jaye, don't mention your real name or mine or the pike will have your blood."

"Blue Vervain isn't your real name, is it?"

The girl looked again toward the river, and then she sighed.

"No," she said, "it isn't. It's Ayelish, but if that name ever passes your lips, it will be bad for you."

Hector Brown left the crossroads, crossed the bridge by the frog pond, where the peep frogs had gone quiet and walked to the banks of the river. He followed the road downstream to the place where the river mist hung thick over a moonless night, and a narrow old dock stretched out into darkness.

The shoe of his first foot on that dock began to shine; the scuffs and age and wear melting away into new tooled leather and gloss. The second followed, and his clothing became a fine suit, his worn satchel a suitcase; the lock of hair on his finger cinched tight, and made him gasp. Ayelish had assured them they were not wed, but the tightening around his finger; he could not fear a comparison less apt.

The dock creaked, and beneath his weight, he could hear the old worn-silver wood shedding splinters as he passed. The dark of night melted into the mute gray of mist as he went, and, at the end of the dock, where a podium and a book stood, Hector felt as though he had walked the length of the dock for the hours from midnight until morning.

There was an inkwell and a pen standing at the podium, the page open, bearing the heading **GUEST BOOK**. Hector took the pen, and with a moment's hesitation, he wrote the name he'd been instructed into the ledger.

For another moment, nothing happened; then the water began to boil.

A great fish head rose up from the water with a long, sharp-tapered snout and a great, copper-tinged eye, big around as a wagon wheel on either side.

"Cody Jaye," said the pike, his voice deep and dark and gravel on a breath that reeked of river bottom.

"I am, sir," said Hector, and, without his volition, his tongue continued, "Cody Jaye of the Blue Hill Jayes."

"We know this," said the pike, "we've seen your face before, in two places, and welcomed one upon our boat before."

"In two places?" asked Hector. "Do you mean to say someone else has been using my face?"

"Interesting that you should come to that conclusion," said the pike, "for it is the correct one. I've heard your name and face have been taken up by a no-account, yellow-eyed bastard named Hector Brown, conceived by rape in a bed that was wet with murder before the sun rose."

Hector held his tongue and showed the pike the face he wore at cards.

"He's yet to do any violence to your reputation, and I assure you, he will be found before he gets the opportunity. How fares your sister?"

"You must mean my sister-in-law, Maryanne?" said Hector, not fully appreciating, until now, how the words had gotten into his head. "For as you know, I've three brothers, but no sisters save those gotten in marriage. It was a difficult delivery, but both she and my new nephew pulled through, thank God."

"Ah, yes," said the pike, "I misspoke. Welcome to my boat; your stateroom is prepared and your accounts will be made available to you by the purser."

Hector could see lights, gold and red, through the mist now, hear the churn of the engines, and a smaller craft, rowed by four men in Askance's slate-colored livery was approaching. He let them take his luggage and stepped aboard.

The riverboat was tall and painted red and yellow, with black whorls and swoops detailing the hull; it was hung with electric bulbs and exotic red paper lanterns. Hector could hear music floating across the deck, chamber music; he found himself listening for the pick of the banjo, shook his head. Somewhere in the back there, in the dark of his mind, he could hear his own voice whispering that name, Ayelish, that strange name, trying it out; tasting it.

"Rachel," he said in his mind as he climbed the ladder to the deck.

Cody Jaye's stateroom was big as such things go, dark wood, red velvet, a painting on the wall of bathing goddesses. Hector was still weary, but he was not ready to sleep; he would see the tables, and most of all, he would see Rachel again, before he rested. He opened up his suitcase, changed into what he found within and went out on deck where the tables were.

He did not seek her out directly, no; that would not do. More importantly, it would not work. Hector checked on the state of Cody Jaye's accounts with the purser and brought some to a table where the dealer had the head of a plumed heron, and sat down to play. If he opened up enough seats at the table, he knew, Rachel would sit at one of them and play.

His understanding with the cards and his understanding of the players at his table held him through many hands, and the sun rose over the Indigo River, patrons came and left, but mostly they left their money to Hector. He was doing well; he set traps and sprung them, faced down the players and the dealer alike, and had a fine mountain in front of him when Rachel switched by his table and he caught her scent.

She had a blue dress on, still, but this one was much finer than the one she'd worn when she took his money the last time; she was tall and fair, and Hector couldn't see her face, she'd been there and gone before he could catch it, but he felt the track of her eyes, where they'd brushed him.

Hector lost three hands and a lot of money; he was on his way to losing a fourth, but something, the sound of his own voice in the back of his mind drew him back to the table. It was still playing with that girl's name, his sponsor; still mouthing it, and the sound of the name had come from whisper to murmur. The ring of her hair cinched up again, and the cards began to fall his way. Still, the other players were wary of him, now, and it took the rest of the day to make up what he had lost in those three hands.

Rachel came to the table between the lighting of the lanterns and the lighting of the electric lights, when the sun was sinking red on the west bank of the Indigo. She sat down next to him, and there was not a breath that Hector took that did not hold her scent. In his mind, the voice saying the banjo-playing girl's name had risen to a conversational tone; distracting, maybe, but he found the distraction his only defense against being so near to Rachel that when she turned her head, her hair sometimes brushed against him. He embraced the distraction; if he was going to win that chip with the heart in the center, this was the only way.

Hector played; his understanding with the cards grew to a full partnership, and the dealer with his blood-red eyes made a nervous glance at Rachel. At ten o'clock, she drew out the white chip with the heart inscribed in the center and placed it in the pile. She won that hand, and Hector spent an hour regaining what he lost.

The voice in his head had grown to the volume of a conversation where the parties were slightly drunk and passionate about their topic, but it helped him win, and the tension around his finger kept him focused. At eleven o'clock, Rachel put out the chip again, and she won the hand.

Now, her shoulder was rubbing against his, and the voice in his head raised itself to the level of an argument, a you-see-here that repeated the name of the girl at the river. He wished it would shut up, but the moment he did, it quieted to a whisper and Hector nearly lost his hand, not before he wished it up higher, louder than it had been, now projecting in his head like a stump speech. At midnight, Rachel put the chip in the center again, but this time, Hector had her, and when the cards were turned, he reached across the table and pulled them in.

Rachel smiled at him. She offered him her hand. He took it, and the two of them stood up from the table. The purser had time to count his winnings before he left the table and declared a sum that was exactly nine times what Hector had sat down holding. Hector barely heard. His head was now shouting the name.

Hector took Rachel to his stateroom. In the cramped place, they kissed, and the voice in his head would not quit yelling that name at him. They kissed, and they touched and they left his fine suit and her fine dress in a pile in the strip of floor between the door and the bed, but the name would not go out of his head, and when Hector's moment arrived, he did not know which name to call, so he said nothing. When they were spent, Hector turned his face to the wall and fell asleep. He dreamed, but not about the girl next to him.

Rachel awoke before dawn, and sat, watching the light filter in through the high little window. She sat up looking at the back of the man who'd won her, grateful that he was pretty, grateful that he was, if not gentle or kind, at least no thug. Little gratitudes that some say should be bitter things, but were sincere in the girl's heart. Then she found a black hair, long and straight, plastered to his back.

Rachel narrowed her eyes. There was one stuck to her breast as well; two more she could find in the bedclothes without looking for them. Both she and the sleeping Cody Jaye had fine, fair hair. Little gratitudes went like flashpaper. Rachel reached out and shook him awake.

Hector rolled over to see a strange look on his lover's face, he spoke a name. Hector could feel his eyes widen, he ran his memory over the taste of the name and it made his breath snag in his throat.

Rachel felt a panic and a rage wash over her like a witch's spell; the young man had a dagger with him, sitting by the bed, it had been sheathed when she helped him have off his belt, but now it was drawn. With both hands wrapped around the hilt, she drove it straight through Hector's breast bone. Blood filled the room, and the young man opened his mouth one last time. In a gurgling, bloody voice, he repeated the name.

Rachel sat on the bed for another moment, heart beating to break against her ribs. She was covered in blood. She was covered, too, in long black hairs, from the other one. She picked at them, trying to pull them off her body, wipe them off her hands, but she only seemed to pick up more. Rachel redoubled her efforts, but panic did no better than deliberation.

A dark hair fell across her forehead, bisected her sight and curled in, between her lips. Rachel screamed. She burst from the stateroom and ran through the decks, naked, trailing bloody footprints. She leaped overboard when she reached the railing up above. The paddlewheel found her body and her blood blossomed out into the river.

Askance tasted it on the river bottom; he tasted her blood and the blood of Hector Brown, he tasted a single strand of hair, straight and dark, and knew then that he'd been duped. He'd been plundered. Askance rose off the river bottom in rush. He stove in the hull of his riverboat with a slap from his mighty tail and tipped it into the water. The boiler exploded, the boat burned and then it sank. The luckier ones burned or drowned before the pike got to them.

The people on the river dragged the waters for the bodies; those who died on the boat were gentlemen and ladies, after all, but only a few were ever recovered. They kept it up for more than a month, partly for the rewards offered, but mostly for the encouragement they got, a girl sitting on a little boat of her own singing for the crews and playing on a banjo with a ghostwood neck.

THE ROAD TO LEVINSHIR

PATRICK ROTHFUSS

I

I was walking one of those long, lonely stretches of road that you only find in the low hills of eastern Vintas, far from civilization. I was, as my father used to say, on the edge of the map. I had passed only one or two travelers all day, and not a single inn. The thought of sleeping outdoors wasn't a particularly troubling one, but I had been eating from my pockets for a couple days, and a warm meal would have been a welcome thing.

Night had nearly fallen and I had given up hope of something decent in my stomach when I spotted a line of white smoke trailing into the darkening sky ahead of me. I took it for a farmhouse at first. Then I heard a faint strain of music in the distance and my hopes for a bed and a hearth hot meal began to rise again. But as I came around a curve in the road I found a surprise better than any roadside inn.

Through the trees, about fifty feet from the road, there was a tall campfire flickering between two achingly familiar wagons. Men and women lounged about talking. One strummed a lute, another tapped a tabor idly against his leg. Others were pitching a tent between two trees while an older woman set up a tripod next to the fire. One of the men laughed.

Troupers. What's better, I recognized familiar markings on the side of one of the wagons. I won't tell you what they are, but they meant these were true troupers. My family, the Edema Ruh.

As I stepped from the trees, one of the men gave a shout, and before I could draw breath to speak there were three swords pointing at me. The sudden stillness after the music and chatter was more than a little unnerving.

A handsome man with a black beard and a silver earring took a slow step forward, never taking the point of his sword off my eye. "Otto!" He shouted into the woods over my shoulder, "If you've fallen asleep I swear on my mother's milk I'll gut you." He focused back on me, his expression fierce. "Who the hell are you?"

Before I could respond a voice came from the trees behind me, "I'm right here, Alleg, as . . . Who's that? How in the hell did he get past me?"

When they'd drawn their swords on me, I'd raised my hands. It's a good habit to have whenever anyone points something sharp at you. It sets them at ease. Nevertheless, I smiled as I spoke. "Sorry to startle you, Alleg . . . ."

"Save it," he said coldly. "If your hand moves toward that sword of yours, things are going to be come very uncomfortable for you. As it is, you only have one breath left to tell me why you were sneaking around our camp."

I had no intention of laying a hand on Caesura at all. My recent training had taught me how to use a sword, but more importantly it had taught me the extent of my abilities. Even with Felurian's cloak and my sword, fighting three men at once would be nothing but foolishness.

But of course I had no need to fight at all, instead I turned so that everyone by the fire could see the lute case slung across my back.

The change in Alleg's attitude was immediate, he relaxed and sheathed his sword. The others followed suit as he smiled and approached me, laughing.

I laughed too. "One family."

"One family." He shook my hand, and turning to the fire he shouted, "Best behavior everyone. We have a guest tonight!" There was a low cheer, and everyone went busily back to whatever they had been doing before I arrived.

A thick-bodied man wearing a sword came stomping out of the trees. "I'll be damned if he came past me, Alleg. He's probably from . . . ."

"He's from our family," Alleg interjected smoothly.

"Oh," Otto said, obviously taken aback. He looked at my lute. "Welcome then."

"I didn't go past you actually," I lied, not wanting to get him in any trouble. "I heard the music and circled around. I thought you might be a different troupe, and I was hoping to surprise them."

Otto gave Alleg a pointed look, then turned and stomped back into the woods.

Alleg laughed again and put his arm around my shoulders. "You'll have to forgive him. He's been irritable for weeks. Myself, I think he's constipated, but he won't admit to it. Might I offer you a drink?"

"A little water, if you can spare it."

"No guest drinks water by our fire," he protested. "Only our best wine will touch your lips."

"The water of the Edema is sweeter than wine to those who have been upon the road." I smiled at him.

"Then have water and wine, each according to your desire." He led me to one of the wagons, where there was a water barrel.

Following a tradition older than time, I drank a ladle of water, and used a second ladle to wash my hands and face. Patting my face dry with the sleeve of my shirt, I looked up at him and smiled. "It's good to be home again."

He clapped me on the back. "Come. Let me introduce you to the rest of your family."

First were two men of about twenty or so, with scruffy not-quite beards. "Fren and Josh are our two best singers, excepting myself of course." I shook their hands.

Next were the two men with instruments by the fire. "Gaskin plays lute. Manst does pipes and tabor." They both smiled at me, Manst giving the tabor a shake.

"There's Tim," Alleg pointed across the fire to a tall man with a deeply pockmarked face, "and Otto, who you've already met. They're our strong arm. They keep us from falling into danger on the road." Tim was as tall as Otto was large. He nodded at me, looking up briefly from oiling a well-notched sword.

"Here is Anne," Alleg gestured to an older woman with a pinched expression and a grey bun of hair. "She keeps us fed and dressed, and plays mother to us all." Anne continued to cut carrots for the stew, ignoring the both of us.

"And far from last is our own sweet Kete, who holds the keys to all our hearts." Kete had hard eyes and a mouth like a thin line, but her expression softened a little when I kissed her hand.

"And that is all of us," Alleg said with a smile and a little bow. "Your name is?"

"Kvothe."

"Welcome, Kvothe. Rest yourself and be at your ease. Is there anything we can do for you?"

"One thing perhaps."

Alleg looked at me curiously.

"A bit of that wine you mentioned earlier?" I smiled.

He touched the heel of his hand to his forehead, "Of course! Or would you prefer ale? We were getting ready to crack a keg when you surprised us."

"Ale would be fine." He returned in a minute or two with a sizable mug. "Excellent." I complimented him, seating myself on a convenient stump.

He tipped an imaginary hat. "Thank you. We were lucky enough to nick it on our way through Levinshir a couple days ago. How has the road been treating you of late?"

I stretched backwards and sighed, "Not bad for a lone minstrel. I play whatever they pay me to, then after they drink themselves nearly to sleep . . . ." I shrugged, "I take advantage of what opportunities present themselves. A purse or two when I can. Two span ago I stole the virtue from the mayor's wife. But that's about all. I have to be careful since I'm alone."

Alleg nodded wisely. "The only safety we have is in numbers," he admitted, then nodded to my lute. "Would you favor us with a bit of a song while we're waiting for Anne to finish dinner?"

"Certainly," I said, setting down my drink. "What would you like to hear?"

"Can you play *Leave the Town Tinker*?"

"Can I? You tell me." I lifted my lute from its case and began to play. By the chorus, everyone stopped what they were doing to listen, a wonderfully attentive audience. I even caught sight of Otto near the edge of the trees as he left his lookout to peer toward the fire.

When I was done, everyone applauded enthusiastically. "You can play it," Alleg laughed. Then his expression became serious and he tapped a finger to his mouth, thoughtfully, "How would you like to walk the road with us for a while?" He asked after a moment. "We could use another player."

I took a long moment to consider it. "I have been away from the family for a long while," I admitted, looking around at everyone sitting in the firelight. "But . . . ."

"One is a bad number for an Edema on the road," Alleg said persuasively, running a finger along the edge of his dark beard.

I sighed. "Ask me again in the morning."

He slapped my knee, grinning. "Good! That means we have all night to convince you."

I replaced my lute and excused myself for a call of nature. Coming back, I stopped at the fire and knelt next to Anne who still stooped by the fire. "What are you making for us, mother?" I asked.

"Stew," she said shortly.

I smiled. "What's in it?"

She squinted at me. "Lamb," she said, as if daring me to challenge the fact.

"It's been a great long while since I've had lamb, mother. Could I have a taste?"

"You'll wait, same as everyone else," she said sharply.

"Not even a small taste?" I wheedled, giving her my best ingratiating smile.

She drew a breath, then darted a look at Alleg. He was watching her from across the fire. "Oh, fine," she said throwing up her hands. "It won't be your fault if your stomach sets to aching."

I laughed, "No, mother. It won't be your fault." I reached for the long handled wooden spoon and drew it out. After blowing on it, I took a bite. "Mother!" I exclaimed. "You've done better on the road than wives hope for in their homes. This is the best thing to touch my lips in a full year."

"Hmmmph," she said.

"It's the first truth, mother," I said earnestly. "Anyone who does not enjoy this fine stew is hardly one of the Ruh in my opinion."

She turned back to stir the pot and shooed me away, but her expression wasn't as sharp as it had been before.

I returned to my seat next to Alleg. Gaskin leaned forward "You've given us a song. Is there anything you'd like to hear?" He asked solicitously.

"How about *Piper Wit*?" I asked.

His brow furrowed, "I don't recognize that one. Maybe I know it by a different name . . . ?"

"It's about a clever Ruh who outwits a farmer."

Gaskin shook his head. "I'm afraid not."

I bent to pick up my lute. "Let me, it's a song every one of us should know."

"Pick something else," Manst protested. "I'll play you something on the pipes. You've played for us once already tonight."

I smiled at him. "I forgot you piped. You'll like this one." I assured him, "Piper's the hero. I don't mind. You're feeding my belly, I'll feed your ears." Before they could raise any more objections, I started to play, quick and light.

They laughed through the whole thing. From the beginning when Piper kills the farmer, to the end when Piper seduces the dead man's wife and daughter. I left off the last two verses where the townsfolk kill Piper. No one noticed my omission, or, if they did, they approved and didn't comment on it.

Manst wiped his eyes after I was done. "Heh. You're right, Kvothe. I'm better off knowing that one. Besides," He shot a look at Kete where she sat across the fire, "It's an honest song. Women can't keep their hands off a piper."

Kete snorted derisively and turned away.

Alleg laughed and pushed more ale on me. I accepted, and we talked of small things until Anne announced the stew was done. Everyone fell to, breaking the silence only to complement Anne on her cooking.

"Honestly, Anne," Alleg pleaded after his second bowl. "Tell me. Did you lift a little pepper back in Levinshir?" Anne looked pleased at all the praise, but didn't say anything.

As we were eating, I asked Alleg, "Have times been good for you and yours?"

"Oh certainly," he said between mouthfuls. "Three days ago Levinshir was especially good to us." He winked. "You'll see how good later."

"I'm glad to hear it."

"In fact," he leaned forward conspiratorially. "We've done so well that I feel quite generous. I'd like to offer you anything you'd like. Anything at all. It's yours already of course, being family and all. But still, ask anything of us and it is yours."

He leaned closer and made a loud stage whisper, "I want you to know that this is a blatant attempt to bribe you into staying on with us. We would make a thick purse off that voice of yours."

"Not to mention the songs he could teach us," Gaskin chimed in.

Alleg gave a mock snarl, "Don't help him bargain, boy. I have the feeling this is going to be hard enough as it is."

I gave it a little thought. "I suppose I could stay . . . ." I let myself trail off uncertainly.

Alleg gave a knowing smile. "But . . . "

"But I would ask for three things."

"Hmmmm, three things." He looked me up and down. "Just like in one of the stories."

"It only seems right," I urged.

He gave a hesitant nod. "I suppose it does. And how long would you travel with us?"

"Until no one objects to my leaving."

"Does anyone have any problem with this?" Alleg looked around.

"What if he asks for one of the wagons?" Tim asked. His voice startled me, harsh and rasping, like a two bricks grating together.

"It won't matter, as he'll be traveling with us," Alleg argued. "They belong to all of us anyway, and he'll be staying with us for as long as we like." He winked at me. "And not one minute more."

There were no more objections. Alleg and I shook hands on it, and there was a small cheer.

Gaskin held up his glass, "To Kvothe and his songs. I have a feeling he will be worth whatever he costs us."

Everyone drank, and I held up my own glass, "I swear on my mother's milk, none of you will ever make a better deal than the one you made with me tonight." This evoked more enthusiastic cheer and everyone drank again.

Wiping his mouth, Alleg looked me in the eye. "So, what is the first thing you want from us?"

I lowered my head, "It's a little thing really. But I lost my tent when I was chased out of a town a couple weeks ago. I could use a new one."

Alleg smiled and waved his glass like a king granting a boon. "Certainly, you'll have mine, piled with furs and blankets a foot deep." He made a gesture over the fire to where Fren and Josh sat. "Go set it up for him."

"That's all right," I protested. "I can manage it myself."

"Hush, it's good for them. Makes them feel useful. Speaking of which," he made another gesture at Tim, "Bring them out, would you?"

Tim stood and pressed a hand to his stomach, "I'll do it in a quick minute." He turned to walk off into the woods. "I don't feel very good."

"That's what you get for eatin' like you're at a trough!" Otto called after him. Then he turned back to the rest of us. "Someday he'll realize he can't eat more'n me and not feel sick afterward."

"Since Tim's busy painting a tree, I'll go get them," Manst said with thinly veiled eagerness.

"I'm on guard tonight," Otto said. "I'll go get 'em."

"*I'll* get them," Alleg said firmly, and stared the other two back into their seats. He walked behind the wagon on my left.

Josh and Fren came out of the other wagon with a tent, ropes, and stakes. "Where do you want it?" Josh asked.

"That's not a question you usually have to ask a man, is it, Josh?" Fren joked, nudging his friend with an elbow.

"I tend to snore," I warned them. "You'll want me away from everyone else." I pointed. "Over between those two trees would be fine."

"I mean, with a man, you normally know where they want it, don't you, Josh?" Fren continued as they wandered off in the direction that I had pointed and began to string up the tent.

Alleg returned a minute later with a pair of lovely young girls. One had a lean body and face, with straight, black hair cut short like a boy's. The other was more generously rounded with curling golden hair. They both had hopeless expressions. They both looked to be about sixteen.

"Meet Krin and Ell." Alleg smiled. "They are one of the ways in which Levinshir was generous to us. Tonight, one of them will be keeping you warm. My gift to you, as the new member in our family." He made a show of looking them over. "Which one would you like?"

I looked from one to the other. "That's a hard choice. Let me think on it a little while."

Alleg sat them down near the edge of the fire and put a bowl of stew in each of their hands. The girl with the golden hair, Ell, ate woodenly for a few bites, then slowed to a stop like a toy winding down. Her eyes looked almost blind, as if she were watching something none of us could see. Krin's eyes, on the other hand, were focused fiercely into the fire. She sat stiffly with her bowl in her lap.

"Girls," Alleg chided. "Don't you know that things will get better as soon as you start cooperating?" Ell took another slow bite, then stopped. Krin stared stiffly into the fire.

Alleg sighed and knelt beside them. "Girls, it is time to eat. You're going to eat, aren't you?" His expression was calm but his tone was hard and flat. The response was the same as before. One slow bite. One stiff rebellion.

Gritting his teeth, Alleg took the dark haired girl firmly by the chin.

"Don't," I urged. "They'll eat when they get hungry enough." Alleg looked up at me curiously. "I know what I'm talking about," I reassured him. "Give them something to drink instead."

Alleg looked for a moment as if he might continue anyway, then shrugged and let go of Krin's jaw. "We'll try it your way. I'm sick of force-feeding this one. Let her starve if she wants." He left, and returned with a clay cup for each of them, and set it in their unresisting hands.

"Water?" I asked.

"Ale," he said. "It'll be better for them if they aren't eating."

I stifled my protest. Ell drank in the same vacant manner in which she had eaten. Krin moved her eyes from the fire to the cup, to me. I felt an almost physical shock seeing her resemblance to Denna. Still looking at me, she drank. Her hard eyes were like mirrors, and revealed nothing of what she might be thinking.

"Bring them over to sit by me," I said. "It might help me to make up my mind."

Ell was docile. Krin was stiff. They both allowed themselves to be led.

Tim came back to the fire looking a little pale. He sat down and Otto gave him a little shove. "Want some more stew?" he asked maliciously.

"Sod off," Tim rasped.

"A little ale might settle your stomach," I advised.

He nodded, seeming eager for anything that might help him. Gaskin fetched him a fresh mug.

By this time the girls were sitting on either side of me, facing the fire. Closer, I saw things that I had missed before. Red marks on their wrists told me that they had been tied. I saw a bruise on the back of Krin's neck, just beginning to fade from purple to a dark green. Surprisingly, they both smelled clean. I guessed that Kete had been taking care of them.

They were also much more lovely up close. I reached out to touch their shoulders. Krin flinched, then stiffened. Ell didn't react at all.

From off in the direction of the trees Fren called out. "It's done. Do you want us to light a lamp for you?"

"Yes, please," I called back. I looked from one girl to the other and then to Alleg. "I cannot decide between the two," I told him honestly. "So I will have both."

Alleg laughed incredulously, then seeing I was serious, he protested, "Oh come now. That's hardly fair to the rest of us. Besides, you can't possibly . . . ."

I gave him a frank look.

"Well," he hedged, "Even if you can. It . . . "

"This is the second thing I ask for," I said formally. "Both of them."

Otto made a cry of protest that was echoed in the expressions of Gaskin and Manst.

I smiled reassuringly at them. "Only for tonight."

Fren and Josh came back from setting up my tent. "Be thankful that he didn't ask for you, Otto," Fren said to the big man. "That's what Josh would have asked for, isn't it, Josh?"

"Shut your hole, Fren," Otto said in an exasperated tone. "Now *I* feel ill."

I stood and slung my lute over one shoulder. Then I led both girls, one golden, one dark, toward my tent.

II

Fren and Josh had done a good job with the tent. It was tall enough to stand in, but it was still crowded with me and both girls standing. I gave the golden haired one, Ell, a gentle push toward the bed of thick blankets. "Sit down," I said gently.

When she didn't respond I took her by the shoulders and eased her into a sitting position. She let herself be moved, but her blue eyes were wide and vacant. I checked her for any signs of a head wound. Not finding any, I guessed she was in deep shock, recognizing the symptoms from my time in the Medica.

I dug through my travel sack and brought out a few heavy glass bottles. Then I shook some powdered leaf into my traveling cup, added potash and sugar and water from my waterskin. After swirling it around in the cup to mix it, I set the cup into Ell's hands.

She took hold of it absently. "Drink it," I encouraged, trying to pitch my voice between gentle encouragement and firm parental command.

It may have worked, or perhaps she was just thirsty. Whatever the reason, Ell drained the cup to the bottom. Her eyes never lost their faraway look.

I shook another measure of the powdered leaf into the cup, refilled it with water, and held it out for the dark haired girl to drink.

We stayed there for several minutes, my arm outstretched, her arms motionless at her sides. Finally she blinked, her eyes focusing on me. "What did you give her?" she asked.

"Crushed velia," I said gently, not bothering to mention the rest. "It's a counter-toxin. There was poison in the stew."

Her eyes told me she didn't believe me. "I didn't eat any of the stew."

"It was in the ale, too. I saw you drink that."

"Good," she said, "I want to die."

I gave a deep sigh. "It won't kill you. It'll just make you miserable. You'll throw up and be weak for a day or two." I raised the cup, offering it to her.

"Why do you care if they kill me?" she asked tonelessly. "If they don't do it now they'll do it later. I'd rather die . . . ." she clenched her teeth before she finished the sentence.

"They didn't poison you. I poisoned them and you happened to get some of it. I'm sorry, but this will help you over the worst of it."

Krin's gaze wavered for a second, then became iron hard again. She looked at the cup, then fixed her gaze on me. "If it's harmless, you drink it."

"I can't drink it," I explained. "It would put me to sleep, and I have things to do tonight."

Krin's eyes darted to the bed of blankets and furs laid out on the floor of the tent.

I smiled my gentlest, saddest smile. "Not those sort of things."

Still she didn't move. We stood there for a long while. I heard a muted retching sound from off in the woods. I sighed and lowered the cup. Looking down I saw that Ell had already curled up and gone to sleep. Her face looked almost peaceful. I took a deep breath and looked back up at Krin.

"You don't have any reason to trust me," I said looking straight into her eyes. "Not after what has happened to you. But I hope you will." I held out the cup again.

She met my eyes without blinking, and, after a long moment, reached for the cup. She drank it off in one swallow, choked a little, and sat down. Her eyes stayed hard as marble as she stared at the wall of the tent. I sat down, slightly apart from her.

In ten minutes she was asleep. I covered the two of them with a blanket and watched their faces. In sleep they were even more beautiful than before. I reached out to brush a strand of hair from Krin's cheek. To my surprise, she opened her eyes and stared at me. Not the cold marble stare she had given me before, she looked at me with the eyes of a young Denna.

I froze with my hand on her cheek. We watched each other for a second. Then her eyes drew closed again. I couldn't tell if it was the drug pulling her under or her own will surrendering to sleep.

I pulled Felurian's cloak around me and for the first time since I had received it, the strange, soft warmth of it did nothing to comfort me. After a moment I settled myself at the entrance of the tent and lay Caesura across my knees. I felt rage like a fire inside me, the sight of the two sleeping girls was like a strong wind fanning the coals. I set my teeth and forced myself to think of what had happened here, letting the fire burn fiercely, letting the heat of it fill me. I drew deep breaths, tempering myself for what was to come.

I waited for three hours, listening to the sounds of the camp. Muted conversation drifted toward me for a while, shapes of sentences with no individual words. Before long they faded, mixing with soft cursing and the sounds of people being ill. I made the circle breath as Tempi had shown me, relaxing my body. Slowly counting my exhalations to mark the passing time.

Then, opening my eyes, I looked at the stars and judged the time to be right. I slowly unfolded myself from my sitting position and made a long, slow stretch. There was a half-moon and everything was very bright around me.

I approached the campfire slowly. It had fallen to sullen coals that did nothing to light the space between the two wagons. Otto was there, his huge body slumped against one of the wheels. I smelled vomit. "Is that you, Kvothe?" he asked blurrily.

"Yes," I continued my slow walk toward him.

"That bitch Anne didn't let the lamb cook through," he moaned. "I swear to holy god I've never been this sick before." He looked up at me. "Are you all right?"

Caesura leapt, caught the moonlight briefly on her blade, and tore his throat. He staggered to one knee, then toppled to his side with his hands staining black as they clutched his neck. I left him bleeding darkly in the moonlight, unable to cry out, dying but not dead.

Manst startled me as I came around the wagon. He made a surprised noise as he saw me walk around the corner with my naked sword. But the poison had made him sluggish and he had barely managed to raise his hands before Caesura took him in the chest. He choked a scream as he fell backward, twisting on the ground.

None of them had been sleeping soundly, and Manst's cry set them pouring from the wagons and tents, staggering and looking around wildly. Two indistinct shapes that I knew must be Josh and Fren leapt from the open back of the wagon closest to me. I struck one in the eye before he hit the ground and tore the belly from the other.

Everyone saw, and now there were screams in earnest. Most of them began to run drunkenly into the trees, some falling as they went. But the tall shape of Tim hurled itself at me. The heavy sword he had been oiling and sharpening all evening glinted silver in the moonlight.

But I was ready, I slid a long, brittle piece of iron into my hand, and muttered a binding. I concentrated and felt the cold leech into my arm. Just as he came close enough to strike I snapped the iron sharply between my fingers. His sword shattered with the sound of a broken bell, the pieces falling brightly to disappear in the dark grass.

Even so, he made a good accounting of himself, and held me at bay for the better part of a minute. I took off his hand as quickly as I could, and left him, knowing that every moment was vital.

I ran in the direction I had seen one of the dark shapes stagger, and I was careless, so when Alleg threw himself on me from the shadow of a tree I wasn't ready. There was no sword, only a slender knife flashing in the moonlight as he dove at me. But a knife is enough to kill a man. He stabbed me in the stomach as we rolled to the ground. I struck the side of my head against a root and tasted blood.

I fought my way to my feet before he did and cut the hamstring on his leg. Then I stabbed him in the stomach and left him cursing on the ground as I went to hunt the rest of them. I held one hand tight across my stomach. I couldn't feel it yet, but I knew the pain would hit me soon. After that, depending on how deep the wound was, I knew I might not have long to live.

It was a long night, and I will not trouble you with any further details. I found all the rest of them as they made their way through the forest: Gaskin, Anne, Kete, and Tim. Anne had broken her leg in her reckless flight, and Tim made it nearly a mile despite the loss of his hand. Each of them begged for mercy as I stalked them through the forest, but nothing they said could appease me. It was a terrible night, but I found them all. There was no honor to it, no glory. But there was justice of a sort, and blood, and in the end I brought their bodies back.

I came back to my tent as the sky was beginning to color to a familiar blue. A sharp, hot line of pain burned a few inches below my navel, and I could tell from the unpleasant tugging when I moved that dried blood had matted my shirt to the wound. I ignored the feeling as best I could, knowing that I could do nothing for myself with my hands shaking and no decent light to see by. Soon I would have light enough to see how badly I was hurt.

I tried not to think of what I knew from my work in the Media. Any deep wound to the gut was a virtual guarantee of a long, painful trip to the grave. A skilled physicker with the right equipment could make a difference, but I couldn't be farther from civilization. I might as well wish for a piece of the moon.

I wiped my sword, sat in the wet grass in front of the tent, and began to think.

III

I had been busy for more than an hour when the sun finally peered over the tops of the trees and began to burn the dew from the grass. I had found a flat rock and a hammer and was proceeding to pound a spare horseshoe I'd found into a different shape. Above the fire a pot of oats was boiling.

I was just putting the finishing touches on the horseshoe when I saw a flicker of movement from the corner of my eye. It was Krin peeking around the corner of the wagon. I guessed I'd woken her with the sound of hammering iron.

"Oh my god." Her hand went to her mouth and she took a couple stunned steps out from behind the wagon. "You killed them."

"Yes," I said simply, my voice sounding dead in my ears.

Her eyes ran up and down my body, staring at my torn and bloody shirt. "Are . . ." her voice caught in her throat and she swallowed. "Are you alright?"

I nodded silently. When I had finally worked up the courage to look, I discovered that Felurian's cloak had saved my life for the first time that night, turning aside the knife as well as any armored coat. Alleg had given me a long shallow cut across my belly hardly breaking the skin. He had also ruined a perfectly good shirt, but I had a hard time feeling bad about it, all things considered.

I examined the horseshoe that I had hammered into a rough circular shape and decided it was close enough. I tied it firmly to the end of a long, straight branch I had cut, then thrust the horseshoe into the coals of the fire.

Seeming to recover from some of her shock, Krin slowly approached, eyeing the row of bodies I had laid on the other side of the fire. I had done nothing other than lay them out in a rough line. It wasn't tidy. Blood stained the corpses bodies and their clothes, and their wounds gaped openly. After coming within a couple feet of them, Krin stopped and stared as if she were afraid they might start to move again.

"What are you doing?" she asked finally.

In answer, I pulled the now-hot horseshoe from the coals and approached the nearest body. It was Tim. I pressed the hot iron against the back of his remaining hand. The skin smoked and hissed and stuck to the hot metal. After a moment I pulled it away, leaving a black burn against his white skin. A broken circle. I moved back to the fire and began to heat the iron again.

Krin stood mutely, still a little too stunned to react normally. Not that there could be a normal way to react in a situation like this. But she didn't scream or run off as I thought she might. She simply looked at the broken circle and asked again, "What are you doing?"

I thought for a long moment before responding, when I finally spoke, my voice sounded strange to my own ears. "All of the Edema Ruh are one family, like a closed circle. It doesn't matter if some of us are strangers to others, we are still family, still close. We have to be this way, because we are scattered, and people hate us.

"We have laws. Rules we follow. When one of us does a thing that cannot be forgiven or mended, if he jeopardizes the safety or the honor of the Edema Ruh, he is branded with the broken circle to show that he is no longer one of us. It is rarely done. There is rarely a need."

I pulled the iron from the fire and walked to the next body. Otto. I pressed it to the back of his hand and listened to it hiss. "These men were *not* Edema Ruh. But they made themselves out to be. They did things that no Edema would do, so I am making sure the world knows that they were not part of our family. The Ruh do not do the sort of things these men did."

"But the wagons," she protested, "the instruments."

"They were not Edema Ruh." I said firmly. "They probably weren't even real troupers, just a group of thieves who killed a band of Ruh performers and thought that they could take their place."

"But . . . how?"

"I am curious about that myself," I said. Pulling the broken circle from the fire again, I moved to Alleg and pressed it onto his palm.

The false trouper jerked and screamed himself awake.

"He isn't dead!" Krin exclaimed shrilly.

I had examined the wound earlier. "He's dead," I said coldly. "He just hasn't stopped moving yet." I turned to look him in the eye. "How about it, Alleg? How did you come by a pair of Edema wagons?"

"Ruh bastard," he cursed at me with blurry defiance.

"Yes," I said, "I am. And you are not. So how did you learn my family's signs and customs?"

"How did you know?" he asked. "We knew the words, the handshake. We knew water and wine and songs before supper. How did you know?"

"Ruh don't do what you did. Ruh don't steal, don't kidnap girls."

He shook his head with a mocking smile. There was blood on his teeth. "Everyone knows what you people do . . . ."

My temper exploded. "Everyone thinks they know! They think rumor is the truth! Ruh don't do this!" I gestured wildly around me. "People only think those things because of people like you!" My anger flared even hotter and I found myself screaming. "Now tell me what I want to know or god will weep when he hears what I've done to you!"

He paled, and had to swallow before he found his voice. "There was an old man and his wife and a couple other players. I traveled guard with them for a while and they kind of took me in . . . " He ran out of breath and gasped a bit as he tried to get it back.

He'd said enough. "So you killed them."

He shook his head. "No. . . . were attacked on the road. I showed the others afterward . . . acting like a troupe." He gaped again, trying to draw a breath against the pain. " . . . good life."

I turned away, disgusted. He was one of us, in a way. One of our adopted family. Somehow it made everything ten times worse knowing that. I pushed the circle into the coals of the fire again, then looked to the girl as it heated. Her eyes had gone to flint again as she watched Alleg.

Not sure if it was the right thing to do, I offered her the brand. Her face went hard and she took it.

Alleg didn't seem to understand what was about to happen until she had the hot iron against his chest. He shrieked and twisted but lacked the strength to get away as she pressed it hard against him. She grimaced as he struggled weakly against the iron, her eyes brimming with angry tears.

After a long minute she pulled the iron away and stood, crying quietly. I let her be.

Alleg looked up at her and somehow managed to find his voice. "Ah girl, we had some good times, didn't we?" She stopped crying and looked at him. "Don't—"

I kicked him sharply in the side before he could say anything else. He stiffened in mute pain and then spat blood at me. I landed another kick and he went limp. Not knowing what else to do, I took back the brand and began heating it again.

There was a long silence. "Is Ell still asleep?"

Krin nodded.

"Do you think it would help for her to see this?"

She thought about it, wiping at her face with a hand. "I don't think so," she said finally. "I don't think she *could* see it right now. She's not right in her head."

I nodded. "The two of you are from Levinshir?" I asked to keep the silence at arm's length.

"My family farms just north of Levinshir," Krin said. "Ell's father is mayor."

"When did they come into your town?" I asked as I set the brand to the back of another hand. The smell of burned flesh was becoming thick in the air.

"What day is it?"

I counted in my head, "Luten."

"They came into town on Theden," she paused. "Five days ago?" Her voice tinged with disbelief. "We were glad to have the chance to see a play, hear the news from far off. Listen to some music." Her voice choked off for a moment, and she looked down. "They were camped on the east edge of town. When I came by to get my fortune read they told me to come back that night. They seemed so friendly, so exciting." She looked away, back at the tent. "I guess Ell got an invitation too."

I finished branding the backs of their hands. I had been planning to do their faces too, but the iron was slow to heat in the fire, and I was quickly growing sick of this work. I hadn't slept that night and the anger that had burned so hot for so long was in its final flicker, leaving me feeling cold and numb.

I made a gesture to the pot of oats I'd pulled off the fire. "Are you hungry?"

"Yes," she said, then darted a look toward the bodies. "No."

I gave a faint smile. "Me neither. Go wake up Ell and we can get you home."

Krin hurried off to the tent. After she disappeared inside, I turned to the line of bodies. "I have taken the third piece of my payment," I said formally. "Does anyone object to my leaving the troupe?"

None of them did. So I left.

IV

It was an hour's work to drive the wagons into a thick piece of forest and hide them. I destroyed their Edema markings and unhitched the horses. There was only one saddle, so I loaded the other two horses with food and whatever other portable valuables I could find.

When I returned with the horses, Krin and Ell were waiting for me. More precisely, Krin was waiting for me and Ell was standing nearby. Her expression vacant, her eyes empty.

"Do you know how to ride?" I asked Krin. She nodded and I handed her the reins to the saddled horse. She got one foot in the stirrup and seemed to change her mind. "I'll walk."

"Do you think Ell would stay on a horse?"

Krin looked over to where the blonde girl was standing. One of the horses nuzzled her curiously and got no response. "Probably. But I don't think it would be good for her. After . . . ."

I nodded in understanding. "We'll all walk then."

"What is the heart of the way?" I asked Tempi.

"Success and right action."

"Which is the more important, success or rightness?"

"They are the same. If you act rightly, success follows."

"But others may succeed by doing wrong things," I pointed out.

"Wrong things never lead to success," Tempi said firmly. "If a man acts wrongly and succeeds, that is not the way. Without the way there is no true success."

Sir? A voice called. "Sir?"

My eyes focused on Krin. Her hair was windblown, her young face tired. She looked at me timidly. "Sir? It's getting dark."

I looked around and saw twilight creeping in from the east. I was bone weary and had fallen into a walking doze after we had stopped for a rest and lunch at midday.

"Just call me Kvothe, Krin. And thanks for waking me up, my mind was somewhere else."

Krin and I set up camp. She gathered wood and started a fire. I unsaddled the horses, fed them and rubbed them down. Then I took a few minutes to set up the tent. Normally I don't bother with a tent, but there had been room for it on the horses and I guessed the girls weren't used to sleeping out of doors.

After I finished with the tent I realized that in my distracted, weary state, I'd neglected to load the blankets and furs that had filled the tent the night before. In fact, I'd only brought one extra blanket from the troupe's supplies. There would be a chill tonight too, if I was any judge of the weather.

"Dinner's ready," I heard Krin call. So I tossed my blanket and the spare one into the tent and headed back to where she was finishing up. She'd done a good job with what was available. Potato soup with bacon and toasted bread. There was a green summer squash nestled into in the coals of the fire as well.

Ell sat blankly by the fire, staring into nothing. She worried me. She had been the same all day. Walking listlessly, never speaking or responding to anything Krin or I said to her. Her eyes would follow things, but there was no thought behind them. Krin and I had discovered the hard way that if left to herself she would stop walking, or wander off the road if something in the trees caught her eye.

Krin handed me a bowl and spoon as I sat down. "It smells good." I complimented her.

She half-smiled as she dished a second bowl for herself. She started to fill a third bowl, then hesitated, realizing that Ell couldn't feed herself.

"Would you like some soup, Ell?" I asked in normal tones. "It smells good."

She gave no response. Her eyes reflected the dancing patterns of the fire.

"Do you want to share mine?" I asked as if it were the most natural thing in the world. I moved closer to where she sat, and blew on a spoonful to cool it. "Here you go."

She ate it mechanically. I blew on another spoonful. "It's Ellie, isn't it?" I asked her, then looked to Krin. "Is it short for Ellie?"

Krin nodded. I fed Ellie another mouthful.

"It sure was a long walk today," I said conversationally. "How do your feet feel, Krin?"

She continued to watch me with her serious dark eyes. "A little sore."

"Mine too. I can't wait to get my shoes off. Are your feet sore, Ellie?"

No response. I fed her another bite.

"It was pretty hot too. It should cool off tonight, though. Good sleeping weather. Won't that be nice, Ellie?"

No response. Krin continued to watch me from the other side of the fire. I took a bite of soup for myself. "This is truly fine, Krin." I said earnestly, then turned back to the vacant girl. "It's a good thing we have Krin to cook for us, Ellie. Everything I cook tastes like horseshit."

On her side of the fire, Krin laughed with a mouthful of soup with predictable results. I thought a saw a flicker in Ellie's eyes. "If I had some horse apples I could make us a horse apple pie for desert," I offered. "I could make some tonight if you want . . . " I trailed off, making it a question.

Ell gave the slightest frown, a small wrinkle creased her forehead.

"You're probably right," I said. "It wouldn't be very good. Would you like more soup instead?"

The barest nod. I gave her a spoonful.

"It's a little salty, though. You probably want some water."

Another nod. I handed her the waterskin and she lifted it to her lips. She drank for a long minute. She was probably parched from our long walk today. I would have to watch her more closely tomorrow to make sure she drank enough.

"Would you like a drink, Krin?"

"Yes please," Krin said, her eyes fixed on Ellie's face.

Moving automatically, Ellie held the waterskin out toward Krin, holding it directly over the fire with the shoulder strap dragging in the coals. Krin grabbed it as quickly as she could, then added a belated, "Thank you, Ellie."

I kept the slow stream of conversation going through the whole meal. Ellie fed herself toward the end of it, and though her eyes were clearer, it was as if she were looking out through a thick pane of frosted glass, seeing but not seeing. Still, it was an improvement.

After she ate two bowls of soup and half a loaf of bread, her eyes began to bob closed. "Would you like to go to bed, Ellie?" I asked.

A more definite nod.

"Should I carry you to the tent?"

Her eyes snapped open at this and she shook her head firmly, once.

"Maybe Krin would help you get ready for bed if you asked her."

Ellie turned to look in Krin's direction. Her mouth moved in a slight, vague way. Krin darted a glance at me and I nodded.

"Let's go and get tucked in then," Krin said, sounding every bit the older sister. She came over and took Ellie's hand, helping her to her feet. As they went into the tent, I finished off what the soup and ate a piece of bread that had been too badly burnt for either of the girls to want.

Before too long Krin came back to the fire. "Is she sleeping?" I asked.

"Before she hit the pillow. Do you think she will be all right?"

She was in shock, her mind had stepped through the doors of madness to protect itself from what was happening. "It's probably just a matter of time," I said tiredly, hoping it was the truth. "The young heal quickly." I chuckled humorlessly as I realized that she was probably about the same age as me. I felt every year twice tonight, some of them three times.

Despite the fact that I felt covered in lead, I forced myself to my feet and helped Krin clean the dishes. I sensed her growing unease as we finished cleaning up, then repicketed the horses to a new piece of grazing. Her tension grew worse as we approached the tent. I stopped and held the flap open for her. "I'll sleep out here tonight."

Her relief was tangible. "Are you sure?"

I nodded. She slipped inside and I let the flap fall closed behind her. Her head poked back out almost immediately, followed by a hand holding a blanket.

I shook my head. "You'll need them both, there'll be a chill tonight." I pulled my cloak around me and lay directly in front of the tent. I didn't want Ellie wandering out during the night and getting lost or hurt.

"But won't you . . . "

"I'll be fine," I said. My cloak was warm and soft, but it hardly mattered, I was tired enough to sleep on a running horse. I was tired enough to sleep *under* a running horse.

Krin ducked her head back into the tent. Soon I heard her nestling into the blankets. Then everything was quiet.

I remembered the startled look on Otto's face as I cut his throat. I heard Alleg struggle weakly and curse me as I dragged him back to the wagons. I remembered the blood. The way it had felt against my hands. The thickness of it.

I had never killed anyone like that before. Not coldly, not close up. I remembered how warm their blood had been. I remembered they way Kete had cried as I stalked her through the woods. "It was them or me!" She had screamed hysterically. "I didn't have a choice. It was them or me!"

I lay awake a long while. When I finally slept, the dreams were worse.

V

We made poor time the next day. Krin and I were obliged to lead the three horses as well as Ellie. Luckily, the horses were well behaved, as Edema-trained horses tend to be. I thank my luck for that, if they had been as wayward as the poor mayor's daughter, we might have never made it to Levinshir at all.

Krin and I did our best to keep Ellie engaged in conversation as we walked. It seemed to help a bit. And by the time our noon meal came around she seemed almost aware of what was going on around her. Almost.

I had an idea as we were getting ready to set out again after lunch. I lead our dappled grey mare over to where Ellie stood. Her golden hair was one great tangle and she was trying to run one of her hands through it while her eyes wandered around in a distracted way, as if she didn't quite understand where she was.

"Ellie," she turned to look. "Have you met Greytail?" I gestured to the mare.

A faint, confused shake of the head.

"I need your help leading her. Have you led a horse before?"

A nod.

"She needs someone to take care of her. Can you do it?" Greytail looked at me with one large eye, as if to let me know she needed leading as much as I needed wheels to walk. But then she lowered her head a bit and nuzzled Ell in a motherly way. The girl reached out a hand to pet her grey nose almost automatically. Ellie nodded to my question, and actually reached to take the reins from me.

"Do you think that's a good idea?" Krin asked when I came back to pack the other horses.

"Greytail is gentle as a lamb."

"Just because Ell is witless as a sheep," Krin said archly, "doesn't make them a good pairing."

I cracked a smile at that. "We'll watch them close for an hour or so. If it doesn't work, it doesn't. But sometimes the best help a person can find is helping someone else."

Since I had slept poorly, I was twice as weary today. My stomach was vaguely sour, and I felt gritty, like someone had roughly sanded the first two layers of my skin away. I was almost tempted to ride the horse and doze in the saddle, but I couldn't bring myself to ride while the girls walked. It didn't seem right.

So I plodded along, leading my horse and nodding on my feet. But today I couldn't fall into the comfortable half-sleep I tend to use when walking. I was plagued with thoughts of Alleg, wondering if he was still alive.

I knew from my time in the Medica that the gut wound I had given him was fatal. I also knew it was a slow death. Slow and painful. With proper care it might be weeks before he died. Even alone in the middle of nowhere, with no medical attention at all, he could live for days with such a wound.

Not pleasant days. He would grow delirious with fever as the infection set in. Every movement would tear the wound open again. He couldn't walk on his hamstrung leg. So if he wanted to move he'd have to crawl. He would be cramped with hunger and burning with thirst by now.

But not dead from thirst. No. I had left a full waterskin nearby. I had laid it at his side before we had left. Not out of kindness. Not to make his last hours more bearable. I had left it because I knew that with water he would live longer, suffer more.

Leaving that waterskin was the most terrible thing I had ever done, and now that my anger had cooled to ashes I regretted it. I wondered how much longer he would live because of it. A day? Two? Certainly no more than two. I tried not to think what those two days would be like.

But even when I forced thoughts of Alleg from my mind, I had other demons to fight. I remembered bits and pieces of that night, the things the false troupers had said as I cut them down. The sounds my sword had made as it dug into them. The smell of their skin as I had branded them. I had killed two women. What would Tempi think of my actions? What would anyone think?

Exhausted from worry and lack of sleep. My thoughts spun in these circles for the remainder of the day. I set camp from force of habit and kept up a conversation with Ellie through an effort of will. The time for sleep came before I was ready and I found myself rolled in my cloak laying in the front of the girl's tent. I was dimly aware that Krin had started giving me the same vaguely worried look she had been giving Ellie for the past two days.

I lay open-eyed for an hour before falling asleep, wondering about Alleg.

When I slept I dreamt of the night I had killed them. In my dream I stalked the forest like grim death, unwavering.

But it was different this time. I killed Otto, his blood spattered my hands like hot grease. Then I killed Manst and Josh, and Tim. They moaned and screamed, twisting on the ground. Their wounds were horrible, but I could not look away.

But then the faces changed and I was killing Taren, the bearded ex-mercenary in my troupe. Then I killed Trip. Then I was chasing Shandi through the forest, my sword naked in my hand. She was crying out, weeping in fear. When I finally caught her she clutched at me, knocking me to the ground, burying her face in my chest, sobbing. "No no no." She begged. "No no no."

I came awake. I laying on my back, terrified and not knowing where my dream ended and the world began. After a brief moment I realized the truth. Ellie had crawled from the tent and lay curled against me. Her face pressed against my chest, her hand grasping desperately at my arm.

"No no," she choked out, "No no no no no." Her body shook with helpless sobs when she couldn't say it any more. My shirt was wet with hot tears. My arm was bleeding where she clutched it. I made consoling noises and brushed at her hair with my hand. After a long while she quieted and eventually fell into an exhausted sleep, still clinging tightly to my chest.

I lay very still, not wanting to wake her. My teeth were clenched. I thought of Alleg and Otto and all the rest, I remembered the blood and screaming and the smell of burning skin. I remembered it all and dreamed of worse things I could have done to them.

I never had the nightmares again. Sometimes I think of Alleg and I smile.

We made it to Levinshir the next day. Ellie had come to her senses but remained quiet and withdrawn. Still, things went quicker now that she was truly with us. The girls decided they had recovered enough to take turns riding the tall roan with the saddle.

We covered eight miles before we stopped at midday. The girls became increasingly excited as they began to recognize turnings in the road. The shape of hills in the distance. A crooked tree by the wayside.

But as we grew closer still, they grew quiet, almost frightened.

"It's just over the hill here," Krin said, getting down off the roan. "You ride from here, Ellie."

Ellie looked from her, to me, to her feet. She shook her head.

I watched them. "Are the two of you okay?"

"My father's going to kill me," Krin's voice was barely a whisper, her face full of serious fear.

"Your father will be one of the happiest men in the world tonight," I said. Then, realizing it was best to be honest, I added. "He might be angry, too. But that's only because he's been scared out of his mind for the last eight days."

Krin seemed slightly reassured. But then Ellie burst out crying. Krin put her arms around her, making gentle words. When she had calmed a bit, I asked her what was the matter.

"No one will marry me," Ellie sobbed. "I was going to marry Jason Waterson and help him run his store. He won't marry me now. No one will."

I looked up to Krin and saw the same fear reflected in her wet eyes. But Krin's eyes were angry while Ellie's held nothing but despair.

"Any man who thinks that way is a fool," I said, weighting my voice with all the conviction I could bring to bear. "And the two of you are too clever to be marrying fools."

It seemed to calm Ellie somewhat, her eyes turning up at me as if looking for something to believe.

"It's the truth," I said. "And none of this was your fault. Make sure you remember that for these next couple days."

"I hate them!" Ellie spat, surprising me with her sudden rage. "I hate men!" Her knuckles were white as she gripped Greytail's reigns. Her face twisted into a mask of anger. Krin moved to put her arms around her, but when she looked at me I saw the sentiment reflected quietly in her dark eyes.

"You have every right to hate them," I said, feeling more anger and helplessness than ever before in my life. "But remember that it was a man who helped you when the time came. Not all of us are like that."

We stayed there for a while, not more than a half-mile from their town. We had a drink of water and a small bite to settle our nerves. Then I took them home.

Levinshir wasn't a big town. Two hundred people lived there, maybe three hundred if you counted the families in the outlying farms. It was mealtime when we rode in, and the dirt road that split the town in half was empty and still. Ellie told me her parent's house was on the far side of town. I hoped to get the girls there without being seen. They were worn down and distraught, the last thing they needed was to face a mob of gossipy neighbors.

But it wasn't meant to be. We were halfway through the town when I saw a flicker of movement in a window. Then a woman's voice cried out, "*Ellie!*" and in ten seconds people began to spill from every doorway in sight.

The women were the quickest, and inside a minute a dozen of them had formed a protective knot around the two girls, talking and crying and hugging one another. The girls didn't seem to mind. Perhaps it was better this way, a warm welcome home might do a lot to heal them.

The men held back, knowing that they were useless in situations like this. Most watched from doorways or porches, six or eight came down onto the street. Moving slowly and eyeing up the situation. These were cautious men, farmers and friends of farmers. They knew the names of everyone within ten miles of their homes. There were no strangers in a town like Levinshir, except for me.

None of the men were close relatives to the girls. Even if they were, they knew they wouldn't get near the girls for at least an hour, maybe as much as a day. So they held back and let their wives and sisters take care of things. With nothing else to occupy them, their attention wandered briefly past the horses and settled onto me.

I motioned over a boy of ten or so. "Go tell the mayor that his daughter's back. Run!" He tore off in a cloud of road dust, his bare feet flying.

The men moved slowly closer to me. Their natural suspicion of strangers made ten times worse by recent events. A boy of fourteen or so wasn't as cautious as the rest and came right up to me, eyeing my sword, my cloak.

I sprung a question on him before he could do the same to me. "What's your name?"

"Pete."

"Can you ride a horse, Pete?"

He looked insulted. "S'nuf."

"Do you know where the Walker farm is?"

He nodded. "'Bout north two miles by the millway."

I stepped sideways and handed him the reins to the roan. "Go tell them their daughter's home. Then let them use the horse to come back to town."

He had a leg over the horse before I could offer him a hand up. I kept a hand on the reins long enough to shorten the stirrups so he wouldn't kill himself on the way there.

"If you make it there and back without breaking your head or my horse's leg, I'll give you a penny," I said.

"You'll give me two," he said.

I laughed. He wheeled the horse around and was gone.

The men had wandered closer in the meantime. Closing around me in a loose circle.

A tall, balding fellow with a permanent scowl and a grizzled beard seemed to appoint himself the leader. "So who're you?" he asked. His tone speaking more clearly than his words, *Who the hell are you?*

"Kvothe," I answered pleasantly. "And yourself?"

"Don't know as that's any of your business," he growled. "What are you doing here? *What the hell are you doing here with our two girls?*"

"God's mother, Jake," an older man said to him. "You don't have the sense god gave a dog. That's no way to talk to the . . . "

"Don't give me any of your lip Benjamin," the scowling man bristled back. "I don't got to take it from you. We got a good right to know who he is." He turned to me and took a few steps in front of everyone else. He eyed the lute that was slung over my shoulder. "You one of those trouper bastards what came through here?"

I shook my head and attempted to look harmless. "No."

"I think you are. I think you look kinda like one of them Ruh. You got them eyes." The men around him craned to get a better look at my face.

"God, Jake," the old fellow chimed in again. "None of them had red hair. You remember hair like that. He ain't one of 'em."

"Why would I bring them back if I'd been one of the men who took them?" I pointed out.

His expression grew darker and he continued his slow advance. "You gettin' smart with me, boy? Maybe you think all us are stupid here? You think if you bring 'em back you'll get a reward or mebbe we won't send anyone else out after you?" He was almost within arm's reach of me now, scowling furiously.

I looked around and saw the same anger lurking in the faces of all the men who stood there. It was the sort of anger that comes to slow boil inside the hearts of good men who want justice, and finding it out of their grasp, decide on vengeance as a substitute.

I tried to think of a way to diffuse the situation, but before I could do anything I heard Krin's voice lash out from behind me. "Jake, you get away from him!"

Jake paused, his hands half raised against me. "Now . . ."

Krin was already stepping toward him. The knot of women loosened to release her, but stayed close. "He saved us, Jake," she shouted furiously, "You stupid shit-eater, *he* saved us. Where the hell were all of you? Why didn't you come get us?"

He backed away from me as anger and shame fought their way across his face. Anger won. "We came," he shouted back. "After we found out what happened we went after 'em. They shot out Bil's horse from under him, and he got his leg crushed. Jim got his arm stabbed, and old Cupper still ain't waked up from the thumping they give him. They almost killed us."

I looked again and saw anger on the men's faces. Saw the real reason for it. The helplessness they had felt, unable to defend their town from the false troupe's rough handling. Worse yet the failure to reclaim the daughters of their friends and neighbors had shamed them.

"Well, it wasn't good enough!" Krin shouted back hotly, her eyes burning. "He came and got us because he's a real man. Not like the rest of you who left us to die!"

The anger leapt out of a young man to my left, a farmboy, about seventeen. "None of this would have happened if you hadn't been running around like some Ruh whore!"

I broke his arm before I quite realized what I was doing. He screamed as he fell to the ground.

I pulled him to his feet by the scruff of his neck. "What's your name?" I snarled into his face.

"My arm!" He gasped, his eyes showing me their whites.

I shook him like a rag doll. "Name!"

"Jason," he blurted. "God's mother, my arm . . ."

I took his chin in my free hand and turned his face toward Krin and Ellie. "Jason," I hissed quietly in his ear. "I want you to look at those girls. And I want you to think about the hell that they've been through in these past days, tied hand and foot in the back of a wagon. And I want you to ask yourself what's worse. A broken arm, or getting kidnapped by a stranger and raped three times a night?"

Then, I turned his face toward me and spoke so quiet that even an inch away it was hardly a whisper. "After you've thought of that, I want you to pray to god to forgive you for what you just said. And if you mean it, Tehlu grant your arm heal straight and true." His eyes were terrified and wet. "After that, if you ever think an unkind thought about either of them, your arm will ache like there's hot iron in the bone. And if you ever say anything unkind, it will go to fever and slow rot and they'll have to cut it off to save your life."

I tightened my grip on him watching his eyes widen, his face covered in a sheen of sweat. "And if you ever do anything to either of them, I'll know. I will come here, and kill you, and leave your broken body hanging in a tree."

There were tears on his face now, although whether from shame or fear or pain I couldn't guess. "Now you tell her you're sorry for what you said." I let go of him after making sure he had his feet under him and pointed him in the direction of Krin and Ellie. The women stood around them like a protective cocoon.

He clutched his arm weakly. "I shouldn'ta said that, Ellie," he sobbed, sounding more wretched and repentant than I would have thought possible, broken arm or no. "It was a demon talkin' out of me. I swear though, I been sick worryin'. We all been. And we did try come get you, but they was a lot of them and they jumped us on the road, then we had to bring Bil home or he'd died from his leg."

Something tickled my memory about the boy's name. Jason? I suddenly suspected that I had just broken Ellie's boyfriend's arm. Somehow I couldn't feel bad for it just now. Best thing for him, really.

Looking around I saw the anger bleed out of the faces of the men around me. As if I'd used up the whole town's supply in a sudden, furious flash. Instead they watched Jason, looking slightly embarrassed, as if he were apologizing for the lot of them.

Then I saw a big, healthy looking man running down the street followed by a dozen other townsfolk. From the look on his face I guess it was Ellie's father, the mayor. He forced his way into the knot of women, gathered his daughter up in his arms and swung her around.

You find two types of mayor in small towns like this. The first type are balding, older men of considerable girth who are good with money and tend to wring their hands a great deal when anything unexpected happens. The second type are tall, broad-shouldered men whose families have grown slowly prosperous and strong because they have worked like angry bastards behind a plow for twenty generations. Ellie's father was the second sort.

He walked over to me, keeping one arm around his daughter's shoulders. "I understand I have you to thank for bringing our girls back." He reached out to shake my hand and I saw that one of his arms was bandaged up tight. His grip was solid in spite of it. He smiled the widest smile I'd seen since I left Simmon at the University. "My name's Jim."

"How's the arm?" I asked, not realizing how it would sound. His smile faded a little, and I was quick to add. "I've had some training as a physicker. And I know that those sort of things can be tricky to deal with when you're away from home." *When you're living in a country that thinks mercury is a cure-all*, I thought to myself.

His smile came back from behind its cloud and he flexed his fingers. "It's stiff, but that's all. Just a little meat. They caught us by surprise. I got my hands on one of them, but he stuck me and got away. How did you end up getting the girls away from those godless Ruh bastards?" He spat.

"They weren't Edema Ruh," I said, my voice sounding more strained than I would have liked. "They weren't even real troupers."

The smile began to fade again. "What do you mean?"

"They weren't Edema Ruh. We don't do the things that they did."

"Listen," he said plainly, his temper starting to rise a bit. "I know damn well what they do and don't do. They came in all sweet and nice, played a little music, made a penny or two. Then they started to make trouble around town. When we told them to leave they took my girl." He almost breathed fire as he said the last words.

"*We?*" Someone said faintly behind me, "Jim, he said *we.*"

Jake scowled around the side of the Mayor to get a look at me again, "I told you he looked like one," he said triumphantly. Then dropped his voice to a hush. "I know 'em. You can always tell by their eyes."

"Hold on," the mayor with slow incredulity. "Are you telling me that you're one of *them*?" His expression grew dangerous.

Before I could explain myself. Ellie had grabbed his arm. "Oh, don't make him mad, Daddy," she said quickly, holding onto his good arm as if to pull him away from me. "Don't say anything to get him angry. You don't know what he's like. He's not with them. He brought me back, he saved me."

The mayor seemed somewhat mollified by this, but his former congeniality was gone. "Explain yourself," he said grimly.

I sighed inside, realizing what I mess I'd made of this. "They weren't troupers, and they certainly weren't Edema Ruh troupers. They were bandits who had killed some of my family and stolen their wagons. They were only pretending to be performers."

"Why would anyone pretend to be Ruh?" he asked as if the thought were incomprehensible.

"So they could do what they did," I snapped. "You let them into your town and they abused that trust. That is something no Edema Ruh would ever do."

"You never did answer my question," he said. "How did you get the girls away?"

"I took care of things," I said simply.

"He killed them," Krin said loudly enough for everyone to hear. "He killed them all."

I could feel everyone looking at me. Half of them were thinking, *All of them? He killed seven men? The other half were thinking, There were two women with them, does he mean them too?*

"Well, then." Jim looked down at me for a long moment. "Good," he said as if he had just made up his mind. "That's good. The world's a better place for it."

I felt everyone relax slightly. "These are their horses." I pointed to the two horses that had been carrying our baggage. "They belong to the girls now. About thirty miles east on the road you'll find the wagons. Krin can show you where they're hidden. They belong to the girls too."

"They'll fetch a good price in a bigger city," Jim mused.

"Together with the instruments inside and the clothes and such. They'll fetch a heavy penny," I agreed. "Split two ways, it'll make a fine dowry," I said firmly.

He met my eyes, nodded slowly as if understanding. "That it will."

"What about the things they stole from us?" A stout, balding man in an apron protested. "They smashed up my place and stole two barrels of my best ale!"

"Do you have any daughters?" I asked him calmly. The sudden, stricken look on his face told me that he did. I met his eye, held it. "Then I think you came away from this pretty well."

The mayor looked around and finally noticed Jason clutching his broken arm. "What happened to you?"

Jason looked at his feet. There was tense silence for a moment. Jake spoke up for him. "He said some things he shouldn't've."

The mayor looked around and saw that getting more of an answer than that would involve an ordeal. He shrugged and let it go.

"I could splint it for you," I said easily.

"No!" Jason said too quickly. Then backpedaled. "I'd rather go to Gran."

I gave a sideways look to the mayor. "Gran?"

He gave a fond smile. "Everyone's grandma. When we scrape our knees Gran patches us back up again."

"Would Bil be there?" I asked. "The man with the crushed leg?"

He nodded. "She won't let him out of her sight. Not for another span of days if I know her."

"I'll walk you over to her house," I said to the sweating boy who was carefully cradling his arm against his chest. "I'd like to watch her work."

Judging from the way she dealt with Jason's broken arm, Gran was worth more than several students I could name in the Medica. We talked shop for a while, and after a small amount of persuasion she let me see Bil, who was in a small room at the back of her home.

His leg was ugly, broken in several places and broken messily. Swollen and discolored as it was, it was healing. Gran had done everything to mend it that I could have, and then some. He wasn't fevered or infected, and it looked like he would probably keep the leg. How much use it would be was another matter. He might come away with nothing more than a heavy limp. But I wouldn't bet on him ever running again.

"What sort of folk shoot a man's horse?" he asked me as I looked at his leg. "It ain't right."

It had been his horse, and you know as well as I do how expensive horses are. This wasn't the sort of town where people had horses to spare. Bil was a young man with a new wife and his own small farm, and he might never walk again because he had tried to do what he thought was the right thing. It hurt to think about it.

When I came outside the crowd had swelled considerably. Krin's father and mother had ridden in on the roan. Pete was there too, having run back to town. He offered up his unbroken head for my inspection and demanded his two pennies for services rendered.

I was warmly thanked by Krin's parents. They seemed to be good people. Most people are if given the chance to be. I managed to get hold of the roan, and using him as a sort of portable wall, managed to get a few minutes of relatively private conversation with Krin.

Her dark eyes were a little red around the edges, but her face was bright and happy. "Make sure you get Burrback," I said, nodding to one of the horses. "He's yours." The mayor's daughter would have a fair dowry no matter what, so I'd loaded Krin's horse with the more valuable goods, as well as most of the money the false troupers had.

Her expression grew serious as she met my eyes, and again she reminded me of a young Denna. "You're leaving," she said.

I guess I was. I nodded. She didn't try to convince me to stay, and instead surprised me with a sudden, emotional embrace. After kissing me on the cheek she whispered in my ear, "Thank you."

We stepped away from each other, knowing that propriety would only allow so much. "Don't sell yourself short and marry some fool," I said, feeling as if I should say something.

"Don't you either," she said, her sad, dark eyes mocking me gently.

I unpacked my lutecase and travelsack from Greytail and led the roan over to where the mayor stood. He was alone, off to one side, watching the crowd in a proprietary way. I handed him the reigns and he cocked an eyebrow at me.

"You'd be doing me a favor if you took care of him until Bil is up and about," I said. "Or taking it to his farm, if he's got family taking care of it."

"You leaving?" He asked, not sounding too surprised, or too disappointed for that matter. I nodded. "Without your horse?" He asked.

"He's just lost his." I shrugged. "And we Ruh are used to walking. I wouldn't know what to do with a horse, anyway," I said half-honestly.

He took the reins and gave me a good long look, as if he wasn't quite sure what to make of me. "Is there anything we can do for you?" he asked at last.

"Remember that it was bandits that took them," I said as I turned to leave. "And remember it was one of the Edema Ruh who brought them back."

FIXING HANOVER

JEFF VANDERMEER

When Shyver can't lift it from the sand, he brings me down from the village. It lies there on the beach, entangled in the seaweed, dull metal scoured by the sea, limpets and barnacles stuck to its torso. It's been lost a long time, just like me. It smells like rust and oil still, but only a tantalizing hint.

"It's good salvage, at least," Shyver says. "Maybe more."

"Or maybe less," I reply. Salvage is the life's blood of the village in the off-season, when the sea's too rough for fishing. But I know from past experience, there's no telling what the salvagers will want and what they discard. They come from deep in the hill country abutting the sea cliffs, their needs only a glimmer in their savage eyes.

To Shyver, maybe the thing he'd found looks like a long box with a smaller box on top. To me, in the burnishing rasp of the afternoon sun, the last of the winter winds lashing against my face, it resembles a man whose limbs have been torn off. A man made of metal. It has lamps for eyes, although I have to squint hard to imagine there ever being an ember, a spark, of understanding. No expression defiles the broad pitted expanse of metal.

As soon as I see it, I call it "Hanover," after a character I had seen in an old movie back when the projector still worked.

"Hanover?" Shyver says with a trace of contempt.

"Hanover never gave away what he thought," I reply, as we drag it up the gravel track toward the village. Sandhaven, they call it, simply, and it's carved into the side of cliffs that are sliding into the sea. I've lived there for almost six years, taking on odd jobs, assisting with salvage. They still know next to nothing about me, not really. They like me not for what I say or who I am, but for what I do: anything mechanical I can fix, or build something new from poor parts. Someone reliable in an isolated place where a faulty water pump can be devastating. That means something real. That means you don't have to explain much.

"Hanover, whoever or whatever it is, has given up on more than thoughts," Shyver says, showing surprising intuition. It means he's already put a face on Hanover, too. "I think it's from the Old Empire. I think it washed up from the Sunken City at the bottom of the sea."

Everyone knows what Shyver thinks, about everything. Brown-haired, green-eyed, gawky, he's lived in Sandhaven his whole life. He's good with a boat, could navigate a cockleshell through a typhoon. He'll never leave the village, but why should he? As far as he knows, everything he needs is here.

Beyond doubt, the remains of Hanover are heavy. I have difficulty keeping my grip on him, despite the rust. By the time we've made it to the courtyard at the center of Sandhaven, Shyver and I are breathing as hard as old men. We drop our burden with a combination of relief and self-conscious theatrics. By now, a crowd has gathered, and not just stray dogs and bored children.

First law of salvage: what is found must be brought before the community. Is it scrap? Should it be discarded? Can it be restored?

John Blake, council leader, all unkempt black beard, wide shoulders, and watery turquoise eyes, stands there. So does Sarah, who leads the weavers, and the blacksmith Growder, and the ethereal captain of the fishing fleet: Lady Salt as she is called—she of the impossibly pale, soft skin, the blonde hair in a land that only sees the sun five months out of the year. Her eyes, ever-shifting, never settling—one is light blue and one is fierce green, as if to balance the sea between calm and roiling. She has tiny wrinkles in the corners of those eyes, and a wry smile beneath. If I remember little else, fault the eyes. We've been lovers the past three years, and if I ever fully understand her, I wonder if my love for her will vanish like the mist over the water at dawn.

With the fishing boats not launching for another week, a host of broad-faced fisher folk, joined by lesser lights and gossips, has gathered behind us. Even as the light fades: shadows of albatross and gull cutting across the horizon and the roofs of the low houses, huddled and glowing a deep gold-and-orange around the edges, framed by the graying sky.

Blake says, "Where?" He's a man who measures words as if he had only a few given to him by Fate; too generous a syllable from his lips, and he might fall over dead.

"The beach, the cove," Shyver says. Blake always reduces him to a similar terseness.

"What is it?"

This time, Blake looks at me, with a glare. I'm the fixer who solved their well problems the season before, who gets the most value for the village from what's sold to the hill scavengers. But I'm also Lady Salt's lover, who used to be his, and depending on the vagaries of his mood, I suffer more or less for it.

I see no harm in telling the truth as I know it, when I can. So much remains unsaid that extra lies exhaust me.

"It is part of a metal man," I say.

A gasp from the more ignorant among the crowd. My Lady Salt just stares right through me. I know what she's thinking: in scant days she'll be on the open sea. Her vessel is as sleek and quick and buoyant as the water, and she likes to call it *Seeker*, or sometimes *Mist*, or even just *Cleave*. Salvage holds little interest for her.

But I can see the gears turning in Blake's head. He thinks awhile before he says more. Even the blacksmith and the weaver, more for ceremony and obligation than their insight, seem to contemplate the rusted bucket before them.

A refurbished water pump keeps delivering from the aquifers; parts bartered to the hill people mean only milk and smoked meat for half a season. Still, Blake knows that the fishing has been less dependable the past few years, and that if we do not give the hill people something, they will not keep coming back.

"Fix it," he says.

It's not a question, although I try to treat it like one.

Later that night, I am with the Lady Salt, whose whispered name in these moments is Rebecca. "Not a name men would follow," she said to me once. "A land-ish name."

In bed, she's as shifting as the tides, beside me, on top, and beneath. Her mouth is soft but firm, her tongue curling like a question mark across my body. She makes little cries that are so different from the orders she barks out ship-board that she might as well be a different person. We're all different people, depending.

Rebecca can read. She has a few books from the hill people, taught herself with the help of an old man who remembered how. A couple of the books are even from the Empire—the New Empire, not the old. Sometimes I want to think she is not the Lady Salt, but the Lady Flight. That she wants to leave the village. That she seeks so much more. But I look into those eyes in the dimness of half-dawn, so close, so far, and realize she would never tell me, no matter how long I live here. Even in bed, there is a bit of Lady Salt in Rebecca.

When we are finished, lying in each other's arms under the thick covers, her hair against my cheek, Rebecca asks me, "Is that thing from your world? Do you know what it is?"

I have told her a little about my past, where I came from—mostly bed-time stories when she cannot sleep, little fantasies of golden spires and a million thronging people, fables of something so utterly different from the village that it must exist only in dream. *Once upon a time there was a foolish man. Once upon a time there was an Empire.* She tells me she doesn't believe me, and there's freedom in that. It's a strange pillow talk that can be so grim.

I tell her the truth about Hanover: "It's nothing like what I remember." If it came from Empire, it came late, after I was already gone.

"Can you really fix it?" she asks.

I smile. "I can fix anything," and I really believe it. If I want to, I can fix anything. I'm just not sure yet I want Hanover fixed, because I don't know what he is.

But my hands can't lie—they tremble to *have at it*, to explore, impatient for the task even then and there, in bed with Blake's lost love.

I came from the same sea the Lady Salt loves. I came as salvage, and was fixed. Despite careful preparation, my vessel had been damaged first by a storm, and then a reef. Forced to the surface, I managed to escape into a raft just before my creation drowned. It was never meant for life above the waves, just as I was never meant for life below them. I washed up near the village, was found, and eventually accepted into their community; they did not sell me to the hill people.

I never meant to stay. I didn't think I'd fled far enough. Even as I'd put distance between me and Empire, I'd set traps, put up decoys, sent out false rumors. I'd done all I could to escape that former life, and yet some nights, sleepless, restless, it feels as if I am just waiting to be found.

Even failure can be a kind of success, my father always said. But I still don't know if I believe that.

Three days pass, and I'm still fixing Hanover, sometimes with help from Shyver, sometimes not. Shyver doesn't have much else to do until the fishing fleet goes out, but that doesn't mean he has to stay cooped up in a cluttered workshop with me. Not when, conveniently, the blacksmithy is next door, and with it the lovely daughter of Growder, who he adores.

Blake says he comes in to check my progress, but I think he comes to check on me. After the Lady Salt left him, he married another—a weaver—but she died in childbirth a year ago, and took the baby with her. Now Blake sees before him a different past: a life that might have been, with the Lady Salt at his side.

I can still remember the generous Blake, the humorous Blake who would stand on a table with a mug of beer made by the hill people and tell an amusing story about being lost at sea, poking fun at himself. But now, because he still loves her, there is only me to hate. Now there is just the brambly fence of his beard to hide him, and the pressure of his eyes, the pursed, thin lips. *If I were a different man. If I loved the Lady Salt less. If she wanted him.*

But instead it is him and me in the work room, Hanover on the table, surrounded by an autopsy of gears and coils and congealed bits of metal long past their purpose. Hanover up close, over time, smells of sea grasses and brine along with the oil. I still do not *know* him. Or what he does. Or why he is here. I think I recognize some of it as the work of Empire, but I can't be sure. Shyver still thinks Hanover is merely a sculpture from beneath the ocean. But no one makes a sculpture with so many moving parts.

"Make it work," Blake says. "You're the expert. Fix it."

Expert? I'm the only one with any knowledge in this area. For hundreds, maybe thousands, of miles.

"I'm trying," I say. "But then what? We don't know what it does."

This is the central question, perhaps of my life. It is why I go slow with

Hanover. My hands already know where most of the parts go. They know most of what is broken, and why.

"Fix it," Blake says, "or at the next council meeting, I will ask that you be sent to live with the hill people for a time."

There's no disguising the self-hatred in his gaze. There's no disguising that he's serious.

"For a time? And what will that prove? Except to show I can live in caves with shepherds?" I almost want an answer.

Blake spits on the wooden floor. "No use to us, why should we feed you? House you . . . "

Even if I leave, she won't go back to you.

"What if I fix it and all it does is blink? Or all it does is shed light, like a whale lamp? Or talk in nonsense rhymes? Or I fix it and it kills us all."

"Don't care," Blake says. "Fix it."

The cliffs around the village are low, like the shoulders of a slouching giant, and caulked with bird shit and white rock, veined through with dark green bramble. Tough, thick lizards scuttle through the branches. Tiny birds take shelter there, their dark eyes staring out from shadow. A smell almost like mint struggles through. Below is the cove where Shyver found Hanover.

Rebecca and I walk there, far enough beyond the village that we cannot be seen, and we talk. We find the old trails and follow them, sometimes silly, sometimes serious. We don't need to be who we are in Sandhaven.

"Blake's getting worse," I tell her. "More paranoid. He's jealous. He says he'll exile me from the village if I don't fix Hanover."

"Then fix Hanover," Rebecca says.

We are holding hands. Her palm is warm and sweaty in mine, but I don't care. Every moment I'm with her feels like something I didn't earn, wasn't looking for, but don't want to lose. Still, something in me rebels. It's tiring to keep proving myself.

"I can do it," I say. "I know I can. But . . . "

"Blake can't exile you without the support of the council," Lady Salt says. I know it's her, not Rebecca, because of the tone, and the way her blue eye flashes when she looks at me. "But he can make life difficult if you give him cause." A pause, a tightening of her grip. "He's in mourning. You know it makes him not himself. But we need him. We need him back."

A twinge as I wonder how she means that. But it's true: Blake has led Sandhaven through good times and bad, made tough decisions and cared about the village.

Sometimes, though, leadership is not enough. What if what you really need is the instinct to be fearful? And the thought as we make our way back to the village: *What if Blake is right about me?*

So I begin to work on Hanover in earnest. There's a complex balance to him that I admire. People think engineering is about practical application of science, and that might be right, if you're building something. But if you're fixing something, something you don't fully understand—say, you're fixing a Hanover—you have no access to a schematic, to a helpful context. Your work instead becomes a kind of detection. You become a kind of detective. You track down clues—cylinders that fit into holes in sheets of steel, that slide into place in grooves, that lead to wires, that lead to understanding.

To do this, I have to stop my ad hoc explorations. Instead, with Shyver's reluctant help, I take Hanover apart systematically. I document where I find each part, and if I think it truly belongs there, or has become dislodged during the trauma that resulted in his "death." I note gaps. I label each part by what I believe it contributed to his overall function. In all things, I remember that Hanover has been made to look like a man, and therefore his innards roughly resemble those of a man in form or function, his makers consciously or subconsciously unable to ignore the implications of that form, that function.

Shyver looks at the parts lying glistening on the table, and says, "They're so different out of him." So different cleaned up, greased with fresh fish oil. Through the window, the sun's light sets them ablaze. Hanover's burnished surface, whorled with a patina of greens, blues, and rust red. The world become radiant.

When we remove the carapace of Hanover's head to reveal a thousand wires, clockwork gears, and strange fluids, even Shyver cannot think of him as a statue anymore.

"What does a machine like this *do*?" Shyver says, who has only rarely seen anything more complex than a hammer or a watch.

I laugh. "It does whatever it wants to do, I imagine."

By the time I am done with Hanover, I have made several leaps of logic. I have made decisions that cannot be explained as rational, but in their rightness set my head afire with the absolute certainty of Creation. The feeling energizes me and horrifies me all at once.

It was long after my country became an Empire that I decided to escape. And still I might have stayed, even knowing what I had done. That is the tragedy of everyday life: when you are in it, you can never see your self clearly.

Even seven years in, Sandhaven having made the Past the past, I still had nightmares of gleaming rows of airships. I would wake, screaming, from what had once been a blissful dream, and the Lady Salt and Rebecca both would be there to comfort me.

Did I deserve that comfort?

Shyver is there when Hanover comes alive. I've spent a week speculating on ways to bypass what look like missing parts, missing wires. I've experimented with a hundred different connections. I've even identified Hanover's independent power source and recharged it using a hand-cranked generator.

Lady Salt has gone out with the fishing fleet for the first time and the village is deserted. Even Blake has gone with her, after a quick threat in my direction once again. If the fishing doesn't go well, the evening will not go any better for me.

Shyver says, "Is that a spark?"

A spark?

"Where?"

I have just put Hanover back together again for possibly the twentieth time and planned to take a break, to just sit back and smoke a hand-rolled cigarette, compliments of the enigmatic hill people.

"In Hanover's . . . eyes."

Shyver goes white, backs away from Hanover, as if something monstrous has occurred, even though this is what we wanted.

It brings memories flooding back—of the long-ago day steam had come rushing out of the huge iron bubble and the canvas had swelled, and held, and everything I could have wished for in my old life had been attained. That feeling had become addiction—I wanted to experience it again and again—but now it's bittersweet, something to cling to and cast away.

My assistant then had responded much as Shyver is now: both on some instinctual level knowing that something unnatural has happened.

"Don't be afraid," I say to Shyver, to my assistant.

"I'm not afraid," Shyver says, lying.

"You should be afraid," I say.

Hanover's eyes gain more and more of a glow. A clicking sound comes from him. Click, click, click. A hum. A slightly rumbling cough from deep inside, a hum again. We prop him up so he is no longer on his side. He's warm to the touch.

The head rotates from side to side, more graceful than in my imagination.

A sharp intake of breath from Shyver. "It's alive!"

I laugh then. I laugh and say, "In a way. It's got no arms or legs. It's harmless."

It's harmless.

Neither can it speak—just the click, click, click. But no words.

Assuming it is trying to speak.

John Blake and the Lady Salt come back with the fishing fleet. The voyage seems to have done Blake good. The windswept hair, the salt-stung face—he looks relaxed as they enter my workshop.

As they stare at Hanover, at the light in its eyes, I'm almost jealous. Standing side by side, they almost resemble a King and his Queen, and suddenly I'm acutely aware they were lovers, grew up in the village together. Rebecca's gaze is distant; thinking of Blake or of me or of the sea? They smell of mingled brine and fish and salt, and somehow the scent is like a knife in my heart.

"What does it do?" Blake asks.

Always, the same kinds of questions. Why should everything have to have a function?

"I don't know," I say. "But the hill folk should find it pretty and perplexing, at least."

Shyver, though, gives me away, makes me seem less and less from this place: "He thinks it can talk. We just need to fix it *more*. It might do all kinds of things for us."

"It's fixed," I snap, looking at Shyver as if I don't know him at all. We've drunk together, talked many hours. I've given him advice about the blacksmith's daughter. But now that doesn't matter. He's from here and I'm from *there*. "We should trade it to the hill folk and be done with it."

Click, click, click. Hanover won't stop. And I just want it over with, so I don't slide into the past.

Blake's calm has disappeared. I can tell he thinks I lied to him. "Fix it," he barks. "I mean really fix it. Make it talk."

He turns on his heel and leaves the workshop, Shyver behind him.

Lady Salt approaches, expression unreadable. "Do as he says. Please. The fishing . . . there's little enough out there. We need every advantage now."

Her hand on the side of my face, warm and calloused, before she leaves.

Maybe there's no harm in it. If I just do what they ask, this one last time—the last of many times—it will be over. Life will return to normal. I can stay here. I can still find a kind of peace.

Once, there was a foolish man who saw a child's balloon rising into the sky and thought it could become a kind of airship. No one in his world had ever created such a thing, but he already had ample evidence of his own genius in the things he had built before. Nothing had come close to challenging his engineering skills. No one had ever told him he might have limits. His father, a biology teacher, had taught him to focus on problems and solutions. His mother, a caterer, had shown him the value of attention to detail and hard work.

He took his plans, his ideas, to the government. They listened enough to give him some money, a place to work, and an assistant. All of this despite his youth, because of his brilliance, and in his turn he ignored how they talked about their enemies, the need to thwart external threats.

When this engineer was successful, when the third prototype actually worked, following three years of flaming disaster, he knew he had created something that had never before existed, and his heart nearly burst with pride. His wife had left him because she never saw him except when he needed sleep, the house was a junk yard, and yet he didn't care. He'd done it.

He couldn't know that it wouldn't end there. As far as he was concerned, they could take it apart and let him start on something else, and his life would have been good because he knew when he was happiest.

But the government's military advisors wanted him to perfect the airship. They asked him to solve problems that he hadn't thought about before. How to add weight to the carriage without it serving as undue ballast, so things could be dropped from the airship. How to add "defensive" weapons. How to make them work without igniting the fuel that drove the airship. A series of challenges that appealed to his pride, and maybe, too, he had grown used to the rich life he had now. Caught up in it all, he just kept going, never said no, and focused on the gears, the wires, the air ducts, the myriad tiny details that made him ignore everything else.

This foolish man used his assistants as friends to go drinking with, to sleep with, to be his whole life, creating a kind of cult there in his workshop that had become a gigantic hangar, surrounded by soldiers and barbed wire fence. He'd become a national hero.

But I still remembered how my heart had felt when the prototype had risen into the air, how the tears trickled down my face as around me men and women literally danced with joy. How I was struck by the image of my own success, almost as if I were flying.

The prototype wallowed and snorted in the air like a great golden whale in a harness, wanting to be free: a blazing jewel against the bright blue sky, the dream made real.

I don't know what the Lady Salt would have thought of it. Maybe nothing at all.

One day, Hanover finally speaks. I push a button, clean a gear, move a circular bit into place. It is just me and him. Shyver wanted no part of it.

He says, "Command water the sea was bright with the leavings of the fish that there were now going to be."

Clicks twice, thrice, and continues clicking as he takes the measure of me with his golden gaze and says, "Engineer Daniker."

The little hairs on my neck rise. I almost lose my balance, all the blood rushing to my head.

"How do you know my name?"

"You are my objective. You are why I was sent."

"Across the ocean? Not likely."

"I had a ship once, arms and legs once, before your traps destroyed me."

I had forgotten the traps I'd set. I'd almost forgotten my true name.

"You will return with me. You will resume your duties."

I laugh bitterly. "They've found no one to replace me?"

Hanover has no answer—just the clicking—but I know the answer. Child prodigy. Unnatural skills. An unswerving ability to focus in on a problem and solve it. Like . . . building airships. I'm still an asset they cannot afford to lose.

"You've no way to take me back. You have no authority here," I say.

Hanover's bright eyes dim, then flare. The clicking intensifies. I wonder now if it is the sound of a weapons system malfunctioning.

"Did you know I was here, in this village?" I ask.

A silence. Then: "Dozens were sent for you—scattered across the world."

"So no one knows."

"I have already sent a signal. They are coming for you."

Horror. Shock. And then anger—indescribable rage, like nothing I've ever experienced.

When they find me with Hanover later, there isn't much left of him. I've smashed his head in and then his body, and tried to grind that down with a pestle. I didn't know where the beacon might be hidden, or if it even mattered, but I had to try.

They think I'm mad—the soft-spoken blacksmith, a livid Blake, even Rebecca. I keep telling them the Empire is coming, that I am the Empire's chief engineer. That I've been in hiding. That they need to leave now—into the hills, into the sea. *Anywhere but here . . .*

But Blake can't see it—he sees only me—and whatever the Lady Salt thinks, she hides it behind a sad smile.

"I said to fix it," Blake roars before he storms out. "Now it's no good for anything!"

Roughly I am taken to the little room that functions as the village jail, with the bars on the window looking out on the sea. As they leave me, I am shouting, "I created their airships! They're coming for me!"

The Lady Salt backs away from the window, heads off to find Blake, without listening.

After dark, Shyver comes by the window, but not to hear me out—just to ask why I did it.

"We could at least have sold it to the hill people," he whispers. He sees only the village, the sea, the blacksmith's daughter. "We put so much work into it."

I have no answer except for a story that he will not believe is true.

Once, there was a country that became an Empire. Its armies flew out from the center and conquered the margins, the barbarians. Everywhere it inflicted itself on the world, people died or came under its control, always under the watchful, floating gaze of the airships. No one had ever seen anything like them before. No one had any defense for them. People wrote poems about them and cursed them and begged for mercy from their attentions.

The chief engineer of this atrocity, the man who had solved the problems, sweated the details, was finally called up by the Emperor of the newly-minted Empire fifteen years after he'd seen a golden shape float against a startling blue sky. The Emperor was on the far frontier, some remote place fringed by desert where the people built their homes into the sides of hills and used tubes to spit fire up into the sky.

They took me to His Excellency by airship, of course. For the first time, except for excursions to the capital, I left my little enclave, the country I'd created for myself. From on high, I saw what I had helped create. In the conquered lands, the people looked up at us in fear and hid when and where they could. Some, beyond caring, threw stones up at us: an old woman screaming words I could not hear from that distance, a young man with a bow, the arrows arching below the carriage until the airship commander opened fire, left a red smudge on a dirt road as we glided by from on high.

This vision I had not known existed unfurled like a slow, terrible dream, for we were like languid Gods in our progress, the landscape revealing itself to us with a strange finality.

On the fringes, war still was waged, and before we reached the Emperor I saw my creations clustered above hostile armies, raining down *my* bombs onto stick figures who bled, screamed, died, were mutilated, blown apart . . . all as if in a silent film, the explosions deafening us, the rest reduced to distant pantomime narrated by the black humored cheer of our airship's officers.

A child's head resting upon a rock, the body a red shadow. A city reduced to rubble. A man whose limbs had been torn from him. All the same.

By the time I reached the Emperor, received his blessing and his sword, I had nothing to say; he found me more mute than any captive, his instrument once more. And when I returned, when I could barely stand myself any more, I found a way to escape my cage.

Only to wash up on a beach half a world away.

Out of the surf, out of the sand, dripping and half-dead, I stumble and the Lady Salt and Blake stand there, above me. I look up at them in the half-light of morning, arm raised against the sun, and wonder whether they will welcome me or kill me or just cast me aside.

The Lady Salt looks doubtful and grim, but Blake's broad face breaks into a smile. "Welcome stranger," he says, and extends his hand.

I take it, relieved. In that moment, there's no Hanover, no pain, no sorrow, nothing but the firm grip, the arm pulling me up toward them.

They come at dawn, much faster than I had thought possible: ten airships, golden in the light, the humming thrum of their propellers audible over the crash of the sea. From behind my bars, I watch their deadly, beautiful approach across the slate-gray sky, the deep-blue waves, and it is as if my children are returning to me. If there is no mercy in them, it is because I never thought of mercy when I created the bolt and canvas of them, the fuel and gears of them.

Hours later, I sit in the main cabin of the airship *Forever Triumph*. It has mahogany tables and chairs, crimson cushions. A platter of fruit upon a dais. A telescope on a tripod. A globe of the world. The scent of snuff. All the debris of the real world. We sit on the window seat, the Lady Salt and I. Beyond, the rectangular windows rise and fall just slightly, showing cliffs and hills and sky; I do not look down.

Captain Evans, aping civilized speech, has been talking to us for several minutes. He is fifty and rake-thin and has hooded eyes that make him mournful forever. I don't really know what he's saying; I can't concentrate. I just feel numb, as if I'm not really there.

Blake insisted on fighting what could not be fought. So did most of the others.

I watched from behind my bars as first the bombs came and then the troops. I heard Blake die, although I didn't see it. He was cursing and screaming at them; he didn't go easy. Shyver was shot in the leg, dragged himself off moaning. I don't know if he made it.

I forced myself to listen—to all of it.

They had orders to take me alive, and they did. They found the Lady Salt with a gutting knife, but took her too when I told the Captain I'd cooperate if they let her live.

Her presence at my side is something unexpected and horrifying. What can she be feeling? Does she think I could have saved Blake but chose not to? Her eyes are dry and she stares straight ahead, at nothing, at no one, while the Captain continues with his explanations, his threats, his flattery.

"Rebecca," I say. "Rebecca," I say.

The whispered words of the Lady Salt are everything, all, the Chief Engineer could have expected: *"Some day I will kill you and escape to the sea."*

I nod wearily and turn my attention back to the Captain, try to understand what he is saying.

Below me, the village burns as all villages burn, everywhere, in time.

"Suffering's going to come to everyone someday."
—*The Willard Grant Conspiracy*

BOOJUM

ELIZABETH BEAR AND SARAH MONETTE

The ship had no name of her own, so her human crew called her the *Lavinia Whateley*. As far as anyone could tell, she didn't mind. At least, her long grasping vanes curled—affectionately?—when the chief engineers patted her bulkheads and called her "Vinnie," and she ceremoniously tracked the footsteps of each crew member with her internal bioluminescence, giving them light to walk and work and live by.

The *Lavinia Whateley* was a Boojum, a deep-space swimmer, but her kind had evolved in the high tempestuous envelopes of gas giants, and their offspring still spent their infancies there, in cloud-nurseries over eternal storms. And so she was streamlined, something like a vast spiny lionfish to the earth-adapted eye. Her sides were lined with gasbags filled with hydrogen; her vanes and wings furled tight. Her color was a blue-green so dark it seemed a glossy black unless the light struck it; her hide was impregnated with symbiotic algae.

Where there was light, she could make oxygen. Where there was oxygen, she could make water.

She was an ecosystem unto herself, as the captain was a law unto herself. And down in the bowels of the engineering section, Black Alice Bradley, who was only human and no kind of law at all, loved her.

Black Alice had taken the oath back in '32, after the Venusian Riots. She hadn't hidden her reasons, and the captain had looked at her with cold, dark, amused eyes and said, "So long as you carry your weight, cherie, I don't care. Betray me, though, and you will be going back to Venus the cold way." But it was probably that—and the fact that Black Alice couldn't hit the broad side of a space freighter with a ray gun—that had gotten her assigned to Engineering, where ethics were less of a problem. It wasn't, after all, as if she was going anywhere.

Black Alice was on duty when the *Lavinia Whateley* spotted prey; she felt the shiver of anticipation that ran through the decks of the ship. It was an odd sensation, a tic Vinnie only exhibited in pursuit. And then they were underway, zooming down the slope of the gravity well toward Sol, and the screens all around Engineering—which Captain Song kept dark, most of the time, on the theory that swabs and deckhands and coal-shovelers didn't need to know where they were, or what they were doing—flickered bright and live.

Everybody looked up, and Demijack shouted,"There! There!" He was right: the blot that might only have been a smudge of oil on the screen moved as Vinnie banked, revealing itself to be a freighter, big and ungainly and hopelessly outclassed. Easy prey. Easy pickings.

We could use some of them, thought Black Alice. Contrary to the e-ballads and comm stories, a pirate's life was not all imported delicacies and fawning slaves. Especially not when three-quarters of any and all profits went directly back to the *Lavinia Whateley*, to keep her healthy and happy. Nobody ever argued. There were stories about the *Marie Curie*, too.

The captain's voice over fiberoptic cable—strung beside the *Lavinia Whateley's* nerve bundles—was as clear and free of static as if she stood at Black Alice's elbow. "Battle stations," Captain Song said, and the crew leapt to obey. It had been two Solar since Captain Song keelhauled James Brady, but nobody who'd been with the ship then was ever likely to forget his ruptured eyes and frozen scream.

Black Alice manned her station, and stared at the screen. She saw the freighter's name—the *Josephine Baker*—gold on black across the stern, the Venusian flag for its port of registry wired stiff from a mast on its hull. It was a steelship, not a Boojum, and they had every advantage. For a moment she thought the freighter would run.

And then it turned, and brought its guns to bear.

No sense of movement, of acceleration, of disorientation. No pop, no whump of displaced air. The view on the screens just flickered to a different one, as Vinnie skipped—apported—to a new position just aft and above the *Josephine Baker*, crushing the flag mast with her hull.

Black Alice felt that, a grinding shiver. And had just time to grab her console before the *Lavinia Whateley* grappled the freighter, long vanes not curling in affection now.

Out of the corner of her eye, she saw Dogcollar, the closest thing the *Lavinia Whateley* had to a chaplain, cross himself, and she heard him mutter, like he always did, *Ave, Grandaevissimi, morituri vos salutant*. It was the best he'd be able to do until it was all over, and even then he wouldn't have the chance to do much. Captain Song didn't mind other people worrying about souls, so long as they didn't do it on her time.

The Captain's voice was calling orders, assigning people to boarding parties port and starboard. Down in Engineering, all they had to do was monitor the *Lavinia Whateley's* hull and prepare to repel boarders, assuming the freighter's crew had the gumption to send any. Vinnie would take care of the rest—until the time came to persuade her not to eat her prey before they'd gotten all the valuables off it. That was a ticklish job, only entrusted to the chief engineers, but Black Alice watched and listened, and although she didn't expect she'd ever get the chance, she thought she could do it herself.

It was a small ambition, and one she never talked about. But it would be a hell of a thing, wouldn't it? To be somebody a Boojum would listen to?

She gave her attention to the dull screens in her sectors, and tried not to crane her neck to catch a glimpse of the ones with the actual fighting on them. Dogcollar was making the rounds with sidearms from the weapons locker, just in case. Once the *Josephine Baker* was subdued, it was the junior engineers and others who would board her to take inventory.

Sometimes there were crew members left in hiding on captured ships. Sometimes, unwary pirates got shot.

There was no way to judge the progress of the battle from Engineering. Wasabi put a stopwatch up on one of the secondary screens, as usual, and everybody glanced at it periodically. Fifteen minutes on-going meant the boarding parties hadn't hit any nasty surprises. Black Alice had met a man once who'd been on the *Margaret Mead* when she grappled a freighter that turned out to be carrying a divisions-worth of Marines out to the Jovian moons. Thirty minutes on-going was normal. Forty-five minutes, upward of an hour on-going, and people started double-checking their weapons. The longest battle Black Alice had ever personally been part of was six hours, forty-three minutes, and fifty-two seconds. That had been the last time the *Lavinia Whateley* worked with a partner, and the double-cross by the *Henry Ford* was the only reason any of Vinnie's crew needed. Captain Song still had Captain Edwards' head in a jar on the bridge, and Vinnie had an ugly ring of scars where the *Henry Ford* had bitten her.

This time, the clock stopped at fifty minutes, thirteen seconds. The *Josephine Baker* surrendered.

Dogcollar slapped Black Alice's arm. "With me," he said, and she didn't argue. He had only six weeks seniority over her, but he was as tough as he was devout, and not stupid either. She checked the Velcro on her holster and followed him up the ladder, reaching through the rungs once to scratch Vinnie's bulkhead as she passed. The ship paid her no notice. She wasn't the captain, and she wasn't one of the four chief engineers.

Quartermaster mostly respected crew's own partner choices, and as Black Alice and Dogcollar suited up—it wouldn't be the first time, if the *Josephine Baker*'s crew decided to blow her open to space rather than be taken captive—he came by and issued them both tag guns and x-ray pads, taking a retina scan in return. All sorts of valuable things got hidden inside of bulkheads, and once Vinnie was done with the steelship there wouldn't be much chance of coming back to look for what they'd missed.

Wet pirates used to scuttle their captures. The Boojums were more efficient.

Black Alice clipped everything to her belt and checked Dogcollar's seals.

And then they were swinging down lines from the *Lavinia Whateley*'s belly to the chewed-open airlock. A lot of crew didn't like to look at the ship's face, but Black Alice loved it. All those teeth, the diamond edges worn to a glitter, and a few of the ship's dozens of bright sapphire eyes blinking back at her.

She waved, unselfconsciously, and flattered herself that the ripple of closing eyes was Vinnie winking in return.

She followed Dogcollar inside the prize.

They unsealed when they had checked atmosphere—no sense in wasting your own air when you might need it later—and the first thing she noticed was the smell.

The *Lavinia Whateley* had her own smell, ozone and nutmeg, and other ships never smelled as good, but this was . . . this was . . .

"What did they kill and why didn't they space it?" Dogcollar wheezed, and Black Alice swallowed hard against her gag reflex and said, "One will get you twenty we're the lucky bastards that find it."

"No takers," Dogcollar said.

They worked together to crank open the hatches they came to. Twice they found crew members, messily dead. Once they found crew members alive.

"Gillies," said Black Alice.

"Still don't explain the smell," said Dogcollar and, to the gillies: "Look, you can join our crew, or our ship can eat you. Makes no never mind to us."

The gillies blinked their big wet eyes and made fingersigns at each other, and then nodded. Hard.

Dogcollar slapped a tag on the bulkhead. "Someone will come get you. You go wandering, we'll assume you changed your mind."

The gillies shook their heads, hard, and folded down onto the deck to wait.

Dogcollar tagged searched holds—green for clean, purple for goods, red for anything Vinnie might like to eat that couldn't be fenced for a profit—and Black Alice mapped. The corridors in the steelship were winding, twisty, hard to track. She was glad she chalked the walls, because she didn't think her map was quite right, somehow, but she couldn't figure out where she'd gone wrong. Still, they had a beacon, and Vinnie could always chew them out if she had to.

Black Alice loved her ship.

She was thinking about that, how, okay, it wasn't so bad, the pirate game, and it sure beat working in the sunstone mines on Venus, when she found a locked cargo hold. "Hey, Dogcollar," she said to her comm, and while he was turning to cover her, she pulled her sidearm and blastered the lock.

The door peeled back, and Black Alice found herself staring at rank upon rank of silver cylinders, each less than a meter tall and perhaps half a meter wide, smooth and featureless except for what looked like an assortment of sockets and plugs on the surface of each. The smell was strongest here.

"Shit," she said.

Dogcollar, more practical, slapped the first safety orange tag of the expedition beside the door and said only, "Captain'll want to see this."

"Yeah," said Black Alice, cold chills chasing themselves up and down her spine. "C'mon, let's move."

But of course it turned out that she and Dogcollar were on the retrieval detail, too, and the captain wasn't leaving the canisters for Vinnie.

Which, okay, fair. Black Alice didn't want the *Lavinia Whateley* eating those things, either, but why did they have to bring them *back*?

She said as much to Dogcollar, under her breath, and had a horrifying thought: "She knows what they are, right?"

"She's the captain," said Dogcollar.

"Yeah, but—I ain't arguing, man, but if she doesn't know . . ." She lowered her voice even farther, so she could barely hear herself: "What if somebody *opens* one?"

Dogcollar gave her a pained look. "Nobody's going to go opening anything. But if you're really worried, go talk to the captain about it."

He was calling her bluff. Black Alice called his right back. "Come with me?"

He was stuck. He stared at her, and then he grunted and pulled his gloves off, the left and then the right. "Fuck," he said. "I guess we oughta."

For the crew members who had been in the boarding action, the party had already started. Dogcollar and Black Alice finally tracked the captain down in the rec room, where her marines were slurping stolen wine from broken-necked bottles. As much of it splashed on the gravity plates epoxied to the *Lavinia Whateley*'s flattest interior surface as went into the marines, but Black Alice imagined there was plenty more where that came from. And the faster the crew went through it, the less long they'd be drunk.

The captain herself was naked in a great extruded tub, up to her collarbones in steaming water dyed pink and heavily scented by the bath bombs sizzling here and there. Black Alice stared; she hadn't seen a tub bath in seven years. She still dreamed of them sometimes.

"Captain," she said, because Dogcollar wasn't going to say anything. "We think you should know we found some dangerous cargo on the prize."

Captain Song raised one eyebrow. "And you imagine I don't know already, cherie?"

Oh shit. But Black Alice stood her ground. "We thought we should be *sure*."

The captain raised one long leg out of the water to shove a pair of necking pirates off the rim of her tub. They rolled onto the floor, grappling and clawing, both fighting to be on top. But they didn't break the kiss. "You wish to be sure," said the captain. Her dark eyes had never left Black Alice's sweating face. "Very well. Tell me. And then you will know that I know, and you can be *sure*."

Dogcollar made a grumbling noise deep in his throat, easily interpreted: *I told you so.*

Just as she had when she took Captain Song's oath and slit her thumb with a razorblade and dripped her blood on the *Lavinia Whateley*'s decking so the ship might know her, Black Alice—metaphorically speaking—took a breath and jumped. "They're brains," she said. "Human brains. Stolen. Black-market. The Fungi—"

"Mi-Go," Dogcollar hissed, and the Captain grinned at him, showing extraordinarily white strong teeth. He ducked, submissively, but didn't step back, for which Black Alice felt a completely ridiculous gratitude.

"Mi-Go," Black Alice said. Mi-Go, Fungi, what did it matter? They came from the outer rim of the Solar System, the black cold hurtling rocks of the Öpik-Oort Cloud. Like the Boojums, they could swim between the stars. "They collect them. There's a black market. Nobody knows what they use them for. It's illegal, of course. But they're. . . alive in there. They go mad, supposedly."

And that was it. That was all Black Alice could manage. She stopped, and had to remind herself to shut her mouth.

"So I've heard," the captain said, dabbling at the steaming water. She stretched luxuriously in her tub. Someone thrust a glass of white wine at her, condensation dewing the outside. The captain did not drink from shattered plastic bottles. "The Mi-Go will pay for this cargo, won't they? They mine rare minerals all over the system. They're said to be very wealthy."

"Yes, captain," Dogcollar said, when it became obvious that Black Alice couldn't.

"Good," the captain said. Under Black Alice's feet, the decking shuddered, a grinding sound as Vinnie began to dine. Her rows of teeth would make short work of the *Josephine Baker*'s steel hide. Black Alice could see two of the gillies—the same two? she never could tell them apart unless they had scars—flinch and tug at their chains. "Then they might as well pay us as someone else, wouldn't you say?"

Black Alice knew she should stop thinking about the canisters. Captain's word was law. But she couldn't help it, like scratching at a scab. They were down there, in the third subhold, the one even sniffers couldn't find, cold and sweating and with that stench that was like a living thing.

And she kept wondering. Were they empty? Or were there brains in there, people's brains, going mad?

The idea was driving her crazy, and finally, her fourth off-shift after the capture of the *Josephine Baker*, she had to go look.

"This is stupid, Black Alice," she muttered to herself as she climbed down the companion way, the beads in her hair clicking against her earrings. "Stupid, stupid, stupid." Vinnie bioluminesced, a traveling spotlight, placidly unconcerned whether Black Alice was being an idiot or not.

Half-Hand Sally had pulled duty in the main hold. She nodded at Black Alice and Black Alice nodded back. Black Alice ran errands a lot, for Engineering and sometimes for other departments, because she didn't smoke hash and she didn't cheat at cards. She was reliable.

Down through the subholds, and she really didn't want to be doing this, but she was here and the smell of the third subhold was already making her sick, and maybe if she just knew one way or the other, she'd be able to quit thinking about it.

She opened the third subhold, and the stench rushed out.

The canisters were just metal, sealed, seemingly airtight. There shouldn't be any way for the aroma of the contents to escape. But it permeated the air nonetheless, bad enough that Black Alice wished she had brought a rebreather.

No, that would have been suspicious. So it was really best for everyone concerned that she hadn't, but oh, gods and little fishes the stench. Even breathing through her mouth was no help; she could taste it, like oil from a fryer, saturating the air, oozing up her sinuses, coating the interior spaces of her body.

As silently as possible, she stepped across the threshold and into the space beyond. The *Lavinia Whateley* obligingly lit the space as she entered, dazzling her at first as the overhead lights—not just bioluminescent, here, but LEDs chosen to approximate natural daylight, for when they shipped plants and animals— reflected off rank upon rank of canisters. When Black Alice went among them, they did not reach her waist.

She was just going to walk through, she told herself. Hesitantly, she touched the closest cylinder. The air in this hold was so dry there was no condensation—the whole ship ran to lip-cracking, nosebleed dryness in the long weeks between prizes—but the cylinder was cold. It felt somehow grimy to the touch, gritty and oily like machine grease. She pulled her hand back.

It wouldn't do to open the closest one to the door—and she realized with that thought that she was planning on opening one. There must be a way to do it, a concealed catch or a code pad. She was an engineer, after all.

She stopped three ranks in, lightheaded with the smell, to examine the problem.

It was remarkably simple, once you looked for it. There were three depressions on either side of the rim, a little smaller than human fingertips but spaced appropriately. She laid the pads of her fingers over them and pressed hard, making the flesh deform into the catches.

The lid sprang up with a pressurized hiss. Black Alice was grateful that even open, it couldn't smell much worse. She leaned forward to peer within. There was a clear membrane over the surface, and gelatin or thick fluid underneath. Vinnie's lights illuminated it well.

It was not empty. And as the light struck the grayish surface of the lump of tissue floating within, Black Alice would have sworn she saw the pathetic unbodied thing flinch.

She scrambled to close the canister again, nearly pinching her fingertips when it clanked shut. "Sorry," she whispered, although dear sweet Jesus, surely the thing couldn't hear her. "Sorry, sorry." And then she turned and ran, catching her hip a bruising blow against the doorway, slapping the controls to make it fucking *close* already. And then she staggered sideways, lurching to her knees, and vomited until blackness was spinning in front of her eyes and she couldn't smell or taste anything but bile.

Vinnie would absorb the former contents of Black Alice's stomach, just as she absorbed, filtered, recycled, and excreted all her crew's wastes. Shaking, Black Alice braced herself back upright and began the long climb out of the holds.

In the first subhold, she had to stop, her shoulder against the smooth, velvet slickness of Vinnie's skin, her mouth hanging open while her lungs worked. And she knew Vinnie wasn't going to hear her, because she wasn't the captain or a chief engineer or anyone important, but she had to try anyway, croaking, "Vinnie, water, please."

And no one could have been more surprised than Black Alice Bradley when Vinnie extruded a basin and a thin cool trickle of water began to flow into it.

Well, now she knew. And there was still nothing she could do about it. She wasn't the captain, and if she said anything more than she already had, people were going to start looking at her funny. Mutiny kind of funny. And what Black Alice did *not* need was any more of Captain Song's attention and especially not for rumors like that. She kept her head down and did her job and didn't discuss her nightmares with anyone.

And she had nightmares, all right. Hot and cold running, enough, she fancied, that she could have filled up the captain's huge tub with them.

She could live with that. But over the next double dozen of shifts, she became aware of something else wrong, and this was worse, because it was something wrong with the *Lavinia Whateley*.

The first sign was the chief engineers frowning and going into huddles at odd moments. And then Black Alice began to feel it herself, the way Vinnie was . . . she didn't have a word for it because she'd never felt anything like it before. She would have said *balky*, but that couldn't be right. It couldn't. But she was more and more sure that Vinnie was less responsive somehow, that when she obeyed the captain's orders, it was with a delay. If she were human, Vinnie would have been dragging her feet.

You couldn't keelhaul a ship for not obeying fast enough.

And then, because she was paying attention so hard she was making her own head hurt, Black Alice noticed something else. Captain Song had them cruising the gas giants' orbits—Jupiter, Saturn, Neptune—not going in as far as the asteroid belt, not going out as far as Uranus. Nobody Black Alice talked to knew why, exactly, but she and Dogcollar figured it was because the captain wanted to talk to the Mi-Go without actually getting near the nasty cold rock of their planet. And what Black Alice noticed was that Vinnie was less balky, less *unhappy*, when she was headed out, and more and more resistant the closer they got to the asteroid belt.

Vinnie, she remembered, had been born over Uranus.

"Do you want to go home, Vinnie?" Black Alice asked her one late-night shift when there was nobody around to care that she was talking to the ship. "Is that what's wrong?"

She put her hand flat on the wall, and although she was probably imagining it, she thought she felt a shiver ripple across Vinnie's vast side.

Black Alice knew how little she knew, and didn't even contemplate sharing her theory with the chief engineers. They probably knew exactly what was wrong and exactly what to do to keep the *Lavinia Whateley* from going core meltdown like the *Marie Curie* had. That was a whispered story, not the sort of thing anybody talked about except in their hammocks after lights out.

The *Marie Curie* had eaten her own crew.

So when Wasabi said, four shifts later, "Black Alice, I've got a job for you,"

Black Alice said, "Yessir," and hoped it would be something that would help the *Lavinia Whateley* be happy again.

It was a suit job, he said, replace and repair. Black Alice was going because she was reliable and smart and stayed quiet, and it was time she took on more responsibilities. The way he said it made her first fret because that meant the Captain might be reminded of her existence, and then fret because she realized the Captain already had been.

But she took the equipment he issued, and she listened to the instructions and read schematics and committed them both to memory and her implants. It was a ticklish job, a neural override repair. She'd done some fiber optic bundle splicing, but this was going to be a doozy. And she was going to have to do it in stiff, pressurized gloves.

Her heart hammered as she sealed her helmet, and not because she was worried about the EVA. This was a chance. An opportunity. A step closer to chief engineer.

Maybe she had impressed the captain with her discretion, after all.

She cycled the airlock, snapped her safety harness, and stepped out onto the *Lavinia Whateley*'s hide.

That deep blue-green, like azurite, like the teeming seas of Venus under their swampy eternal clouds, was invisible. They were too far from Sol—it was a yellow stylus-dot, and you had to know where to look for it. Vinnie's hide was just black under Black Alice's suit floods. As the airlock cycled shut, though, the Boojum's own bioluminescence shimmered up her vanes and along the ridges of her sides—crimson and electric green and acid blue. Vinnie must have noticed Black Alice picking her way carefully up her spine with barbed boots. They wouldn't *hurt* Vinnie—nothing short of a space rock could manage that—but they certainly stuck in there good.

The thing Black Alice was supposed to repair was at the principal nexus of Vinnie's central nervous system. The ship didn't have anything like what a human or a gilly would consider a brain; there were nodules spread all through her vast body. Too slow, otherwise. And Black Alice had heard Boojums weren't supposed to be all that smart—trainable, sure, maybe like an Earth monkey.

Which is what made it creepy as hell that, as she picked her way up Vinnie's flank—though *up* was a courtesy, under these circumstances—talking to her all the way, she would have sworn Vinnie was talking back. Not just tracking her with the lights, as she would always do, but bending some of her barbels and vanes around as if craning her neck to get a look at Black Alice.

Black Alice carefully circumnavigated an eye—she didn't think her boots would hurt it, but it seemed discourteous to stomp across somebody's field of vision—and wondered, only half-idly, if she had been sent out on this task not because she was being considered for promotion, but because she was expendable.

She was just rolling her eyes and dismissing that as borrowing trouble when she came over a bump on Vinnie's back, spotted her goal—and all the ship's lights went out.

She tongued on the comm. "Wasabi?"

"I got you, Blackie. You just keep doing what you're doing."

"Yessir."

But it seemed like her feet stayed stuck in Vinnie's hide a little longer than was good. At least fifteen seconds before she managed a couple of deep breaths—too deep for her limited oxygen supply, so she went briefly dizzy—and continued up Vinnie's side.

Black Alice had no idea what inflammation looked like in a Boojum, but she would guess this was it. All around the interface she was meant to repair, Vinnie's flesh looked scraped and puffy. Black Alice walked tenderly, wincing, muttering apologies under her breath. And with every step, the tendrils coiled a little closer.

Black Alice crouched beside the box, and began examining connections. The console was about three meters by four, half a meter tall, and fixed firmly to Vinnie's hide. It looked like the thing was still functional, but something—a bit of space debris, maybe—had dented it pretty good.

Cautiously, Black Alice dropped a hand on it. She found the access panel, and flipped it open: more red lights than green. A tongue-click, and she began withdrawing her tethered tools from their holding pouches and arranging them so that they would float conveniently around.

She didn't hear a thing, of course, but the hide under her boots vibrated suddenly, sharply. She jerked her head around, just in time to see one of Vinnie's feelers slap her own side, five or ten meters away. And then the whole Boojum shuddered, contracting, curved into a hard crescent of pain the same way she had when the *Henry Ford* had taken that chunk out of her hide. And the lights in the access panel lit up all at once—red, red, yellow, red.

Black Alice tongued off the *send* function on her headset microphone, so Wasabi wouldn't hear her. She touched the bruised hull, and she touched the dented edge of the console. "Vinnie," she said, "does this *hurt*?"

Not that Vinnie could answer her. But it was obvious. She was in pain. And maybe that dent didn't have anything to do with space debris. Maybe—Black Alice straightened, looked around, and couldn't convince herself that it was an accident that this box was planted right where Vinnie couldn't . . . quite . . . reach it.

"So what does it *do*?" she muttered. "Why am I out here repairing something that fucking hurts?" She crouched down again and took another long look at the interface.

As an engineer, Black Alice was mostly self-taught; her implants were secondhand, black market, scavenged, the wet work done by a gilly on Providence Station. She'd learned the technical vocabulary from Gogglehead Kim before he bought it in a stupid little fight with a ship named the *V. I. Ulyanov*, but what she relied on were her instincts, the things she knew without being able to say. So she *looked* at that box wired into Vinnie's spine and all its red and yellow lights, and then she tongued the comm back on and said, "Wasabi, this thing don't look so good."

"Whaddya mean, don't look so good?" Wasabi sounded distracted, and that was just fine.

Black Alice made a noise, the auditory equivalent of a shrug. "I think the node's inflamed. Can we pull it and lock it in somewhere else?"

"No!" said Wasabi.

"It's looking pretty ugly out here."

"Look, Blackie, unless you want us to all go sailing out into the Big Empty, we are *not* pulling that governor. Just fix the fucking thing, would you?"

"Yessir," said Black Alice, thinking hard. The first thing was that Wasabi knew what was going on—knew what the box did and knew that the *Lavinia Whateley* didn't like it. That wasn't comforting. The second thing was that whatever was going on, it involved the Big Empty, the cold vastness between the stars. So it wasn't that Vinnie wanted to go home. She wanted to go *out*.

It made sense, from what Black Alice knew about Boojums. Their infants lived in the tumult of the gas giants' atmosphere, but as they aged, they pushed higher and higher, until they reached the edge of the envelope. And then—following instinct or maybe the calls of their fellows, nobody knew for sure—they learned to skip, throwing themselves out into the vacuum like Earth birds leaving the nest. And what if, for a Boojum, the solar system was just another nest?

Black Alice knew the *Lavinia Whateley* was old, for a Boojum. Captain Song was not her first captain, although you never mentioned Captain Smith if you knew what was good for you. So if there *was* another stage to her life cycle, she might be ready for it. And her crew wasn't letting her go.

Jesus and the cold fishy gods, Black Alice thought. Is this why the *Marie Curie* ate her crew? Because they wouldn't let her go?

She fumbled for her tools, tugging the cords to float them closer, and wound up walloping herself in the bicep with a splicer. And as she was wrestling with it, her headset spoke again. "Blackie, can you hurry it up out there? Captain says we're going to have company."

Company? She never got to say it. Because when she looked up, she saw the shapes, faintly limned in starlight, and a chill as cold as a suit leak crept up her neck.

There were dozens of them. Hundreds. They made her skin crawl and her nerves judder the way gillies and Boojums never had. They were man-sized, roughly, but they looked like the pseudoroaches of Venus, the ones Black Alice still had nightmares about, with too many legs, and horrible stiff wings. They had ovate, corrugated heads, but no faces, and where their mouths ought to be sprouting writing tentacles

And some of them carried silver shining cylinders, like the canisters in Vinnie's subhold.

Black Alice wasn't certain if they saw her, crouched on the Boojum's hide with only a thin laminate between her and the breathsucker, but she was certain of something else. If they did, they did not care.

They disappeared below the curve of the ship, toward the airlock Black Alice had exited before clawing her way along the ship's side. They could be a trade delegation, come to bargain for the salvaged cargo.

Black Alice didn't think even the Mi-Go came in the battalions to talk trade.

She meant to wait until the last of them had passed, but they just kept coming. Wasabi wasn't answering her hails; she was on her own and unarmed. She fumbled with her tools, stowing things in any handy pocket whether it was where the tool went or not. She couldn't see much; everything was misty. It took her several seconds to realize that her visor was fogged because she was crying.

Patch cables. Where were the fucking patch cables? She found a two-meter length of fiberoptic with the right plugs on the end. One end went into the monitor panel. The other snapped into her suit comm.

"Vinnie?" she whispered, when she thought she had a connection. "Vinnie, can you hear me?"

The bioluminescence under Black Alice's boots pulsed once.

Gods and little fishes, she thought. And then she drew out her laser cutting torch, and started slicing open the case on the console that Wasabi had called the *governor*. Wasabi was probably dead by now, or dying. Wasabi, and Dogcollar, and. . . well, not dead. If they were lucky, they were dead.

Because the opposite of lucky was those canisters the Mi-Go were carrying.

She hoped Dogcollar was lucky.

"You wanna go *out*, right?" she whispered to the *Lavinia Whateley*. "Out into the Big Empty."

She'd never been sure how much Vinnie understood of what people said, but the light pulsed again.

"And this thing won't let you." It wasn't a question. She had it open now, and she could see that was what it did. Ugly fucking thing. Vinnie shivered underneath her, and there was a sudden pulse of noise in her helmet speakers: screaming. People screaming.

"I know," Black Alice said. "They'll come get me in a minute, I guess." She swallowed hard against the sudden lurch of her stomach. "I'm gonna get this thing off you, though. And when they go, you can go, okay? And I'm sorry. I didn't know we were keeping you from . . . " She had to quit talking, or she really was going to puke. Grimly, she fumbled for the tools she needed to disentangle the abomination from Vinnie's nervous system.

Another pulse of sound, a voice, not a person: flat and buzzing and horrible. "We do not bargain with thieves." And the scream that time—she'd never heard Captain Song scream before. Black Alice flinched and started counting to slow her breathing. Puking in a suit was the number one badness, but hyperventilating in a suit was a really close second.

Her heads-up display was low-res, and slightly miscalibrated, so that everything had a faint shadow-double. But the thing that flashed up against her own view of her hands was unmistakable: a question mark.

<?>

"Vinnie?"

Another pulse of screaming, and the question mark again.

<?>

"Holy shit, Vinnie! . . . Never mind, never mind. They, um, they collect people's brains. In canisters. Like the canisters in the third subhold."

The bioluminescence pulsed once. Black Alice kept working.

Her heads-up pinged again: <ALICE> A pause. <?>

"Um, yeah. I figure that's what they'll do with me, too. It looked like they had plenty of canisters to go around."

Vinnie pulsed, and there was a longer pause while Black Alice doggedly severed connections and loosened bolts.

<WANT> said the *Lavinia Whateley.* <?>

"Want? Do I *want* . . . ?" Her laughter sounded bad. "um, no. No, I don't want to be a brain in a jar. But I'm not seeing a lot of choices here. Even if I went cometary, they could catch me. And it kind of sounds like they're mad enough to do it, too."

She'd cleared out all the moorings around the edge of the governor; the case lifted off with a shove and went sailing into the dark. Black Alice winced. But then the processor under the cover drifted away from Vinnie's hide, and there was just the monofilament tethers and the fat cluster of fiber optic and superconductors to go.

<HELP>

"I'm doing my best here, Vinnie," Black Alice said through her teeth.

That got her a fast double-pulse, and the *Lavinia Whateley* said, <HELP> And then, <ALICE>

"You want to help *me?*" Black Alice squeaked.

A strong pulse, and the heads-up said, <HELP ALICE>

"That's really sweet of you, but I'm honestly not sure there's anything you can do. I mean, it doesn't look like the Mi-Go are mad at *you*, and I really want to keep it that way."

<EAT ALICE> said the *Lavinia Whateley.*

Black Alice came within a millimeter of taking her own fingers off with the cutting laser. "Um, Vinnie, that's um . . . well, I guess it's better than being a brain in a jar." Or suffocating to death in her suit if she went cometary and the Mi-Go *didn't* come after her.

The double-pulse again, but Black Alice didn't see what she could have missed. As communications went, *EAT ALICE* was pretty fucking unambiguous.

<HELP ALICE> the *Lavinia Whateley* insisted. Black Alice leaned in close, unsplicing the last of the governor's circuits from the Boojum's nervous system. <SAVE ALICE>

"By eating me? Look, I know what happens to things you eat, and it's not . . . " She bit her tongue. Because she *did* know what happened to things the *Lavinia Whateley* ate. Absorbed. Filtered. Recycled. "Vinnie . . . are you saying you can save me from the Mi-Go?"

A pulse of agreement.

"By eating me?" Black Alice pursued, needing to be sure she understood.

Another pulse of agreement.

Black Alice thought about the *Lavinia Whateley*'s teeth. "How much *me* are we talking about here?"

<ALICE> said the *Lavinia Whateley*, and then the last fiber-optic cable parted, and Black Alice, her hands shaking, detached her patch cable and flung the whole mess of it as hard as she could straight up. Maybe it would find a planet with atmosphere and be some little alien kid's shooting star.

And now she had to decide what to do.

She figured she had two choices, really. One, walk back down the *Lavinia Whateley* and find out if the Mi-Go believed in surrender. Two, walk around the *Lavinia Whateley* and into her toothy mouth.

Black Alice didn't think the Mi-Go believed in surrender.

She tilted her head back for one last clear look at the shining black infinity of space. Really, there wasn't any choice at all. Because even if she'd misunderstood what Vinnie seemed to be trying to tell her, the worst she'd end up was dead, and that was light-years better than what the Mi-Go had on offer.

Black Alice Bradley loved her ship.

She turned to her left and started walking, and the *Lavinia Whateley*'s bioluminescence followed her courteously all the way, vanes swaying out of her path. Black Alice skirted each of Vinnie's eyes as she came to them, and each of them blinked at her. And then she reached Vinnie's mouth and that magnificent panoply of teeth.

"Make it quick, Vinnie, okay?" said Black Alice, and walked into her leviathan's maw.

Picking her way delicately between razor-sharp teeth, Black Alice had plenty of time to consider the ridiculousness of worrying about a hole in her suit. Vinnie's mouth was more like a crystal cave, once you were inside it; there was no tongue, no palate. Just polished, macerating stones. Which did not close on Black Alice, to her surprise. If anything, she got the feeling the Vinnie was holding her . . . breath. Or what passed for it.

The Boojum was lit inside, as well—or was making herself lit, for Black Alice's benefit. And as Black Alice clambered inward, the teeth got smaller, and fewer, and the tunnel narrowed. Her throat, Alice thought. I'm inside her.

And the walls closed down, and she was swallowed.

Like a pill, enclosed in the tight sarcophagus of her space suit, she felt rippling pressure as peristalsis pushed her along. And then greater pressure, suffocating, savage. One sharp pain. The pop of her ribs as her lungs crushed.

Screaming inside a space suit was contraindicated, too. And with collapsed lungs, she couldn't even do it properly.

alice.

She floated. In warm darkness. A womb, a bath. She was comfortable.

An itchy soreness between her shoulderblades felt like a very mild radiation burn.

alice.

A voice she thought she should know. She tried to speak; her mouth gnashed, her teeth ground.

alice. talk here.

She tried again. Not with her mouth, this time.

Talk. . . here?

The buoyant warmth flickered past her. She was . . . drifting. No, swimming. She could feel currents on her skin. Her vision was confused. She blinked and blinked, and things were shattered.

There was nothing to see anyway, but stars.

alice talk here.

Where am I?

eat alice.

Vinnie. Vinnie's voice, but not in the flatness of the heads-up display anymore. Vinnie's voice alive with emotion and nuance and the vastness of her self.

You ate me, she said, and understood abruptly that the numbness she felt was not shock. It was the boundaries of her body erased and redrawn.

!

Agreement. Relief.

I'm. . . in you, Vinnie?

=/=

Not a "no." More like, this thing is not the same, does not compare, to this other thing. Black Alice felt the warmth of space so near a generous star slipping by her. She felt the swift currents of its gravity, and the gravity of its satellites, and bent them, and tasted them, and surfed them faster and faster away.

I am you.

!

Ecstatic comprehension, which Black Alice echoed with passionate relief. Not dead. Not dead after all. Just, transformed. Accepted. Embraced by her ship, whom she embraced in return.

Vinnie. Where are we going?

out, Vinnie answered. And in her, Black Alice read the whole great naked wonder of space, approaching faster and faster as Vinnie accelerated, reaching for the first great skip that would hurl them into the interstellar darkness of the Big Empty. They were going somewhere.

Out, Black Alice agreed and told herself not to grieve. Not to go mad. This sure beat swampy Hell out of being a brain in a jar.

And it occurred to her, as Vinnie jumped, the brainless bodies of her crew already digesting inside her, that it wouldn't be long before the loss of the *Lavinia Whateley* was a tale told to frighten spacers, too.

THE DIFFICULTIES OF EVOLUTION

KAREN HEULER

"I want to save this one," Franka said, stroking Yagel, her youngest. The child sat in Franka's lap, her dark eyes following the doctor happily. She chattered and waved her small hands around.

"She's my second," Franka added. Her hand rubbed the spot on Yagel's ribs where it was thickening.

"Ah, yes," Dr. Bennecort said. "Evan. What was he—ten or so—when it started?"

"Yes. I thought, at her age, it was too early, there should be lots of time."

"You know it can happen at any point. I had a patient who was sixty . . . "

"Yes, you told me," Franka said impatiently, and stopped herself. She took a moment to calm herself, and the doctor waited. He was good—patient, professional—and Franka hoped that he could help. She wanted to say, "I'm imagining the worst," and have him reply, "The worst won't happen." She knew better, but she was hoping to hear it nevertheless.

It had happened suddenly. Franka was bathing her daughter the week before, cooing at the smiling, prattling wonder of her life. After the shock of watching Evan go, she knew she was a little possessive. Franka smoothed the washcloth over the toddler's skin, gently swirling water over the perfect limbs, the wrinkles at the joints, the plum calves and shoulders. She felt a thickening at the ribs—an area that, surely, just the day before had been soft and pliant.

She automatically talked back as Yagel babbled, but she felt her face freeze and Yagel noticed the difference in her touch and grew concerned, her legs pumping impatiently.

And Franka couldn't keep her hands off her, touching, touching the spots that were changing, until Yagel began to bruise, and Simyon told her to go to the doctor. He said it coldly. He felt the spots that Franka felt, and he holed himself up deep inside, leaving Franka to find out the truth alone.

"She's my second," Franka whispered to the doctor. He'd been highly recommended by Deirdre, who had three emerald beetles tethered to her house, buzzing and smacking the picture window when the family sat down to watch TV. "We know their favorite shows," Dierdre said. "We know when they're happy."

Franka didn't want Yagel to end up like that, a child-sized insect swooping to her and away, eating from her palm. She wanted Yagel to end up a little girl.

"Time will tell," Dr. Bennecort said. Time, and blood tests. Yagel screamed when the needle went in, but she forgot it all when given a lollipop. Maybe everything was still all right.

A month to get the results. And packets of information, numbers of people to talk to, a video explaining the process. He forgot she already had all this, from when Evan changed.

She didn't look at any of it, and neither did Simyon.

"I don't want this to happen," Franka whispered to her daughter, day and night. Yagel cooed back.

"Don't you think you could love her, no matter what?" Deirdre asked cruelly when she came to lend her support. She so seldom left her home; she preferred to stay close to her emerald boys. Some people let their children go when they changed, gave in and released them. Took the ones that swam to the sea, and the ones that flew to the hills. The lucky ones kept the cats and dogs as pets—not such a change, after all—and put the ponies in the yard. You could wish for the higher orders; you could wish for the softer, cuddlier evolutions, but you couldn't change what was meant to be.

"But whatever they are, you love them, still," Deirdre said.

The three emerald beetles were about the size of a five-year-old child. They lifted and fluttered up and hit the window sometimes three at a time, with whirring thuds, they pulled to the ends of their cords, their green wings pulsing.

"My dears, my sweets," Deirdre thought as she stood on the inside of the picture window, her fingertips touching the glass as they swooped towards her, their hard black eyes intent. "My all, my all, my all."

She put out bowls for them, rotted things mixed with honey and vitamins, her own recipe, and rolled down the awning in case it rained, and went to Franka's house when she called, where she found her friend with her child in her arms.

"Feel this," Franka said. She rubbed a spot along Yagel's ribs. "It's thicker, isn't it? Not like the rest of her skin."

Deirdre took her fingers and delicately felt the spot. It felt like a piece of tape under the skin—less resilient, forming a kind of half-moon. "Yes," Deirdre said. "Maybe. It could be anything."

"Evan was ten," Franka whispered. "And she's only three. Your boys—did it happen at the same age for each?"

Deirdre shook her head. "Every one was different," she said, trying to find the right thing to say. "They're always different."

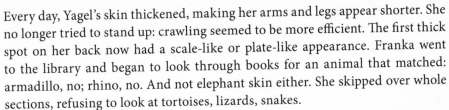

Every day, Yagel's skin thickened, making her arms and legs appear shorter. She no longer tried to stand up: crawling seemed to be more efficient. The first thick spot on her back now had a scale-like or plate-like appearance. Franka went to the library and began to look through books for an animal that matched: armadillo, no; rhino, no. And not elephant skin either. She skipped over whole sections, refusing to look at tortoises, lizards, snakes.

They were taught evolution as children, of course—the intimate, intricate link of the stages of life. Ameba, fish, crawling fish, reptile; pupa, insect; egg, bird; chimp, ape, human; all the wonderful trigonometry of form and function. The beauty of it was startling. However life started, it changed. You were a baby once, then you're different. Each egg had its own calling; no one stopped.

How beautiful it was to watch as characteristics became form, as the infant with a lithe crawl became a cat; as the toddler with the steady gaze became an owl, as the child who ran became a horse. It was magnificent. Her own brother had soared into the sky finally, a remarkable crow (always attracted to sparkle, rawkishly rowdy). She had envied him—his completion. She had stayed a child.

Still. Maybe it was less than magnificent when it was your own child. Or it was some deficit of her own. Simyon told her gruffly, "Babies grow up, Franka. You know they change. You don't decide when it's time for them to go; they do. When it's right for them. Not for you."

He was not a sympathetic man—but had that always been true? No. He used to be interested in her worries; he used to want to soothe her rather than lecture. Although—she told herself—he was dealing with it, too. Both children evolving; leaving. So quickly gone. Of course it was hard for him, too.

She remembered her own brother's meta-morphosis as a magical time—she had leapt up out of bed each morning to see the change in him overnight: a pouty mouth to a beak; dark fuzz on his shoulders into feathers; the way his feet cramped into claws; the tilt of his head and the glitter of his eye. It had been wonderful to see him fly, leaning out the window one minute, through it the next.

Even in the memory of it she heard her mother's faltering cry. How stodgy her mother had seemed.

She leaned over Yagel. "I will always love you," she confided to the child's tender ear. Yagel poked her tongue out, clamped her arms to her side. "Always, Franka repeated. "Always." She kissed her on the neck and bit her ear tenderly.

Her neighbor Phoebe had two girls, neither of them evolved. She looked pregnant again and Franka went over to talk to her. "I think Yagel is evolving," she said. "You're so lucky." Of course it was wrong not to accept her children as they were, but she felt it in her, a deep reluctance to let go.

Phoebe nodded. "It's so nice to have them at home for so long, yes. Of course there's so much beauty in the changes—you know Hildy's girl?" Franka nodded. "A lunar moth. Elegant, curved wings. Extraordinary. Trembling on the roof.

Hildy's taken photos and made an incredible silkscreen image. It's haunting. I look at some of the changes and it feels almost religious."

Phoebe's face looked dutiful and Franka knew a lie when she heard one: the false sincerity, the false envy. It was always better to have children who stayed children, and not some phenomenal moth. And when they changed, there was always a judgment. No one really said it, but it was there. The mothers of sharks would always weep. Children who didn't evolve were more of a blessing, no matter how basic it was to evolve.

"You're too possessive," Simyon said, hunched over his dinner. He was eating quickly, tearing at his food. "Life is change." He finished his meal and prowled down the hall, going into his daughter's room, sniffing and blinking. "Reptile," he said, coming back. "Cold blood." He went off to watch his TV.

She drove around the next day, slowly. There were cages everywhere, some of them immense and gothic. There were new ponds, and short bursts of trees. A huge, exquisite ceramic beehive stood next to a garage. She heard the trumpet of an elephant down the next road, and the scream of a peacock.

As she drove, heads poked from the corners of garages and from behind gazebos, some of them not yet completely determined. She made a mental note to remember where they were, in case she needed them. For Yagel.

Sometimes the changes were slow, and sometimes the changes were fast. Yagel stood up again and walked like a little girl—stubby, but a little girl. She described every event of her day, repeating the things the other little girls had done, describing how one of them grew a bandit mask on her face and sometimes washed her food before eating.

"She's all right," Simyon said stubbornly.

"I'm afraid for her," she said, and her voice sounded thick. Simyon's hard, bushy eyes stared at her, ticking down her body, studying her.

Maybe Yagel would never change; maybe this was just her version of a little girl. Some evolved early; some evolved late. Every morning she counted Yagel's fingers and toes, and then she counted her own. She longed for nighttime and the rise of the wind, for the moment of freshness at the start of a storm.

She was beginning to sense her own change and was surprised one day to look at Yagel and consider how fragile she was, how available and simple her neck looked, how fatty her arms and how ample her thighs. She caught new angles when she saw her face in the mirror, a starkness that hadn't been there and now struck her as cunning. She went to the top of the stairs and stared down them; she looked out the windows and her eyes caught the blur and skitter of countless beings, hiding behind and under things. She no longer cooked her food and finally Simyon coaxed her out with promises of meat, and locked the door against her.

She had skin stretched tight across the bones that pulled out from her shoulders, a hard elastic that wrinkled only when she pulled in her elbows firm against her ribs. When she stretched her arms out it was not possible to fight the tug, stronger than blood, that lifted her, or dropped her from great heights when she'd already been lifted. When she fell, it was with a liquid plummet, streamlined and terrible, her jaw slicing the air, her eyes tricking out every detail. Each movement in the air was adrenaline: she was pure and fast and vastly hungry. When she sighted her prey she started out silent and swift but just before she struck a large chaotic cry burst from her, turning the prey's eyes up, freezing their limbs. Just like that, food.

Small and furry; fat and hairy; clothed and crying; it didn't matter. The power was hers and in the air and right; what she could take was meant to be taken. High up, on the tips of the buildings, she could feel it all move beneath her, each little tiny patter, each needless drumming word. They soon took to rifles and guns and arrows, and she slipped behind buildings, faster than they were, and took them out when they pointed to where she'd been. As if she would ever stay where she once had been.

This was what she was meant to be and she filled her throat with the joy of it.

CATHERINE DREWE

PAUL CORNELL

Hamilton could hear, from the noises outside the window, that the hunters had caught up with their prey. There was a particular noise that Derbyshire Man Hounds made seconds before impact. A catch in their cries that told of their excitement, the shift in breathing as they prepared to leap at the neck of the quarry the riders had run in for them. He appreciated that sound.

He looked back to where Turpin was sitting in a wing chair, the volume of Butriss he'd taken from Sanderton's library in the early stages of the hunt still open on his lap. The skin on Turpin's face was a patchwork of different shades, from fair new freckles that would have put an Irishman to shame to the richer tones of a mulatto. This was common in the higher ranks of the military, a sign that parts of Turpin's body had been regrown and grafted back on many different occasions. Hamilton saw it as an affectation, though he would never have said so. He had asked for his own new right arm to match the rest of his body completely. He'd expected Turpin, or one of the other ranking officers who occasionally requested his services, to ask about it, but they never had.

The noise from outside reached a crescendo of cries and horns and the sudden high howl of one dog claiming the prey and then being denied more than a rip at it. Turpin opened his eyes. "Damn," he said. He managed a slight smile. "Still, five hours. They got their exercise."

Hamilton reflected the smile back at him, shifting his posture so that he mirrored Turpin's nonchalant air more exactly. "Yes, sir."

Turpin closed the book. "I thought they had me an hour ago, which is why I sent for you. How's your weekend been? Has Sanderton been keeping you in the style to which you're accustomed?" Turpin had arrived unannounced and unexpected, as he often did, late last night, sitting down at the end of the dinner table as the gentlemen were about to adjourn and talking only about the forthcoming day's hunting, including asking his host for Hamilton to be excepted from it.

"It's been a most enjoyable house party, sir. Dinner was excellent."

"I heard you bagged your share of poultry."

Hamilton inclined his head. He was waiting for Turpin to get to the point, but it wouldn't be for a while yet. Indeed, Turpin spent the next twenty minutes and thirty-three seconds asking after Hamilton's family, and going into some of the details of his genealogy. This happened a lot, Hamilton found. Every now and then it occurred to him that it was because he was Irish. The thought registered again now, but did not trouble him. He had considerable love for the man who had ordered him to return home from Constantinople when it became clear the only good he could do there was to remind the Kaiser that every disturbance to the peace of Europe had consequences, that every action was paid for in blood. Hamilton would have done it, obviously, but it was one fewer weight to drag up the hill when he woke each morning.

"So." Turpin got up and replaced the book on the library shelf. "We've seen you're fit, and attended to your conversation, which rang like a bell with the white pudding crowd. We have a job for you, Major. Out of uniform."

Hamilton took that to be the royal *we*. He found that a healthy smile had split his lips. "Yes, sir. Thank you, sir."

Turpin touched his finger to the surface of the table, where the imprint glowed with bacterial phosphorescence. Hamilton leaned over and made the same gesture, connecting the receptors in his skin with the package.

"Nobody else knows about this," said Turpin.

The information rolled into Hamilton. It exhilarated him. He felt his nostrils flare at the smells and pictures of a land he'd never been to. New territory. Low white newly grown wood buildings, less than a day old by the look of them, with the banners of imperial Russia fluttering gallant. That is, fluttering not entirely through the progression of an atmosphere past them. Near darkness. Was it dawn? Not unpleasant.

And there was the woman. She stood on a bluff, looking down into a dark grey canyon, looking at a prize. He couldn't see what she was looking at; the emotion came with the package, and Hamilton reacted to it, making himself hate her and her prize for a moment, so if anything like this moment came in the world, he would be in charge of it.

She wore her hair green, but bundled in the knots that suggested she rarely had to unfurl it and take the benefit. Her neck was bare in the manner that said she was ready for the guillotine, the black collar of her dress emphasising her defiance. Hamilton let himself admire that bravery, as he did the martial qualities of all those he met in his work. Her gown was something that had been put together in the narrow hell of the foundry streets of Kiev, tiny blue veins of enforcement and supply across Imperial white, with the most intricate parchment wrinkles. It looked like she was wearing a map.

Her hands were clasped before her, and she was breathing hard, controlling her posture through an immense effort of will. She wanted to exult, to raise herself in triumph.

Hamilton found himself wishing she would turn around.

But the information froze there, and the rare data tumbled into his mind. He sent most of it into various compartments, for later examination, keeping only the index in the front of his attention.

"Catherine Drewe," said Turpin. "Ever meet her?"

Just because they were both Irish? Hamilton killed the thought. "No."

"Good. We got that emotional broadcast image by accident. From someone standing behind her—a bodyguard, we think. One of our satellites happened to be passing over the Valles Marineris at the right moment, three days ago."

Hamilton had already realised. "The Russians are on Mars."

Turpin nodded. "Terrifying, isn't it?"

"Is her army—?"

"Down there with her, because if so, we're acting with a criminal disregard for the safety of our allies in the Savoy court?"

Hamilton acknowledged Turpin's smile. "Thought you might be ahead of me, sir."

"We hope not. And we don't see how. So we're not getting Chiamberi involved as yet. She's probably down there on her own, either negotiating a rate to take the Russian side in whatever their long-term plans against the House of Savoy might be, or already part of those plans, possibly as a consultant. Now, the mercenary armies alarm us all, but the good thing about them is that we've sometimes been able to use them as passive aggregators of intelligence, allowing them to serve a side to the point where they're trusted, and then buying them off, netting all they know in the process."

"Is that the mission, sir?"

"No. We've created and are ready to plant chaotic information of an unbreakable nature strongly suggesting that this has already happened, that we have paid Miss Drewe in advance for her dalliance with the bear. Your front cover will be as a serf, your inside cover as a deniable asset of the Okhranka. Your mission is to kill her and any associates in one move."

Hamilton felt himself take another deep breath. "So the world will think the Russians discovered her treachery and covertly executed her."

"And botched the cover, which the world will enjoy working out for itself. Miss Drewe's mercenaries are tremendously loyal to her. Many of them declare themselves to be in love with her. Doubtless, several of them are actually her lovers. They will not proceed with any contract should she die in this way. Moreover, they may feel obliged to expose the Russian presence on Mars—"

"Without us having been involved in exposing it."

"So the czar's state visit at Christmas and the superconductor trade talks won't have any awkwardness hanging over them. Savoy won't ask and won't tell. They'll be able to bring pressure to bear before the Russians are anywhere near ready to tussle. There will be no shooting war, the balance will be preserved, and even better—"

"Miss Drewe's disaffected mercenaries may actually give us the information on Russian arms and intentions that we're alleging she did."

"And other such groups, irked at Russian gall, will be less disposed to aid them. It *is* rather beautiful, isn't it?" Turpin held out his hand, the ring finger crooked, and Hamilton touched fingertip to fingertip, officially taking on the orders and accepting them. "Very good. You leave in three days. Come in tomorrow for the covers and prep."

There was a knock on the door. Turpin called enter, and in marched a hearty group of hunters, led by Sanderton, the mud still on their boots. At the front of the pack came a small girl, Sanderton's daughter. She'd been blooded across the cheeks, and in her right hand she held, clutched by the hair, Turpin's deceased head. "Do you want to eat it, Uncle?" she asked.

Turpin went to her, ruffled her hair, and inspected the features of his clone. "Yes, I'll take my prion transmitters back, Augusta. Can't be spendthrift with them at my age."

Sanderton advised him that his chef was used to the situation, and would prepare the brain as a soup.

Hamilton caught the eye of the girl as she hefted the head onto a plate provided by a servant. She was laughing at the blood that was falling onto the carpet, trying to save it with her hand.

Hamilton found that he was sharing her smile.

Hamilton made his apologies to his host, and that night drove to Oxford in his motor carriage, a Morgan SixtySix. The purr of the electrical motor made him happy. Precision workings. Small mechanisms making the big ones tick over.

It was a clear run up St. Giles, but glancing at his watch, Hamilton knew he wasn't going to make it in time for the start of the service. He tore down the Banbury Road, and slowed down at the last moment to make the turn into Parks, enjoying the spectacle of the Pitt Rivers, lit up with moving displays for some special exhibition. The Porters, in all their multitudes, ran out of their lodge as he cut the engine and sailed into the quad, but the sight of the Fourth Dragoons badge had them doffing their caps and applauding. After a few words of greeting had been exchanged, Loftus, the head porter, came out and swore at Hamilton in her usual friendly fashion, and had her people boost the carriage onto the gravel just beyond the lodge.

Hamilton walked across the quad in the cold darkness, noticing with brief pleasure that new blades had appeared in neon scrawl on the wall of his old staircase. The smells of cooking and the noise of broadcast theatric systems in students' rooms were both emphasised by the frost. The food and music belonged to Musselmen and Hindus and the registered Brethren of the North American protectorates. Keble continued its cosmopolitan tradition.

He headed for the chapel. As he passed the main doors, the bells that had been sounding from inside fell silent. He put his hand to the wood, then hesitated, and went to sit in the hallway outside the side door. He listened to the start of the service, and found his heart lifted by the words, and by the voice that was saying them. "Your world turns as the solar system turns as the universe turns, every power in balance, for every action an opposite, a rotation and equalisation that stands against war and defeats death, and the mystery of what may happen in any moment or in any space will continue. . . . "

He waited an hour, until the service was over, enjoying the cold, listening to that voice through the wood of the door, intimate and distant.

As the congregation came out, Hamilton stepped through the mass of them, unnoticed, and past churchwardens putting out candles and gathering hymn books. There she was. She had her back to him. Annie. In the gleaming vault of the chapel interior, dominated by the giant depiction of God with a sword for a tongue, reaching across time and space with his Word.

She turned at the sound of his footsteps. She was as lovely as he remembered. "Jonathan," she whispered, "why are you here?"

He took her hand and put it to his face and asked for a blessing.

The blessing only gave him an edge of 0.2 percent. Annie checked again, in his head behind his eyes, and for a moment he thought how splendid it would be to show her all his old covers, to share. But no. He could not. Not until this part of his life was over.

"It's a very slight effect," she said. "Your prayers have hardly provoked the field. Are you contemplating murder?"

Hamilton laughed in a way that said of course not. But really his laugh was about the irony. It wasn't the first time the balance had stood against he who sought only to maintain it.

They went into the side chapel where *The Light of the World* by William Holman Hunt was kept, the one on display to the empire's gawkers in St. Paul's being a copy.

Places like this, to Hamilton, were where the sons of empire returned to after they had done terrible things, the clockwork pivots about which their dangerous world turned, where better people could keep the civilisation that they did those things for. Annie, his old tutors like Hartridge and Parrish, the architecture and custom, the very ground were why he went to work. On his way from here, he would look in on the Lamb and Flag and drink a half of a beer with the hope that he would return to drink the other half. As had many before him, for all the centuries.

After the churchwardens had left, Annie did him a certain service behind the altar, and Hamilton returned the favour.

And then he left holy ground, and went out into the world that wasn't England, equipped only with a tiny and ironic blessing.

At the square, anonymous offices off Horse Guards Parade, they armed him and briefed him. He looked out from the secret part of his mind and saw that he was now Miquel Du Pasonade, a bonded serf of three generations. He let Miquel walk to the door and bid farewell, only leaning forward to take over during weapons familiarisation.

He let his cover take the overnight to Woomera, switching off completely, waking only as he was paying in Californian rubles for a one-way ticket up the needle.

Hamilton always preferred to watch the continents drop below him as he ascended. He mentally picked out the shapes of the great European Empires, their smaller allies, colonies, and protectorates. The greater solar system reflected those nations like a fairground mirror, adding phantom weight to some of the smaller states through their possessions out there in the dark, shaming others with how little they'd reached beyond the world.

Hamilton waited at Orbital for two days, letting his cover hang around the right inns, one of the starving peasantry. He let himself be drunk one night, and that was when they burst in, the unbreachable doors flapping behind them, solid men who looked like they should be in uniform, but were conspicuously not.

His cover leapt up.

Hamilton allowed himself a moment of hidden pride as they grabbed his hair and put their fingers onto his face. And then that was that.

Hamilton woke up pressed into service, his fellows all around him celebrating their fate with their first good meal in weeks. They sat inside a hull of blue and white.

His cover didn't know where they were heading.

But Hamilton knew.

Normally on arriving at Mars, Hamilton would have booked into the Red Savoy Raffles, a tantalising distance from Mons, as the gauche advertising put it, and spent the evening arguing the toss of the wine list with Signor Harakita. Serfdom to the Bear offered a different prospect. The hull the serfs were kept in smelt of unaltered body. During the passage, they did the tasks that would have needed continual expensive replacements had mechanisms been assigned to them: maintaining the rocket motors, repairing the ship's life-support infrastructure. There were two fatalities in the three weeks Hamilton was on board.

They didn't take the serfs on face value. All of them were run through an EM scan. Hamilton watched it register the first level of his cover. It accepted it. The deeper cover would only be noticed once that print was sent, hopefully long after the fact when inquiries and excuses were the order of the day, to the cracking centres in the hives of St. Petersburg. It had also, to more deadly effect, been registered in public with the authorities at Orbital, and would thus also be cracked by every empire's mind men in every capital.

But that was not all that the EM scanner did. It suddenly went deeper. But not searching, Hamilton realised—

Cutting!

Hamilton winced at the distant sight of some of the higher functions of his cover's mind dissolving.

From that point on, it was like sitting on the shoulders of a drunkard, and Hamilton had to intervene a couple of times to stop his body getting into danger. That was all right. The serfs also smoked tobacco, and he declined that as well. A cover couldn't look too perfect.

The serfs were strapped in as the Russian space carriage aerobraked around Mars's thin atmosphere, then started its angled descent towards the surface. This was the first surprise. The carriage was taking a completely conventional course: it would be visible from every lighthouse. This must, realised Hamilton, wishing for a window, be a scheduled flight. And by now they must be very close to whatever their destination was, the resorts of Tharsis, perhaps—

Then there came a roar, a sudden crash, and the giddy sensation of falling. Hamilton's stomach welcomed it. He knew himself to be more at home in freefall than the majority of those he encountered. It was the sea welcoming the shark.

He could feel the different momentum: they must have been jettisoned from the main carriage, at a very narrow angle, under the sensor shadow of some mountain range—

The realisation came to him like the moment when Isaac Newton had seen that tiny worm and started thinking about the very small.

Hamilton started to curl into the crash position—

Then with an effort of will he forced himself not to. Too perfect!

His seat broke from its fastenings, and he flew at the ceiling.

The quality of the air felt strange. Not enough! It felt like hell. And the smell. For a moment Hamilton thought he was in a battle. So where were the noises?

They pulled the darkness from around him. They were rough. There were bright lights, and a curt examination, his body being turned right and left. Hamilton had a sudden moment of fear for his body, not belonging to him now, carelessly damaged by the puppet he'd leant it to! He wanted to fight! To let his fists bite into their faces!

He held it in. Tried to breathe.

He struggled out of their grasp for a moment, only to look round.

A serf barracks, turned into a makeshift hospital. Bunks growing out of packed -down mud, providing their own sawdust. Bright Russian guard uniforms, blue and white with epaulettes gleaming, polished, ceremonial helmets off indoors. All wearing masks and oxygen supplies. All ceramics, no metal. Afraid of detectors. A Russian military medic, in his face again, flashing a torch into his eye. Masked too.

There was a rectangle of light shining in through the doorway. They were pushed from their beds, one by one, and sent stumbling towards it. Still couldn't breathe. That was where the smell of battle was coming from—

No, not battle. A mixture. Bodies from in here. From out there—

Gunpowder.

Soil with a high mineral content.

He moved into the light and put a hand up.

He felt his skin burning and yelled. He threw himself forward into a welcome sliver of dark, shielding his eyes from a glare that could have blinded him.

He lay in shadow on the gunpowder-grey ground, with laughter from behind him, the sun refracting off angled rock, through a blurred sky, like a cold furnace.

He was in the Mariner Valley, the deepest gorge in the solar system, with the sun flaring low in the west, rebounding off the white buildings. There was hard UV in the sky. His lungs were hoiking on tiny breaths. Frost was already burning his fingers. And he wasn't wearing any kind of protective equipment.

They made the serfs march along the shaded side of the valley. At least they gave them gloves.

An enormous wind would suddenly blast across the column of men, like a blow to the ground, sloughing them with rock dust, and then it would be gone again. It was a shock that breathing was even possible. Hamilton stole glances from the shade as he struggled to adjust, looking upwards to the nearest escarpment. In the valley proper, you wouldn't necessarily assume you were in a gorge; the vast depression stretched from horizon to horizon. So this must be one of the minor valleys that lay inside the great rift. They could be six miles deep here. Given the progress of terraforming on the rest of the Martian globe, the air pressure might just be enough.

He realised, at a shout from the overseer in the Russian uniform, that he had slowed down, letting his fellow serfs march past him. But his cover was pushing his body to move as fast as it could.

He realised: he was different to the others.

He was finding physical action more difficult than they were. Why?

He looked at the man next to him, and was met with a disinterested misty expression.

The mental examination! They hadn't ripped out the higher functions of the serfs purely in order to make them docile; they'd shut down brain processes that required oxygen!

Hamilton added his own mental weight to that of his cover, and made the body step up its march. He could feel his lungs burning. The serfs had perhaps a couple of months of life before this exposure caught up with them. It felt like he had a week.

He considered, for a moment, the exit strategy. The personal launcher waiting in a gulley—he checked his internal map—sixteen miles away.

That was closer than it might have been. But it was still out of the question without the oxygen supply that previously had been standard for serfs working in such conditions. If he was going to get out of this, he would need to steal such equipment, the quicker the better, before his body weakened.

On the other hand, if he stayed and died, after having made his kills, the mission would be successfully completed. The cover would still be planted.

He decided. He would not leave quickly while there was still a chance of success.

He took care to think of Annie and the quad and the noise of the Morgan's engine. Then he did not think of those things again.

In the days that followed Hamilton was put to work alongside the other serfs. He mentally rehearsed that Raffles wine list. He remembered the mouth feels and tastes. He considered a league table of his favourites. Although the details changed, it was headed every day by the 2003 Leoville Las Cases.

Meanwhile, his body was collapsing: blisters forming on his exposed, sunburnt, and windburnt skin; deep aches and cramps nagging at his every muscle; headaches that brought blood from his nose. And the worst of it was he hadn't seen Catherine Drewe.

His work crew were using limited ceramic and wooden tools to install growing pit props into what was obviously a mine shaft. Other serfs were digging, fed off nutrient bath growths that had been thrown up the walls of the valley. There was a sense of urgency. The digging was being directed precisely, according to charts.

These were not fortifications that were being dug. Turpin's conclusions had been rational, but wrong. This was not a military offensive. The Russians gave the impression of sneak thieves, planning to smash and grab and run.

So what was this? Hamilton had only seen one mercenary uniform, bearing the coat of arms of Drewe's Army. The badge displayed the typically amateur and self-aggrandising heraldry of the mercenary bands. It claimed spurious (and now nonexistent) Irish aristocracy, but had nods to all the major courts of Europe, nothing that would inflame the temper of even the most easily offended monarch. The badge irked Hamilton. It was a bastard thing that revealed nothing and too much.

The emblem had been on the sleeve of some sort of bodyguard, a man with muscle structure that had been designed to keep going having taken some small arms fire. He moved awkwardly in the lower gravity. Hamilton felt a surge of odd fellow feeling, and knew this was the man from whom the emotional broadcast had originated.

He and his mistress would doubtless appear together at some point.

After three days, Hamilton's crew swapped tasks with the other group, and were put to dig at the rock face down the tunnel. Hamilton welcomed it: the air pressure was slightly greater here.

He had started to hallucinate. In his mind, he saw great rolling clockworks against a background of all the imperial flags. Armies advanced as lines across maps, and those lines broke into sprays of particles, every advance countered to keep the great system going. He himself walked one of the lines, firing at imaginary assailants. Women spun in their own orbits, the touch of their hands, the briefest of kisses before they were swept away maintaining the energy of the whole merry-go-round.

And at the centre of it all . . . He didn't know; he couldn't see. The difference of accident, the tiny percentage effect that changed the impossible into the everyday. He bowed his head amongst the infinite cogwheels and prayed for grace.

He was broken out of his stupor by the sudden noise in front of him. There had been a fall of rocks. The whole working face in front of him had given way.

Something, maybe the pebbles beneath their feet, was making the serfs working with him sway and stumble. One beside him fell. The Russian overseer bent to check on the man's condition, then took out a gun, thought better of the expense, and instead used a ceramic knife to slit the serf's throat. The body was carried out to be bled over the nutrient baths, the overseer calling out orders as he walked with the man back towards the exit.

Hamilton put his face close to the rock wall that had been revealed. It felt different. It looked blacker. Iconic. Like a wall that was death ought to look. He thought he could hear something in there. That he was being called. Or was that the thought he wasn't allowing himself, the chapel and Annie inside?

A voice broke that terrible despair that would have led him away. "There!"

Hamilton turned and smiled in relief to see her at last. Catherine Drewe. Face-to-face. Her hair was dark with dust, her face powdered around her oxygen mask in a way that looked almost cosmetic. Her eyes were certain and terrified. The other serfs were staring at her. Behind her came the bodyguard, his bulk filling the tunnel.

Hamilton's right hand twitched.

She pushed past him and put her ear to the rock.

He decided not to kill her yet.

"You," she said, turning to point at one of the serfs, "go and tell Sizlovski that we've hit a snag. The rest of you, get out of here, you're relieved."

The serfs, barely understanding, took a moment to down tools and start following the first towards the light.

Hamilton let his cover open his mouth in blank surprise and kept it there. He stayed put.

The bodyguard tapped her shoulder, and Drewe turned to look at him, puzzled. "I said you're finished."

Hamilton detected something urgent in her voice, something he'd heard in the moments before other situations had got rough. This was no setback, no sighing pause.

He crumpled his cover into the darkness of his mind.

He slammed his palm against the wall beside her head.

The bodyguard moved—

But she put up a hand and he stopped.

He let out his Irish accent. "You've got a problem, Miss Drewe," he said.

She considered that for a moment.

He smelt the edge of the ceramic knife as it split molecules an inch from his eye.

He flathanded the wrist of her knife hand into the wall, his other hand catching the gun she'd pulled at his stomach, his finger squashing hers into firing it pointblank into the bodyguard. His face exploded and he fell and Hamilton ripped aside the weapon and threw it.

There was a shout from behind.

Hamilton grabbed the Webley Collapsar 2 mm handgun from the folded dimensions in his chest, spun into firing stance, and blasted a miniature black hole into the skull of a Russian officer, sending the man's brains flying into another universe.

He spun back to catch Drewe pulling another device from her boot.

He grabbed her wrist.

He knew intuitively how to snap her neck from this posture.

In moments, the gunfire would bring many soldiers running. Killing the overseer had compromised Hamilton's mission but slightly. It was still something that a Russian assassin might do, to give his cover credibility. He had completed half his mission now.

But why had she pulled *that*, instead of something to kill him with?

He looked into her eyes.

"Do what you were going to do," said Hamilton.

He let go.

Drewe threw the device at the overseer's body, grabbed Hamilton, and heaved him with her through the rock wall.

The thump of the explosion and the roar of the collapsing tunnel followed them into the chamber, but no dust or debris did. It was a vaulted cavern, sealed off, with something glowing. . . .

Hamilton realised, as he didn't need to take a breath, that the air was thick in here. He started to cough, doubling up. Precious air! Thick air that he gulped down, that made his head swim.

When he straightened up, Drewe was pointing a gun at him. She looked shocked and furious. But that was contained. She was military, all right.

He let his gun arm fall to his side. "Well?" he said.

"Who are you?"

Hamilton carefully pulled out his uniform tag identification.

"British. All right. I assume you're here for that?" She nodded towards the glow.

He looked. Something was protruding from the rock in the centre of the chamber. A silver spar that shone in an unnatural way. It seemed to be connected to something that was lodged—no, that was in some way *part of* the rocks all around it. There were blazing rivulets threaded in and out of the mass. It was like someone had thrown mercury onto pumice stone.

It was like something trapped. And yet it looked whole and obvious. It seemed apt that it had formed a place where they could live, and a wall they could step through. It spoke of uneasy possibilities.

"What is it?"

She cocked her head to one side, surprised he didn't know. "A carriage."

"Some carriage."

"You don't know. That wasn't your mission."

"I was just having a poke around. I didn't expect a non-Russian here. You're Catherine Drewe, aren't you? What's *your* mission?"

She considered, until he was sure she wasn't going to tell him. But then—"I saw this thing. In my prayers. I spent a week in an isolation tank in Kyoto. You see, lately I've started to think there's something wrong with the balance—"

"Everyone always thinks that."

She swore at him. "You have no idea. Inside your empires. You know what that is?"

"No."

"A new arrival."

"From—?"

"Another universe."

Hamilton looked back to the object. He was already on his way to the punchline.

"I followed it calling," Drewe continued, "via a steady and demonstrable provocation of the field. I proved the path led to Mars. I used my rather awe-inspiring political clout to whisper all this into Czar Richard's ear. By which I mean: his ear."

"Why choose the Russians?"

She ignored the question. "I dreamed before I set off that only two people would find it, that their motives would be different. I took Aaron into my confidence. He was motivated only by art, by beauty. But you killed him."

"How do you feel?"

She bared her teeth in a grim smile, her gaze darting all over his face, ready for any provocation. "I'm strongly inclined to return the compliment."

"But you won't." He slowly replaced his gun in its dimensional fold. "Destiny says it's two people."

She kept him waiting another moment. Then she slipped her own gun back into the folds of that dangerous gown.

They looked at each other for a moment. Then they stepped over to the glowing object together. "That glow worries me," she said. "Have you heard of nuclear power?"

Hamilton shook his head.

"Energy produced by the radioactive decay of minerals. An alternative technology. It's poisonous like hard UV. A dead end. One of the outsider sciences something like this might bring in."

Hamilton consulted his internal register, holding in a shudder at the damage he'd already taken. He hadn't anything designed to log radioactivity, but he changed the spectrum on his UV register, and after a moment he was satisfied.

"I'm not seeing *any* radiation. Not even ..." He stopped. He wasn't even detecting that light he could see with his own eyes. But somehow he doubted that what he was seeing would allow him to come to harm.

Drewe put a hand on the apparently shining limb, deploying sensors of her own. "There's nobody in here, no passenger or driver. But . . . I'm getting requests for information. Pleas. Greetings. Quite . . . eccentric ones." She looked at him as if he were going to laugh at her.

In a civilian, Hamilton thought, it would have been endearing. He didn't laugh. "A mechanism intelligence? Not possible."

"By our physics. But it opened a door for us through solid rock. And let me know it had. And there's air in here."

Hamilton put his own hand on the object, realised his sensors weren't up to competing with that dress, and took it away in frustration. "All right. But this is beside the point."

"The point being—"

"This thing will tip the balance. You can't be the only one who's intuited it's here. Whoever gets it gains a decisive advantage. It'll be the end of the Great Game—"

"The start of a genuine war for the world, one not fought by proxies like you and me. All the great nations give lip service to the idea of the balance, but—"

"So how much are you going to ask? Couple of Italian dukedoms?"

"Not this time. You asked why I used the Russians to get me here." She reached into the gown. She produced another explosive device. A much larger one. "Because they're the empire I detest the most."

Hamilton licked his lips quickly.

"I don't think mere rocks can hold this being. I was called here because it got caught in . . . this mortal coil. It has to be freed. For its own sake, and for the sake of the balance."

Hamilton looked at the object again. Either of them could pull their gun and put down the other one in a moment. He wondered if he was talking to a zealot, a madwoman. He had pretty vague ideas about God and his pathway through the field, and the line that connected his holy ground to the valley of death. He'd never interrogated those ideas. And he wasn't about to start now.

But here were answers! Answers those better than him would delight in. That could protect the good people of his empire better than he could!

There was a noise from outside. They'd started digging.

Drewe met his gaze once more.

"You say it can be reasoned with. . . . "

"Not to get itself out of here. That's not what it wants."

Hamilton looked around the chamber, once and conclusively, with every sense at his disposal. No way out.

"You have to decide."

Hamilton reached into the hidden depths of his heart once more. He produced his own explosives. "No, I don't," he said. "Thank God."

Drewe had an exit strategy of her own. She had a launcher waiting, she said, lying under fractal covers in the broken territory of a landslide, two miles east of the Russian encampment.

It was again like walking through a door. As soon as they had both set the timers on their explosives to commit, in that otherwise inescapable room, an act of faith as great as any Hamilton had experienced—

The room turned inside out, and they took that simple step, and found themselves on the surface again.

Hamilton gasped as the air went. His wounds caught up with him at once. He fell.

Drewe looked down at him.

Hamilton looked back up at her. There was auburn hair under the green.

She pulled her gun while his hand was still sailing slowly towards his chest. "I think God is done with you," she said. "We'll make a balance."

"Oh we must," said Hamilton, letting his accent slip into the Irish once more. He was counting in his head, doing the mathematics. And suddenly he had a feeling that he hadn't been the only one. "But your calculations are out."

The amusement in his voice made her hesitate. "How so?"

"By about . . . point-two percent."

The force of the explosion took Drewe, and she was falling sideways.

Hamilton rolled, got his feet on the ground.

A wall of dust and debris filled the canyon ahead of them—

And then was on them, racing over them, folding them into the surface until they were just two thin streaks of history, their mortal remains at the end of comet trails.

There was silence.

Hamilton burst out of his grave, and stumbled for where the launcher lay, bright in the dust, its covers burst from it.

He didn't look back. He limped with faith and no consideration. With an explosion that size there would be nothing left of the encampment. His mission had not succeeded. But he felt his own balance was intact.

He hit a codebreaker release code on his palm onto the craft's fuselage, and struggled into the cockpit. He was aware of his own silhouette against the dying light.

He looked back now. There she was. Only now staggering to her feet.

In this second and only this second, he could draw and shoot her down and with a little adjustment of leaks and revelations his mission would be done.

He thought about the grace that had been afforded him.

He hit the emergency toggle, the cockpit sealed, and he was slammed back in his seat as the launcher sailed up into the Martian sky.

He thought of a half pint of beer. And then let himself be taken into darkness again.

SILENT AS DUST

JAMES MAXEY

—◆—

The Company I Keep. I'm judging a talent show in the attic of Seven Chimneys. The theatre is a maze of cardboard boxes, gray with grime. The moonlight through the round window serves as our spotlight.

First up is Dan, a deer head with five-point antlers and a startled look in his glass eyes. Dan sings "Jailhouse Rock" as if it were a blue grass ballad, accompanied by Binky, a sock monkey with a quilted banjo.

Next comes Professor Wink, a 65-year-old teddy bear with one eye and half his original fur. Professor Wink is a juggler, keeping aloft a crochet mallet, a broken lava lamp, and the ceramic manger from the Christmas decorations. When all three items are in the air, he grabs an old bowling ball and tosses it into the mix with a cool grace that earns him points.

The last act is Tulip. She's a baby doll with no left leg. Her act is to climb high into the lofty rafters of this old Victorian attic, then leap. She unpins the threadbare dishtowel someone diapered her with long ago and flips it into a parachute. She drifts toward the floor, reciting the Gettysburg Address. For her finale she lets go, and plummets to a safe landing in a white plastic bucket.

Tulip is an unusually talented baby. Also, alas, a noisy one. She lands with a loud clatter.

I hold my breath.

Darcy's voice from the room below: "Don't tell me you didn't hear that."

"Ish muffin," Eric mumbles, sounding as if he were on the verge of sleep. The mattress creaks. Then he says, "It's an old house. It has noises."

"Something's moving in the attic," Darcy says.

"Maybe," Eric concedes. "Don't worry about it."

"What if it's a raccoon?" she asks. "They carry rabies."

The light flips on beneath me. Thin pencils of light shoot up through cracks in the corners of their ceiling. I creep across the rafters, light as a breath, placing my weight with practiced precision on joists I know will not creak. I hear Eric and Darcy in the hallway, near the pull-down stairs. I reach the main chimney and slither behind it, into the shaft that leads to the basement.

The springs twang as the attic steps are lowered. Light chases me as I drop into the passage and wedge myself against the bricks. I go corpse quiet. I've taught myself not to cough, fart, belch, gurgle, or sneeze. My breathing is soft and silent as cotton gauze.

Eric has clicked on the single light bulb, with its dangling chain. The bulb is coated in cobwebs; a burning smell wafts across the attic. I'm upside down in the shaft, behind five feet of brick. The yoga practice pays off. I don't feel strained. I'm free to follow the conversation as Eric pokes around the attic, griping to Darcy, still in the hall. A bright beam flickers around the top of the shaft. He's got a flashlight to supplement the bulb. If he looks in the hole behind the chimney, my presence will be difficult to explain. As he draws closer I see the ancient red brick surrounding me. I normally make this journey in utter darkness.

"This is stupid," he says, mere feet above me. On the surface, he's talking about the search. But I hear the subtext in his voice. For two weeks they've been arguing about having a baby. Darcy's ready, Eric isn't. Every conversation now is colored by this central disagreement.

"Keep looking, please," she says. My sensitive ears place her at the foot of the stairs.

"What if I find something?" Eric grumbles. The light diminishes as he turns away. "Suppose there *is* a raccoon up here. Then what?"

"Stomp on it," she says, half-joking, I think.

"It's not a spider," he says, exasperated. He's moving around, nudging boxes with his feet. "It's not anything. I stand by my original opinion. It's the house. It's old. It creaks."

"I know what I heard," she says. "It wasn't the house."

"Maybe it's one of the ghosts," Eric says, moving closer to the chimney again. "I don't recall anyone dying in the attic, but it's easy to lose track."

Suddenly, there's enough light in the shaft I can see my shadow spilling down the long wall before me. This is it. "Oh my God!" he shouts, as the light jerks away. "You won't believe what I just found!"

"What?" Darcy asks, sounding scared.

"My old sock monkey! Mr. Bojangles!"

Oh, right. The monkey *was* named Bojangles. Where did I get Binky from?

"I'm coming down. An army of raccoons could hide up here. We'll call an exterminator tomorrow. Have him put out traps, if it makes you feel better."

"Okay," says Darcy.

The light clicks off.

My breath slides out of me in a long, gentle release. I loosen my grip on the brick and slink my way back down the shaft toward the cellar. I'm tempted to go back to the attic. That stupid Tulip and her noisy landing almost got me caught. I'd like to pull out her other leg. Fortunately, there's still a sane person sharing my brain that knows, deep down, I was the one who threw Tulip into the bucket. I was having one of my spells again. From time to time, boredom puts me in tight spots.

My name is Steven Cooper. I'm a Seven Chimneys' ghost. I've haunted the place for three years.

If haunted is the right word. Since, you know . . . I'm not *technically* dead.

Could Have Been a Tour Guide. It can get confusing talking about Seven Chimneys. There's the town of Seven Chimneys, a little speck on the map an hour's drive outside Charlotte. The town has barely two thousand people, most living in mobile homes or old millhouses. In contrast to the modest surroundings, the core of Seven Chimneys is a picturesque village that reached its prime a century ago, with a main street dominated by a dozen Victorian mansions restored to top condition by wealthy Charlotte refugees looking for the laid-back, small town life.

The grandest of these mansions is Seven Chimneys, the house. Thirteen-thousand square feet of towers, wraparound porches, and decorative woodwork. Seven Chimneys isn't a true Victorian home, since the building started shortly after the Revolutionary War. Three brothers, the Corbens, released from George Washington's army, traveled to the then-nameless town and built homes close together on a single acre lot. The Corbens prospered, churning out doctors and lawyers and inventors over the coming decades. The three homesites began to sprawl as slave quarters were built, kitchens added on, and, eventually, the houses merged together into a single Frankenstein's monster mansion with seven chimneys . . . thus, the name.

Sometime before World War I, Franklin Corben, the railroad king, prettied up the place with a Victorian facade and extensive remodeling on the interior, adding electricity, plumbing, etc. Parts of the house in poor repair were walled off.

The hidden rooms, the dead spaces, became useful during prohibition. Behind a secret panel in the library, there's a room with a well-stocked bar and a slate pool table that I don't think Eric knows about. He does, however, know about the wine cellar that had its entrance bricked over, with only a hidden trap door inside a pantry to give access. He was the first person to show me the coal chute at the rear of the house that leads to a furnace, and behind the furnace the narrow tunnel that leads to a room with a bathtub in which actual bathtub gin was fermented. The place is covered in dust and spider webs now, forgotten by history. But not by me.

A Close Call. I'm down in the root cellar doing yoga with Professor Wink. I'm naked; I haven't worn clothes in two years. My pants got snagged once in the chimney and I was stuck for two days. Up above, I can hear a bustle of activity. Eric is kind enough to let the locals hold weddings at Seven Chimneys. The floor boards thud and bump with their movements. It makes it hard for me to stay tuned into Eric and Darcy's conversation. They're talking about getting a puppy. Although, of course, the puppy conversation is only a substitute for the whole baby thing.

I've warmed up with the Cobbler's pose. Now I bend into the once impossible Camel pose as if I'm made of rubber. Professor Wink, even boneless, can't hold this pose.

"It's not like we're here most of the time," Eric argues. "A puppy needs attention. It needs time that we don't have."

"We can make time," Darcy says. "There's more to life than work. A dog will keep us focused on what's important."

Eric counters with, "Maybe after my schedule changes, but that's no time soon. Look, the world will still be full of puppies a year from now. Let's think about it then."

Someone heavy walks overhead and I miss Darcy's response.

The artfully named "Half Lord of the Fishes" pose has me twisting my torso around to the point I can see my bony, callused butt. It's hard to believe I learned everything I know about yoga from a picture book I swiped from the library.

After a few minutes I realize I've completely lost Eric and Darcy's voices. I'll have to wait to find out if they've decided anything.

I finish my routine in the so-called Corpse pose, flat as a flounder, every muscle in my body in a state of utter release. Professor Wink is good at this one.

Then I realize someone else is here. I look toward the stairs and find a little girl standing there, staring. She's wearing a white, frilly dress; she looks like a flower girl. She's quiet, quieter than me.

We stare at each other for an uncomfortably long time. I'm anticipating her scream. Any second, adults will rush down the steps.

Then, to my great relief, she silently turns and walks up the steps, vanishing back into the shadows. Probably, she'll tell people about the naked yoga ghost in the cellar. I'll be part of the folklore. It's a living.

How I Use The Bathroom. I'm not always hiding in the attic or under floorboards. Thirteen-thousand square feet, occupied by two people, means a lot of the house never gets looked at on a daily basis. Eric and Darcy have three housekeepers and a crew of landscapers, but none live onsite. Eric's an ER surgeon; he works insane shifts at Charlotte General. Darcy's a corporate acquisitions attorney and is out of town half the time. If they did get a puppy, they'd probably hire someone to watch after it.

Once the cleaning crew finishes their daily duties, I'm free to climb up from the cellar and roam around the main part of the house. I use the bathroom in the small toilet near the library. Since it's Tuesday, I shower. I stopped shaving when I moved in. Now, a pale, wild-haired man stares back at me from the mirror. I'm thin as Ghandi. My body has become a grand collection of calluses. It's a yogi's body, the body of a holy man, limber and tough and purposeful.

They've Never Noticed My Gleaning. I'm not hungry tonight, but I eat anyway. Eric and Darcy's refrigerator sports an assortment of half-eaten Chinese takeout.

After my meal, I creep into the library. My senses expand to cover all of Seven Chimneys. I'm tuned to Darcy's breathing as she sleeps in the master bedroom on the third floor. Eric didn't come home tonight; on his busier days, he sleeps at the hospital. I worry Eric is putting his career ahead of his marriage. Darcy deserves better. I read in the library until the predawn hours. When Darcy's breathing shifts the slight way it does every morning before her alarm goes off, I carefully reshelve the books. I tiptoe to the kitchen, slip through the hidden passage in the pantry, then wiggle through the narrow gaps in the floor joists that lead to the main cellar, and the base of the big chimney.

Exactly the way I remember doing as a child.

Eric and I Go Way Back. I've been listening to Darcy and Eric argue about the damn puppy again. As usual, Eric prevails. Eric always prevails. The world has bent to his will since we were kids.

Eric and I have a bond that dates back over twenty years. Eric Corben was born to the wealth and privilege that accompanies his family name. I was born in a crumbling shotgun shack. Eric's father was an attorney and mayor of Seven Chimneys, the town, for five terms. My father was an unemployed drunk. My mother cleaned the bathrooms of Seven Chimneys, the house. I would come with her. Eric and I would play. We explored all the spooky corridors of Seven Chimneys. Or, so we thought. We never knew about the hidden bar. We found the shaft behind the chimney, but never had the courage to climb it.

Until we started school, Eric and I weren't really aware of the class differences between us. Alas, in kindergarten, cliques formed. Eric was part of the cool crowd, wearing new clothes and showing off the latest hot toys. I was the same age, but several inches shorter, and went to school wearing Eric's hand-me-downs. We would have grown apart if not for a tragic coincidence. When we were both eight, Eric's mother and my father died in separate car crashes. We didn't really talk about this shared bond. But, from then on, we had each other's back.

In fairness, Eric had my back more than I had his. He'd make sure I wasn't the last kid picked for the kickball team. He let the school bullies know I was off limits. I returned the favor in high school by letting him cheat off tests and writing papers for him. Eric wasn't a dummy, by any means. If anything, public school bored him. By sixth grade, he was already weighing his college choices. He let me write his report on *Huckleberry Finn* because his attention was focused on James Joyce's *Ulysses*.

Eventually, college separated us. Eric went off to Harvard. I stayed home and attended Corben Community College. He graduated and went to medical school. I graduated and landed a job as assistant manager at a convenience store. I still had hopes and dreams . . . until Mom came down with breast cancer. I stayed home to care for her. Mom fought cancer for six years.

In a second coincidence, Eric's father had a heart attack while attending Eric's graduation from medical school. He turned blue and died surrounded by five hundred doctors. On the same day, my mother passed away in ICU, after three weeks of unconsciousness. I was holding her hand as she passed.

I went to Eric's father's funeral. He came to Mom's. I met Darcy for the first time. I learned that Eric had just accepted the position in Charlotte; he'd been planning on buying a condo, but now he and Darcy had decided it made more sense to move to Seven Chimneys and commute.

After the funerals, Eric went home to Seven Chimneys, now the richest man in the county. I went back to the 1960s era silver Jetstream trailer I'd been renting after the bank foreclosed on Mom's place. I was three months behind on rent. When I pulled into the driveway, I saw the padlock. My landlord had taken the opportunity of my mother's funeral to lock me out.

My Art Museum Breathes. In the middle of the night, I tiptoe into the master bedroom. I like to look at Darcy while she sleeps. That sounds creepy but I'm not a pervert. What I am is a man with a decent mind who never escaped the shackles of poverty. I've never traveled to Italy for a summer, like Eric has. I've never been to Paris, where they honeymooned. All I know of the great art of the world I know from books, and from the Corben art collection, which boasts a Renoir, three Wyeths, and a Rembrandt.

None are as lovely as Darcy. She's art, given breath. My time spent at her bedside, staring at her face, is the closest I will ever get to the Louvre. Her eyes are moving beneath her eyelids. She's dreaming. Of Eric, I wonder? Or puppies? Or ghosts?

Her breathing stills and her eyelids flutter. She turns in her sleep. Catlike, silent, I slink to the doorway as her eyes open. I'm halfway down the hallway before she can possibly focus. I don't know how the rest of the world can be satisfied by art that doesn't have the possibility of looking back.

Ordinarily I Like Dogs. Friday, Darcy brought home a puppy. For the last seventy hours, the dog has barked. If I'm in the attic, he barks at the ceiling. If I'm in the cellar, he barks at the floorboards. He pauses from time to time to eat or nap, but even in his sleep, he growls. Eric and Darcy are practically in tears, not knowing what to do about their insane little dog.

On Monday, Darcy skipped work to take Yippy to the vet. She tells Eric that the puppy didn't make a peep at the vet's office. The second he's returned to Seven Chimney's, he's back at the main chimney, barking, staring, as if there's some unseen stranger lurking behind the wall.

Maybe I should shower more often.

The first few days, I hoped the dog would get used to me. Now, I don't think he will.

"I told you a puppy was a bad idea," Eric says.

"You always have to be right, don't you?" Darcy snaps. I hear in her voice the beginning of the end. It would break my heart if they got divorced because of this.

On Tuesday, they both leave for work. The housekeepers go out to lunch with the ground crew. I'm alone with the puppy.

I feel bad about what I did to shut Yippy up. He had such sad eyes. Professor Wink tries to console me with the idea that maybe I saved Eric's marriage. But maybe I haven't. I don't have a track record of getting things right.

My Life as an Action Movie. I was drunk on vodka. I was driving in the mountains in my 1982 Dodge Omni, taking curves at sixty miles an hour in a driving rain. I was coming up on the White River Gorge. I wasn't wearing my seat belt. This was three years ago.

My Omni went through the guardrail. I went through the windshield.

For a long moment I hung in the air, weightless. The rain-slick hood of my car floated before me, close enough to touch. Slowly, our arcs diverged. The car dropped toward the swollen river a hundred feet below. I fell toward the tip of a tall pine, twenty feet down. I imagined I might impale myself on the tree. Instead, I tangled in the upper branches and the whole tree bowed, carrying me at decreasing speed another thirty feet until the trunk snapped, dropping me into a thick cluster of branches in a neighboring pine. I slid across the soggy needles, falling into the limbs of yet a third tree. I dropped in a painful series of snags and snaps, until I landed, crotch first, on a long bough that sagged beneath my weight, lowering me gently to the moss softened rocks by the riverside.

I stood there, stunned, as I watched the twisted scrap metal of the Omni vanish into the floodwaters. I was bleeding from a hundred scratches. My clothes were little more than tatters.

I leaned against a tree trunk, going limp, slipping down until I was flat against the soggy earth. I think I was crying; quite possibly I was laughing. As best I can remember, I said then, of my attempted suicide, "Son of a bitch. I can't do anything right." Maybe I'm imagining that. It seems suspiciously cool-headed, in retrospect.

Darcy's Pregnant. It's a chilly March morning when I hear Darcy break the news on the phone to her mother. I do the math; the last time they made love was on February second. Probably they fooled around on Valentine's Day, but they flew to Bermuda that weekend, so I can't be sure. There's a chance this baby will be born on Halloween. I wonder if they'll open the house for the ghost tour this year.

I don't know if Eric will be a good father. He's not the best husband. Yes, he's caring, and Lord knows he's rich, and movie star handsome. But, he's never around. He only thinks of his career. He's not the sort of person who would give up six years of his life to care for his dying mother. I wonder if he'll tell Darcy to have an abortion.

Ghost Stories. There's a picture of me in the paper. I've been careless again. I was in the attic Saturday, looking out the window, watching the tourists who invade the town for the Apple Festival on Main Street. Lots of people take pictures of Seven Chimneys. I forgot to duck.

I'm clearly visible in the window. You can make out my long hair and beard, and my sunken, skeletal eyes. If you stare at the picture long enough, it's easy to reinterpret my face as the reflection of clouds on wavy glass.

The paper recounts the civil war legend of Crispus Matherton, a union soldier who'd been left for dead on the battlefield, only to stagger into town days later, disoriented, his wounds riddled with maggots. The sheriff was going to jail him, until Anne Corben intervened. Anne took the stranger home, saying even a Yankee shouldn't suffer so grievously. She bathed his wounds, dressed him in fresh linen, and fed him a hearty meal of red beans and cornbread.

That night, she smothered him with a pillow. Her husband, Colonel Randolf

Corben, had been decapitated by a Yankee shell at Petersburg six months earlier.

A half dozen other ghosts keep Matherton company. Franklin Corben, the railroad guy, choked on a cocktail olive. He's been spotted by firelight in the library, reading the first edition of *Leaves of Grass* normally on display in the glass case. Sometimes, the book is missing from the case, and found on the coffee table beside the leather couch. I admit, I've moved the book a time or two, pausing to study the priceless words.

I give you fair warning before you attempt me further,
I am not what you supposed, but far different.

Sometimes, in the gravelike silence of the predawn house, I wonder: Perhaps I *am* Franklin Corben, and my whole life is some odd afterlife fantasy. Perhaps I am also Alicia Corben, the six-year-old girl who was raped and strangled in the cellar. Or maybe I'm Anthony Adams, the convict who swore revenge against Judge Harlan Corben and was blamed for Alicia's death. Adams supposedly wanders the grounds looking for his head after he was lynched by an angry mob. They dropped him too far. He dangled only a few minutes before his head came off.

There's also the possibility that I'm old Cyrus Washington, the slave who saved Anne Corben from the fire that destroyed the kitchen. He was rewarded with his freedom, but never moved away. He lived in the main house in a private room for decades until he died of carbon-monoxide poisoning from a malfunctioning gas lamp. They say he was a hundred and twelve. Supposedly, his ghost dialed the fire department in 1987 when the wiring in the back bedroom went kablooey and set the wallpaper on fire.

John Arthur Corben drowned at Pearl Harbor. His spirit found its way home when his medals were sent back to his mother. He was a gifted piano player, and sometimes, in the quiet of the night, the soft strains of Mozart are faintly heard from the grand piano. Perhaps I'm him.

Or perhaps I'm Steven Cooper, a man whose life made no impact at all upon the world. A man forgotten, unworthy of ghostly legend, a man who did nothing of significance with the breaths of air he drew. A man who lives like dust under the floor of another man's life.

A Long Walk in a Cold Rain. When I walked back to town the night I drove off the bridge, I felt invisible. The fire truck and a dozen police cars raced past me. You might have thought that they would ask the bleeding man in torn clothing what he knew about the accident. In their defense, the night was dark. After the rain stopped, the clouds hid the moon and stars. The responsible thing to do would have been to call someone and tell them not to waste time dragging the river.

I never made the phone call. Instead I walked to Seven Chimneys and pounded on the front door at five in the morning. Eric wasn't home. He'd gone to Boston to take care of some business, though I didn't know that at the time. I was soaked. I was turning blue from the bruises. I felt dreamy and numb;

busting through the windshield had left the whole world with a gentle clockwise spin. When I closed my eyes, I felt weightless.

I crawled into the cellar through the window that doesn't latch. I found some Tylenol in a guest bathroom, and went to sleep on a bed stuffed with goose feathers, snuggled beneath two musty old quilts. I slept for what seemed like days.

I'd been living in Eric's house for two weeks when he and Darcy moved in permanently. I thought about revealing myself, telling my story, but, at the time, it struck me as a fairly pathetic tale. What's more, I knew Eric would say something wise and caring, something perfect, the way he always does. I worried that Darcy, who I'd only met at the funerals, would look at me with pitying eyes and wonder how her new husband had managed to befriend such a loser. So, I didn't find the courage to come out of my hiding place in the cellar that first day. Or the first week. By the time I'd been living side by side with them for a month, unseen, unheard, unsuspected, revealing my presence would have been awkward.

My Days Are Numbered. Of course, Eric reacts to Darcy's pregnancy perfectly. He's thrilled, you can hear it in his voice. Any doubts he might have had are gone. A white spike of jealously pins me to the attic floor. Eric lives a charmed life. He's not a parasite living off the crumbs of his childhood friend. He's married, building a career, and now he's going to pass on his genes to a new generation, fulfilling his highest biological purpose. The great wheel of life turns, and he's riding that wheel. I'm somewhere beneath the tread, crushed out of existence.

Only, I do exist. I have a life, of sorts. And that life is going to get complicated. Darcy's decided to leave her job. She's going to do consulting work from home. Her mother is coming down to help when she's further along. The house is never going to be empty. Darcy's always the one who hears me when I slip up. If her mother is half as sensitive, I'll never be able to relax.

They sound so happy down below. I hug Professor Wink, needing the company. I look into his dark, wise eye and silently ask where my life went wrong. *Oh, right.* The cancer mom and the deadbeat dad. The vodka and the White River Gorge. The fact I make a better ghost than person.

Suddenly, Professor Wink gets a gleam in his eye. He's thought of a fiendish plan.

The Fiendish Plan. The key, of course, is to make Seven Chimneys more haunted. Gamble that Darcy won't raise her child in a gateway for spooks.

I leave the Whitman book on the table almost every night. They put a new lock on the case. It takes me three nights to pick it. I have time on my hands. For good measure, I occasionally build a roaring fire in the fireplace. I leave a half-finished martini on the coffee table.

There's an ancient Victrola in the attic, and a cobwebbed collection of warped records. The Victrola doesn't work. I take it apart. I fix a broken gear with crazy glue and a paper clip. At four in the morning, on the night of July Fourth, Eric and Darcy are awakened to the warbling strains of Mozart. They come upstairs to find John Arthur Corben's army uniform unfolded beside the Victrola. I've soaked the uniform in salt water for three days. It smells like the sea.

Alicia Corben's room has barely been opened in seventy years. I normally steer clear of the place. There's an air of melancholy that hangs over the ceramic dolls lined neatly on the shelf above the small bed. When I enter the room, I catch a glimpse in the mirror. In the dim light, through the fog of dust, the whole room looks ghostly, me most of all. I'm only thirty, but my blonde hair looks colorless and gray. The face that peeks from behind my whiskers is gaunt. My body is more skeleton than muscles; my skin sags on my bones. I'm guessing I've lost fifty pounds, and I wasn't fat before.

I shake off the reflection and search Alicia's closet for a dress. I find the perfect one, all frills and pink ribbons, the color bleached with age. It's September; they've designated the room beside theirs as the baby's room. They already have a crib set up.

I leave the dress in the crib.

One of the maids finds it the next morning. Her scream is so loud, I scan the newspaper the next day for reports of earthquakes and tsunamis.

Cooler Minds Prevail. In my cleverness, I overlooked the possibility of third party interference. It's mid-October. By now, I had hoped Eric and Darcy would be long gone, moved to a new McMansion nearer to the hospital, a place fresh built and free of ghosts. It is not to be.

Eric is blasé about the whole affair. He's grown up with the ghosts and the legends; he's heard creaks that sound like footsteps, the wind playing in the chimneys that sound like human whispers. He admits to Darcy, yes, he thinks the house *is* haunted. It's been haunted for generations, and the ghosts haven't hurt a soul, and have actually been useful, assuming Cyrus Washington really did call the fire department. Eric thinks it's kind of cool. I hate him.

Darcy's mother, Marsha, has arrived in time to take the opposite approach. She's a devout atheist; it's an article of faith that the house is ghostless. What the house isn't, she argues, is secure. The slapped together architecture of Seven Chimney's makes the alarm system installed in the seventies a joke. Marsha doesn't believe in ghosts; she does believe in pranksters. She thinks local kids are finding a way into the house and pulling these stunts. She's persuasive. Even I start thinking she might be right.

Marsha proposes a simple, obvious idea. Put security cameras throughout the house.

I am so screwed.

Fortunately, one of the maids claims to have a psychic aunt. The maid's name is Rosa; her aunt is the oddly named Tia Tomato. At least I think she said Tomato. Her accent is hard to follow. Rosa tells Marsha that sometimes the dead have unfinished business. Sometimes they don't even know they are dead, and linger on, confused and lost, growing increasingly warped and frustrated. For a reasonable fee, she'll bring Tia Tomato around to try to explain the situation to the ghost and/or ghosts.

Marsha fires her on the spot. All my months of hard work, down the drain, because now even Darcy is convinced that Rosa was staging the haunting in a scheme to shake them down for money. I'm pissed at Rosa, though I know she should be pissed with me. I have to remind myself Rosa really wasn't guilty of anything; she's out of a job due to my mischief.

In the aftermath, I lay low. I want the talk of installing video cameras put on the back burner. Darcy goes into labor a few weeks later. She's whisked off to Charlotte. I have the house to myself. I take a long, hot shower. For the first time in years, I shave. I cut my hair, cropping it short to the scalp. I gather up all my trimmings in a plastic grocery bag. There's a lot of me to throw away.

In the mirror, I see the man I used to be. Do I see the man I might be again?

Crib Death. The baby's been home for two weeks. It cries a lot; it's almost as bad as the puppy. I get some relief when they take it out to the car and drive around the neighborhood. Apparently, the baby sleeps like a baby when they drive.

In fairness, it dozes off at other times as well. Starting at two in the morning, the baby can reliably be counted on to slumber for at least a few hours. During this time, Eric, Darcy, and Marsha sleep like corpses.

It's three in the morning on a Saturday. I'm at the foot of the crib, staring at the infant. They've named him Franklin. Franky, he'll be called. If he's anything like Eric, by the time he's six, he's going to explore every inch of this house. He's going to take a flashlight and poke around the cellars. He'll spend hours in the attic, clawing through two centuries of clutter. He'll play with Tulip and Professor Wink and Bojangles.

I'm afraid of Franky.

Kids know all the best hiding places. Kids imagine their house is full of hidden panels and trap doors and secret passages—and this particular kid will be right. One day, he's going to find me.

Approximately one baby in a thousand dies from Sudden Infant Death Syndrome. They pass away quietly in their sleep for no reason at all. This is today, with modern medicine. Think about this house, dating back to Colonial times, when babies had the mortality rate of goldfish. I don't know of actual numbers, but I'm guessing a dozen babies have died in Seven Chimneys. A hundred, maybe.

It's a dark thing to stand beside a crib contemplating a hundred dead babies.

I reach out my hand, holding it inches over Franky's pink little face.

I linger a moment, my hand unable to move closer, as if an invisible hand has caught my wrist and holds it with supernatural strength.

I can't swallow. My mouth is dry.

I can't do it. A puppy is one thing. If I do this, though, I'll cross a line. I'll no longer be a ghost.

I'll be a monster.

I release my breath, silent as dust.

Franky really is a cute baby.

No longer blocked by the moral barrier, I lower my hand to stroke his pink, plump cheek.

Again, my fingers stop short. It's not my imagination. Something is holding my wrist.

"I'm not going to hurt him," I mumble, saying it half to myself, half to the unseen thing gripping my arm.

I watch as dust swirls in the dim moonlight, and a second shadow appears on the wall beside my own. Bony old fingers the color of coffee materialize on my wrist. My eyes follow the arm upward, to find a skeletal old man, his face dark beneath a halo of white hair. His expression is stern; his eyes are thin slits.

"Cyrus?" I ask.

He says nothing.

"I won't hurt him," I say.

Then, a third shadow, and a fourth. A soldier stands beside me, gray and grainy as old film. He's soaked. Water pours from his clothes, chilling my bare feet.

Beside the soldier, a little girl with sad eyes shakes her head slowly. She looks familiar; was she the girl in the cellar? She's little more than mist; I can see right through her to the mirror on the back of the door.

Then I realize I'm seeing only a sweater over a chair in the mirror; in the moonlight, it drapes like a girl's dress. My feet are cold—it's an October night in a house with hardwoods like ice—but they are dry. The soldier was nothing more than the shadow of a tree.

And Cyrus? Cyrus is still standing there, now solid oak, and he whispers, in a voice of rustling leaves: "We're watching you, boy."

He vanishes as the headlights of a passing car sweep across the room.

I rub my wrist. My whole arm is numb. I decide that Franklin's chubby little cheeks are best left uncaressed.

After a quick trip to the attic, I go to the laundry room and steal some clothes. Eric's jeans invoke a certain sense of deja vu; it's not the first time I've worn his used pants. His old tennis shoes are too big for me; I compensate with two pairs of socks.

Then, I'm out the door, into the open sky. Leaves crunch beneath my feet as I walk across the lawn. On the front porch, a line of Jack-o-lantern's grin, a few still faintly glowing with the last flickers of their candles. I reach the end of the sidewalk and glance back one last time at Seven Chimneys, before crossing the road and taking my return step into the wider world.

Beneath my arm, I cradle Professor Wink.

I can tell he's going to miss the place.

Me, not so much. Even with thirteen-thousand square feet, some places are just too crowded.

EVIL ROBOT MONKEY

MARY ROBINETTE KOWAL

Sliding his hands over the clay, Sly relished the moisture oozing around his fingers. The clay matted down the hair on the back of his hands making them look almost human. He turned the potter's wheel with his prehensile feet as he shaped the vase. Pinching the clay between his fingers he lifted the wall of the vase, spinning it higher.

Someone banged on the window of his pen. Sly jumped and then screamed as the vase collapsed under its own weight. He spun and hurled it at the picture window like feces. The clay spattered against the Plexiglas, sliding down the window.

In the courtyard beyond the glass, a group of school kids leapt back, laughing. One of them swung his arms aping Sly crudely. Sly bared his teeth, knowing these people would take it as a grin, but he meant it as a threat. Swinging down from his stool, he crossed his room in three long strides and pressed his dirty hand against the window. Still grinning, he wrote SSA. Outside, the letters would be reversed.

The student's teacher flushed as red as a female in heat and called the children away from the window. She looked back once as she led them out of the courtyard, so Sly grabbed himself and showed her what he would do if she came into his pen.

Her naked face turned brighter red and she hurried away. When they were gone, Sly rested his head against the glass. The metal in his skull thunked against the window. It wouldn't be long now, before a handler came to talk to him.

Damn.

He just wanted to make pottery. He loped back to the wheel and sat down again with his back to the window. Kicking the wheel into movement, Sly dropped a new ball of clay in the center and tried to lose himself.

In the corner of his vision, the door to his room snicked open. Sly let the wheel spin to a halt, crumpling the latest vase.

Vern poked his head through. He signed, "You okay?"

Sly shook his head emphatically and pointed at the window.

"Sorry." Vern's hands danced. "We should have warned you that they were coming."

"You should have told them that I was not an animal."

Vern looked down in submission. "I did. They're kids."

"And I'm a chimp. I know." Sly buried his fingers in the clay to silence his thoughts.

"It was Delilah. She thought you wouldn't mind because the other chimps didn't."

Sly scowled and yanked his hands free. "I'm not like the other chimps." He pointed to the implant in his head. "Maybe Delilah should have one of these. Seems like she needs help thinking."

"I'm sorry." Vern knelt in front of Sly, closer than anyone else would come when he wasn't sedated. It would be so easy to reach out and snap his neck. "It was a lousy thing to do."

Sly pushed the clay around on the wheel. Vern was better than the others. He seemed to understand the hellish limbo where Sly lived–too smart to be with other chimps, but too much of an animal to be with humans. Vern was the one who had brought Sly the potter's wheel which, by the Earth and Trees, Sly loved. Sly looked up and raised his eyebrows. "So what did they think of my show?"

Vern covered his mouth, masking his smile. The man had manners. "The teacher was upset about the 'evil robot monkey.' "

Sly threw his head back and hooted. Served her right.

"But Delilah thinks you should be disciplined." Vern, still so close that Sly could reach out and break him, stayed very still. "She wants me to take the clay away since you used it for an anger display."

Sly's lips drew back in a grimace built of anger and fear. Rage threatened to blind him, but he held on, clutching the wheel. If he lost it with Vern–rational thought danced out of his reach. Panting, he spun the wheel trying to push his anger into the clay.

The wheel spun. Clay slid between his fingers. Soft. Firm and smooth. The smell of earth lived in his nostrils. He held the world in his hands. Turning, turning, the walls rose around a kernel of anger, subsuming it.

His heart slowed with the wheel and Sly blinked, becoming aware again as if he were slipping out of sleep. The vase on the wheel still seemed to dance with life. Its walls held the shape of the world within them. He passed a finger across the rim.

Vern's eyes were moist. "Do you want me to put that in the kiln for you?"

Sly nodded.

"I have to take the clay. You understand that, don't you?"

Sly nodded again staring at his vase. It was beautiful.

Vern scowled. "The woman makes me want to hurl feces."

Sly snorted at the image, then sobered. "How long before I get it back?"

Vern picked up the bucket of clay next to the wheel. "I don't know." He stopped at the door and looked past Sly to the window. "I'm not cleaning your mess. Do you understand me?"

For a moment, rage crawled on his spine, but Vern did not meet his eyes and kept staring at the window. Sly turned.

The vase he had thrown lay on the floor in a pile of clay.

Clay.

"I understand." He waited until the door closed, then loped over and scooped the clay up. It was not much, but it was enough for now.

Sly sat down at his wheel and began to turn.

IF ANGELS FIGHT

RICHARD BOWES

1.

Outside the window, the blue water of the Atlantic danced in the sunlight of an early morning in October. They're short, quiet trains, the ones that roll through Connecticut just after dawn. I sipped bad tea, dozed off occasionally and awoke with a start.

Over the last forty years, I've ridden the northbound train from New York to Boston hundreds of times. I've done it alone, with friends and lovers, going home for the holidays, setting out on vacations, on my way to funerals.

That morning, I was with one who was once in some ways my best friend and certainly my oldest. Though we had rarely met in decades, it seemed that a connection endured. Our mission was vital and we rode the train by default: a terrorist threat had closed traffic at Logan Airport in Boston the night before.

I'd left messages canceling an appointment, letting the guy I was going out with know I'd be out of town briefly for a family crisis. No need to say it was another, more fascinating, family disrupting my life, not mine.

The old friend caught my discomfort at what we were doing and was amused.

A bit of Shakespeare occurred to me when I thought of him:
Not all the water in the rough rude sea
Can wash the balm off from an anointed king

He was quiet for a while after hearing those lines. It was getting toward twenty-four hours since I'd slept. I must have dozed because suddenly I was in a dark place with two tiny slits of light high above. I found hand and foot holds and crawled up the interior wall of a stone tower. As I got to the slits of light, a voice said, "New Haven. This stop New Haven."

2.

Carol Bannon had called me less than two weeks before. "I'm going to be down in New York the day after tomorrow," she said. "I wondered if we could get together." I took this to mean that she and her family wanted to get some kind of fix on the present location and current state of her eldest brother, my old friend Mark.

Over the years when this had happened it was Marie Bannon, Mark and Carol's mother, who contacted me. Those times I'd discovered channels through which she could reach her straying son. This time, I didn't make any inquiries before meeting Carol, but I did check to see if certain parties still had the same phone numbers and habits that I remembered.

Thinking about Marky Bannon, I too wondered where he was. He's always somewhere on my mind. When I see a photo of some great event, a reception, or celebrity trial, a concert or inauguration—I scan the faces wondering if he's present.

I'm retired these days, with time to spend. But over the years, keeping tabs on the Bannons was an easy minor hobby. The mother is still alive though not very active now. The father was a longtime Speaker of the Massachusetts House and a candidate for governor who died some years back. An intersection in Dorchester and an entrance to the Boston Harbor tunnel are still named for him.

Carol, the eldest daughter, got elected to the City Council at the age of twenty-eight. Fourteen years later she gave up a safe U.S. House seat to run the Commerce Department for Clinton. Later she served on the 9/11 commission and is a perennial cable TV talking head. She's married to Jerry Simone who has a stake in Google. Her brother Joe is a leading campaign consultant in D.C. Keeping up the idealistic end of things, her little sister Eileen is a member of Doctors Without Borders. My old friend Mark is the tragic secret without which no Irish family would be complete.

Carol asked me to meet her for tea uptown in the Astor Court of the St. Regis Hotel. I got there a moment after four. The Astor Court has a blinding array of starched white tablecloths and gold chandeliers under a ceiling mural of soft, floating clouds.

Maybe her choice of meeting places was intentionally campy. Or maybe because I don't drink anymore she had hit upon this as an amusing spot to bring me.

Carol and I always got along. Even aged ten and eleven I was different enough from the other boys that I was nice to my friends' little sisters.

Carol has kept her hair chestnut but allowed herself fine gray wings. Her skin and teeth are terrific. The Bannons were what was called dark Irish when we were growing up in Boston in the 1950s. That meant they weren't so white that they automatically burst into flames on their first afternoon at the beach.

They're a handsome family. The mother is still beautiful in her eighties. Marie Bannon had been on the stage a bit before she married. She had that light and charm, that ability to convince you that her smile was for you alone that led young men and old to drop everything and do her bidding.

Mike Bannon, the father, had been a union organizer before he went nights to law school, then got into politics. He had rugged good looks, blue eyes that would look right into you, and a fine smile that he could turn on and off and didn't often waste on kids.

"When the mood's upon him, he can charm a dog off a meat wagon," I remember a friend of my father's remarking. It was a time and place where politicians and race horses alike were scrutinized and handicapped.

The Bannon children had inherited the parents' looks and, in the way of politicians' kids, were socially poised. Except for Mark, who could look lost and confused one minute, oddly intense the next, with eyes suddenly just like his father's.

Carol rose to kiss me as I approached the table. It seemed kind of like a Philip Marlowe moment: I imagined myself as a private eye, tough and amused, called in by the rich dame for help in a personal matter.

When I first knew Carol Bannon, she wore pigtails and cried because her big brother wouldn't take her along when we went to the playground. Recently there's been speculation everywhere that a distinguished Massachusetts senator is about to retire before his term ends. Carol Bannon is the odds-on favorite to be appointed to succeed him.

Then, once she's in the Senate, given that it's the Democratic Party we're talking about, who's to say they won't go crazy again and run one more Bay State politician for President in the wild hope that they've got another JFK?

Carol said, "My mother asked me to remember her to you." I asked Carol to give her mother my compliments. Then we each said how good the other looked and made light talk about the choices of teas and the drop-dead faux Englishness of the place. We reminisced about Boston and the old neighborhood.

"Remember how everyone called that big overgrown vacant lot, 'Fitzie's' ?" I asked. The nickname had come from its being the site where the Fitzgerald mansion, the home of 'Honey Fitz,' the old mayor of Boston, once stood. His daughter, Rose, was mother to the Kennedy brothers.

"There was a marble floor in the middle of the trash and weeds," I said, "And everybody was sure the place was haunted.

"The whole neighborhood was haunted," she said. "There was that little old couple who lived down Melville Avenue from us. They knew my parents. He was this gossipy elf. He had held office back in the old days and everyone called him, 'The Hon Hen,' short for 'the Honorable Henry.' She was a daughter of Honey Fitz. They were aunt and uncle of the Kennedys."

Melville Avenue was and is a street where the houses are set back on lawns and the garages are converted horse barns. When we were young, doctors and prosperous lawyers lived there along with prominent saloon owners and politicians like Michael Bannon and his family.

Suddenly at our table in the Astor Court, the pots and plates, the Lapsang and scones, the marmalade, the clotted cream and salmon finger sandwiches appeared. We were silent for a little while and I thought about how politics had seemed a common occupation for kids' parents in Irish Boston. Politicians' houses tended to be big and semi-public with much coming and going and loud talk.

Life at the Bannons' was much more exciting than at my house. Mark had his own room and didn't have to share with his little brother. He had a ten-year-old's luxuries: electronic football, enough soldiers to fight Gettysburg if you didn't mind that the Confederates were mostly Indians, and not one but two electric train engines, which made wrecks a positive pleasure. Mark's eyes would come alive when the cars flew off the tracks in a rainbow of sparks.

"What are you smiling at?" Carol asked.

And I cut to the chase and said, "Your brother. I remember the way he liked to leave his room. That tree branch right outside his window: he could reach out, grab hold of it, scramble hand over hand to the trunk."

I remembered how the branches swayed and sighed and how scared I was every time I had to follow him.

"In high school," Carol said, "at night he'd sneak out when he was supposed to be in bed and scramble back inside much later. I knew and our mother, but no one else. One night the bough broke as he tried to get back in the window. He fell all the way to the ground, smashing through more branches on the way.

"My father was down in the study plotting malfeasance with Governor Furcolo. They and everyone else came out to see what had happened. We found Mark lying on the ground laughing like a lunatic. He had a fractured arm and a few scratches. Even I wondered if he'd fallen on his head."

For a moment I watched for some sign that she knew I'd been right behind her brother when he fell. I'd gotten down the tree fast and faded into the night when I saw lights come on inside the house. It had been a long, scary night and before he laughed, Mark had started to sob.

Now that we were talking about her brother, Carol was able to say, almost casually, "My mother has her good days and her bad days. But for thirty years she's hinted to me that she had a kind of contact with him. I didn't tell her that wasn't possible because it obviously meant a lot to her."

She was maintaining a safe zone, preserving her need not to know. I frowned and fiddled with a sliver of cucumber on buttered brown bread.

Carol put on a full court press, "Mom wants to see Mark again and she thinks it needs to be soon. She told me you knew people and could arrange things. It would make her so happy if you could do whatever that was again."

I too kept my distance. "I ran some errands for your mother a couple of times that seemed to satisfy her. The last time was fourteen years ago and at my age I'm not sure I can even remember what I did."

Carol gave a rueful little smile, "You were my favorite of all my brother's friends. You'd talk to me about my dollhouse. It took me years to figure out why that was. When I was nine and ten years old I used to imagine you taking me out on dates."

She reached across the table and touched my wrist. "If there's any truth to any of what Mom says, I could use Mark's help too. You follow the news.

"I'm not going to tell you the current administration wrecked the world all by themselves or that if we get back in it will be the second coming of Franklin Roosevelt and Abe Lincoln all rolled into one.

"I am telling you I think this is end game. We either pull ourselves together in the next couple of years or we become Disney World."

I didn't tell her I thought we had already pretty much reached the stage of the U.S. as theme park.

"It's not possible that Mark's alive," she said evenly. "But his family needs him. None of us inherited our father's gut instincts, his political animal side. It may be a mother's fantasy, but ours says Mark did."

I didn't wonder aloud if the one who had been Marky Bannon still existed in any manifestation we'd recognize.

Then Carol handed me a very beautiful check from a consulting firm her husband owned. I told her I'd do whatever I could. Someone had said about Carol, "She's very smart and she knows all the rules of the game. But I'm not sure the game these days has anything to do with the rules."

3.

After our little tea, I thought about the old Irish-American city of my childhood and how ridiculous it was for Carol Bannon to claim no knowledge of Mark Bannon. It reminded me of the famous Bolger brothers of South Boston.

You remember them: William Bolger was first the President of the State Senate and then the President of the University of Massachusetts. Whitey Bolger was head of the Irish mob, a murderer and an FBI informant gone bad. Whitey was on the lam for years. Bill always claimed, even under oath, that he never had any contact with his brother.

That had always seemed preposterous to me. The Bolgers' mother was alive. And a proper Irish mother will always know what each of her children is doing no matter how they hide. And she'll bombard the others with that information no matter how much they don't want to know. I couldn't imagine Mrs. Bannon not doing that.

What kept the media away from the story was that Mark had—in all the normal uses of the terms—died, been waked and memorialized some thirty-five years ago.

I remembered how in the Bannon family the father adored Carol and her sister Eileen. He was even a tiny bit in awe of little Joe who at the age of six already knew the name and political party of the governor of each state in the union. But Michael Bannon could look very tired when his eyes fell on Mark.

The ways of Irish fathers with their sons were mysterious and often distant. Mark was his mother's favorite. But he was, I heard it whispered, dull normal, a step above retarded.

I remembered the way the Bannons' big house could be full of people I didn't know and how all the phones—the Bannons were the only family I knew with more than one phone in their house—could be ringing at once.

Mike Bannon had a study on the first floor. One time when Mark and I went past, I heard him in there saying, "We got the quorum. Now who's handling the seconding speech?" We went up to Mark's room and found two guys there. One sat on the bed with a portable typewriter on his lap, pecking away. The other stood by the window and said, " . . . real estate tax that's fair for all."

"For everybody," said the guy with the typewriter, "Sounds better." Then they noticed we were there and gave us a couple of bucks to go away.

Another time, Mark and I came back from the playground to find his father out on the front porch talking to the press who stood on the front lawn. This, I think, was when he was elected Speaker of the Lower House of the Great and General Court of the Commonwealth of Massachusetts, as the state legislature was called.

It was for moments like these that Speaker Bannon had been created. He smiled and photographers' flashes went off. Then he glanced in his son's direction, the penetrating eyes dimmed, the smile faded. Remembering this, I wondered what he saw.

After it was over, when his father and the press had departed, Mark went right on staring intently at the spot where it had happened. I remember thinking that he looked kind of like his father at that moment.

One afternoon around then the two of us sat on the rug in the TV room and watched a movie about mountain climbers scaling the Himalayas. Tiny black and white figures clung to ropes, made their way single file across glaciers, huddled in shallow crevices as high winds blew past.

It wasn't long afterward that Mark, suddenly intense, led me and a couple of other kids along a six-inch ledge that ran around the courthouse in Codman Square.

The ledge was a couple of feet off the ground at the front of the building. We sidled along, stumbling once in a while, looking in the windows at the courtroom where a trial was in session. We turned the corner and edged our way along the side of the building. Here we faced the judge behind his raised desk. At first he didn't notice. Then Mark smiled and waved.

The judge summoned a bailiff, pointed to us. Mark sidled faster and we followed him around to the back of the building. At the rear of the courthouse was a sunken driveway that led to a garage. The ledge was a good sixteen feet above the cement. My hands began to sweat but I was smart enough not to look down.

The bailiff appeared, told us to halt and go back. The last kid in line, eight years old where the rest of us were ten, froze where he was and started to cry.

Suddenly the summer sunshine went gray and I was inching my way along an icy ledge hundreds of feet up a sheer cliff.

After a moment that vision was gone. Cops showed up, parked their car right under us to cut the distance we might fall. A crowd, mostly kids, gathered to watch the fire department bring us down a ladder. When we were down, I turned to Mark and saw that his concentration had faded.

"My guardian angel brought us out here," he whispered.

The consequences were not severe. Mark was a privileged character and that extended to his confederates. When the cops drove us up to his house, Mrs. Bannon came out and invited us all inside. Soon the kitchen was full of cops drinking spiked coffee like it was St. Patrick's Day and our mothers all came by to pick us up and laugh about the incident with Mrs. Bannon.

Late that same summer, I think, an afternoon almost at the end of vacation, the two of us turned onto Melville Avenue and saw Cadillacs double-parked in front of the Hon Hen's house. A movie camera was set up on the lawn. A photographer stood on the porch. We hurried down the street.

As we got there, the front door flew open and several guys came out laughing. The cameraman started to film, the photographer snapped pictures. Young Senator Kennedy was on the porch. He turned back to kiss his aunt and shake hands with his uncle.

He was thin with reddish brown hair and didn't seem entirely adult. He winked as he walked past us and the cameras clicked away. A man in a suit got out of a car and opened the door, the young senator said, "Okay, that's done."

As they drove off, the Hon Hen waved us up onto the porch, brought out dishes of ice cream. It was his wife's birthday and their nephew had paid his respects.

A couple of weeks later, after school started, a story with plenty of pictures appeared in the magazine section of the *Globe*: a day in the life of Senator Kennedy. Mark and I were in the one of him leaving his aunt's birthday. Our nun, Sister Mary Claire, put the picture up on the bulletin board.

The rest of the nuns came by to see. The other kids resented us for a few days. The Cullen brothers, a mean and sullen pair, motherless and raised by a drunken father, hated us for ever after.

I saw the picture again a few years ago. Kennedy's wearing a full campaign smile, I'm looking at the great man, open mouthed. Mark stares at the camera so intently that he seems ready to jump right off the page.

4.

The first stop on my search for Mark Bannon's current whereabouts was right in my neighborhood. It's been said about Greenwich Village that here time is all twisted out of shape like an abstract metal sculpture: past, present, and future intertwine.

Looking for that mix, the first place I went was Fiddler's Green way east on Bleecker Street. Springsteen sang at Fiddler's and Madonna waited tables before she became Madonna. By night it's a tourist landmark and a student magnet but during the day it's a little dive for office workers playing hooky and old village types in search of somewhere dark and quiet.

As I'd hoped, "Daddy Frank" Parnelli, with eyes like a drunken hawk's and sparse white hair cropped like a drill sergeant's, sipped a beer in his usual spot at the end of the bar. Once the legend was that he was where you went when you wanted yesterday's mistake erased or needed more than just a hunch about tomorrow's market.

Whether any of that was ever true, now none of it is. The only thing he knows these days is his own story and parts of that he can't tell to most people. I was an exception.

We hadn't talked in a couple of years but when he saw me he grimaced and asked, "Now what?" like I pestered him every day.

"Seemed like you might be here and I thought I'd stop by and say hello."

"Real kind of you to remember an old sadist."

I'm not that much younger than he is but over the years, I've learned a thing or two about topping from Daddy Frank. Like never giving a bottom an even break. I ordered a club soda and pointed for the bartender to fill Daddy Frank's empty shot glass with whatever rye he'd been drinking.

Daddy stared at it like he was disgusted then took a sip and another. He looked out the window. Across the street, a taxi let out an enormously fat woman with a tiny dog. Right in front of Fiddler's a crowd of smiling Japanese tourists snapped pictures of each other.

A bearded computer student sat about halfway down the bar from us with a gin and tonic and read what looked like a thousand-page book. A middle-aged man and his wife studied the signed photos on the walls while quietly singing scraps of songs to each other.

Turning back to me with what might once have been an enigmatic smile, Daddy Frank said, "You're looking for Mark Bannon."

"Yes."

"I have no fucking idea where he is," he said. "Never knew him before he appeared in my life. Never saw him again when he was through with me."

I waited, knowing this was going to take a while. When he started talking, the story wasn't one that I knew.

"Years ago, in sixty-nine, maybe seventy, it's like, two in the afternoon on Saturday, a few weeks before Christmas. I'm in a bar way west on Fourteenth Street near the meat-packing district. McNally's maybe or the Emerald Gardens, one of them they used to have over there that all looked alike. They had this bartender with one arm, I remember. He'd lost the other one on the docks."

"Making mixed drinks must have been tough," I said.

"Anyone asked for one, he came at them with a baseball bat. Anyway, the time I'm telling you about, I'd earned some money that morning bringing discipline to someone who hadn't been brought up right. I was living with a bitch in Murray Hill. But she had money and I saw no reason to share.

"I'm sitting there and this guy comes in wearing an overcoat with the collar pulled up. He's younger than me but he looks all washed out like he's been on a long complicated bender. No one I recognized, but people there kind of knew him."

I understood what was being described and memory supplied a face for the stranger.

"He sits down next to me. Has this piece he wants to unload, a cheap thirty-two. It has three bullets in it. He wants ten bucks. Needs the money to get home to his family. I look down and see I still have five bucks left."

I said, "A less stand-up guy might have wondered what happened to the other three bullets."

"I saw it as an opportunity. As I look back I see, maybe, it was a test. I offer the five and the stranger sells me the piece. So now I have a gun and no money. All of a sudden the stranger comes alive, smiles at me, and I feel a lot different. With a purpose, you know?

"With the buzz I had, I didn't even wonder why this was. All I knew was I needed to put the piece to use. That was when I thought of Klein's. The place I was staying was over on the East Side and it was on my way home. You remember Klein's Department Store?"

"Sure, on Union Square. 'Klein's on the Square' was the motto and they had a big neon sign of a right angle ruler out front."

"Great fucking bargains. Back when I was six and my mother wanted to dress me like a little asshole, that's where she could do it cheap. As a kid I worked there as a stock boy. I knew they kept all the receipts, whatever they took in, up on the top floor and that they closed at six on Saturdays."

As he talked, I remembered the blowsy old Union Square, saw the tacky Christmas lights, the crowds of women toting shopping bags and young Frank Parnelli cutting his way through them on his way to Klein's.

"It's so simple I do it without thinking. I go up to the top floor like I have some kind of business. It's an old-fashioned store way back when people used cash. Security is one old guy wearing glasses. I go in the refund line and when I get up to the counter, I pull out the gun. The refunds ladies all soil their panties

"I clean the place out. Thousands of bucks in a shopping bag and I didn't even have to go out of my way. I run down the stairs and nobody stops me. It's dark outside and I blend in with the crowd. As I walk down Fourteenth, the guy from the bar who sold me the gun is walking beside me.

"Before he looked beat. Now it's like the life has been sucked out of him and he's the living dead. But you know what? I have a locker at Grammercy Gym near Third Ave. I go in there so I can change from my leathers into a warm-up jacket and a baseball cap. Like it's the most natural thing, I give the guy a bunch of bills. He goes off to his family. I don't ever see him again.

"I'm still drunk and amazed. That night I'm on a plane. Next day I'm in L.A. Both of those things for the first time. After that I'm not in this world half the time. Not this world like I thought it was anyway. And somewhere in those first days, I realized I wasn't alone inside my own head. A certain Mark Bannon was in there too."

I looked down the bar. The student was drinking his gin, turning his pages. The couple had stopped singing and were sitting near the window. The bartender was on his cell phone. I signaled and he refilled Frank's glass.

"It was a wild ride for a few years," Daddy Frank said, "We hitched up with

Red Ruth who ran us both ragged. She got us into politics in the Caribbean: Honduras, Nicaragua, stuff I still can't talk about, Ruth and me and Bannon.

"Then she got tired of us, I got tired of having Mark Bannon on the brain and he got tired of me being me. It happens."

He leaned his elbow on the bar and had one hand over his eyes. "What is it? His mother looking for him again? I met her that first time when she had you find him. She's a great lady."

"Something like that," I said. "Anyone else ask you about Mark Bannon recently?"

"A couple of weeks ago someone came around asking questions. He said he has like a news show on the computer. Paul Revere is his name? Something like that. He came on like he knew something. But a lot smarter guys than him have tried to mix it up with me."

"No one else has asked?"

He shook his head.

"Anything you want me to tell Marky if I should see him?"

Without taking his hand away from his eyes, Daddy Frank raised the other, brought the glass to his lips, and drained it. "Tell him it's been thirty years and more and I was glad when he left but I've been nothing but a bag of muscles and bones ever since."

5.

As evening falls in the South Village, the barkers come out. On opposite corners of the cross streets they stand with their spiels and handbills.

"Come hear the brightest song writers in New York," said an angry young man, handing me a flyer.

A woman with snakes and flowers running up and down her arms and legs insisted, "You have just hit the tattoo jackpot!"

"Sir, you look as if you could use a good . . . laugh," said a small African-American queen outside a comedy club.

I noticed people giving the little sidelong glances that New Yorkers use when they spot a celebrity. But when I looked, the person was no one I recognized. That happens to me a lot these days.

Thinking about Mark Bannon and Frank Parnelli, I wondered if he just saw Frank as a vehicle with a tougher body and a better set of reflexes than his own? Did he look back with fondness when they parted company? Was it the kind of nostalgia you might have for a favorite horse or your first great car?

It was my luck to have known Mark when he was younger and his "guardian angel" was less skilled than it became. One Saturday when we were fourteen or so, going to different high schools and drifting apart, he and I were in a hockey free-for-all down on the Neponset River.

It was one of those silver and black winter Saturday afternoons when nothing was planned. A pack of kids from our neighborhood was looking for ice to play on. Nobody was ever supposed to swim or skate on that water so that's where a dozen of us headed.

We grabbed a stretch of open ice a mile or so from where the Neponset opens onto the Nantasket Roads, the stretch of water that connects Boston Harbor to the Atlantic Ocean. Our game involved shoving a battered puck around and plenty of body checks. Mark was on my team but seemed disconnected like he was most of the time.

The ice was thick out in the middle of the river but old and scarred and rutted by skates and tides. Along the shore where it was thin, the ice had been broken up at some points.

Once I looked around and saw that some kids eight or nine years old were out on the ice in their shoes jumping up and down, smashing through it and jumping away laughing when they did. There was a whir of skates behind me and I got knocked flat.

I was the smallest guy my age in the game. Ice chips went up the legs of my jeans and burned my skin. When I got my feet under me again, the little kids were yelling. One of them was in deep water holding onto the ice which kept breaking as he grabbed it.

Our game stopped and everyone stood staring. Then Mark came alive. He started forward and beckoned me, one of the few times he'd noticed me that afternoon. As I followed him, I thought I heard the words "Chain-Of-Life." It was a rescue maneuver that, maybe, boy scouts practiced but I'd never seen done.

Without willing it, I suddenly threw myself flat and was on my stomach on the ice. Mark was down on the ice behind me and had hold of my ankles. He yelled at the other guys for two of them to grab his ankles and four guys to grab theirs. I was the point of a pyramid.

Somehow I grabbed a hockey stick in my gloved hands. My body slithered forward on the ice and my arms held the stick out toward the little kid. Someone else was moving my body.

The ice here was thin. There was water on top of it. The kid grabbed the stick. I felt the ice moving under me, hands pulled my legs.

I gripped the stick. At first the kid split the ice as I pulled him along. I wanted to let go and get away before the splitting ice engulfed me too.

But I couldn't. I had no control over my hands. Then the little kid reached firm ice. Mark pulled my legs and I pulled the kid. His stomach bounced up onto the ice and then his legs. Other guys grabbed my end of the stick, pulled the kid past me.

I stood and Mark was standing also. The little boy was being led away, soaked and crying, water sloshing in his boots. Suddenly I felt the cold—the ice inside my pants and up the sleeves of my sweater—and realized what I'd done.

Mark Bannon held me up, pounded my back. "We did it! You and me!" he said. His eyes were alive and he looked like he was possessed. "I felt how scared you were when the ice started to break." And I knew this was Mark's angel talking.

The other guys clustered around us yelling about what we'd done. I looked up at the gray sky, at a freighter in the distance sailing up the Roads toward Boston Harbor. It was all black and white like television and my legs buckled under me.

Shortly afterward as evening closed in, the cops appeared and ordered everybody off the ice. That night, a little feverish, I dreamed and cried out in my sleep about ice and TV.

No adult knew what had happened but every kid did. Monday at school, ones who never spoke to me asked about it. I told them even though it felt like it had happened to someone else. And that feeling, I think, was what the memory of his years with Mark Bannon must have been like for Daddy Frank.

6.

As soon as Frank Parnelli started talking about Paul Revere, I knew who he meant and wasn't surprised. I called Desmond Eliot and he wasn't surprised to hear from me either. Back when I first knew Des Eliot he and Carol Bannon went to Amherst and were dating each other. Now he operates the political blog, *Midnight Ride: Spreading the Alarm*.

A few days later, I sat facing Eliot in his home office in suburban Maryland. I guess he could work in his pajamas if he wanted to. But, in fact, he was dressed and shaved and ready to ride.

He was listening to someone on the phone and typing on a keyboard in his lap. Behind him were a computer and a TV with the sound turned off. The screen showed a runway in Jordan where the smoking ruins of a passenger plane were still being hosed down with chemicals. Then a Republican senator with presidential ambitions looked very serious as he spoke to reporters in Washington.

A brisk Asian woman, who had introduced herself as June, came into the office, collected the outgoing mail, and departed. A fax hummed in the corner. Outside, it was a sunny day and the trees had just begun to turn.

"Yes, I saw the dustup at the press conference this morning," he said into the phone. "The White House, basically, is claiming the Democrats planted a spy in the Republican National Committee. If I thought anyone on the DNC had the brains and chutzpah to do that I'd be cheering."

At that moment Des was a relatively happy man. *Midnight Ride* is, as he puts it, "A tool of the disloyal opposition," and right now things are going relatively badly for the administration.

He hung up and told me, "Lately every day is a feast. This must be how the right wing felt when Clinton was up to his ass in blue dresses and cigars." As he spoke he typed on a keyboard, probably the very words he was uttering.

He stopped typing, put his feet up on a coffee table, and looked out over his half-frame glasses. His contacts with the Bannons go way back. It bothers him that mine go back further.

"You come all the way down here to ask me about Mark Bannon," he said. "My guess is it's not for some personal memoir like you're telling me. I think the family is looking for him and thinks I may have spotted him like I did with Svetlanov."

I shook my head like I didn't understand.

"Surely you remember. It was twenty years ago. No, a bit more. Deep in the Reagan years. Glasnost and Perestroika weren't even rumors. The Soviet Union was the Evil Empire. I was in Washington, writing for *The Nation,* consulting at a couple of think tanks, going out with Lucia, an Italian sculptress. Later on I was married to her for about six months.

"There was a Goya show at the Corcoran that Lucia wanted to see. We'd just come out of one of the galleries and there was this guy I was sure I'd never seen before, tall, prematurely gray.

"There was something very familiar about him. Not his looks, but something. When he'd talk to the woman he was with, whatever I thought I'd recognized didn't show. Then he looked my way and it was there again. As I tried to place him, he seemed like he was trying to remember me.

"Then I realized it was his eyes. At moments they had the same uncanny look that Mark Bannon's could get when I first knew him. Of course by then Mark had been dead for about thirteen years.

"Lucia knew who this was: a Russian art dealer named Georgi Svetlanov, the subject of rumors and legends. Each person I asked about him had a different story: he was a smuggler, a Soviet agent, a forger, a freedom fighter."

Eliot said, "It stuck with me enough that I mentioned it the next time I talked to Carol. She was planning a run for congress and I was helping. Carol didn't seem that interested.

"She must have written the name down, though. I kept watch on Svetlanov. Even aside from the Bannon connection he was interesting.

Mrs. Bannon must have thought so too. He visited her a few times that I know of."

Marie Bannon had gotten in touch with me and mentioned this Russian man someone had told her about. She had the name and I did some research, found out his itinerary. At a major opening at the Shifrazi Gallery in Soho, I walked up to a big steely-haired man who seemingly had nothing familiar about him at all.

"Mark Bannon," I said quietly but distinctly.

At first the only reaction was Svetlanov looking at me like I was a bug. He sneered and began to turn away. Then he turned back and the angel moved behind his eyes. He looked at me hard, trying to place me.

I handed him my card. "Mark Bannon, your mother's looking for you," I said. "That's her number on the back." Suddenly eyes that were very familiar looked right into mine.

Des told me, "I saw Svetlanov after that in the flesh and on TV. He was in the background at Riga with Reagan and Gorbachev. I did quite a bit of research and discovered Frank Parnelli among other things. My guess is that Mark Bannon's . . . spirit or subconscious or whatever it is—was elsewhere by nineteen-ninety-two when Svetlanov died in an auto accident. Was I right?"

In some ways I sympathized with Eliot. I'd wondered about that too. And lying is bad. You get tripped by a lie more often than by the truth.

But I looked him in the face and said, "Mark wasn't signaling anybody from deep inside the skull of some Russian, my friend. You were at the wake, the funeral, the burial. Only those without a drop of Celtic blood believe there's any magic in the Irish."

He said, "The first time I noticed you was at that memorial service. Everyone else stood up and tiptoed around the mystery and disaster that had been his life. Then it was your turn and you quoted Shakespeare. Said he was a ruined king. You knew he wasn't really dead."

"Des, it was 1971. Joplin, Hendrix. Everyone was dying young. I was stoned, I was an aspiring theater person and very full of myself. I'd intended to recite Dylan Thomas's 'Do Not Go Gentle' but another drunken Mick beat me to that.

"So I reared back and gave them *Richard the Second,* which I'd had to learn in college. Great stuff:
'Not all the water in the rough rude sea
Can wash the balm off from an anointed king;
The breath of worldly men cannot depose
The deputy elected by the Lord'

"As I remember," I said, "the contingent of nuns who taught Mark and me in school was seated down front. When I reached the lines:
. . . if angels fight,
Weak men must fall . . .

"They looked very pleased about the angels fighting. Booze and bravura is all it was," I said.

Partly that was true. I'd always loved the speech, maybe because King Richard and I share a name. But also it seemed so right for Mark. In the play, a king about to lose his life and all he owns on Earth invokes royal myth as his last hope.

"When I was dating Carol I heard the legends," Des told me. "She and her sister talked about how the family had gotten him into some country club school in New Jersey. He was expelled in his third week for turning the whole place on and staging an orgy that got the college president fired.

"They said how he'd disappear for weeks and Carol swore that once when he came stumbling home, he'd mumbled to her months before it happened that King and Bobby Kennedy were going to be shot.

"Finally, I was at the Bannons with Carol when the prodigal returned and it was a disappointment. He seemed mildly retarded, a burnout at age twenty-five. I didn't even think he was aware I existed.

"I was wrong about that. Mark didn't have a license or a car anymore. The second or third day he was back, Carol was busy. I was sitting on the sun porch, reading. He came out, smiled this sudden, magnetic smile just like his old man's and asked if that was my Ford two-door at the end of the driveway.

"Without his even asking I found myself giving him a lift. A few days later I woke up at a commune in the Green Mountains in New Hampshire with no clear idea of how I'd gotten there. Mark was gone and all the communards could tell me was, 'He enters and leaves as he wishes.'

"When I got back to Boston, Carol was pissed. We made up but in a lot of ways it was never the same. Not even a year or two later when Mike Bannon ran for governor and I worked my ass off on the campaign.

"Mark was back home all the time then, drinking, taking drugs, distracting the family, especially his father, at a critical time. His eyes were empty and no matter how long everyone waited, they stayed that way. After the election he died, maybe as a suicide. But over the years I've come to think that didn't end the story."

It crossed my mind that Eliot knew too much. I said, "You saw them lower him into the ground."

"It's Carol who's looking this time, isn't it?" he asked. "She's almost there as a national candidate. Just a little too straight and narrow. Something extra needs to go in the mix. Please tell me that's going to happen."

A guy in his fifties looking for a miracle is a sad sight. One also sporting a college kid's crush is sadder still.

"Just to humor you, I'll say you're right," I told him. "What would you tell me my next step should be?"

The smile came off his face. "I have no leads," he said. "No source who would talk to me knows anything."

"But some wouldn't talk to you," I said.

"The only one who matters won't. She refuses to acknowledge my existence. It's time you went to see Ruth Vega."

7.

I was present on the night the angel really flew.

It was in the summer of '59 when they bulldozed the big overgrown lot where the Fitzgerald mansion had once stood. Honey Fitz's place had burned down just twenty years before. But to kids my age, "Fitzie's" was legendary ground, a piece of untamed wilderness that had existed since time out of mind.

I was finishing my sophomore year in high school when they cleared the land. The big old trees that must have stood on the front lawn, the overgrown apple orchard in the back were chopped down and their stumps dug up.

The scraggly new trees, the bushes where we hid smeared in war paint on endless summer afternoons waiting for hapless smaller kids to pass by and get massacred, the half flight of stone stairs that ended in midair, the marble floor with moss growing through the cracks, all disappeared.

In their place a half-dozen cellars were dug and houses were built. We lost the wild playground but we'd already outgrown it. For that one summer we had half-finished houses to hide out in.

Marky and I got sent to different high schools outside the neighborhood and had drifted apart. Neither of us did well academically and we both ended up in the same summer school. So we did hang out one more time. Nights especially we sat with a few guys our age on unfinished wood floors with stolen beer and cigarettes and talked very large about what we'd seen and done out in the wide world.

That's what four of us were up to in a raw wood living room by the light of the moon and distant street lamps. Suddenly a flashlight shone in our faces and someone yelled, "Hands over your heads. Up against the wall."

For a moment, I thought it was the cops and knew they'd back off once they found out Marky was among us. In fact it was much worse: the Cullen brothers and a couple of their friends were there. In the dim light I saw a switchblade.

We were foul-mouthed little twerps with delusions of delinquency. These were the real thing: psycho boys raised by psycho parents. A kid named Johnny Kilty was the one of us nearest the door. Teddy—the younger, bigger, more rabid Cullen brother—pulled Johnny's T-shirt over his head, punched him twice in the stomach, and emptied his pockets.

Larry, the older, smarter, scarier Cullen, had the knife and was staring right at Marky. "Hey, look who we got!" he said in his toneless voice. "Hands on your head, faggot. This will be fucking hilarious."

Time paused as Mark Bannon stared back slack-jawed. Then his eyes lit up and he smiled like he saw something amazing.

As that happened, my shirt got pulled over my head. My watch was taken off my wrist. Then I heard Larry Cullen say without inflection, "This is no good. Give them their stuff back. We're leaving."

The ones who held me let go; I pulled my T-shirt back on.

"What the fuck are you talking about?" Teddy asked.

"I gotta hurt you before you hear me?" Larry asked in dead tones. "Move before I kick your ass."

They were gone as suddenly as they appeared, though I could hear Teddy protesting as they went through the construction site and down the street. "Have you gone bird shit, stupid?" he asked. I didn't hear Larry's reply.

We gathered our possessions. The other guys suddenly wanted very badly to be home with their parents. Only I understood that Mark had saved us. When I looked, he was staring vacantly. He followed us out of the house and onto the sidewalk.

"I need to go home," he whispered to me like a little kid who's lost. "My angel's gone," he said.

It was short of midnight though well past my curfew when I walked Marky home. Outside of noise and light from the bars in Codman Square, the streets were quiet and traffic was sparse. I tried to talk but Marky shook his head. His shoes seemed to drag on the pavement. He was a lot bigger than me but I was leading him.

Lights were on at his place when we got there and cars were parked in the driveway. "I need to go in the window," he mumbled and we went around back. He slipped as he started to climb the tree and it seemed like a bad idea. But up he went and I was right behind him.

When the bough broke with a crack, he fell, smashing through other branches, and I scrambled back down the trunk. The lights came on but I got away before his family and the governor of the Commonwealth came out to find him on the ground laughing hysterically.

The next day, I was in big trouble at home. But I managed to go visit Mark. On the way, I passed Larry Cullen walking away from the Bannons' house. He crossed the street to avoid me.

Mark was in bed with a broken wrist and a bandage on his leg. The light was on in his eyes and he wore the same wild smile he'd had when he saw Larry Cullen. We both knew what had happened but neither had words to describe it. After that Mark and I tended to avoid each other.

Then my family moved away from the neighborhood and I forgot about the Bannons pretty much on purpose. So it was a surprise years later when I came home for Christmas that my mother said Mark Bannon wanted to speak to me.

"His mother called and asked about you," she said. "You know I've heard that Mark is in an awful way. They say Mike Bannon's taken that harder than losing the governorship.

My father looked up from the paper and said, "Something took it out of Bannon. He sleepwalked through the campaign. And when it started he was the favorite."

Curiosity, if nothing else, led me to visit Mark. My parents now lived in the suburbs and I lived in New York. But the Bannons were still on Melville Avenue.

Mrs. Bannon was so sad when she smiled and greeted me that I would have done anything she asked.

When I saw Mark, one of the things he said was, "My angel's gone and he's not coming back." I thought of the lost, scared kid I'd led home from Fitzie's that night. I realized I was the only one, except maybe his mother, who he could tell any of this to.

I visited him a few times when I'd be up seeing my family. Mostly he was stoned on pills and booze and without the angel he seemed lobotomized. Sometimes we just watched television like we had as kids.

He told me about being dragged through strange and scary places in the world. "I guess he wasn't an angel. Or not a good one." Doctors had him on tranquilizers. Sometimes he slurred so badly I couldn't understand him.

Mike Bannon, out of office, was on committees and commissions and was a partner in a law firm. But he was home in his study a lot and the house was very quiet. Once as I was leaving, he called me in, asked me to sit down, offered me a drink.

He wondered how his son was doing. I said he seemed okay. We both knew this wasn't so. Bannon's face appeared loose, sagging.

He looked at me and his eyes flashed for a moment. "Most of us God gives certain . . . skills. They're so much a part of us we use them by instinct. We make the right move at the right moment and it's so smooth it's like someone else doing it.

"Marky had troubles but he also had moments like that. Someone told me the other day you and he saved a life down on the river when you were boys because he acted so fast. He's lost it now, that instinct. It's gone out like a light." It seemed he was trying to explain something to himself and I didn't know how to help him.

Mark died of an overdose, maybe an intentional one, and they asked me to speak at the memorial service. A few years later, Big Mike Bannon died. Someone in tribute said, "A superb political animal. Watching him in his prime rounding up a majority in the lower chamber was like seeing a cheetah run, an eagle soar . . . "

" . . . a rattlesnake strike," my father added.

8.

A couple of days after my meeting with Des Eliot, I flew to Quebec. A minor border security kerfuffle between the U.S. and Canada produced delays at both Newark International and Jean Lesage International.

It gave me a chance to think about the first time I'd gone on one of these quests. Shortly after her husband's death Mrs. Bannon had asked me to find Mark's angel.

A few things he'd told me when I'd visited, a hint or two his mother had picked up, allowed me to track one Frank Parnelli to the third floor of a walk-up in Washington Heights.

I knocked on the door, the eyehole opened and a woman inside asked, "Who is it?"

"I'm looking for Ruth Vega."

"She's not here."

"I'm looking for Mark Bannon."

"Who?"

"Or for Frank Parnelli."

The eyehole opened again. I heard whispers inside. "This will be the man we had known would come," someone said and the door opened.

Inside were statues and pictures and books everywhere: a black and white photo of Leon Trotsky, a woman's bowling trophy, and what looked like a complete set of Anna Freud's *The Psychoanalytic Study of the Child*.

A tiny old woman with bright red hair and a hint of amusement in her expression stood in the middle of the room looking at me. "McCluskey, where have you been?"

"That's not McCluskey, Mother," said a much larger middle-aged woman in a tired voice.

"McCluskey from the Central Workers Council! Where's your cigar?" Suddenly she looked wise. "You're not smoking because of my big sister Sally, here. She hates them. I like a man who smokes a cigar. You were the one told me Woodrow Wilson was going to be president when I was a little kid. When it happened I thought you could foretell the future. Like I do."

"Why don't you sit down," the other woman said to me. "My niece is the one you're looking for. My mother's a little confused about past and present. Among other things."

"So, McCluskey," said the old woman, "who's it going to be next election? Roosevelt again, that old fascist?" I wondered whether she meant Teddy or FDR.

"I know who the Republicans are putting up," she said. It was 1975 and Gerald Ford was still drawing laughs by falling down stairs. I tried to look interested.

"That actor," she said. "Don Ameche. He'll beat the pants off President Carter." At that moment I'd never heard of Carter. "No, not Ameche, the other one."

"Reagan?" I asked. I knew about him. Some years before he'd become governor of California, much to everyone's amusement.

"Yes, that's the one. See. Just the same way you told me about Wilson, you've told me about Reagan getting elected president."

"Would you like some tea while you wait?" asked the daughter, looking both bored and irritated.

We talked about a lot of things that afternoon. What I remembered some years later, of course, was the prediction about Reagan. With the Vega family there were always hints of the paranormal along with a healthy dose of doubletalk.

At that moment the door of the walk-up opened and a striking couple came in. He was a thug who had obviously done some boxing, with a nicely broken nose and a good suit. She was tall and in her late twenties with long legs in tight black pants, long red hair drawn back, a lot of cool distance in her green eyes.

At first glance the pair looked like a celebrity and her bodyguard. But the way Ruth Vega watched Frank Parnelli told me that somehow she was looking after him.

Parnelli stared at me. And a few years after I'd seen Marky Bannon's body lowered into the ground, I caught a glimpse of him in a stranger's eyes.

That was what I remembered when I was east of Quebec walking uphill from the Vibeau Island Ferry dock.

Des knew where Ruth was, though he'd never actually dared to approach her. I believed if she wanted to stop me from seeing her, she would already have done it.

At a guess, Vibeau Island looked like an old fishing village that had become a summer vacation spot at some point in the mid-twentieth century and was now an exurb. Up here it was chilly even in the early afternoon.

I saw the woman with red hair standing at the end of a fishing pier. From a distance I thought Ruth Vega was feeding the ducks. Then I saw what she threw blow out onto the Saint Lawrence and realized she was tearing up papers and tossing them into the wind. On first glance, I would have said she looked remarkably as she had thirty years before.

I waited until I was close to ask, "What's wrong, Ms. Vega, your shredder broken?"

"McCluskey from the Central Workers Council," she said, and when she did, I saw her grandmother's face in hers. "I remember that first time we met, thinking that Mark's mother had chosen her operative well. You found her son and were very discreet about it."

We walked back to her house. It was a cottage with good sight lines in all directions and two large black schnauzers snarling in a pen.

"That first time was easy." I replied. "He remembered his family and wanted to be found. The second time was a few years later and that was much harder."

Ruth nodded. We sat in her living room. She had a little wine, I had some tea. The décor had a stark beauty, nothing unnecessary: a gun case, a computer, a Cy Twombly over the fireplace.

"The next time Mrs. Bannon sent me out to find her son, it was because she and he had lost touch. Frank Parnelli when I found him was a minor Village character. Mark no longer looked out from behind his eyes. He had no idea where you were. Your grandmother was a confused old woman wandering around her apartment in a nightgown.

"I had to go back to Mrs. Bannon and tell her I'd failed. It wasn't until a couple of years later that Svetlanov turned up."

"Mark and I were in love for a time," Ruth said. "He suggested jokingly once or twice that he leave Parnelli and come to me. I didn't want that and in truth he was afraid of someone he wouldn't be able to control.

"Finally being around Parnelli grew thin and I stopped seeing them. Not long afterward Mark abandoned Parnelli and we both left New York for different destinations. A few years later, I was living in the Yucatan and he showed up again. This time with an old acquaintance of mine.

"When I lived with Grandmother as a kid," Ruth said, "she was in her prime and all kinds of people were around. Political operatives, prophetesses, you name it. One was called Decker, this young guy with dark eyes and long dark hair like classical violinists wore. For a while he came around with some project on which he wanted my grandmother's advice. I thought he was very sexy. I was ten.

"Then he wasn't around the apartment. But I saw him: coming out of a bank, on the street walking past me with some woman. Once on a school trip to the United Nations Building, I saw him on the subway in a naval cadet's uniform.

"I got home that evening and my grandmother said, 'Have you seen that man Decker recently?' When I said yes, she told me to go do my homework and made a single very short phone call. Decker stopped appearing in my life.

"Until one night in Mexico a knock came on my door and there he stood looking not a day older than when I'd seen him last. For a brief moment, there was a flicker in his eyes and I knew Mark was there but not in control.

"Decker could touch and twist another's mind with his. My grandmother, though, had taught me the chant against intrusive thoughts. Uncle Dano had taught me how to draw, aim, and fire without even thinking about it.

"Killing is a stupid way to solve problems. But sometimes it's the only one. After Decker died I played host to Mark for about an hour before I found someone else for him to ride. He was like a spark, pure instinct unfettered by a soul. That's changed somewhat."

When it was time for my ferry back to the city, Ruth rose and walked down to the dock with me.

"I saw his sister on TV the other night when they announced she would be appointed to the Senate. I take it she's the one who's looking for him?"

I nodded and she said, "Before too long idiot senators will be trying to lodge civil liberty complaints after martial law has been declared and the security squads are on their way to the capital to throw them in jail. Without Mark she'll be one of them."

Before I went up the gangplank, she hugged me and said, "You think you're looking for him but he's actually waiting for you."

After a few days back in New York memories of Vibeau Island began to seem preposterous. Then I walked down my block late one night. It was crowded with tourists and college kids, barkers and bouncers. I saw people give the averted celebrity glance.

Then I spotted a black man with a round face and a shaven head. I did recognize him: an overnight hip-hop millionaire. He sat in the back of a stretch limo with the door open. Our eyes met. His widened then dulled and he sank back in his seat.

At that moment, I saw gray winter sky and felt the damp cold of the ice-covered Neponset. *On old familiar ground,* said a voice inside me and I knew Mark was back.

9.

Some hours later passengers found seats as our train pulled out of New Haven.

"Ruth said you were waiting for me," I told Mark silently.

And Red Ruth is never wrong.

"She told me about Decker."

I thought I had selected him. But he had selected me. Once inside him I was trapped. He was a spider. I couldn't control him. Couldn't escape. I led him to Ruth as I was told.

He showed me an image of Ruth pointing an automatic pistol, firing at close range.

I leaped to her as he died. She was more relentless than Decker in some ways. I had to promise to make my existence worthwhile. To make the world better.

"If angels fight, weak men must fall."

Not exactly an angel. Ego? Id? Fragment? Parasite?

I thought of how his father had something like an angel himself.

His body, soul, and mind were a single entity. Mine weren't.

I saw his memory of Mike Bannon smiling and waving in the curved front windows of his house at well-wishers on the snowy front lawn. Bannon senior never questioned his own skills or wondered what would have happened if they'd been trapped in a brain that was mildly damaged. Then he saw it happen to his son.

Once I understood that, he showed me the dark tower again with two tiny slits of light high above. I found hand-and foot-holds and crawled up the interior stone walls. This time I looked through the slits of light and saw they were the eyeholes of a mask. In front of me were Mike and Marie Bannon looking very young and startled by the sudden light in the eyes of their troublingly quiet little boy.

When the train approached Boston, the one inside me said, *Let's see the old neighborhood.*

We took a taxi from Back Bay and drove out to Dorchester. We saw the school we'd gone to and the courthouse and place where I'd lived and the houses that stood where Fitzie's had once been.

My first great escape.

That night so long ago came back. Larry Cullen, seen through the eyeholes of a mask, stood with his thin psycho smile. In a flash I saw Mark Bannon slack-jawed and felt Cullen's cold fear as the angel took hold of his mind and looked out through his eyes.

Cullen's life was all horror and hate. His father was a monster. It should have taught me something. Instead I felt like I'd broken out of jail. After each time away from my own body it was harder to go back.

Melville Avenue looked pretty much the way it always did. Mrs. Bannon still lived in the family house. We got out of the car and the one inside me said, *When all this is over, it won't be forgotten that you brought me back to my family.*

In the days since then, as politics has become more dangerous, Carol Bannon has grown bolder and wilier. And I wonder what form the remembering will take.

Mrs. Bannon's caregiver opened the door. We were expected. Carol stood at the top of the stairs very much in command. I thought of her father.

"My mother's waiting to see you," she said. I understood that I would spend a few minutes with Mrs. Bannon and then depart. Carol looked right into my eyes and kissed me. Her eyes flashed and she smiled.

In that instant the one inside my head departed. The wonderful sharpness went out of the morning and I felt a touch of the desolation that Mark Bannon and all the others must have felt when the angel deserted them.

SPIDERHORSE

LIZ WILLIAMS

—◆—

I was born dead on a midwinter's night. I remember my mother, wailing. They wrapped me in a linen cloth and I remember that, too—the softness of it over my unbreathing mouth. Then they put me in a yew box to contain any evil that might rise like swamp mist from my skin, and that evening, near dusk with the last flash of a late sun reddening the thorn branches on the high slopes of Heimfell, my father carried me up to the crossroads and put my on the mounting block. The dead can't hear anything except the wind but I know that his face was wet, as he bade me goodbye.

Then I waited.

I knew they'd come. I'd been told they would, before they squeezed me into channels of blood and struts of bone, slid me between earth and sky and walls of flesh, confined me in something small and dead.

"If you don't breathe in the first minutes of light," they said in their one-voice-that-was-three, "then the Hunt will come for you."

It didn't sound so bad. I did not like what I'd heard of the mid-world, it sounded lumpy and clotted like sour mild, earth always clinging to your feet, weighing you down. And I didn't want to leave the Hall. I said so.

"That's the problem," they said. "You've been here too long. The Hall's growing into you and you're growing into it." The Eldest took my hand and held it above the cauldron's smoke to a shaft of starlight. "See?"

I suppose she was right. Now that she mentioned it, I could see the green threads of holly and ivy and oak, twining around what would have been my sinews. And I suppose my arms and fingers did look more like twigs and branches. But I was happy here. The Hall was my home. I liked living in its forest eaves, high in its canopy near the sun and the moon. I didn't see why I had to be rooted in human flesh but they said that everything had to be planted in earth if it was to grow.

And so I sank down into a room of flesh, but I didn't like it, and when at last I was shoved forth into midnight I held my breath and hoped to be hauled back up again to the Hall. I didn't really believe that they'd just leave me there, in my dead baby body.

Instead, I stayed stuck in chilly stiffness, waiting for the Hunt.

I knew when they came. I knew it must be them, from the voices in the wind, an old, cold breath.

"Another! There's another!"

Cries and laughter, and then a whispering voice like the sound the dead leaves made, rustling on the crossroad's earth. "A child made of dead flesh. Yes. We'll take her as a gift to us."

I, leaf-light, lifted up onto the saddle of a horse and secured with a leather thing. I got my first glimpse of them then: horses of shadow, of sinew and bone, with something writhing at the head of the herd—two horses? No, one, spide-legged and with a long hand holding the reins from beneath the night billow of a cloak. The ones who rode alongside all smiled and their teeth and eyes were bright as moonlight. As the horse that carried me leaped up from the crossroad I took my first breath and it burned into my lungs like smoke.

It wasn't the Hall. But it wasn't as bad as a life spent looking after pigs, either.

They made much of me. I grew fast, and I had skin like new milk, bloodless and smooth. They crowned me with mistletoe and gave me catskin gloves to wear. Even the one with the hood, the one who rode Spiderhorse, gave me more than a passing glance and stuck a feather from a raven's wing behind my ear. The feather told me things and sometimes it made me laugh out loud. I had waterfall hair and the other women showed me how to braid it into plaits, which brushed the ground as I walked and made it ring out like frost.

I earned a reputation for being somewhat heartless.

I missed the Hall at first, and the Tree, and the Three, but as I grew the memories became small and dim like the far stars and adult things took their place. I rode at the end of the Hunt, on something brown with a coat that was the texture of moss. It tried to bite me in the leg, but it only did that once. It did not seem to enjoy sky-riding—I don't know where they found it, but Holda, one of the women who helped me braid my hair, said that it had come from the bottom of a lake. I could believe this easily enough. Sometimes it seemed to shift underneath me, turning from horse to otter, and then to a mass that stank of waterweed and smelled of mud.

My waterfall hair reached to its thick heels when I stood beside it. I didn't want to be stuck riding a waterweed thing all my life, or what passed for it. I liked Frigga's tuft-eared cat, or Holda's black mare with her glittering starlit eyes. But most of all, I wanted to ride Spiderhorse.

It was just a wish, nothing more than that. But wishes are like thistledown seeds when the Hunt rides: they get blown on the wind of horses' hooves, and take root in odd places.

I certainly didn't mean to steal Wotan's horse. It just worked out that way.

It was my tenth hunt, or thereabouts. Easy enough to count: the warriors gave me a silver bracelet every time I rode. They asked for a different kind of ride in exchange, but I didn't mind that. It was as much fun as the waterweed steed, and the feather whispered to me all night long while the warriors snored.

On that tenth Hunt, we rode out over Heimfell. It was winter again, not long after Yule, and even in a land which rang with church bells there was still enough room for us: still holly and ivy round the lintel, still the midnight crossroads' gifts. The long back of Heimfell glittered with snow and my waterweed pony plodded on the sparkling air as if we were trotting across mud. When I dug my heels in, so did it. I looked all the way up the curve of the Hunt and saw Spiderhorse prance and dance as the ravens' wings blotted out the moon and I thought: *that's what I want.*

I didn't mean to say it out loud. No one heard me except Waterweed—and the feather, which caught on a sudden gust of icy air and fluttered down. I grabbed at it and almost fell. I watched it spiral down, down, through the hooves of the Hunt to the summit of Heimfell, where it arrowed into the snow and quivered into stillness. I saw the feather vanish and a shadowy stain spread out across the snow. I didn't know what it meant at the time. I should have remembered about wishes.

Wotan started to take more of an interest in me after that, and this should have worried me more than it did, too. But I was a girl, and popular, and wanting to be so, and of course it turned my head.

And Wotan was—well, Wotan. It's hard to describe his kind, because it's hard to look at them closely, or for long. Think of someone dark and sparkling, with an amber eye and wolf's pelt hair. Think of someone who can blot out the moon.

It didn't take long and I knew it would only be the once. He was gentle, at first. He gave me mead in a glass cup and a comb made of human bone to clasp my hair. But lying with him was not like lying with a warrior, or with a human man (what? I'd had an experimental phase). He was ice cold and when he entered me it burned and hurt. I was too proud to cry out and I think he liked that, though eventually I did so, but with the pleasure behind the pain.

I thought he'd probably got me pregnant. He usually did, with his girls, and quite often they lived through the birth. He did not go to sleep like a warrior, did not sprawl snoring. He lay on his back, still as stone, and I saw the reflection of his amber eye upon the ceiling, like a little coal. Gradually the reflection faded, and when I dared to look I saw that the eye had faded from amber to shadow, although it was still open. I reached down between my legs and found that I was mistletoe-sticky, but there was no blood. That, Holda had told me before I went to Wotan's chamber, was a very good sign.

I thought: *I want this child. But I want to ride Spiderhorse, too.*

Well, no time like the present.

I slid from the whispering sheets. Wotan's ravens were sitting on the bedposts: I hadn't seen them when I came in. But when I sought a closer look, fearing immediate betrayal, I saw that they were nothing more than rough carvings of black wood. So I kept silent and slipped on. One of the advantages of being born dead is that you still need to breathe, but not often. I barely stirred the shadows as I went through the door and down the hall, and through the mead-hall where the dogs and the warriors muttered in meat-soaked sleep, and out into the night to where the horses were stabled.

My pony was kept at the end nearest to the mead-hall. Water that smelled of pond-weed leaked from under the door. I went on, along the row of doors to the far end, the end closest to the edge of things. The stars seemed very close, here, and the moonlight fell hard on my skin. I looked down at my fingers, still sticky with mistletoe, and they gleamed silver. I could feel Spiderhorse inside his stall. I heard him stamp one of his eight feet, that are said to be shod with human bone to enable his master to ride the sky-roads, and it rang on the floor of the stable like church bells. I shivered to hear it, but I still walked on to the furthest stable, where everything stopped. I looked out onto a black sea, star-speckled. Very far away, out across the edge of things, I thought I could see the trunk of the Tree, a column of dark against dark, but I wasn't sure. I'd ride there, I thought to myself, and take a look. Maybe I'd even drop in on the Hall, and I smiled at the little, rooty thing I had once been as I looked down at my milky hands. Strong enough to hold Sleipnir's bridle? I hoped so. Time to find out. I could almost hear the beat of ravens' wings at my back, catch the gleam of a wolf's eye, wakening.

I opened the stable door. Spiderhorse seemed a lot bigger, close to. It was hard to see how the eight legs joined his body; the muscles seemed to be in constant movement, sliding beneath the shining skin. Impossible to tell what colour he was, too: sometimes he looked as black as the night sea, or as grey as the winter dusk, and then a clear glistening white like wet bone. I blinked, and there was only an eight-legged moving shadow, brown as ash-wood. Spiderhorse arched a long neck and looked at me and his eyes were like a man's eyes, filled with a wicked knowing.

I didn't give myself time to think, or I would have turned and fled. I snatched the saddle from the wall—made of warriors' skins, or so they said, and heavy enough to make my knees buckle. I threw it over Spiderhorse's back and drew the girth tight. The horse did nothing, but he watched me all the while. Then the bridle—made of women's braids, or so they said, and it snaked in my hands like lightning. Over the horse's head, and then it was time to put my foot in the stirrup and leap, a jump that felt sun-high. Spiderhorse stamped his foot, once, and I turned him and rode him through the door and out over the edge. He gave a long shrieking cry as we went and his eight hooves rang out across the star road –I could see it now a little way below, many packed points of light, grain scattered across the heavens' floor. I risked a glance over my shoulder and saw that far behind us, the lights were indeed going on. Wotan's hall had woken up. I took a deep breath, and rode on.

What was it like, riding Spiderhorse? It was more pleasure than any I've known, speed and power running through me like water, stronger than the pleasure of the warrior's ride, stronger than the pleasure of killing. I would have ridden Sleipnir to the end of time, to Ragnarok, forever, if I'd had the chance.

But the chance wasn't to come. Something brushed my face and I looked up to see the first leaves of the Tree. Then there was the sharpness of pain and when I put my hand to my cheek, it came away bloody. Spiderhorse charged through the leaves, and I ducked, leaning low over the horse's steaming neck as we went on, past the vast column of the Trunk and through the other side. If my old Hall was there, I did not see it. But I did see Mid-Earth below, a tapestry of silver and black with the hard ball of the moon hanging over it, and then a burst of blinding light as the sun rolled up over the world's edge. The light blinded me so that I cast my arm in front of my face, just in time to see Wotan's Hunt ride up behind me, with a yellow eye gleaming from under the hood of someone standing at the prow of Freya's cat chariot.

I shouldn't have let go of the reins.

Of course, Spiderhorse reared.

Of course, I fell.

I saw the whole length of the Tree as I went, crown to trunk to root, with the sun's light striking off the leaves as the morning world roared to meet me. A winter world still, with the waterfalls frozen, and the land bitter under the frost. And as I fell, I felt myself grow small, dwindling down, my hair streaming behind me like a comet's tail and then evaporating into fire as my flesh burned painlessly away and I grew yet smaller, soft as a frog.

I went straight through a roof, sending the snow that covered it hissing into steam, and landed somewhere dark and hot and wet. I didn't realise what had happened at first, until I couldn't get out, and then I tried to scream, with my frog mouth, and could not.

I did get out eventually. It took nine months, of chafing and regrets and pleading and cursing, until nature took its course and took pity on me. No one else was listening, after all. My new hostess squeezed me out into a midwife's hands, into a hovel's smoky air.

I'd already planned what to do. I'd done it before. But as I came into Mid-world for the second time, I opened my eyes and there was Wotan, standing on the other side of the fire. The yellow eye flared in the firelight with a bitter burn and it frightened me so much that I opened my mouth and shrieked.

That was that. The Hunt only ever take the dead.

And that was seventeen years ago, now. I still dream of my root-life in the Hall, and of my time spent riding on the waterweed steed in the wake of the Hunt. But most of all, as I trudge the slopes of Heimfell after the pigs, I dream of riding Spiderhorse, especially in the spring when the black hooves of the ash-trees start springing new leaves.

I have never been touched by a man. I'm just as beautiful as I used to be in Wotan's mead hall, so there's been no lack of offers. But I've had to ask my father to turn them all down. He's indulged me so far, but the pregnancy—still concealed—is growing on. It's taken seventeen years, so far, to get to this point.

I don't know how long it has to go, or what I will give birth to. Wotan's child, deep within, is silent, and tells me nothing. But when it is born, I know exactly what I will do. I'll take it to the midnight crossroads, in winter when the moon is dark, and together we'll wait for the beat of eight hooves, and the breath of cold on the wind.

THE TEAR

IAN McDONALD

Ptey, sailing

On the night that Ptey voyaged out to have his soul shattered, eight hundred stars set sail across the sky. It was an evening at Great Winter's ending. The sunlit hours raced toward High Summer, each day lavishly more full of light than the one before. In this latitude, the sun hardly set at all after the spring equinox, rolling along the horizon, fat and idle and pleased with itself. Summer-born Ptey turned his face to the sun as it dipped briefly beneath the horizon, closed his eyes, enjoyed its lingering warmth on his eyelids, in the angle of his cheekbones, on his lips. To the summer-born, any loss of the light was a reminder of the terrible, sad months of winter and the unbroken, encircling dark.

But we have the stars, his father said, a Winter-born. *We are born looking out into the universe.*

Ptey's father commanded the little machines that ran the catamaran, trimming sail, winding sheets, setting course by the tumble of satellites; but the tiller he held himself. The equinoctial gales had spun away to the west two weeks before and the catboat ran fast and fresh on a sweet wind across the darkening water. Twins hulls cut through the ripple-reflections of gas-flares from the Temejveri oil platforms. As the sun slipped beneath the huge dark horizon and the warmth fell from the hollows of Ptey's face, so his father turned his face to the sky. Tonight, he wore his Steris Aspect. The ritual selves scared Ptey, so rarely were they unfurled in Ctarisphay: births, namings, betrothals and marriages, divorces and deaths. And of course, the Manifoldings. Familiar faces became distant and formal. Their language changed, their bodies seemed slower, heavier. They became possessed by strange, special knowledges. Only Steris possessed the language for the robots to sail the catamaran and, despite the wheel of positioning satellites around tilted Tay, the latitude and longitude of the Manifold House. The catamaran itself was only run out from its boathouse, to strong songs heavy with clashing harmonies, when a child from Ctarisphay on the edge of adulthood sailed out beyond the outer mole and the fleet of oil platforms to have his or her personality unfolded into eight.

Only two months since, Cjatay had sailed out into the oily black of a late winter afternoon. Ptey was Summer-born, a Solstice boy; Cjatay a late Autumn. It was considered remarkable that they shared enough in common to be able to speak to each other, let alone become the howling boys of the neighborhood, the source of every broken window and borrowed boat. The best part of three seasons between them, but here was only two moons later, leaving behind the pulsing gas flares and maze of pipe work of the sheltering oil-fields, heading into the great, gentle oceanic glow of the plankton blooms, steering by the stars, the occupied, haunted stars. The Manifolding was never a thing of moons and calendars, but of mothers' watchings and grandmothers' knowings and teachers' notings and fathers' murmurings, of subtly shifted razors and untimely lethargies, of deep-swinging voices and stained bedsheets.

On Etjay Quay, where the porcelain houses leaned over the landing, Ptey had thrown his friend's bag down into the boat. Cjatay's father had caught it and frowned. There were observances. Ways. Forms.

"See you," Ptey had said.

"See you." Then the wind caught in the catamaran's tall, curved sails and carried it away from the rain-wet, shiny faces of the houses of Ctarisphay. Ptey had watched the boat until it was lost in the light dapple of the city's lamps on the winter-dark water. See Cjatay he would, after his six months on the Manifold House. But only partially. There would be Cjatays he had never known, never even met. Eight of them, and the Cjatay with whom he had stayed out all the brief Low Summer nights of the prith run on the fishing staithes, skinny as the piers' wooden legs silhouetted against the huge sun kissing the edge of the world, would be but a part, a dream of one of the new names and new personalities. Would he know him when he met him on the great floating university that was the Manifold House?

Would he know himself?

"Are they moving yet?" Steris called from the tiller. Ptey shielded his dark-accustomed eyes against the pervasive glow of the carbon-absorbing plankton blooms and peered into the sky. *Sail of Bright Anticipation* cut two lines of liquid black through the gently undulating sheet of biolight, fraying at the edges into fractal curls of luminescence as the sheets of microorganisms sought each other.

"Nothing yet."

But it would be soon, and it would be tremendous. Eight hundred stars setting out across the night. Through the changes and domestic rituals of his sudden Manifolding, Ptey had been aware of sky-watch parties being arranged, star-gazing groups setting up telescopes along the quays and in the campaniles, while day on day the story moved closer to the head of the news. Half the world—that half of the world not blinded by its extravagant axial tilt—would be looking to the sky. Watching Steris rig *Sail of Bright Anticipation*, Ptey had felt cheated, like a sick child confined to bed while festival raged across the boats lashed beneath his window. Now, as the swell of the deep dark of his world's girdling ocean lifted the twin prows of *Sail of Bright Anticipation*, on his web of shock-plastic mesh ahead of the mast, Ptey felt his excitement lift with it. A carpet of lights below, a sky of stars above: all his alone.

They were not stars. They were the eight hundred and twenty six space habitats of the Anpreen Commonweal, spheres of nano-carbon ice and water five hundred kilometers in diameter that for twice Ptey's lifetime had adorned Bephis, the ringed gas giant, like a necklace of pearls hidden in a velvet bag, far from eye and mind. The negotiations fell into eras. The Panic; when the world of Tay became aware that the gravity waves pulsing through the huge ripple tank that was their ocean-bound planet were the bow-shocks of massive artifacts decelerating from near light-speed. The Denial, when Tay's governments decided it was Best Really to try and hide the fact that their solar system had been immigrated into by eight hundred-and-some space vehicles, each larger than Tay's petty moons, falling into neat and proper order around Bephis. The Soliciting, when it became obvious that Denial was futile—but on our terms, our terms. A fleet of space probes was dispatched to survey and attempt radio contact with the arrivals—as yet silent as ice. And, when they were not blasted from space or vaporized or collapsed into quantum black holes or any of the plethora of fanciful destructions imagined in the popular media, the Overture. The Sobering, when it was realized that these star-visitors existed primarily as swarms of free-swimming nano-assemblers in the free-fall spherical oceans of their eight hundred and some habitats, one mind with many forms; and, for the Anpreen, the surprise that these archaic hominiforms on this backwater planet were many selves within one body. One thing they shared and understood well. Water. It ran through their histories, it flowed around their ecologies, it mediated their molecules. After one hundred and twelve years of near-light speed flight, the Anpreen Commonweal was desperately short of water; their spherical oceans shriveled almost into zero gravity teardrops within the immense, nano-tech-reinforced ice shells. Then began the era of Negotiation, the most prolonged of the phases of contact, and the most complex. It had taken three years to establish the philosophical foundations: the Anpreen, an ancient species of the great Clade, had long been a colonial mind, arranged in subtle hierarchies of self-knowledge and ability, and did not know who to talk to, whom to ask for a decision, in a political system with as many governments and nations as there were islands and archipelagos scattered across the world ocean of the fourth planet from the sun.

Now the era of Negotiation had become the era of Open Trade. The Anpreen habitats spent their last drops of reaction mass to break orbit around Bephis and move the Commonweal in-system. Their destination was not Tay, but Tejaphay, Tay's sunward neighbor, a huge waterworld of unbroken ocean one hundred kilometers deep, crushing gravity, and endless storms. A billion years before the seed-ships probed the remote star system, the gravitational interplay of giant worlds had sent the least of their number spiraling sunwards. Solar wind had stripped away its huge atmosphere and melted its mantle of water ice into a planetary ocean, deep and dark as nightmares. It was that wink of water in the system-scale interferometers of the Can-Bet-Merey people, half a million years before, that had inspired them to fill their night sky with solar sails as one hundred thousand slow seed-ships rode out on flickering launch lasers toward the new system. An evangelically pro-life people were the Can-Bet-Merey, zealous for the Clade's implicit dogma that intelligence was the only force in the universe capable of defeating the physical death of space-time.

If the tens of thousand of biological packages they had rained into the world-ocean of Tejaphay had germinated life, Tay's probes had yet to discover it. The Can-Bet-Merey did strike roots in the afterthought, that little blue pearl next out from the sun, a tear spun from huge Tejaphay.

One hundred thousand the years ago, the Can-Bet-Merey had entered the post-biological phase of intelligence and moved to that level that could no longer communicate with the biological life of Tay, or even the Anpreen.

"Can you see anything yet?" A call from the tiller. *Sail of Bright Anticipation* had left behind the carbon-soaked plankton bloom, the ocean was deep dark and boundless. Sky and sea blurred; stars became confused with the riding lights of ships close on the horizon.

"Is it time?" Ptey called back.

"Five minutes ago."

Ptey found a footing on the webbing, and, one hand wrapped in the sheets, stood up to scan the huge sky. Every child of Tay, crazily tilted at 48 degrees to the ecliptic, grew up conscious that her planet was a ball rolling around the sun and that the stars were far, vast and slow, almost unchanging. But stars could change; Bephis, that soft smudge of light low in the south-east, blurred by the glow of a eight hundred moon-sized space habitats, would soon be once again the hard point of light by which his ancestors had steered to their Manifoldings.

"Give it time," Ptey shouted. Time. The Anpreen were already voyaging; had switched on their drives and pulled out of orbit almost an hour before. The slow light of their embarkation had still not reached Tay. He saw the numbers spinning around in his head, accelerations, vectors, space and time all arranged around him like fluttering carnival banners. It had taken Ptey a long time to understand that not everyone could see numbers like him and reach out and make them do what they wanted.

"Well, I'll be watching the football," Cjatay had declared when Teacher Deu had declared a Special Class Project in conjunction with the Noble Observatory of Pteu to celebrate the Anpreen migration. "We're all jumping up and down, Anpreen this, Anpreen that, but when it comes down to it, they aliens and we don't know what they really want, no one does."

"They're not aliens," Ptey had hissed back. "There *are* no aliens, don't you know that? We're all just part of the one big Clade."

Then Teacher Deu had shouted at them quiet you boys and they had straightened themselves at their kneeling-desks, but Cjatay had hissed,

"So if they're our cousins, why don't they give us their star-crosser drive?"

Such was the friendship between Ptey and Cjatay that they would argue over nodes of free-swimming nanotechnology orbiting a gas giant.

"Look! Oh look!"

Slowly, very slowy, Bephis was unraveling into a glowing smudge, like one of the swarms of nuchpas that hung above the waves like smoke on High Summer mornings. The fleet was moving. Eight hundred worlds. The numbers in his skull told Ptey that the Anpreen Commonweal was already at ten percent of lightspeed. He tried to work out the relativistic deformations of space-time but there were too many numbers flocking around him too fast. Instead, he watched Bephis unfurl into a galaxy, that cloud of stars slowly pull away from the bright mote of the gas giant. Crossing the ocean of night. Ptey glanced behind him. In the big dark, his father's face was hard to read, especially as Steris, who was sober and focused, and, Ptey had learned, not particularly bright. He seemed to be smiling.

It is a deep understanding, the realization that you are cleverer than your parents, Ptey thought. Behind that first smirking, satisfied sense of your own smartness comes a more profound understanding; that smart is only smart at some things, in some situations. Clever is conditional: Ptey could calculate the space-time distortion of eight hundred space habitats, plot a course across the dark, steepening sea by the stars in their courses, but he could never harness the winds or whistle the small commands to the machines, all the weather-clevernesses of Steris. That is how our world has shaped our intelligences. A self for every season.

The ravel of stars was unwinding, the Anpreen migration flowing into a ribbon of sparkles, a scarf of night beyond the veils of the aurora. Tomorrow night, it would adorn Tejaphay, that great blue guide star on the edge of the world, that had become a glowing smudge, a thumbprint of the alien. Tomorrow night, Ptey would look at that blue eye in the sky from the minarets of the Manifold House. He knew that it had minarets; every child knew what the Manifold House and its sister houses all round the world, looked like. Great hulks of grey wood gone silvery from salt and sun, built over upon through within alongside until they were floating cities. Cities of children. But the popular imaginations of Teacher Deu's Grade Eight class never painted them bright and loud with voices; they were dark, sooty labyrinths sailing under a perpetual cloud of black diesel smoke that poured from a thousand chimneys, taller even than the masts and towers. The images were sharp in Ptey's mind, but he could never see himself there, in those winding wooden staircases loud with the cries of sea birds, looking out from the high balconies across the glowing sea. Then his breath caught. All his imaginings and failures to imagine were made true as lights disentangled themselves from the skein of stars of the Anpreen migration: red and green stars, the riding lights of the Manifold House. Now he could feel the thrum of its engines and generators through the water and the twin hulls. Ptey set his hand to the carbon nanofiber mast. It sang to deep harmonic. And just as the stars are always further than you think, so Prey saw that the lights of the Manifold House were closer than he thought, that he was right under them, that *Sail of Bright Anticipation* was slipping through the outer buoys and nets, and that the towers and spires and minarets, rising in his vision, one by one, were obliterating the stars.

⋐═══⋑

Nejben, swimming

Beneath a sky of honey, Nejben stood hip deep in water warm as blood, deep as forgetting. This High Summer midnight, the sun was still clear from the horizon, and in its constant heat and light, the wood of the Manifold House's old, warped spires seemed to exhale a spicy musk, the distilled pheromone of centuries of teenage hormones and sexual angsts and identity crises. In cupped hands, Nejben scooped up the waters of the Chalybeate Pool and let them run, gold and thick, through his fingers. He savored the sensuality, observed the flash of sunlight through the falling water, noted the cool, deep plash as the pool received its own. A new Aspect, Nejben; old in observation and knowledge, for the body remained the same though a flock of selves came to roost in it, fresh in interpretation and experience.

When Nejben first emerged, shivering and anoxic, from the Chalybeate Pool, to be wrapped in silvery thermal sheets by the agisters, he had feared himself mad. A voice in his head, that would not go away, that would not be shut up, that seemed to know him, know every part of him.

"It's perfectly normal," said agister Ashbey, a plump, serious woman with the blackest skin Nejben had ever seen. But he remembered that every Ritual Aspect was serious, and in the Manifold House the agisters were never in any other Aspect. None that the novices would ever see. "Perfectly natural. It takes time for your Prior, your childhood Aspect, to find its place and relinquish the control of the higher cognitive levels. Give it time. Talk to him. Reassure him. He will feel very lost, very alone, like he has lost everything that he ever knew. Except you, Nejben."

The time-free, sun-filled days in the sunny, smoggy yards and cloisters of the First Novitiate were full of whisperings; boys and girls like himself whispering goodbye to their childhoods. Nejben learned his Prior's dreads, that the self that had been called Ptey feared that the numbers, the patterns between them, the ability to reduce physical objects to mathematics and see in an instant their relationships and implications, would be utterly lost. He saw also that Nejben in himself scared Ptey: the easy physicality, the unselfconscious interest in his own body, the awareness of the hormones pumping like tidewater through his tubes and cells; the ever-present, ever-tickling nag of sex; everywhere, everywhen, everyone and thing. Even as a child-self, even as shadow, Ptey knew that the first self to be birthed at the Manifold House was the pubescent self, the sexual self, but he felt this growing, aching youth to be more alien than the disembodied, mathematical Anpreen.

The tiers led down into the palp pool. In its depths, translucencies shifted. Nejben shivered in the warm High Summer midnight.

"Hey! Ptey!"

Names flocked around the Manifold House's towers like sun-gulls. New selves, new identities unfolded every hour of every day and yet old names clung. Agister Ashbey, jokey and astute, taught the social subtleties by which adults knew what Aspect and name to address and which Aspect and name of their own to wear in response. From the shade of the Poljeri Cloister, Puzhay waved. Ptey had found girls frightening, but Nejben liked them, enjoyed their company and the little games of admiring insult and flirting mock-animosity he played with them. He reckoned he understood girls now. Puzhay was small, still boy-figured, her skin Winterborn-pale, a Janni from Bedenderay, where at midwinter the atmosphere froze. She had a barbarous accent and continental manners, but Nejben found himself thinking often about her small, flat boy-breasts with their big, thumbable nipples. He had never thought when he came to the Manifold House that there would be people here from places other than Ctarisphay and its archipelago sisters. People—girls—from the big polar continent. Rude girls who cursed and openly called boys' names.

"Puzhay! What're you doing?"

"Going in."

"For the palps?"

"Nah. Just going in."

Nejben found and enjoyed a sudden, swift swelling of his dick as he watched Puzhay's breasts taunten as she raised her arms above her head and dived, awkward as a Bedenderay land-girl, into the water. Water hid it. Sun dapple kept it secret. The he felt a shiver run over him and he dived down, deep down. Almost he let the air rush out of him in a gasp as he felt the cool cool water close around his body; then he saw Puzhay in her tight swim-shorts that made her ass look so strong and muscley turn in the water, tiny bubbles leaking from her nose, to grin and wave and beckon him down. Nejben swam down past the descending tiers of steps. Green opened before him, the bottomless emerald beyond the anti-skray nets where the Chalybeate pond was refreshed by the borderless sea. Between her pale red body and the deep green sea was the shimmering curtains of the palps.

They did not make them we did not bring them they were here forever. Ten thousand years of theology, biology, and xenology in that simple kinder-group rhyme. Nejben—all his people—had always known their special place; stranger to this world, spurted into the womb of the world-sea as the star-sperm, the seed of sentience. Twenty million drops of life-seed swam ashore and became humanity, the rest swam out to sea and met and smelled and loved the palps, older than forever. Now Nejben turned and twisted like an eel past funny, flirting, heartbreaking Puzhay, turning to show the merest glimpse of his own sperm-eel, down toward the palps. The curtain of living jelly rippled and dissolved into their separate lives. Slick, cold, quivering jelly slid across his sex-warm flesh.

Nejben shivered, quivered; repelled yet aroused in a way that was other than sex. The water took on a prickle, a tickle, a tang of salt and fear and ancient ancient lusts, deep as his first stiff dream. Against sense, against reason, against three million years of species wisdom, Nejben employed the tricks of agister Ashbey and opened his mouth. He inhaled. Once he gagged, twice he choked, then he felt the jellied eeling of the palps squirm down his throat: a choke, and into the lungs. He inhaled green salt water. And then, as the palps demurely unraveled their nano-tube outer integuments and infiltrated them into his lungs, his bronchial tubes, his bloodstream, he *became*. Memories stirred, invoked by olfactory summonings, changed as a new voice, a new way of seeing, a new interpretation of those memories and experiences, formed. Nejben swam down, breathing memory-water, stroke by stroke unraveling. There was another down there, far below him, swimming up not through water but through the twelve years of his life. A new self.

—◆—

Puzhay, against the light of a three o'clock sky. Framed in the arch of a cell window, knees pulled up to her chest. Small budding breasts; strong, boy jawline, fall and arc of hair shadow against lilac. She had laughed, throwing her head back. That first sight of her was cut into Nejben's memory, every line and trace, like the paper silhouettes the limners would cut of friends and families and enemies for Autumn Solstice. That first stirring of sex, that first intimation in the self of Ptey of this then-stranger, now-familiar Nejben.

As soon as he could, he had run. After he had found out where to put his bag, after he had worked out how to use the ancient, gurgling shit-eater, after agister Ashbey had closed the door with a smile and a blessing on the wooden cell—his wooden cell—that still smelled of fresh-cut timber after hundreds of years on the world-ocean of Tay. In the short season in which photosynthesis was possible, Bedenderay's forests grew fast and fierce, putting on meters in a single day. Small wonder the wood still smelled fresh and lively. After the midnight walk along the ceramic lanes and up the wooden staircases and through the damp-smelling cloisters, through the gently undulating quadrangles with the sky-train of the Anpreen migration bright overhead, holding on, as tradition demanded, to the bell-hung by a chain from his agister's waist; after the form filling and the photographings and the registering and the this-is-your-ident-card this is your map I've tattooed onto the back of your hand trust it will guide you and I am your agister and we'll see you in the east Refectory for breakfast; after the climb up the slimy wooden stairs from *Sail of Bright Anticipation* on to the Manifold House's quay, the biolights green around him and the greater lamps of the great college's towers high before him; when he was alone in this alien new world where he would become eight alien new people: he ran.

Agister Ashbey was faithful; the tattoo, a clever print of smart molecules and nanodyes, was meshed into the Manifold House's network and guided him through the labyrinth of dormitories and cloisters and Boy's Pavilions and Girlhearths by the simple, aversive trick of stinging the opposite side his map-hand to the direction in which he was to turn.

Cjatay. Sea-sundered friend. The only other one who knew him, knew him the moment they had met outside the school walls and recognized each other as different from the sailing freaks and fishing fools. Interested in geography, in love with numbers, with the wonder of the world and the worlds, as the city net declared, beyond. Boys who looked up at the sky.

As his burning hand led him left, right, up this spiral staircase under the lightening sky, such was Ptey's impetus that he never thought, would he know Cjatay? Cjatay had been in the Manifold House three months. Cjatay could be—*would* be—any number of Aspects now. Ptey had grown up with his father's overlapping circles of friends, each specific to a different Aspect, but he had assumed that it was a grown up thing. That couldn't happen to him and Cjatay! Not them.

The cell was one of four that opened off a narrow oval at the head of a tulip-shaped minaret—the Third Moon of Spring Tower, the legend on the back of Ptey's hand read. Cells were assigned by birth-date and season. Head and heart full of nothing but seeing Cjatay, he pushed open the door—no door in the Manifold House was ever locked.

She was in the arched window, dangerously high above the shingled roofs and porcelain domes of the Vernal Equinox division. Beyond her, only the wandering stars of the Anpreen. Ptey had no name for the sudden rush of feelings that came when he saw Puzhay throw back her head and laugh at some so-serious comment of Cjatay's. Nejben did.

It was only at introductory breakfast in the East Refectory, where he met the other uncertain, awkward boys and girls of his intake, that Ptey saw past the dawn seduction of Puzhay to Cjatay, and saw him unchanged, exactly as he had had been when he had stepped down from Etjay Quay into the catamaran and been taken out across the lagoon to the waste gas flares of Temejveri.

⇒⊱

She was waiting crouched on the wooden steps where the water of the Chalybeate Pool lapped, knees pulled to her chest, goose flesh pimpling her forearms and calves in the cool of after-midnight. He knew this girl, knew her name, knew her history, knew the taste of a small, tentative kiss stolen among the crowds of teenagers pushing over 12th Canal Bridge. The memory was sharp and warm, but it was another's.

"Hi there."

He dragged himself out of the water onto to the silvery wood, rolled away to hide his nakedness. In the cloister shadow, Ashbey waited with a sea-silk robe.

"Hi there." There was never any easy way to tell someone you were another person from the one they remembered. "I'm Serejen." The name had been there, down among the palps, slipped into him with their mind-altering neurotransmitters.

"Are you?"

"All right. Yes, I'm all right." A tickle in the throat made him cough, the cough amplified into a deep retch. Serejen choked up a lungful of mucus-stained palp-jelly. In the early light, it thinned and ran, flowed down the steps to rejoin its shoal in the Chalybeate Pool. Agister Ashbey took a step forward. Serejen waved her away.

"What time is it?"

"Four thirty."

Almost five hours.

"Serejen." Puzhay looked coyly away. Around the Chalybeate Pool, other soul-swimmers were emerging, coughing up lungfuls of palp, shivering in their thermal robes, growing into new Aspects of themselves. "It's Cjatay. He needs to see you. Dead urgent."

Waiting Ashbey folded new-born Serejen in his own thermal gown, the intelligent plastics releasing their stored heat to his particular body temperature.

"Go to him," his agister said.

"I thought I was supposed to . . . "

"You've got the rest of your life to get to know Serejen. I think you should go."

Cjatay. A memory of fascination with starry skies, counting and numbering and betting games. The name and the face belonged to another Aspect, another life, but that old lust for numbers, for discovering the relationships between things, stirred a deep welling of joy. It was as rich and adult as the swelling of his dick he found in the bright mornings, or when he thought about Puzhay's breasts in his hands and the tattooed triangle of her sex. Different; no less intense.

The shutters were pulled close. The screen was the sole light in the room. Cjatay turned on hearing his lockless door open. He squinted into the gloom of the stair head, then cried excitedly,

"Look at this look at this!"

Pictures from the observation platforms sent to Tejaphay to monitor the doings of the Anpreen. A black-light plane of stars, the blinding blue curve of the water world stopped down to prevent screen-burn. The closer habitats showed a disc, otherwise it was moving lights. Patterns of speed and gravity.

"What am I looking at?"

"Look look, they're building a space elevator! I wondered how they were going to get the water from Tejaphay. Simple, duh! They're just going to vacuum it up! They've got some kind of processing unit in stationary orbit chewing up one of those asteroids they brought with them, but they using one of their own habitats to anchor it."

"At twice stationary orbit," Serejen said. "So they're going to have to build down and up at the same time to keep the elevator in tension." He did not know where the words came from. They were on his lips and they were true.

"It must be some kind of nano-carbon compound," Cjatay said, peering at the screen for some hint, some elongation, some erection from the fuzzy blob of the construction asteroid. "Incredible tensile strength, yet very flexible. We have to get that; with all our oil, it could change everything about our technology. It could really make us a proper star-faring people." Then, as if hearing truly for the first time, Cjatay turned from the screen and peered again at the figure in the doorway. "Who are you?" His voice was high and soft and plaintive.

"I'm Serejen."

"You sound like Ptey."

"I was Ptey. I remember him."

Cjatay did a thing with his mouth, a twisting, chewing movement that Serejen recalled from moments of unhappiness and frustration. The time at his sister's nameday party, when all the birth family was gathered and he had shown how it was almost certain that someone in the house on Drunken Chicken Lane had the same nameday as little Sezjma. There had been a long, embarrassed silence as Cjatay had burst into the adult chatter. Then laughter. And again, when Cjatay had worked out how long it would take to walk a light-year and Teacher Deu has asked the class *does anyone understand this?* For a moment, Serejen thought that the boy might cry. That would have been a terrible thing; unseemly, humiliating. Then he saw the bag on the unkempt bed, the ritual white clothes thrust knotted and fighting into it.

"I think what Cjatay wants to say is that he's leaving the Manifold House," agister Ashbey said, in the voice that Serejen understood as the one adults used when they had uncomfortable things to say. In that voice was a hidden word that Ashbey would not, that Serejen and Puzhay could not, and that Cjatay never would speak.

There was one in every town, every district. Kentlay had lived at the bottom of Drunken Chicken Lane, still at fortysomething living with his birth-parents. He had never married, though then-Ptey had heard that some did, and not just others like them. Normals. Multiples. Kentlay had been a figure that drew pity and respect alike; equally blessed and cursed, the Lonely were granted insights and gifts in compensation for their inability to manifold into the Eight Aspects. Kentlay had the touch for skin diseases, warts, and the sicknesses of birds. Ptey had been sent to see him for the charm of a dangling wart on his chin. The wart was gone within a week. Even then, Ptey had wondered if it had been through unnatural gifts or superstitious fear of the alien at the end of the wharf.

Cjatay. Lonely. The words were as impossible together as *green sun* or *bright winter.* It was never to be like this. Though the waters of the Chalybeate Pool would break them into many brilliant shards, though there would be other lives, other friends, even other wives and husbands, there would always be aspects of themselves that remembered trying to draw birds and fishes on the glowing band of the Mid Winter Galaxy that hung in the sky for weeks on end, or trying to calculate the mathematics of the High Summer silverlings that shoaled like silver needles in the Lagoon, how they kept together yet apart, how they were many but moved as one. *Boiling rain. Summer ice. A morning where the sun wouldn't rise. A friend who would always, only be one person.* Impossibilities. Cjatay could not be abnormal. Dark word. A vile word that hung on Cjatay like an oil-stained tarpaulin.

He sealed his bag and slung it over his shoulder.

"I'll give you a call when you get back."

"Yeah. Okay. That would be good." Words and needs and sayings flocked to him, but the end was so fast, so sudden, that all Serejen could do was stare at his feet so that he would not have to see Cjatay walk away. Puzhay was in tears. Cjatay's own agister, a tall, dark-skinned Summer-born, put his arm around Cjatay and took him to the stairs.

"Hey. Did you ever think?" Cjatay threw back the line from the top of the spiral stair. "Why are they here? The Anpreen." Even now, Serejen realized, Cjatay was hiding from the truth that he would be marked as different, as not fully human, for the rest of his life, hiding behind stars and ships and the mystery of the alien. "Why did they come here? They call it the Anpreen Migration, but where are they migrating *to*? And what are they migrating *from*? Anyone ever ask that? Ever think about that, eh?"

Then agister Ashbey closed the door on the high tower-top cell.

"We'll talk later."

Gulls screamed. Change in the weather coming. On the screen behind him, stars moved across the face of the great water.

Serejen could not bear to go down to the quay, but watched *Sail of Bright Anticipation* make sail from the cupola of the Bright Glance Netball Hall. The Manifold House was sailing through a plankton-bloom and he watched the ritual catamaran's hulls cut two lines of bioglow through the carpet of carbon-absorbing microlife. He stood and followed the sails until they were lost among the hulls of huge ceramic oil tankers pressed low to the orange smog-glow of Ctarisphay down under the horizon. Call each other. They would always forget to do that. They would slip out of each other's lives—Serejen's life now vastly more rich and populous as he moved across the social worlds of his various Aspects. In time, they would slip out of each other's thoughts and memories. So it was that Serejen Nejben ex-Ptey knew that he was not a child any longer. He could let things go.

After morning Shift class, Serejen went down to the Old Great Pool, the ancient flooded piazza that was the historic heart of the Manifold House, and used the techniques he had learned an hour before to effortlessly transfer from Serejen to Nejbet. Then he went down into the waters and swam with Puzhay. She was teary and confused, but the summer-warmed water and the physical exercise brightened her. Under a sky lowering with the summer storm that the gulls had promised, they sought out the many secret flooded colonnades and courts where the big groups of friends did not go. There, under the first crackles of lightning and the hiss of rain, he kissed her and she slipped her hand into his swimsuit and cradled the comfortable swell of his cock.

Serejen, loving.

Night, the aurora and sirens. Serejen shivered as police drones came in low over the Conservatorium roof. Through the high, arched windows, fires could still be seen burning on Yaskaray Prospect. The power had not yet been restored, the streets, the towering apartment blocks that lined them, were still dark. A stalled tram sprawled across a set of points, flames flickering in its rear carriage. The noise of the protest had moved off, but occasional shadows moved across the ice beneath the mesmerism of the aurora; student rioters, police security robots. It was easy to tell the robots by the sprays of ice crystals thrown up by their needle-tip, mincing legs.

"Are you still at that window? Come away from there, if they see you they might shoot you. Look, I've tea made."

"Who?"

"What?"

"Who might shoot me? The rioters or the police?"

"Like you'd care if you were dead."

But he came and sat at the table and took the bowl of thin, salty Bedenderay maté.

"But sure I can't be killed."

Her name was Seriantep. She was an Anpreen Prebendary ostensibly attached to the College of Theoretical Physics at the Conservatorium of Jann. She looked like a tall, slim young woman with the dark skin and blue-black hair of a Summer-born Archipelagan, but that was just the form that the swarm of Anpreen nano-processor motes had assumed. She hived. Reris Orhum Fejannan Kekjay Prus Rejmer Serejen Nejben wondered how close you had to get before her perfect skin resolved into a blur of microscopic motes. He had had much opportunity to make this observation. As well as being his notional student—though what a functionally immortal hive-citizen who had crossed one hundred and twenty light years could learn from a fresh twenty-something meat human was moot—she was his occasional lover.

She drank the tea. Serejen watched the purse of her lips around the delicate porcelain bowl decorated with the ubiquitous Lord of the Fishes motif, even in high, dry continental Jann. The small movement of her throat as she swallowed. He knew a hundred such tiny, intimate movements, but even as she cooed and giggled and gasped to the stimulations of the Five Leaves, Five Fishes ritual, the involuntary actions of her body had seemed like performances. Learned responses. Performances as he made observations. Actor and audience. That was the kind of lover he was as Serejen.

"So what is it really like to fuck a pile of nano-motes?" Puzhay had asked as they rolled around with wine in the cosy warm fleshiness of the Thirteenth Window Coupling Porch at the ancient, academic Ogrun Menholding. "I'd imagine it feels . . . fizzy." And she'd squeezed his cock, holding it hostage, *watch what you say boy.*

"At least nano-motes never get morning breath," he'd said, and she'd given a little shriek of outrage and jerked his dick so that he yelped, and then they both laughed and then rolled over again and buried themselves deep into the winter-defying warmth of the piled quilts.

I should be with her now, he thought. The months-long winter nights beneath the aurora and the stars clouds of the great galaxy were theirs. After the Manifold House, he had gone with her to her Bedenderay and her home city of Jann. The City Conservatorium had the world's best theoretical physics department. It was nothing to do with small, boyish, funny Puzhay. They had formalised a partnering six months later. His parents had complained and shivered through all the celebrations in this cold and dark and barbarous city far from the soft elegance of island life. But ever after winter, even on the coldest mornings when carbon dioxide frost crusted the steps of the Tea Lane Ladyhearth where Puzhay lived, was their season. He should call her, let her know he was still trapped but that at the first sign, the very first sign, he would come back. The cell net was still up. Even an email. He couldn't. Seriantep didn't know. Seriantep wouldn't understand. She had not understood that one time when he tried to explain it in abstracts; that different Aspects could—should—have different relationships with different partners, love separately but equally. *That as Serejen, I love you, Anpreen Prebendary Seriantep, but as Nejben, I love Puzhay.* He could never say that. For an immortal, starcrossing hive of nano motes, Seriantep was very singleminded.

Gunfire cracked in the crystal night, far and flat.

"I think it's dying down," Seriantep said.

"I'd give it a while yet."

So strange, so rude, this sudden flaring of anti-alien violence. In the dreadful dead of winter too, when nothing should rightfully fight and even the trees along Yaskaray Prospect drew down to their heartwood and turned to ice. Despite the joy of Puzhay, Serejen knew that he would always hate the Bedenderay winter. *You watch out now,* his mother had said when he had announced his decision to go to Jann. *They all go dark-mad there.* Accidie and suicide walked the frozen canals of the Winter City. No surprise then that madness should break out against the Anpreen Prebendaries. Likewise inevitable that the popular rage should be turned against the Conservatorium. The university had always been seen as a place apart from the rest of Jann, in summer aloof and lofty above the sweltering streets, like an over-grand daughter; in winter a parasite on this most marginal of economies. Now it was the unofficial alien embassy in the northern hemisphere. There were more Anpreen in its long, small-windowed corridors than anywhere else in the world.

There are no aliens, Serejen thought. *There is only the Clade. We are all family. Cjatay had insisted that.* The ship had sailed over the horizon, they hadn't called, they had drifted from each other's lives. Cjatay's name occasionally impinged on Serejen's awareness through radio interviews and opinion pieces. He had developed a darkly paranoid conspiracy theory around the Anpreen Presence. Serejen, high above the frozen streets of Jann in deeply abstract speculation about the physical reality of mathematics, occasionally mused upon the question of at what point the Migration had become a Presence. The Lonely often obsessively took up narrow, focused interests. Now the street was listening, acting. Great Winter always was a dark, paranoid season. *Here's how to understand*, Serejen thought. *There are no aliens after you've had sex with them.*

Helicopter blades rattled from the walls of the College of Theoretical Physics and then retreated across the Central Canal. The silence in the warm, dimly-lit little faculty cell was profound. At last, Serejen said, "I think we could go now."

On the street, cold stabbed even through the quilted layers of Serejen's great-coat. He fastened the high collar across his throat and still he felt the breath crackle into ice around his lips. Seriantep stepped lightly between the half bricks and bottle shards in nothing more than the tunic and leggings she customarily wore around the college. Her motes gave her full control over her body, including its temperature.

"You should have put something on," Serejen said. "You're a bit obvious."

Past shuttered cafés and closed up stores and the tall brick faces of the student Hearths. The burning tram on the Tunday Avenue junction blazed fitfully, its bitter smoke mingling with the eternal aromatic hydrocarbon smog exhaled by Jann's power plants. The trees that lined the avenue's centre strip were folded down into tight fists, dreaming of summer. Their boot heels rang loud on the street tiles.

A darker shape upon the darkness moved in the narrow slit of an alley between two towering tenement blocks. Serejen froze, his heart jerked. A collar turned down, a face studying his—Obredajay from the Department of Field Physics.

"Safe home."

"Aye. And you."

The higher academics all held apartments within the Conservatorium and were safe within its walls; most of the research staff working late would sit it out until morning. Tea and news reports would see them through. Those out on the fickle streets had reasons to be there. Serejen had heard that Obredajay was head-over-heels infatuated with a new manfriend.

The dangers we court for little love.

On the intersection of Tunday Avenue and Yaskaray Wharf, a police robot stepped out of the impervious dark of the arches beneath General Gatoris Bridge. Pistons hissed it up to its full three meters; green light flicked across Serejen's retinas. Seriantep held up her hand, the motes of her palm displaying her immunity as a Prebendary of the Clade. The machine shrank down, seemingly dejected, if plastic and pumps could display such an emotion.

A solitary tea-shop stood open on the corner of Silver Spider Entry and the Wharf, its windows misty with steam from the simmering urns. Security eyes turned and blinked at the two fleeing academics.

On Tannis Lane, they jumped them. There was no warning. A sudden surge of voices rebounding from the stone staircases and brick arches broke into a wave of figures lumbering around the turn of the alley, bulky and shouldering in their heavy winter quilts. Some held sticks, some held torn placards, some were empty handed. They saw a man in a heavy winter coat, breath frosted on his mouth-shield. They saw a woman almost naked, her breath easy, unclouded. They knew in an instant what she saw. The hubbub in the laneway became a roar.

Serejen and Seriantep were already in flight. Sensing rapid motion, the soles of Serejen's boots extended grips into the rime. As automatically, he felt the heart-numbing panic-rush ebb, felt himself lose his grip on his body and grow pale. Another was taking hold, his flight-or-fight Aspect; his cool, competent emergency service Fejannen.

He seized Seriantep's hand.

"With me. Run!"

Serejen-Fejannen saw the change of Aspect flicker across the tea-shop owner's face like weather as they barged through his door, breathless between his stables. Up to his counter with its looming, steaming urns of hot hot water. This tea-man wanted them out, wanted his livelihood safe.

"We need your help."

The tea-man's eyes and nostrils widened at the charge of rioters that skidded and slipped around the corner in to Silver Spider Entry. Then his hand hit the button under the counter and the shutters rolled down. The shop boomed, the shutters bowed to fists striking them. Rocks banged like gunfire from metal. Voices rose and joined together, louder because they were unseen.

"I've called the police," Seriantep said. "They'll be here without delay."

"No, they won't," Fejannen said. He pulled out a chair from the table closest the car and sat down, edgily eying the grey slats of the shutter. "Their job is to restore order and protect property. Providing personal protection to aliens is far down their list of priorities."

Seriantep took the chair opposite. She sat down wary as a settling bird.

"What's going on here? I don't understand. I'm very scared."

The café owner set two glasses of maté down on the table. He frowned, then his eyes opened in understaidng. An alien at his table. He returned to the bar and leaned on it, staring at the shutters beyond which the voice of the mob circled.

"I thought you said you couldn't be killed."

"That's not what I'm scared of. I'm scared of you, Serejen."

"I'm not Serejen. I'm Fejannen."

"Who, what's Fejannen?"

"Me, when I'm scared, when I'm angry, when I need to be able to think clearly and coolly when a million things are happening at once, when I'm playing games or hunting or putting a big funding proposal together."

"You sound . . . different."

"I *am* different. How long have you been on our world?"

"You're hard. And cold. Serejen was never hard.."

"I'm not Serejen."

A huge crash—the shutter bowed under a massive impact and the window behind it shattered.

"Right, that's it, I don't care what happens, you're going." The tea-man leaped from behind his counter and strode towards Seriantep. Fejannen was there to meet him.

"This woman is a guest in your country and requires your protection."

"That's not a woman. That's a pile of . . . insects. Things. Tiny things."

"Well, they look like mighty scared tiny things."

"I don't think so. Like you said, like they say on the news, they can't really die."

"They can hurt. *She* can hurt."

Eyes locked, then disengaged. The maté-man returned to his towering silos of herbal mash. The noise from the street settled into a stiff, waiting silence. Neither Fejannen nor Seriantep believed that it was true, that the mob had gone, despite the spearing cold out there. The lights flickered once, twice.

Seriantep said suddenly, vehemently, "I could take them."

The tea-man looked up.

"Don't." Fejannen whispered.

"I could. I could get out under the door. It's just a reforming."

The tea-man's eyes were wide. A demon, a winter-grim in his prime location canal-side tea shop!

"You scare them enough as you are," Fejannen said.

"Why? We're only here to help, to learn from you."

"They think, what have you got to learn from *us*? They think that you're keeping secrets from us."

"Us?"

"Them. Don't scare them any more. The police will come, eventually, or the Conservatorium proctors. Or they'll just get bored and go home. These things never really last."

"You're right." She slumped back into her seat. "This fucking world . . . Oh, why did I come here?" Seriantep glanced up at the inconstant lumetubes, beyond to the distant diadem of her people's colonies, gravid on decades of water. It was a question, Fejannen knew, that Serejen had asked himself many times. A post-graduate scholar researching space-time topologies and the cosmological constant. A thousand-year-old post-human innocently wearing the body of a twenty-year-old woman, playing the student. She could learn nothing from him. All the knowledge the Anpreen wanderers had gained in their ten thousands year migration was incarnate in her motes. She embodied all truth and she lied with every cell of her body. Anpreen secrets. No basis for a relationship, yet Serejen loved her, as Serejen could love. But was it any more for her than novelty; a tourist, a local boy, a brief summer loving?

Suddenly, vehemently, Seriantep leaned across the table to take Fejannen's face between her hands.

"Come with me."

"Where? Who?"

"Who?" She shook her head in exasperation. "Ahh! Serejen. But it would be you as well, it has to be you. To my place, to the Commonweal. I've wanted to ask you for so long. I'd love you to see my worlds. Hundreds of worlds, like jewels, dazzling in the sun. And inside, under the ice, the worlds within worlds within worlds . . . I made the application for a travel bursary months ago, I just couldn't ask."

"Why? What kept you from asking?" A small but significant traffic of diplomats, scientists, and journalists flowed between Tay and the Anpreen fleet around Tejaphay. The returnees enjoyed global celebrity status, their opinions and experiences sought by think-tanks and talk shows and news-site columns, the details of the faces and lives sought by the press. Serejen had never understood what it was the people expected from the celebrity of others but was not so immured behind the fortress walls of the Collegium, armoured against the long siege of High Winter, that he couldn't appreciate its personal benefits. The lights seemed to brighten, the sense of the special hush outside, that was not true silence but waiting, dimmed as Serejen replaced Fejannen. "Why didn't you ask?"

"Because I though you might refuse."

"Refuse?" The few, the golden few. "Turn down the chance to work in the Commonweal? Why would anyone do that, what would I do that?"

Seriantep looked long at him, her head cocked slightly, alluringly, to one side, the kind of gesture an alien unused to a human body might devise,

"You're Serejen again, aren't you?"

"I am that Aspect again, yes."

"Because I thought you might refuse because of *her*. That other woman. Puzhay."

Serejen blinked three times. From Seriantep's face, he knew that she expected some admission, some confession, some emotion. He could not understand what.

Seriantep said, "I know about her. We know things at the Anpreen Mission. We check whom we work with. We have to. We know not everyone welcomes us, and that more are suspicious of us. I know who she is and where she lives and what you do with her three times a week when you go to her. I know where you were intending to go tonight, if all this hadn't happened."

Three times again, Serejen blinked. Now he was hot, too hot in his winter quilt in this steamy, fragrant tea-shop.

"But that's a ridiculous question. *I* don't love Puzhay. *Nejben* does."

"Yes, but you *are* Nejben."

"How many times do I have to tell you . . . ." Serejen bit back the anger. There were Aspects hovering on the edge of his consciousness like the hurricane-front angels of the Bazjendi Psalmody; selves inappropriate to Seriantep. Aspects that in their rage and storm might lose him this thing, so finely balanced now in this tea-shop. "It's our way," he said weakly. "It's how we are."

"Yes, but . . . " Seriantep fought for words. "It's *you*, there, that body. You say it's different, you say it's someone else and not you, not Serejen, but how do I know that? How *can* I know that?"

You say that, with your body that in this tea-shop you said could take many forms, any form, Serejen thought. Then Fejannen, shadowed but never more than a thought away in this besieged, surreal environment, heard a shift in the silence outside. The tea-man glanced up. He had heard it too. The difference between *waiting* and *anticipating*.

"Excuse me, I must change Aspects."

A knock on the shutter, glove-muffled. A voice spoke Fejannen's full name. A voice that Fejannen knew from his pervasive fear of the risk his academic Aspect was taking with Seriantep and that Serejen knew from those news reports and articles that broke through his vast visualisations of the topology of the universe and that Nejben knew from a tower top cell and a video screen full of stars.

"Came I come in?"

Fejannen nodded to the tea-man. He ran the shutter up high enough for the bulky figure in the long quilted coat and boots to duck under. Dreadful cold blew around Fejannen.

Cjatay bowed, removed his gloves, banging rime from the knuckles and made the proper formalities to ascertain which Aspect he was speaking to.

"I have to apologise; I only recently learned that it was you who were caught here."

The voice, the intonations and inflections, the over-precisions and refine-ments—no time might have passed since Cjatay walked out of Manifold House. In a sense, no time *had* passed; Cjatay was caught, inviolable, unchangeable by anything other than time and experience. Lonely.

"The police will be here soon," Seriantep said.

"Yes, they will," Cjatay said mildly. He looked Seriantep up and down, as if studying a zoological specimen. "They have us well surrounded now. These things are almost never planned; what we gain in spontaneity of expression we lose in strategy. But when I realised it was you, Fejannen-Nejben, I saw a way that we could all emerge from this intact."

"Safe passage," Fejannen said.

"I will personally escort you out."

"And no harm at all to you, politically."

"I need to distance myself from what has happened tonight."

"But your fundamental fear of the visitors remains unchanged?"

"I don't change. You know that. I see it as a virtue. Some things are solid, some things endure. Not everything changes with the seasons. But fear, you said. That's clever. Do you remember, that last time I saw you, back in the Manifold House. Do you remember what I said?"

"Nejben remembers you asking, where are they migrating to? And what are they migrating from?"

"In all your seminars and tutorials and conferences, in all those questions about the shape of the universe—oh, we have our intelligences too, less broad than the Anpreen's, but subtler, we think—did you ever think to *ask* that question: why have you come here?" Cjatay's chubby, still childish face was an accusation. "You are fucking her, I presume?"

In a breath, Fejannen had slipped from his seat into the Third Honorable Offense Stance. A hand on his shoulder; the teashop owner. No honor in it, not against a Lonely. Fejannen returned to his seat, sick with shuddering rage.

"Tell him," Cjatay said.

"It's very simple," Seriantep said. "We are refugees. The Anpreen Commonweal is the surviving remnant of the effective annihilation of our sub-species of Panhumanity. Our eight hundred habitats are such a minuscule percentage of our original race that, to all statistical purposes, we are extinct. Our habitats once englobed an entire sun. We're all that's left."

"How? Who?"

"Not so much *who*, as *when*," Cjatay said gently. He flexed cold-blued fingers and pulled on his gloves.

"They're coming?"

"We fear so," Seriantep said. "We don't know. We were careful to leave no traces, to cover our tracks, so to speak, and we believe we have centuries of a headstart on them. We are only here to refuel our habitats, then we'll go, hide ourselves in some great globular cluster."

"But why, *why* would anyone do this? We're all the same species, that's what you told us. The Clade, Panhumanity."

"Brothers disagree," Cjatay said. "Families fall out, families feud within themselves. No animosity like it."

"Is this true? How can this be true? Who knows about this?" Serejen strove with Fejannen for control and understanding. One of the first lessons the Agisters of the Manifold House had taught was the etiquette of transition between conflicting Aspects. A war in the head, a conflict of selves. He could understand sibling strife on a cosmic scale. But a whole species?

"The governments," Cjatay said. To the tea-man, "Open the shutter again. You be all right with us. I promise." To Serejen, "Politicians, some senior academics, and policy makers. And us. Not you. But we all agree, we don't want to scare anyone. So we question the Anpreen Prebendaries on our world, and question their presence in our system, and maybe sometimes it bubbles into xenophobic violence, but that's fine, that's the price, that's nothing compared to what would happen if we realised that our guests might be drawing the enemies that destroyed them to our homes. Come on. We'll go now."

The tea-man lifted the shutter. Outside, the protestors stood politely aside as Cjatay led the refugees out on to the street. There was not a murmur as

Seriantep, in her ridiculous, life-threatening house-clothes, stepped across the cobbles. The great Winter Clock on the tower of Alajnedeng stood at twenty past five. The morning shift would soon be starting, the hot-shops firing their ovens and fry-pots.

A murmur in the crowd as Serejen took Seriantep's hand.

"Is it true?" he whispered.

"Yes," she said. "It is."

He looked up at the sky that would hold stars for another three endless months. The aurora coiled and spasmed over huddling Jann. Those stars were like crystal spearpoints. The universe was vast and cold and inimical to humanity, the greatest of Great Winters. He had never deluded himself it would be otherwise. Power had been restored, yellow street light glinted from the helmets of riot control officers and the carapaces of counterinsurgency drones. Serejen squeezed Seriantep's hand.

"What you asked."

"When?"

"Then. Yes. I will. Yes."

Torben, melting.

The Anpreen shatter-ship blazed star-bright as it turned its face to the sun. A splinter of smart-ice, it was as intricate as a snow-flake, stronger than any construct of Taynish engineering. Torben hung in free-fall in the observation dome at the centre of the cross of solar vanes. The Anpreen, being undifferentiated from the motes seeded through the hull, had no need for such architectural fancies. Their senses were open to space; the fractal shell of the ship was one great retina. They had grown the blister—pure and perfectly transparent construction-ice—for the comfort and delight of their human guests.

The sole occupant of the dome, Torben was also the sole passenger on this whole alien, paradoxical ship. Another would have been good. Another could have shared the daily, almost hourly shocks of strange and new and wonder. His other Aspects had felt with Torben the breath-catch of awe, and even greater privilege, when he had looked from the orbital car of the space elevator—the Anpreen's gift to the peoples of Tay—and seen the shatter-ship turn out of occultation in a blaze of silver light as it came in to dock. They had felt his glow of intellectual vindication as he first swam clumsily into the star-dome and discovered, with a shock, that the orbital transfer station was no more than a cluster of navigation lights almost lost in the star fields beyond. No sense of motion. His body had experienced no hint of acceleration. He had been correct. The Anpreen could adjust the topology of spacetime. But there was no one but his several selves to tell it to. The Anpreen crew—Torben was not sure whether it was one or many, or if that distinction had any meaning—was remote and alien. On occasion, as he swam down the live-wood panelled corridors, monoflipper and web-mittens pushing thick, humid air, he had glimpsed a swirl of silver motes twisting and knotting like a captive waterspout. Always they had dispersed in his presence. But the ice beyond those wooden walls, pressing in around him, felt alive, crawling, aware.

Seriantep had gone ahead months before him.

"There's work I have to do."

There had been a party; there was always a party at the Anpreen Mission among the ever-green slopes of generous, volcanic Sulanj. Fellow academics, press and PR from Ctarisphay, politicians, family members, and the Anpreen Prebendaries, eerie in their uniform loveliness.

"You can do the research work on *Thirty-Third Tranquil Abode*, that's the idea," Seriantep had said. Beyond the paper lanterns hung in the trees and the glow of the carbon-sink lagoon, the lights of space-elevator cars rose up until they merged with the stars. She would ride that narrow way to orbit within days. Serejen wondered how he would next recognise her.

"You have to go." Puzhay stood in the balcony of the Tea Lane Ladyhearth, recently opened to allow spring warmth into rooms that had sweated and stifled and stunk all winter long. She looked out at the shooting, uncoiling fresh green of the trees along Uskuben Avenue. Nothing there you have not seen before, Nejben thought. Unless it is something that is the absence of me.

"It's not forever," Nejben said. "I'll be back in year, maybe two years." *But not here*, he thought. He would not say it, but Puzhay knew it. As a returnee, the world's conservatoriums would be his. Bright cities, sun-warmed campuses far from the terrible cold on this polar continent, the winter that had driven them together.

All the goodbyes, eightfold goodbyes for each of his Aspects. And then he took sail for the ancient hospice of Bleyn, for sail was the only right way to come to those reefs of ceramic chapels that had clung to the Yesger atoll for three thousand hurricane seasons.

"I need . . . another," he whispered in the salt-breezy, chiming cloisters to Shaper Rejmen. "The curiosity of Serejen is too naive, the suspicion of Fejannen is too jagged, and the social niceties of Kekjay are too too eager to be liked."

"We can work this for you," the Shaper said. The next morning, he went down into the sweet, salt waters of the Othering Pots and let the programmed palps swarm over him, as he did for twenty mornings after. In the thunder-heavy gloaming of a late spring night storm, he awoke to find he was Torben. Clever, inquisitive, wary, socially adept and conversationally witty Torben. Extreme need and exceptional circumstances permitted the creation of Nineths, but only, always. temporarily. Tradition as strong as an incest taboo demanded that the number of Aspects reflect the eight phases of Tay's manic seasons.

The Anpreen shatter-ship spun on its vertical axis and Torben Reris Orhum Fejannan Kekjay Prus Rejmer Serejen Nejben looked on in wonder. Down, up, forward: his orientation shifted with every breath of air in the observation dome. An eye, a monstrous eye. Superstition chilled him, childhood stories of the Dejved whose sole eye was the eye of the storm and whose body was the storm entire. Then he unfolded the metaphor. An anti-eye. Tejaphay was a shield of heartbreaking blue, streaked and whorled with perpetual storms. The Anpreen space habitat *Thirty-Third Tranquil Abode*, hard-docked these two years past to the anchor end of the space elevator, was a blind white pupil, an anti-pupil, an unseeing opacity. The shatter-ship was approaching from Tejaphay's axial plane, the mechanisms of the orbital pumping station were visible beyond the habitat's close horizon. The space elevator was a cobweb next to the habitat's three-hundred kilometre bulk, less even than a thread compared to enormous Tejaphay, but as the whole assemblage turned into daylight, it woke sparkling, glittering as sun reflected from its billions of construction-ice scales. A fresh metaphor came to Torben: the sperm of the divine. *You're swimming the wrong way!* he laughed to himself, delighted at this infant Aspect's unsuspected tendency to express in metaphor what Serejen would have spoken in math, Kekjay in flattery, and Fejannen not at all. No, it's our whole system it's fertilising, he thought.

The Anpreen ship drew closer, manipulating space-time on the centimetre scale. Surface details resolved from the ice glare. The hull of *Thirty-Third Tranquil Abode* was a chaotic mosaic of sensors, docks, manufacturing hubs, and still less comprehensible technology, all constructed from smart-ice. A white city. A flight of shatter-ships detached from docking arms like a flurry of early snow. Were some of those icy mesas defensive systems; did some of those ice canyons, as precisely cut as a skater's figures, conceal inconceivable weapons? Had the Anpreen ever paused to consider that to all cultures of Tay, white was the colour of distrust, the white of snow in the long season of dark?

Days in free-gee had desensitised Torben sufficiently so that he was aware of the subtle pull of nanogravity in his belly. Against the sudden excitement and the accompanying vague fear of the unknown, he tried to calculate the gravity of *Thirty-Third Tranquil Abode*, changing every hour as it siphoned up water from Tejaphay. While he was still computing the figures, the shatter-ship performed another orientation flip and came in to dock at one of the radial elevator heads, soft as a kiss to a loved face.

On tenth days, they went to the falls, Korpa and Belej, Sajhay and Hannaj, Yetger and Torben. When he stepped out of the elevator that had taken him down through thirty kilometres of solid ice, Torben had imagined something like the faculty of Jann; wooden-screen cloisters and courts roofed with ancient painted ceilings, thronged with bright, smart, talkative students boiling with ideas and vision. He found Korpa and Belej, Sajhay, Hannaj, and Yetger all together in a huge, windy construct of cells and tunnels and abrupt balconies and netted-in ledges, like a giant wasps' nest suspended from the curved ceiling of the interior hollow.

"Continuum topology is a tad specialised, I'll admit that," Belej said. She was a sting-thin quantum-foam specialist from Yeldes in the southern archipelago of Ninnt, gone even thinner and bonier in the attenuated gravity of *Thirty-Third Tranquil Abode*. "If it's action you're looking for, you should get over to *Twenty Eighth*. They're sociologists."

Sajhay had taught him how to fly.

"There are a couple of differences from the transfer ship," he said as he showed Torben how to pull up the fish-tail mono-tights and how the plumbing vents worked. "It's lo-gee, but it's not *no*-gee, so you will eventually come down again. And it's easy to build up too much delta-vee. The walls are light but they're strong and you will hurt yourself. And the nets are there for a reason. Whatever you do, don't go through them. If you end up in that sea, it'll take you apart."

That sea haunted Torben's unsettled, nanogee dreams. The world-sea, the two hundred and twenty-kilometer diameter sphere of water, its slow, huge nanogee waves forever breaking into globes and tears the size of clouds. The seething, dissolving sea into which the Anpreen dissipated, many lives into one immense, diffuse body which whispered to him through the paper tunnels of the Soujourners' house. Not so strange, perhaps. Yet he constantly wondered what it would be like to fall in there, to swim against the tiny but non-negligible gravity and plunge slowly, magnificently, into the boil of water-borne motes. In his imagination, there was never any pain, only the blissful, light-filled losing of self. So good to be free from the unquiet parliament of selves.

Eight is natural, eight is holy, the Bleyn Shaper Yesger had whispered from behind ornate cloister grilles. *Eight arms, eight seasons. Nine must always be unbalanced.*

Conscious of each other's too-close company, the guest scholars worked apart with their pupils. Seriantep met daily with Torben in a bulbous chapter house extruded from the mother nest. Tall hexagon-combed windows opened on the steeply downcurving horizons of *Thirty-Third Tranquil Abode*, stippled with the stalactite towers of those Anpreen who refused the lure of the sea. Seriantep flew daily from such a tower down around the curve of the world to alight on Torben's balcony. She wore the same body he had known so well in the Jann Conservatorium, with the addition of a pair of functional wings in her back. She was a vision, she was a marvel, a spiritual creature from the aeons-lost motherworld of the Clade: an *angel*. She was beauty, but since arriving in *Thirty Third Tranquil Abode*, Torben had only had sex with her twice. It was not the merman-angel thing, though that was a consideration to metaphor-and-ludicrous-conscious Torben. He didn't love her as Serejen had. She noticed, she commented.

"You're not . . . the same."

Neither are you. What he *said* was, "I know. I couldn't be. Serejen couldn't have lived here. Torben can. Torben is the only one who can." *But for how long, before he splits into his component personalities?*

"Do you remember the way you . . . he . . . used to see numbers?"

"Of course I do. And before that, I remember how Ptey used to see numbers. He could look up into the night sky and tell you without counting, just by *knowing*, how many stars there were. He could see numbers. Serejen could make them *do* things. For me, Torben; the numbers haven't gone away, I just see them differently. I see them as clearly, as absolutely, but when I see the topospace transformations, I see them as words, as images and stories, as analogies. I can't explain it any better than that."

"I think, no matter how long I try, how long any of us try, we will never understand how your multiple personalities work. To us, you seem a race of partial people, each a genius, a savant, in some strange obsessive way."

Are you deliberately trying to punish me? Torben thought at the flicker-wing angel hovering before the ice-filled windows.

True, he was making colossal intuitive leaps in his twisted, abstruse discipline of spacetime geometry. Not so abstruse: the Anpreen space drives, that Taynish physicists said broke the laws of physics, reached into the elevenspace substrate of the universe to locally stretch or compress the expansion of spacetime—foreshortening ahead of the vehicle, inflating it behind. Thus the lack of any measurable acceleration, it was the entire continuum within and around the shatter-ship that had moved. Snowflakes and loxodromic curves had danced in Torben's imagination: he had it, he had it. The secret of the Anpreen: relativistic interstellar travel, was now open to the peoples of Tay.

The *other* secret of the Anpreen, that was.

For all his epiphanies above the spherical ocean, Torben knew that seminars had changed. The student had become the teacher, the master the pupil. *What is you want from us?* Torben asked himself. *Truly want, truly need?*

"Don't know, don't care. All I know is, if I can find a commercial way to bubble quantum black holes out of elevenspace and tap the evaporation radiation, I'll have more money than God," said Yetger, a squat, physically uncoordinated Oprann islander who relished his countrymen's reputation for boorishness, though Torben found him an affable conversationalist and a refined thinker. "You coming to the Falls on Tennay?"

So they set off across the sky, a little flotilla of physicists with wine and sweet biscuits to dip in it. Those older and less sure of their bodies used little airscooter units. Torben flew. He enjoyed the exercise. The challenge of a totally alien language of movement intrigued him, the fish-tail flex of the flipper-suit. He liked what it was doing to his ass muscles.

The Soujourners'-house's western windows gave distant views of the Falls, but the sense of awe began twenty kilometres out when the thunder and shriek became audible over the constant rumble of sky traffic. The picnic party always flew high, close to the ceiling among the tower roots, so that long vistas would not spoil their pleasure. A dense forest of inverted trees, monster things grown kilometres tall in the nanogee, had been planted around the Falls, green and mist-watered by the spray. The scientists settled on to one of the many platforms sculpted from the boulevard-wide branches. Torben gratefully peeled off his fin-tights, kicked his legs free, and spun to face the Falls.

What you saw, what awed you, depended on how you looked at it. Feet down to the world-sea, head up to the roof, it was a true fall, a cylinder of falling water two hundred metres across and forty kilometres long. Feet up, head down, it was even more terrifying, a titanic geyser. The water was pumped through from the receiving station at near supersonic speeds, where it met the ocean-bead the joined waters boiled and leaped kilometres high, broke into high looping curls and crests and globes, like the fantastical flarings of solar prominences. The roar was terrific. But for the noise-abatement properties of the nanoengineered leaves, it would have meant instant deafness. Torben could feel the tree branch, as massive as any buttress wall of Jann fortress-university, shudder beneath him.

Wine was opened and poured. The biscuits, atavistically hand-baked by Hannaj, one of whose Aspects was a master pastry chef, were dipped into it and savoured. Sweet, the light sharpness of the wine and the salt mist of another world's stolen ocean tanged Torben's tongue.

There were rules to Tennays by the Falls. No work. No theory. No relationships. Five researchers made up a big enough group for family jealousy, small enough for cliquishness. Proper topics of conversation looked homeward; partnerships ended, children born, family successes and sicknesses, gossip, politics, and sports results.

"Oh. Here." Yetger sent a message flake spinning lazily through the air. The Soujourners'-house exfoliated notes and message from home onto slips of whisper-thin paper that peeled from the walls like eczema. The mechanism was poetic but inaccurate; intimate messages unfurled from unintended walls to turn and waft in the strange updrafts that ran through the nest's convoluted tunnels. It was the worst of forms to read another's message-scurf.

Torben unfolded the rustle of paper. He read it once, blinked, read it again. Then he folded precisely in eight and folded it away in his top pocket.

"Bad news?" For a broad beast of a man, Yetger was acute to emotional subtleties. Torben swallowed.

"Nothing strange or startling."

Then he saw where Belej stared. Her gaze drew his, drew that of everyone in the picnic party. The Falls were failing. Moment by moment, they dwindled, from a deluge to a river, from a river to a stream to a jet, a hiding shrieking thread of water. On all the platforms on all the trees, Anpreen were rising into the air, hovering in swarms, as before their eyes the Falls sputtered and ceased. Drops of water, fat as storms, formed around the lip of the suddenly exposed nozzle to break and drift, quivering, down to the spherical sea. The silence was profound. Then the trees seemed to shower blossoms as the Anpreen took to the air in hosts and choirs, flocking and storming.

Numbers and images flashed in Torben's imagination. The fuelling could not be complete, was weeks from being complete. The ocean would fill the entire interior hollow, the stalactite cities transforming into strange reef communities. Fear gripepd him and he felt Fejannen struggle to free himself from the binding into Torben. *I need you here, friend,* Torben said to himself, and saw the others had made the same calculations.

They flew back, a ragged flotilla strung across kilometres of airspace, battling through the ghostly aerial legions of Anpreen. The Soujourners' house was filled with fluttering, gusting message slips shed from the walls. Torben snatched one from the air and against all etiquette read it.

Sajhay are you all right what's happening? Come home, we are all worried about you. Love Mihenj.

The sudden voice of Suguntung, the Anpreen liaison, filled every cell of the nest, an order—polite, but an order—to come to the main viewing lounge, where an important announcement would be made. Torben had long suspected that Suguntung never left the Soujourners' house, merely deliquesced from hominiform into airborne motes, a phase transition.

Beyond the balcony nets, the sky seethed, an apocalypse of insect humanity and storm clouds back as squid ink rolling up around the edge of the world ocean.

"I have grave news," Suguntung said. He was a grey, sober creature, light and lithe and androgynous, without any salting of wit or humour. "At 12:18 Taynish Enclave time, we detected gravity waves passing through the system. These are consistent with a large numbers of bodies decelerating from relativistic flight."

Consternation. Voices shouting. Questions questions questions. Suguntung held up a hand and there was quiet.

"On answer to your questions, somewhere in the region of thirty eight thousand objects. We estimate them at a range of seventy astronomical units beyond the edge of the Kuiper belt, decelerating to ten percent lightspeed for system transition."

"Ninety three hours until they reach us," Torben said. The numbers, the coloured numbers, so beautiful, so distant.

"Yes," said Suguntung.

"Who are they?" Belej asked.

"I know," Torben said. "Your enemy."

"We believe so," Suguntung answered. "There are characteristic signatures in the gravity waves and the spectral analysis."

Uproar. By a trick of the motes, Suguntung could raise his voice to a roar that could shout down a crowd of angry physicists.

"The Anpreen Commonweal is making immediate preparations for departure. As a matter of priority, evacuation for all guests and visitors has been arranged and will commence immediately. A transfer ship is already waiting. We are evacuating the system not only for our own protection, but to safeguard you as well. We believe that the Enemy has no quarrel with you."

"*Believe?*" Yetger spat. "Forgive me if I'm less than completely reassured by that!"

"But you haven't got enough water," Torben said absently, mazed by the numbers and pictures swimming around in his head, as the message leaves of concern and hope and come-home-soon fluttered around. "How many habitats are fully fuelled? Five hundred, five hundred and fifty? You haven't got enough, even this one is at eighty percent capacity. What's going to happen to them?"

"I don't give a fuck what happens to them!" Hannaj had always been the meekest and least assertive of men, brilliant but forever hamstrung by self-doubt. Now, threatened, naked in space, pieced through and through by the gravity waves of an unknowable and power, his anger burned. "I want to know what's going to happen to *us*."

"We are transferring the intelligences to the interstellar-capable habitats." Suguntung spoke to Torben alone.

"Transferring; you mean copying," Torben said. "And the originals that are left, what happens to them?"

Suguntung made no answer.

Yetger found Torben floating in the exact centre of the viewing lounge, moving his tail just enough to maintain him against the microgee.

"Where's your stuff?"

"In my cell."

"The shatter-ship's leaving in an hour."

"I know."

"Well, maybe you should, you know . . ."

"I'm not going."

"You're *what*?"

"I'm not going, I'm staying here."

"Are you insane?"

"I've talked to Suguntung and Seriantep. It's fine. There are a couple of others on the other habitats."

"You have to come home, we'll need you when they come . . ."

"Ninety hours and twenty five minutes to save the world? I don't think so."

"It's home, man."

"It's not. Not since *this*." Torben flicked the folded note of his secret pocket, offered it to Yetger between clenched fingers.

"Oh."

"Yes."

"You're dead. We're all dead, you know that."

"Oh, I know. In the few minutes it takes me to reach wherever the Anpreen Migration goes next, you will have aged and died many times over. I know that, but it's not home. Not now."

Yetger ducked his head in sorrow that did not want to be seen, then in a passion hugged Torben hugely to him, kissed him hard.

"Goodbye. Maybe in the next one."

"No, I don't think so. One is all we get. And that's a good enough reason to go out there where none of our people have ever been before, I think."

"Maybe it is." Yetger laughed, the kind of laughter that is on the edge of tears. Then he spun and kicked off up through the ceiling door, his duffel of small possessions trailing from his ankle.

For an hour now, he had contemplated the sea and thought that he might just be getting the way of it, the fractal patterns of the ripples, the rhythms and the micro-storms that blew up in squalls and waves that sent globes of water quivering into the air that, just as quickly, were subsumed back into the greater sea. He understood it as music, deeply harmonised. He wished one of his Aspects had a skill for an instrument. Only choirs, vast ensembles, could capture the music of the water bead.

"It's ready now."

All the while Torben had calculated the music of the sea, Seriantep had worked on the smart-paper substrate of the Soujourners'-house. Now the poll was complete, a well in the floor of the lounge. *When I leave, will it revert?* Torben thought, the small, trivial wit that fights fear. *Will it go back to whatever it was before, or was it always only just Suguntung?* The slightest of gestures and Seriantep's wisp-dress fell from her, The floor ate it greedily. Naked and wingless now in this incarnation, she stepped backward into the water, never for an instant taking her eyes from Torben.

"Whenever you're ready," she said. "You won't be hurt."

She lay back into the receiving water. Her hair floated out around her, coiled and tangled as she came apart. There was nothing ghastly about it, no decay into meat and gut and vile bone, no grinning skeleton fizzing apart in the water like sodium. A brightness, a turning to motes of light. The hair was the last to go. The pool seethed with motes. Torben stepped out of his clothes.

I'm moving on. It's for the best. Maybe not for you. For me. You see, I didn't think I'd mind, but I did. You gave it all up so easily, just like that, off into space. There is someone else. It's Cjatay. I heard what he was saying, and as time went by, as I didn't hear from you, it made sense. I know I'm reacting. I think I owe you that, at least. We're all right together. With him, you get everything, I find I can live with that. I think I like it,. I'm sorry Torben, but this is what I want.

The note sifted down through the air like a falling autumn leaf to join the hundreds of others that lay on the floor. Torben's feet kicked up as he stepped down into the water. He gasped at the electrical tingle, then laughed, and, with a great gasp, emptied his lungs and threw himself under the surface. The motes swarmed and began to take him apart. As the *Thirty-Third Tranquil Abode* broke orbit around Tejaphay, the abandoned space elevator coiling like a severed artery, the bottom of the Soujourners'-house opened, and, like a tear, the mingled waters fell to the sea below.

Jedden, running.

Eighty years Jedden had fallen, dead as a stone, silent as light. Every five years, a few subjective minutes so close to light-speed, he woke up his senses and sent a slush of photons down his wake to see if the hunter was still pursuing.

Redshifted to almost indecipherability, the photons told him, *Yes, still there, still gaining.* Then he shut down his senses, for even that brief wink, that impact of radiation blueshifted to gamma frequencies on the enemy engine field, betrayed him. It was decades since he had risked the scalarity drive. The distortions it left in space-time advertised his position over most of a quadrant. Burn quick, burn hot and fast, get to lightspeed if it meant reducing his reaction mass perilously close to the point where he would not have sufficient ever to brake. Then go dark, run silent and swift, coasting along in high time dilation where years passed in hours.

Between wakings, Jedden dreamed. He dreamed down into the billions of lives, the dozens of races and civilizations that the Anpreen had encountered in their long migration. The depth of their history had stunned Jedden, as if he were swimming and, looking down, discovered beneath him not the green water of the lagoon but the clear blue drop of the continental shelf. Before they englobed their sun with so many habitats that it became discernible only as a vast infra-red glow, before even the wave of expansion that had brought them to that system, before even they became motile, when they wore mere bodies, they had been an extroverted, curious race, eager for the similarities and differences of other sub-species of PanHumanity. Records of the hundreds of societies they had contacted were stored in the spin-states of the quantum-ice flake that comprised the soul of Jedden. Cultures, customs, ways of being human were simulated in such detail that, if he wished, Jedden could have spend aeons living out their simulated lives. Even before they had reached the long-reprocessed moon of their homeworld, the Anpreen had encountered a light-sail probe of the Ekkad, three hundred years out on a millennium-long survey of potential colony worlds. As they converted their asteroid belts into habitat rings, they had fought a savage war for control of the high country against the Okranda asteroid colonies that had dwelled there, hidden and unsuspected, for twenty thousand years. The doomed Okranda had, as a final, spiteful act, seared the Anpreen homeworld to the bedrock, but not before the Anpreen had absorbed and recorded the beautiful, insanely complex hierarchy of caste, classes, and societies that had evolved in the baroque cavities of the sculpted asteroids. Radio transmission had drawn them out of their Oort cloud across two hundred light years to encounter the dazzling society of the Jad. From them, the Anpreen had learned the technology that enabled them to pload themselves into free-flying nanomotes and become a true Level Two civilization.

People and beasts, machines and woods, architectures and moralities, and stories beyond counting. Among the paraphernalia and marginalia of a hundred races, were the ones who had destroyed the Anpreen, who were now hunting Jedden down over all the long years, closing metre by metre.

So he spent hours and years immersed in the great annual eisteddfod of the Barrant-Hoj, where one of the early generation of seed ships (early in that it was seed of the seed of the seed of the first flowering of mythical Earth) had been drawn into the embrace of a fat, slow hydrocarbon-rich gas giant and birthed a brilliant, brittle airborne culture, where blimp-cities rode the edge of storms wide enough to drown whole planets and the songs of the contestants—gas-bag-spider creatures huge as reefs, fragile as honeycomb—belled in infrasonic wavefronts kilometers between crests and changed entire climates. It took Barrant-Hoj two hominiform lifetimes to circle its sun—the Anpreen had chanced upon the songspiel, .preserved it, hauled it out of the prison of gas giant's gravity well, and given it to greater Clade.

Jedden blinked back into interstellar flight. He felt—he imagined—tears on his face as the harmonies reverberated within him. Cantos could last days, chorales entire weeks. Lost in music. A moment of revulsion at his body, this sharp, unyielding thing of ice and energies. The hunter's ramscoop fusion engine advertised its presence across a thousand cubic light-years. It was inelegant and initially slow, but, unlike Jedden's scalarity drive, was light and could live off the land. The hunter would be, like Jedden, a ghost of a soul impressed on a Bose-condensate quantum chip, a mote of sentience balanced on top of a giant drive unit. The hunter was closing, but was no closer than Jedden had calculated. Only miscalculation could kill you in interstellar war. The equations were hard but they were fair.

Two hundred and three years to the joke point. It would be close, maybe close enough for the enemy's greed to blind him. Miscalculation and self-deception, these were the killers in space. And luck. Two centuries. Time enough for a few moments rest.

Among all the worlds was one he had never dared visit: the soft blue tear of Tay. There, in the superposed spin states, were all the lives he could have led. The lovers, the children, the friends and joys and mudanities. Puzhay was there, Cjatay too. He could make of them anything he wanted: Puzhay faithful, Cjatay Manifold, no longer Lonely.

Lonely. He understood that now, eighty light years out and decades to go before he could rest.

Extraordinary, how painless it had been. Even as the cells of Torben's body were invaded by the motes into which Seriantep had dissolved, even as they took him apart and rebuilt him, even as they read and copied his neural mappings, there was never a moment where fleshly Torben blinked out and nanotechnological Torben winked in, there was no pain. Never pain, only a sense of wonder, of potential racing away to infinity on every side, of a new birth—or, it seemed to him, an anti-birth, a return to the primal, salted waters. As the globe of mingled motes dropped slow and quivering and full as a breast toward the world-ocean, Torben still thought of himself as Torben, as a man, an individual, as a body. Then they hit and burst and dissolved into the sea of seething motes, and voices and selves and memories and personalities rushed in on him from every side, clamouring, a sea-roar. Every life in every detail. Senses beyond his native five brought him impression upon impression upon impression. Here was intimacy beyond anything he had ever known with Seriantep. As he communed, he was communed with. He knew that the Anpreen government—now he understood the reason for the protracted and ungainly negotiations with Tay : the two representations had almost no points of communication—were unwrapping him to construct a deep map of Tay and its people—rather, the life and Aspects of one under-socialised physics researcher. Music. All was music. As he understood this, Anpreen Commonweal Habitat *Thirty Third Tranquil Abode*, with its five hundred and eighty two companions, crossed one hundred and nineteen light years to the Milius 1183 star system.

One hundred and nineteen light years, eight months subjective, in which Torben Reris Orhum Fejannan Kekjay Prus Rejmer Serejen Nejben ceased to exist. In the mote-swarm, time, like identity, could be anything you assigned it to be. To the self now known as Jedden, it seemed that he had spent twenty years of re-subjectivized time in which he had grown to be a profound and original thinker in the Commonweal's physics community. Anpreen life had only enhanced his instinctive ability to see and apprehend number. His insights and contributions were startling and creative. Thus it had been a pure formality for him to request a splinter-ship to be spun off from *Thirty Third Tranquil Abode* as the fleet entered the system and dropped from relativistic flight at the edge of the Oort cloud. A big fat splinter ship with lots of fuel to explore space-time topological distortions implicit in the orbital perturbations of inner Kuiper Belt cubewanos for a year, a decade, a century, and then come home.

So he missed the annihilation.

Miscalculation kills. Lack of circumspection kills. Blind assumption kills. The Enemy had planned their trap centuries ahead. The assault on the Tay system had been a diversion; the thirty-eight thousand drive signatures mostly decoys; propulsion units and guidance systems and little else scattered among a handful of true battleships dozens of kilometres long. Even as lumbering, barely mobile Anpreen habitats and Enemy attack drones burst across Tay's skies, so bright they even illuminated the sun-glow of high summer, the main fleet was working around Milius 1183. A work of decades, year upon year of slow modifications, staggering energies, careful careful concealment and camouflage, as the Enemy sent their killing hammer out on its long slow loop.

Blind assumption. The Anpreen saw a small red sun at affordable range to the ill-equpped fleet. They saw there was water there, water; worlds of water to re-equip the Commonweal and take it fast and far beyond the reach of the Enemy in the great star clouds that masked the galactic core. In their haste, they failed to note that Milius 1183 was a binary system, a tired red dwarf star and a companion neutron star in photosphere-grazing eight hour orbit. Much less then did they notice that the neutron star was missing.

The trap was perfect and complete. The Enemy had predicted perfectly. Their set-up was flawless. The hunting fleet withdrew to the edges of system, all that remained were the relays and autonomous devices. Blindsided by sunglare, the Anpreen sensoria had only milliseconds of warning before the neutron star impacted Milius 1183 at eight percent light speed.

The nova would in time be visible over a light-century radius. Within its spectrum, careful astronomers might note the dark lines of hydrogen, oxygen, and smears of carbon. Habitats blew away in sprays of plasma. The handful of stragglers that survived battled to reconstruct their mobility and life-support systems. Shark-ships hidden half a century before in the rubble of asteroid belts and planetary ring systems woke from their long sleeps and went a-hunting.

Alone in his splinter ship in the deep dark, Jedden, his thoughts outwards to the fabric of space-time and at the same time inwards to the beauty of number, the song within him, saw the system suddenly turn white with death light. He heard five hundred billion sentients die. All of them, all at once, all their voices and hearts. He heard Seriantep die, he heard those other Taynish die, those who had turned away from their home world in the hope of knowledge and experience beyond anything their world could offer. Every life he had ever touched, that had ever been part of him, that had shared number or song or intimacy beyond fleshly sex. He heard the death of the Anpreen migration. Then he was alone. Jedden went dark for fifty years. He contemplated the annihilation of the last of the Anpreen. He drew up escape plans. He waited. Fifty years was enough. He lit the scalarity drive. Space-time stretched. Behind him, he caught the radiation signature of a fusion drive igniting and the corresponding electromagnetic flicker of a scoopfield going up. Fifty years was not enough.

That would be his last miscalculation.

Twenty years to bend his course away from Tay. Another ten to set up the deception. *As you deceived us, so I will fool you*, Jedden thought as he tacked ever closer to lightspeed. *And with the same device, a neutron star.*

Jedden awoke from the sleep that was beyond dreams, a whisper away from death, that only disembodied intelligences can attain. The magnetic vortex of the hunter's scoopfield filled half the sky. Less than the diameter of a light-minute separated them. Within the next ten objective years, the Enemy ship would overtake and destroy Jedden. Not with physical weapons or even directed energy, but with information: skullware and dark phages that would dissolve him into nothingness or worse, isolate him from any external sense or contact, trapped in unending silent, nerveless darkness.

The moment, when it came, after ninety light-years, was too fine-grained for hominiform-intelligence. Jedden's sub-routines, the autonomic responses that controlled the ship that was his body, opened the scalarity drive and summoned the dark energy. Almost instantly, the Enemy responded to the course change, but that tiny relativistic shift, the failure of simultaneity, was Jedden's escape and life.

Among the memories frozen into the heart of the Bose-Einstein condensate were the star-logs of the Cush Né, a fellow migrant race the Anpreen had encountered—by chance, as all such meets must be—in the big cold between stars. Their star maps charted a rogue star, a neutron dwarf ejected from its stellar system and wandering dark and silent, almost invisible, through deep space. Decades ago, when he felt the enemy ramfield go up and knew that he had not escaped, Jedden had made the choice and the calculations. Now he turned his flight, a prayer short of light-speed, towards the wandering star.

Jedden had long ago abolished fear. Yet he experienced a strange psychosomatic sensation in that part of the splinter-ship that corresponded to his testicles.

Balls tightening. The angle of insertion was so precise that Jedden had had to calculate the impact of stray hydroxyl radicals on his ablation field. One error would send him at relativistic speed head on into a neutron star. But he did not doubt his ability, he did not fear, and now he understood what the sensation in his phantom testicles was. Excitement.

The neutron star was invisible, would always be invisible, but Jedden could feel its gravity in every part of his body, a quaking, quailing shudder, a music of a hundred harmonies as different parts of the smart-ice hit their resonant frequencies. A chorale in ice and adrenaline, he plunged around the neutron star. He could hope that the hunting ship would not survive the passage, but the Enemy, however voracious, was surely never so stupid as to run a scoop ship through a neutron star's terrifying magnetic terrain with the drive field up. That was not his strategy anyway. Jedden was playing the angles. Whipping tight around the intense gravity well, even a few seconds of slowness would amplify into light-years of distance, decades of lost time. Destruction would have felt like a cheat. Jedden wanted to win by geometry. By calculation, we live.

He allowed himself one tiny flicker of a communication laser. Yes. The Enemy was coming. Coming hard, coming fast, coming *wrong*. Tides tore at Jedden, every molecule of his smart-ice body croaked and moaned, but his own cry rang louder and he sling-shotted around the neutron. *Yes!* Before him was empty space. The splinter-ship would never fall of its own accord into another gravity well. He lacked sufficient reaction mass to enter any Clade system. Perhaps the Enemy had calculated this in the moments before he too entered the neutron star's transit. An assumption. In space, assumptions kill. Deep in his quantum memories, Jedden knew what was out there. The slow way home.

Fast Man, slowly

Kites, banners, pennants, and streamers painted with the scales and heads of ritual snakes flew from the sun rigging on the Festival of Fast Children. At the last minute, the climate people had received budgetary permission to shift the prevailing winds lower. The Clave had argued that the Festival of Fast Children seemed to come round every month and a half, which it did, but the old and slow said, *not to the children it doesn't.*

Fast Man turned off the dust road on to the farm track. The wooden gate was carved with the pop-eyed, O-mouthed hearth-gods, the chubby, venal guardians of agricultural Yoe Canton. As he slowed to Parent Speed, the nodding heads of the meadow flowers lifted to a steady metronome tick. The wind-rippled grass became a restless choppy sea of current and cross-currents. Above him, the clouds raced down the face of the sun-rod that ran the length of the environment cylinder, and in the wide yard before the frowning eaves of the ancient earthen manor, the children, preparing for the ritual Beating of the Sun-lines, became plumes of dust.

For three days, he had walked up the eternal hill of the cylinder curve, through the tended red forests of Canton Ahaea. Fast Man liked to walk. He walked at Child-Speed and they would loop around him on their bicycles and ped-cars and then pull away shouting, you're not so fast, Fast Man! He could have caught them, of course, he could have easily outpaced them. They knew that, they knew he could on a wish take the form of a bird, or a cloud, and fly away from them up to the ends of the world. Everyone in the Three Worlds knew Fast Man. He needed neither sleep nor food, but he enjoyed the taste of the highly seasoned, vegetable-based cuisine of the Middle Cantons and their light but fragrant beer, so he would call each night at a hostel or township pub. Then he would drop down into Parent Speed and talk with the locals. Children were fresh and bright and inquiring, but for proper conversation, you needed adults.

The chirping cries of the children rang around the grassy eaves of Toe Yau Manor. The community had gathered, among them the Toe Yau's youngest, a skipping five year-old. In her own speed, that was. She was months old to her parents; her birth still a fresh and painful memory. The oldest, the one he had come about, was in his early teens. Noha and Jehau greeted Fast Man with water and bread.

"God save all here," Fast Man blessed them. Little Nemaha flickered around him like summer evening bugs. He heard his dual-speech unit translate the greeting into Children-Speech in a chip of sound. This was his talent and his fame; that his mind and words could work in two times at once. He was the generational ambassador to three worlds.

The three great cylinders of the Aeo Taea colony fleet were fifty Adult Years along in their journey to the star Sulpees 2157 in the Anpreen categorisation. A sweet little golden star with a gas giant pressed up tight to it, and, around that gas world, a sun-warmed, tear-blue planet. Their big, slow lathe-sculpted asteroids, two hundred kilometres long, forty across their flats, had appeared as three small contacts at the extreme edge of the Commonweal's sensory array. Too far from their flightpath to the Tay system and, truth be told, too insignificant. The galaxy was festering with little sub-species, many of them grossly ignorant that they were part of an immeasurably more vast and glorious Clade, all furiously engaged on their own grand little projects and empires. Races became significant when they could push lightspeed. Ethnologists had noted as a point of curiosity a peculiar time distortion to the signals, as if everything had been slowed to a tenth normal speed. Astrogators had put it down to an unseen gravitational lensing effect and noted course and velocity of the lumbering junk as possible navigation hazards.

That idle curiosity, that moment of fastidiousness of a now-dead, now-vaporised Anpreen who might otherwise have dismissed it, had saved Jedden. There had always been more hope than certainty in the mad plan he had concocted as he watched the Anpreen civilization end in nova light. Hope as he opened up the dark energy that warped space-time in calculations made centuries before that would only bear fruit centuries to come. Hope as he woke up, year upon year in the long flight to the stray neutron star, always attended by doubt. The slightest miscalculation could throw him off by light-years and centuries. He himself could not die, but his reaction mass was all too mortal. Falling forever between stars was worse than any death. He could have abolished that doubt with a thought, but so would the hope have been erased to become mere blind certainty.

Hoping and doubting, he flew out from the slingshot around the neutron star.

Because he could hope, he could weep; smart-ice tears when his long range radars returned three slow-moving images less than five light-hours from the position he had computed. As he turned the last of his reaction mass into dark energy to match his velocity with the Aeo Taea armada, a stray calculation crossed his consciousness. In all his redefinitions and reformations, he had never given up the ability to see numbers, to hear what they whispered to him. He was half a millennium away from the lives he had known on Tay.

For ten days, he broadcast his distress call. *Help, I am a refugee from a star war.* He knew that, in space, there was no rule of the sea, as there had been on Tay's world ocean, no Aspects at once generous, stern, and gallant that had been known as SeaSelves. The Aeo Taea could still kill him with negligence. But he could sweeten them with a bribe.

Like many of the country houses of Amoa ark, Toe Yau Manor featured a wooden belvedere, this one situated on a knoll two fields spinward from the old house. Airy and gracious, woven from genetweak willow plaits, it and its country cousins all across Amoa's Cantons had become a place for Adults, where they could mix with ones of their own speed, talk without the need for the hated speech convertors around their necks, gripe and moan and generally gossip, and, through the central roof iris, spy through the telescope on their counterparts on the other side of the world. Telescope parties were the latest excuse for Parents to get together and complain about their children.

But this was their day—though it seemed like a week to them—the Festival of Fast Children, and this day Noha Toe Yau had his telescope trained not on his counterpart beyond the sun, but on the climbing teams fizzing around the sun-riggings, tens of kilometres above the ground, running out huge monoweave banners and fighting ferocious kite battles high where the air was thin.

"I tell you something, no child of mine would ever be let do so damn fool a thing," Noha Toe Yau grumbled. "I'll be surprised if any of them make it to the Destination."

Fast Man smiled, for he knew that he had only been called because Yemoa Toe Yau was doing something much more dangerous.

Jehau Toe Yau poured chocolate, thick and cooling and vaguely hallucinogenic.

"As long as he's back before Starship Day," she said. She frowned down at the wide green before the manor where the gathered Fast Children of the neighbourhood in their robes and fancies were now hurtling around the long trestles of festival foods. They seemed to be engaged in a high-velocity food fight. "You know, I'm sure they're speeding the days up. Not much, just a little every day, but definitely speeding them up. Time goes nowhere these days."

Despite a surprisingly sophisticated matter-anti-matter propulsion system, the Aeo Taea fleet was limited to no more than ten percent of lightspeed, far below the threshold where time dilation became perceptible. The crossing to the Destination—Aeo Taea was a language naturally given to Portentous Capitalizations, Fast Man had discovered—could only be made by generation ship. The Aeo Taea had contrived to do it in just one generation. The strangely slow messages the Anpreen had picked up from the fleet were no fluke of space-time distortion. The voyagers' bodies, their brains, their perceptions and metabolisms, had been in-vitro engineered to run at one-tenth hominiform normal. Canned off from the universe, the interior lighting, the gentle spin gravity and the slow, wispy climate easily adjusted to a life lived at a snail's pace. Morning greetings lasted hours, that morning a world-week. Seasons endured for what would have been years in the outside universe, vast languorous autumns. The three hundred and fifty years of the crossing would pass in the span of an average working career. Amoa was a world of the middle-aged.

Then Fast Man arrived and changed everything.

"Did he give any idea where he was going?" Fast Man asked. It was always the boys. Girls worked it through, girls could see further.

Jehau pointed down. Fast Man sighed. Rebellion was limited in Amoa, where any direction you ran lead you swiftly back to your own doorstep. The wires that rigged the long sun could take you high, kilometres above it all in your grand indignation. Everyone would watch you through their telescopes, up there high and huffing, until you got hungry and wet and bored and had to come down again. In Amoa, the young soul rebels went *out*.

Fast Man set down his chocolate glass and began the subtle exercise that reconfigured the motes of his malleable body. To the Toe Yaus, he seemed to effervesce slightly, a sparkle like fine silver talc or the dust from a moth's wings. Jehau's eyes widened. All the three worlds knew of Fast Man, who had brought the end of the Journey suddenly within sight, soothed generational squabbles, and found errant children—and so everyone though they knew him personally. Truly, he was an alien.

"It would help considerably if they left some idea of where they were going," Fast Man said. "There's a lot of space out there. Oh well. I'd stand back a little, by the way." He stood up, opened his arms in a little piece of theatre, and exploded into a swarm of motes. He towered to a buzzing cylinder that rose from the iris at the centre of the belvedere. *See this through your telescopes on the other side of the world and gossip.* Then, in a thought, he speared into the earth and vanished.

In the end, the Fast Boy was pretty much where Fast Man reckoned he would be. He came speed-walking up through the salt-dead city-scape of the communications gear just above the convex flaring of the drive shield, and there he was, nova-bright in Fast man's radar sight. A sweet, neat little cranny in the main dish gantry with a fine view over the construction site. Boys and building. His complaining to the Toe Yaus had been part of the curmudgeonly image he liked to project. Boys were predictable things.

"Are you not getting a bit cold up there?" Fast Man said. Yemoa started at the voice crackling in his helmet phones. He looked round, helmet tilting from side to side as he tried to pick the interloper out of the limitless shadow of inter-stellar space. Fast Man increased his surface radiance. He knew well how he must seem; a glowing man, naked to space, toes firmly planted on the pumice-dusted hull and leaning slightly forward against the spin force. He would have terrified himself at that age, but awe worked for the Fast Children as amiable curmudgeon worked for their slow parents.

"Go away."

Fast Man's body-shine illuminated the secret roots. Yemoa Toe Yau was spindly even in the tight yellow and green pressure skin. He shuffled around to turn his back; a deadlier insult among the Aeo Taea than among the Aspects of Tay for all their diverse etiquettes. Fast Man tugged at the boy's safety lanyard. The webbing was unfrayed, the carabiner latch operable.

"Leave that alone."

"You don't want to put too much faith in those things. Cosmic rays can weaken the structure of the plastic: put any tension on them, and they snap just like that, just when you need them most. Yes sir, I've seen people just go sailing out there, right away out there."

The helmet, decorated with bright bird motifs, turned toward Fast Man.

"You're just saying that."

Fast Man swung himself up beside the runaway and settled into the little nest. Yemoa wiggled away as far as the cramped space would permit.

"I didn't say you could come up here."

"It's a free ship."

"It's not *your* ship."

"True," said Fast Man. He crossed his legs and dimmed down his self-shine until they could both look out over the floodlit curve of the star drive works. The scalarity drive itself was a small unit—small by Amoa's vistas; merely the size of a well-established country manor. The heavy engineering that overshadowed it, the towering silos and domes and pipeworks, was the transfer system that converted water and anti-water into dark energy. Above all, the lampships hovered in habitat-stationary orbits, five small suns. Fast Man did not doubt that the site hived with desperate energy and activity, but to his Child Speed perceptions, it was as still as a painting, the figures in their bird-bright skinsuits, the heavy engineers in their long-duration work armour, the many robots and vehicles and little jetting skipcraft all frozen in time, moving so slowly that no individual motion was visible, but when you looked back, everything had changed. A long time even for a Parent, Fast

Man sat with Yemoa. Beyond the construction lights, the stars arced past. How must they seem to the adults, Fast Man thought, and in that thought pushed down into Parent Speed and felt a breathless, deeply internalised gasp of wonder as the stars accelerated into curving streaks. The construction site ramped up into action; the little assembly robots and skippers darting here and there on little puffs of reaction gas.

Ten years, ten grown-up years, since Fast Man had osmsoed through the hull and coalesced out of a column of motes on to the soil of Ga'atu Colony, and still he did not know which world he belonged to, Parent or Fast Children. There had been no Fast Children then, no children at all. That was the contract. When the Destination was reached, that was the time for children, born the old way, the fast way, properly adjusted to their new world. Fast Man had changed all that with the price of his rescue: the promise that the Destination could be reached not in slow years, not even in a slow season, but in hours; real hours. With a proviso; that they detour—a matter of moments to a relativistic fleet—to Fast Man's old homeworld of Tay.

The meetings were concluded, the deal was struck, the Aeo Taea fleet's tight tight energy budget would allow it, just. It would mean biofuels and muscle power for the travellers; all tech resources diverted to assembling the three dark energy scalarity units. But the journey would be over in a single sleep. Then the generous forests and woodlands that carpeted the gently rolling midriffs of the colony cylinders all flowered and released genetweak pollen. Everyone got a cold for three days, everyone got pregnant, and nine Parent months later, the first of the Fast Children was born.

"So where's your clip?"

At the sound of Yemoa's voice, Fast Man geared up into Child Speed. The work on the dazzling plain froze, the stars slowed to a crawl.

"I don't need one, do I?" Fast Man added, "I know exactly how big space is."

"Does it really use dark energy?"

"It does."

Yemoa pulled his knees up to him, stiff from his long vigil in the absolute cold. A splinter of memory pierced Fast Man: the fast-frozen canals of Jann, the months-long dark. He shivered. Whose life was that, whose memory?

"I read about dark energy. It's the force that makes the universe expand faster and faster, and everything in it, you, me, the distance between us. In the end, everything will accelerate away so fast from everything else that the universe will rip itself apart, right down to the quarks."

"That's one theory."

"Every particle will be so far from everything else that it will be in a universe of its own. It will *be* a universe of its own."

"Like I said, it's a theory. Yemoa, your parents . . ."

"You use this as a space drive."

"Your matter/anti-matter system obeys the laws of Thermodynamics, and that's the heat-death of the universe. We're all getter older and colder and more and more distant. Come on, you have to come in. You must be uncomfortable in that suit."

The Aeo Taea skinsuits looked like flimsy dance costumes to don in the empty cold of interstellar space but their hides were clever works of molecular technology, recycling and refreshing and repairing. Still, Fast Man could not contemplate the itch and reek of one after days of wear.

"You can't be here on Starship Day," Fast Man warned. "Particle density is very low out here, but it's still enough to fry you, at lightspeed."

"We'll be the Slow ones then," Yemoa said. "A few hours will pass for us, but in the outside universe, it will be fifty years."

"It's all relative," Fast Man said.

"And when we get there," Yemoa continued, "we'll unpack the landers and we'll go down and it'll be the new world, the big Des Tin Ay Shun, but our Moms and Dads, they'll stay up in the Three Worlds. And we'll work, and we'll build that new world, and we'll have our children, and they'll have children, and maybe we'll see another generation after that, but in the end, we'll die, and the Parents up there in the sky, they'll hardly have aged at all."

Fast Man draped his hands over his knees.

"They love you, you know."

"I know. I know that. It's not that at all. Did you think that? If you think that, you're stupid. What does everyone see in you if you think stuff like that? It's just . . . what's the point?"

None, Fast Man thought. *And everything. You are as much point as the universe needs, in your yellow and green skinsuit and mad-bird helmet and fine rage.*

"You know," Fast Man said, "whatever you think about it, it's worse for them. It's worse than anything I think you can imagine. Everyone they love growing old in the wink of an eye, dying, and they can't touch them, they can't help, they're trapped up there. No, I think it's so very much worse for them."

"Yah," said Yemoa. He slapped his gloved hands on his thin knees. "You know, it is freezing up here."

"Come on then." Fast Man stood up and offered a silver hand. Yemoa took it. The stars curved overhead. Together, they climbed down from the aerial and walked back down over the curve of the world, back home.

Oga, tearing.

He stood on the arch of the old Jemejnay bridge over the dead canal. Acid winds blew past him, shrieking on the honed edges of the shattered porcelain houses. The black sky crawled with suppressed lightning. The canal was a dessicated vein, cracked dry, even the centuries of trash wedged in its cracked silts had rusted away, under the bite of the caustic wind, to scabs and scales of slag. The lagoon was a dish of pure salt shimmering with heat haze. In natural light, it would have been blinding but no sun ever challenged the clouds. In Oga's extended vision, the old campanile across the lagoon was a snapped tooth of crumbling masonry.

A flurry of boiling acid rain swept over Oga as he turned away from the burning vista from the dead stone arch on to Ejtay Quay. His motes sensed and changed mode on reflex, but not before a wash of pain burned through him. Feel it. It is punishment. It is good.

The houses were roofless, floorless; rotted snapped teeth of patinated ceramic,: had been for eight hundred years. Drunken Chicken Street. Here Kentlay the Lonely had sat out in the sun and passed the time of day with his neighbours and visitors come for his gift. Here were the Dilmajs and the vile, cruel little son who had caught birds and pulled their feathers so that they could not fly from his needles and knives, street bully and fat boy. Mrs Supris, a sea-widow, a baker of cakes and sweets, a keeper of mournings and ocean-leavings. All dead. Long dead, dead with their city, their world.

This must be a mock Ctarisphay, a stage, a set, a play-city for some moral tale of a prodigal, an abandoner. A traitor. Memories turned to blasted, glowing stumps. A city of ruins. A world in ruins. There was no sea any more. Only endless poisoned salt. This could not be true. Yet this was his house. The acid wind had no yet totally erased the carved squid that stood over the door. Oga reached up to touch. It was hot, biting hot; everything was hot, baked to an infra-red glow by runaway greenhouse effect. To Oga's carbon-shelled fingertips, it was a small stone prayer, a whisper caught in a shell. If the world had permitted tears, the old, eroded stone squid would have called Oga's. Here was the hall, here the private parlour, curved in on itself like a ceramic musical instrument. The stairs, the upper floors, everything organic had evaporated centuries ago, but he could still read the niches of the sleeping porches cast in the upper walls. How would it have been in the end days, when even the summer sky was black from burning oil? Slow, painful, as year upon year the summer temperatures rose and the plankton blooms, carefully engineered to absorb the carbon from Tay's oil-riches, died and gave up their own sequestered carbon.

The winds keened through the dead city and out across the empty ocean. With a thought, Oga summoned the ship. Ion glow from the re-entry shone through the clouds. Sonic booms rolled across the sterile lagoon and rang from the dead porcelain houses. The ship punched out of the cloud base and unfolded, a sheet of nano motes that, to Oga's vision, called memories of the ancient Bazjendi angels stooping down the burning wind. The ship beats its wings over the shattered campanile, then dropped around Oga like possession. Flesh melted, flesh ran and fused, systems meshed, selves merged. Newly incarnate, Oga kicked off from Ejtay Quay in a pillar of fusion fire. Light broke around the empty houses and plazas, sent shadows racing down the desiccated canals. The salt pan glared white, dwindling to the greater darkness as the light ascended. With a star at his feet, Oga punched up through the boiling acid clouds, up and out until, in his extended shipsight, he could see the infra-glow of the planet's limb curve against space. A tear of blood. Accelerating, Oga broke orbit.

Oga. The name was a festival. Father-of-all-our-Mirths, in subtly inflected Aeo Taea. He was Fast Man no more, no longer a sojourner; he was Parent of a nation. The Clave had ordained three Parent Days of rejoicing as the Aeo Taea colony cylinders dropped out of scalarity drive at the edge of the system. For the children, it had been a month of party. Looking up from the flat end of the cylinder, Oga had felt the light from his native star on his skin, subtle and sensitive in a dozen spectra. He masked out the sun and looked for those sparks of reflected light that were worlds. There Saltpeer, and great Bephis: magnifying his vision, he could see its rings and many moons; there Tejaphay. It too wore a ring now; the shattered icy remnants of the Anpreen Commonweal. And there; there: Tay. Home. Something not right about it. Something missing in its light. Oga had ratcheted up his sight to the highest magnification he could achieve in this form.

There was no water in the spectrum. There was no pale blue dot.

The Clave of Aeo Taea Interstellar Cantons received the message some hours after the surface crews registered the departure of the Anpreen splinter ship in a glare of fusion light: *I have to go home.*

From five A.U.s out, the story became brutally evident. Tay was a silver ball of unbroken cloud. Those clouds comprised carbon dioxide, carbonic, and sulphuric acid and a memory of water vapour. The surface temperature read at two hundred and twenty degrees. Oga's ship-self possessed skills and techniques beyond his hominiform self; he could see the perpetual lighting storms cracking cloud to cloud, but never a drop of pure rain. He could see through those clouds, he could peel them away so that the charred, parched surface of the planet lay open to his sight. He could map the outlines of the continents and the continental shelves lifting from the dried ocean. The chains of archipelagos, once jewels around the belly of a beautiful dancer, were ribs, bones, stark mountain chains glowing furiously in the infra-dark.

As he fell sun-wards, Oga put the story together. The Enemy had struck Tay casually, almost as an afterthought. A lone warship, little larger than the ritual catamaran on which the boy called Ptey had sailed from this quay so many centuries before, had detached itself from the main fleet action and swept the planet with its particle weapons, a spray of directed fire that set the oil fields burning. Then it looped carelessly back out of the system, leaving a world to suffocate. They had left the space elevator intact. There must be a way out. This was judgment, not murder. Yet two billion people, two thirds of the planet's population, had died.

One third had lived. One third swarmed up the life-rope of the space elevator and looked out at space and wondered where they could go. Where they went, Oga went now. He could hear their voices, a low em-band chitter from the big blue of Tejaphay. His was a long, slow chasing loop. It would be the better part of a year before he arrived in parking orbit above Tejaphay. Time presented its own distractions and seductions. The quantum array that was his heart could as easily recreate Tay as any of scores of cultures it stored. The mid-day aurora would twist and glimmer again above the steep-gabled roofs of Jann. He would fish with Cjatay from the old, weather-silvered fishing stands for the spring run of prith. The Sulanj islands would simmer and bask under the midnight sun and Puzhay would again nuzzle against him and press her body close against the hammering cold outside the Tea Lane Womenhearth walls. They all could live, they all would believe they lived, *he* could, by selective editing of his consciousness, believe they lived again. He could recreate dead Tay. But it was the game of a god, a god who could take off his omniscience and enter his own delusion, and so Oga chose to press his perception down into a time flow even slower than Parent Time and watch the interplay of gravity wells around the sun.

On the final weeks of approach, Oga returned to world time and opened his full sensory array on the big planet that hung tantalisingly before him. He had come here before, when the Anpreen Commonweal hung around Tejaphay like pearls, but then he had given the world beneath him no thought, being inside a world complete in itself and his curiosity turned outwards to the shape of the universe. Now he beheld Tejaphay and remembered awe. Three times the diameter of Tay, Tejaphay was the true water world now. Ocean covered it pole to pole, a hundred kilometres deep. Immense weather systems mottled the planet, white on blue. The surviving spine of the Anpreen space elevator pierced the eye of a perpetual equatorial storm system. Wave trains and swells ran unbroken from equator to pole to smash in stupendous breakers against the polar ice caps. Oga drew near in sea meditation. Deep ocean appalled him in a way that centuries of time and space had not. That was distance. This was hostility. This was elementary fury that knew nothing of humanity.

Yet life clung here. Life survived. From two light minutes out, Oga had heard a whisper of radio communication, from the orbit station on the space elevator, also from the planet's surface. Scanning sub Antarctic waters, he caught the unmistakable tang of smart ice. A closer look: what had on first glance seemed to be bergs revealed a more complex structure. Spires, buttresses, domes, and sprawling terraces. Ice cities, riding the perpetual swell. Tay was not forgotten: these were the ancient Manifold Houses reborn, grown to the scale of vast Tejaphay. Closer again: the berg city under his scrutiny floated at the centre of a much larger boomed circle. Oga's senses teemed with life-signs. This was a complete ecosystem, and ocean farm, and Oga began to appreciate what these refugees had undertaken. No glimpse of life had ever been found on Tejaphay. Waterworlds, thawed from ice-giants sent spiralling sunwards by the gravitational play of their larger planetary rivals, were sterile. At the bottom of the hundred-kilometre deep ocean, was pressure ice, five thousand kilometres of pressure ice down to the iron core. No minerals, no carbon ever percolated up through that deep ice. Traces might arrive by cometary impact, but the waters of Tejaphay were deep and pure. What the Taynish had, the Taynish had brought. Even this ice city was grown from the shattered remnants of the Anpreen Commonweal.

A hail from the elevator station, a simple language algorithm. Oga smiled to himself as he compared the vocabulary files to his own memory of his native tongue. Half a millennium had changed the pronunciation and many of the words of Taynish, but not its inner subtleties, the rhythmic and contextual clues as to which Aspect was speaking.

"Attention unidentified ship, this is Tejaphay orbital Tower approach control. Please identify yourself and your flight plan."

"This is the Oga of the Aeo Taea Interstellar Fleet." He toyed with replying in the archaic speech. Worse than a breach of etiquette, such a conceit might give away information he did not wish known. Yet. "I am a representative with authority to negotiate. We wish to enter into communications with your government regarding fuelling rights in this system."

"Hello, Oga, this is Tejaphay Orbital Tower. By the Aeo Taea Interstellar Fleet, I assume you refer to the these objects." A sub-chatter on the data channel identified the cylinders, coasting in-system. Oga confirmed.

"Hello, Oga, Tejaphay Tower. Do not, repeat, do not approach the tower docking station. Attain this orbit and maintain until you have been contacted by Tower security. Please confirm your acceptance."

It was a reasonable request, and Oga's subtler senses picked up missile foramens unfolding in the shadows of the Orbital Station solar array. He was a runner, not a fighter; Tejaphay's defences might be basic fusion warheads and would need sustained precision hits to split open the Aeo Taea colony cans, but they were more than a match for Oga without the fuel reserves for full scalarity drive.

"I confirm that."

As he looped up to the higher ground, Oga studied more closely the berg cities of Tejaphay, chips of ice in the monstrous ocean. It would be a brutal life down there under two gravities, every aspect of life subject to the melting ice and the enclosing circle of the biosphere boom. Everything beyond that was as lifeless as space. The horizon would be huge and far and empty. City ships might sail for lifetimes without meeting another polis. The Taynish were tough. They were a race of the extremes. Their birthworld and its severe seasonal shifts had called forth a social response that other cultures would regard as mental disease, as socialized schizophrenia. Those multiple Aspects—a self for every need—now served them on the hostile vastnesses of Tejaphay's world ocean. They would survive, they would thrive. Life endured. This was the great lesson of the Clade: that life was hope, the only hope of escaping the death of the universe.

"*Every particle will be so far from everything else that it will be in a universe of its own. It will be a universe of its own*, a teenage boy in a yellow spacesuit had said up on the hull of mighty Amoa, looking out on the space between the stars. Oga had not answered at that time. It would have scared the boy, and though he had discovered it himself on the long flight from Milius 1183, he did not properly understand to himself, and in that gap of comprehension, he too was afraid. *Yes,* he would have said. *And in that is our only hope.*

Long range sensors chimed. A ship had emerged around the limb of the planet. Consciousness is too slow a tool for the pitiless mathematics of space. In the split second that the ship's course, design, and drive signature had registered on Oga's higher cognitions, his autonomic systems had plotted course, fuel reserves, and engaged the scalarity drive. At a thousand gees, he pulled away from Tejaphay. Manipulating space time so close to the planet would send gravity waves rippling through it like a struck gong. Enormous slow tides would circle the globe; the space elevator would flex like a crackled whip. Nothing to be done. It was instinct alone and by instinct he lived, for here came the missiles. Twenty nanotoc warheads on hypergee drives, wiping out his entire rearward vision in a white glare of lightweight MaM engines, but not before he had felt on his skin sensors the unmistakable harmonies of an Enemy deep-space scoopfield going up.

The missiles had the legs, but Oga had the stamina. He had calculated it thus. The numbers still came to him. Looking back at the blue speck into which Tejaphay had dwindled, he saw the engine-sparks of the missiles wink out one after the other. And now he could be sure that the strategy, devised in nanoseconds, would pay off. The warship was chasing him. He would lead it away from the Aeo Taea fleet. But this would be no long stern chase over the light decades. He did not have the fuel for that, nor the inclination. Without fuel, without weapons, he knew he must end it. For that, he needed space.

It was the same ship. The drive field harmonics, the spectrum of the fusion flame, the timbre of the radar images that he so gently, kiss-soft, bounced off the pursuer's hull, even the configuration he had glimpsed as the ship rounded the planet and launched missiles. This was the same ship that had hunted him down all the years. Deep mysteries here. Time dilation would compress his planned course to subjective minutes and Oga needed time to find an answer.

The ship had known where he would go even as they bucked the stormy cape of the wandering neutron star. It had never even attempted to follow him; instead, it had always known that it must lay in a course that would whip it round to Tay. That meant that even as he escaped the holocaust at Milius 1183, it had known who he was, where he came from, had seen through the frozen layers of smart-ice to the Torben below. The ship had come from around the planet. It was an enemy ship, but not the Enemy. They would have boiled Tejaphay down to its iron heart. Long Oga contemplated these things as he looped out into the wilderness of the Oort cloud. Out there among the lonely ice, he reached a conclusion. He turned the ship over and burned the last of his reaction in a hypergee deceleration burn. The enemy ship responded immediately, but its ramjet drive was less powerful. It would be months, years even, before it could turn around to match orbits with him. He would be ready then. The edge of the field brushed Oga as he decelerated at fifteen hundred gravities and he used his external sensors to modulate a message on the huge web, a million kilometres across: *I surrender.*

Gigayears ago, before the star was born, the two comets had met and entered into their far, cold marriage. Beyond the dramas and attractions of the dust cloud that coalesced into Tay and Tejaphay and Bephis, all the twelve planets of the solar system, they maintained their fixed-grin gazes on each other, locked in orbit around a mutual centre of gravity where a permanent free-floating haze of ice crystals hovered, a fraction of a Kelvin above absolute zero. Hidden amongst them, and as cold and seemingly as dead, was the splintership. Oga shivered. The cold was more than physical—on the limits of even his malleable form. Within their thermal casing, his motes moved as slowly as Aeo Taea Parents. He felt old as this ice and as weary. He looked up into the gap between ice worlds. The husband-comet floated above his head like a halo. He could have leaped to it in a thought.

Lights against the starlight twinkle of the floating ice storm. A sudden occlusion. The Enemy was here. Oga waited, feeling every targeting sensor trained on him.

No, you won't, will you? Because you have to know.

A shadow detached itself from the black ship, darkest on dark, and looped around the comet. It would be a parliament of self-assembling motes like himself. Oga had worked out decades before that Enemy and Anpreen were one and the same, sprung from the same nanotechnological seed when they attained Class Two status. Theirs was a civil war. *In the Clade, all war was civil war*, Oga thought. Panhumanity was all there was. More like a family feud. Yes, those were the bloodiest fights of all. No quarter and no forgiveness.

The man came walking around the small curve of the comet, kicking up shards of ice crystals from his grip soles. Oga recognised him. He was meant to. He had designed himself so that he would be instantly recognisable, too. He bowed, in the distances of the Oort cloud.

"Torben Reris Orhum Fejannan Kekjay Prus Rejmer Serejen Nejben, sir."

The briefest nod of a head, a gesture of hours in the slow-motion hypercold.

"Torben. I'm not familiar with that name."

"Perhaps we should use the name most familiar to you. That would be Serejen, or perhaps Fejannen, I was in that Aspect when we last met. I would have hoped you still remembered the old etiquette."

"I find I remember too much these days. Forgetting is a choice since I was improved. And a chore. What do they call you now?"

"Oga."

"Oga it shall be, then."

"And what do they call *you* now?"

The man looked up into the icy gap between worldlets. *He has remembered himself well*, Oga thought. *The slight portliness, the child-chubby features, like a boy who never grew up. As he says, forgetting is a chore.*

"The same thing they always have: Cjatay."

"Tell me your story then, Cjatay. This was never your fight, or my fight."

"You left her."

"She left *me*, I recall, and, like you, I forget very little these days. I can see the note still; I could recreate it for you, but it would be a scandalous waste of energy and resources. She went to you."

"It was never me. It was the cause."

"Do you truly believe that?"

Cjatay gave a glacial shrug.

"We made independent contact with them when they came. The Council of governments was divided, all over the place, no coherent approach or strategy. 'Leave us alone. We're not part of this.' But there's no neutrality in these things. We had let them use our system's water. We had the space elevator they built for us, there was the price, there was the blood money. We knew it would never work—our hope was that we could convince them that some of us had always stood against the Anpreen. They torched Tay anyway, but they gave us a deal. They'd let us survive as a species if some of us joined them on their crusade."

"They *are* the Anpreen."

"*Were* the Anpreen. I know. They took me to pieces. They made us into something else. Better, I think. All of us, there were twenty four of us. Twenty four, that was all the good people of Tay, in their eyes. Everyone who was worth saving."

"And Puzhay?"

"She died. She was caught in the Arphan conflagration. She went there from Jann to be with her parents. It always was an oil town. They melted it to slag."

"But you blame me."

"You are all that's left."

"I don't believe that. I think it was always personal. I think it was always revenge."

"You still exist."

"That's because you don't have all the answers yet."

"We know the kind of creatures we've become; what answers can I not know?"

Oga dipped his head, then looked up to the halo moon, so close he could almost touch it.

"Do you want me to show you what they fear so much?"

There was no need for the lift of the hand, the conjuror's gesture; the pieces of his ship-self Oga had seeded so painstakingly through the wife-comet's structure were part of his extended body. *But I do make magic here*, he thought. He dropped his hand. The star-speckled sky turned white, hard painful white, as if the light of every star were arriving at once. *An Olbers sky*, Oga remembered from his days in the turrets and cloisters of Jann. And as the light grew intolerable, it ended. Blackness, embedding, huge and comforting. The dark of death. Then Oga's eyes grew familiar with the dark, and, though it was the plan and always had been the plan, he felt a plaint of awe as he saw ten thousand galaxies resolve out of the Olbers dazzle. And he knew that Cjatay saw the same.

"Where are we? What have you done?"

"We are somewhere in the region of two hundred and thirty million light years outside our local group of galaxies, more precisely, on the periphery of the cosmological galactic supercluster known as the Great Attractor. I made some refinements to the scalarity drive unit to operate in a one dimensional array."

"Faster-than-light travel," Cjatay said, his upturned face silvered with the light of the ten thousand galaxies of the Great Atrractor.

"No, you still don't see it," Oga said, and again turned the universe white. Now when he flicked out of hyperscalarity, the sky was dark and starless but for three vast streams of milky light that met in a triskelion hundreds of millions of light years across.

"We are within the Bootes Supervoid," Oga said. "It is so vast that if our own galaxy were in the centre of it, we would have thought ourselves alone and that our galaxy was the entire universe. Before us are the Lyman alpha-blobs, three conjoined galaxy filaments. These are the largest structures in the universe. On scales larger than this, structure becomes random and grainy. We become grey. These are the last grand vistas, this is the end of greatness."

"Of course, the expansion of space is not limited by lightspeed," Cjatay said.

"Still you don't understand." A third time, Oga generated the dark energy from the ice beneath his feet and focused it into a narrow beam between the wife-comet and its unimaginably distant husband. *Two particles in contact will remain in quantum entanglement no matter how far they are removed*, Oga thought. *And is that true also for lives?* He dismissed the scalarity generator and brought them out in blackness. Complete, impenetrable, all-enfolding blackness, without a photon of light.

"Do you understand where I have brought you?"

"You've taken us beyond the visible horizon," Cjatay said. "You've pushed space so far that the light from the rest of the universe has not had time to reach us. We are isolated from every other part of reality. In a philosophical sense, we are a universe in ourselves."

"That was what they feared? You feared?"

"That the scalarity drive had the potential to be turned into a weapon of unimaginable power? Oh yes. The ability to remove any enemy from reach, to banish them beyond the edge of the universe. To exile them from the universe itself, instantly and irrevocably."

"Yes, I can understand that, and that you did what you did altruistically. They were moral genocides. But our intention was never to use it as a weapon—if it had been, wouldn't we have used it on you?"

Silence in the darkness beyond dark.

"Explain then."

"I have one more demonstration."

The mathematics were critical now. The scalarity generator devoured cometary mass voraciously. If there were not enough left to allow him to return them home . . . Trust number, Oga. You always have. Beyond the edge of the universe, all you have is number. There was no sensation, no way of perceiving when he activated and deactivated the scalarity field, except by number. For an instant, Oga feared number had failed him, a first and fatal betrayal. Then light blazed down on to the dark ice. A single blinding star shone in the absolute blackness.

"What is that?"

"I pushed a single proton beyond the horizon of this horizon. I pushed it so far that space and time tore."

"So I'm looking at . . ."

"The light of creation. That is an entire universe, new born. A new big bang. A young man once said to me, 'Every particle will be so far from everything else that it will be in a universe of its own. It will *be* a universe of its own.' An extended object like this comet, or bodies, is too gross, but in a single photon, quantum fluctuations will turn it into an entire universe-in-waiting."

The two men looked up a long time into the nascent light, the surface of he fireball seething with physical laws and forces boiling out. *Now you understand,* Oga thought. *It's not a weapon. It's the way out. The way past the death of the universe. Out there beyond the horizon, we can bud off new universes, and universes from those universes, forever. Intelligence has the last word. We won't die alone in the cold and the dark.* He felt the light of the infant universe on his face, then said, "I think we probably should be getting back. If my calculations are correct—and there is a significant margin of error—this fireball will shortly undergo a phase transition as dark energy separates out and will undergo catastrophic expansion. I don't think that the environs of an early universe would be a very good place for us to be."

He saw portly Cjatay smile.

"Take me home, then. I'm cold and I'm tired of being a god."

"Are we gods?"

Cjatay nodded at the microverse.

"I think so. No, I know I would want to be a man again."

Oga thought of his own selves and lives, his bodies and natures. Flesh indwelled by many personalities, then one personality—one aggregate of experience and memory—in bodies liquid, starship, nanotechnological. And he *was* tired, so terribly tired beyond the universe, centuries away from all that he had known and loved. All except this one, his enemy.

"Tejaphay is no place for children."

"Agreed. We could rebuild Tay."

"It would be a work of centuries."

"We could use the Aeo Taea Parents. They have plenty of time."

Now Cjatay laughed.

"I have to trust you now, don't I? I could have vaporized you back there, blown this place to atoms with my missiles. And now you create an entire universe . . ."

"And the Enemy? They'll come again."

"You'll be ready for them, like you were ready for me. After all, I am still the enemy."

The surface of the bubble of universe seemed to be in more frenetic motion now. The light was dimming fast.

"Let's go then," Cjatay said.

"Yes," Oga said. "Let's go home."

⊰⊱

Oga, returning

BIOGRAPHIES

Since her first sale in 1987, **Kij Johnson** has sold dozens of short stories to markets including *Amazing Stories, Analog, Asimov's, Duelist Magazine, Fantasy & Science Fiction*, and *Realms of Fantasy*. She has won the Theodore Sturgeon Memorial Award for the best short story and the 2001 Crawford Award for best new fantasy novelist. Her short story "26 Monkeys, Also the Abyss" was a nominee for the 2008 Nebula and Hugo awards.

Her novels include two volumes of the Heian trilogy Love/War/Death: *The Fox Woman* and *Fudoki*. She's also co-written with Greg Cox a Star Trek: The Next Generation novel, *Dragon's Honor*. She is currently researching a third novel set in Heian Japan; and Kylen, two novels set in Georgian Britain.

Elizabeth Bear is an American science fiction and fantasy author, born September 22, 1971 in Hartford, Connecticut. Her first professionally-published fiction appeared in 2003; since then, she has published twelve solo novels (*Hammered, Scardown, Worldwired, Blood and Iron, Whiskey and Water, Ink and Steel, Hell and Earth, Dust, Carnival, New Amsterdam, Undertow*, and *All the Windwracked Stars*), one novel in collaboration with Sarah Monette (*A Companion to Wolves*), and a story collection (*The Chains that You Refuse*). Her web site is at www.elizabethbear.com, and she maintains a popular LiveJournal at matociquala.livejournal.com.

Daryl Gregory lives in State College, PA, where he's a programmer by day and a science fiction writer by later in the day. His stories have appeared in *F&SF, Asimov's, Eclipse 2*, and several year's best anthologies. His first novel, *Pandemonium*, was published by Del Rey Books in 2008. A second, unrelated book is due out in 2009.

Christopher Golden is the author of such novels as *The Boys Are Back in Town, The Myth Hunters, Wildwood Road, Strangewood, Of Saints and Shadows*, and (with Tim Lebbon) *The Map of Moments*. Golden co-wrote the illustrated novel *Baltimore, or, The Steadfast Tin Soldier and the Vampire* with Mike Mignola. He has also written books for teens and young adults, including *Poison Ink, Soulless*, and the upcoming *The Secret Journeys of Jack London*, a new series of hardcover YA fantasy novels co-authored with Tim Lebbon. Golden was born and raised in Massachusetts, where he still lives with his family. His original novels have been published in more than fourteen languages in countries around the world. Please visit him at *www.christophergolden.com*.

Naomi Novik is a Campbell Award winner and the *New York Times*-bestselling author of the Temeraire series from Del Rey, including *His Majesty's Dragon* (UK title *Temeraire*), *Throne of Jade*, *Black Powder War*, *Empire of Ivory*, and *Victory of Eagles*. She lives in New York City with her husband, Charles Ardai, and an extensive brood of computers. Her website and livejournal are at *www.temeraire.org*.

Alice Sola Kim is currently attending graduate school in St. Louis. Her work has appeared in *Rabid Transit: Long Voyages, Great Lies, Lady Churchill's Rosebud Wristlet*, and *Strange Horizons*.

Ted Kosmatka is a complex interaction between genes and environment. Over the year's he's fed tigers, and worked in laboratories and shoveled coke in a steel mill blast furnace. Ted lives with his family on the north coast of the US and earns his living behind the lens of an electron microscope.

Eugene Mirabelli writes novels, short stories, journalistic pieces and book reviews. He's a Nebula Award nominee, and his fiction has been published in Czech, Hebrew, Russian, Sicilian, and Turkish. His most recent work is the novel, *The Goddess in Love with a Horse*. He's old and has a short stiff white beard.

Margo Lanagan lives in Sydney, Australia. Her novel, *Tender Morsels*, was published in the US and Australia in October 2008 to immediate critical success, garnering five starred reviews and appearing in Amazon's Top 100 Editors' Picks and on several Year's Best Books lists, including *Kirkus Reviews* and *Publishers Weekly*. Previously, her collection of speculative fiction short stories, *Black Juice* (Allen & Unwin Australia 2004, HarperCollins US 2005, Orion 2006), was also widely acclaimed, won two World Fantasy Awards, a Victorian Premier's Award, two Ditmars and two Aurealis Awards, and was shortlisted for the Los Angeles Times Book Prize and an honour book in the American Library Association's Michael L. Printz Award. Her third collection, *Red Spikes*, published in Australia in October 2006, was a CBCA Book of the Year, as well as being shortlisted for the Commonwealth Writers Prize and longlisted for the Frank O'Connor International Short Story Award.

Peter S. Beagle was born in New York City in 1939 and raised in the borough of that city known as the Bronx. He originally proclaimed he would be a writer when ten years old: subsequent events have proven him either prescient or even more stubborn than hitherto suspected. Today, thanks to classic works such as

A Fine and Private Place, *The Last Unicorn* (plus its award-winning sequel, "Two Hearts"), *Tamsin*, and *The Innkeeper's Song*, his dazzling storytelling has earned him millions of fans around the world.

In addition to stories and novels Peter has written numerous teleplays and screenplays, including the animated versions of *The Lord of the Rings* and *The Last Unicorn*, plus the fan-favorite "Sarek" episode of *Star Trek: The Next Generation*. His nonfiction book *I See By My Outfit*, which recounts a 1963 journey across America on motor scooter, is considered a classic of American travel writing; and he is also a gifted poet, lyricist, and singer/songwriter.

For more information on Peter and his works, see www.peterbeagle.com or www.conlanpress.com.

Robert Reed has written dozens and dozens of stories, publishing in most markets. His novella, "A Billion Eves," won the Hugo in 2007. He is currently at work on a gigantic and ambitious novel full of vivid characters, death and sex. Reed lives in Lincoln, Nebraska with his wife and daughter.

Delia Sherman's most recent short stories have appeared in the Viking young adult anthologies *The Green Man*, *Fairy Reel*, and *Coyote Road*. Her novels are *Through a Brazen Mirror*, *The Porcelain Dove*, *The Fall of the Kings* (with Ellen Kushner), and *Changeling*, for younger readers. A second novel in the series, *The Magic Mirror of the Mermaid Queen*, is due out in June 2009. *Interfictions: An Anthology of Interstitial Writing*, edited with Theodora Goss, came out in 2007. *Interfictions 2*, edited with Christopher Barzak, is also scheduled for 2009. She lives in New York City with partner Ellen Kushner and writes in cafes of many lands.

Rivka Galchen's essays and stories have appeared in *Zoetrope*, *The New Yorker*, *Believer Magazine*, *Scientific American* and *The New York Times*. Her first novel, *Atmospheric Disturbances* was published by FSG in June 2008.

Jeffrey Ford is the author of The Well Built-City Trilogy from Golden Gryphon Press, and stand alone novels *The Portrait of Mrs. Charbuque*, *The Girl In The Glass*, *The Shadow Year* from Harper Collins. His three short story collections are: *The Fantasy Writer's Assistant*, *The Empire of Ice Cream*, *The Drowned Life*. Ford has the following stories forthcoming in anthologies—"Ganesha" in *The Beastly Bride* (Viking), "The Coral Heart" in *Eclipse* 3 (Night Shade Books), "Down Atsion Road" in *Haunted Legends* (Tor), "Daddy Long Legs of the Evening" in *Naked City* (St. Martin's), "Daltharee" in *Best American Fantasy* 3 (Underland).

James Alan Gardner got his master's degree in applied mathematics (with a thesis on black holes) and then immediately gave up academics for writing. First, it was computer documentation, but now he's devoted to science fiction and fantasy. He has published eight novels and one book of short stories; he's won the Aurora award twice, and has been a finalist for both the Hugo and the Nebula. In addition to writing, Gardner spends his time practicing and teaching kung fu.

Ann Leckie is a graduate of Clarion West. She has published short stories in *Subterranean Magazine* and *Strange Horizons*, and *Andromeda Spaceways Inflight Magazine*, and has work forthcoming in *Realms of Fantasy*. She has worked as a waitress, a receptionist, a rodman on a land-surveying crew, and a recording engineer. She lives in St. Louis, Missouri, with her husband, children, and cats.

Will McIntosh has published stories in *Asimov's, Strange Horizons, Interzone, Postscripts*, and others. By day he is a psychology professor in the Southeastern U.S.

Meghan McCarron's stories have recently appeared in *Strange Horizons, Clarkesworld Magazine*, and *Lady Churchill's Rosebud Wristlet*. She was born in 1983 and currently lives in New York City, where she works a tiny bookstore.

James L. Cambias is originally from New Orleans and graduated from the University of Chicago. His first published story was "A Diagram of Rapture" (*F&SF*, April 2000), and he has followed it with more than a dozen others in magazines and original anthologies. When he isn't writing SF he is a game designer, creating science-based card games for his company Zygote Games, and writing roleplaying game books for various publishers. He lives with his family in western Massachusetts and drinks a lot of coffee.

Charlie Jane Anders blogs about science fiction at io9.com. She's the author of a novel, *Choir Boy*, and co-editor of an anthology, *She's Such A Geek*. She has stories in the anthologies Sex *For America, The McSweeney's Joke Book Of Book Jokes* and *Paraspheres: New Wave Fabulist Fiction*. Her writing has appeared in *Salon.com, the Wall Street Journal, the SF Chronicle, Strange Horizons, ZYZZYVA* and *Lady Churchill's Rosebud Wristlet*.

Holly Phillips is the author most recently of *The Engine's Child*, a dark fantasy novel that "suggests that we've stepped past the boundaries of genre and into literature that knows no boundaries" (*The Agony Column*). She doesn't know if that's true, but she likes the sound of it quite a lot. Holly is also the owner of a cat and the sister of an English professor. These last points are not very relevant, but she's written a lot of bios over the years and is getting a bit silly about it all.

Peter Watts is a reformed marine biologist and failed gel-jock who is nevertheless adept at faking science, just so long as he can mix some characters and plot in amongst the numbers. His latest novel, *Blindsight*, was nominated for several prestigious awards, winning none of them. He nonetheless appears to be a big hit in Poland.

Alex Jeffers's sf, fantasy, and literary stories have been published at wide, unpredictable intervals since 1976. His novel *Safe as Houses*, called "a gay novel about family values" by Edmund White, appeared in 1995. He lives in Rhode Island and, on the web, at www.sentenceandparagraph.com.

Garth Nix was born in 1963 in Melbourne, Australia. A full-time writer since 2001, he has previously worked as a literary agent, marketing consultant, book editor, book publicist, book sales representative, bookseller, and as a part-time soldier in the Australian Army Reserve. Garth's short fiction has appeared in numerous magazines and anthologies. His novels include the award-winning fantasies *Sabriel, Lirael* and *Abhorsen* and the cult favourite YA SF novel *Shade's Children*. His fantasy books for children include *The Ragwitch;* the six books of *The Seventh Tower* sequence; and the seven books of *The Keys to the Kingdom* series. His books have appeared on the bestseller lists of *The New York Times, Publishers Weekly, The Guardian, The Sunday Times* and *The Australian*, and his work has been translated into thirty-seven languages. He lives in a Sydney beach suburb with his wife and two children.

Jay Lake lives in Portland, Oregon, where he works on numerous writing and editing projects. His 2009 novels are *Green* from Tor Books and *Death of a Starship* from MonkeyBrain Books, while his short fiction appears regularly in literary and genre markets worldwide. Jay is a winner of the John W. Campbell Award for Best New Writer, and a multiple nominee for the Hugo and World Fantasy Awards.

Beth Bernobich is a writer, reader, mother, and geek. Her short stories have appeared in *Asimov's, Interzone, Subterranean Online*, and *Postscripts Magazine*, among other places. She's pleased to report that a sequel to "The Golden Octopus" is forthcoming from PS Publishing in 2009, and her first novel is scheduled to appear from Tor Books in early 2010.

Taken broadly, **Erik Amundsen** has had an interesting life; he's been a baker, an itinerant schoolteacher, worked for two governments and gotten in bar fights overseas. He now lives at the foot of a cemetery in central Connecticut where he writes nasty little stories and poems that shuffle around in the night when he's not looking. Or at least he hopes it's them; something's got to be making those noises and it's not the furnace.

Patrick Rothfuss lives in central Wisconsin where he drinks too much coffee and tells lies for a living. He was once described as "a rough, earthy iconoclast with a pipeline to the divine in everyone's subconscious." But honestly, that person was pretty drunk at the time, so you might want to take it with a grain of salt. In his free time, Pat runs writing workshops, practices civil disobedience, and dabbles with alchemy in his basement. He loves words, laughs often, and refuses to dance.

Jeff VanderMeer is an award-winning writer with books published in over twenty countries. He is generally recognized as both one of the world's best SF/ fantasy writers, and one of the internet's next-generation "internet writer-entrepreneurs" along with creators such as Cory Doctorow and John Scalzi. His books have made the year's best lists of *Publishers Weekly, LA Weekly, Amazon, the San Francisco Chronicle*, and many more. VanderMeer has worked with rock band The Church, *30 Days of Night* creator Ben Templesmith, Dark Horse Comics, and Playstation Europe on various multimedia projects, including music soundtracks and short films. His nonfiction appears regularly in the *Washington Post* and on the Amazon book blog. With his wife Ann (together, cited by Boing Boing as a literary "power couple"), he is also an award-winning editor profiled on Wired.com and the NYT blog, whose books include the iconic and bestselling *Steampunk* anthology. Current projects include *Booklife: Survival Tips for Twenty-First Century Writers* and the novel *Finch*.

Sarah Monette grew up in Oak Ridge, Tennessee, one of the three secret cities of the Manhattan Project. Having completed her Ph.D. in English literature, she now lives and writes in a 102-year-old house in the Upper Midwest. Her novels are published by Ace Books. Her short fiction has appeared in many venues, including *Strange Horizons, Weird Tales*, and *Lady Churchill's Rosebud Wristlet*. Visit her online at www.sarahmonette.com

Karen Heuler's odd stories have appeared in over forty publications, ranging from literary to fantasy to horror, and she writes odd novels as well, the latest of which—*Journey to Bom Goody*—concerns fantastic doings in the Amazon. She lives in New York with a very stable cat and a very unstable dog, both of whom make things up.

Paul Cornell is an SF writer who also writes for television (notably Doctor Who) and comics (Wisdom and Captain Britain and MI-13 fo Marvel Comics). He's proud to have stories in the latest volumes of all three ongoing non-theme SF anthologies, and has just adapted Iain M. Banks' "The State of the Art" for Radio 4.

James Maxey lives in Hillsborough, NC, in a cinderblock house on a hilltop that can be easily defended during zombie uprisings. His short fiction has appeared in *Asimov's, IGMS*, and numerous anthologies. His novels include the cult-classic superhero novel *Nobody Gets the Girl* and the Dragon Age trilogy of *Bitterwood, Dragonforge*, and *Dragonseed*. More information about his writing can be found at *dragonprophet.blogspot.com*.

Mary Robinette Kowal is a professional puppeteer who moonlights as a writer. Her short fiction appears *in Strange Horizons, Cosmos* and *CICADA*. In 2008 she received the John W. Campbell Award for Best New Writer. Visit her website *www.maryrobinettekowal.com* for more fiction and puppetry.

Richard Bowes' most recent novel is the Nebula nominated *From the Files of the Time Rangers*. His most recent short fiction collection *Streetcar Dreams And Other Midnight Fancies* appeared from PS Publications in England. He has won the World Fantasy, Lambda, International Horror Guild and Million Writers Awards. Recent and upcoming stories appear *in F&SF, Electric Velocipede, Subterranean, Clarkesworld* and *Fantasy* magazines and in *The Del Rey Book of Science Fiction and Fantasy, Year's Best Gay Stories 2008, Naked City, Best Science Fiction and Fantasy, Beastly Bride, Haunted Legends* and *Lovecraft Unbound* anthologies. Many of these stories are chapters in his novel in progress *Dust Devil on a Quiet Street*. His email is: *rickbowes@earthlink.net*.

Liz Williams is a science fiction and fantasy writer living in Glastonbury, England, where she is co-director of a witchcraft supply business. She is currently published by Bantam Spectra (US) and Tor Macmillan (UK), also Night Shade Press and appears regularly in *Realms of Fantasy, Asimov's* and other magazines. She is the secretary of the Milford SF Writers' Workshop, and also teaches creative writing and the history of science fiction.

Ian McDonald lives in Northern Ireland by the shore of Belfast Lough. From that vantage he's seen the Troubles start and also, he hopes, end. His first story was sold in 1983 to short-lived but very glossy local SFF magazine *Extro*. He bought a guitar with the money. His first novel, *Desolation Road*, came out in 1988 from Bantam Spectra, this year PYR republish it for the first time since then in the US. His most recent novel was the Hugo- and Nebula-nominated *Brasyl*, just out from PYR in the US and Gollancz in the UK is *Cyberabad Days*, a collexction of stories from teh future India of his 2006 novel *River of Gods*, including Hugo-winning novelette *The Djinn's Wife*. In progress is a new novel, *The Dervish House*, set in near-future Turkey. In daylight hours he works as a development producer for a local animation company.

RECOMMENDED READING

Jim Aikin, "Run! Run!" (*F&SF*, September)
William Alexander, "Ana's Tag"
        (*Lady Churchill's Rosebud Wristlet*, November)
Nina Allan, "Angelus" (*Albedo One* #34)
Erik Amundsen, "Turnipseed" (*Fantasy*, March)
Charlie Anders, "Love Might Be Too Strong a Word" (*LCRW*, June)
Charlie Anders, "Suicide Drive" (*Helix*, January)
Nick Antosca, "Soon You Will Be Gone and Possibly Eaten" (*GUD*, Autumn)
Paolo Bacigalupi, "The Gambler" (*Fast Forward* 2)
Kelly Barnhill, "The Men Who Live in Trees" (*Postscripts*, Spring)
Stephen Baxter, "Turing's Apples" (*Eclipse* 2)
Peter S. Beagle, "The Tale of Junko and Sayiri" (*IGMS*, July)
Peter S. Beagle, "Uncle Chaim and Aunt Rifke and the Angel"
        (*Strange Roads*)
Peter S. Beagle, "What Tune the Enchantress Plays" (*A Book of Wizards*)
Elizabeth Bear, "Overkill" (*Shadow Unit* 1.07)
Beth Bernobich, "Air and Angels" (*Subterranean*, Spring)
Terry Bisson, "Private Eye" (*F&SF*, October/November)
Neal Blaikie, "Offworld Friends are Best" (*GUD*, Spring)
Naomi Bloch, "Same Old Story" (*Strange Horizons*, December 8)
Michael Blumlein, "The Big One" (*Flurb* #6)
Sarah Rees Brennan, "An Old-Fashioned Unicorn's Guide to Courtship"
        (*Coyote Wild*, August)
John Brown, "From the Clay of His Heart" (*IGMS*, April)
Alan Campbell, "The Gadgey" (*Strange Horizons*, May 5)
E. L. Chen, "The Story of the Woman and Her Dog" (*Tesseracts* Twelve)
Ted Chiang, "Exhalation" (*Eclipse* Two)
Deborah Coates, "How to Hide a Heart" (*Strange Horizons*, January 31)
Tina Connolly, "The Bitrunners" (*Helix*, Summer)
Constance Cooper, "The Wily Thing" (*Black Gate*, Spring)
Cory Doctorow, "The Things that Make Me Weak and Strange Get
        Engineered Away" (*Tor.com*, August)
Brendan DuBois,Not Enough Stars in the Night" (*Cosmos Online*, May 9)
David Dumitru, "Little Moon, Too, Goes Round" (*Aeon* Thirteen)

Hal Duncan, "The Toymaker's Grief" (*Lone Star Stories,* October)

Hal Duncan, "The Behold of the Eye" (*Lone Star Stories,* August)

Carol Emshwiller, "Master of the Road to Nowhere" (*Asimov's,* March)

Rebecca Epstein, "When We Were Stardust" (*Fantasy,* February)

Charles Coleman Finlay, "The Political Prisoner" (*F&SF,* August)

Charles Coleman Finlay, "The Rapeworm" (*Noctem Aeturnus*)

Carolyn Ives Gilman, "Arkfall" (*F&SF,* September)

Kathleen Ann Goonan, "Memory Dog" (*Asimov's,* April/May)

Peni R. Griffin, "The Singers in the Tower"
    (*Realms of Fantasy,* February)

Merrie Haskell, "The Girl-Prince" (*Coyote Wild,* August)

Merrie Haskell, "The Wedding Dress Parties of 2443"
    (*Quantum Kiss,* October 9)

Nina Kiriki Hoffman, "Trophy Wives" (*Fellowship Fantastic*)

Nina Kiriki Hoffman, "The Trouble with the Truth"
    (*The Dimension Next Door*)

Alex Irvine, "Mystery Hill" (*F&SF,* January)

Paul Jessup, "A World Without Ghosts" (*Fantasy,* April)

Alaya Dawn Johnson, "Down the Well" (*Strange Horizons,* August 4)

John Kessel, "Pride and Prometheus" (*F&SF,* January)

Nicole Kornher-Stace, "Yell Alley" (*Fantasy,* October)

Ted Kosmatka, "N-Words" (*Seeds of Change*)

Nancy Kress, "First Rites" (*Baen's Universe,* October)

Bill Kte'pi, "The End of Tin" (*Strange Horizons*)

Jay Lake, "The Sky that Wraps the World Round,
    Past the Blue and into the Black" (*Clarkesworld,* March)

Jay Lake, "A Water Matter" (*Tor.com,* November)

Margo Lanagan, "Machine Maid" (*Extraordinary Engines*)

Ann Leckie, "The God of Au" (*Helix,* Spring)

Yoon Ha Lee, "Architectural Constants"
    (*Beneath Ceaseless Skies,* October 23)

Rose Lemberg, "Geddarien" (*Fantasy,* December)

Kelly Link, "The Surfer" (*The Starry Rift*)

Ian R. MacLeod, "The Hob Carpet" (*Asimov's,* June)

Bruce McAllister, "Hit" (*Aeon* Thirteen)

Paul McAuley, "The Thought War" (*Postscripts,* Summer)

Todd McAulty, "The Soldiers of Serenity" (*Black Gate,* Spring)

Meghan McCarron, "The Magician's House" (*Strange Horizons,* July 21)

Kirstyn McDermott, "Painlessness" (*GUD,* Spring)

Maureen F. McHugh, "The Kingdom of the Blind" (*Plugged In*)

Will McIntosh, "Linkworlds" (*Strange Horizons,* March 17-24)

Dean McLaughlin, "Tenbrook of Mars" (*Analog,* July/August)

Holly Messinger, "End of the Line" (*Baen's Universe,* February)

Silvia Moreno-Garcia, "Enchantment" (*Reflection's Edge,* November)

David Erik "Nelson,Tucker Teaches the Clockies to Copulate"
(*Paradox*, Spring)
Garth Nix, "Infestation" (*The Starry Rift*)
Paul Park, "The Blood of Peter Francisco" (*Sideways in Crime*)
Richard Parks, "On the Wheel" (*Hub* #41)
Norman Partridge, "Apotropaics" (*Subterranean*, Fall)
Tim Powers, "The Hour of Babel" (*Subterranean: Tales of Dark Fantasy*)
Tom Purdom, "Sepoy Fidelities" (*Asimov's*, March)
Philip Raines and Harvey Welles, "Alice and Bob" (*Albedo One* #34)
David Reagan, "Solitude Ripples from the Past" (*Futurismic*, May)
Robert Reed, "Five Thrillers" (*F&SF*, April)
Robert Reed, "Truth" (*Asimov's*, October/November)
Jessica Reisman, "Flowertongue" (*Farrago's Wainscot*, May)
Kate Riedel, "Pest Control" (*On Spec*, Winter)
Mark Rigney, "Portfolio" (*LCRW*, June)
Mercurio D. Rivera, "Snatch Me Another" (*Abyss and Apex*, First Quarter)
Adam Roberts, "The Man of the Strong Arm" (*Celebration*)
Margaret Ronald, "When the Gentlemen Go By" (*Clarkesworld*, July)
Benjamin Rosenbaum, "Sense and Sensibility"
(*The Ant King and Other Stories*)
Mary Rosenblum, "The Egg Man" (*Asimov's*, February)
Mary Rosenblum, "Horse Racing" (*Asimov's*, September)
Kristine Kathryn Rusch, "G-Men" (*Sideways in Crime*)
Geoff Ryman, "Talk is Cheap" (*Interzone*, June)
Karl Schroeder, "Book, Theatre, and Wheel"
(*The Solaris Book of New Science Fiction*, Volume 2)
David J. Schwartz, "The Sun Inside" (*The Sun Inside*)
Gord Sellar, "Wonjiang and the Madman of Pyongyang" (*Tesseracts* Twelve)
Stacy Sinclair, "The 21st Century Isobel Down" (*Fantasy*, April)
Jeremy Adam Smith, "The Wreck of the Grampus" (*Lone Star Stories*, April)
Sherwood Smith, "The Rule of Engagement" (*Lace and Blade*)
Katherine Sparrow, "The Future is Already Seen" (*Shiny* #3)
William Browning Spencer, "Penguins of the Apocalypse"
(*Subterranean: Tales of Dark Fantasy*)
Brian Stableford, "Following the Pharmers" (*Asimov's*, March)
James Stoddard, "The First Editions" (*F&SF*, April)
Jason Stoddard, "Far Horizon" (*Interzone*, February)
Jason Stoddard, "Willpower" (*Futurismic*, December)
Michael Swanwick, "From Babel's Fall'n Glory We Fled" (*Asimov's*, February)
Chris Szego, "Valiant on the Wing" (*Strange Horizons*, April 14)
Lavie Tidhar, "The Case of the Missing Puskat" (*Chiaroscuro* #35)
Lavie Tidhar, "Blakenjel" (*Apex*, October)
Catherynne M. Valente, "A Buyer's Guide to Maps of Antarctica"
(*Clarkesworld*, May)

James Van Pelt, "Rock House" (*Talebones*, Spring)

John Walker, "The Disappearance of Juliana" (*GUD*, Spring)

Chris Willrich, "The Sword of Loving Kindness"
    (*Beneath Ceaseless Skies*, October 23)

PUBLICATION HISTORY

ABOUT THE EDITOR

RICH HORTON is a software engineer in St. Louis. He is a contributing editor to *Locus*, for which he does short fiction reviews and occasional book reviews; and to *Black Gate*, for which he does a continuing series of essays about SF history. He also contributes book reviews to *Fantasy Magazine*, and to many other publications.